DUEL

WRITTEN BY
JESSIXA BAGLEY

ILLUSTRATED BY
AARON BAGLEY

DEC 2023

Simon & Schuster Books for Young Readers

NEW YORK LONDON TORONTO SYDNEY NEW DELHI

SIMON & SCHUSTER BOOKS FOR YOUNG READERS
An imprint of Simon & Schuster Children's Publishing Division
1230 Avenue of the Americas, New York, New York 10020

Text © 2023 by Jessixa Bagley
Illustration © 2023 by Aaron Bagley
Book design by Aaron Bagley, Tom Daly,
and Chloë Foglia © 2023 by Simon & Schuster, Inc.
Coloring by Guy Major

SIMON & SCHUSTER BOOKS FOR YOUNG READERS
and related marks are trademarks of Simon & Schuster, Inc.
For information about special discounts for bulk purchases, please contact Simon & Schuster Special Sales at 1-866-506-1949 or business@simonandschuster.com.
The Simon & Schuster Speakers Bureau can bring authors to your live event. For more information or to book an event, contact the Simon & Schuster Speakers Bureau at 1-866-248-3049 or visit our website at www.simonspeakers.com.
The text for this book was set in hand-lettered fonts created with Aaron's letters, and Archer.
The illustrations for this book were rendered in ink and digitally colored.
Manufactured in China
0723 SCP
First Edition
2 4 6 8 10 9 7 5 3 1
CIP data for this book is available from the Library of Congress.
ISBN 9781534496545 (paperback)
ISBN 9781534496552 (hardcover)
ISBN 9781534496569 (ebook)

For SiSi—J. B.

For Eddie—A. B.

Chapter 1

Right-of-Way

There are three weapons in the combat sport of fencing: foil, épée, and sabre. All three have different rules that set them apart from one another.

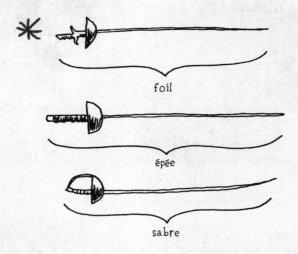

foil

épée

sabre

As you begin your foil training, you must first learn right-of-way. Right-of-way refers to the first person to establish a valid threat to their opponent's target area. Whoever has right-of-way gets awarded the point, and the first fencer to gain fifteen points wins the bout. Establishing right-of-way can be complicated. You might think that your opponent has priority because they are attacking you. But in the blink of an eye you can make a move and suddenly gain the upper hand.

I CAN'T BELIEVE I HAVE TO TAKE THE BUS ON MY FIRST DAY OF MIDDLE SCHOOL.

BUTLER MIDDLE SCHOOL

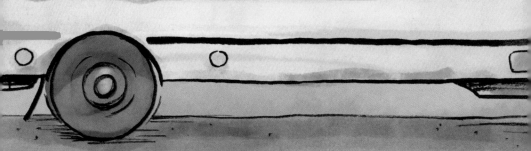

I WISH MOM COULD HAVE DRIVEN ME. PEOPLE ARE GOING TO THINK I'M SUCH A BABY.

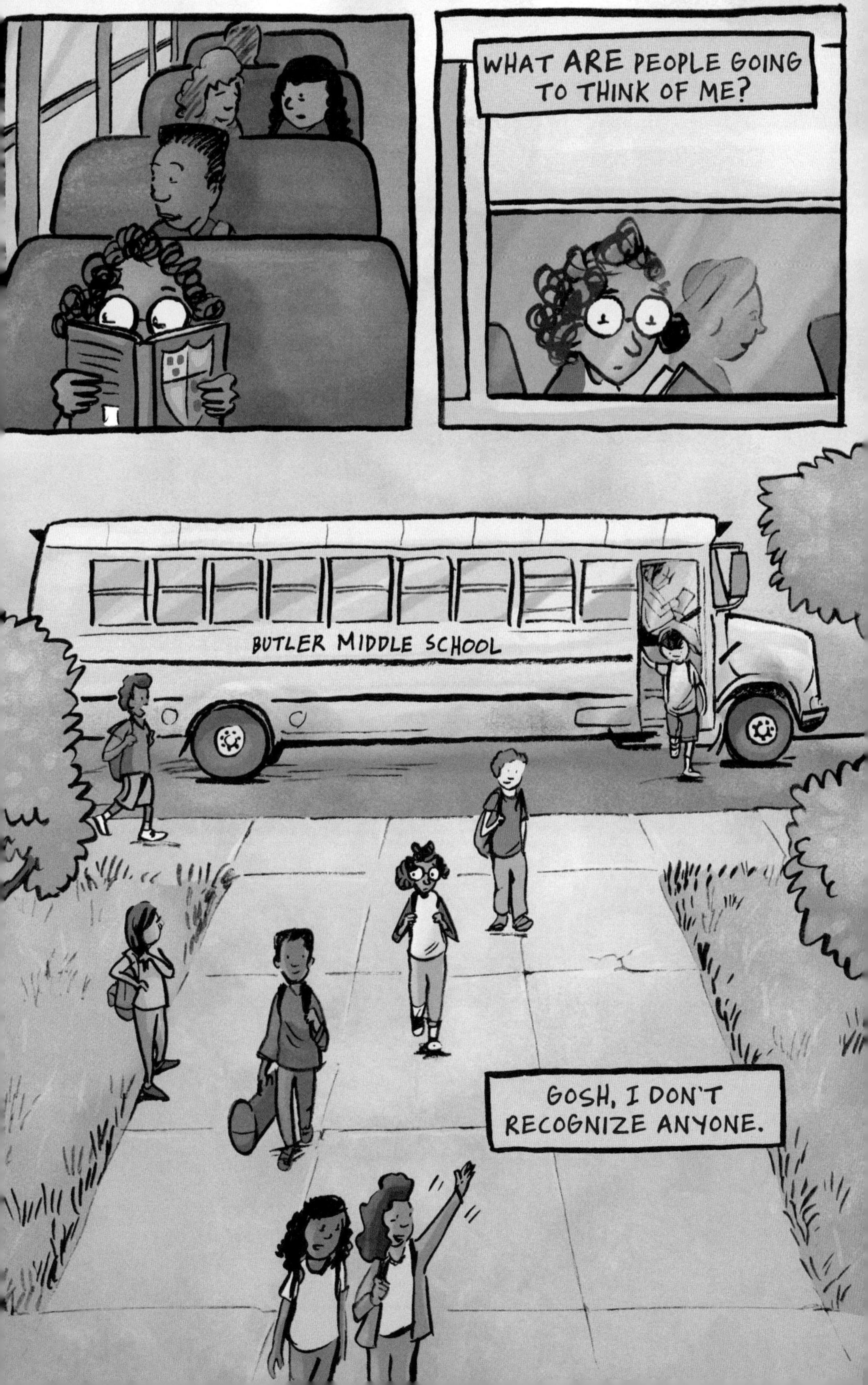
WHAT ARE PEOPLE GOING TO THINK OF ME?
BUTLER MIDDLE SCHOOL
GOSH, I DON'T RECOGNIZE ANYONE.

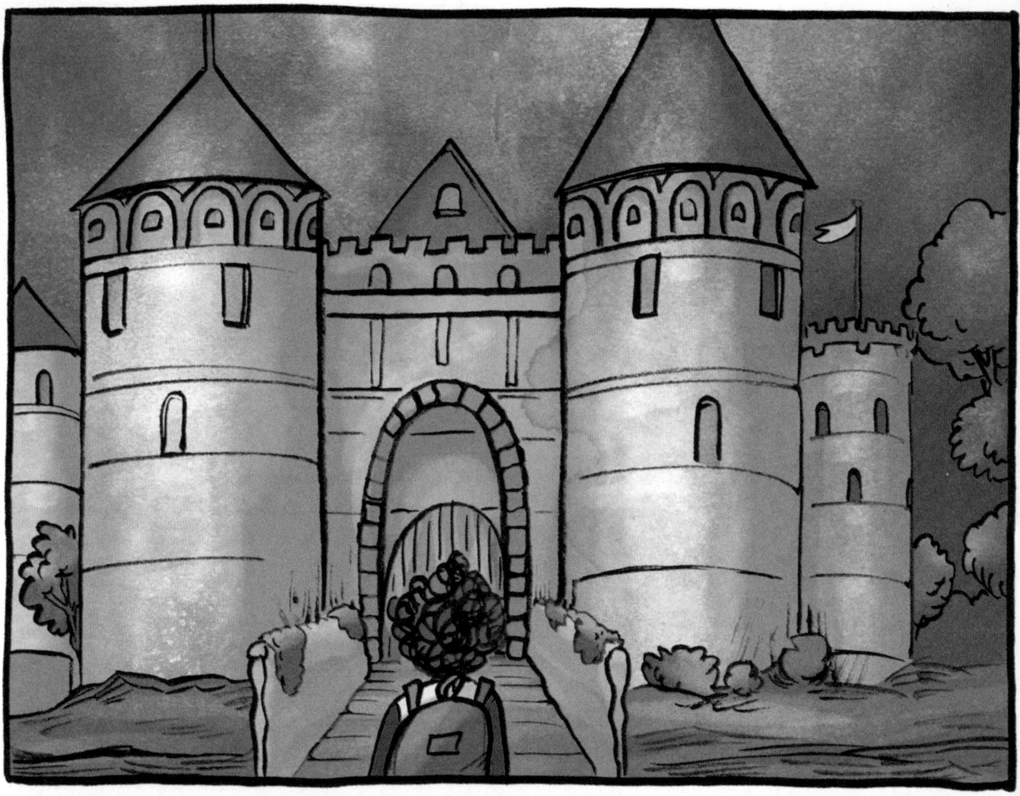

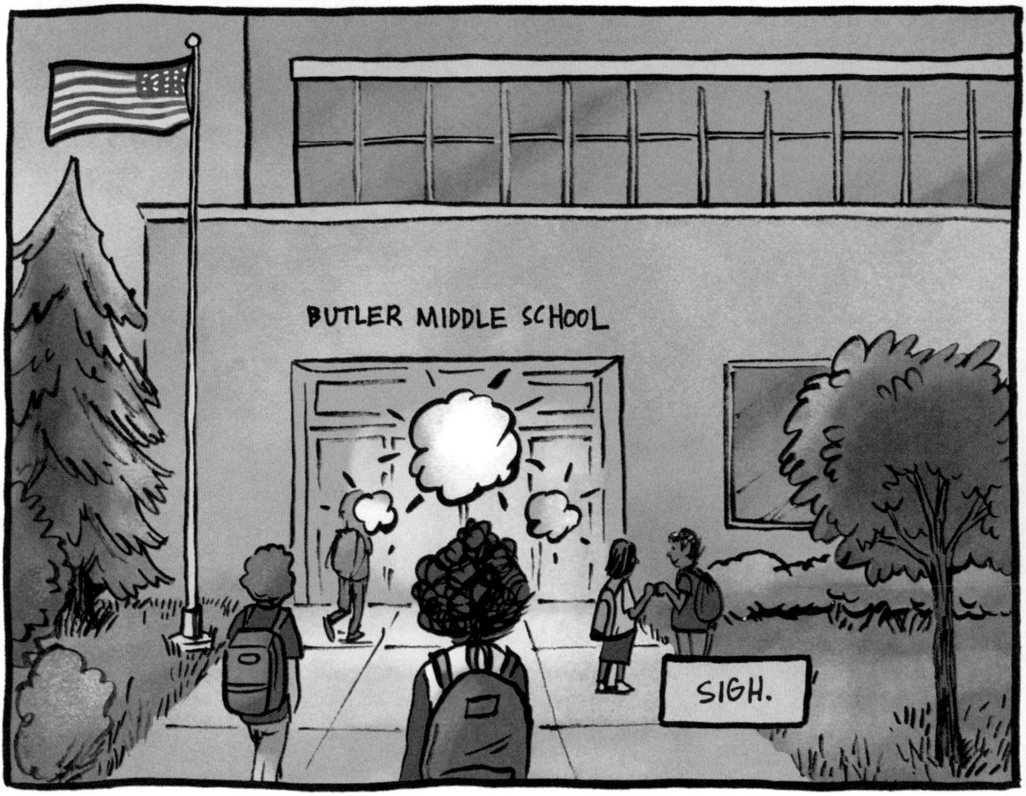
BUTLER MIDDLE SCHOOL
SIGH.

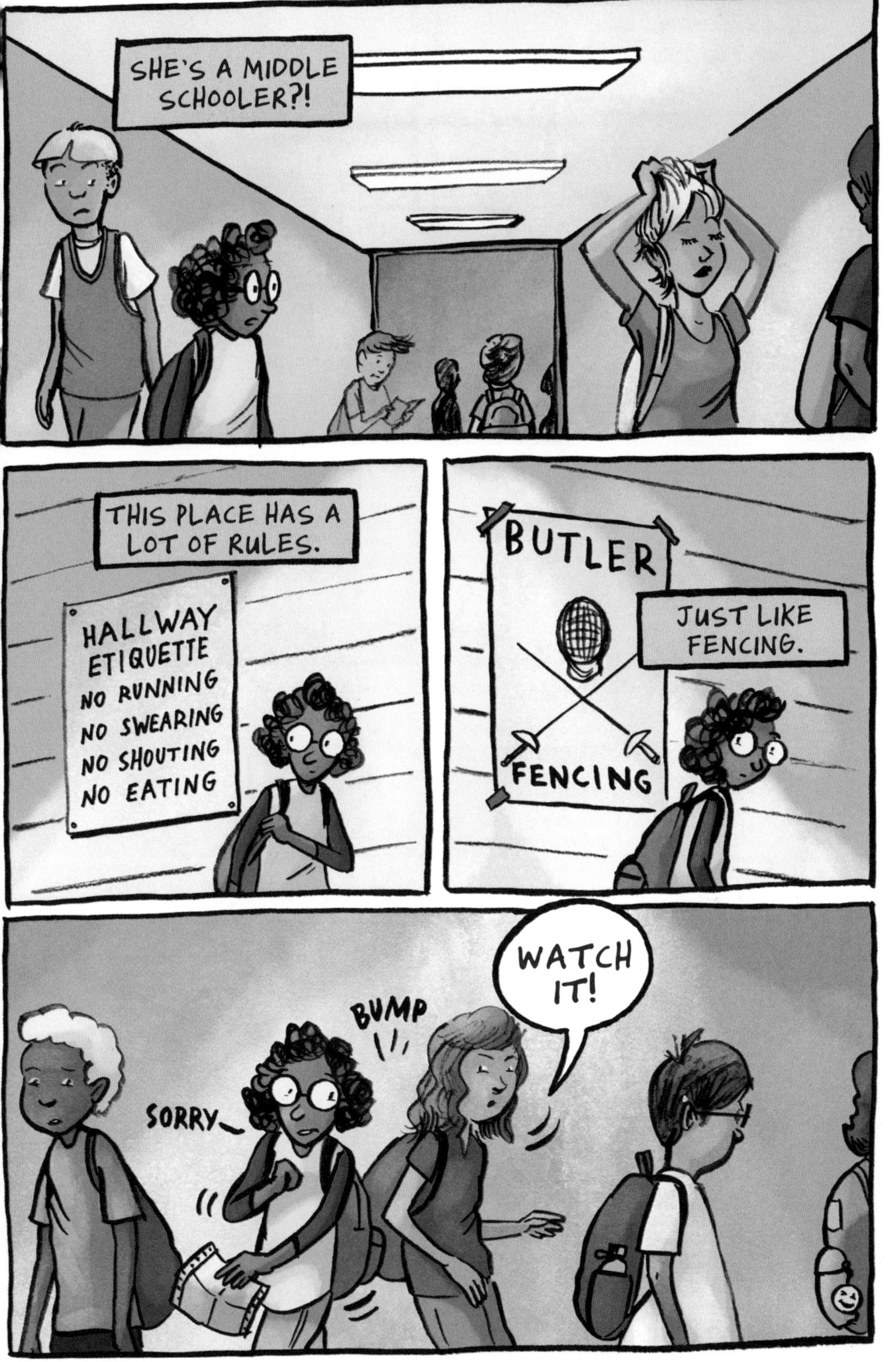
SHE'S A MIDDLE SCHOOLER?!
THIS PLACE HAS A LOT OF RULES.
HALLWAY ETIQUETTE
NO RUNNING
NO SWEARING
NO SHOUTING
NO EATING
BUTLER
FENCING
JUST LIKE FENCING.
BUMP
SORRY
WATCH IT!

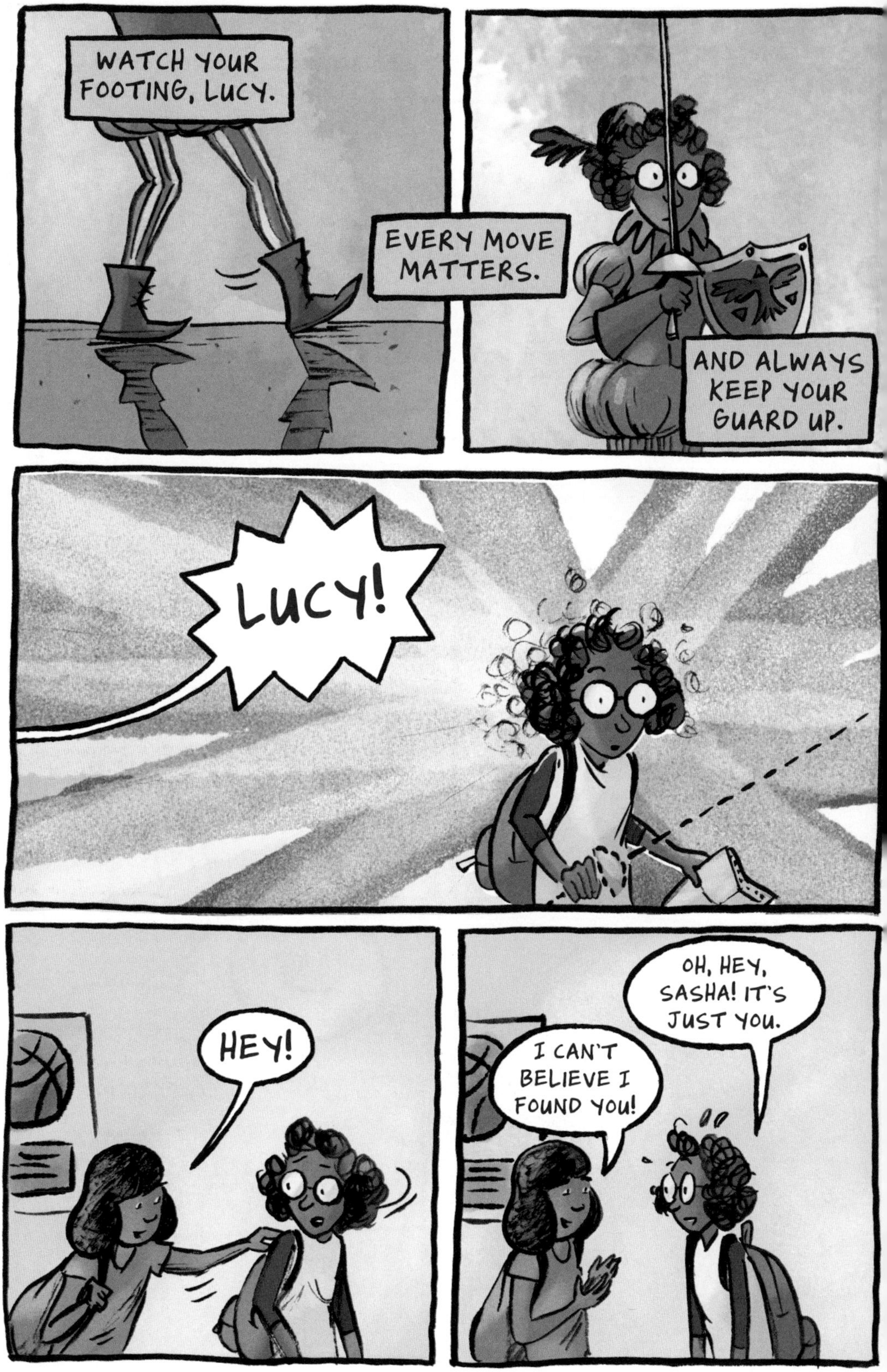
WATCH YOUR FOOTING, LUCY.
EVERY MOVE MATTERS.
AND ALWAYS KEEP YOUR GUARD UP.
LUCY!
HEY!
OH, HEY, SASHA! IT'S JUST YOU.
I CAN'T BELIEVE I FOUND YOU!

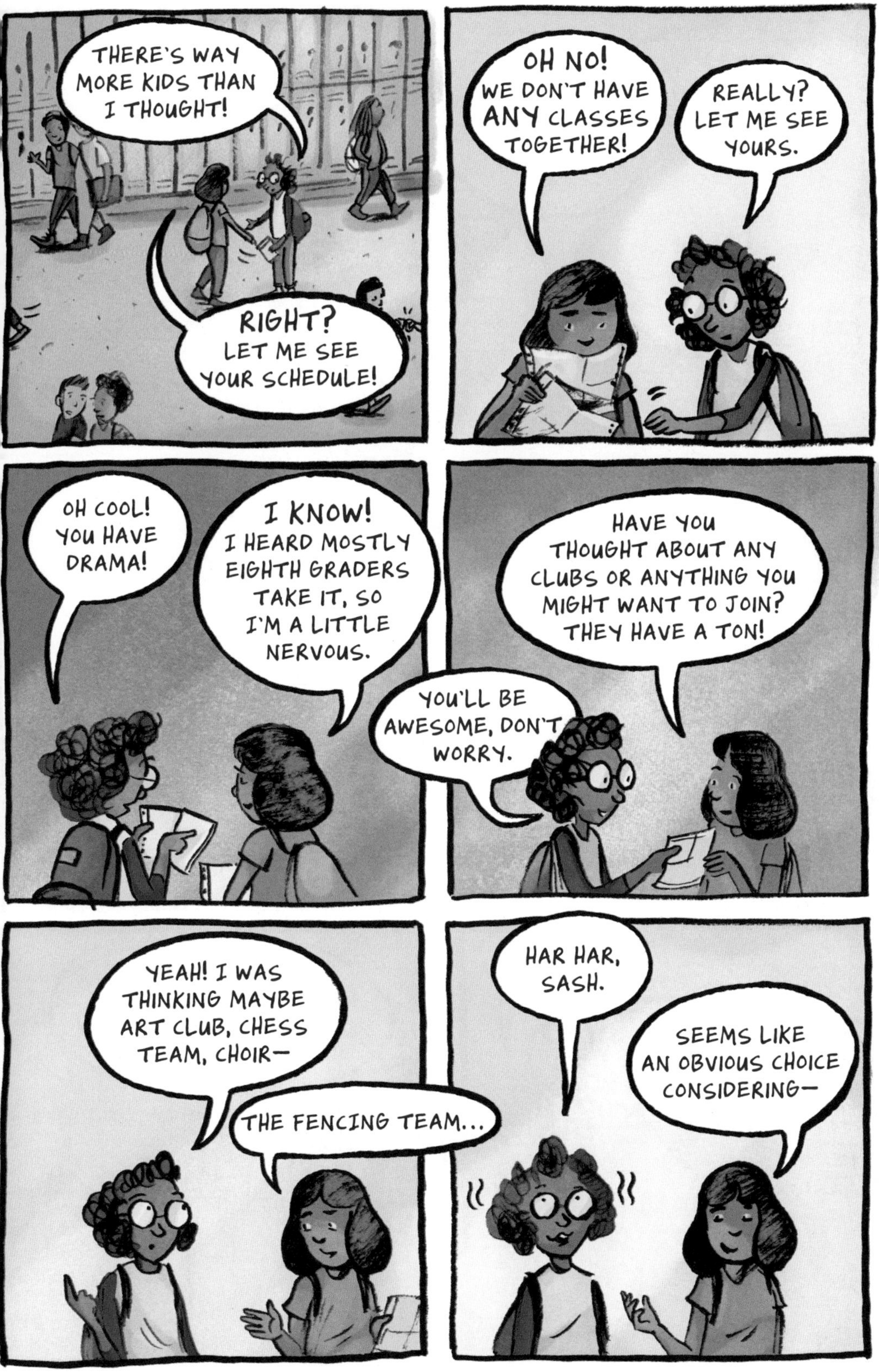
THERE'S WAY MORE KIDS THAN I THOUGHT!
RIGHT? LET ME SEE YOUR SCHEDULE!
OH NO! WE DON'T HAVE ANY CLASSES TOGETHER!
REALLY? LET ME SEE YOURS.
OH COOL! YOU HAVE DRAMA!
I KNOW! I HEARD MOSTLY EIGHTH GRADERS TAKE IT, SO I'M A LITTLE NERVOUS.
YOU'LL BE AWESOME, DON'T WORRY.
HAVE YOU THOUGHT ABOUT ANY CLUBS OR ANYTHING YOU MIGHT WANT TO JOIN? THEY HAVE A TON!
YEAH! I WAS THINKING MAYBE ART CLUB, CHESS TEAM, CHOIR—
THE FENCING TEAM...
HAR HAR, SASH.
SEEMS LIKE AN OBVIOUS CHOICE CONSIDERING—

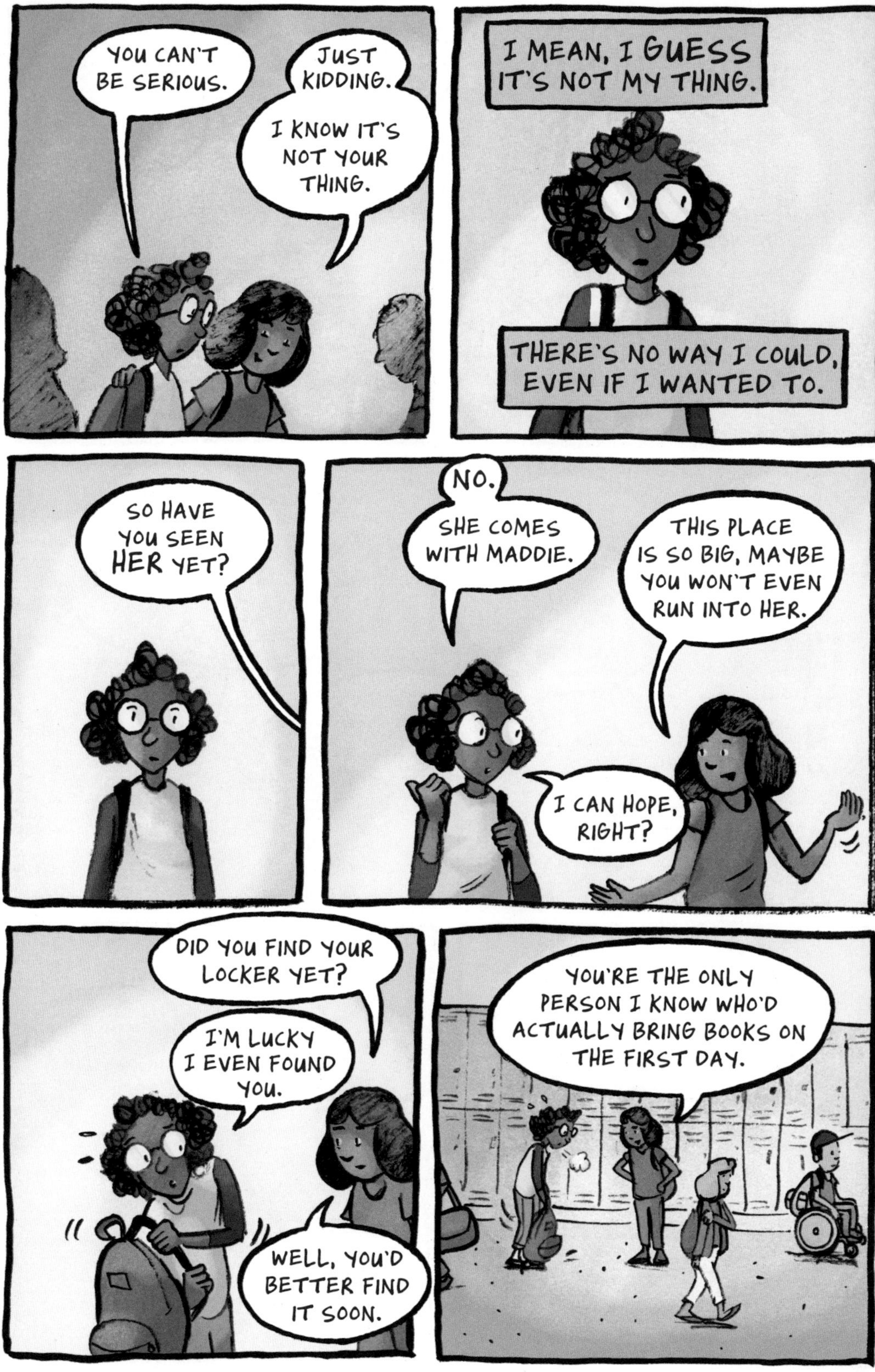
YOU CAN'T BE SERIOUS.
JUST KIDDING.
I KNOW IT'S NOT YOUR THING.
I MEAN, I GUESS IT'S NOT MY THING.
THERE'S NO WAY I COULD, EVEN IF I WANTED TO.
SO HAVE YOU SEEN HER YET?
NO.
SHE COMES WITH MADDIE.
THIS PLACE IS SO BIG, MAYBE YOU WON'T EVEN RUN INTO HER.
I CAN HOPE, RIGHT?
DID YOU FIND YOUR LOCKER YET?
I'M LUCKY I EVEN FOUND YOU.
WELL, YOU'D BETTER FIND IT SOON.
YOU'RE THE ONLY PERSON I KNOW WHO'D ACTUALLY BRING BOOKS ON THE FIRST DAY.

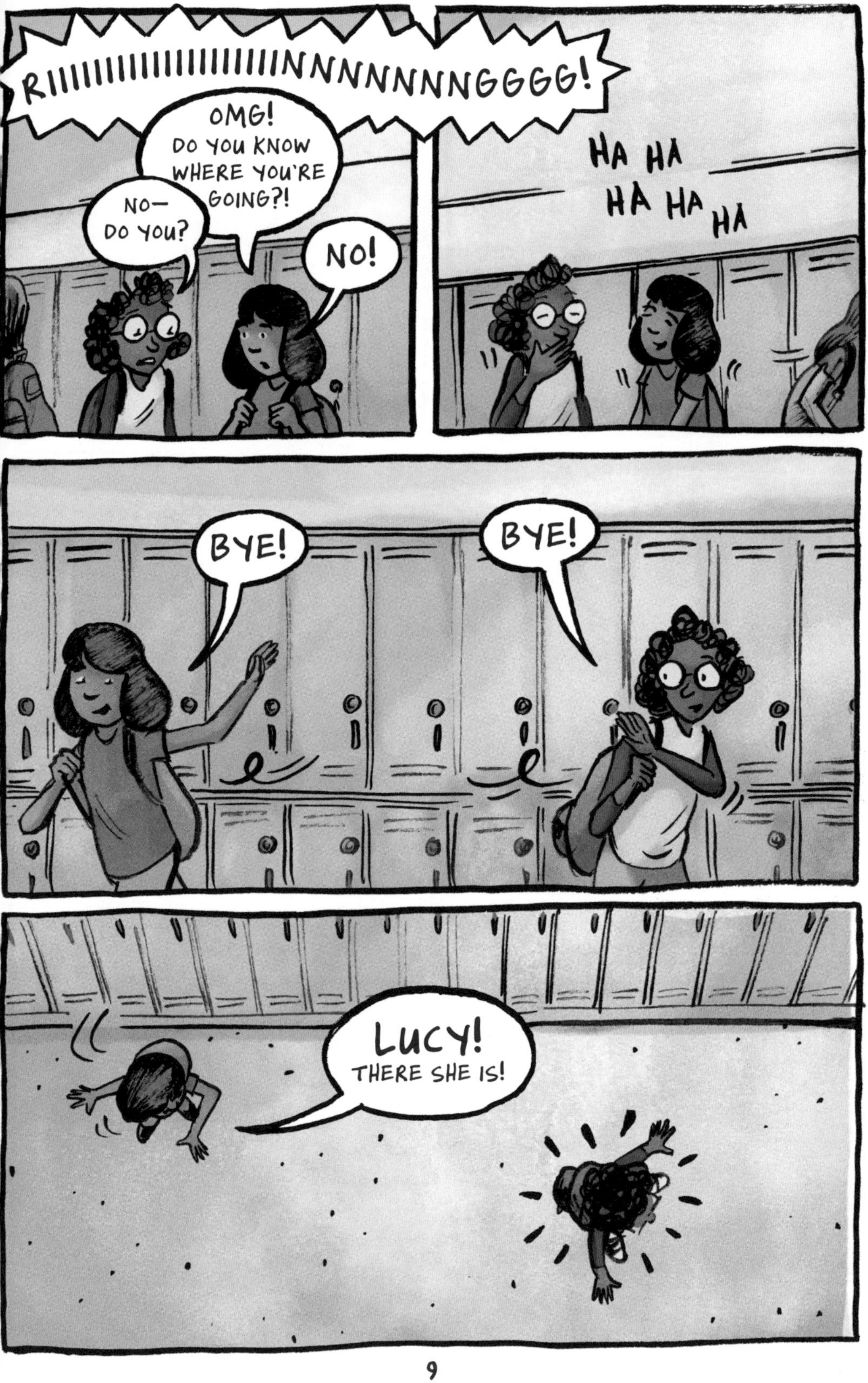
RIIIIIIIIIIIIIIIIIIIIIIINNNNNNNNNNGGGG!
OMG! DO YOU KNOW WHERE YOU'RE GOING?!
NO— DO YOU?
NO!
HA HA HA HA HA
BYE!
BYE!
LUCY! THERE SHE IS!

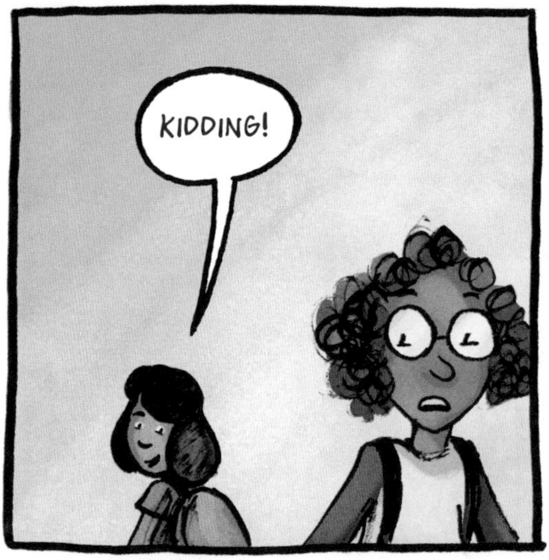
KIDDING!

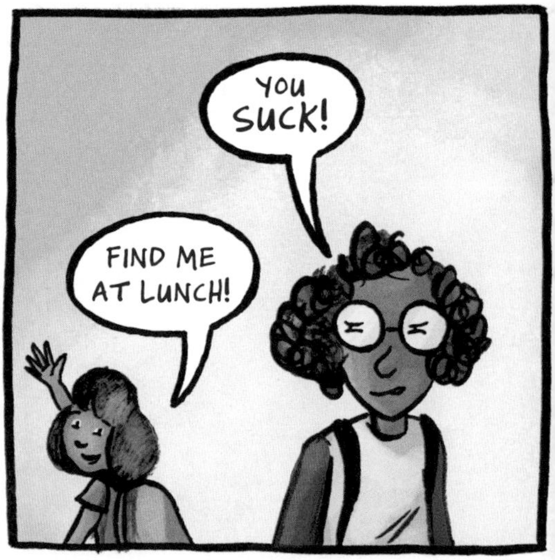
YOU SUCK!
FIND ME AT LUNCH!

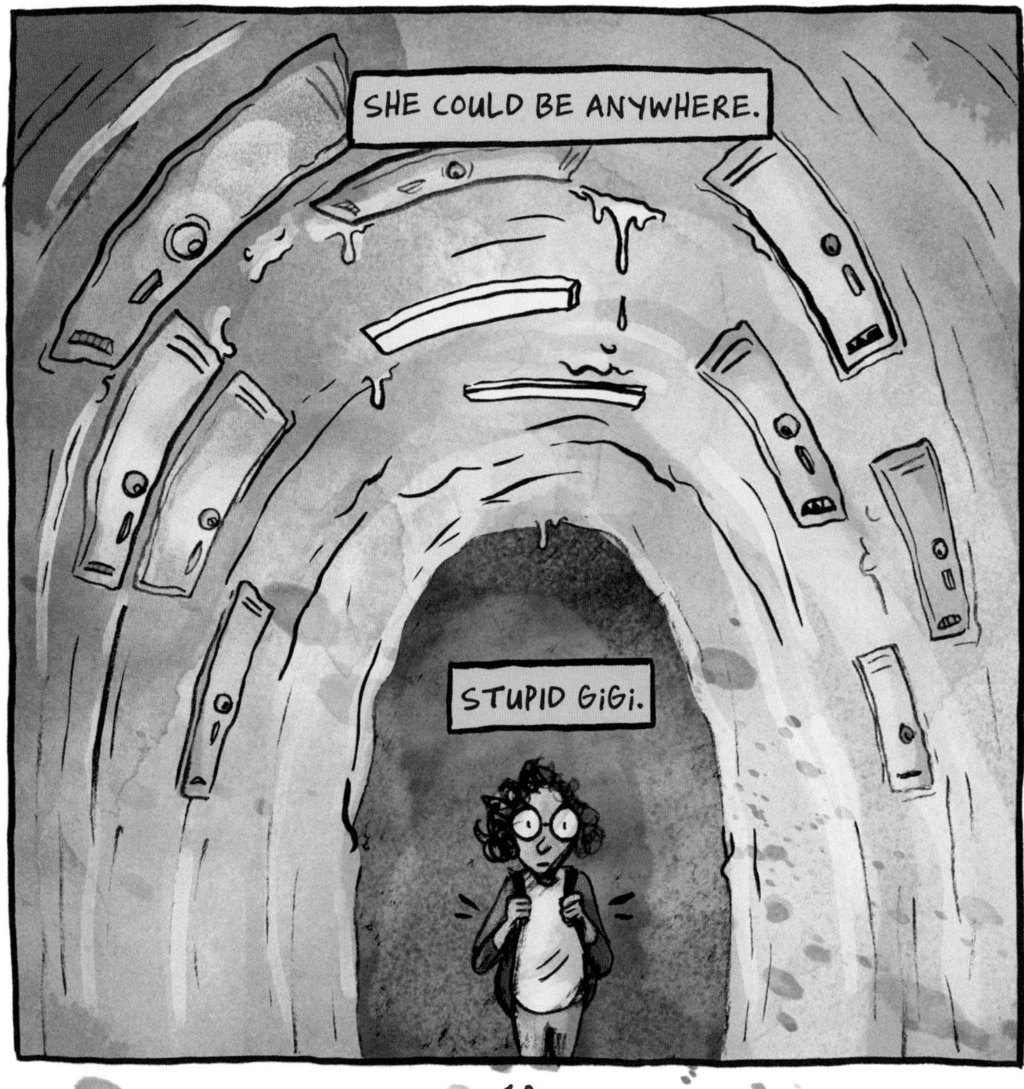
SHE COULD BE ANYWHERE.
STUPID GiGi.

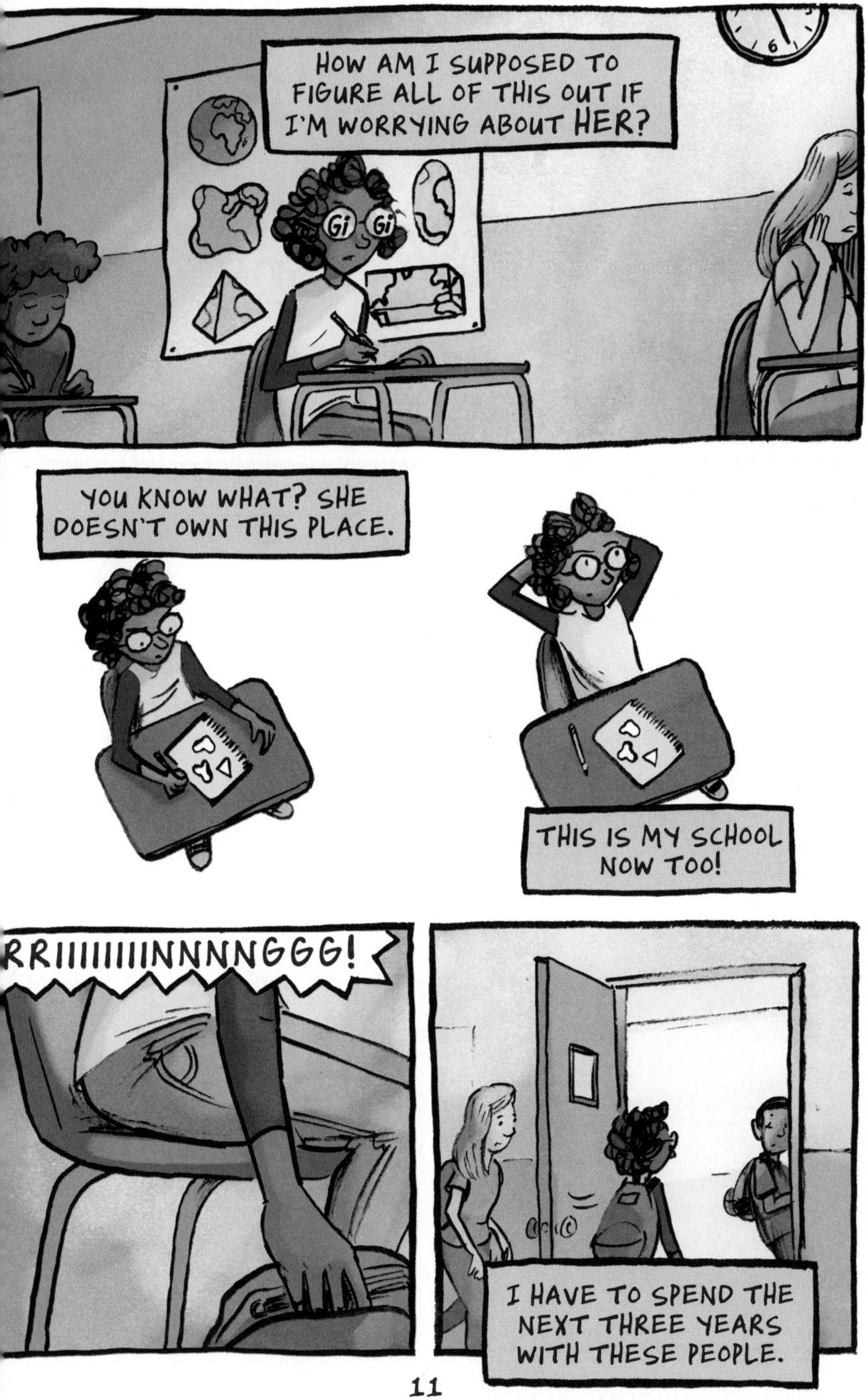
HOW AM I SUPPOSED TO FIGURE ALL OF THIS OUT IF I'M WORRYING ABOUT HER?
Gi Gi
YOU KNOW WHAT? SHE DOESN'T OWN THIS PLACE.
THIS IS MY SCHOOL NOW TOO!
RRIIIIIIIINNNNGGG!
I HAVE TO SPEND THE NEXT THREE YEARS WITH THESE PEOPLE.

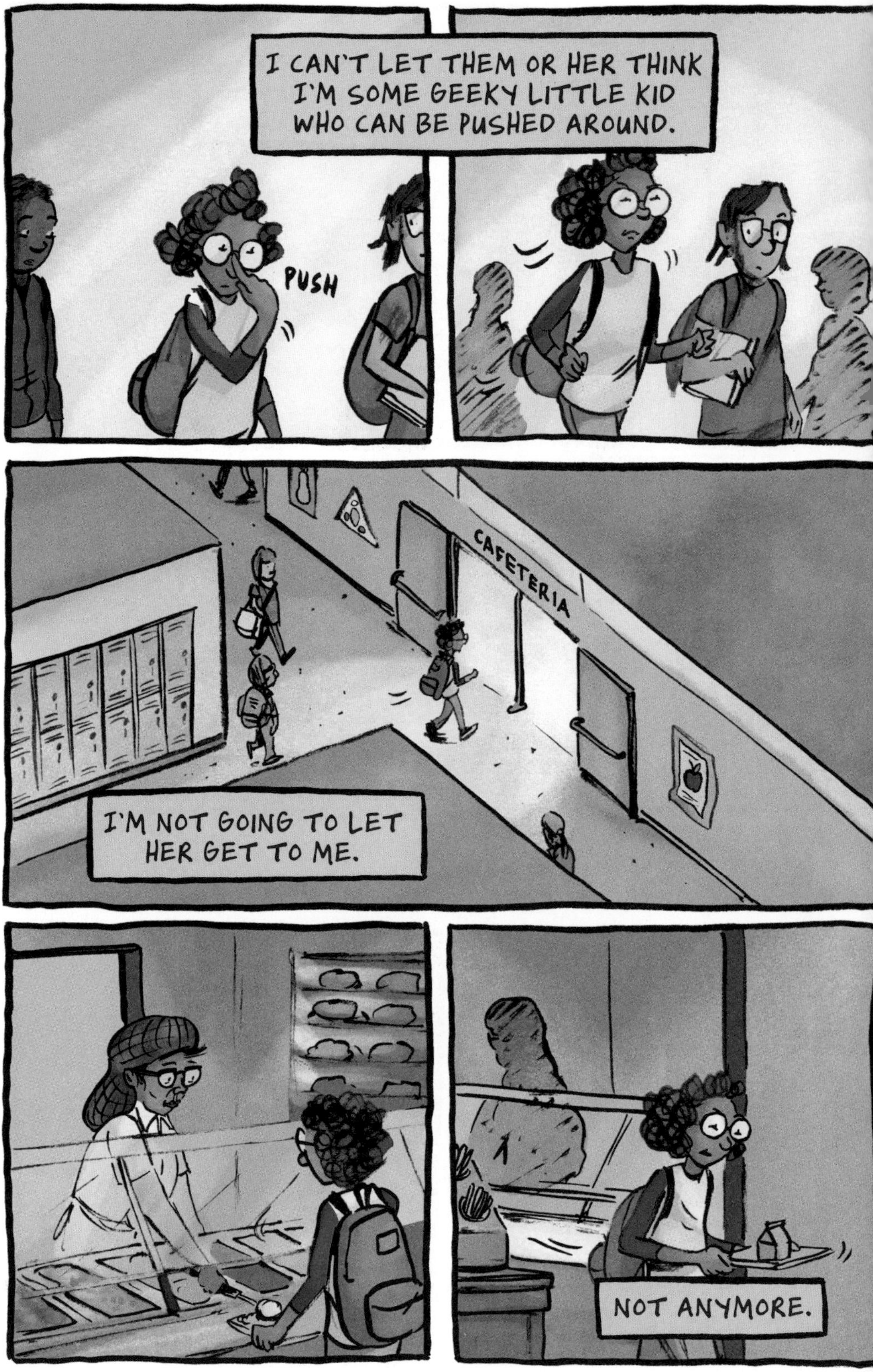
I CAN'T LET THEM OR HER THINK I'M SOME GEEKY LITTLE KID WHO CAN BE PUSHED AROUND.
PUSH
CAFETERIA
I'M NOT GOING TO LET HER GET TO ME.
NOT ANYMORE.

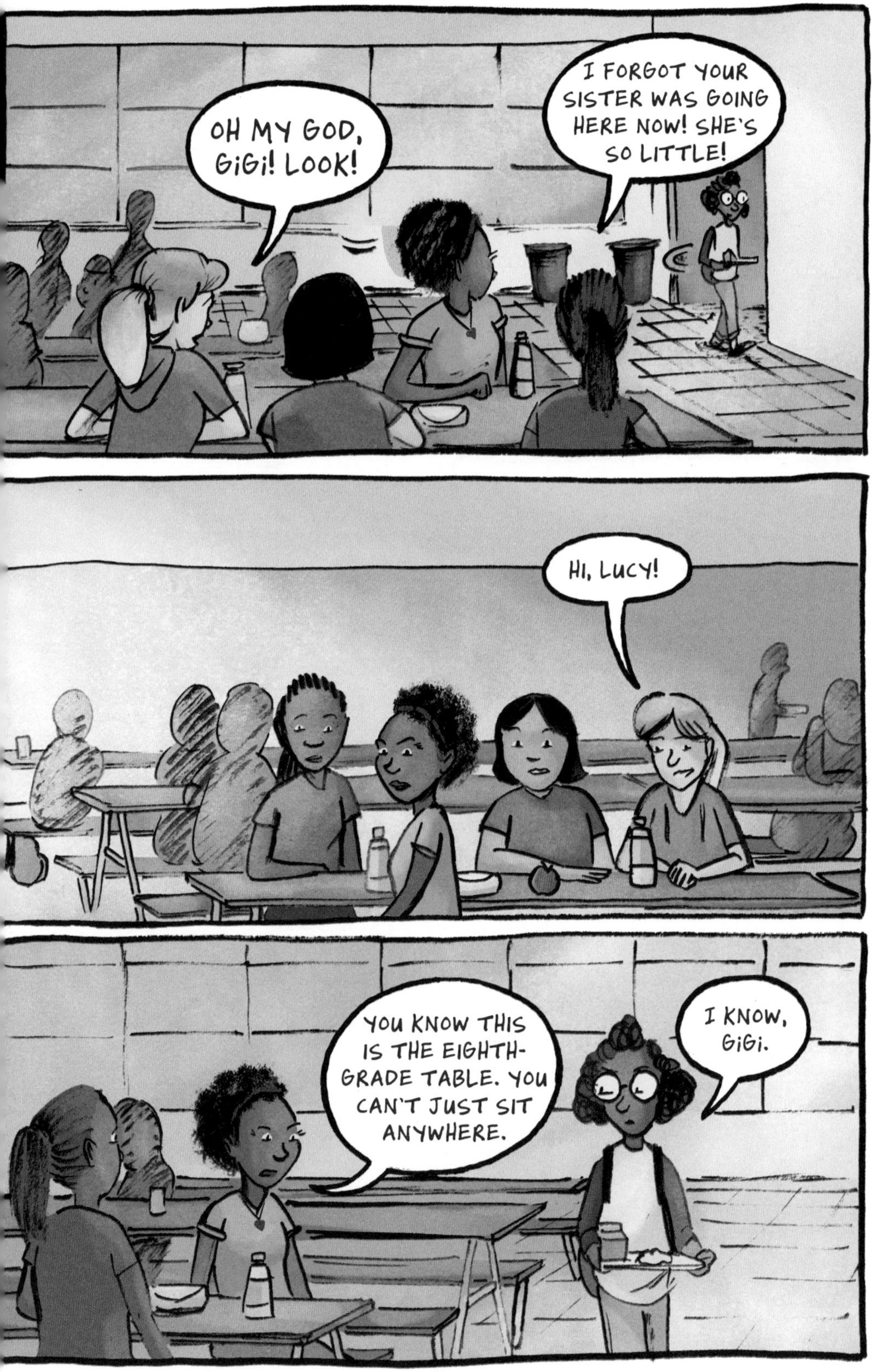
OH MY GOD, GiGi! LOOK!
I FORGOT YOUR SISTER WAS GOING HERE NOW! SHE'S SO LITTLE!
HI, LUCY!
YOU KNOW THIS IS THE EIGHTH-GRADE TABLE. YOU CAN'T JUST SIT ANYWHERE.
I KNOW, GiGi.

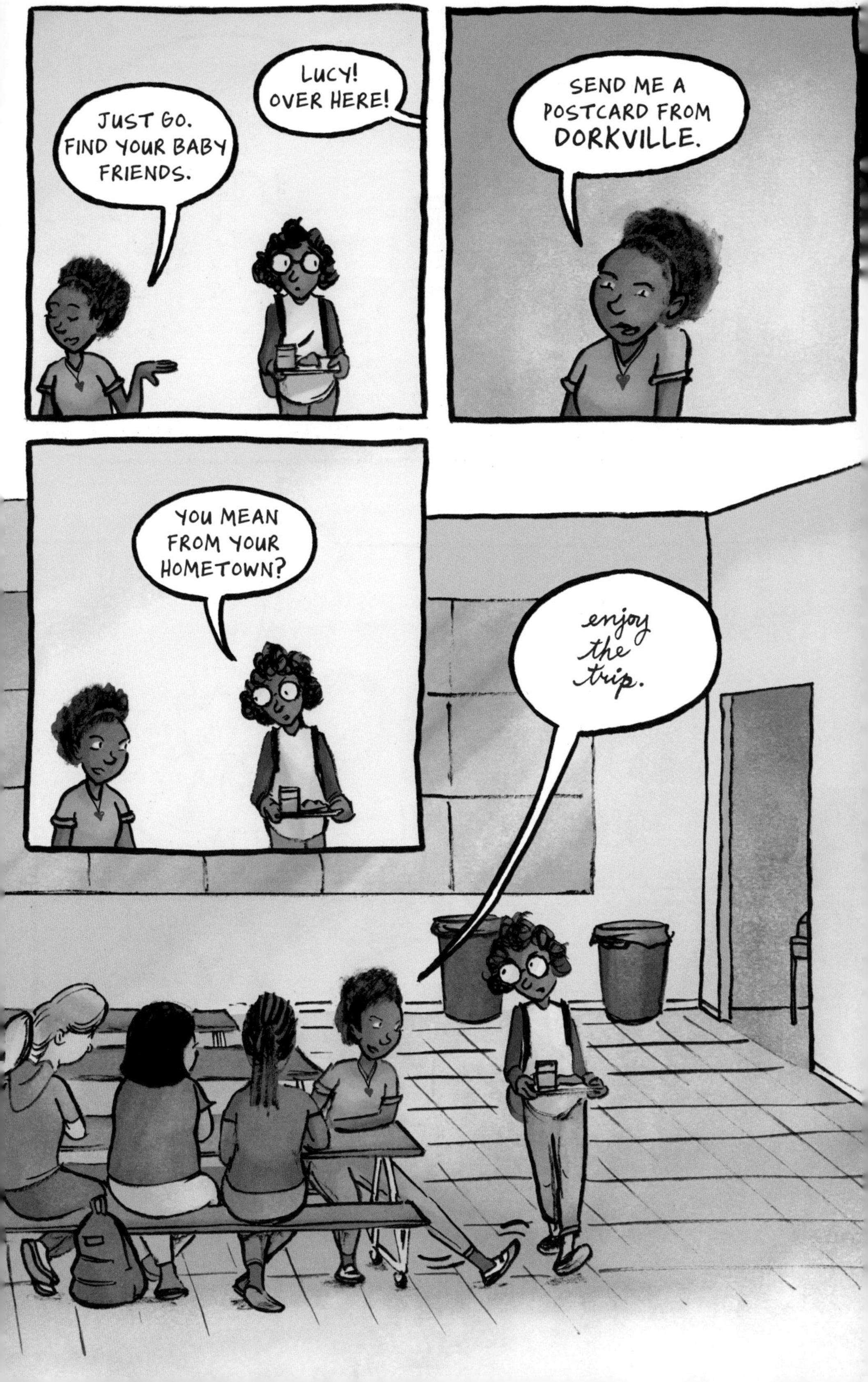
JUST GO. FIND YOUR BABY FRIENDS.
LUCY! OVER HERE!
SEND ME A POSTCARD FROM DORKVILLE.
YOU MEAN FROM YOUR HOMETOWN?
enjoy the trip.

trip

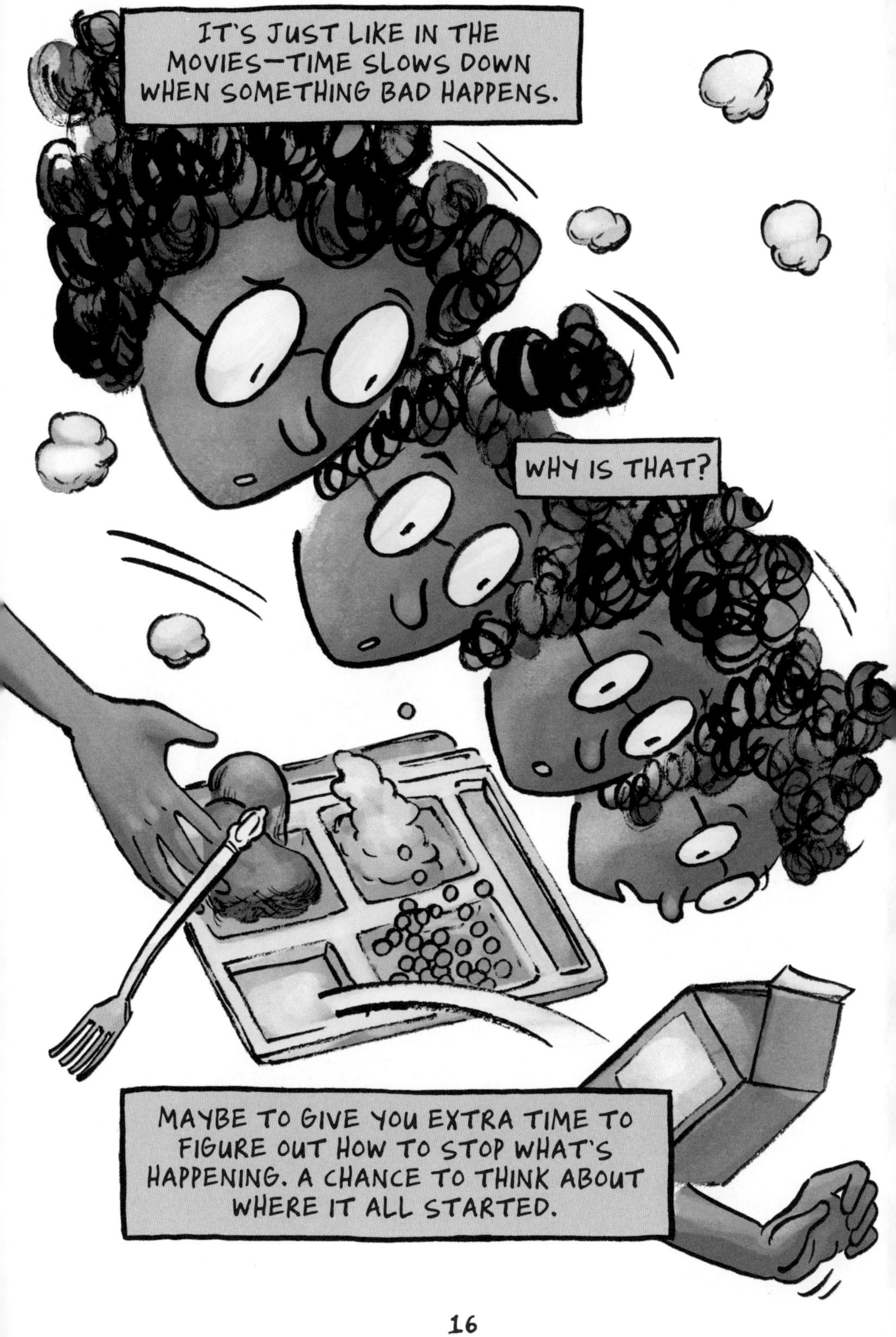
IT'S JUST LIKE IN THE MOVIES—TIME SLOWS DOWN WHEN SOMETHING BAD HAPPENS.
WHY IS THAT?
MAYBE TO GIVE YOU EXTRA TIME TO FIGURE OUT HOW TO STOP WHAT'S HAPPENING. A CHANCE TO THINK ABOUT WHERE IT ALL STARTED.

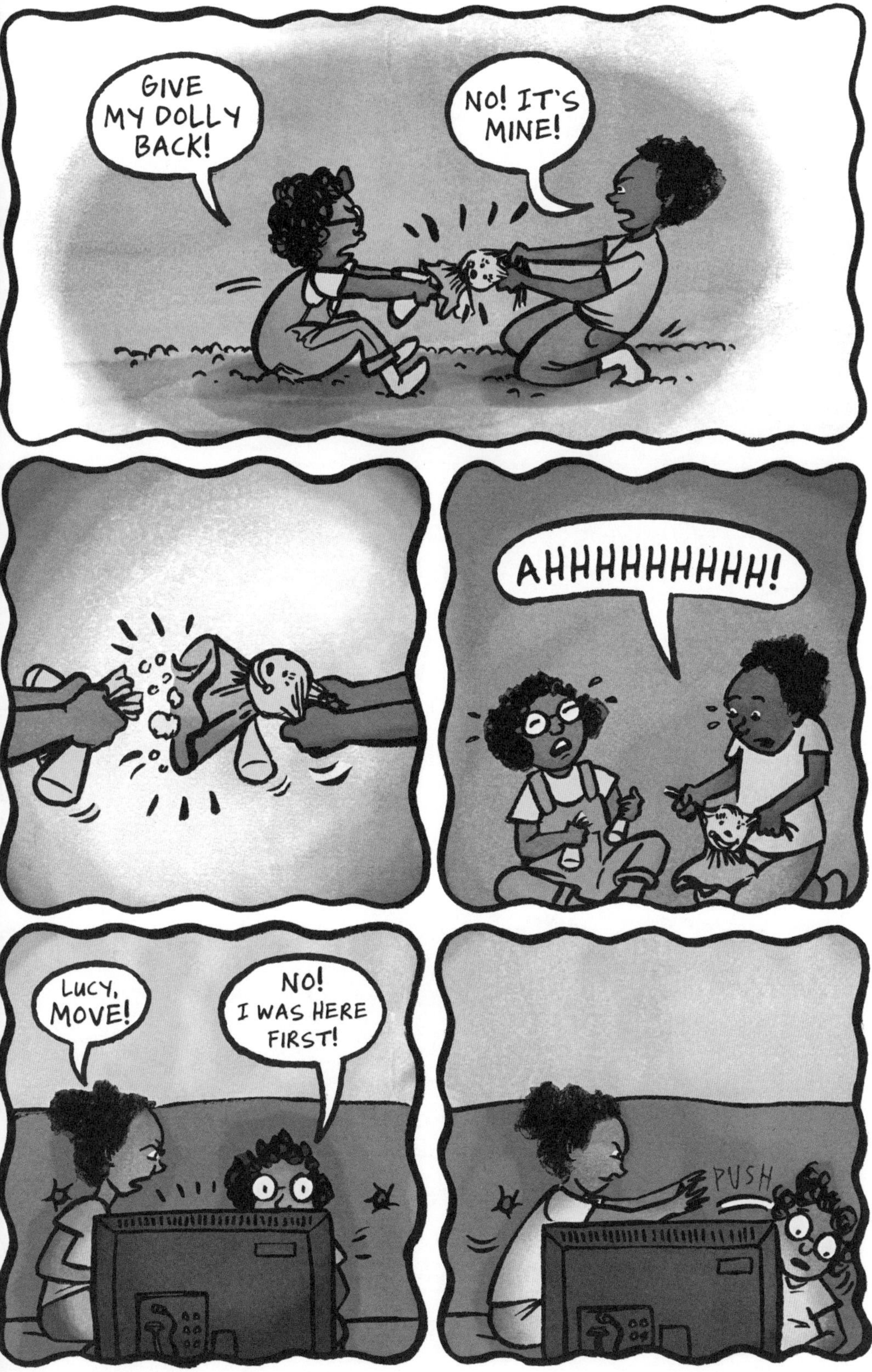
GIVE MY DOLLY BACK!
NO! IT'S MINE!
AHHHHHHHHHH!
LUCY, MOVE!
NO! I WAS HERE FIRST!
PUSH

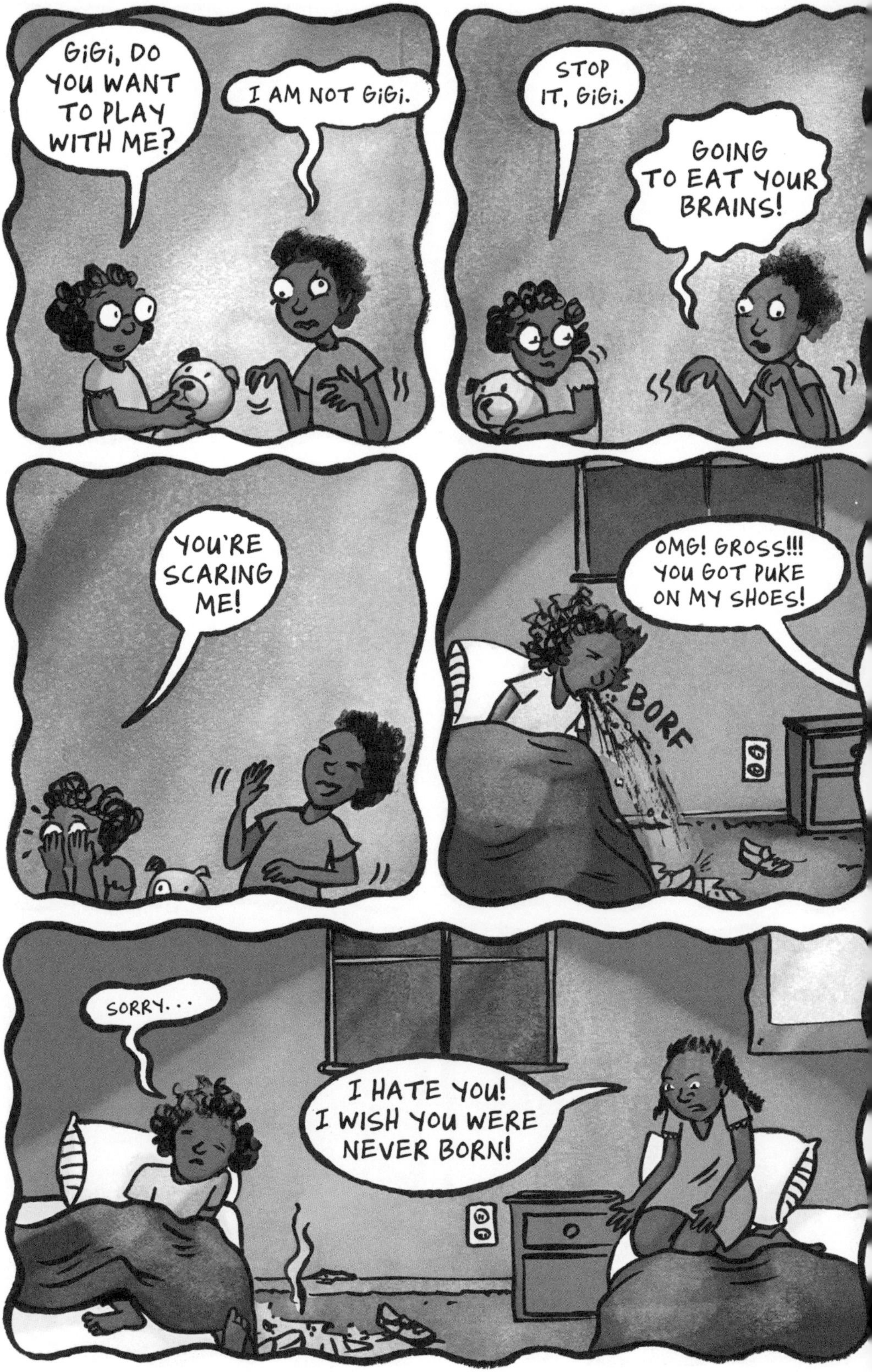
GIGI, DO YOU WANT TO PLAY WITH ME?
I AM NOT GIGI.
STOP IT, GIGI.
GOING TO EAT YOUR BRAINS!
YOU'RE SCARING ME!
OMG! GROSS!!! YOU GOT PUKE ON MY SHOES!
BORF
SORRY...
I HATE YOU! I WISH YOU WERE NEVER BORN!

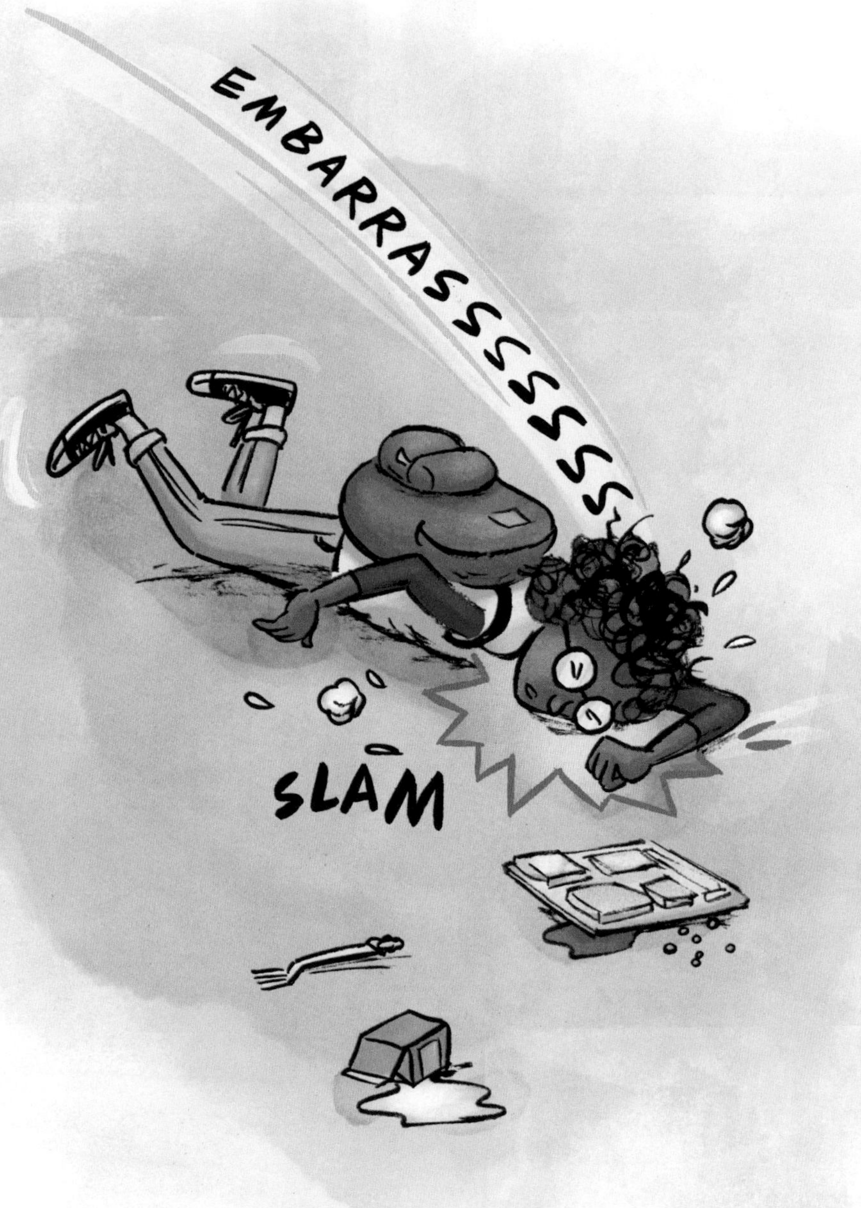
EMBARRASSSSSSS
SLAM

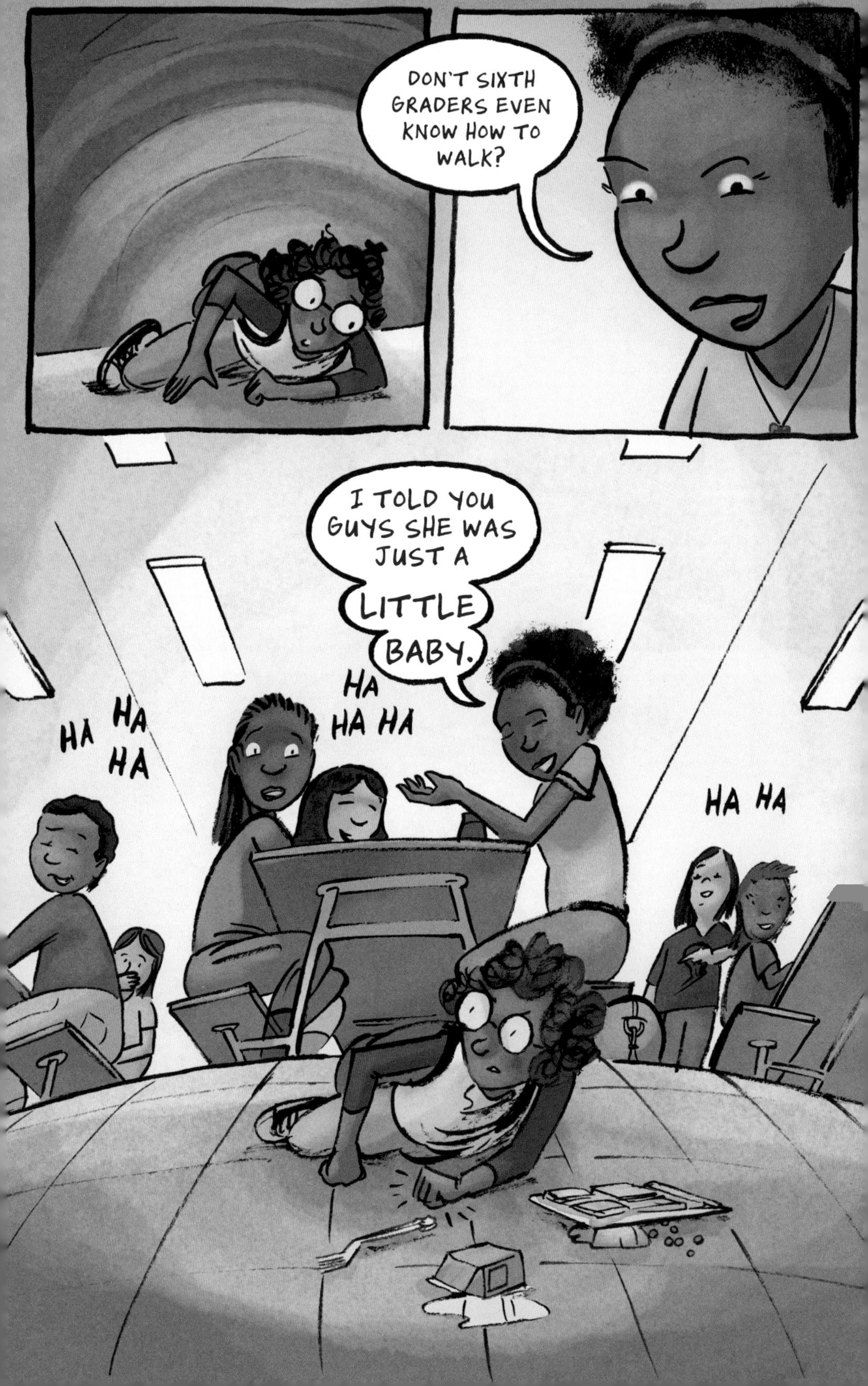
DON'T SIXTH GRADERS EVEN KNOW HOW TO WALK?
I TOLD YOU GUYS SHE WAS JUST A LITTLE BABY.
HA HA HA
HA HA HA
HA HA

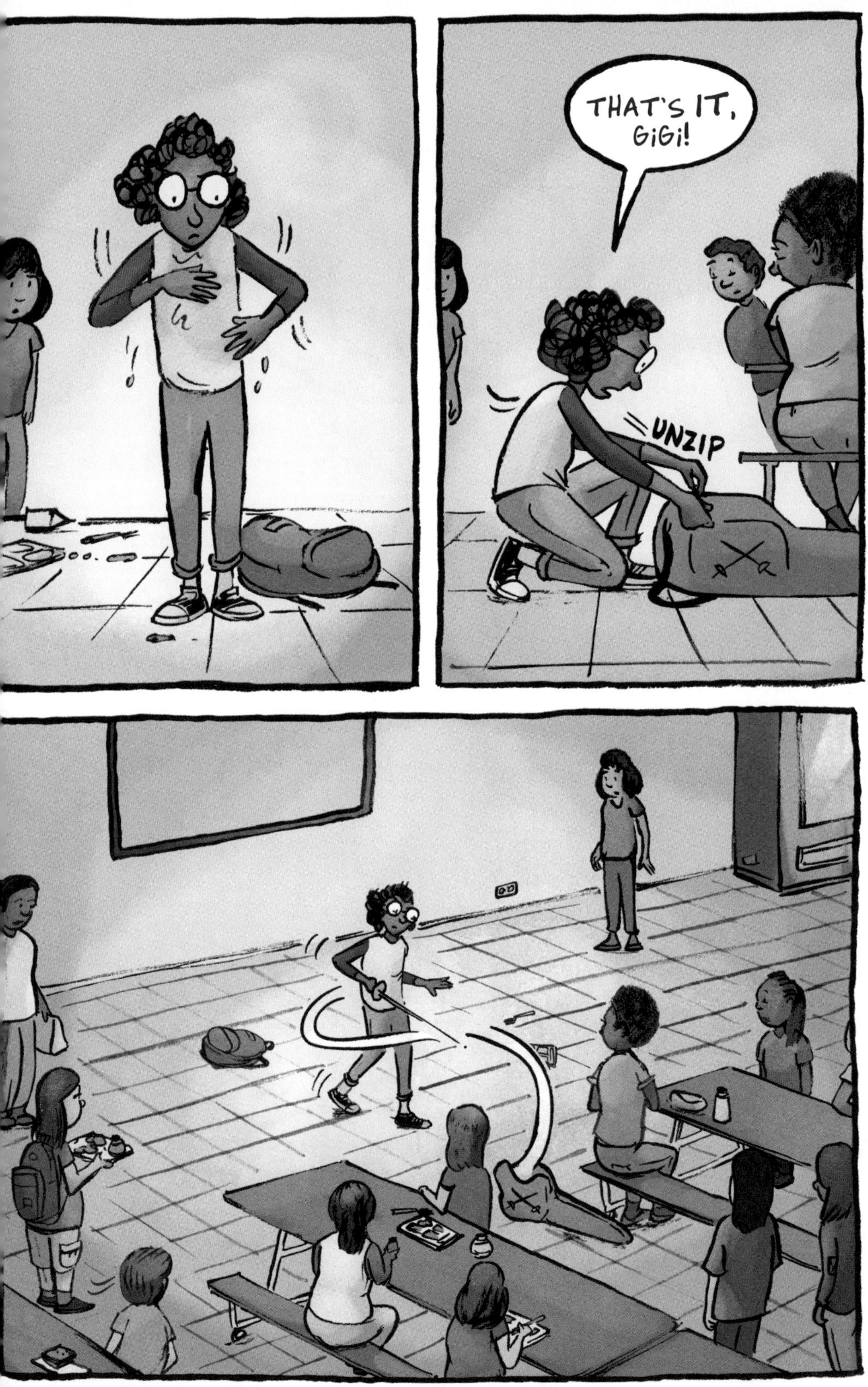
THAT'S IT, GiGi!
UNZIP

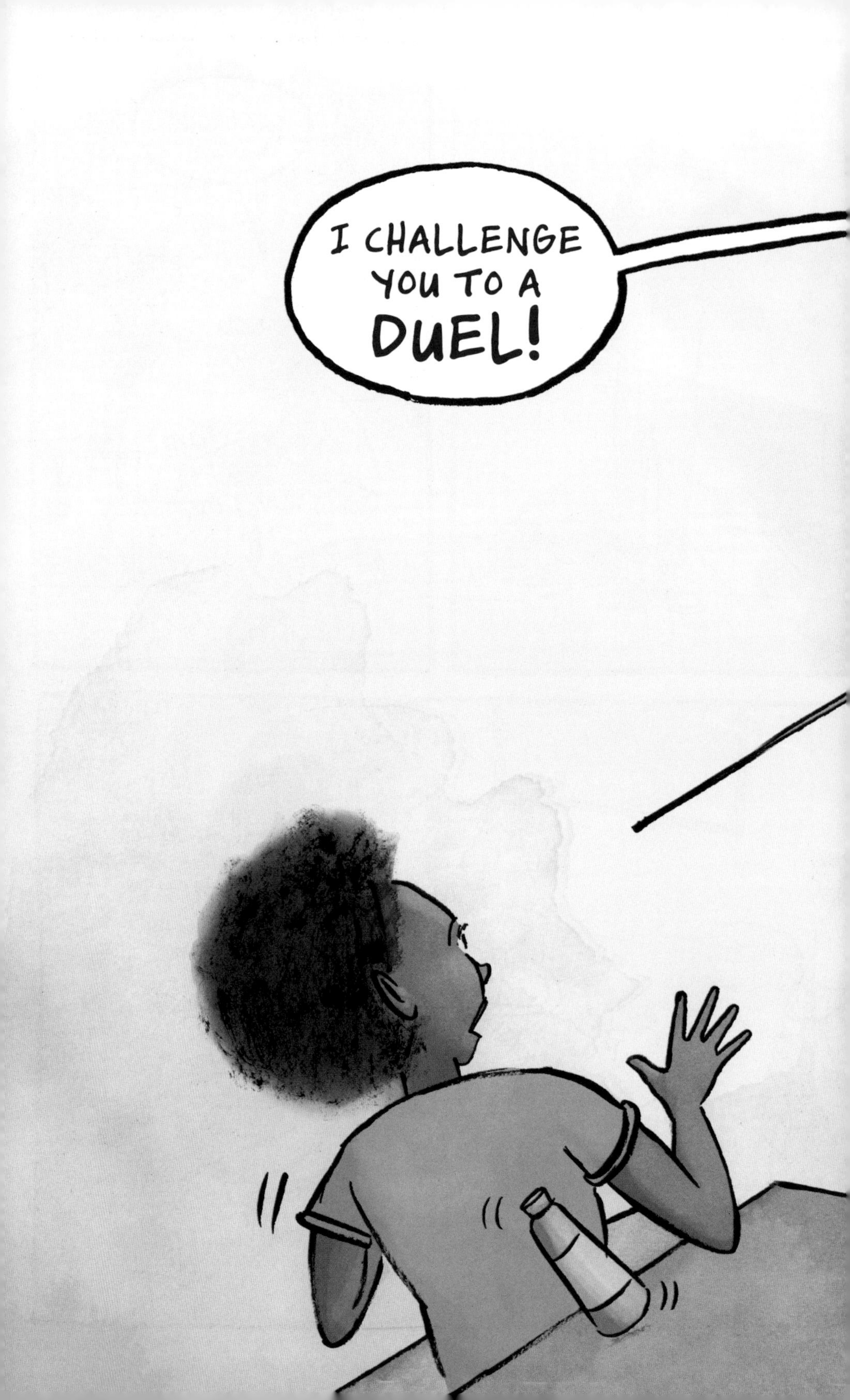
I CHALLENGE YOU TO A DUEL!

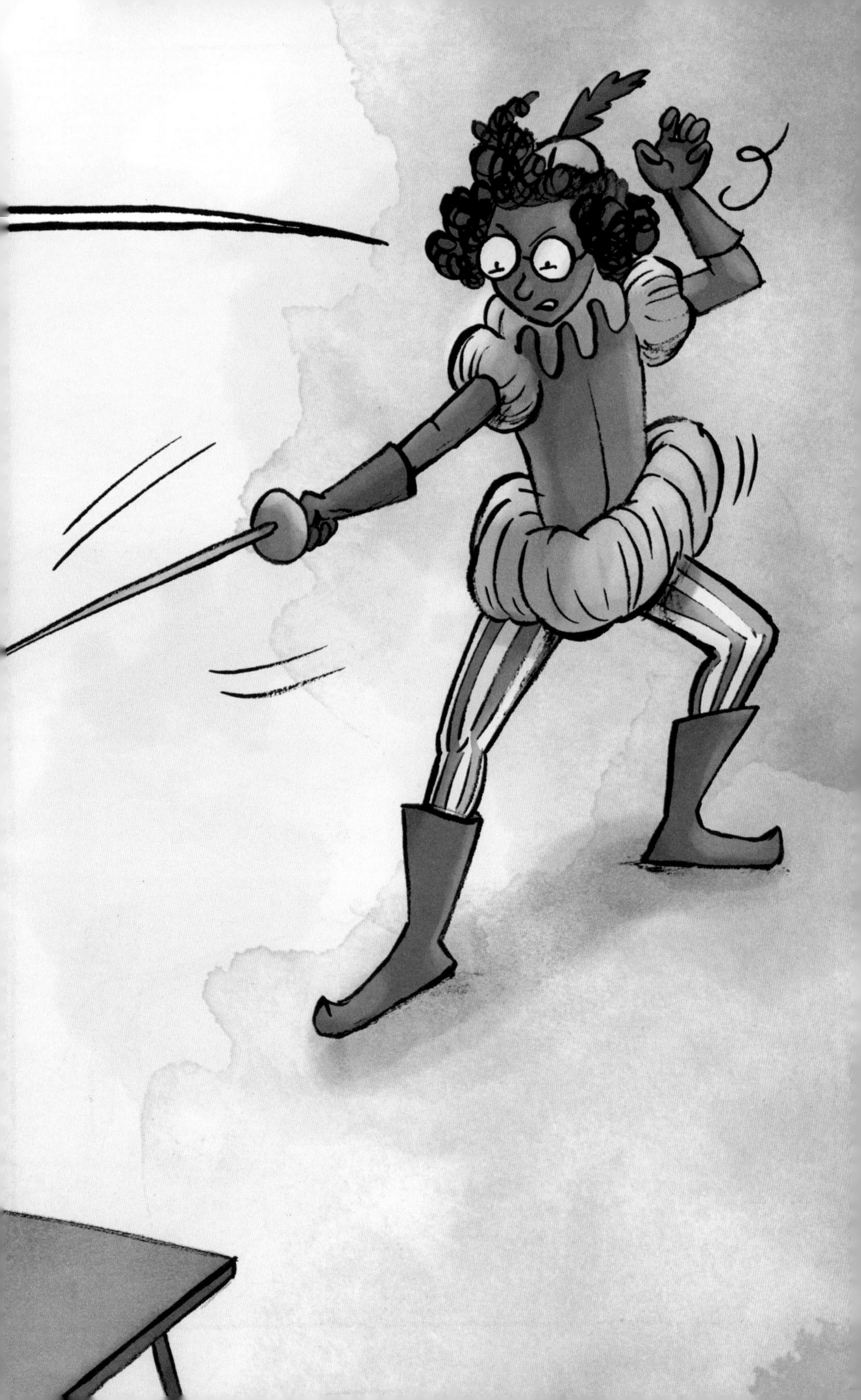

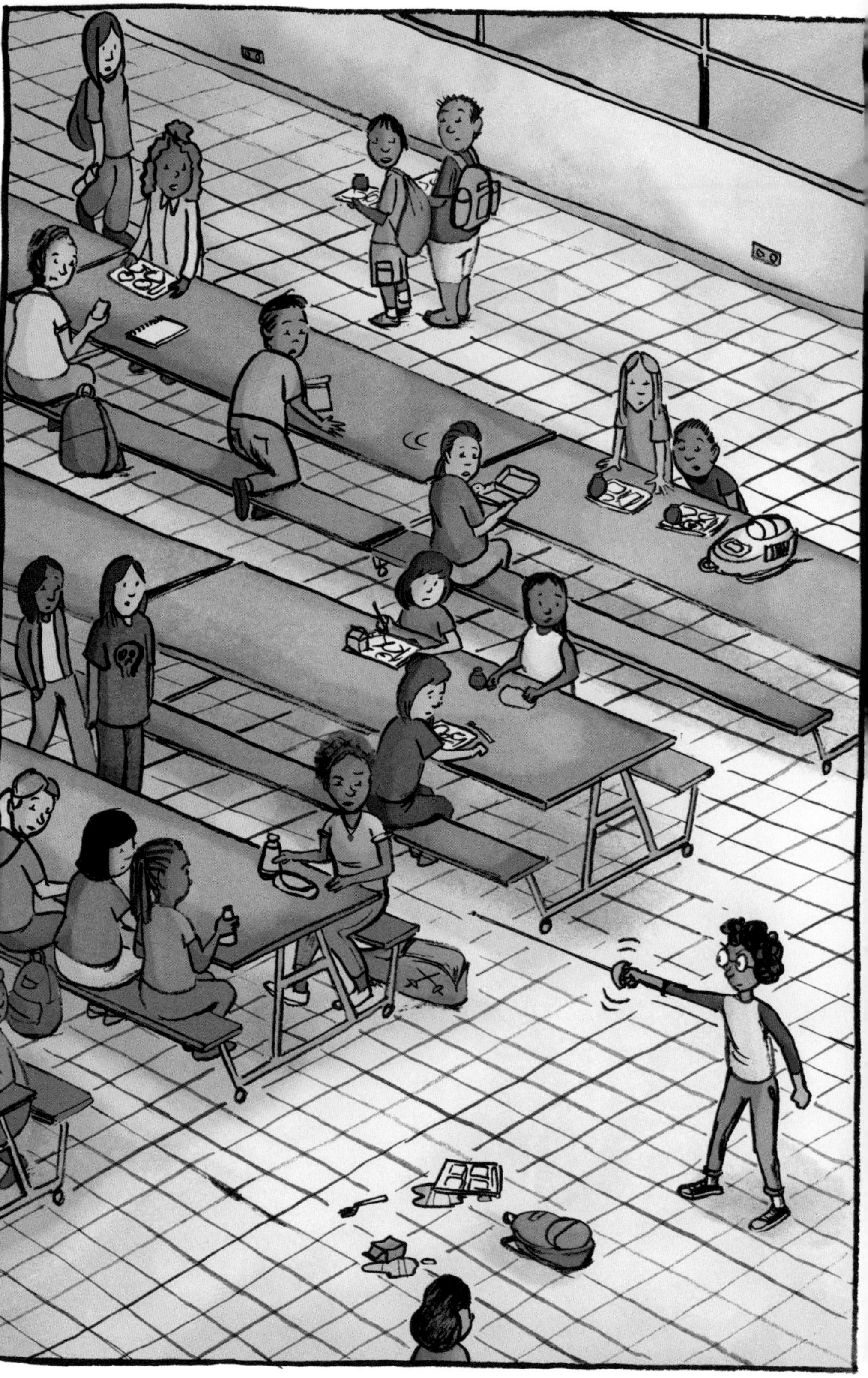

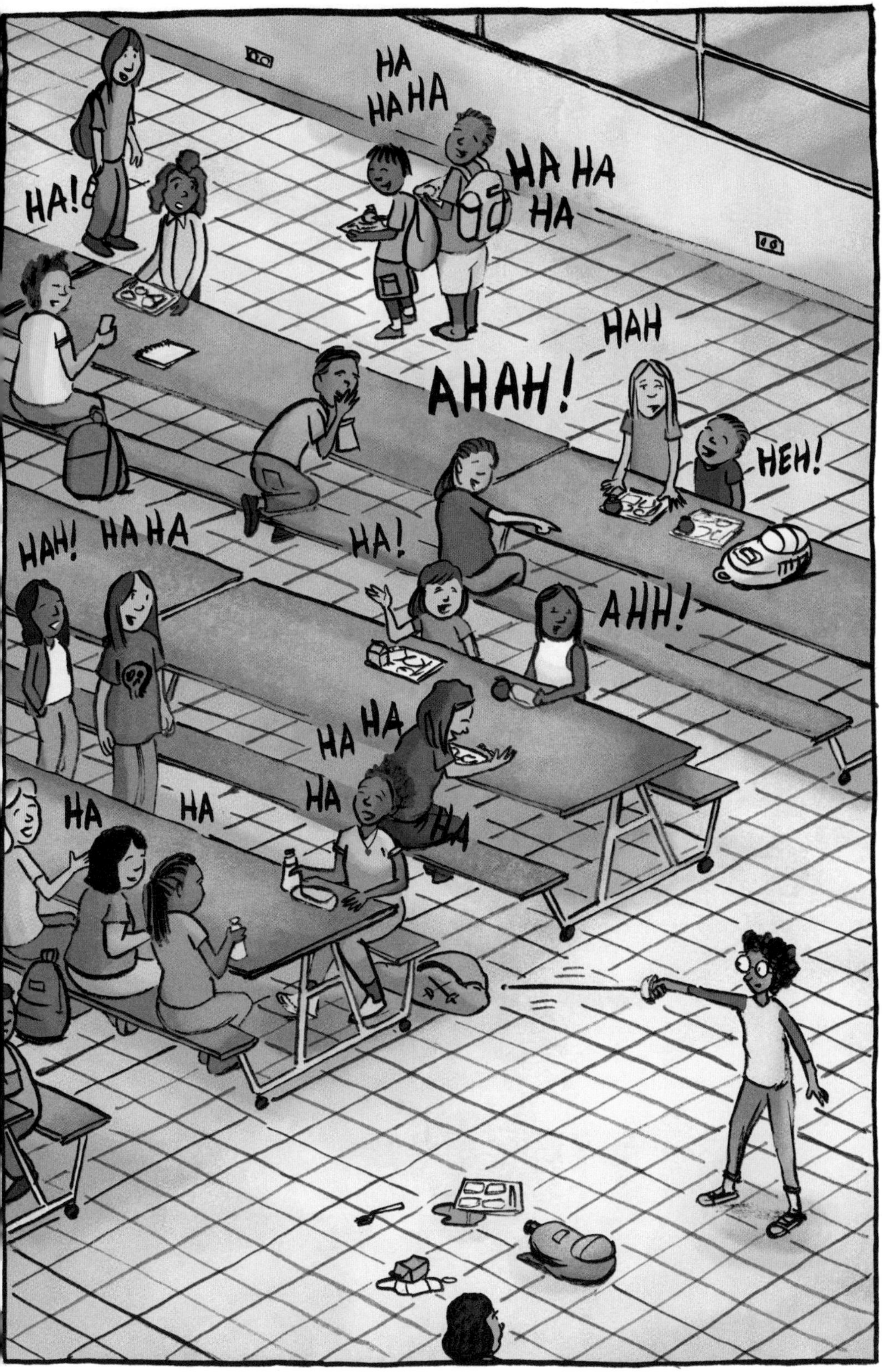
HA HAHA
HA!
HA HA HA
HAH
AHAH!
HEH!
HAH!
HA HA
HA!
AHH!
HA HA
HA
HA
HA
HA

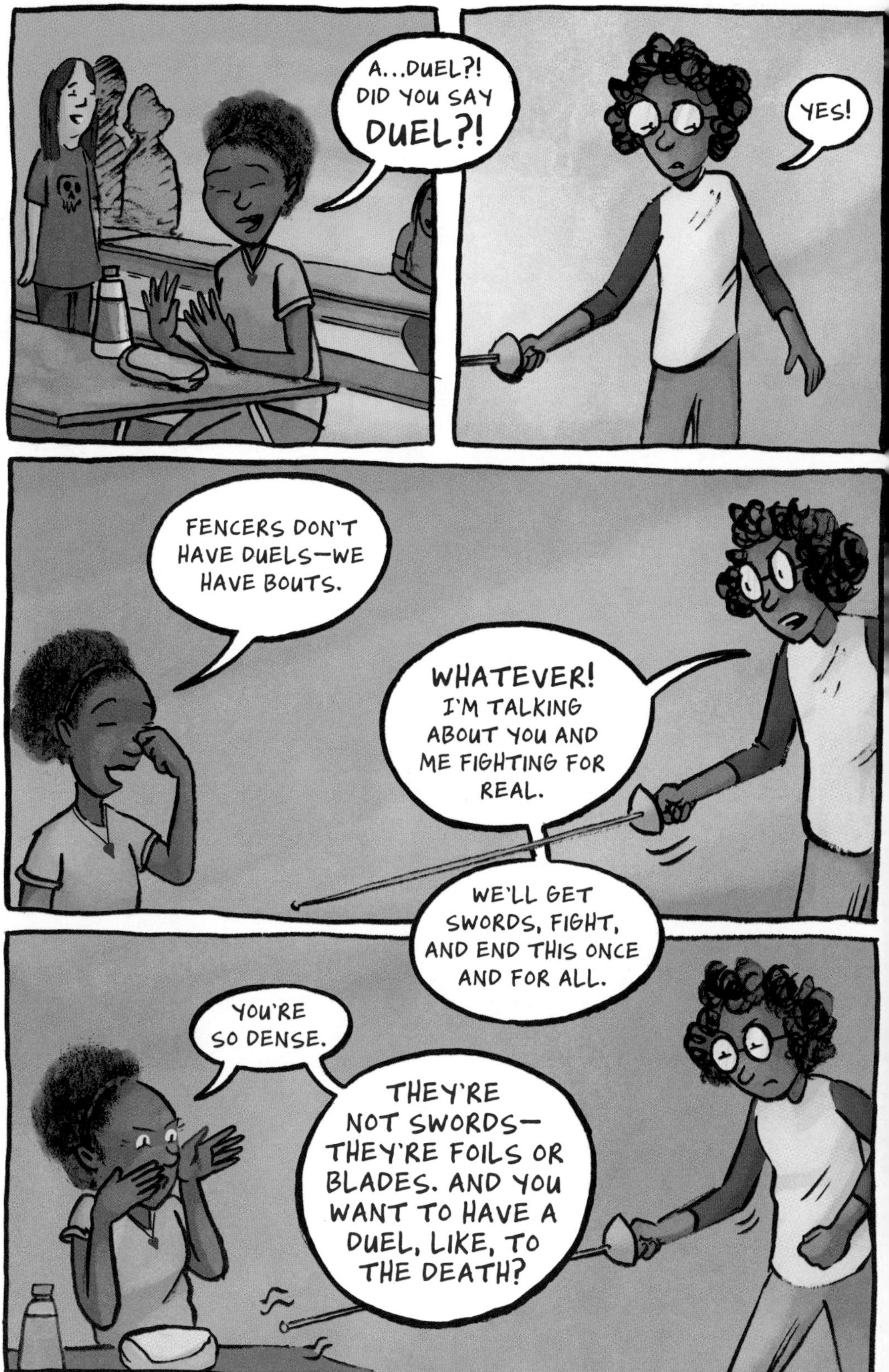

A...DUEL?! DID YOU SAY DUEL?!
YES!
FENCERS DON'T HAVE DUELS—WE HAVE BOUTS.
WHATEVER! I'M TALKING ABOUT YOU AND ME FIGHTING FOR REAL.
WE'LL GET SWORDS, FIGHT, AND END THIS ONCE AND FOR ALL.
YOU'RE SO DENSE.
THEY'RE NOT SWORDS—THEY'RE FOILS OR BLADES. AND YOU WANT TO HAVE A DUEL, LIKE, TO THE DEATH?

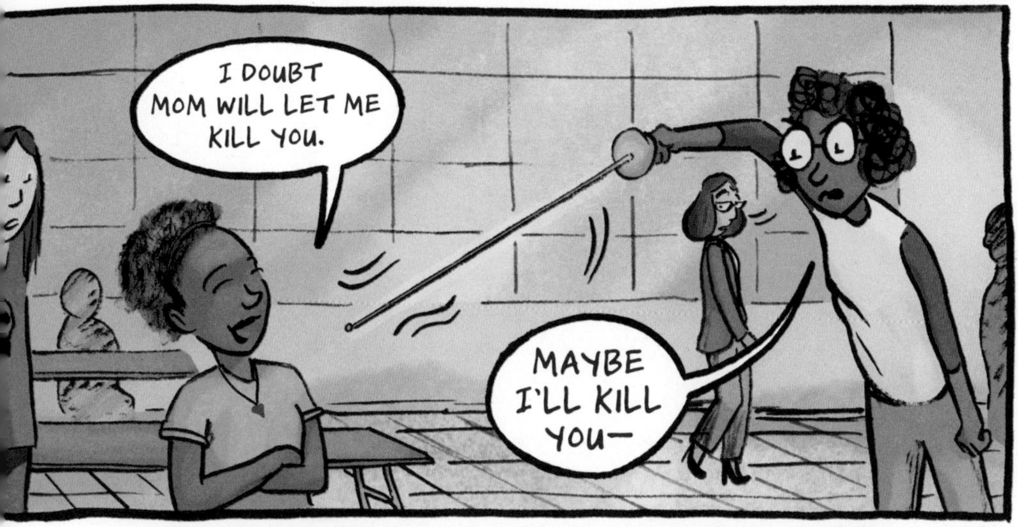
I DOUBT MOM WILL LET ME KILL YOU.
MAYBE I'LL KILL YOU—

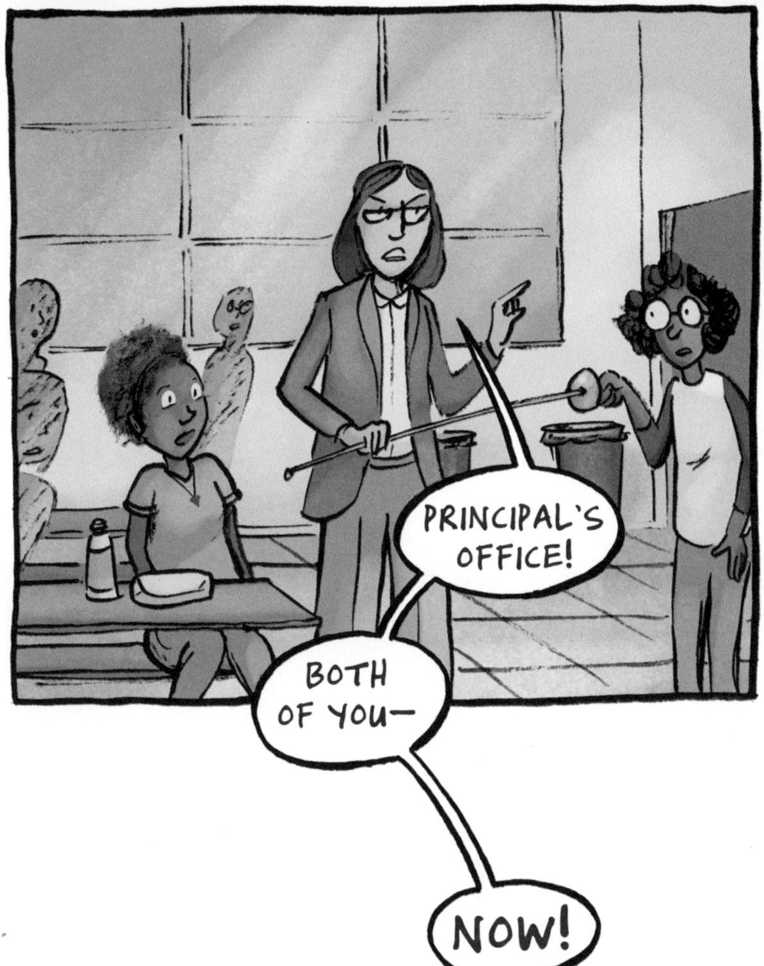
PRINCIPAL'S OFFICE!
BOTH OF YOU—
NOW!

Chapter 2

Salute

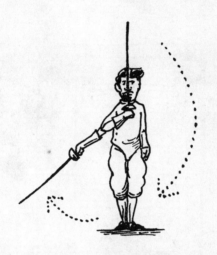

The salute is a blade action performed before the start of a bout in which you acknowledge your opponent, referee, and judges. This act indicates respect and good sportsmanship. The action happens by moving the blade in a sweeping motion across the face or from the face down in a counterclockwise motion in front of the body. Saluting is a required action before fencing will start. If you do not salute, it is a sign of disrespect. And much like the shaking of hands, the salute signifies an agreement between opponents.

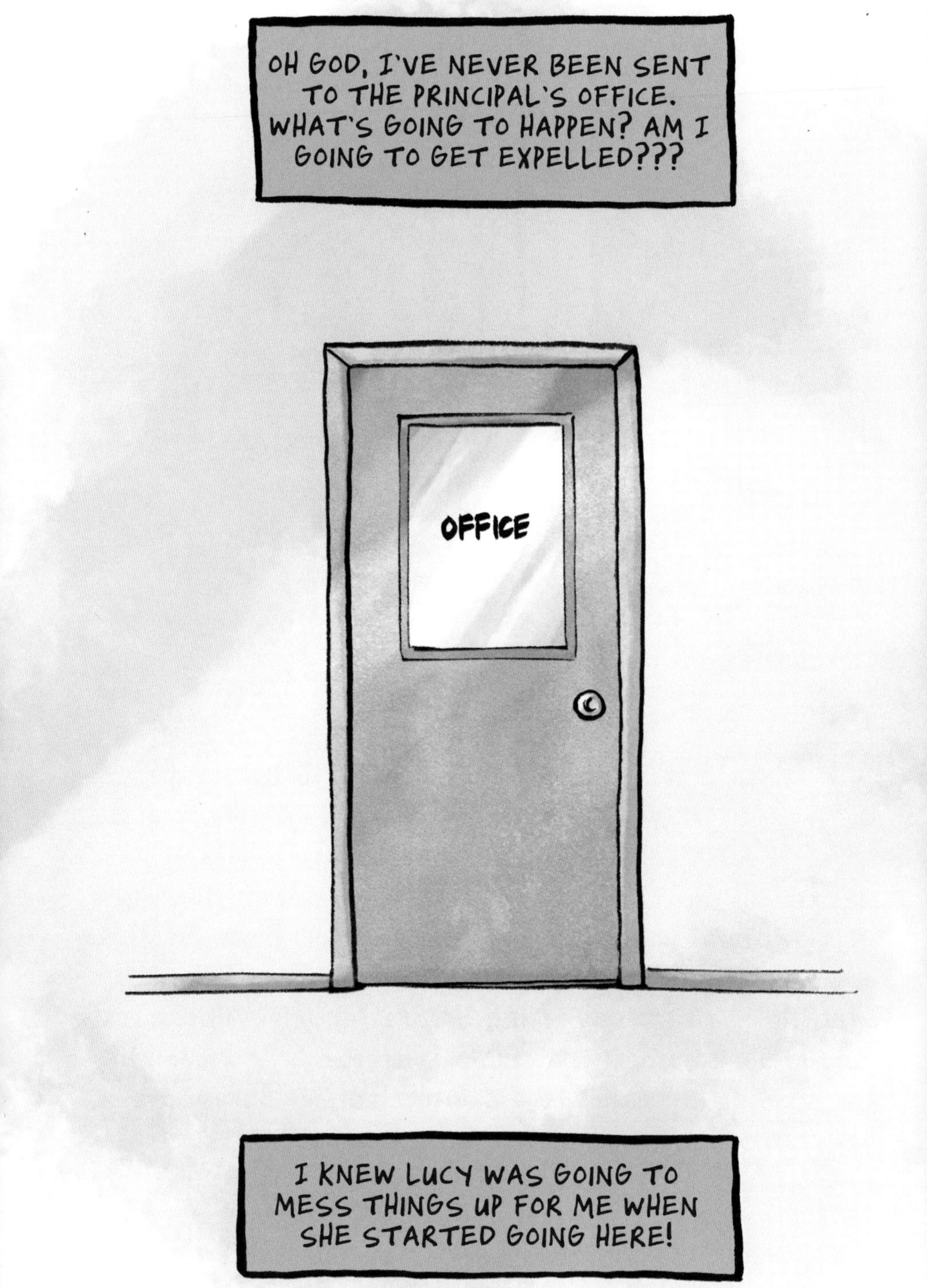
OH GOD, I'VE NEVER BEEN SENT TO THE PRINCIPAL'S OFFICE. WHAT'S GOING TO HAPPEN? AM I GOING TO GET EXPELLED???
OFFICE
I KNEW LUCY WAS GOING TO MESS THINGS UP FOR ME WHEN SHE STARTED GOING HERE!

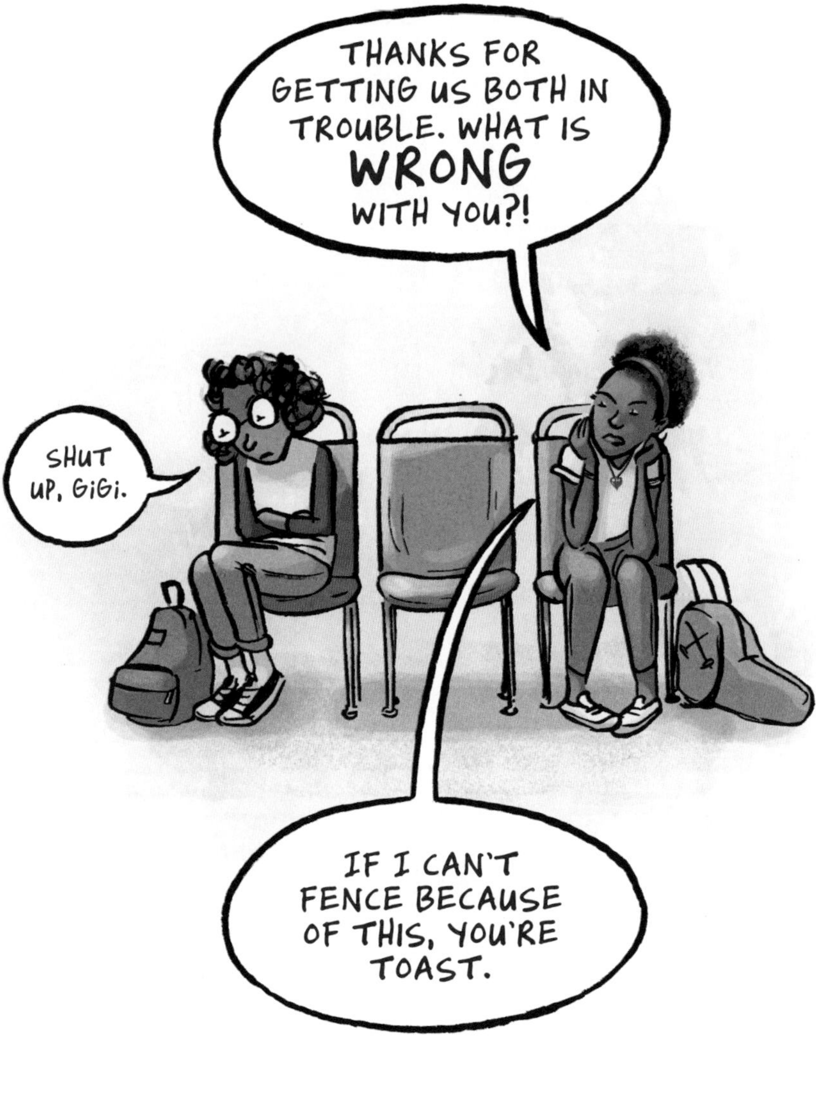
THANKS FOR GETTING US BOTH IN TROUBLE. WHAT IS **WRONG** WITH YOU?!
SHUT UP, GIGI.
IF I CAN'T FENCE BECAUSE OF THIS, YOU'RE TOAST.

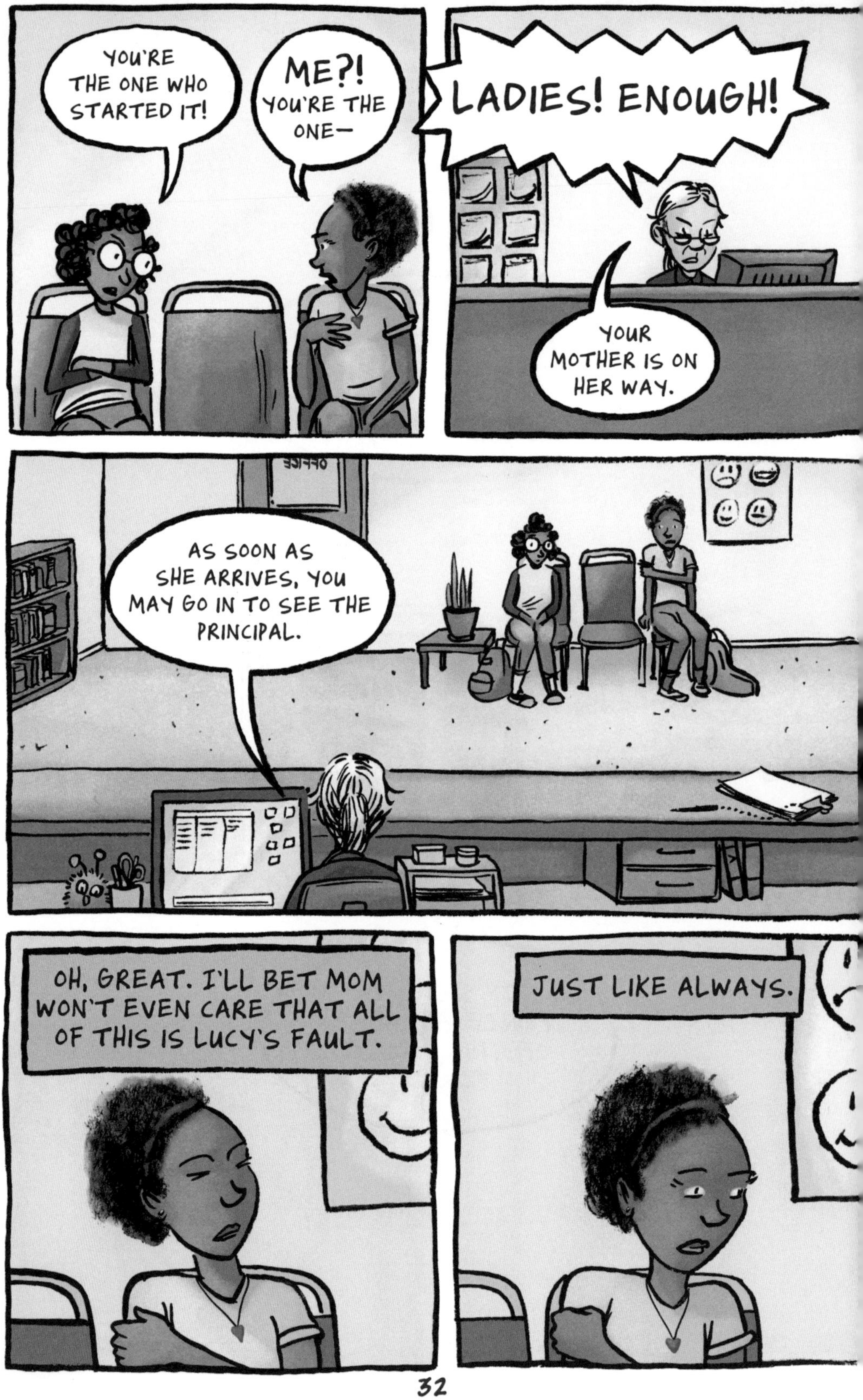
YOU'RE THE ONE WHO STARTED IT!
ME?! YOU'RE THE ONE—
LADIES! ENOUGH!
YOUR MOTHER IS ON HER WAY.
OFFICE
AS SOON AS SHE ARRIVES, YOU MAY GO IN TO SEE THE PRINCIPAL.
OH, GREAT. I'LL BET MOM WON'T EVEN CARE THAT ALL OF THIS IS LUCY'S FAULT.
JUST LIKE ALWAYS.

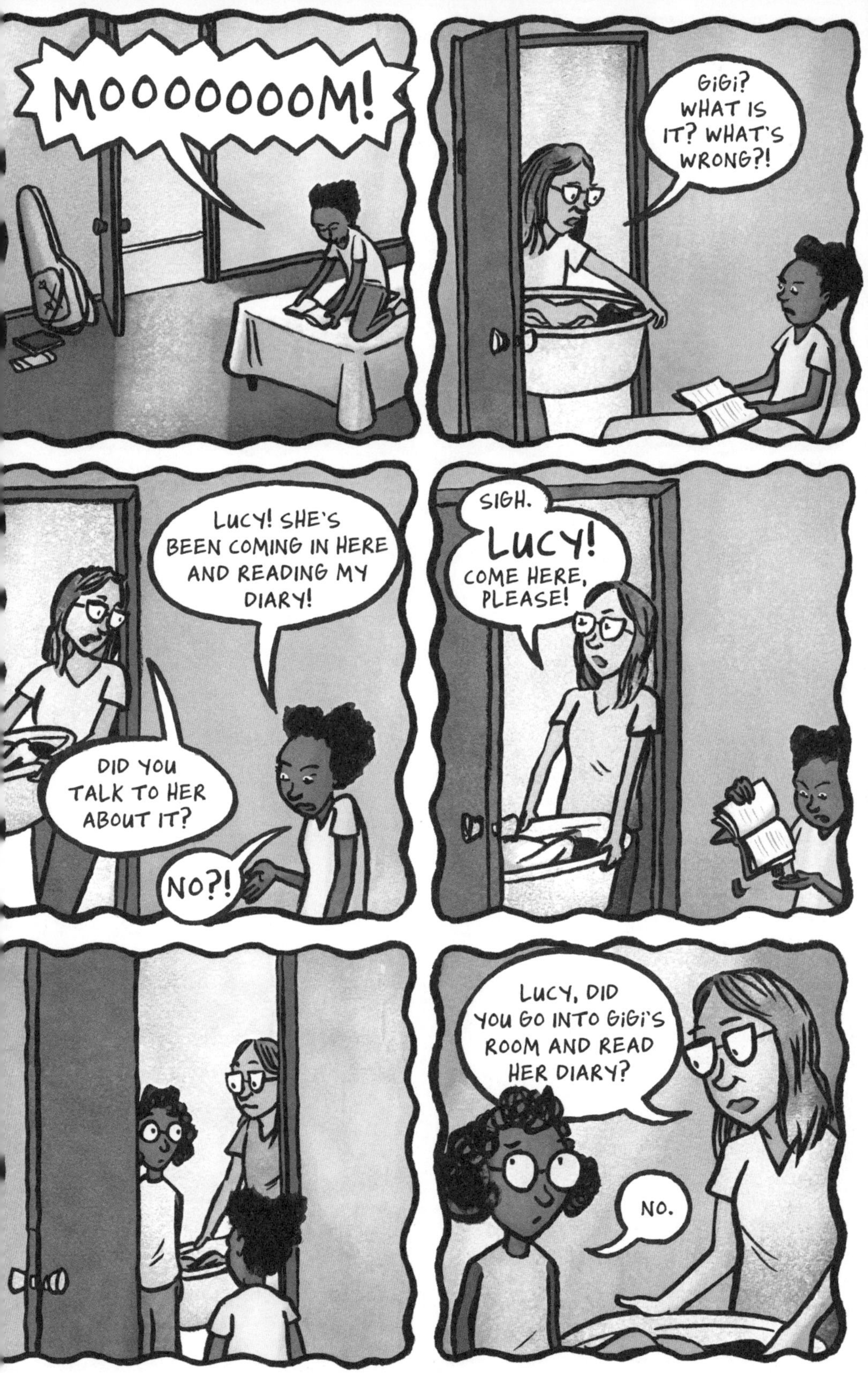
MOOOOOOM!
GIGI? WHAT IS IT? WHAT'S WRONG?!
LUCY! SHE'S BEEN COMING IN HERE AND READING MY DIARY!
DID YOU TALK TO HER ABOUT IT?
NO?!
SIGH.
LUCY!
COME HERE, PLEASE!
LUCY, DID YOU GO INTO GIGI'S ROOM AND READ HER DIARY?
NO.

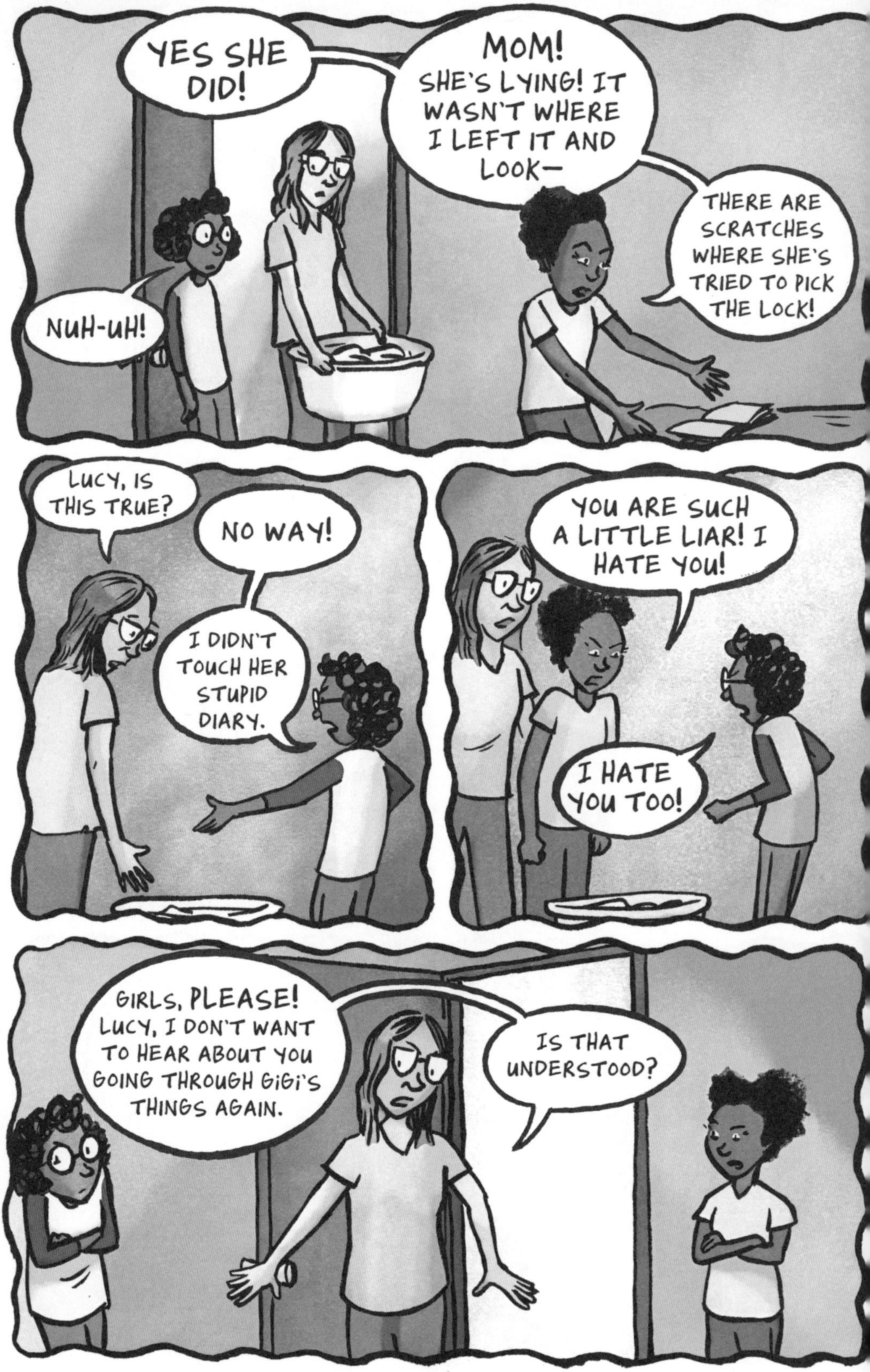
YES SHE DID!
MOM! SHE'S LYING! IT WASN'T WHERE I LEFT IT AND LOOK—
NUH-UH!
THERE ARE SCRATCHES WHERE SHE'S TRIED TO PICK THE LOCK!
LUCY, IS THIS TRUE?
NO WAY!
I DIDN'T TOUCH HER STUPID DIARY.
YOU ARE SUCH A LITTLE LIAR! I HATE YOU!
I HATE YOU TOO!
GIRLS, PLEASE! LUCY, I DON'T WANT TO HEAR ABOUT YOU GOING THROUGH GIGI'S THINGS AGAIN.
IS THAT UNDERSTOOD?

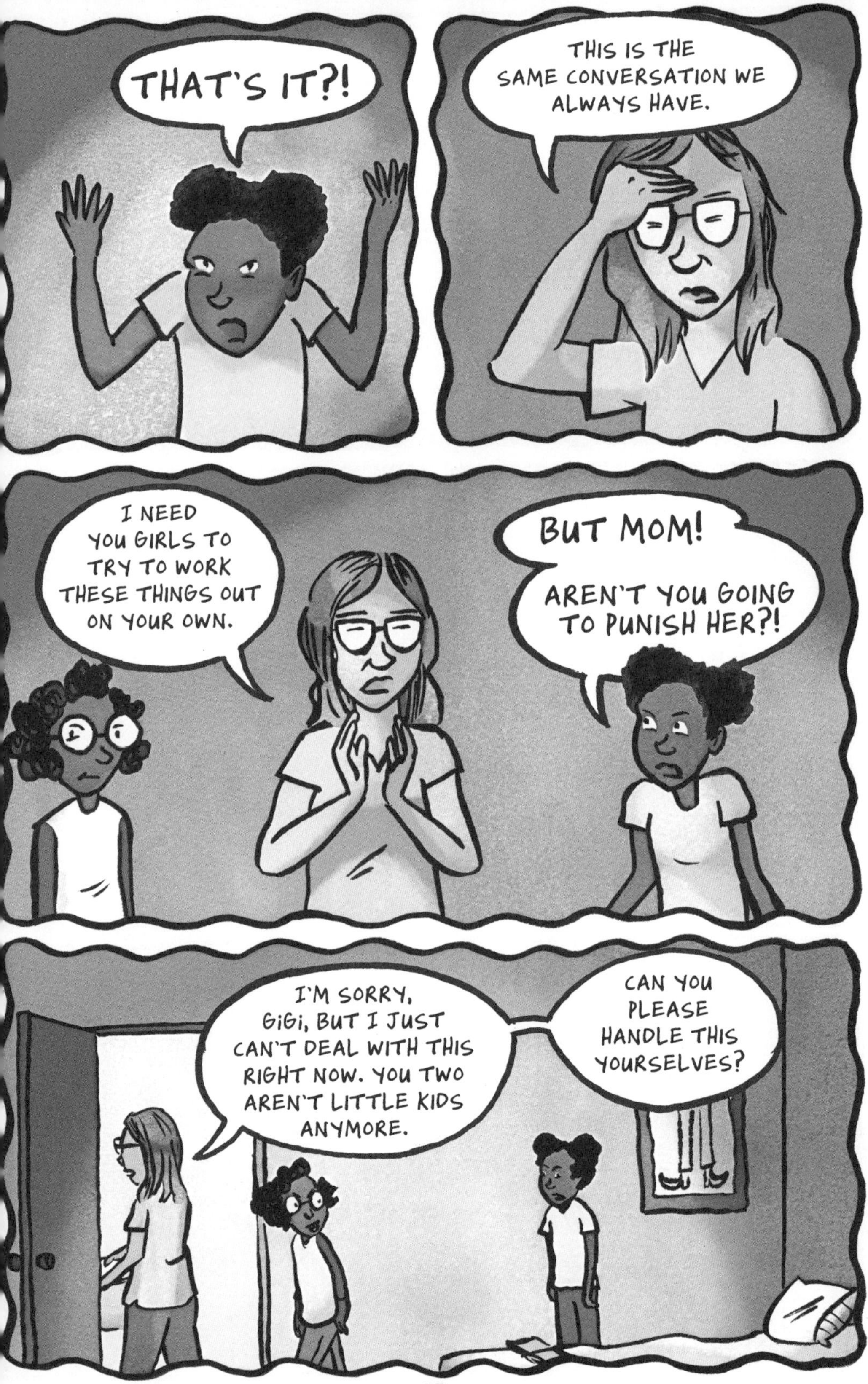
THAT'S IT?!
THIS IS THE SAME CONVERSATION WE ALWAYS HAVE.
I NEED YOU GIRLS TO TRY TO WORK THESE THINGS OUT ON YOUR OWN.
BUT MOM!
AREN'T YOU GOING TO PUNISH HER?!
I'M SORRY, GiGi, BUT I JUST CAN'T DEAL WITH THIS RIGHT NOW. YOU TWO AREN'T LITTLE KIDS ANYMORE.
CAN YOU PLEASE HANDLE THIS YOURSELVES?

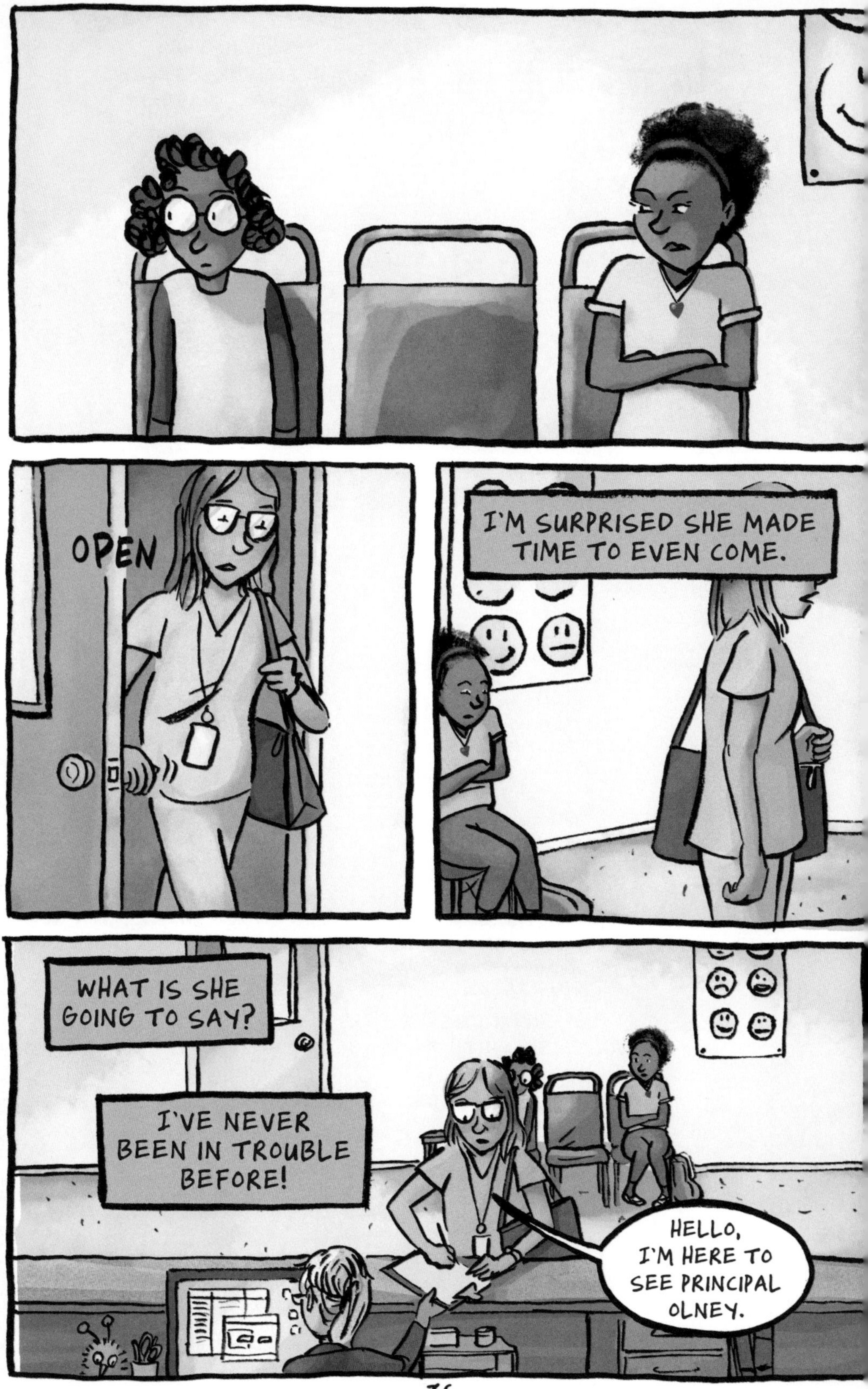
OPEN
I'M SURPRISED SHE MADE TIME TO EVEN COME.
WHAT IS SHE GOING TO SAY?
I'VE NEVER BEEN IN TROUBLE BEFORE!
HELLO, I'M HERE TO SEE PRINCIPAL OLNEY.

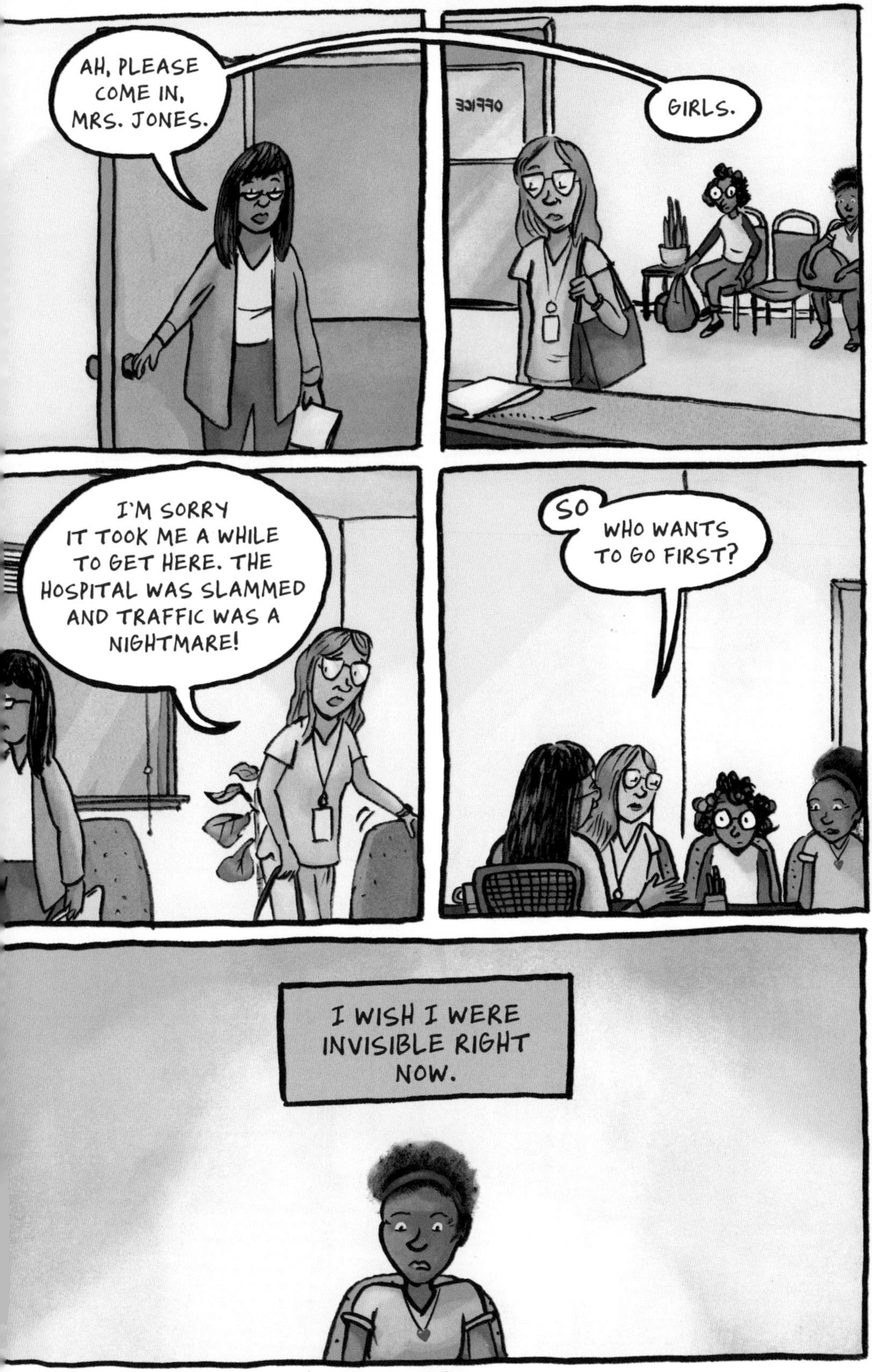
AH, PLEASE COME IN, MRS. JONES.
OFFICE
GIRLS.
I'M SORRY IT TOOK ME A WHILE TO GET HERE. THE HOSPITAL WAS SLAMMED AND TRAFFIC WAS A NIGHTMARE!
SO
WHO WANTS TO GO FIRST?
I WISH I WERE INVISIBLE RIGHT NOW.

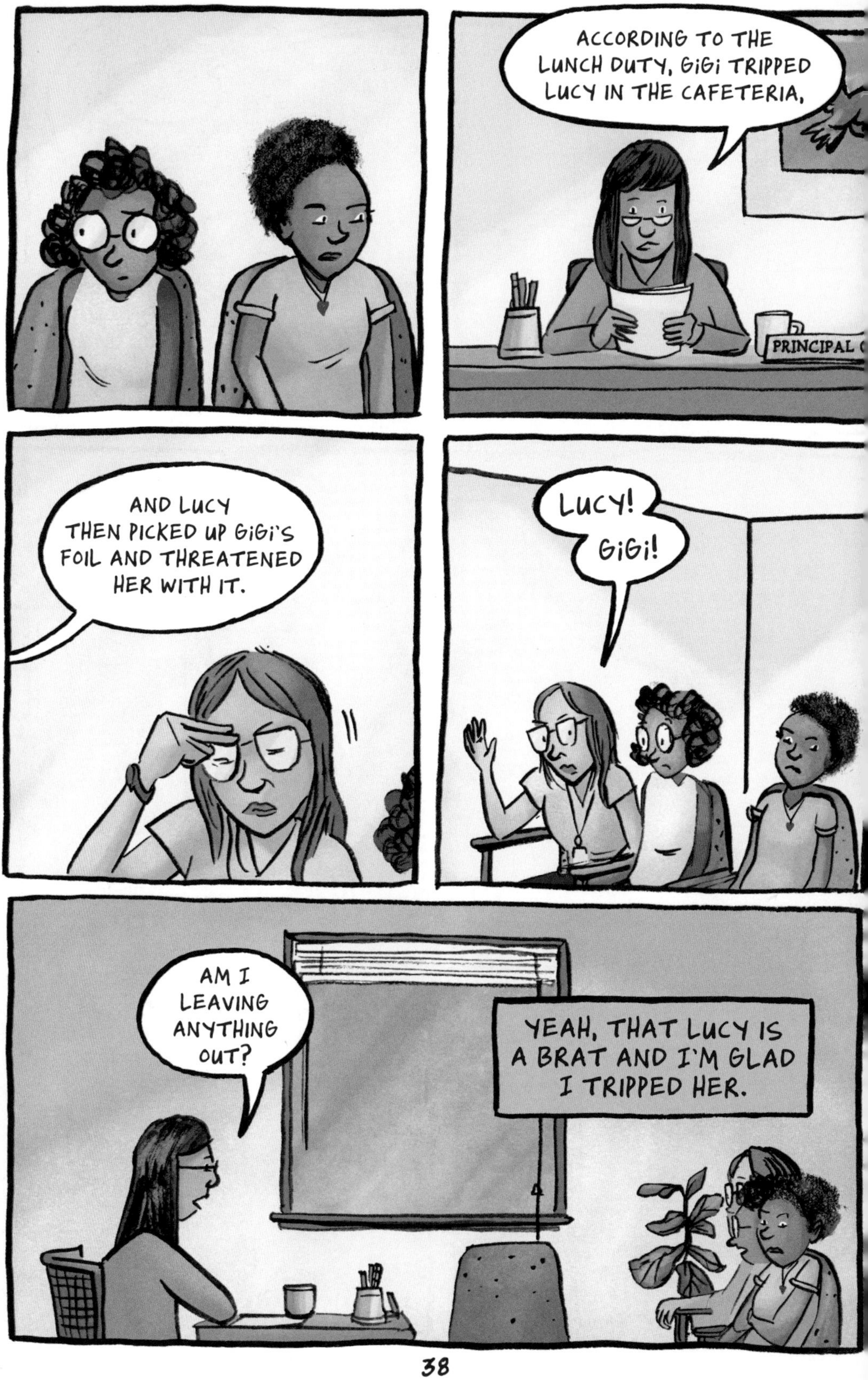
ACCORDING TO THE LUNCH DUTY, GiGi TRIPPED LUCY IN THE CAFETERIA,
PRINCIPAL
AND LUCY THEN PICKED UP GiGi'S FOIL AND THREATENED HER WITH IT.
LUCY!
GiGi!
AM I LEAVING ANYTHING OUT?
YEAH, THAT LUCY IS A BRAT AND I'M GLAD I TRIPPED HER.

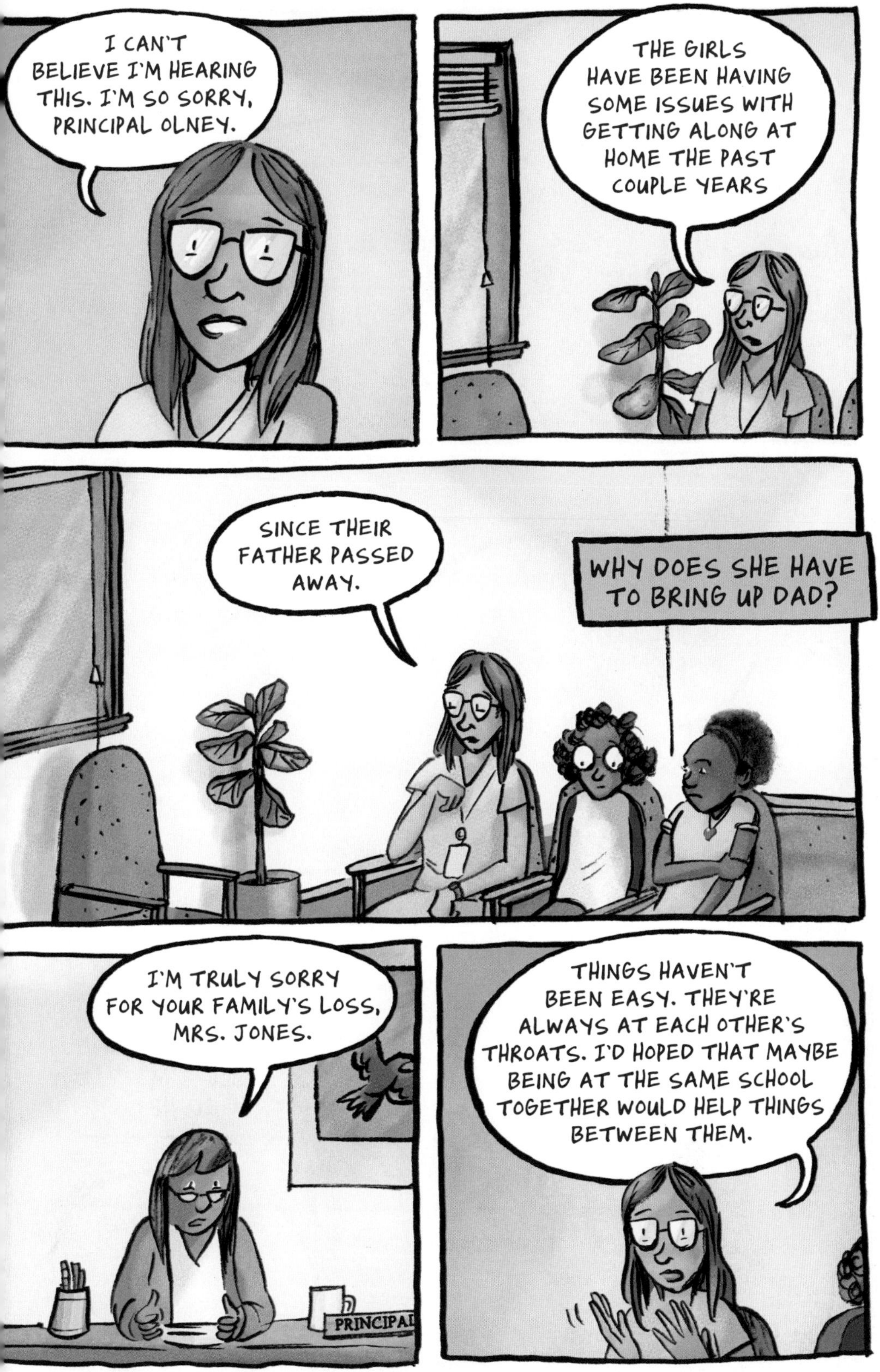
I CAN'T BELIEVE I'M HEARING THIS. I'M SO SORRY, PRINCIPAL OLNEY.
THE GIRLS HAVE BEEN HAVING SOME ISSUES WITH GETTING ALONG AT HOME THE PAST COUPLE YEARS
SINCE THEIR FATHER PASSED AWAY.
WHY DOES SHE HAVE TO BRING UP DAD?
I'M TRULY SORRY FOR YOUR FAMILY'S LOSS, MRS. JONES.
PRINCIPAL
THINGS HAVEN'T BEEN EASY. THEY'RE ALWAYS AT EACH OTHER'S THROATS. I'D HOPED THAT MAYBE BEING AT THE SAME SCHOOL TOGETHER WOULD HELP THINGS BETWEEN THEM.

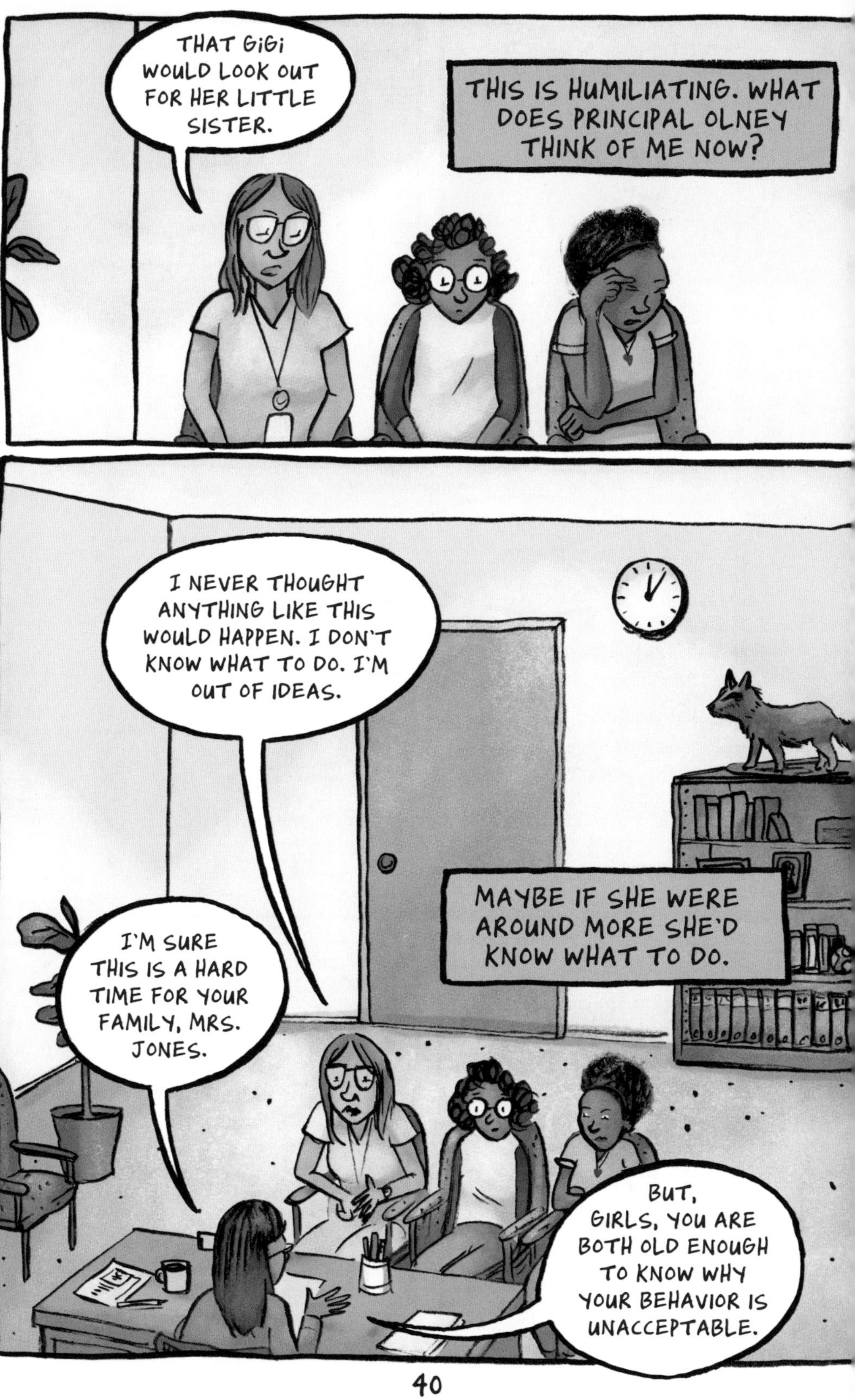
THAT GiGi WOULD LOOK OUT FOR HER LITTLE SISTER.
THIS IS HUMILIATING. WHAT DOES PRINCIPAL OLNEY THINK OF ME NOW?
I NEVER THOUGHT ANYTHING LIKE THIS WOULD HAPPEN. I DON'T KNOW WHAT TO DO. I'M OUT OF IDEAS.
MAYBE IF SHE WERE AROUND MORE SHE'D KNOW WHAT TO DO.
I'M SURE THIS IS A HARD TIME FOR YOUR FAMILY, MRS. JONES.
BUT, GIRLS, YOU ARE BOTH OLD ENOUGH TO KNOW WHY YOUR BEHAVIOR IS UNACCEPTABLE.

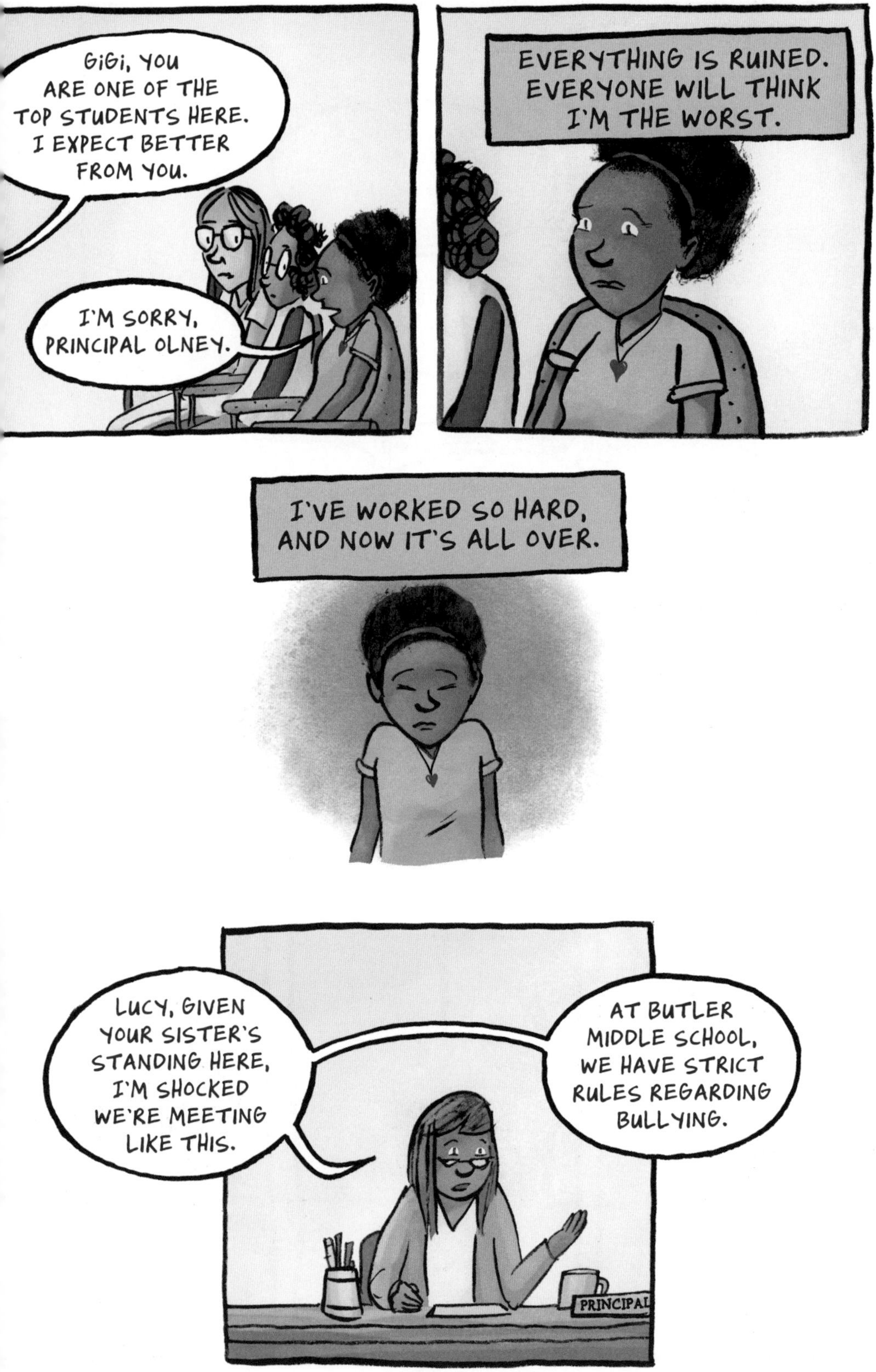
GiGi, YOU ARE ONE OF THE TOP STUDENTS HERE. I EXPECT BETTER FROM YOU.
I'M SORRY, PRINCIPAL OLNEY.
EVERYTHING IS RUINED. EVERYONE WILL THINK I'M THE WORST.
I'VE WORKED SO HARD, AND NOW IT'S ALL OVER.
LUCY, GIVEN YOUR SISTER'S STANDING HERE, I'M SHOCKED WE'RE MEETING LIKE THIS.
AT BUTLER MIDDLE SCHOOL, WE HAVE STRICT RULES REGARDING BULLYING.
PRINCIPAL

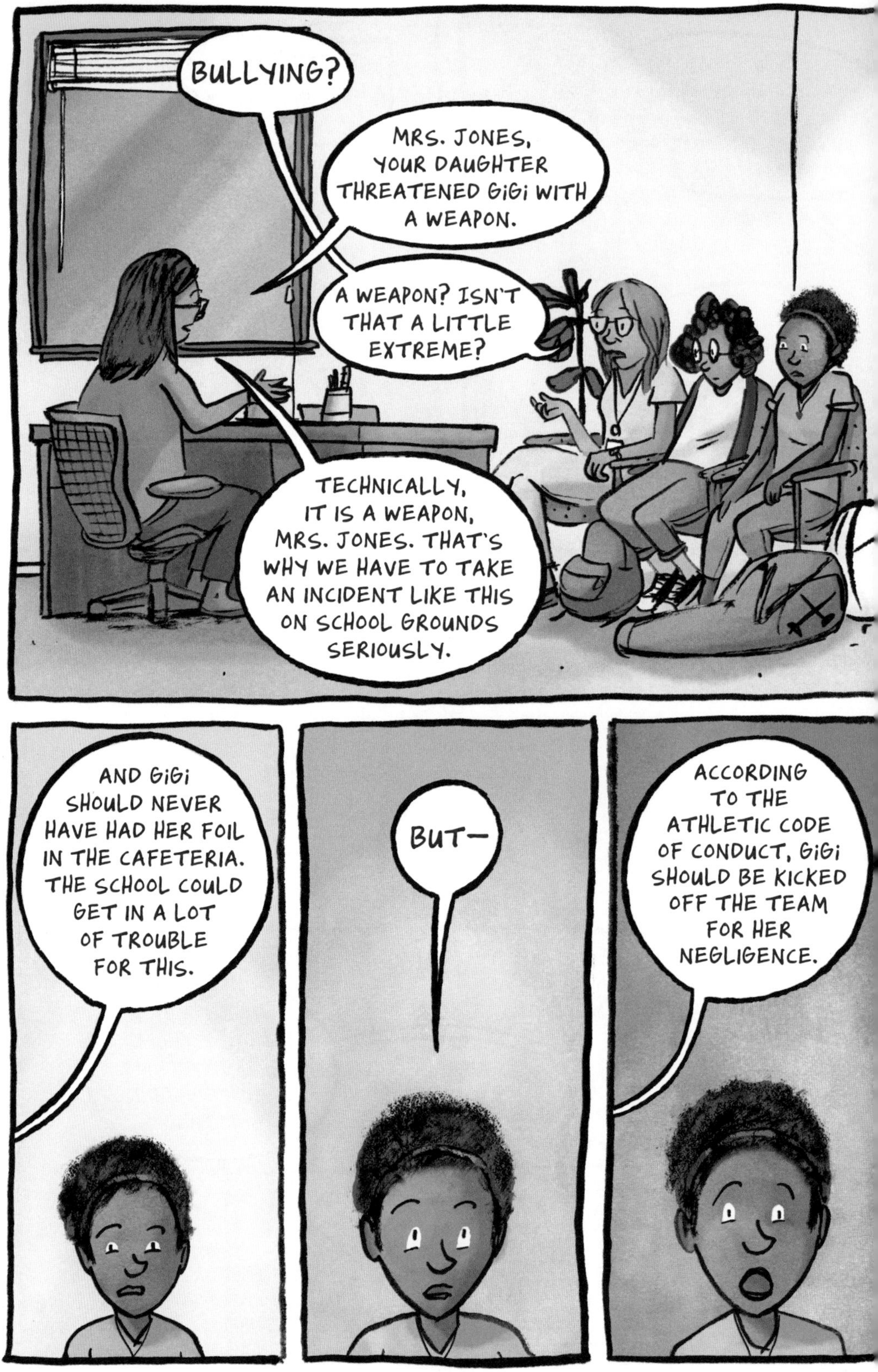
BULLYING?
MRS. JONES, YOUR DAUGHTER THREATENED GiGi WITH A WEAPON.
A WEAPON? ISN'T THAT A LITTLE EXTREME?
TECHNICALLY, IT IS A WEAPON, MRS. JONES. THAT'S WHY WE HAVE TO TAKE AN INCIDENT LIKE THIS ON SCHOOL GROUNDS SERIOUSLY.
AND GiGi SHOULD NEVER HAVE HAD HER FOIL IN THE CAFETERIA. THE SCHOOL COULD GET IN A LOT OF TROUBLE FOR THIS.
BUT—
ACCORDING TO THE ATHLETIC CODE OF CONDUCT, GiGi SHOULD BE KICKED OFF THE TEAM FOR HER NEGLIGENCE.

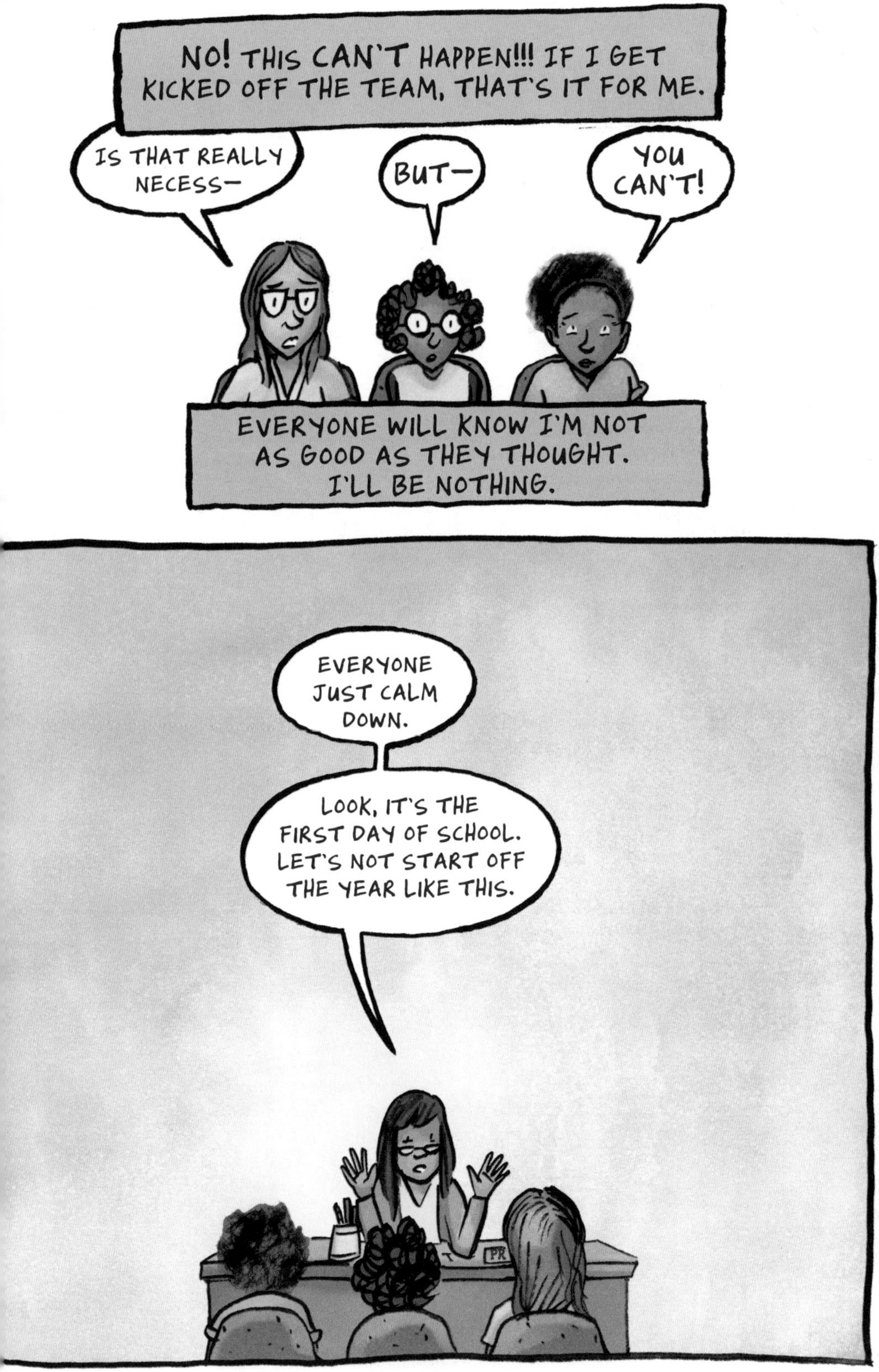
NO! THIS CAN'T HAPPEN!!! IF I GET KICKED OFF THE TEAM, THAT'S IT FOR ME.
IS THAT REALLY NECESS—
BUT—
YOU CAN'T!
EVERYONE WILL KNOW I'M NOT AS GOOD AS THEY THOUGHT. I'LL BE NOTHING.
EVERYONE JUST CALM DOWN.
LOOK, IT'S THE FIRST DAY OF SCHOOL. LET'S NOT START OFF THE YEAR LIKE THIS.

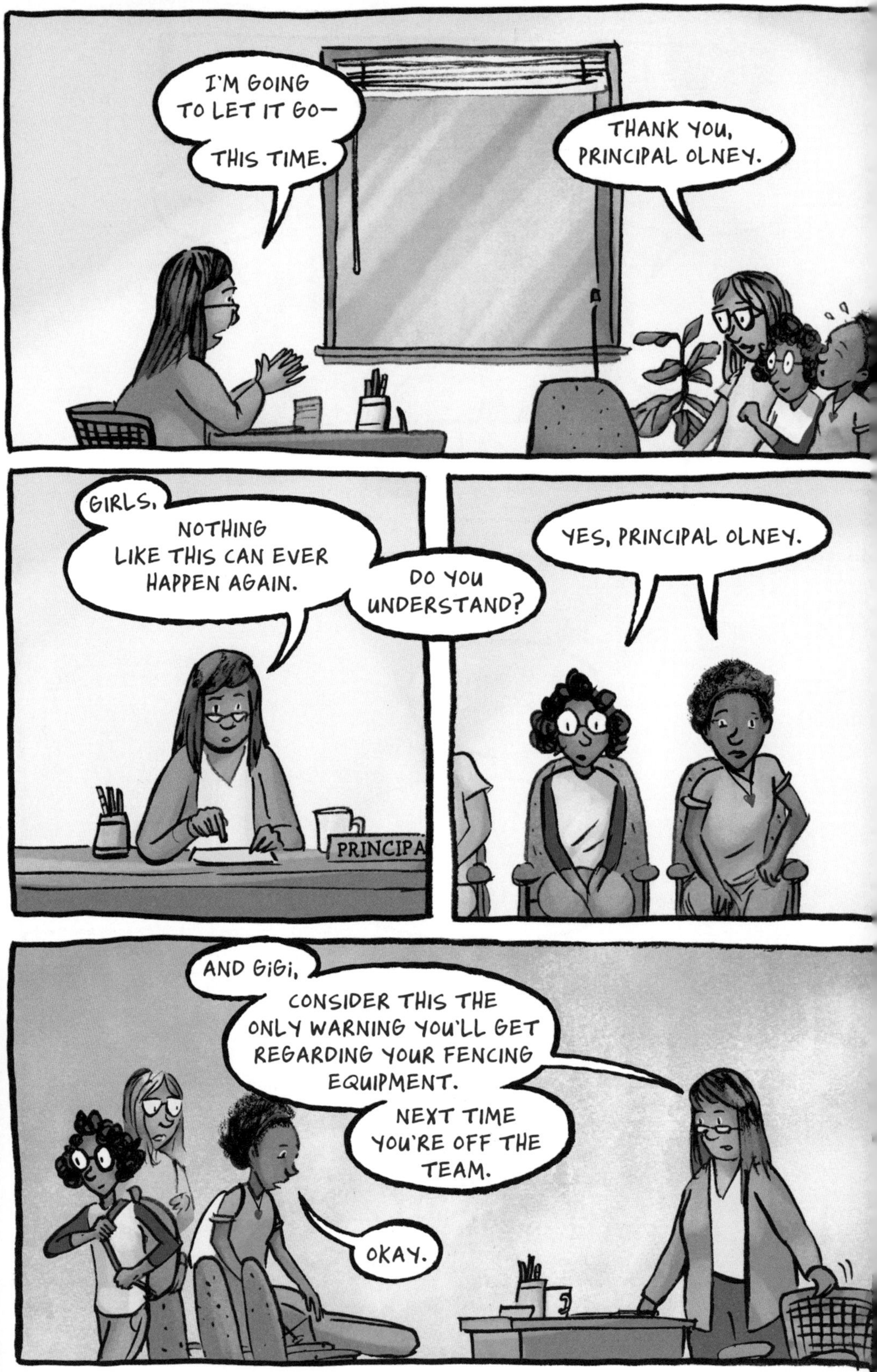
I'M GOING TO LET IT GO—
THIS TIME.
THANK YOU, PRINCIPAL OLNEY.
GIRLS,
NOTHING LIKE THIS CAN EVER HAPPEN AGAIN.
DO YOU UNDERSTAND?
PRINCIPA
YES, PRINCIPAL OLNEY.
AND GiGi,
CONSIDER THIS THE ONLY WARNING YOU'LL GET REGARDING YOUR FENCING EQUIPMENT.
NEXT TIME YOU'RE OFF THE TEAM.
OKAY.

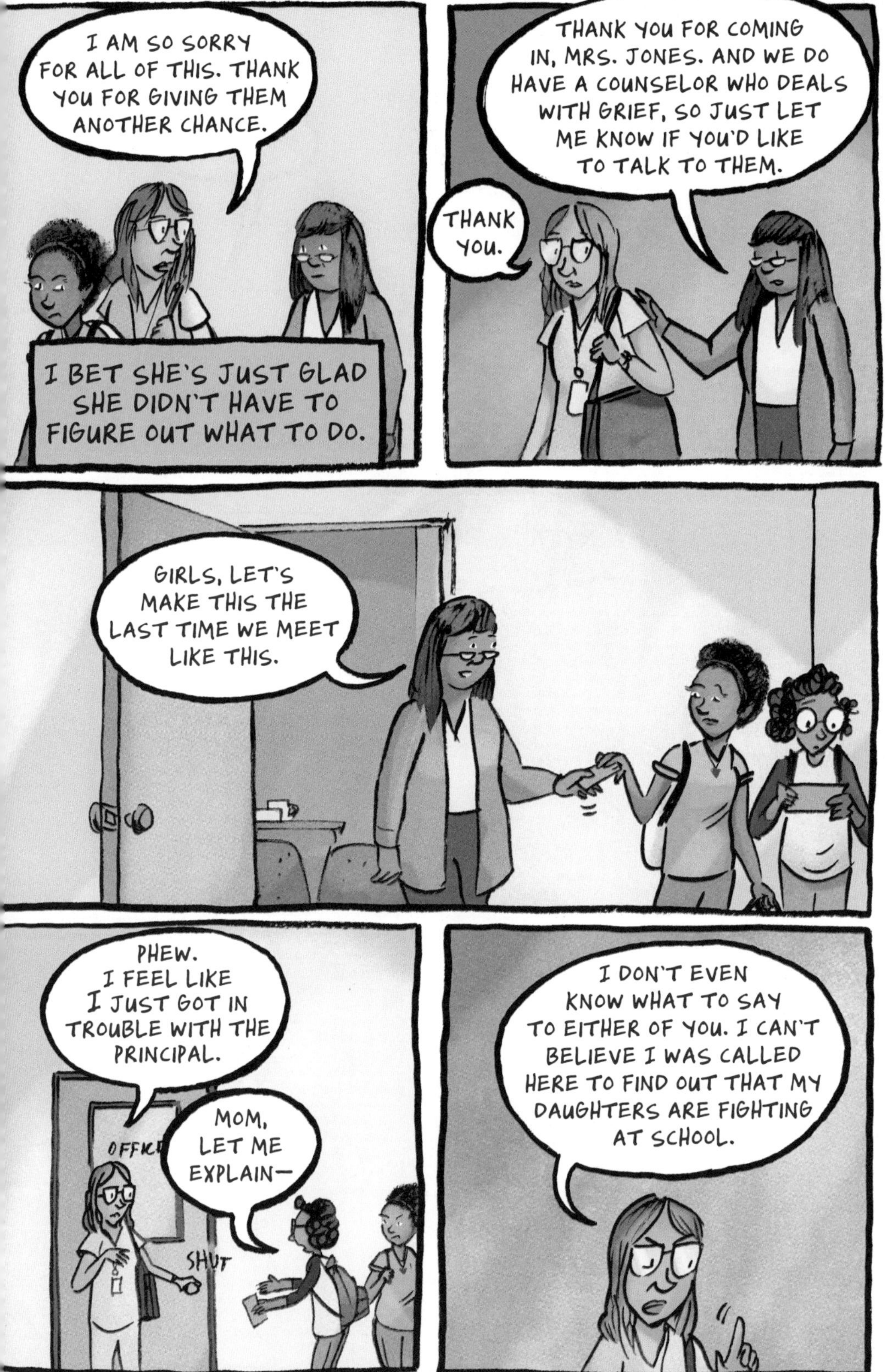
I AM SO SORRY FOR ALL OF THIS. THANK YOU FOR GIVING THEM ANOTHER CHANCE.
I BET SHE'S JUST GLAD SHE DIDN'T HAVE TO FIGURE OUT WHAT TO DO.
THANK YOU FOR COMING IN, MRS. JONES. AND WE DO HAVE A COUNSELOR WHO DEALS WITH GRIEF, SO JUST LET ME KNOW IF YOU'D LIKE TO TALK TO THEM.
THANK YOU.
GIRLS, LET'S MAKE THIS THE LAST TIME WE MEET LIKE THIS.
PHEW. I FEEL LIKE I JUST GOT IN TROUBLE WITH THE PRINCIPAL.
OFFIC
MOM, LET ME EXPLAIN—
SHUT
I DON'T EVEN KNOW WHAT TO SAY TO EITHER OF YOU. I CAN'T BELIEVE I WAS CALLED HERE TO FIND OUT THAT MY DAUGHTERS ARE FIGHTING AT SCHOOL.

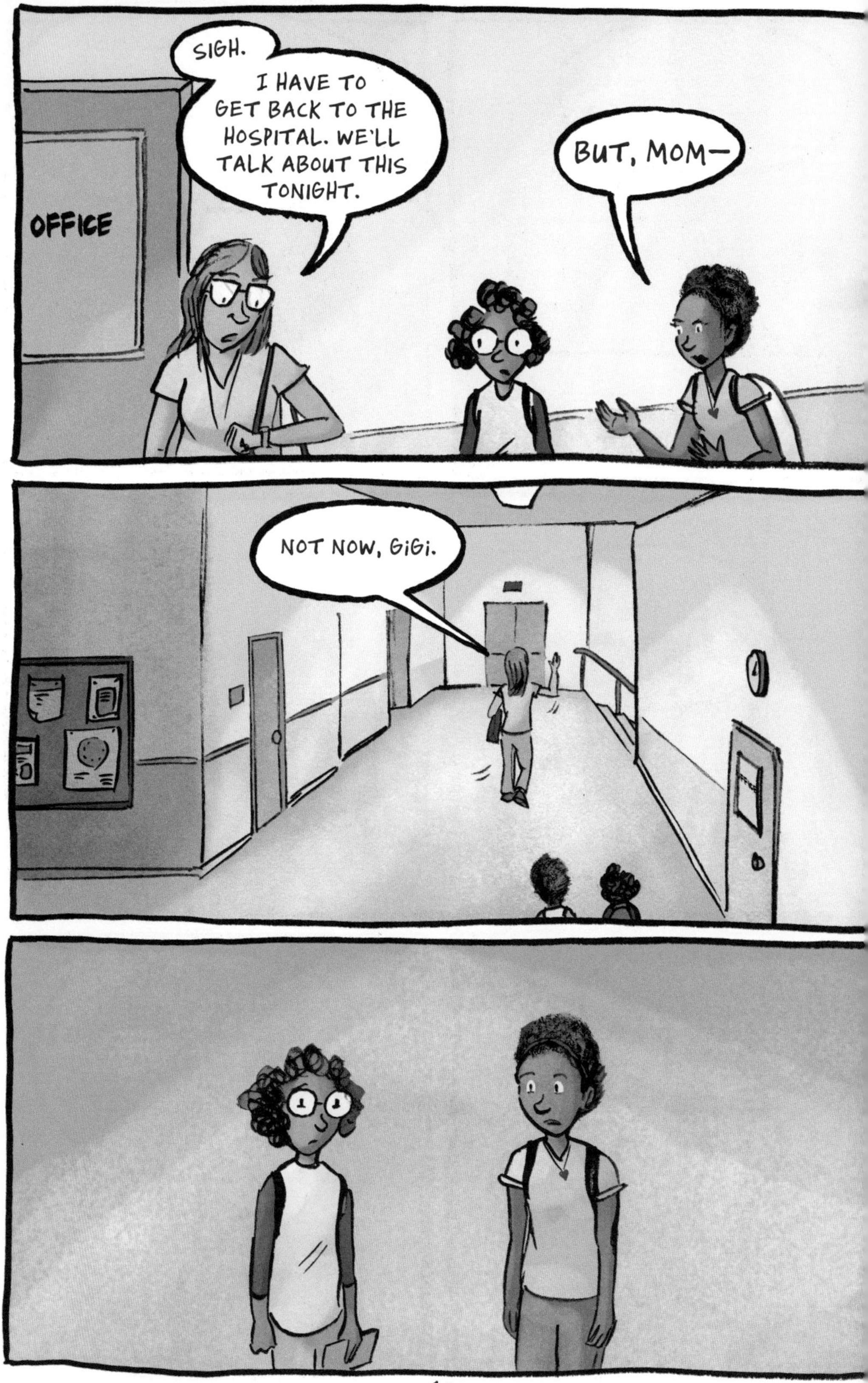
OFFICE
SIGH.
I HAVE TO GET BACK TO THE HOSPITAL. WE'LL TALK ABOUT THIS TONIGHT.
BUT, MOM—
NOT NOW, GiGi.

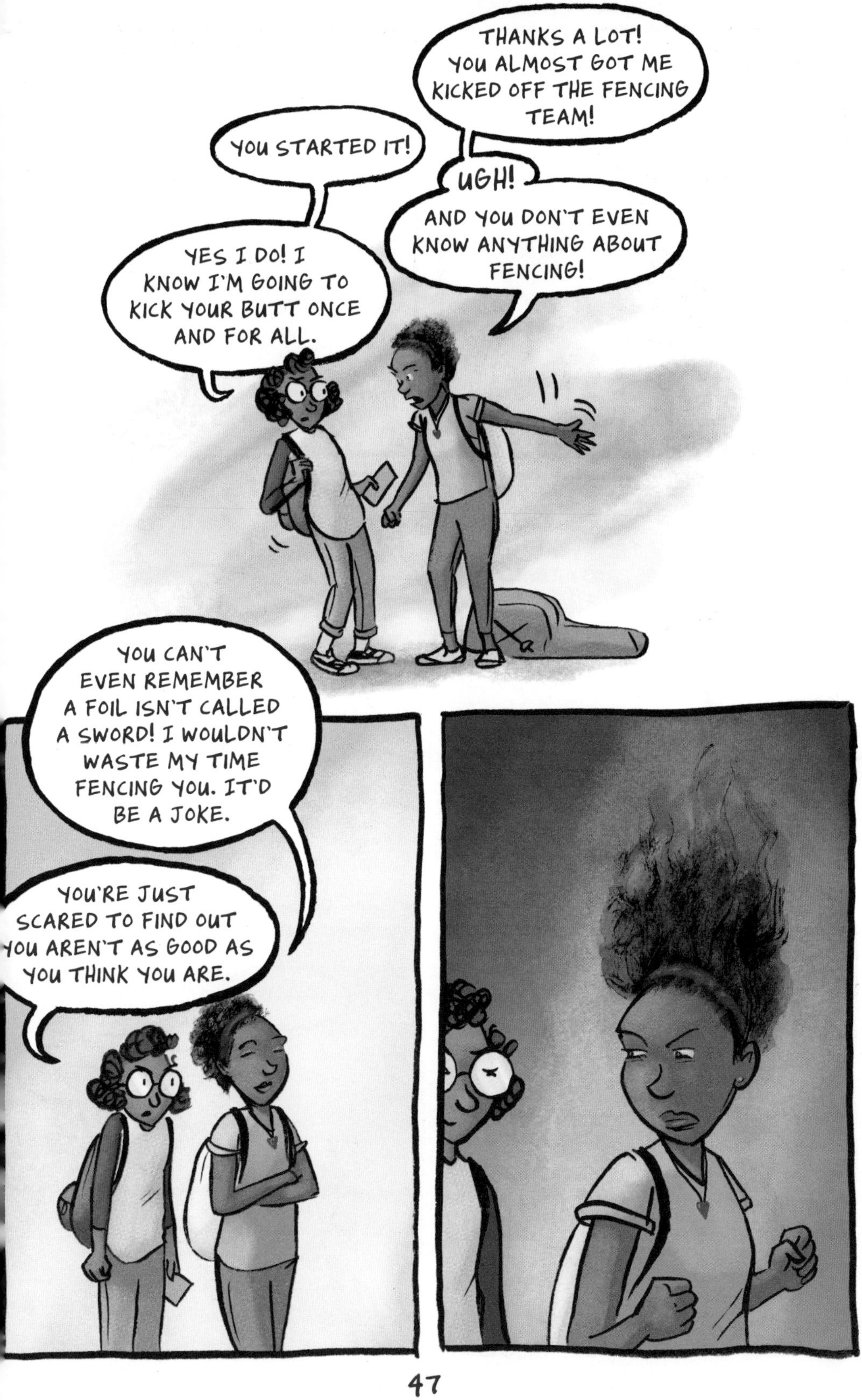
THANKS A LOT! YOU ALMOST GOT ME KICKED OFF THE FENCING TEAM!
YOU STARTED IT!
UGH!
AND YOU DON'T EVEN KNOW ANYTHING ABOUT FENCING!
YES I DO! I KNOW I'M GOING TO KICK YOUR BUTT ONCE AND FOR ALL.
YOU CAN'T EVEN REMEMBER A FOIL ISN'T CALLED A SWORD! I WOULDN'T WASTE MY TIME FENCING YOU. IT'D BE A JOKE.
YOU'RE JUST SCARED TO FIND OUT YOU AREN'T AS GOOD AS YOU THINK YOU ARE.

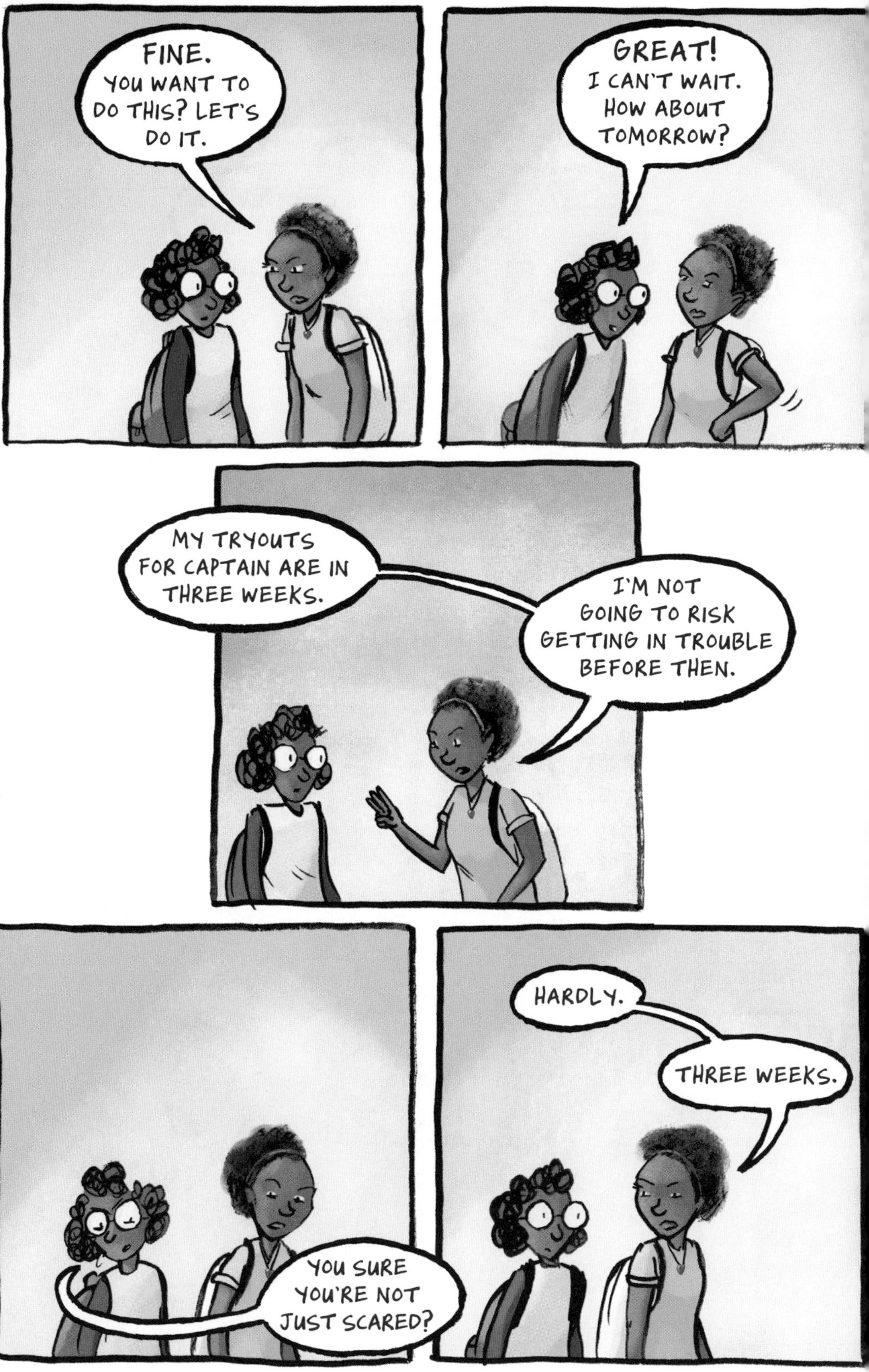
FINE. YOU WANT TO DO THIS? LET'S DO IT.
GREAT! I CAN'T WAIT. HOW ABOUT TOMORROW?
MY TRYOUTS FOR CAPTAIN ARE IN THREE WEEKS.
I'M NOT GOING TO RISK GETTING IN TROUBLE BEFORE THEN.
YOU SURE YOU'RE NOT JUST SCARED?
HARDLY.
THREE WEEKS.

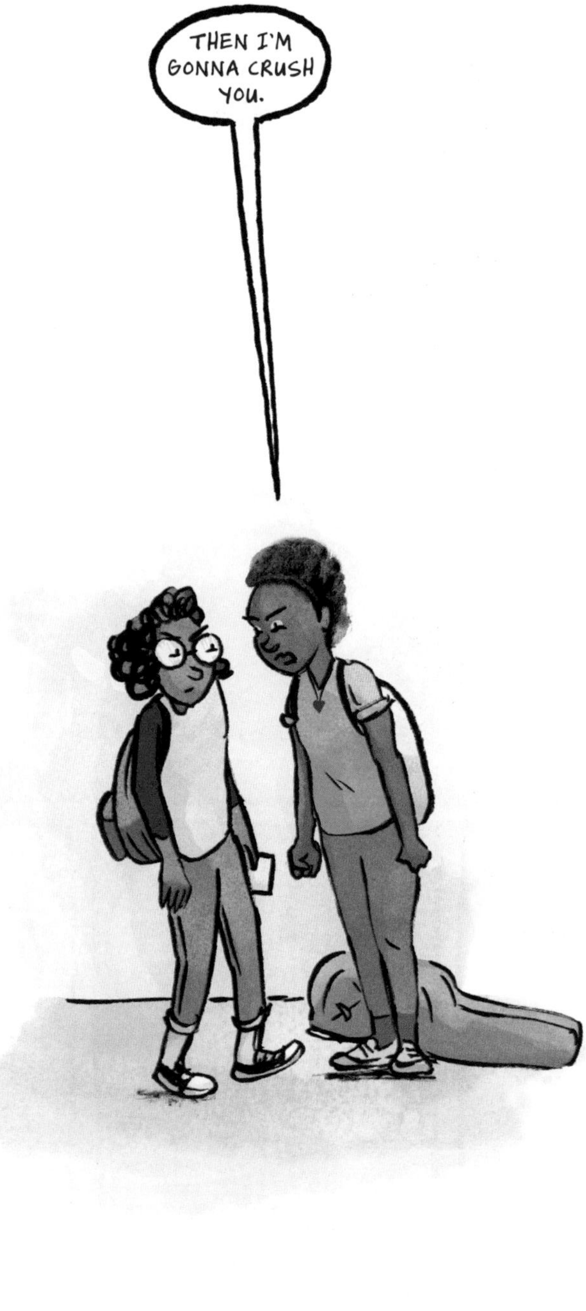
THEN I'M GONNA CRUSH YOU.

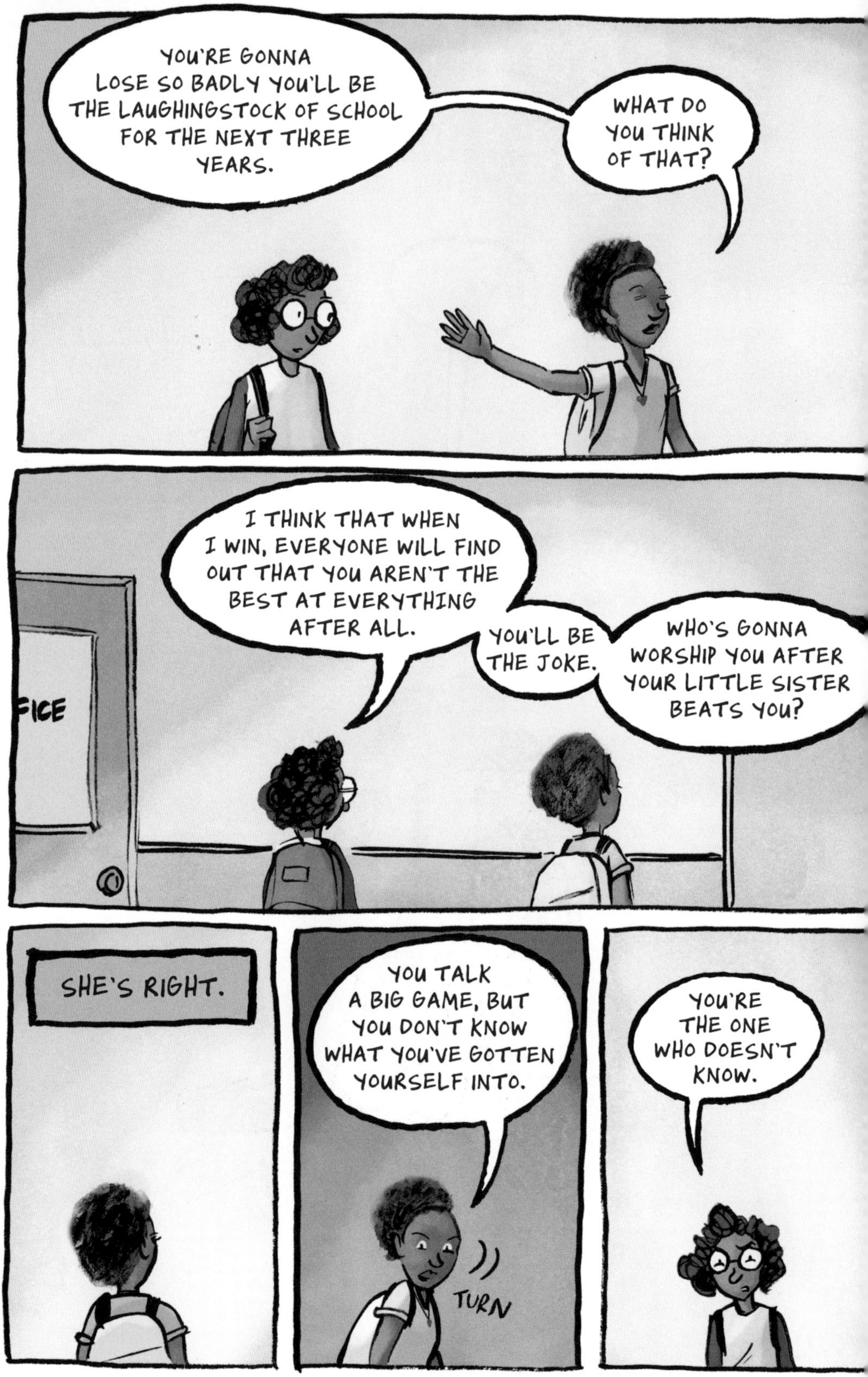
YOU'RE GONNA LOSE SO BADLY YOU'LL BE THE LAUGHINGSTOCK OF SCHOOL FOR THE NEXT THREE YEARS.
WHAT DO YOU THINK OF THAT?
I THINK THAT WHEN I WIN, EVERYONE WILL FIND OUT THAT YOU AREN'T THE BEST AT EVERYTHING AFTER ALL.
YOU'LL BE THE JOKE.
WHO'S GONNA WORSHIP YOU AFTER YOUR LITTLE SISTER BEATS YOU?
FICE
SHE'S RIGHT.
YOU TALK A BIG GAME, BUT YOU DON'T KNOW WHAT YOU'VE GOTTEN YOURSELF INTO.
TURN
YOU'RE THE ONE WHO DOESN'T KNOW.

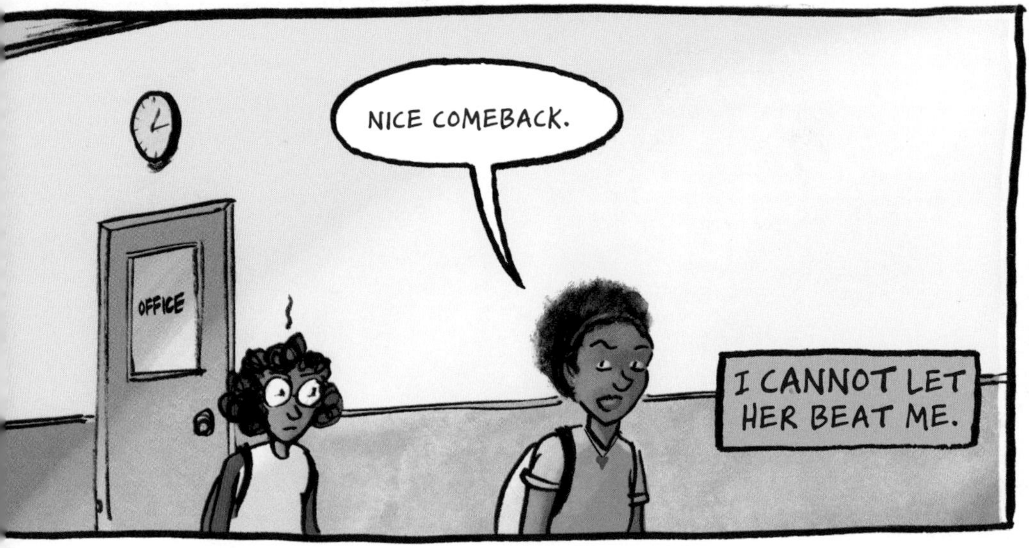
OFFICE
NICE COMEBACK.
I CANNOT LET HER BEAT ME.

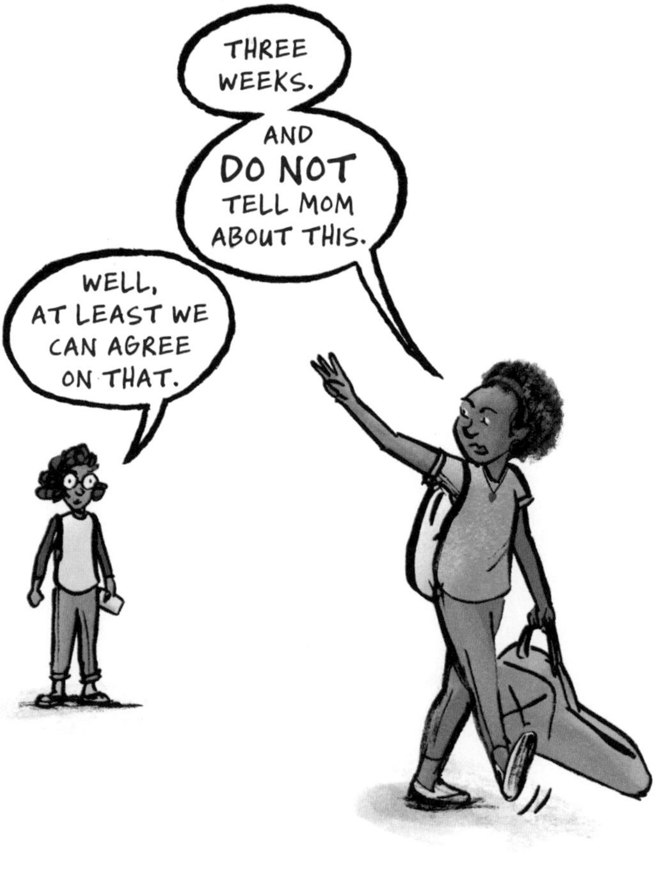
THREE WEEKS.
AND DO NOT TELL MOM ABOUT THIS.
WELL, AT LEAST WE CAN AGREE ON THAT.

Chapter 3

En Garde

As indicated in figure 3.1.a, the fencer is in proper en garde stance: Front foot pointed forward, back foot roughly 2-3ft apart and at a 90 degree angle. The knees should be bent to allow for quick and easy movement. The body is turned and the back arm is comfortably behind the body.

fig. 3.1.a

En garde is French for "on your guard." When two opponents are ready to begin, the referee speaks this phrase to alert fencers to take their positions before fencing commences. To be on guard means to be ready, poised for fighting either for attack or defense.

yes!

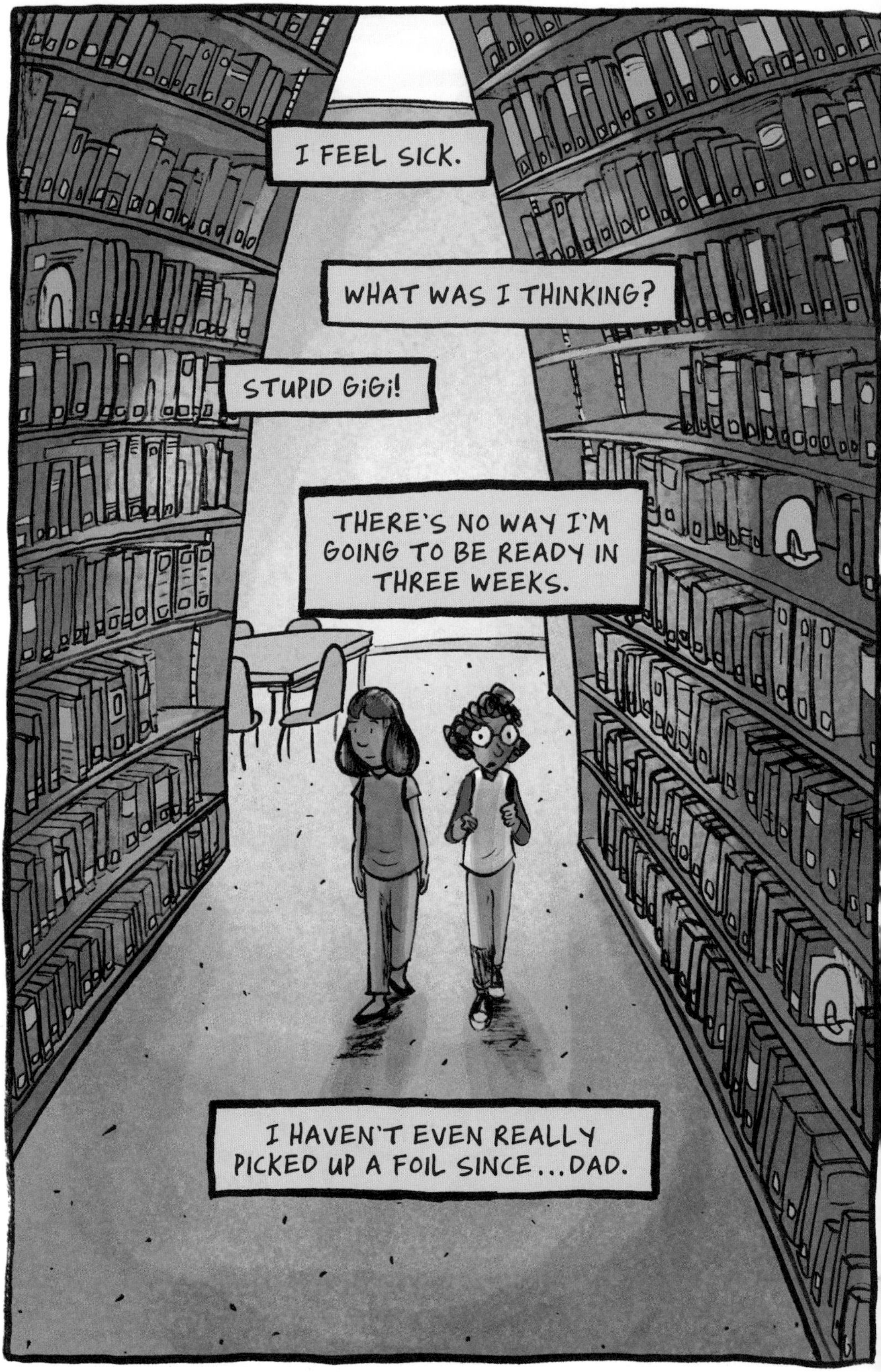
I FEEL SICK.
WHAT WAS I THINKING?
STUPID GIGI!
THERE'S NO WAY I'M GOING TO BE READY IN THREE WEEKS.
I HAVEN'T EVEN REALLY PICKED UP A FOIL SINCE...DAD.

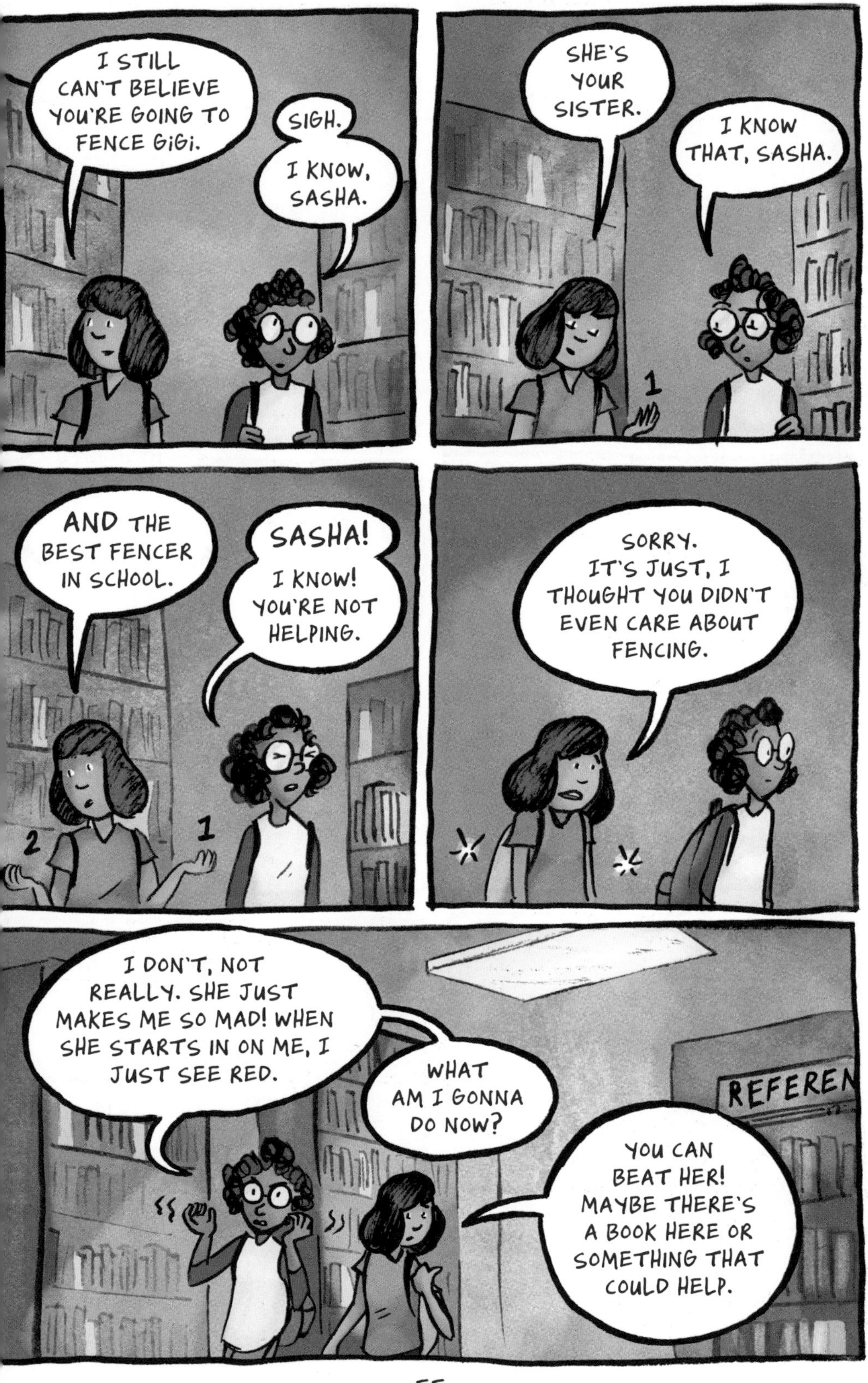
I STILL CAN'T BELIEVE YOU'RE GOING TO FENCE GiGi.
SIGH.
I KNOW, SASHA.
SHE'S YOUR SISTER.
1
I KNOW THAT, SASHA.
AND THE BEST FENCER IN SCHOOL.
2
1
SASHA!
I KNOW! YOU'RE NOT HELPING.
SORRY. IT'S JUST, I THOUGHT YOU DIDN'T EVEN CARE ABOUT FENCING.
I DON'T, NOT REALLY. SHE JUST MAKES ME SO MAD! WHEN SHE STARTS IN ON ME, I JUST SEE RED.
WHAT AM I GONNA DO NOW?
YOU CAN BEAT HER! MAYBE THERE'S A BOOK HERE OR SOMETHING THAT COULD HELP.
REFEREN

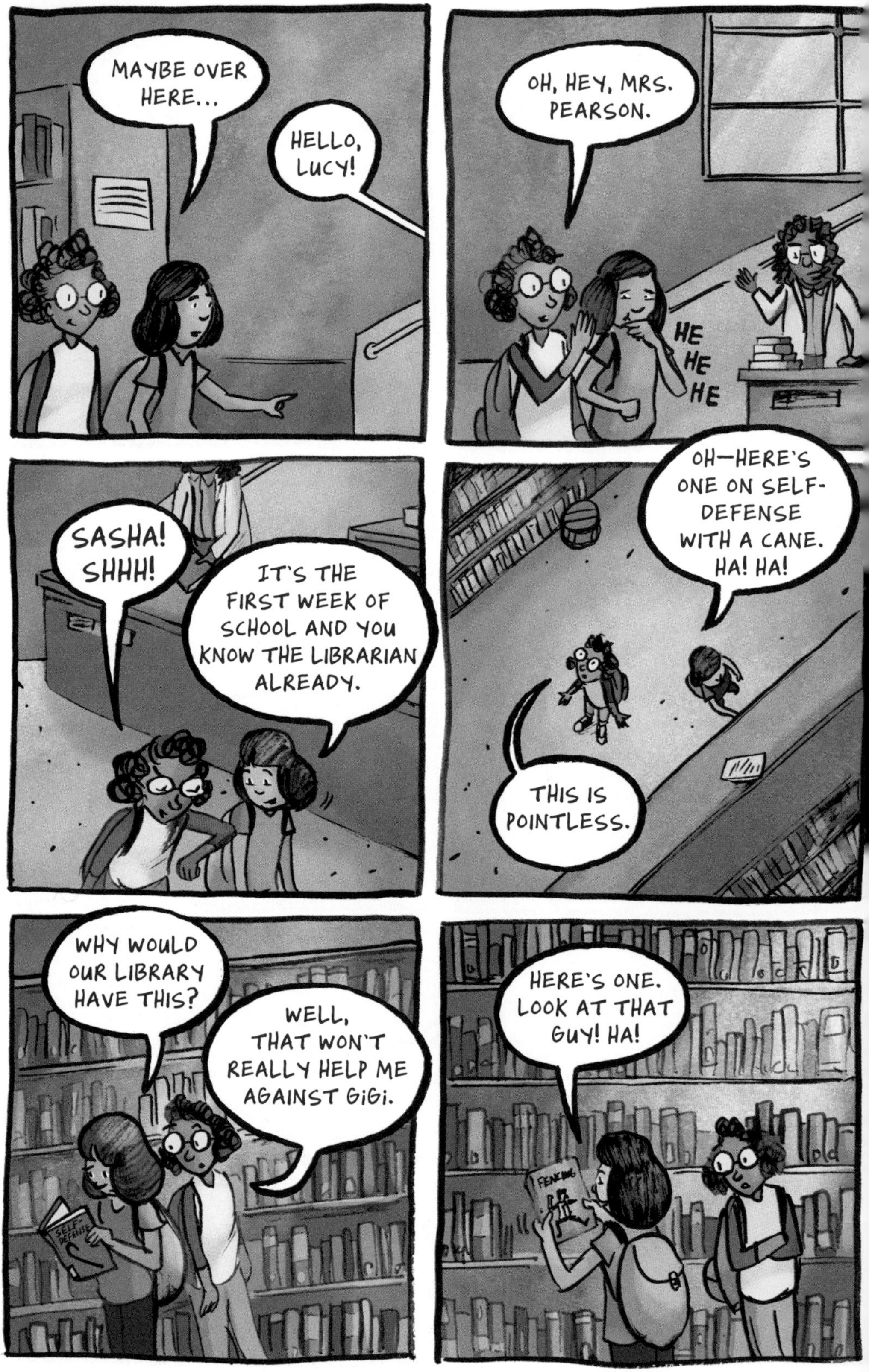
MAYBE OVER HERE...
HELLO, LUCY!
OH, HEY, MRS. PEARSON.
HE HE HE
SASHA! SHHH!
IT'S THE FIRST WEEK OF SCHOOL AND YOU KNOW THE LIBRARIAN ALREADY.
OH—HERE'S ONE ON SELF-DEFENSE WITH A CANE. HA! HA!
THIS IS POINTLESS.
WHY WOULD OUR LIBRARY HAVE THIS?
WELL, THAT WON'T REALLY HELP ME AGAINST GIGI.
SELF-DEFENSE
HERE'S ONE. LOOK AT THAT GUY! HA!
FENCING

WHAT'S WRONG?

UH, NOTHING. THAT'S JUST...MY DAD HAD THAT SAME BOOK.

OH, SORRY, I DIDN'T—

IT'S FINE. HE, UH...HE LOOKS SO RIDICULOUS. THAT'S NOT HOW FENCERS EVEN REALLY STAND.

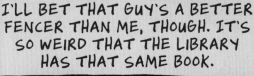

I'LL BET THAT GUY'S A BETTER FENCER THAN ME, THOUGH. IT'S SO WEIRD THAT THE LIBRARY HAS THAT SAME BOOK.

MAYBE THERE'S SOMETHING IN HERE THAT COULD HELP.

"The origins of swordplay and swordsmanship have been recorded as early as the twelfth century in Egypt. Fencing was originally used as both a pastime and in the military in single-person combat. Its popularity grew throughout Europe during the fourteenth century in fencing schools, for entertainment, sport, and combat, but it didn't become an organized competitive sport until the nineteenth century when..."

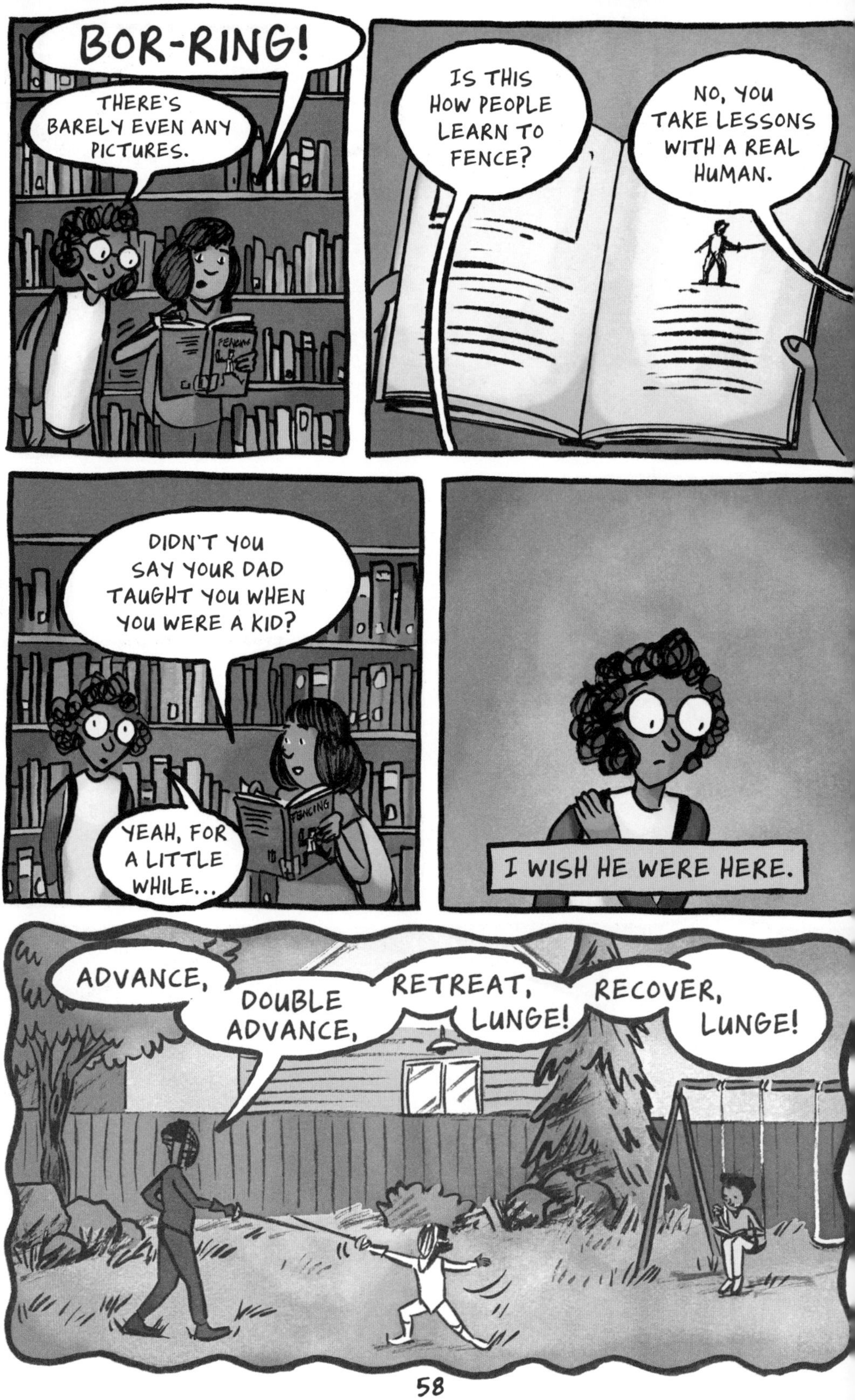
BOR-RING!
THERE'S BARELY EVEN ANY PICTURES.
FENCING
IS THIS HOW PEOPLE LEARN TO FENCE?
NO, YOU TAKE LESSONS WITH A REAL HUMAN.
DIDN'T YOU SAY YOUR DAD TAUGHT YOU WHEN YOU WERE A KID?
YEAH, FOR A LITTLE WHILE...
FENCING
I WISH HE WERE HERE.
ADVANCE,
DOUBLE ADVANCE,
RETREAT,
LUNGE!
RECOVER,
LUNGE!

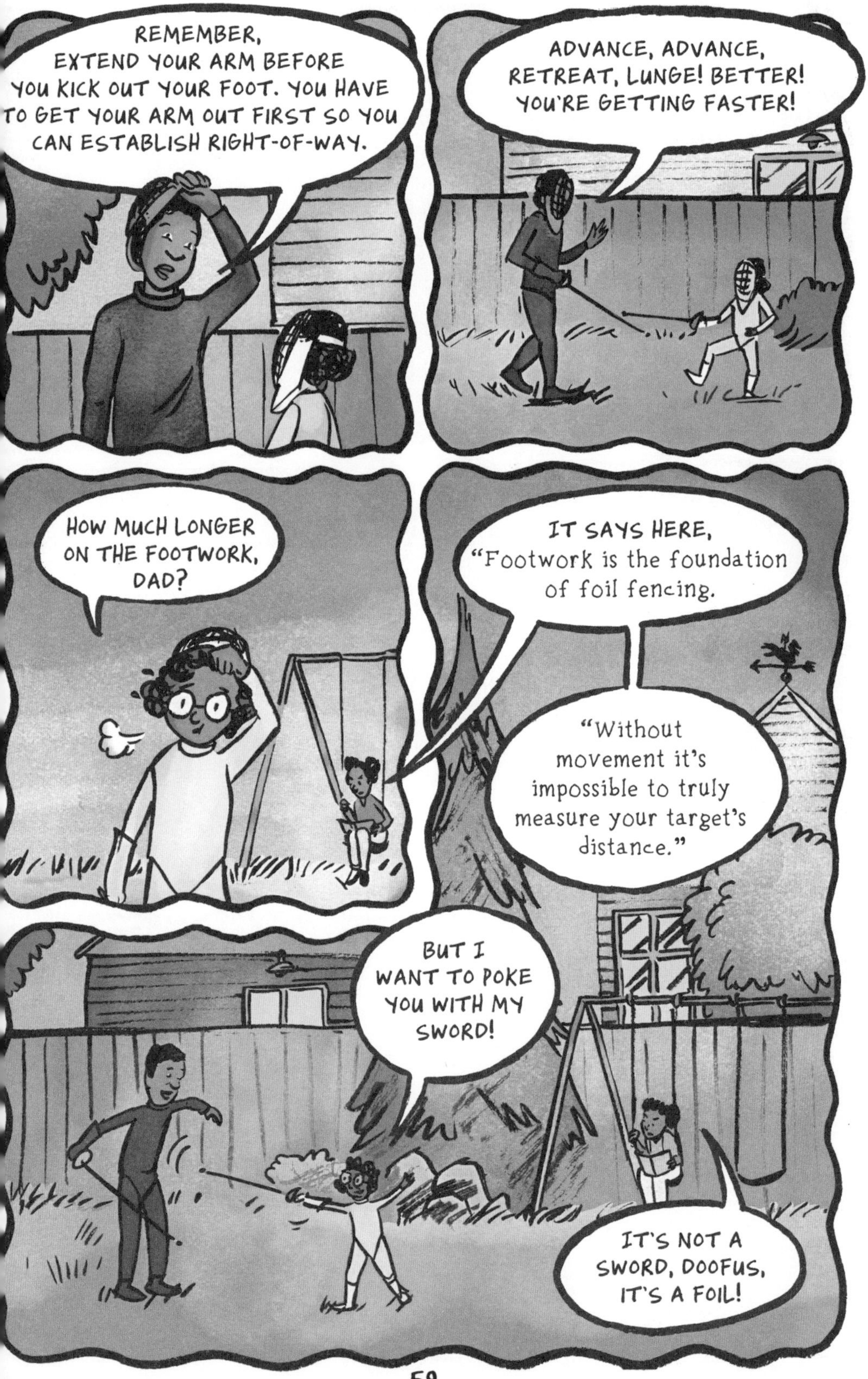
REMEMBER, EXTEND YOUR ARM BEFORE YOU KICK OUT YOUR FOOT. YOU HAVE TO GET YOUR ARM OUT FIRST SO YOU CAN ESTABLISH RIGHT-OF-WAY.
ADVANCE, ADVANCE, RETREAT, LUNGE! BETTER! YOU'RE GETTING FASTER!
HOW MUCH LONGER ON THE FOOTWORK, DAD?
IT SAYS HERE, "Footwork is the foundation of foil fencing.
"Without movement it's impossible to truly measure your target's distance."
BUT I WANT TO POKE YOU WITH MY SWORD!
IT'S NOT A SWORD, DOOFUS, IT'S A FOIL!

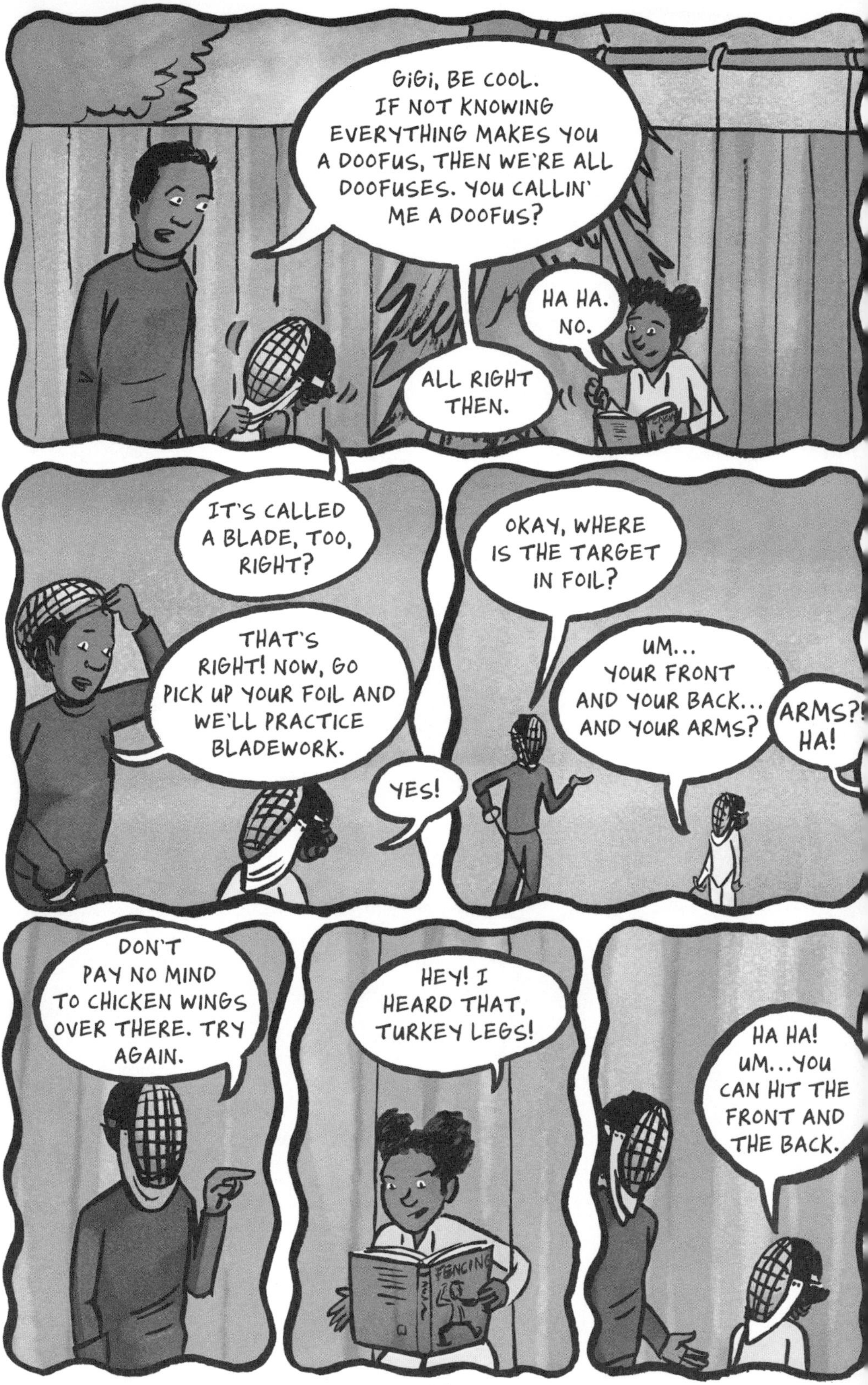

GiGi, BE COOL. IF NOT KNOWING EVERYTHING MAKES YOU A DOOFUS, THEN WE'RE ALL DOOFUSES. YOU CALLIN' ME A DOOFUS?
HA HA. NO.
ALL RIGHT THEN.
IT'S CALLED A BLADE, TOO, RIGHT?
THAT'S RIGHT! NOW, GO PICK UP YOUR FOIL AND WE'LL PRACTICE BLADEWORK.
YES!
OKAY, WHERE IS THE TARGET IN FOIL?
UM... YOUR FRONT AND YOUR BACK... AND YOUR ARMS?
ARMS?! HA!
DON'T PAY NO MIND TO CHICKEN WINGS OVER THERE. TRY AGAIN.
HEY! I HEARD THAT, TURKEY LEGS!
FENCING
HA HA! UM...YOU CAN HIT THE FRONT AND THE BACK.

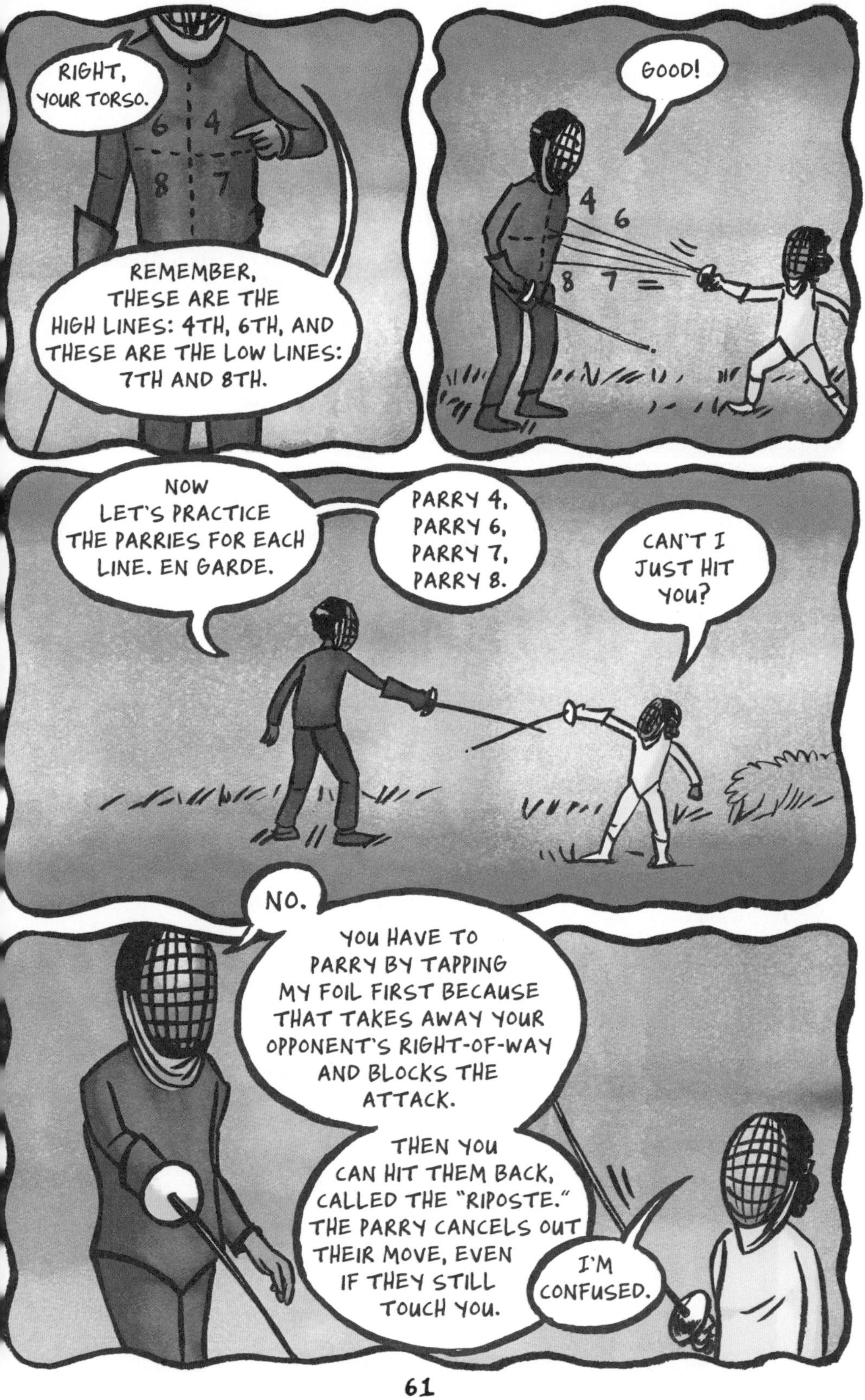
RIGHT, YOUR TORSO.
6 4 8 7
REMEMBER, THESE ARE THE HIGH LINES: 4TH, 6TH, AND THESE ARE THE LOW LINES: 7TH AND 8TH.
GOOD!
4 6 8 7
NOW LET'S PRACTICE THE PARRIES FOR EACH LINE. EN GARDE.
PARRY 4, PARRY 6, PARRY 7, PARRY 8.
CAN'T I JUST HIT YOU?
NO.
YOU HAVE TO PARRY BY TAPPING MY FOIL FIRST BECAUSE THAT TAKES AWAY YOUR OPPONENT'S RIGHT-OF-WAY AND BLOCKS THE ATTACK.
THEN YOU CAN HIT THEM BACK, CALLED THE "RIPOSTE." THE PARRY CANCELS OUT THEIR MOVE, EVEN IF THEY STILL TOUCH YOU.
I'M CONFUSED.

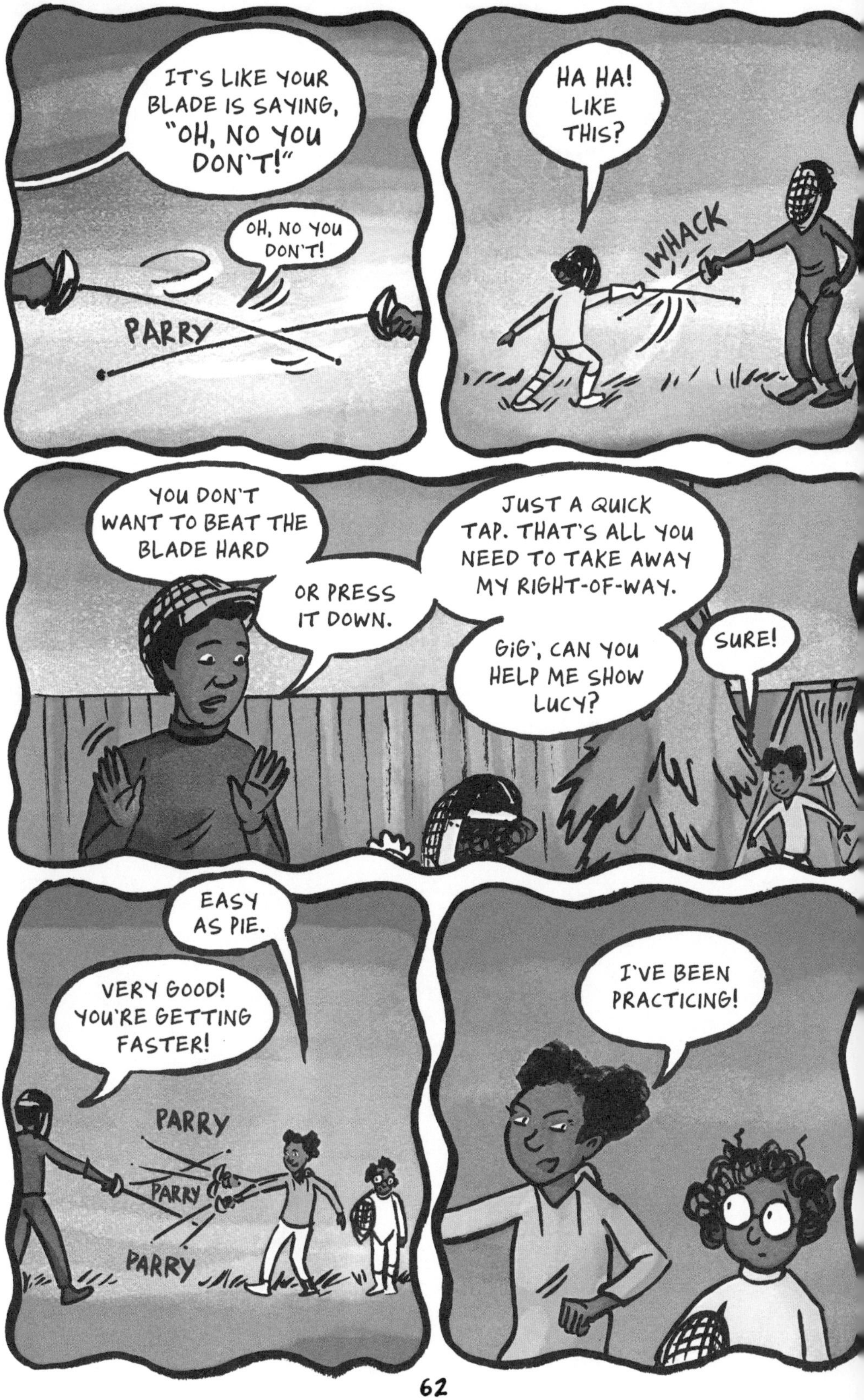
IT'S LIKE YOUR BLADE IS SAYING, "OH, NO YOU DON'T!"
OH, NO YOU DON'T!
PARRY
HA HA! LIKE THIS?
WHACK
YOU DON'T WANT TO BEAT THE BLADE HARD
OR PRESS IT DOWN.
JUST A QUICK TAP. THAT'S ALL YOU NEED TO TAKE AWAY MY RIGHT-OF-WAY.
GIG', CAN YOU HELP ME SHOW LUCY?
SURE!
EASY AS PIE.
VERY GOOD! YOU'RE GETTING FASTER!
PARRY
PARRY
PARRY
I'VE BEEN PRACTICING!

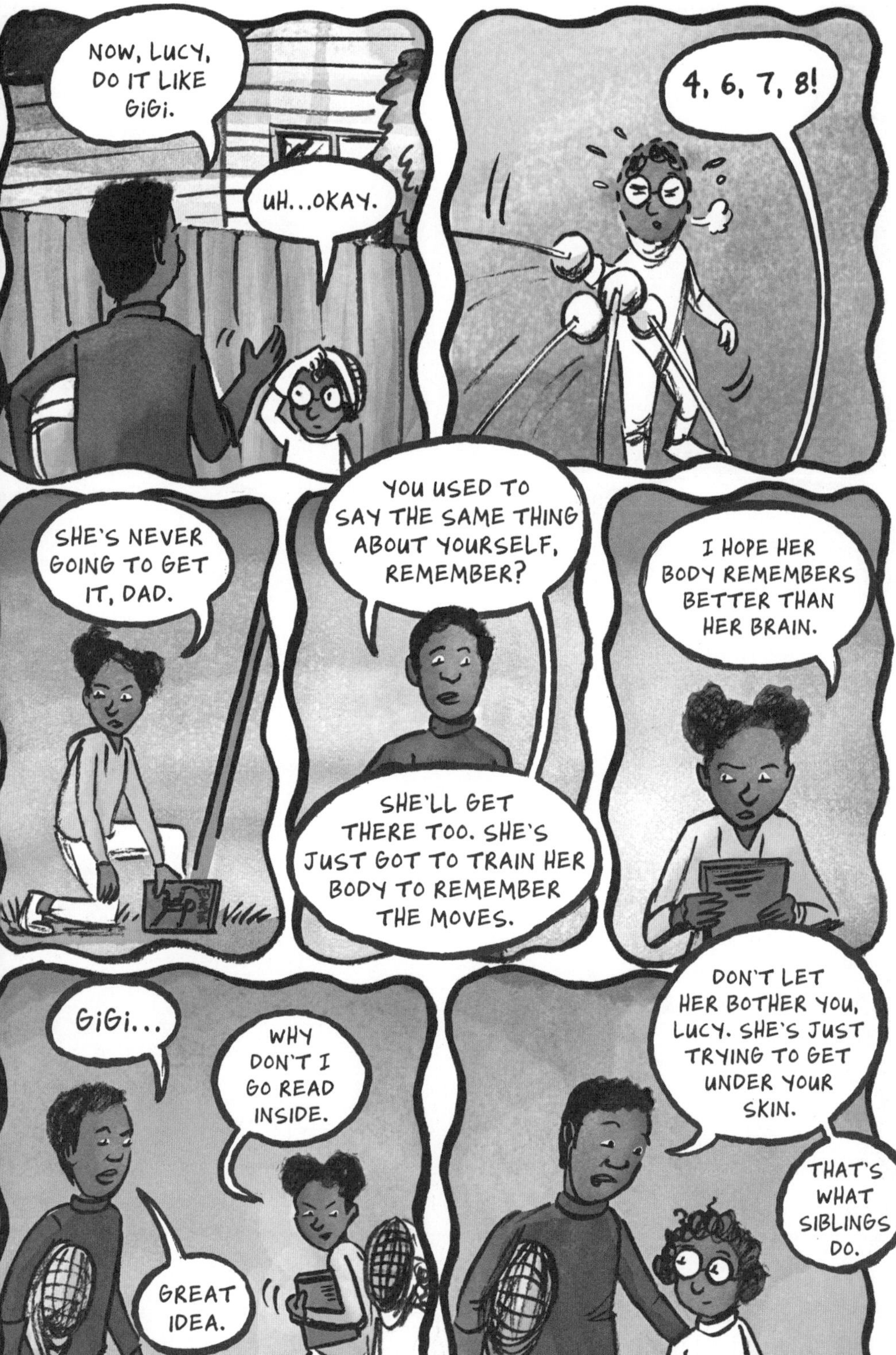
NOW, LUCY, DO IT LIKE GiGi.
UH...OKAY.
4, 6, 7, 8!
SHE'S NEVER GOING TO GET IT, DAD.
YOU USED TO SAY THE SAME THING ABOUT YOURSELF, REMEMBER?
SHE'LL GET THERE TOO. SHE'S JUST GOT TO TRAIN HER BODY TO REMEMBER THE MOVES.
I HOPE HER BODY REMEMBERS BETTER THAN HER BRAIN.
GiGi...
WHY DON'T I GO READ INSIDE.
GREAT IDEA.
DON'T LET HER BOTHER YOU, LUCY. SHE'S JUST TRYING TO GET UNDER YOUR SKIN.
THAT'S WHAT SIBLINGS DO.

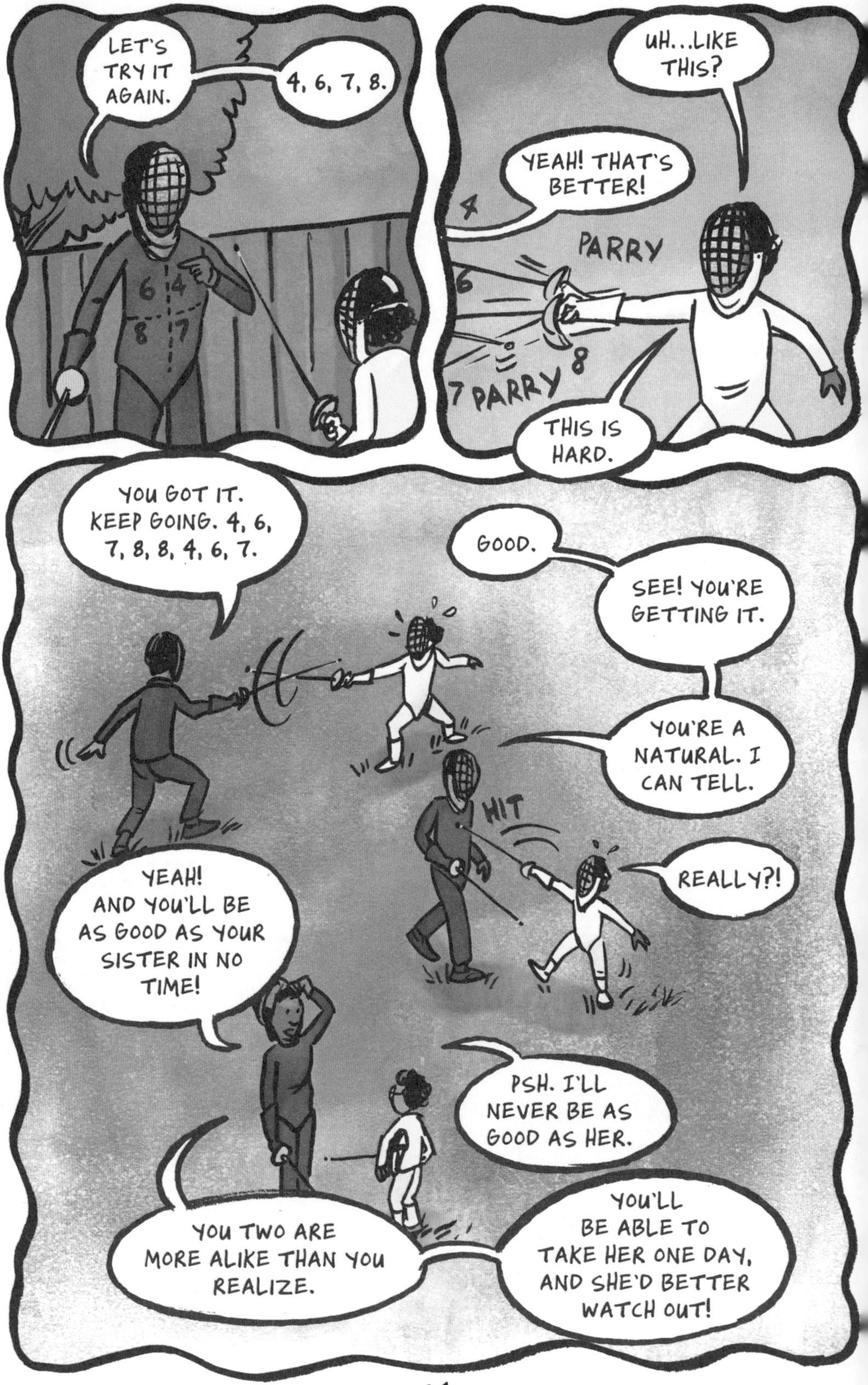

LET'S TRY IT AGAIN.
4, 6, 7, 8.
6 4 8 7
UH...LIKE THIS?
YEAH! THAT'S BETTER!
4
PARRY
6
8
7 PARRY
THIS IS HARD.
YOU GOT IT. KEEP GOING. 4, 6, 7, 8, 8, 4, 6, 7.
GOOD.
SEE! YOU'RE GETTING IT.
YOU'RE A NATURAL. I CAN TELL.
HIT
REALLY?!
YEAH! AND YOU'LL BE AS GOOD AS YOUR SISTER IN NO TIME!
PSH. I'LL NEVER BE AS GOOD AS HER.
YOU TWO ARE MORE ALIKE THAN YOU REALIZE.
YOU'LL BE ABLE TO TAKE HER ONE DAY, AND SHE'D BETTER WATCH OUT!

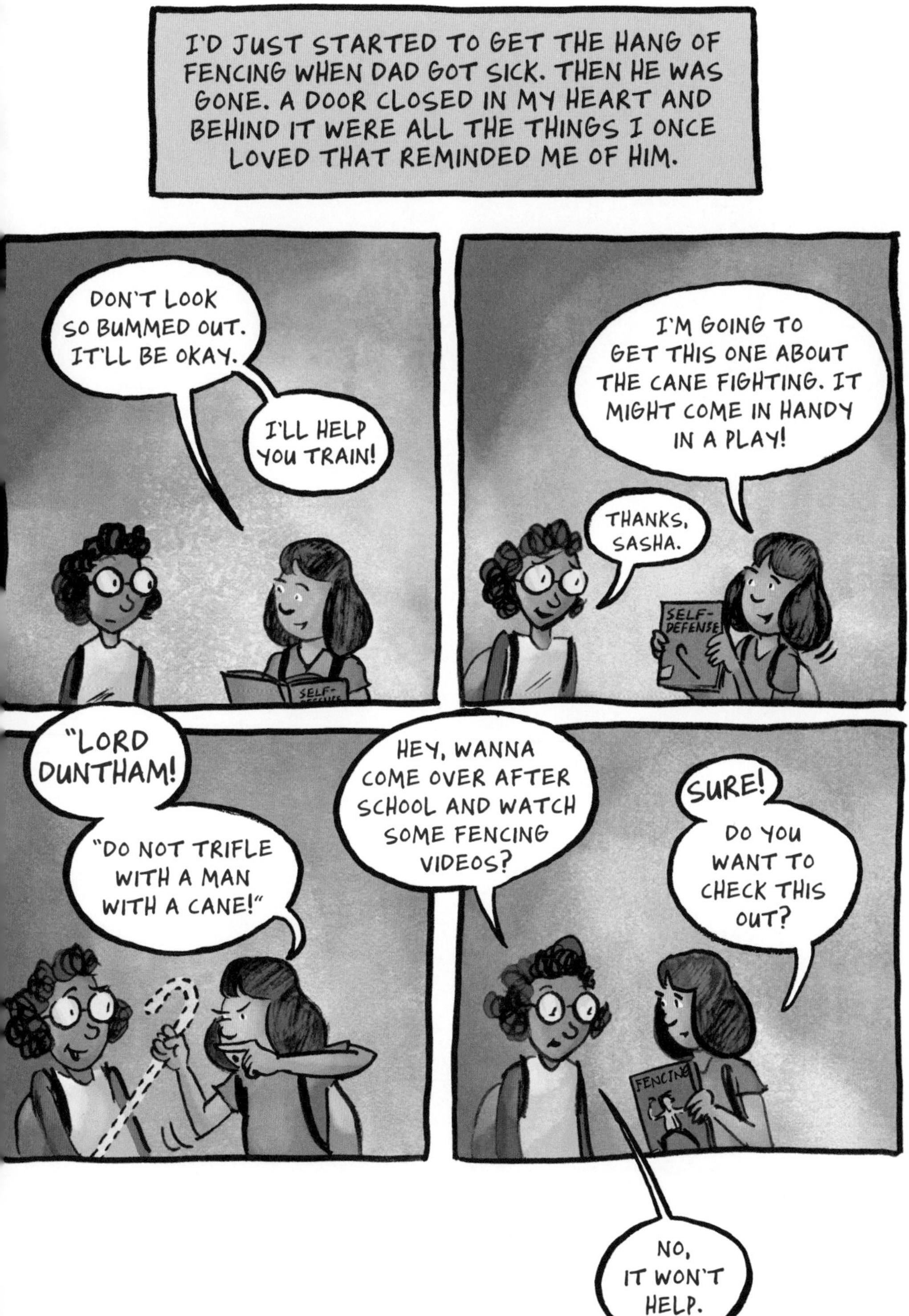
I'D JUST STARTED TO GET THE HANG OF FENCING WHEN DAD GOT SICK. THEN HE WAS GONE. A DOOR CLOSED IN MY HEART AND BEHIND IT WERE ALL THE THINGS I ONCE LOVED THAT REMINDED ME OF HIM.
DON'T LOOK SO BUMMED OUT. IT'LL BE OKAY.
I'LL HELP YOU TRAIN!
I'M GOING TO GET THIS ONE ABOUT THE CANE FIGHTING. IT MIGHT COME IN HANDY IN A PLAY!
THANKS, SASHA.
SELF-DEFENSE
"LORD DUNTHAM!
"DO NOT TRIFLE WITH A MAN WITH A CANE!"
HEY, WANNA COME OVER AFTER SCHOOL AND WATCH SOME FENCING VIDEOS?
SURE!
DO YOU WANT TO CHECK THIS OUT?
FENCING
NO, IT WON'T HELP.

Chapter 4

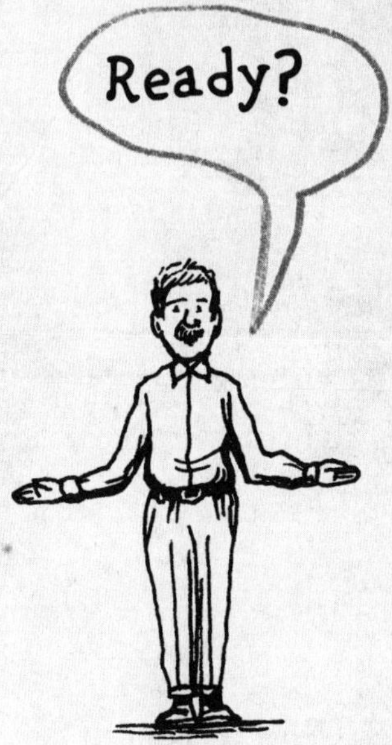
Ready?

After the fencers are in their respective positions to start the bout, the referee (or judge) gives the fencers one final opportunity to mention anything that might suspend the match. They ask the fencers, "Ready?" If neither opponent has any reason to stop proceeding, the bout will commence.

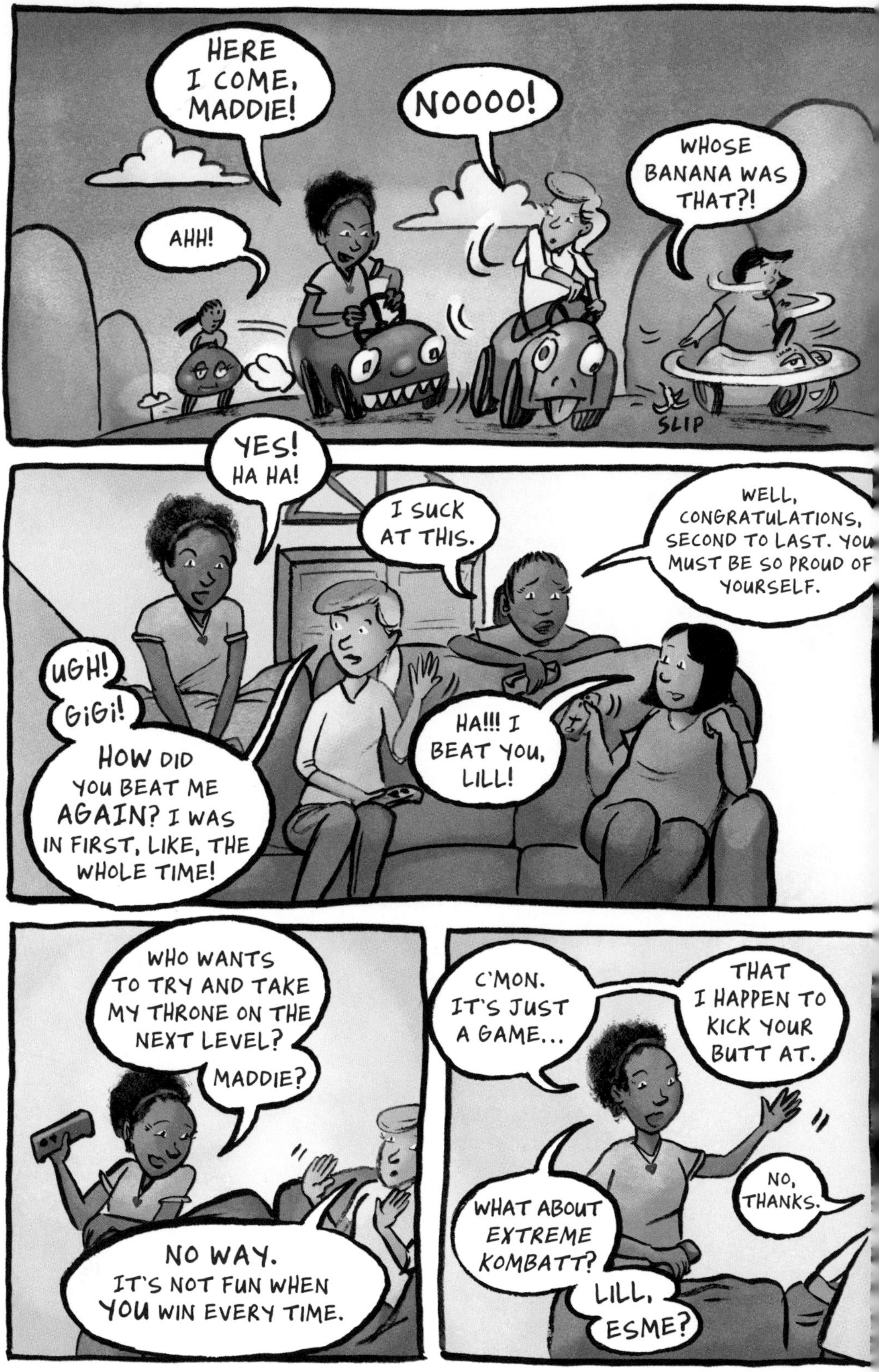
HERE I COME, MADDIE!
AHH!
NOOOO!
WHOSE BANANA WAS THAT?!
SLIP
YES! HA HA!
I SUCK AT THIS.
WELL, CONGRATULATIONS, SECOND TO LAST. YOU MUST BE SO PROUD OF YOURSELF.
UGH!
GiGi!
HOW DID YOU BEAT ME AGAIN? I WAS IN FIRST, LIKE, THE WHOLE TIME!
HA!!! I BEAT YOU, LILL!
WHO WANTS TO TRY AND TAKE MY THRONE ON THE NEXT LEVEL?
MADDIE?
NO WAY. IT'S NOT FUN WHEN YOU WIN EVERY TIME.
C'MON. IT'S JUST A GAME...
THAT I HAPPEN TO KICK YOUR BUTT AT.
WHAT ABOUT EXTREME KOMBATT?
LILL, ESME?
NO, THANKS.

WHEN DO YOU HAVE TIME TO GET SO GOOD AT VIDEO GAMES, GIGI?

YEAH, ALL YOU EVER DO IS FENCE AND STUDY.

THAT'S ALL THEY THINK OF ME.

I NEVER SLEEP.

IT'S NOT FAIR. YOU'RE THE BEST AT EVERYTHING.

I WISH THEY WOULDN'T SAY THAT ALL THE TIME.

PSHHH.

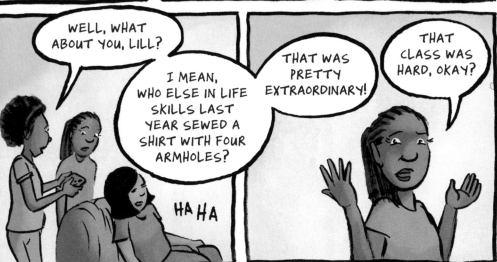

WELL, WHAT ABOUT YOU, LILL?

I MEAN, WHO ELSE IN LIFE SKILLS LAST YEAR SEWED A SHIRT WITH FOUR ARMHOLES?

THAT WAS PRETTY EXTRAORDINARY!

THAT CLASS WAS HARD, OKAY?

HA HA

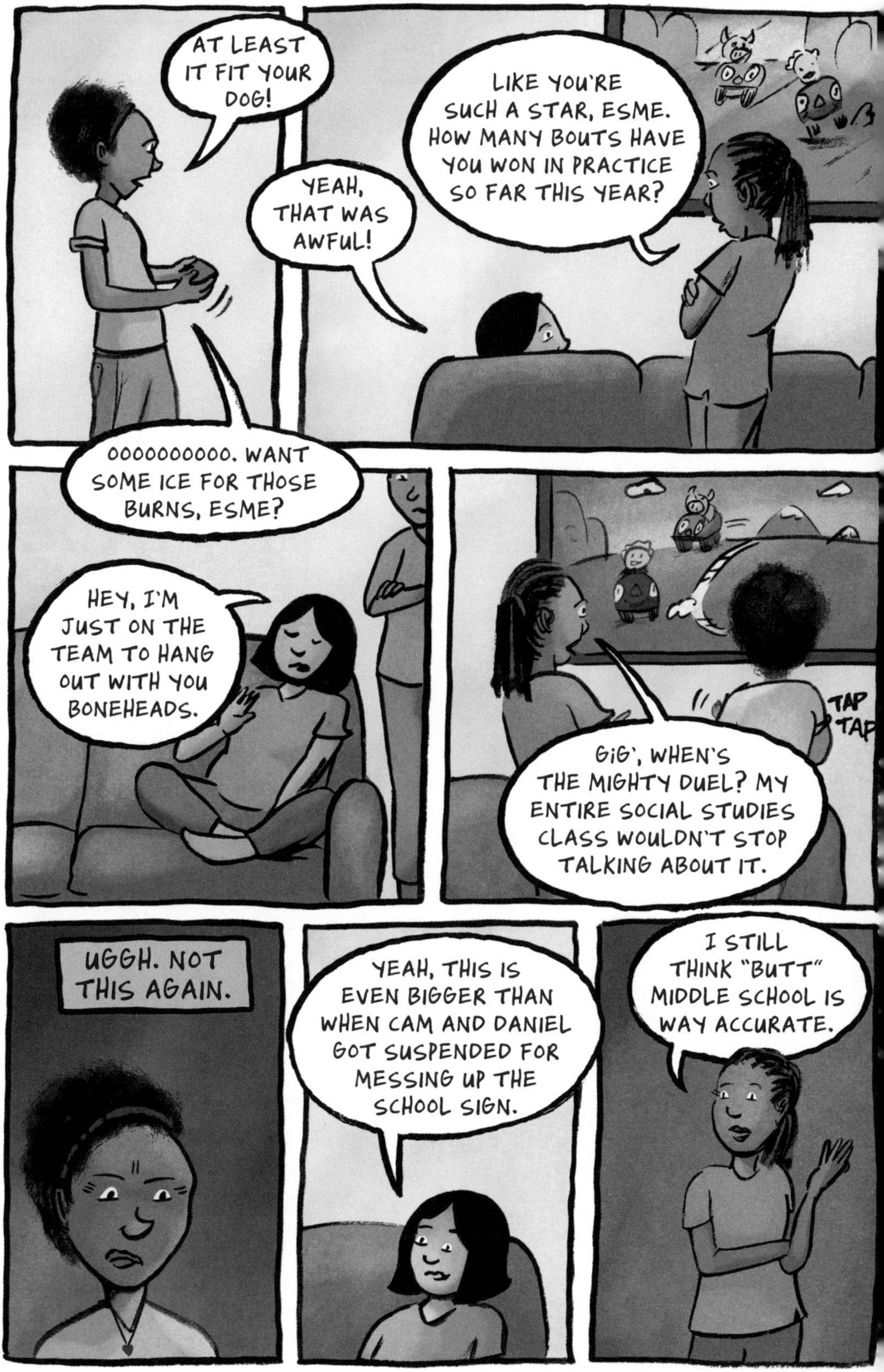
AT LEAST IT FIT YOUR DOG!
YEAH, THAT WAS AWFUL!
LIKE YOU'RE SUCH A STAR, ESME. HOW MANY BOUTS HAVE YOU WON IN PRACTICE SO FAR THIS YEAR?
OOOOOOOOOO. WANT SOME ICE FOR THOSE BURNS, ESME?
HEY, I'M JUST ON THE TEAM TO HANG OUT WITH YOU BONEHEADS.
TAP TAP
GIG', WHEN'S THE MIGHTY DUEL? MY ENTIRE SOCIAL STUDIES CLASS WOULDN'T STOP TALKING ABOUT IT.
UGGH. NOT THIS AGAIN.
YEAH, THIS IS EVEN BIGGER THAN WHEN CAM AND DANIEL GOT SUSPENDED FOR MESSING UP THE SCHOOL SIGN.
I STILL THINK "BUTT" MIDDLE SCHOOL IS WAY ACCURATE.

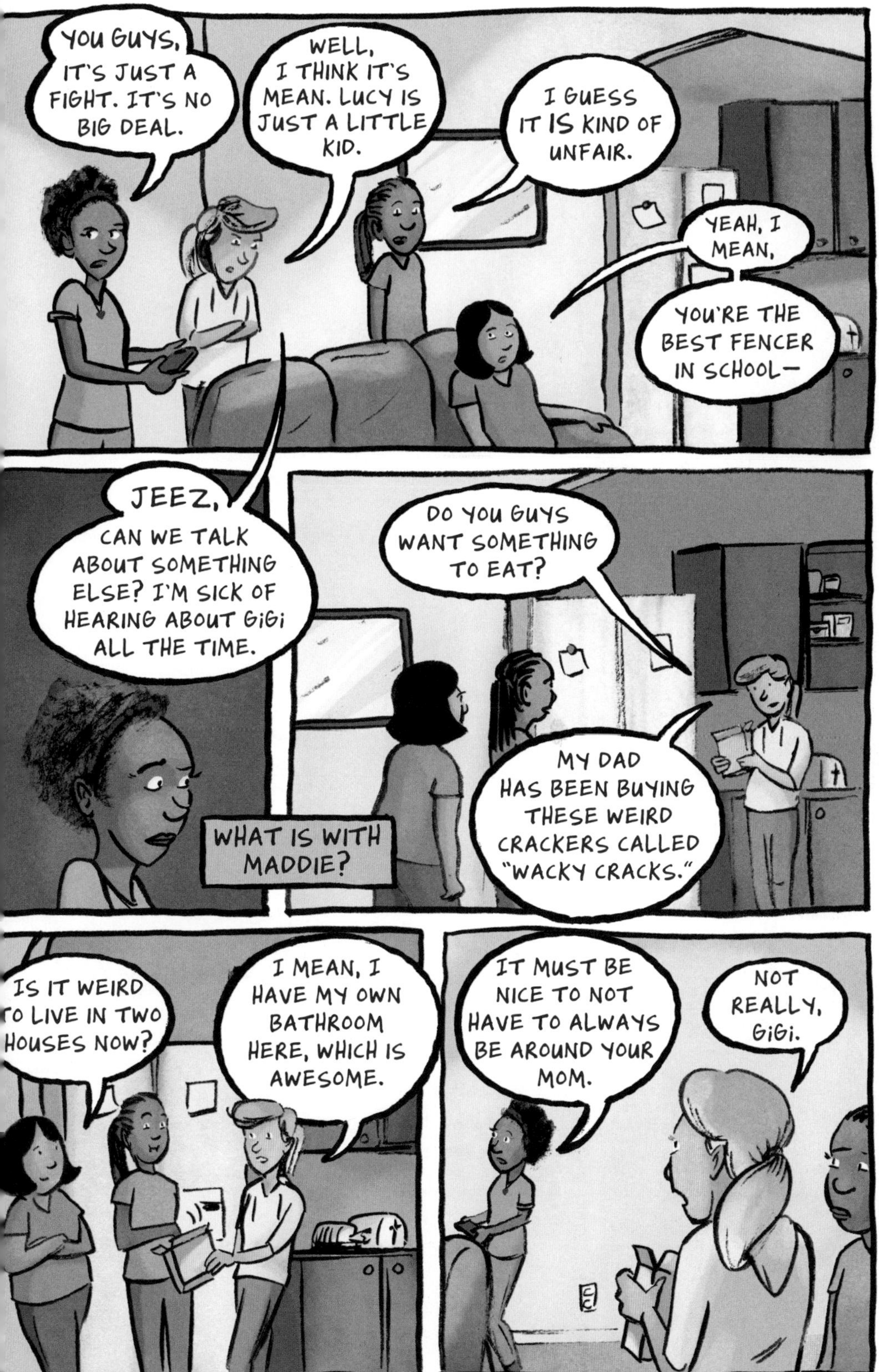
YOU GUYS, IT'S JUST A FIGHT. IT'S NO BIG DEAL.
WELL, I THINK IT'S MEAN. LUCY IS JUST A LITTLE KID.
I GUESS IT IS KIND OF UNFAIR.
YEAH, I MEAN,
YOU'RE THE BEST FENCER IN SCHOOL—
JEEZ, CAN WE TALK ABOUT SOMETHING ELSE? I'M SICK OF HEARING ABOUT GIGI ALL THE TIME.
WHAT IS WITH MADDIE?
DO YOU GUYS WANT SOMETHING TO EAT?
MY DAD HAS BEEN BUYING THESE WEIRD CRACKERS CALLED "WACKY CRACKS."
IS IT WEIRD TO LIVE IN TWO HOUSES NOW?
I MEAN, I HAVE MY OWN BATHROOM HERE, WHICH IS AWESOME.
IT MUST BE NICE TO NOT HAVE TO ALWAYS BE AROUND YOUR MOM.
NOT REALLY, GIGI.

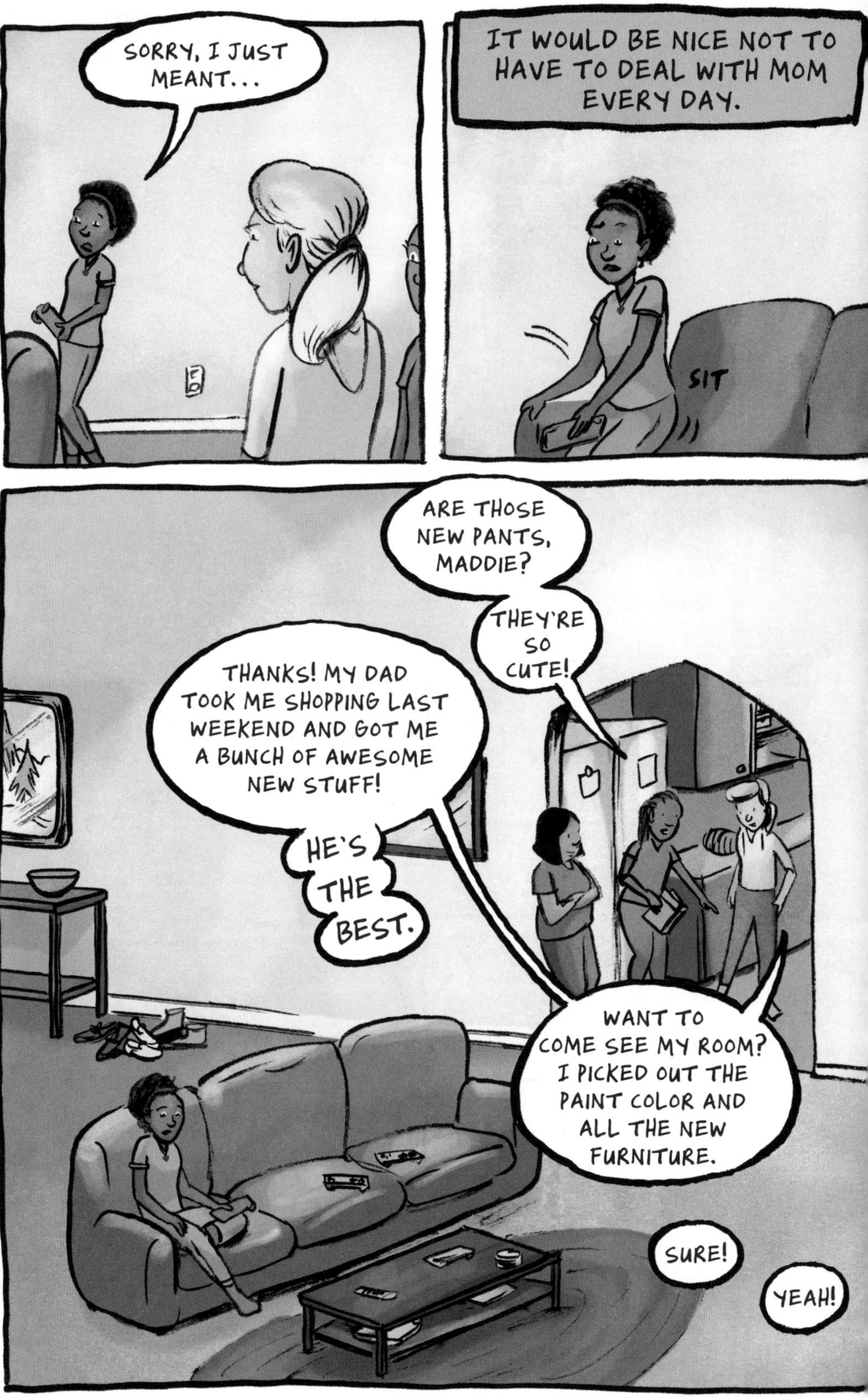
SORRY, I JUST MEANT...
IT WOULD BE NICE NOT TO HAVE TO DEAL WITH MOM EVERY DAY.
SIT
ARE THOSE NEW PANTS, MADDIE?
THEY'RE SO CUTE!
THANKS! MY DAD TOOK ME SHOPPING LAST WEEKEND AND GOT ME A BUNCH OF AWESOME NEW STUFF!
HE'S THE BEST.
WANT TO COME SEE MY ROOM? I PICKED OUT THE PAINT COLOR AND ALL THE NEW FURNITURE.
SURE!
YEAH!

MADDIE CAN BE SUCH A JERK,

LIKE OUT OF NOWHERE.

I DON'T GET IT.

AND WHAT'S WITH HER DEFENDING LUCY?

MASH
MASH
MASH

EVERYONE DEFENDS LUCY.

REDOUBLE, REDOUBLE, REDOUBLE! ALL RIGHT!

PHEW! I NEED A BREAK!

HIGH FIVE! C'MON, DON'T LEAVE ME HANGING!

DA-AD.

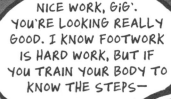

NICE WORK, GIG'. YOU'RE LOOKING REALLY GOOD. I KNOW FOOTWORK IS HARD WORK, BUT IF YOU TRAIN YOUR BODY TO KNOW THE STEPS—

THEY'LL BE AUTOMATIC. YOU TELL ME THIS EVERY TIME.

I GUESS I NEED SOME NEW MATERIAL! THE APPR—

APPRENTICE HAS BECOME THE MASTER.

73

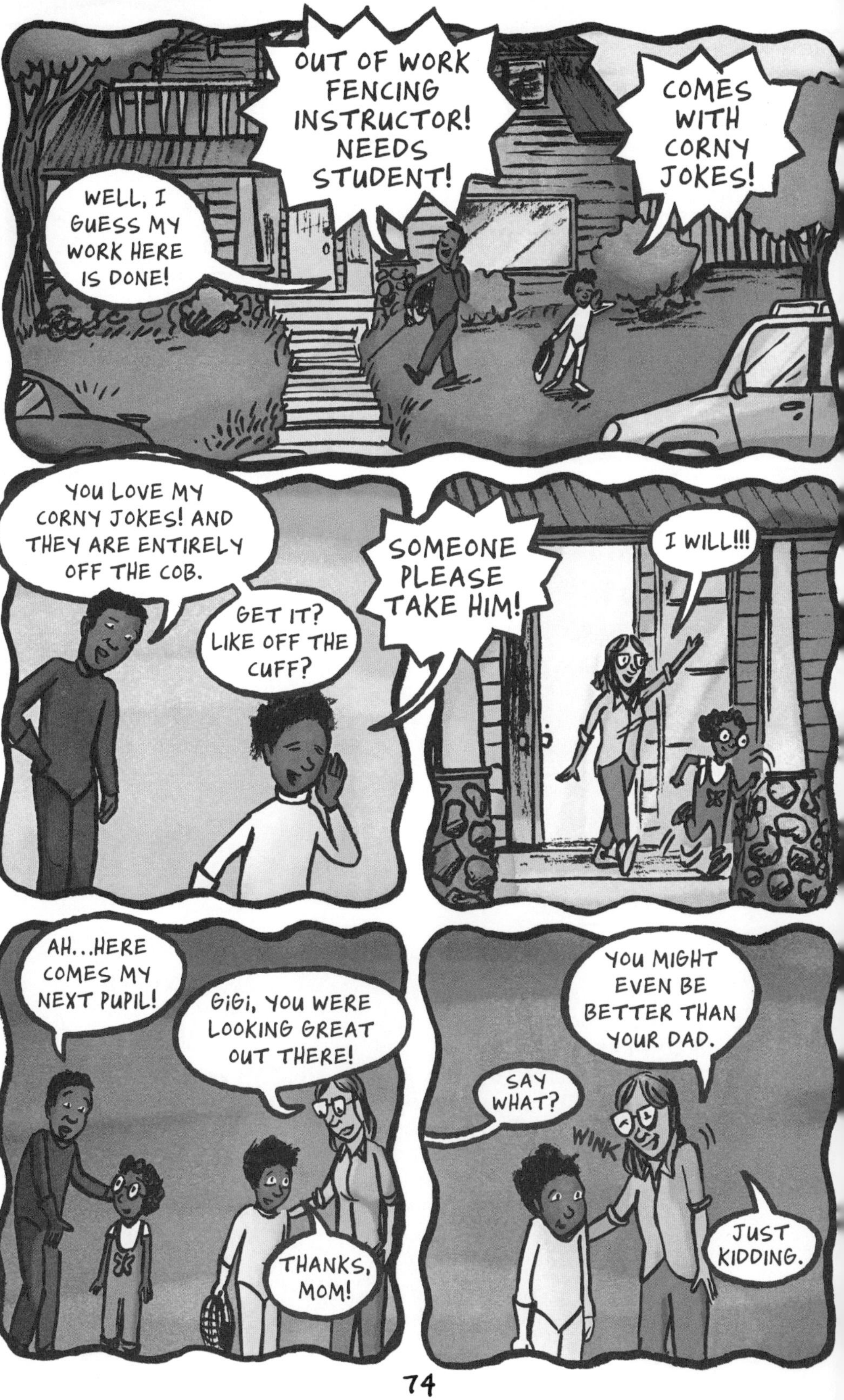
OUT OF WORK FENCING INSTRUCTOR! NEEDS STUDENT!
COMES WITH CORNY JOKES!
WELL, I GUESS MY WORK HERE IS DONE!
YOU LOVE MY CORNY JOKES! AND THEY ARE ENTIRELY OFF THE COB.
GET IT? LIKE OFF THE CUFF?
SOMEONE PLEASE TAKE HIM!
I WILL!!!
AH...HERE COMES MY NEXT PUPIL!
GiGi, YOU WERE LOOKING GREAT OUT THERE!
THANKS, MOM!
YOU MIGHT EVEN BE BETTER THAN YOUR DAD.
SAY WHAT?
WINK
JUST KIDDING.

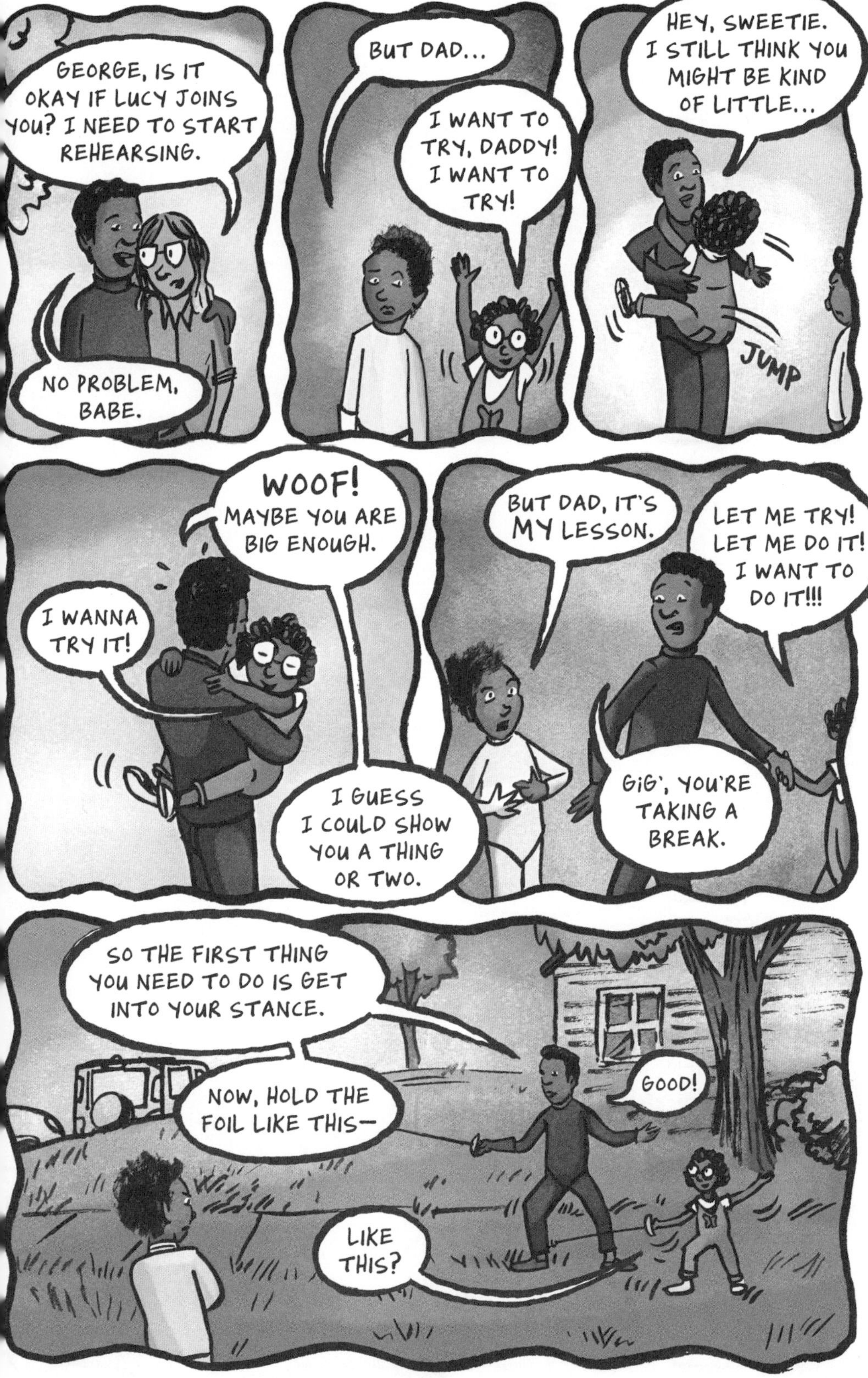
GEORGE, IS IT OKAY IF LUCY JOINS YOU? I NEED TO START REHEARSING.
NO PROBLEM, BABE.
BUT DAD...
I WANT TO TRY, DADDY! I WANT TO TRY!
HEY, SWEETIE. I STILL THINK YOU MIGHT BE KIND OF LITTLE...
JUMP
WOOF! MAYBE YOU ARE BIG ENOUGH.
I WANNA TRY IT!
I GUESS I COULD SHOW YOU A THING OR TWO.
BUT DAD, IT'S MY LESSON.
LET ME TRY! LET ME DO IT! I WANT TO DO IT!!!
GIG', YOU'RE TAKING A BREAK.
SO THE FIRST THING YOU NEED TO DO IS GET INTO YOUR STANCE.
NOW, HOLD THE FOIL LIKE THIS—
GOOD!
LIKE THIS?

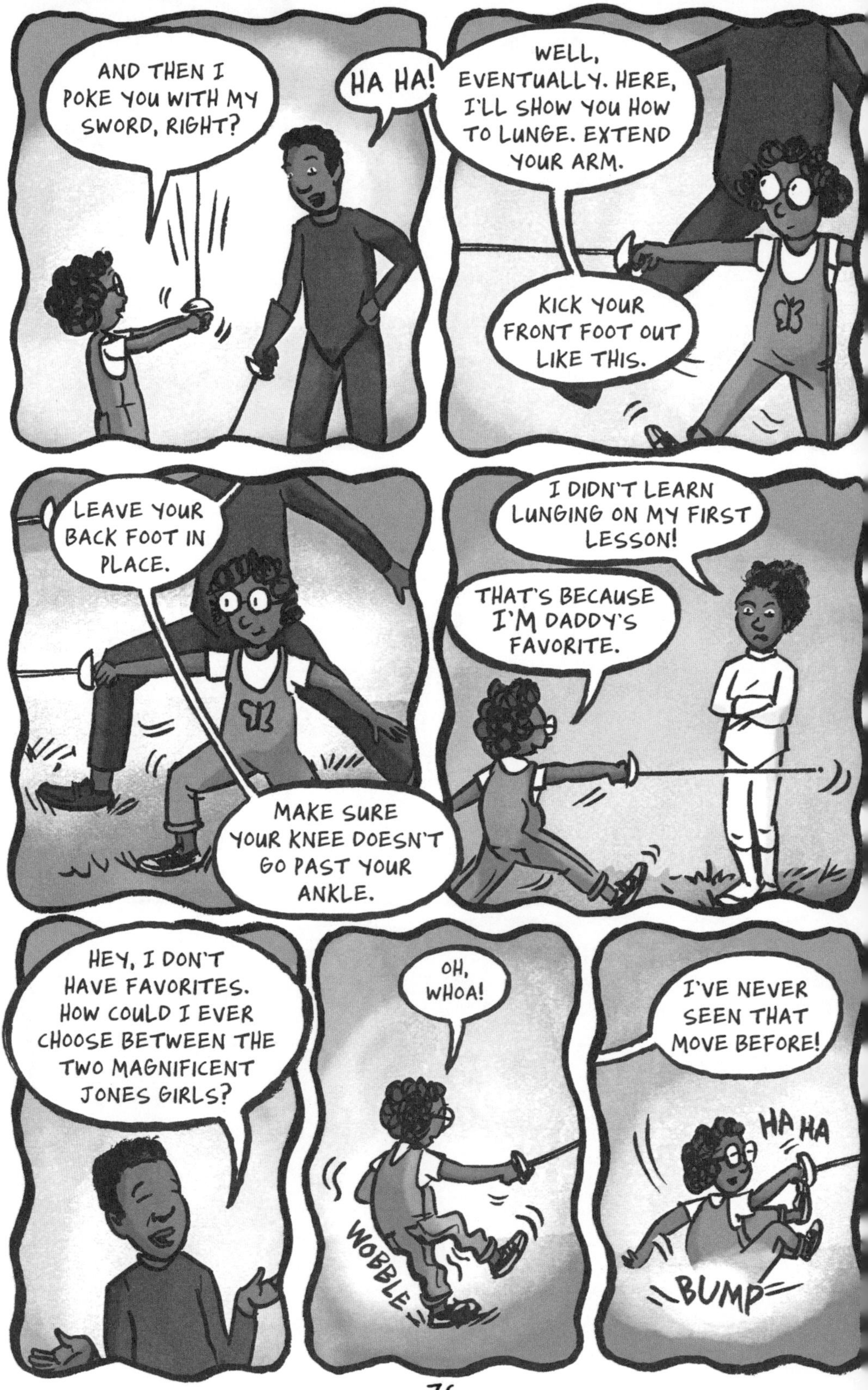
AND THEN I POKE YOU WITH MY SWORD, RIGHT?
HA HA!
WELL, EVENTUALLY. HERE, I'LL SHOW YOU HOW TO LUNGE. EXTEND YOUR ARM.
KICK YOUR FRONT FOOT OUT LIKE THIS.
LEAVE YOUR BACK FOOT IN PLACE.
MAKE SURE YOUR KNEE DOESN'T GO PAST YOUR ANKLE.
I DIDN'T LEARN LUNGING ON MY FIRST LESSON!
THAT'S BECAUSE I'M DADDY'S FAVORITE.
HEY, I DON'T HAVE FAVORITES. HOW COULD I EVER CHOOSE BETWEEN THE TWO MAGNIFICENT JONES GIRLS?
OH, WHOA!
WOBBLE
I'VE NEVER SEEN THAT MOVE BEFORE!
HA HA
BUMP

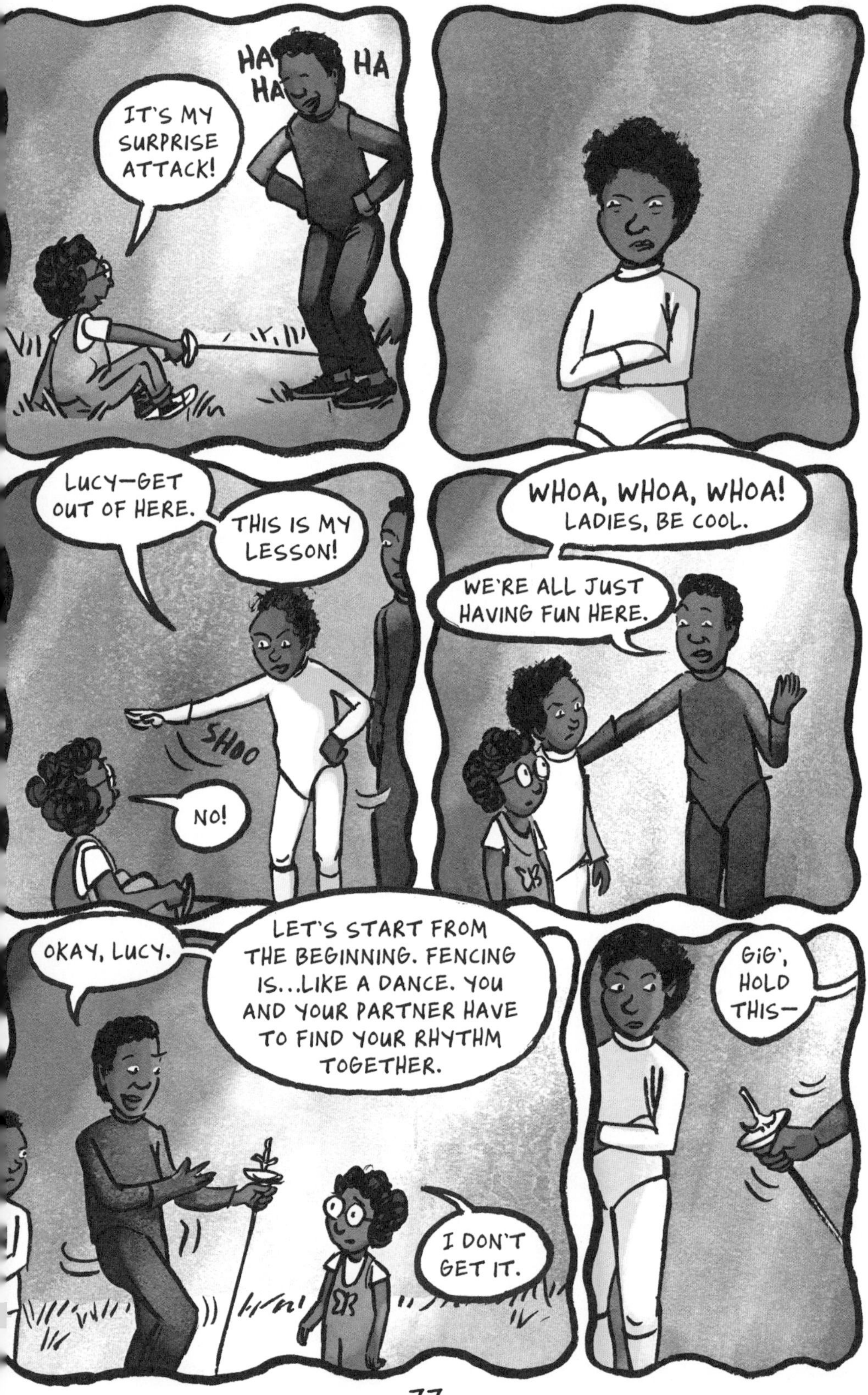
IT'S MY SURPRISE ATTACK!
HA HA HA
LUCY—GET OUT OF HERE.
THIS IS MY LESSON!
SHOO
NO!
WHOA, WHOA, WHOA! LADIES, BE COOL.
WE'RE ALL JUST HAVING FUN HERE.
OKAY, LUCY.
LET'S START FROM THE BEGINNING. FENCING IS...LIKE A DANCE. YOU AND YOUR PARTNER HAVE TO FIND YOUR RHYTHM TOGETHER.
I DON'T GET IT.
GIG', HOLD THIS—

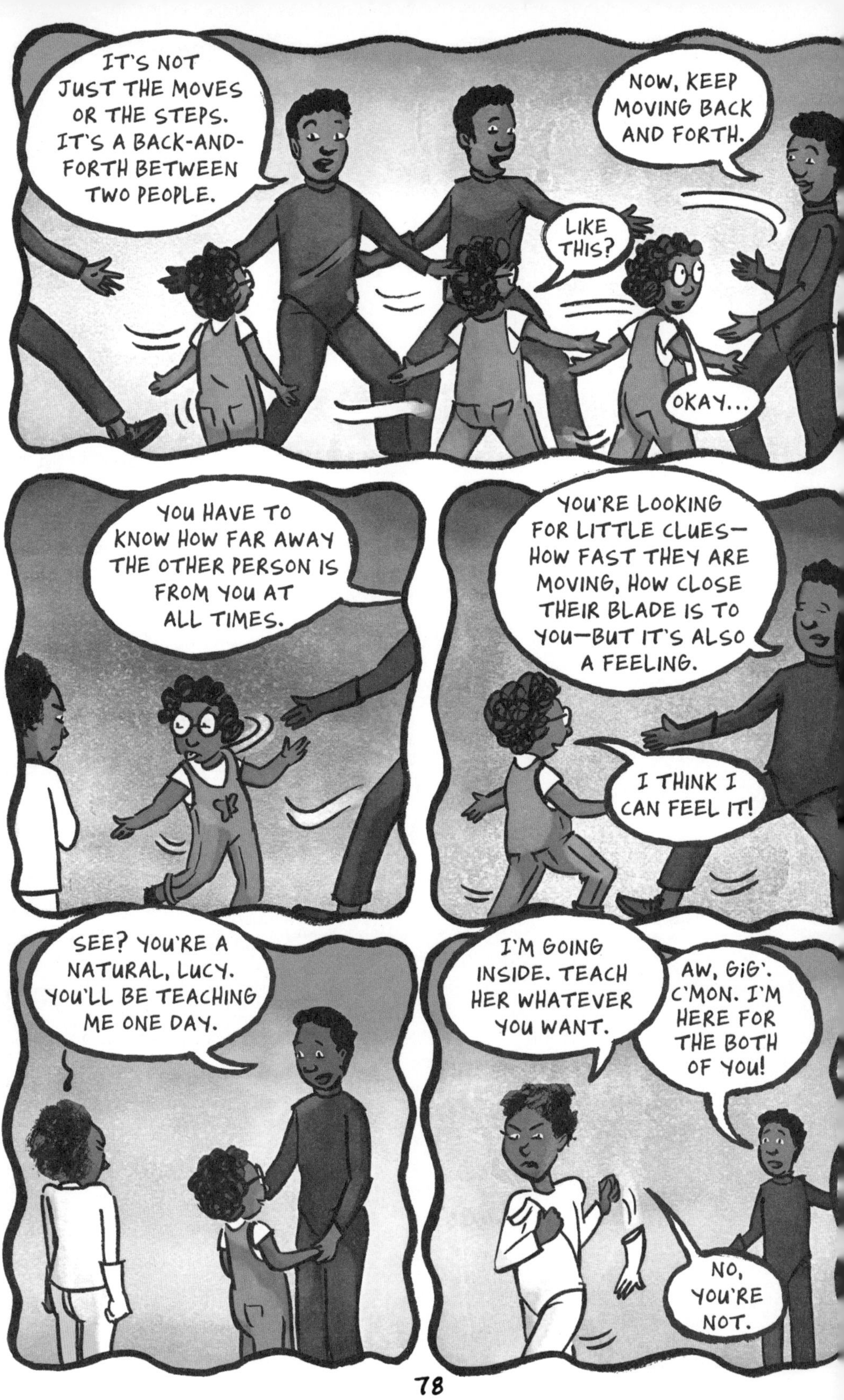
IT'S NOT JUST THE MOVES OR THE STEPS. IT'S A BACK-AND-FORTH BETWEEN TWO PEOPLE.
LIKE THIS?
NOW, KEEP MOVING BACK AND FORTH.
OKAY...
YOU HAVE TO KNOW HOW FAR AWAY THE OTHER PERSON IS FROM YOU AT ALL TIMES.
YOU'RE LOOKING FOR LITTLE CLUES—HOW FAST THEY ARE MOVING, HOW CLOSE THEIR BLADE IS TO YOU—BUT IT'S ALSO A FEELING.
I THINK I CAN FEEL IT!
SEE? YOU'RE A NATURAL, LUCY. YOU'LL BE TEACHING ME ONE DAY.
I'M GOING INSIDE. TEACH HER WHATEVER YOU WANT.
AW, GIG'. C'MON. I'M HERE FOR THE BOTH OF YOU!
NO, YOU'RE NOT.

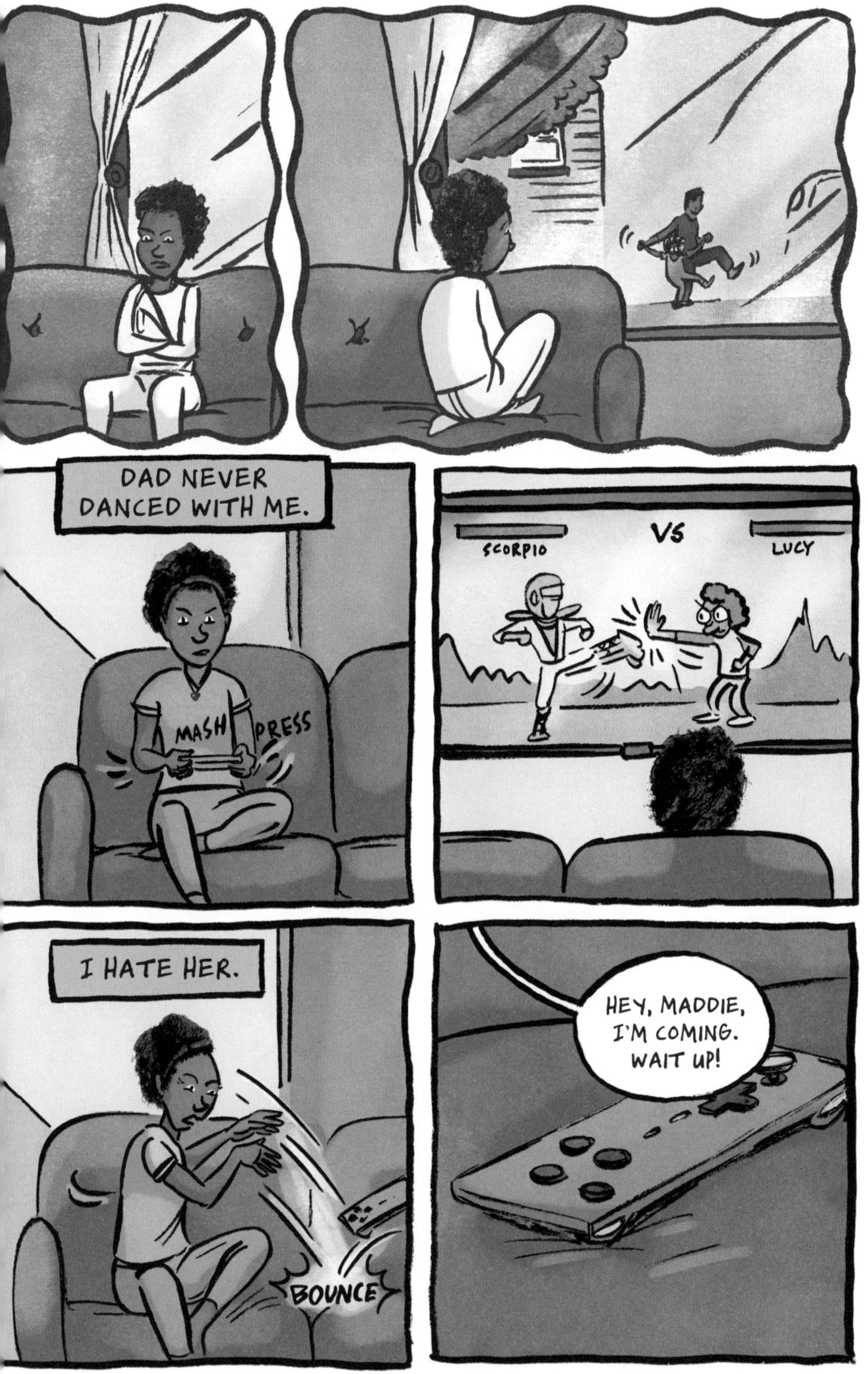
DAD NEVER DANCED WITH ME.
VS
SCORPIO
LUCY
MASH
PRESS
I HATE HER.
BOUNCE
HEY, MADDIE, I'M COMING. WAIT UP!

Chapter 5

Allez!

The style in which a fencer is trained determines the language terminology they will use. In American fencing, the styles are primarily French and Italian in origin. The term *allez* is French, meaning "Go!" The command of *allez* is given by the referee to signify the start of the bout and that action may begin. When a fencer is ready, they must decide if they will attack or defend first, and often their decision is based on the moves of their opponent.

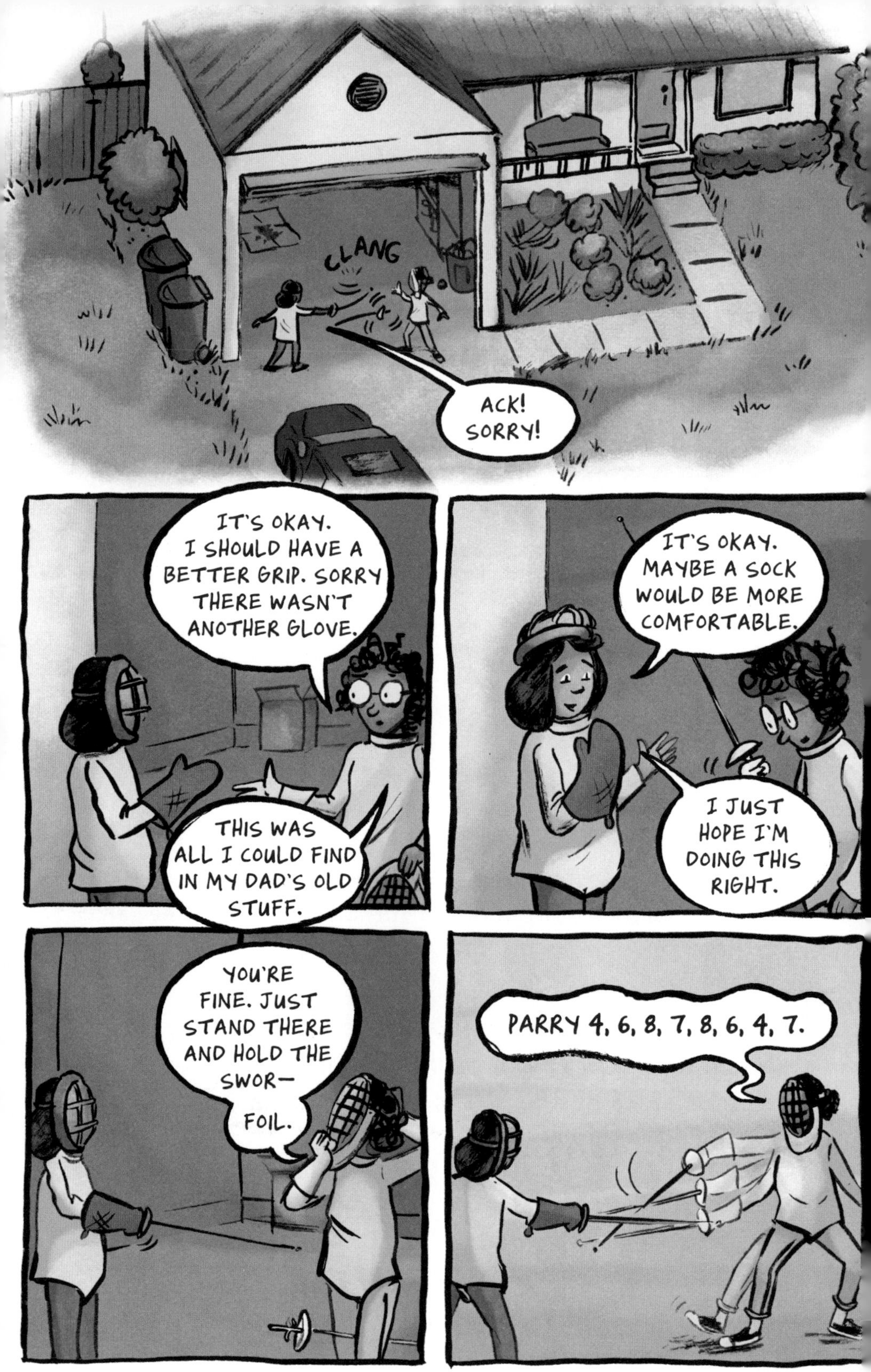
CLANG
ACK! SORRY!
IT'S OKAY. I SHOULD HAVE A BETTER GRIP. SORRY THERE WASN'T ANOTHER GLOVE.
THIS WAS ALL I COULD FIND IN MY DAD'S OLD STUFF.
IT'S OKAY. MAYBE A SOCK WOULD BE MORE COMFORTABLE.
I JUST HOPE I'M DOING THIS RIGHT.
YOU'RE FINE. JUST STAND THERE AND HOLD THE SWOR—
FOIL.
PARRY 4, 6, 8, 7, 8, 6, 4, 7.

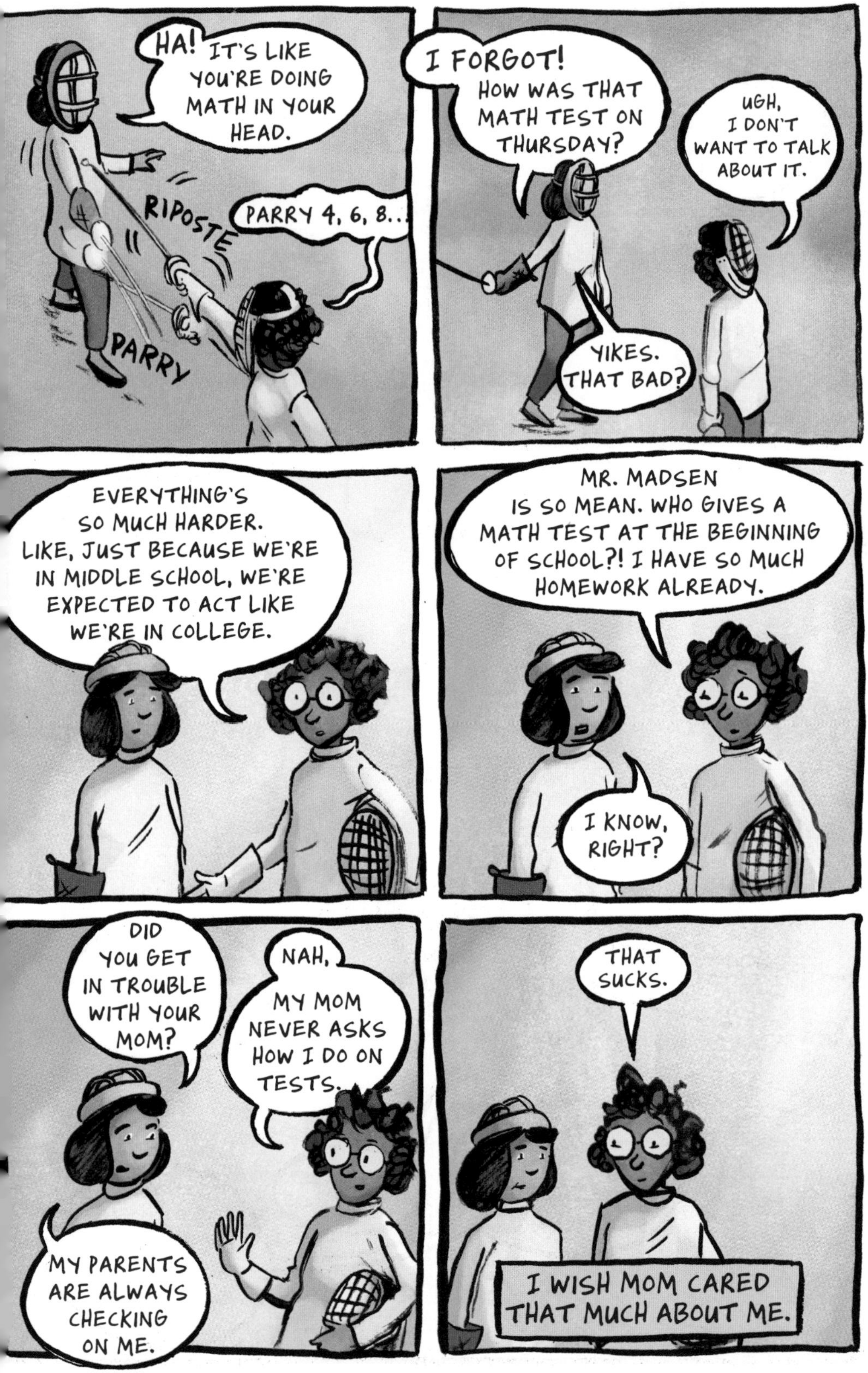
HA! IT'S LIKE YOU'RE DOING MATH IN YOUR HEAD.
RIPOSTE
PARRY
PARRY 4, 6, 8...
I FORGOT! HOW WAS THAT MATH TEST ON THURSDAY?
UGH, I DON'T WANT TO TALK ABOUT IT.
YIKES. THAT BAD?
EVERYTHING'S SO MUCH HARDER. LIKE, JUST BECAUSE WE'RE IN MIDDLE SCHOOL, WE'RE EXPECTED TO ACT LIKE WE'RE IN COLLEGE.
MR. MADSEN IS SO MEAN. WHO GIVES A MATH TEST AT THE BEGINNING OF SCHOOL?! I HAVE SO MUCH HOMEWORK ALREADY.
I KNOW, RIGHT?
DID YOU GET IN TROUBLE WITH YOUR MOM?
NAH,
MY MOM NEVER ASKS HOW I DO ON TESTS.
MY PARENTS ARE ALWAYS CHECKING ON ME.
THAT SUCKS.
I WISH MOM CARED THAT MUCH ABOUT ME.

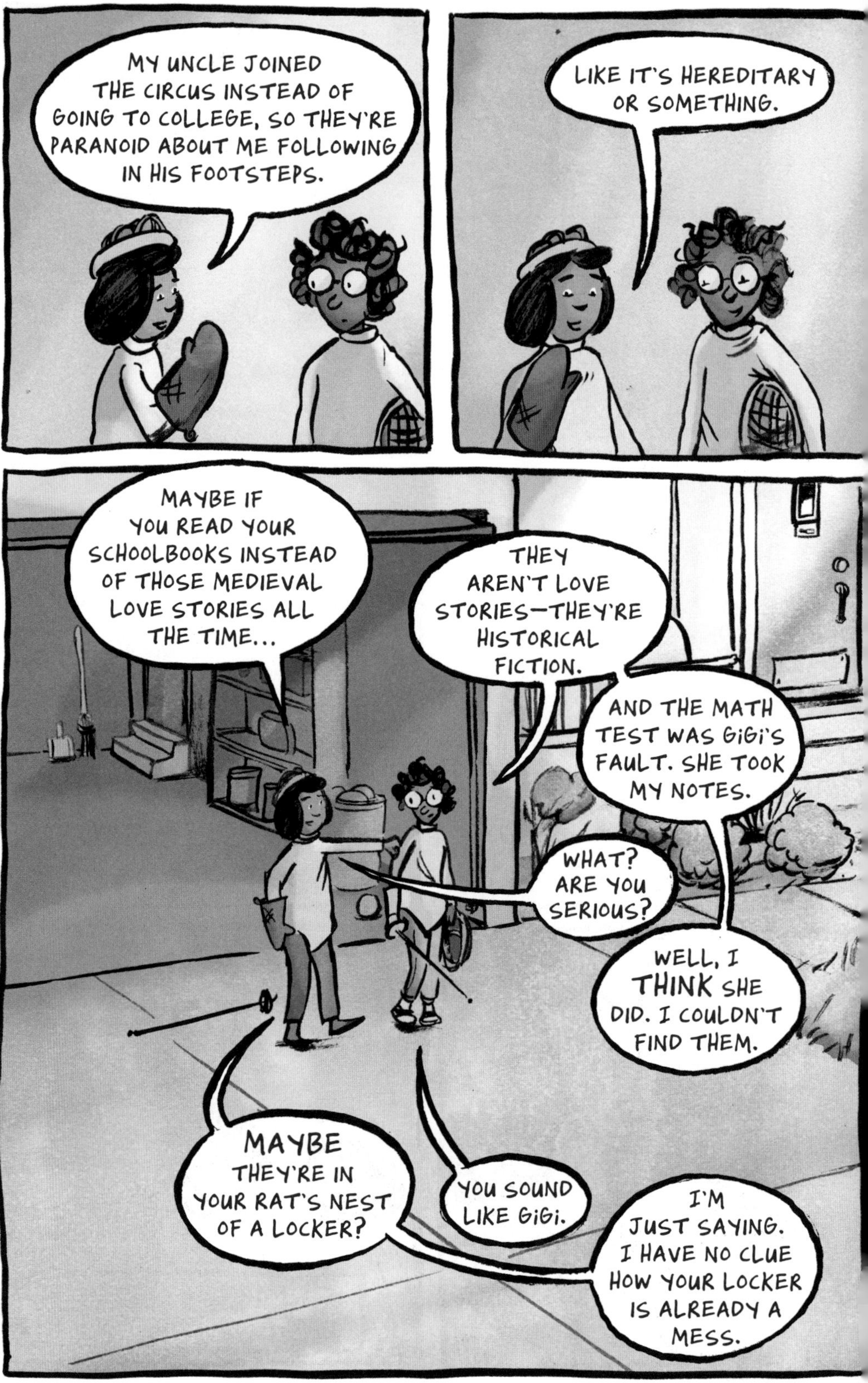
MY UNCLE JOINED THE CIRCUS INSTEAD OF GOING TO COLLEGE, SO THEY'RE PARANOID ABOUT ME FOLLOWING IN HIS FOOTSTEPS.
LIKE IT'S HEREDITARY OR SOMETHING.
MAYBE IF YOU READ YOUR SCHOOLBOOKS INSTEAD OF THOSE MEDIEVAL LOVE STORIES ALL THE TIME...
THEY AREN'T LOVE STORIES—THEY'RE HISTORICAL FICTION.
AND THE MATH TEST WAS GIGI'S FAULT. SHE TOOK MY NOTES.
WHAT? ARE YOU SERIOUS?
WELL, I THINK SHE DID. I COULDN'T FIND THEM.
MAYBE THEY'RE IN YOUR RAT'S NEST OF A LOCKER?
YOU SOUND LIKE GIGI.
I'M JUST SAYING. I HAVE NO CLUE HOW YOUR LOCKER IS ALREADY A MESS.

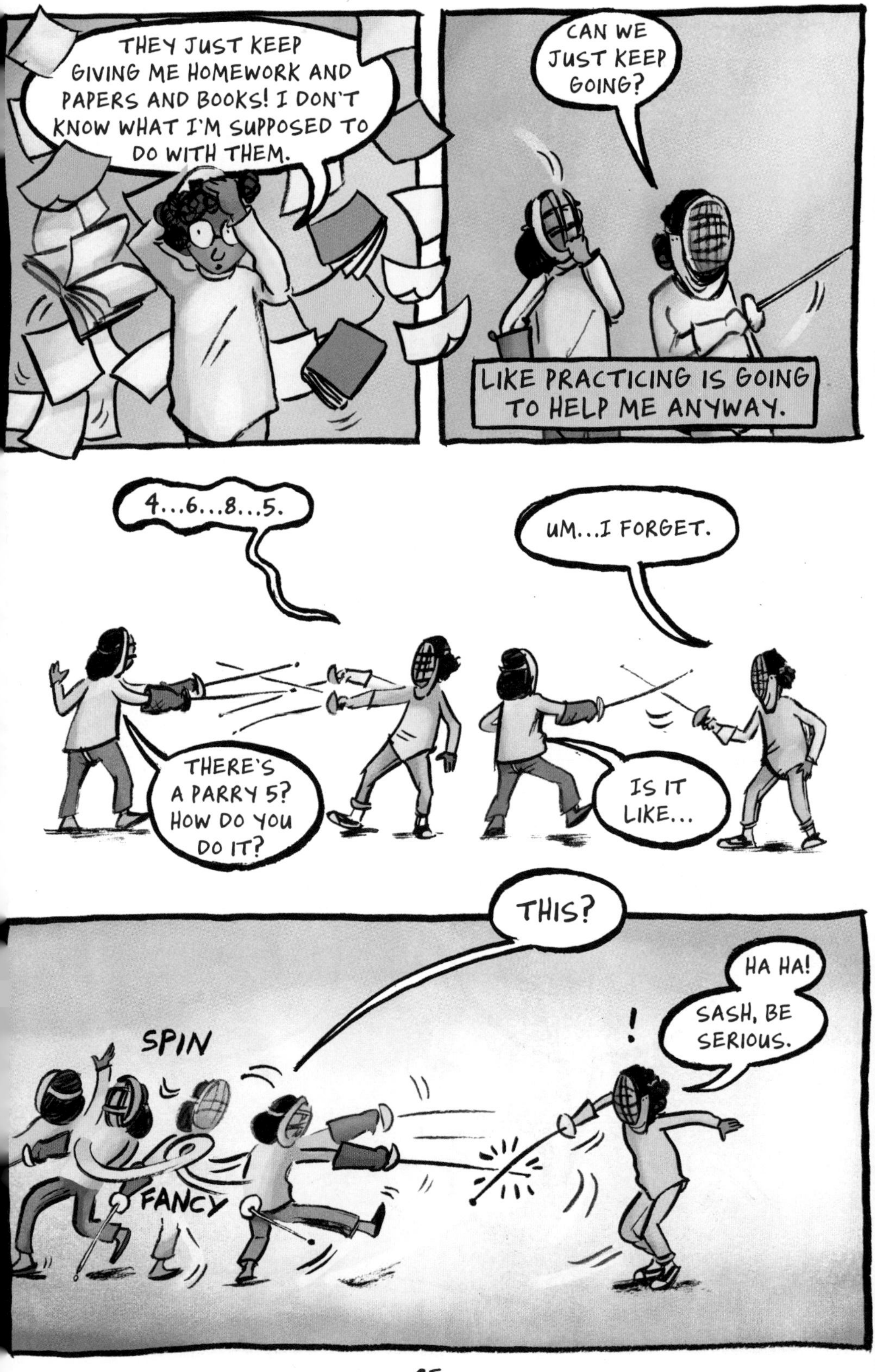
THEY JUST KEEP GIVING ME HOMEWORK AND PAPERS AND BOOKS! I DON'T KNOW WHAT I'M SUPPOSED TO DO WITH THEM.
CAN WE JUST KEEP GOING?
LIKE PRACTICING IS GOING TO HELP ME ANYWAY.
4...6...8...5.
THERE'S A PARRY 5? HOW DO YOU DO IT?
UM...I FORGET.
IS IT LIKE...
THIS?
SPIN
FANCY
!
HA HA!
SASH, BE SERIOUS.

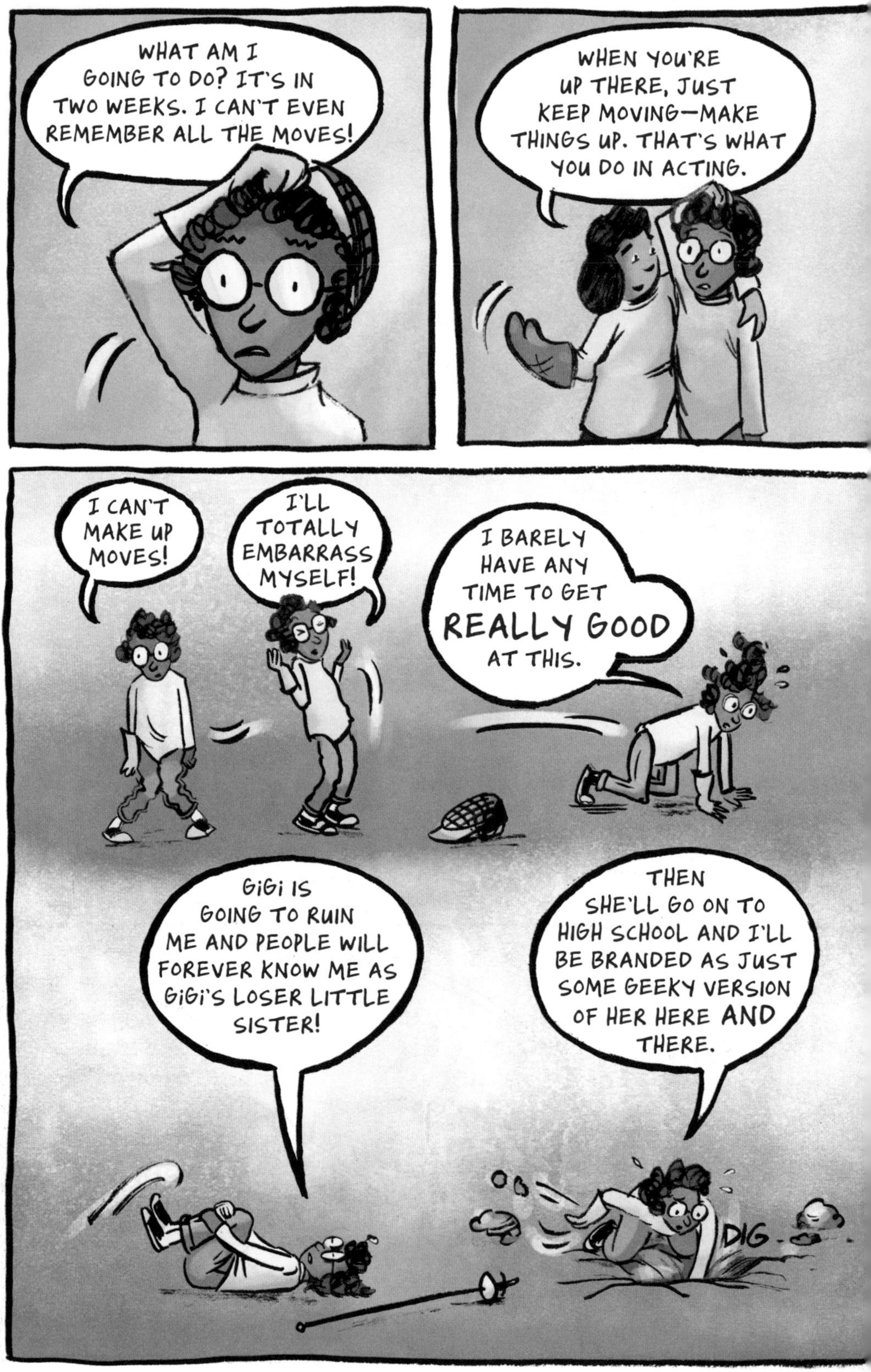

WHAT AM I GOING TO DO? IT'S IN TWO WEEKS. I CAN'T EVEN REMEMBER ALL THE MOVES!
WHEN YOU'RE UP THERE, JUST KEEP MOVING—MAKE THINGS UP. THAT'S WHAT YOU DO IN ACTING.
I CAN'T MAKE UP MOVES!
I'LL TOTALLY EMBARRASS MYSELF!
I BARELY HAVE ANY TIME TO GET REALLY GOOD AT THIS.
GIGI IS GOING TO RUIN ME AND PEOPLE WILL FOREVER KNOW ME AS GIGI'S LOSER LITTLE SISTER!
THEN SHE'LL GO ON TO HIGH SCHOOL AND I'LL BE BRANDED AS JUST SOME GEEKY VERSION OF HER HERE AND THERE.
DIG

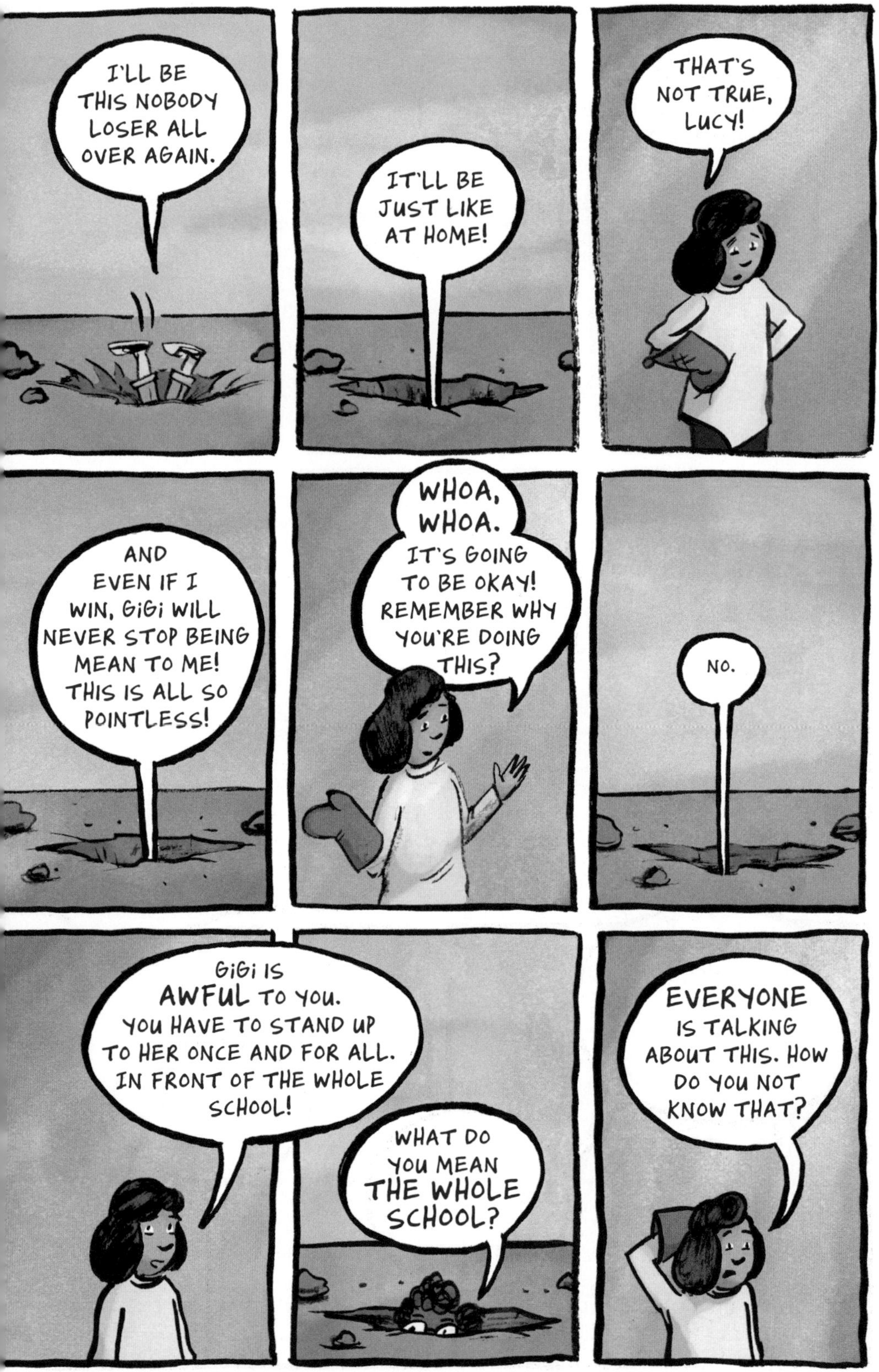
I'LL BE THIS NOBODY LOSER ALL OVER AGAIN.
IT'LL BE JUST LIKE AT HOME!
THAT'S NOT TRUE, LUCY!
AND EVEN IF I WIN, GIGI WILL NEVER STOP BEING MEAN TO ME! THIS IS ALL SO POINTLESS!
WHOA, WHOA.
IT'S GOING TO BE OKAY! REMEMBER WHY YOU'RE DOING THIS?
NO.
GIGI IS AWFUL TO YOU. YOU HAVE TO STAND UP TO HER ONCE AND FOR ALL. IN FRONT OF THE WHOLE SCHOOL!
WHAT DO YOU MEAN THE WHOLE SCHOOL?
EVERYONE IS TALKING ABOUT THIS. HOW DO YOU NOT KNOW THAT?

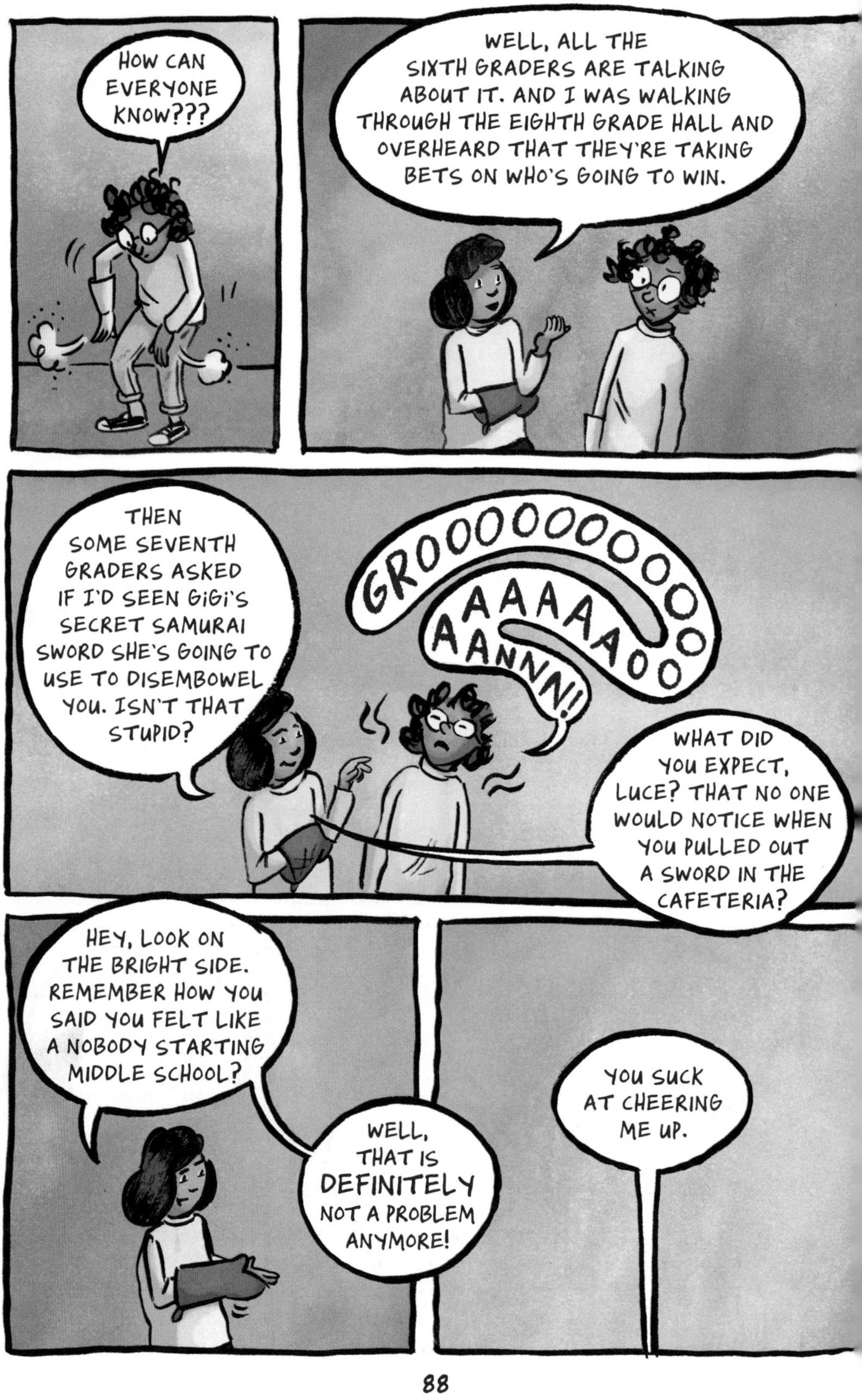
HOW CAN EVERYONE KNOW???
WELL, ALL THE SIXTH GRADERS ARE TALKING ABOUT IT. AND I WAS WALKING THROUGH THE EIGHTH GRADE HALL AND OVERHEARD THAT THEY'RE TAKING BETS ON WHO'S GOING TO WIN.
THEN SOME SEVENTH GRADERS ASKED IF I'D SEEN GIGI'S SECRET SAMURAI SWORD SHE'S GOING TO USE TO DISEMBOWEL YOU. ISN'T THAT STUPID?
GROOOOOOOOOOOAAAAAAAAAANNNN!
WHAT DID YOU EXPECT, LUCE? THAT NO ONE WOULD NOTICE WHEN YOU PULLED OUT A SWORD IN THE CAFETERIA?
HEY, LOOK ON THE BRIGHT SIDE. REMEMBER HOW YOU SAID YOU FELT LIKE A NOBODY STARTING MIDDLE SCHOOL?
WELL, THAT IS DEFINITELY NOT A PROBLEM ANYMORE!
YOU SUCK AT CHEERING ME UP.

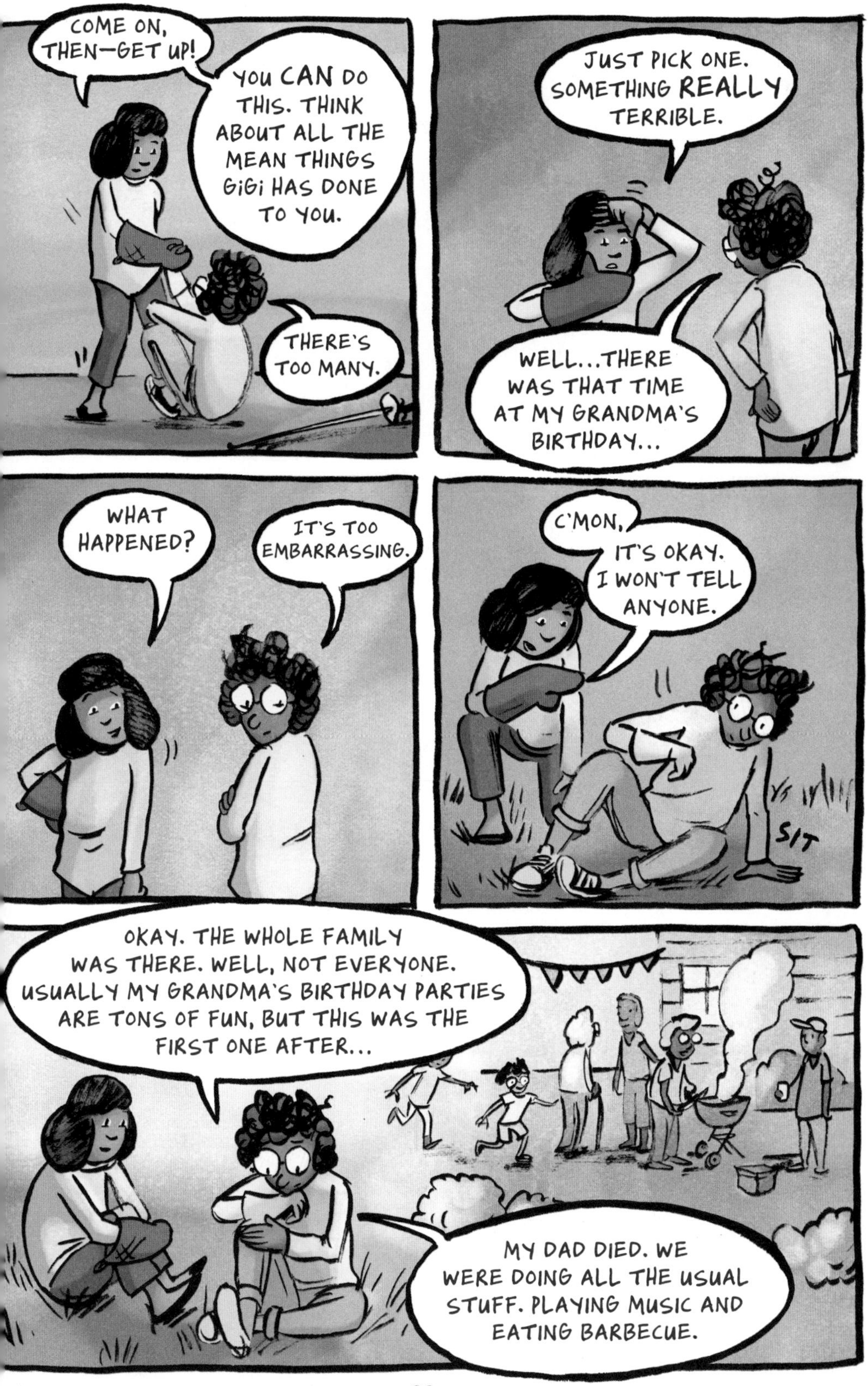
COME ON, THEN—GET UP!
YOU CAN DO THIS. THINK ABOUT ALL THE MEAN THINGS GIGI HAS DONE TO YOU.
THERE'S TOO MANY.
JUST PICK ONE. SOMETHING REALLY TERRIBLE.
WELL...THERE WAS THAT TIME AT MY GRANDMA'S BIRTHDAY...
WHAT HAPPENED?
IT'S TOO EMBARRASSING.
C'MON,
IT'S OKAY. I WON'T TELL ANYONE.
SIT
OKAY. THE WHOLE FAMILY WAS THERE. WELL, NOT EVERYONE. USUALLY MY GRANDMA'S BIRTHDAY PARTIES ARE TONS OF FUN, BUT THIS WAS THE FIRST ONE AFTER...
MY DAD DIED. WE WERE DOING ALL THE USUAL STUFF. PLAYING MUSIC AND EATING BARBECUE.

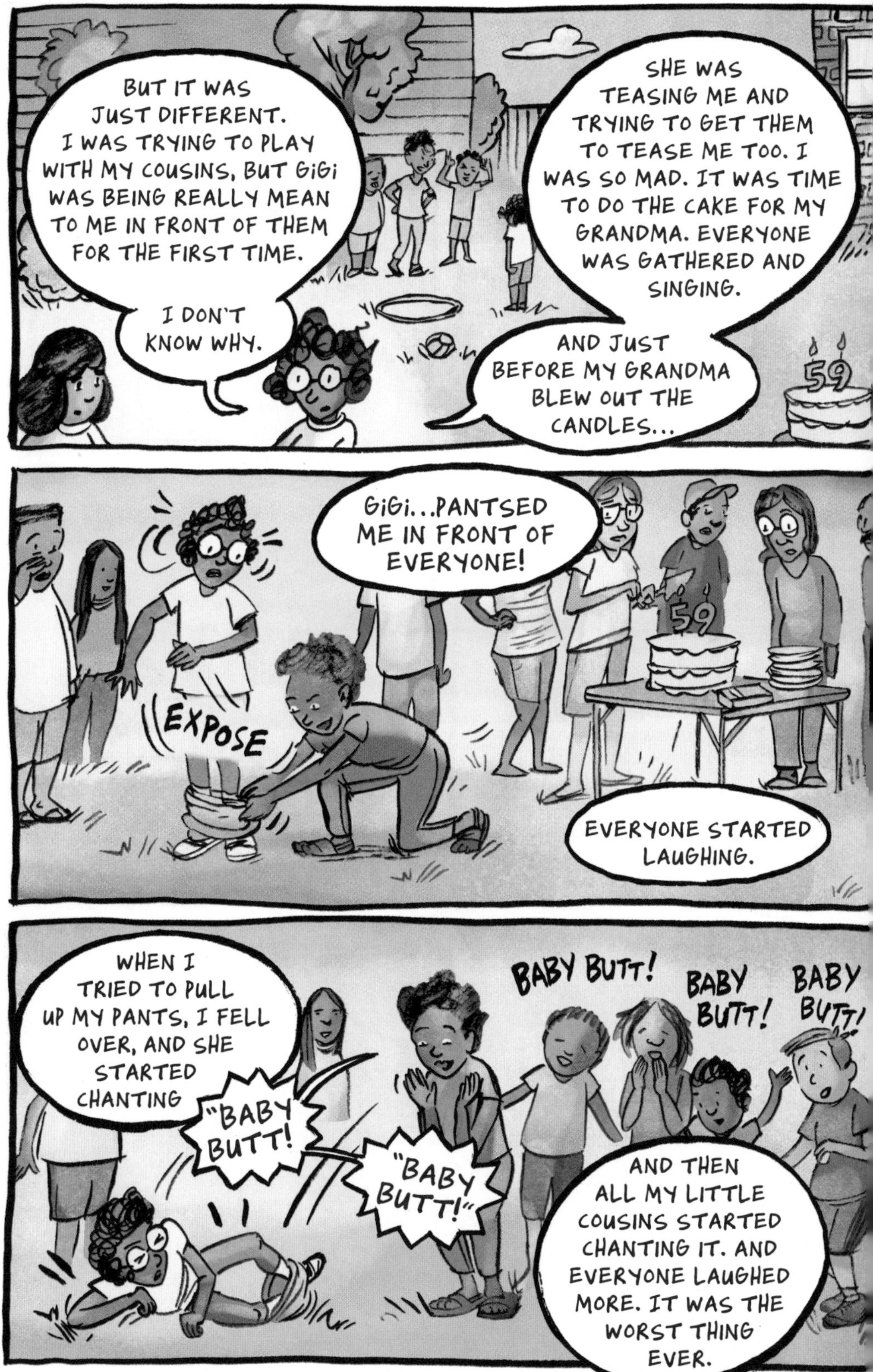
BUT IT WAS JUST DIFFERENT. I WAS TRYING TO PLAY WITH MY COUSINS, BUT GiGi WAS BEING REALLY MEAN TO ME IN FRONT OF THEM FOR THE FIRST TIME.
I DON'T KNOW WHY.
SHE WAS TEASING ME AND TRYING TO GET THEM TO TEASE ME TOO. I WAS SO MAD. IT WAS TIME TO DO THE CAKE FOR MY GRANDMA. EVERYONE WAS GATHERED AND SINGING.
AND JUST BEFORE MY GRANDMA BLEW OUT THE CANDLES...
59
GiGi...PANTSED ME IN FRONT OF EVERYONE!
EXPOSE
59
EVERYONE STARTED LAUGHING.
WHEN I TRIED TO PULL UP MY PANTS, I FELL OVER, AND SHE STARTED CHANTING
"BABY BUTT!
"BABY BUTT!"
BABY BUTT!
BABY BUTT!
BABY BUTT!
AND THEN ALL MY LITTLE COUSINS STARTED CHANTING IT. AND EVERYONE LAUGHED MORE. IT WAS THE WORST THING EVER.

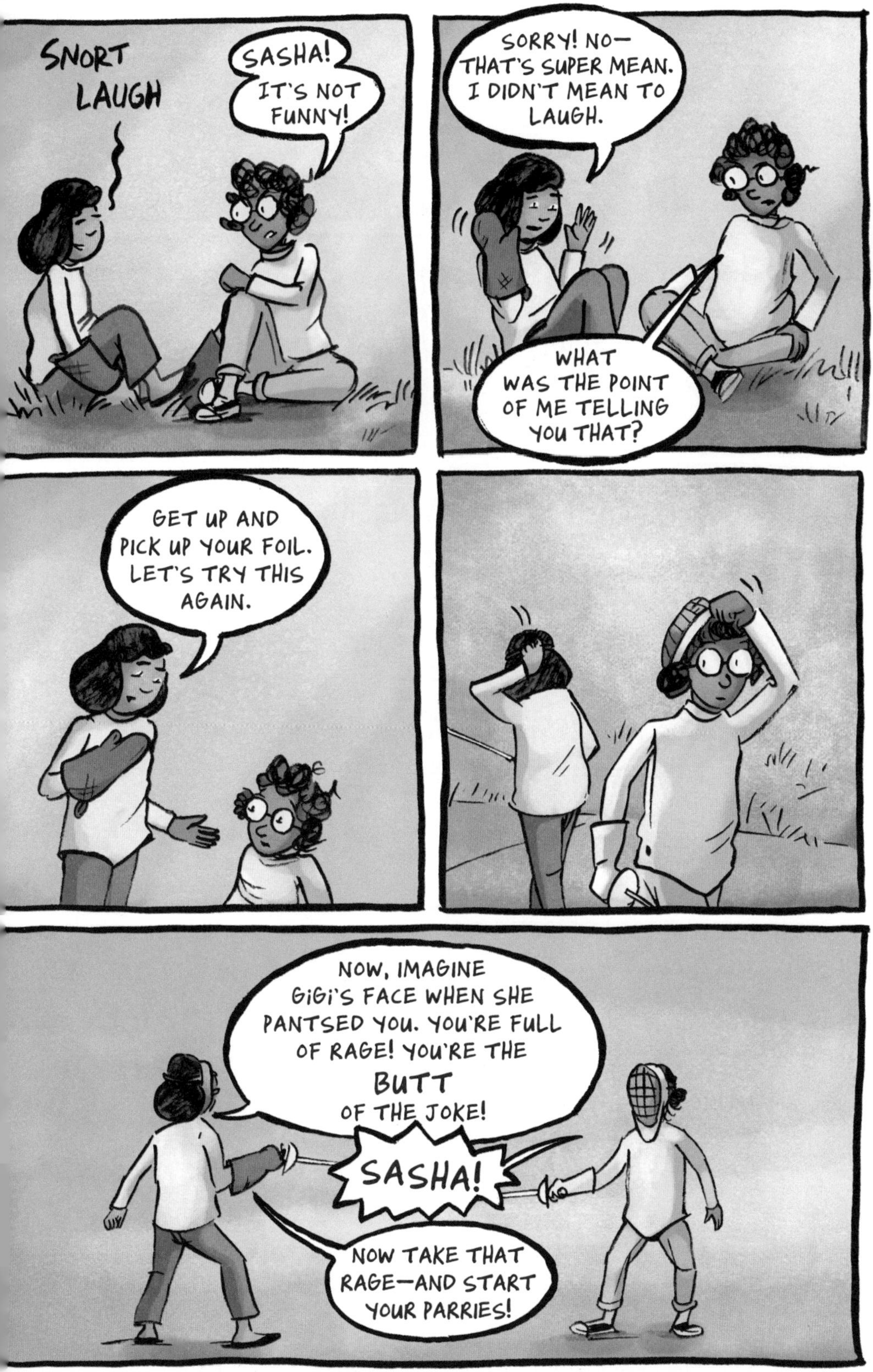
SNORT LAUGH
SASHA! IT'S NOT FUNNY!
SORRY! NO— THAT'S SUPER MEAN. I DIDN'T MEAN TO LAUGH.
WHAT WAS THE POINT OF ME TELLING YOU THAT?
GET UP AND PICK UP YOUR FOIL. LET'S TRY THIS AGAIN.
NOW, IMAGINE GiGi'S FACE WHEN SHE PANTSED YOU. YOU'RE FULL OF RAGE! YOU'RE THE BUTT OF THE JOKE!
SASHA!
NOW TAKE THAT RAGE—AND START YOUR PARRIES!

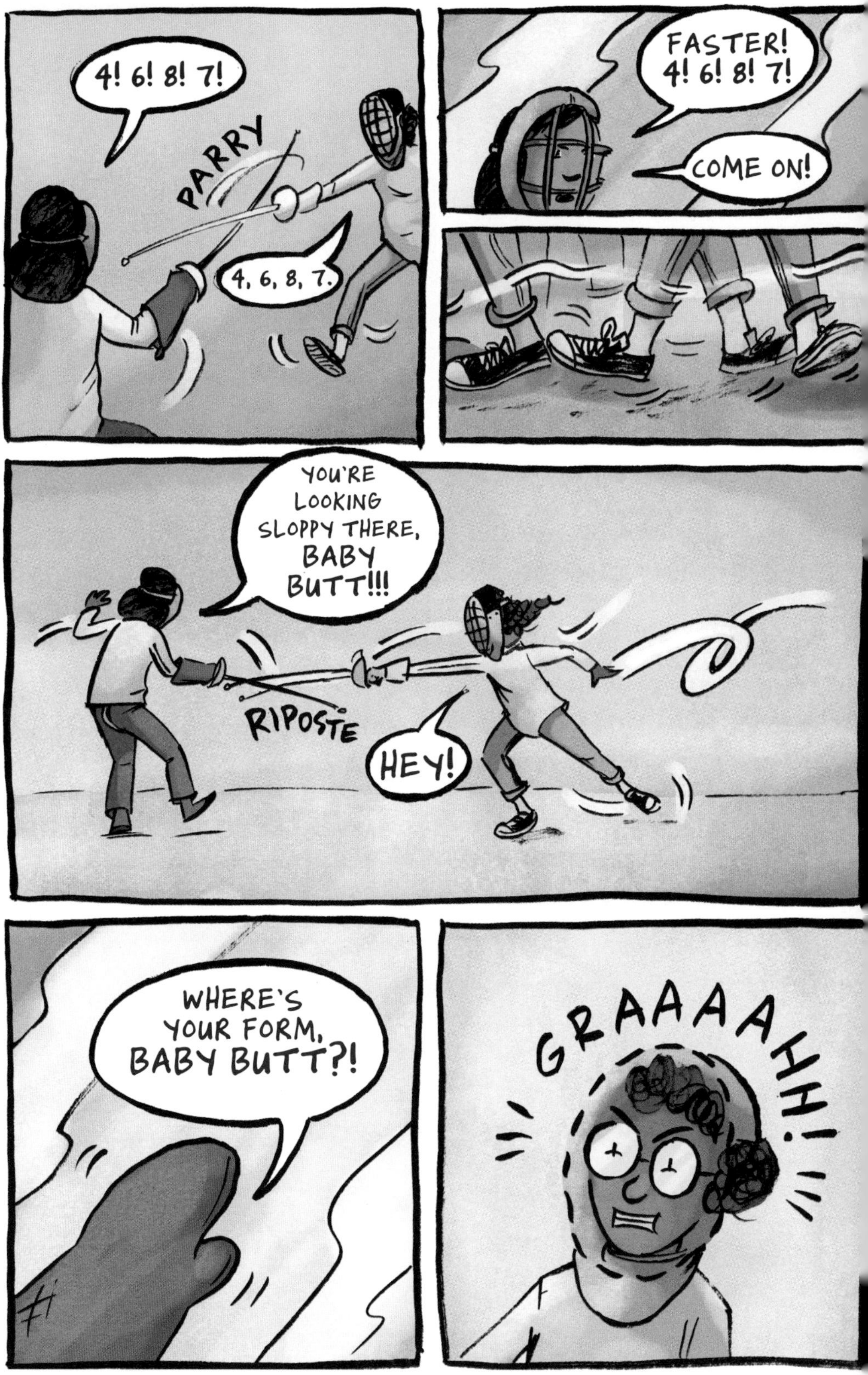
4! 6! 8! 7!
PARRY
4, 6, 8, 7.
FASTER! 4! 6! 8! 7!
COME ON!
YOU'RE LOOKING SLOPPY THERE, BABY BUTT!!!
RIPOSTE
HEY!
WHERE'S YOUR FORM, BABY BUTT?!
GRAAAAHH!

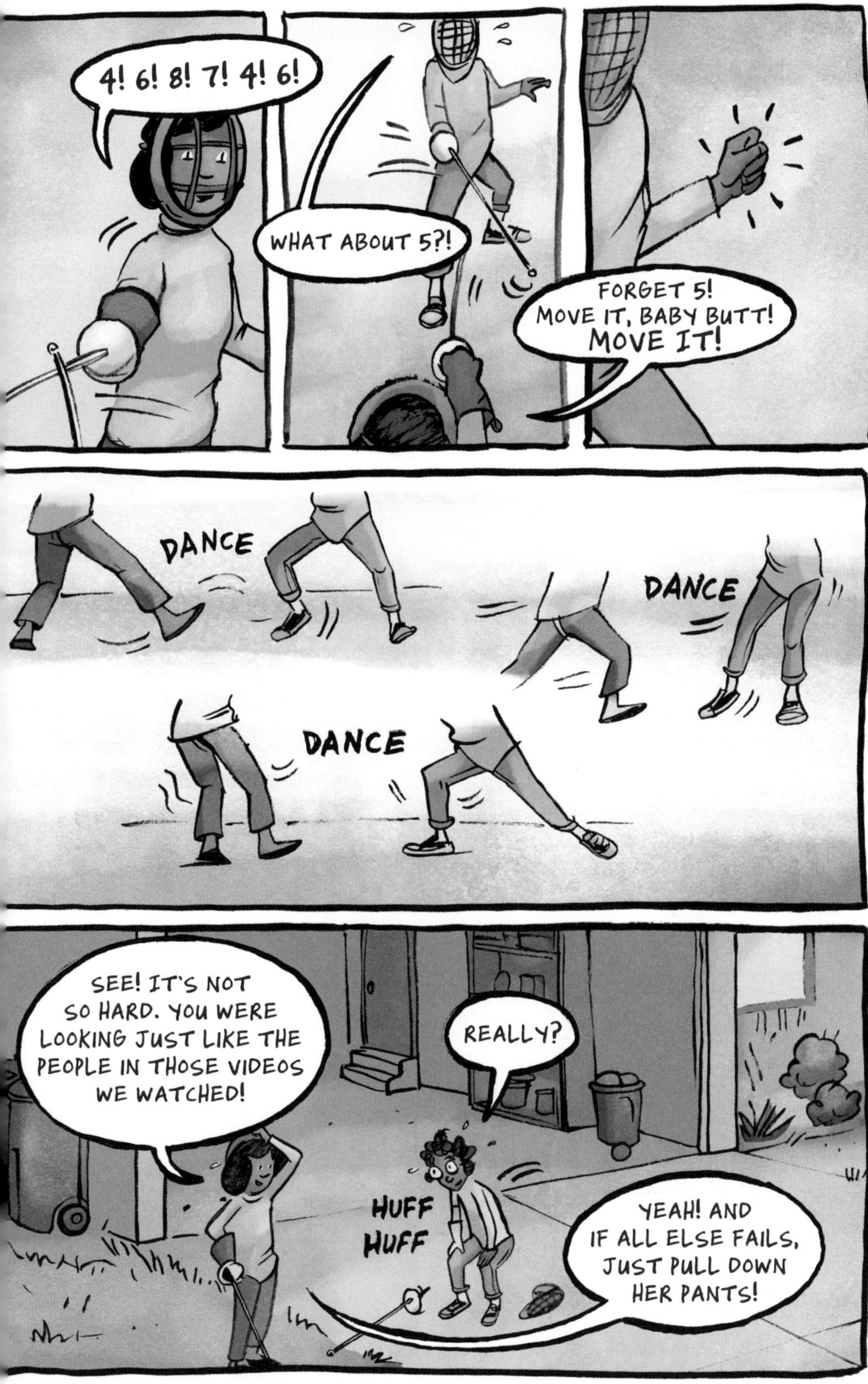

4! 6! 8! 7! 4! 6!
WHAT ABOUT 5?!
FORGET 5! MOVE IT, BABY BUTT! MOVE IT!
DANCE
DANCE
DANCE
SEE! IT'S NOT SO HARD. YOU WERE LOOKING JUST LIKE THE PEOPLE IN THOSE VIDEOS WE WATCHED!
REALLY?
HUFF HUFF
YEAH! AND IF ALL ELSE FAILS, JUST PULL DOWN HER PANTS!

Chapter 6

Advance

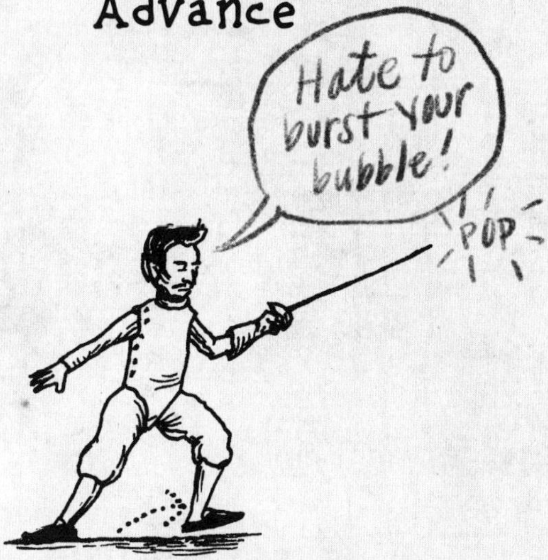
Hate to burst your bubble!
POP

Across all three weapons, foil, épée, and sabre, the foundation of footwork is the same. The advance is the act of taking one step toward your opponent. This distance may vary based upon a person's size, but in general it is the equivalent of a natural comfortable step. To advance, you start in your en garde position, then push off the rear foot while slightly lifting the toes of your front foot. Reach out with your front foot, then bring your back foot forward. The advance is a key move that not only changes the pace and direction of the action, but also moves you closer to your opponent, potentially putting them in striking distance.

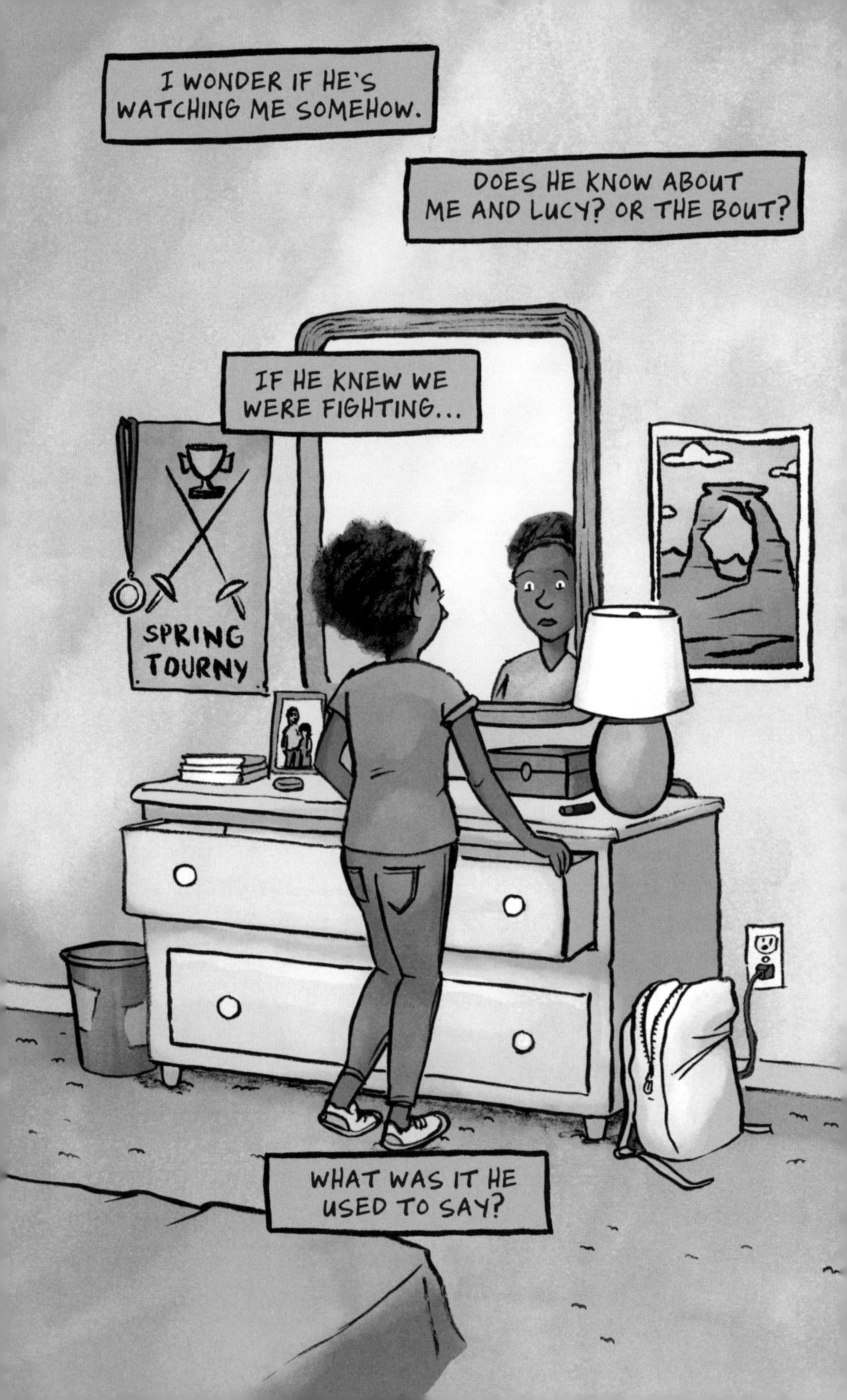
I WONDER IF HE'S WATCHING ME SOMEHOW.
DOES HE KNOW ABOUT ME AND LUCY? OR THE BOUT?
IF HE KNEW WE WERE FIGHTING...
SPRING TOURNY
WHAT WAS IT HE USED TO SAY?

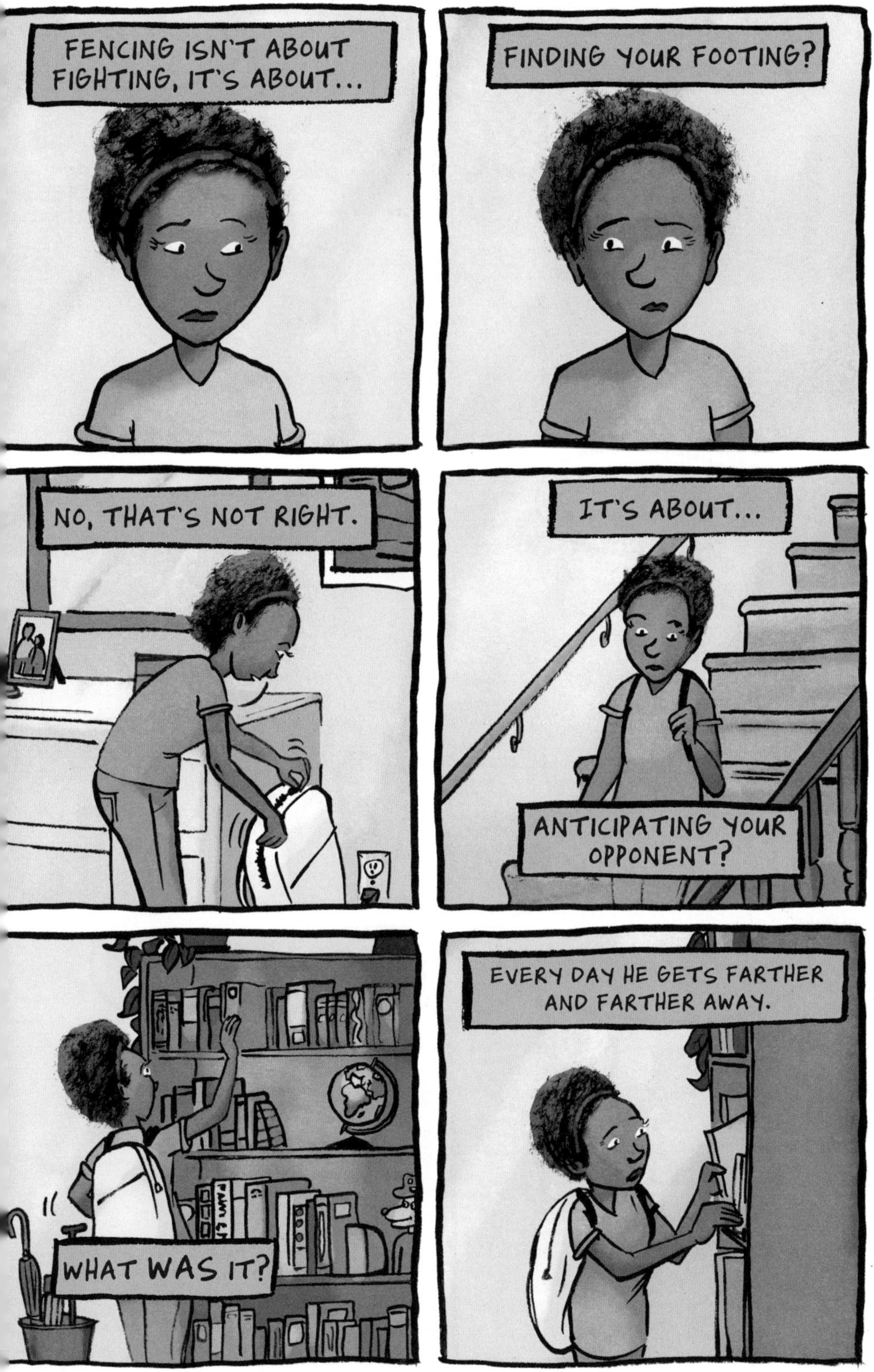
FENCING ISN'T ABOUT FIGHTING, IT'S ABOUT...
FINDING YOUR FOOTING?
NO, THAT'S NOT RIGHT.
IT'S ABOUT...
ANTICIPATING YOUR OPPONENT?
WHAT WAS IT?
EVERY DAY HE GETS FARTHER AND FARTHER AWAY.

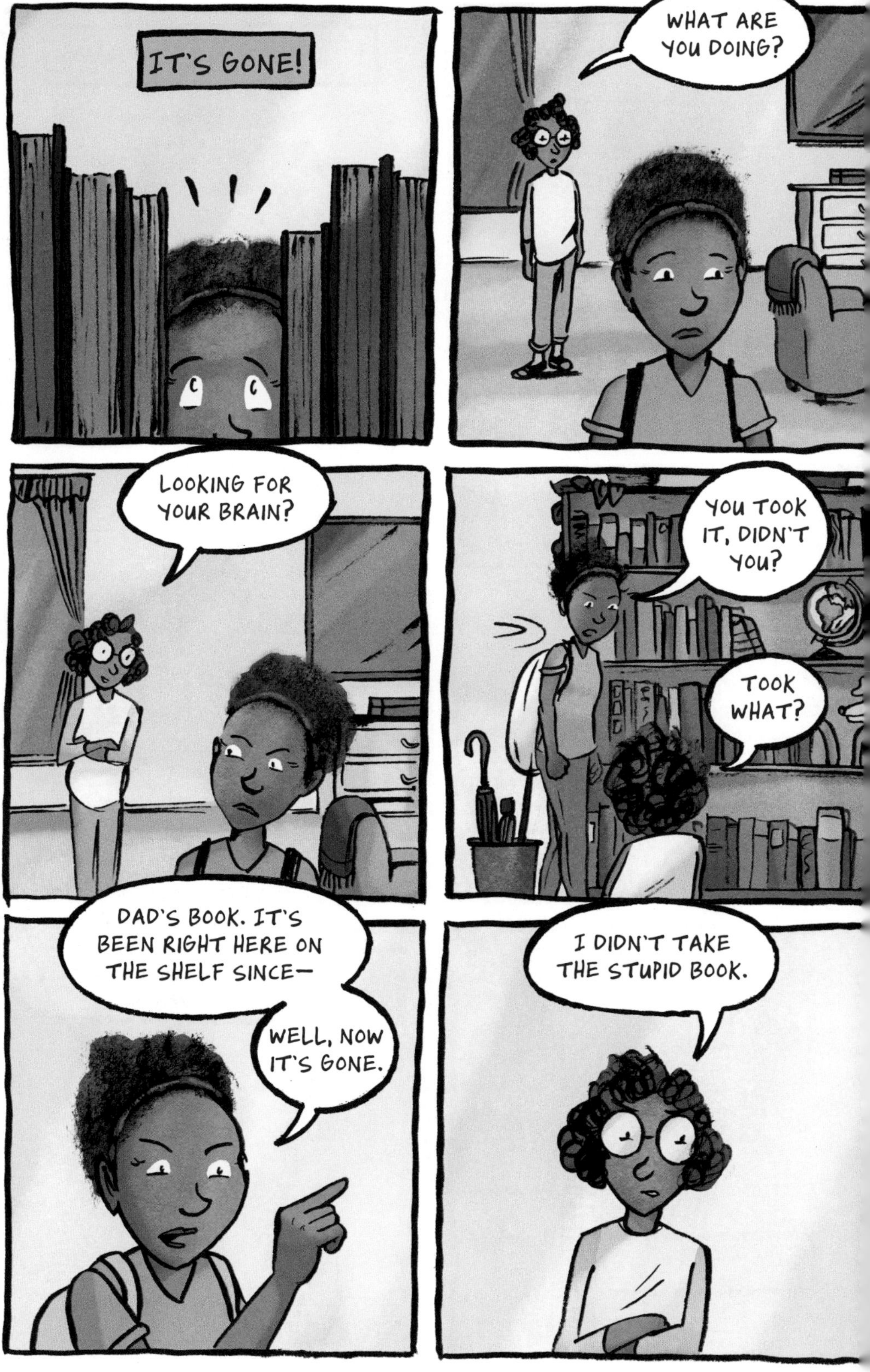
IT'S GONE!
WHAT ARE YOU DOING?
LOOKING FOR YOUR BRAIN?
YOU TOOK IT, DIDN'T YOU?
TOOK WHAT?
DAD'S BOOK. IT'S BEEN RIGHT HERE ON THE SHELF SINCE—
WELL, NOW IT'S GONE.
I DIDN'T TAKE THE STUPID BOOK.

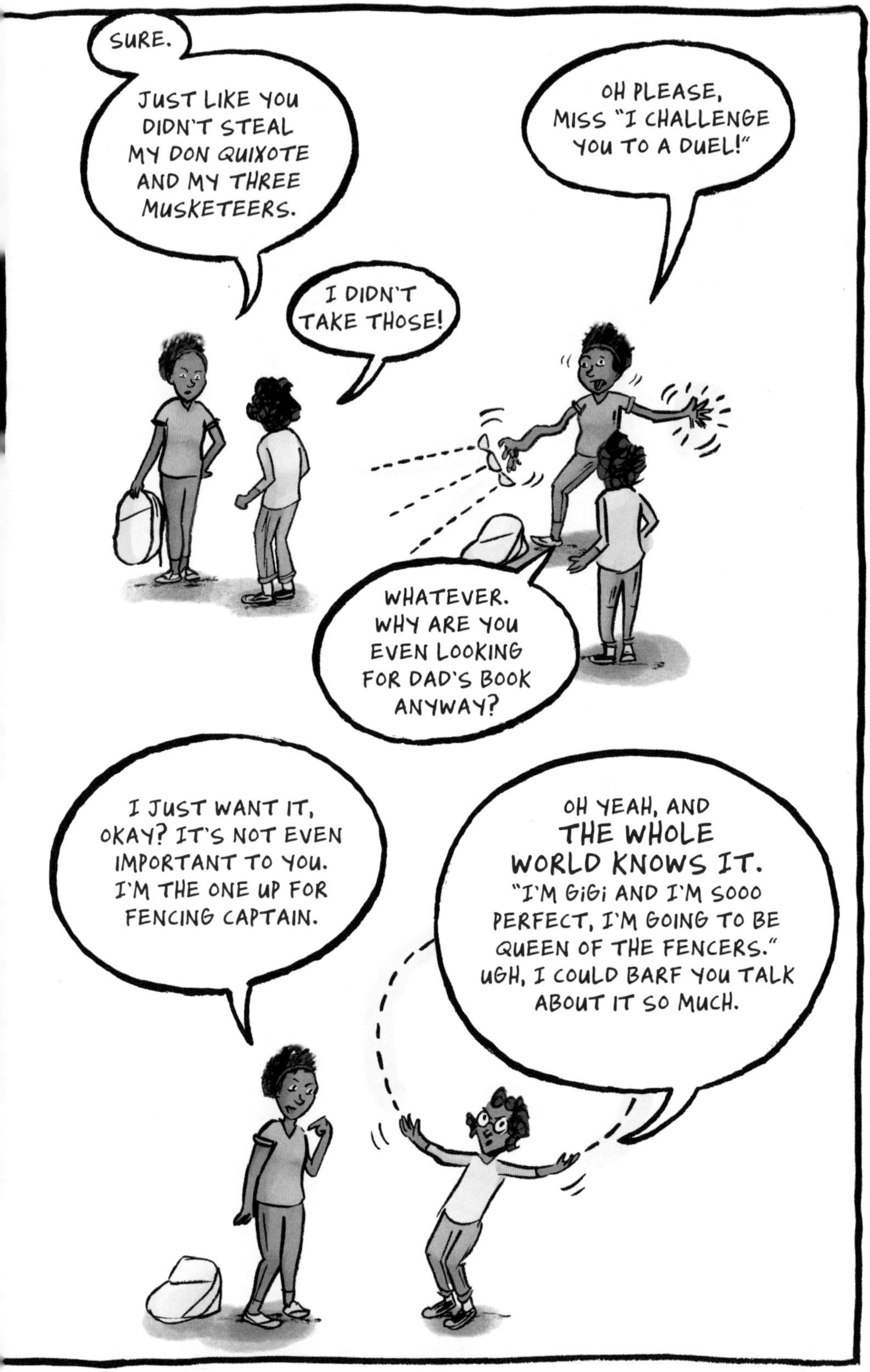
SURE.
JUST LIKE YOU DIDN'T STEAL MY DON QUIXOTE AND MY THREE MUSKETEERS.
I DIDN'T TAKE THOSE!
OH PLEASE, MISS "I CHALLENGE YOU TO A DUEL!"
WHATEVER. WHY ARE YOU EVEN LOOKING FOR DAD'S BOOK ANYWAY?
I JUST WANT IT, OKAY? IT'S NOT EVEN IMPORTANT TO YOU. I'M THE ONE UP FOR FENCING CAPTAIN.
OH YEAH, AND THE WHOLE WORLD KNOWS IT. "I'M GIGI AND I'M SOOO PERFECT, I'M GOING TO BE QUEEN OF THE FENCERS." UGH, I COULD BARF YOU TALK ABOUT IT SO MUCH.

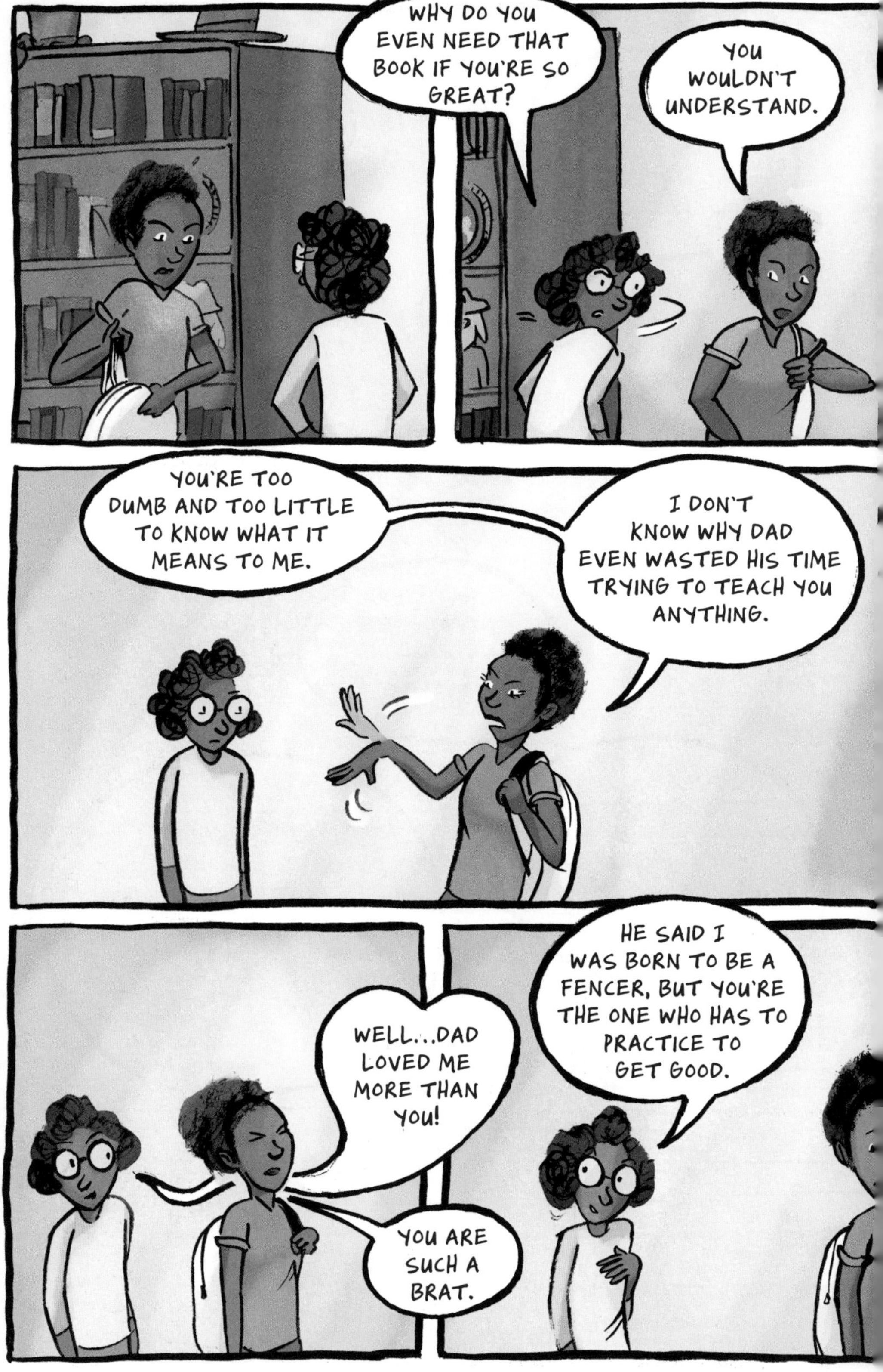

WHY DO YOU EVEN NEED THAT BOOK IF YOU'RE SO GREAT?
YOU WOULDN'T UNDERSTAND.
YOU'RE TOO DUMB AND TOO LITTLE TO KNOW WHAT IT MEANS TO ME.
I DON'T KNOW WHY DAD EVEN WASTED HIS TIME TRYING TO TEACH YOU ANYTHING.
WELL...DAD LOVED ME MORE THAN YOU!
YOU ARE SUCH A BRAT.
HE SAID I WAS BORN TO BE A FENCER, BUT YOU'RE THE ONE WHO HAS TO PRACTICE TO GET GOOD.

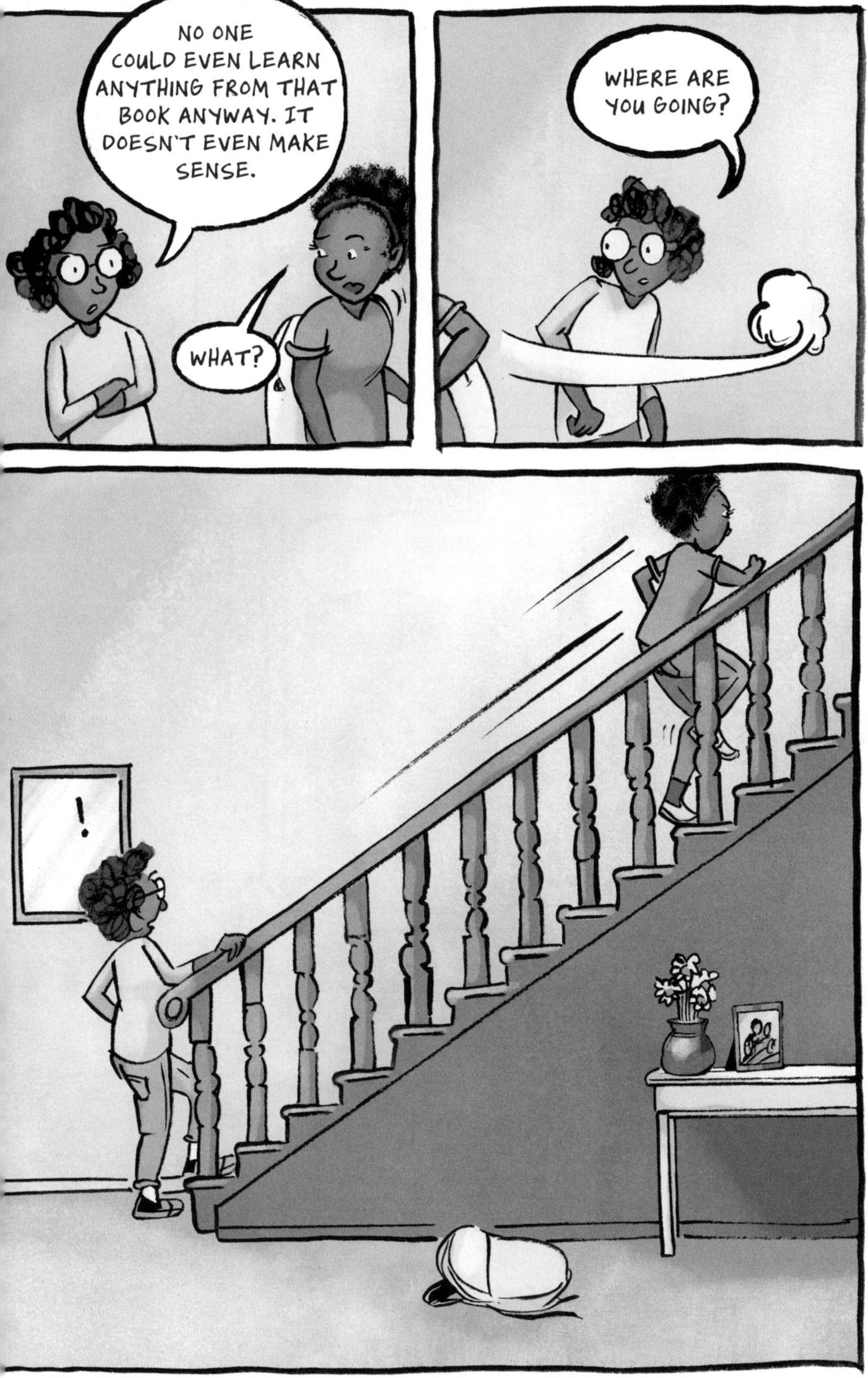
NO ONE COULD EVEN LEARN ANYTHING FROM THAT BOOK ANYWAY. IT DOESN'T EVEN MAKE SENSE.
WHAT?
WHERE ARE YOU GOING?
!

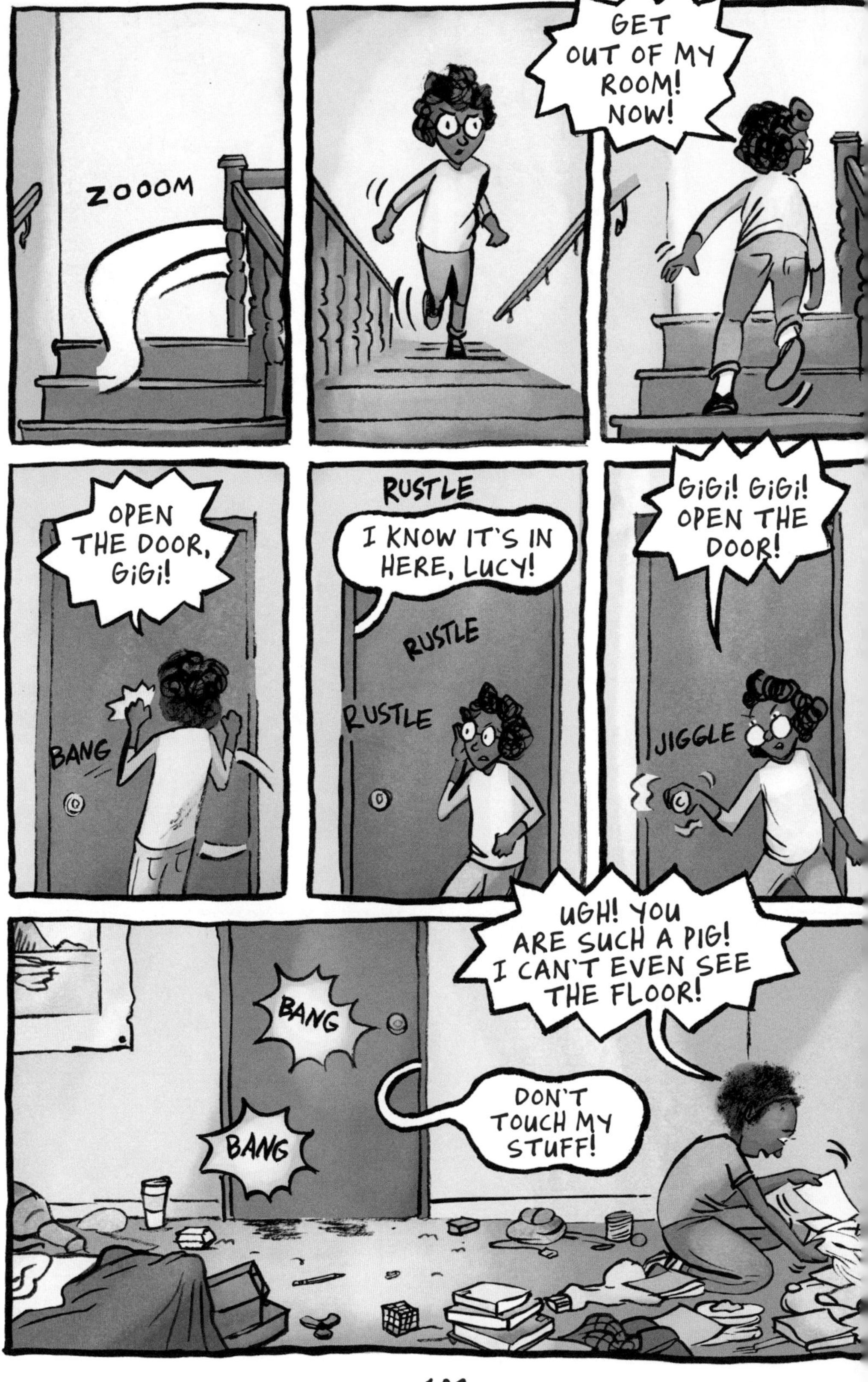
ZOOOM
GET OUT OF MY ROOM! NOW!
OPEN THE DOOR, GiGi!
BANG
RUSTLE
I KNOW IT'S IN HERE, LUCY!
RUSTLE
RUSTLE
GiGi! GiGi! OPEN THE DOOR!
JIGGLE
UGH! YOU ARE SUCH A PIG! I CAN'T EVEN SEE THE FLOOR!
BANG
BANG
DON'T TOUCH MY STUFF!

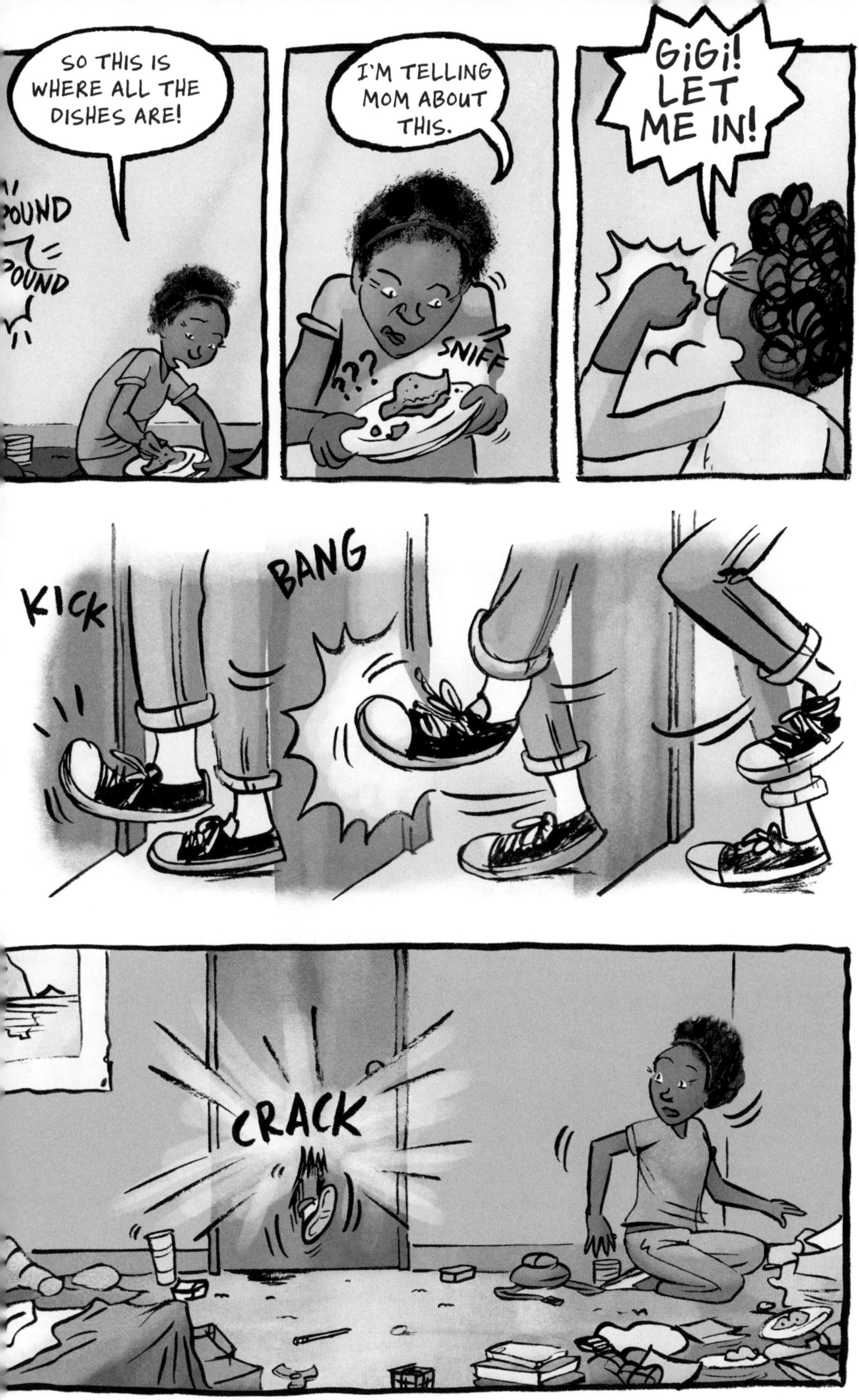
SO THIS IS WHERE ALL THE DISHES ARE!
POUND
POUND
I'M TELLING MOM ABOUT THIS.
???
SNIFF
GiGi! LET ME IN!
KICK
BANG
CRACK

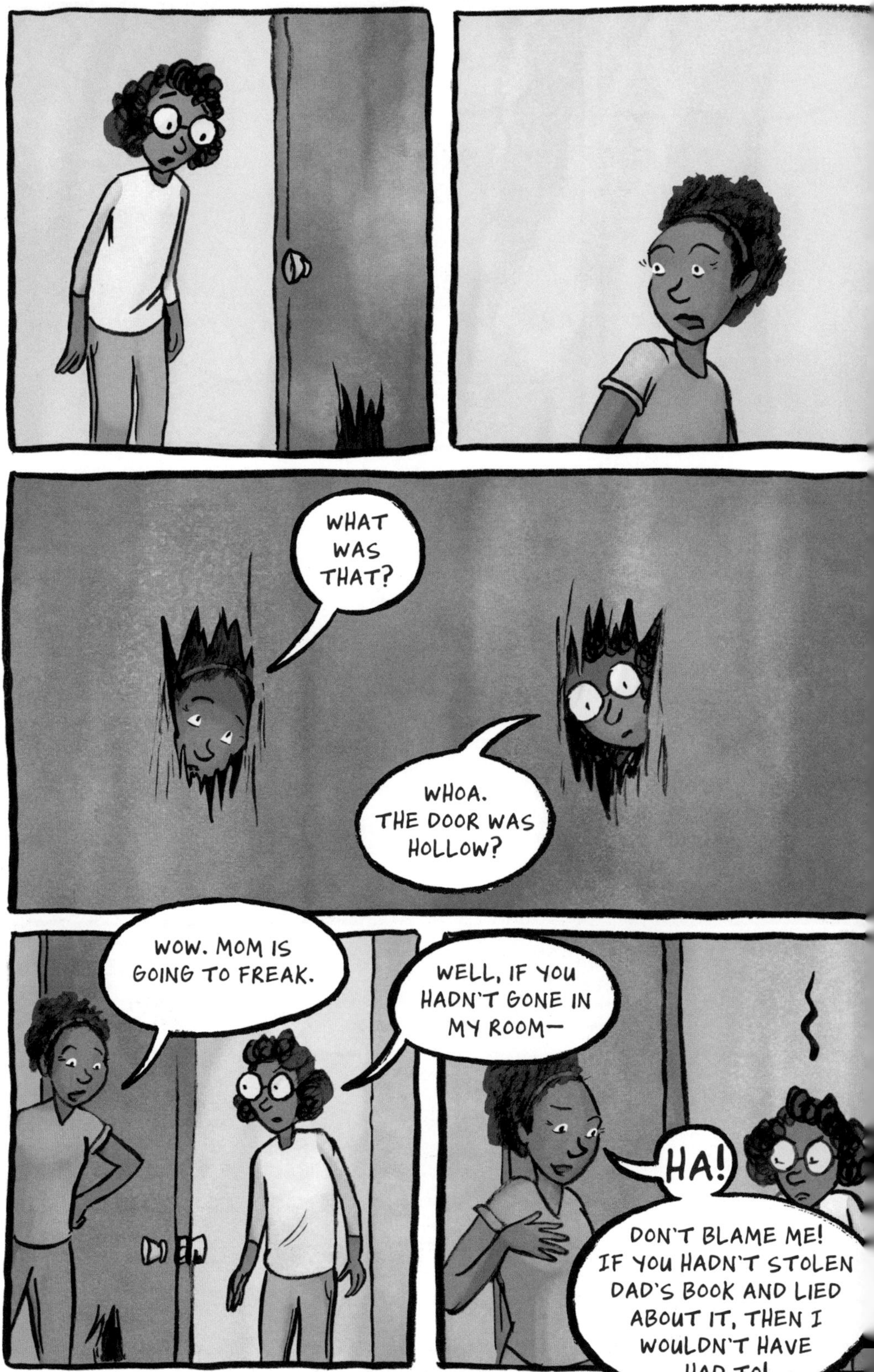
WHAT WAS THAT?
WHOA. THE DOOR WAS HOLLOW?
WOW. MOM IS GOING TO FREAK.
WELL, IF YOU HADN'T GONE IN MY ROOM—
HA!
DON'T BLAME ME! IF YOU HADN'T STOLEN DAD'S BOOK AND LIED ABOUT IT, THEN I WOULDN'T HAVE HAD TO!

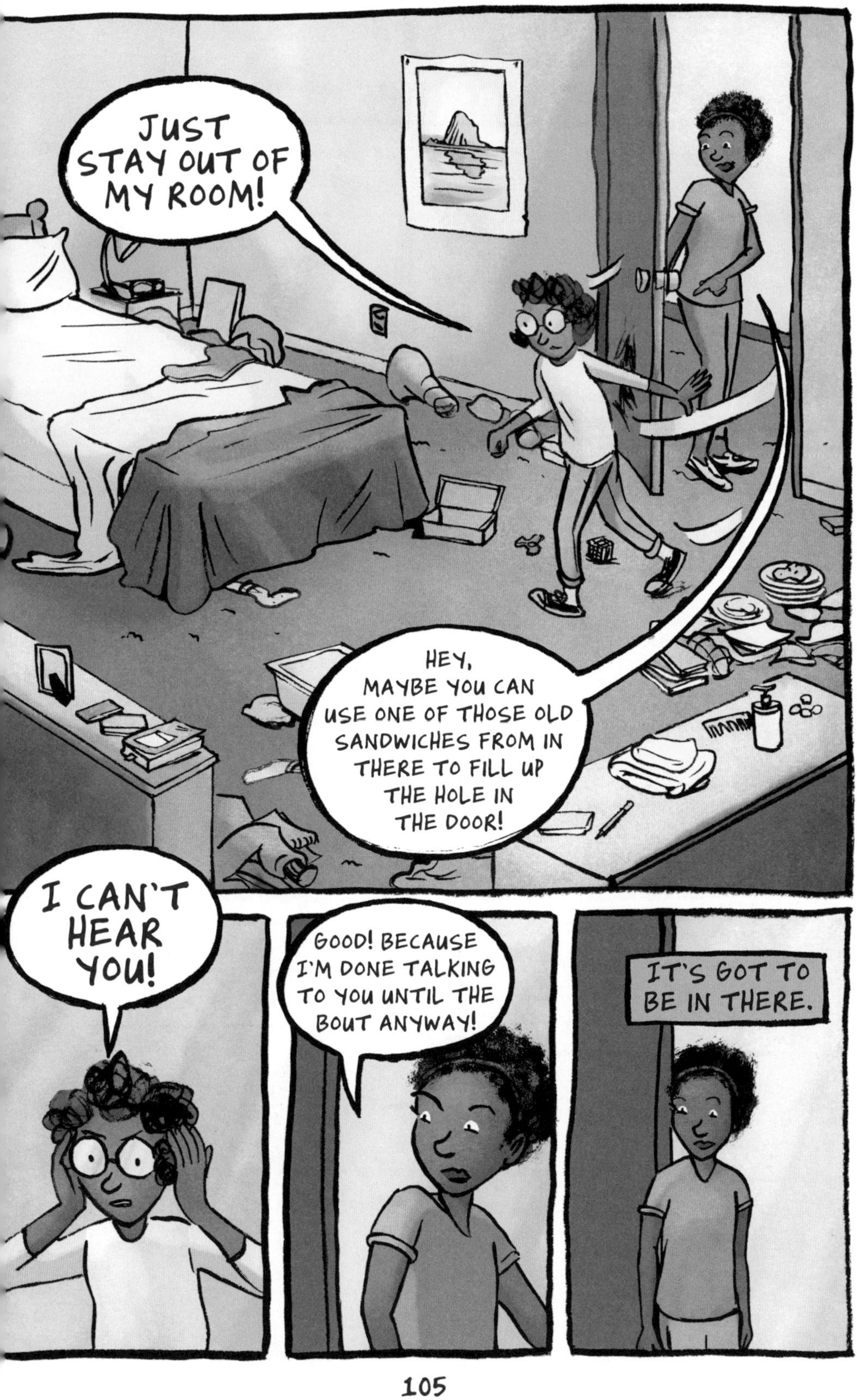
JUST STAY OUT OF MY ROOM!
HEY, MAYBE YOU CAN USE ONE OF THOSE OLD SANDWICHES FROM IN THERE TO FILL UP THE HOLE IN THE DOOR!
I CAN'T HEAR YOU!
GOOD! BECAUSE I'M DONE TALKING TO YOU UNTIL THE BOUT ANYWAY!
IT'S GOT TO BE IN THERE.

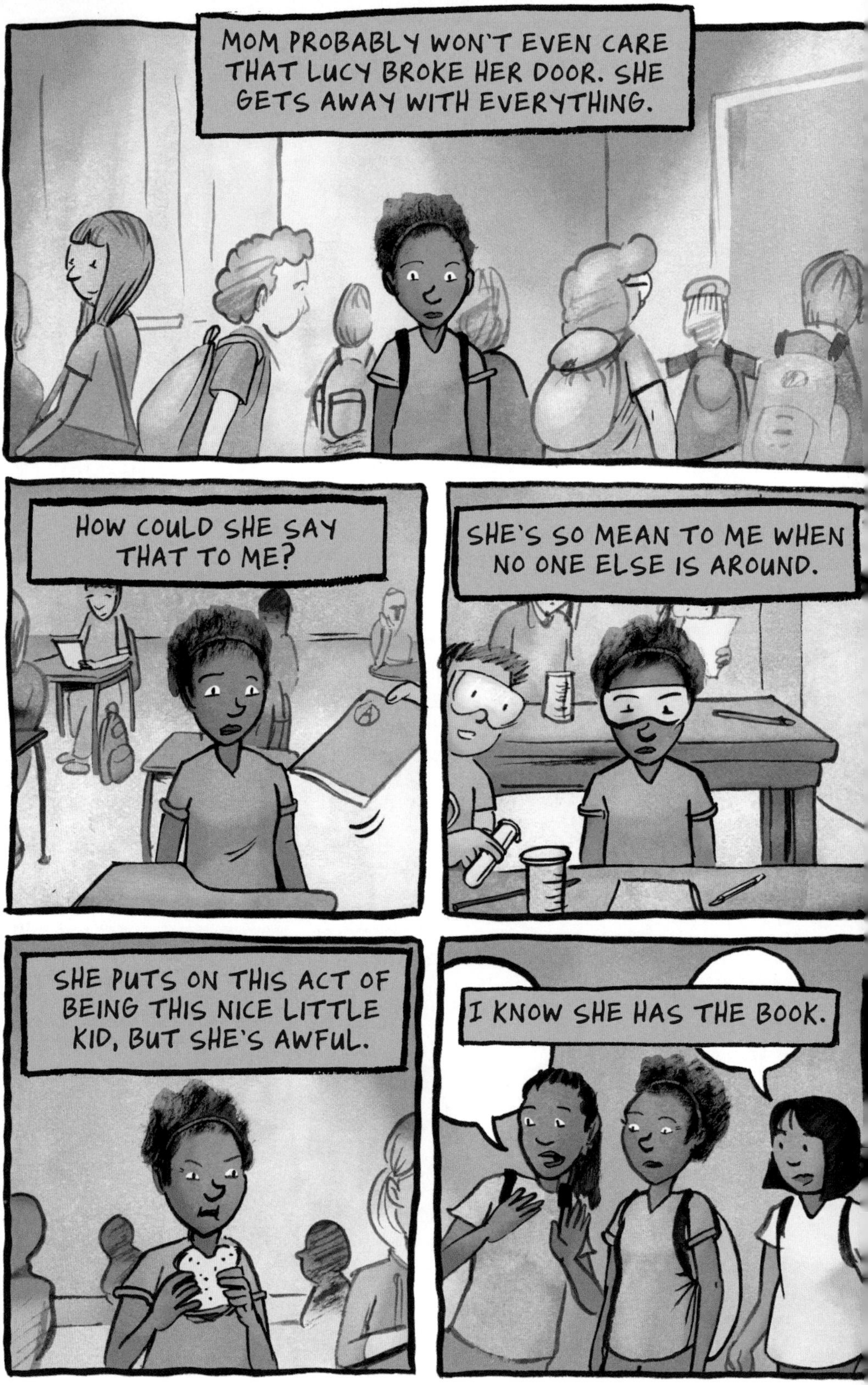
MOM PROBABLY WON'T EVEN CARE THAT LUCY BROKE HER DOOR. SHE GETS AWAY WITH EVERYTHING.
HOW COULD SHE SAY THAT TO ME?
SHE'S SO MEAN TO ME WHEN NO ONE ELSE IS AROUND.
SHE PUTS ON THIS ACT OF BEING THIS NICE LITTLE KID, BUT SHE'S AWFUL.
I KNOW SHE HAS THE BOOK.

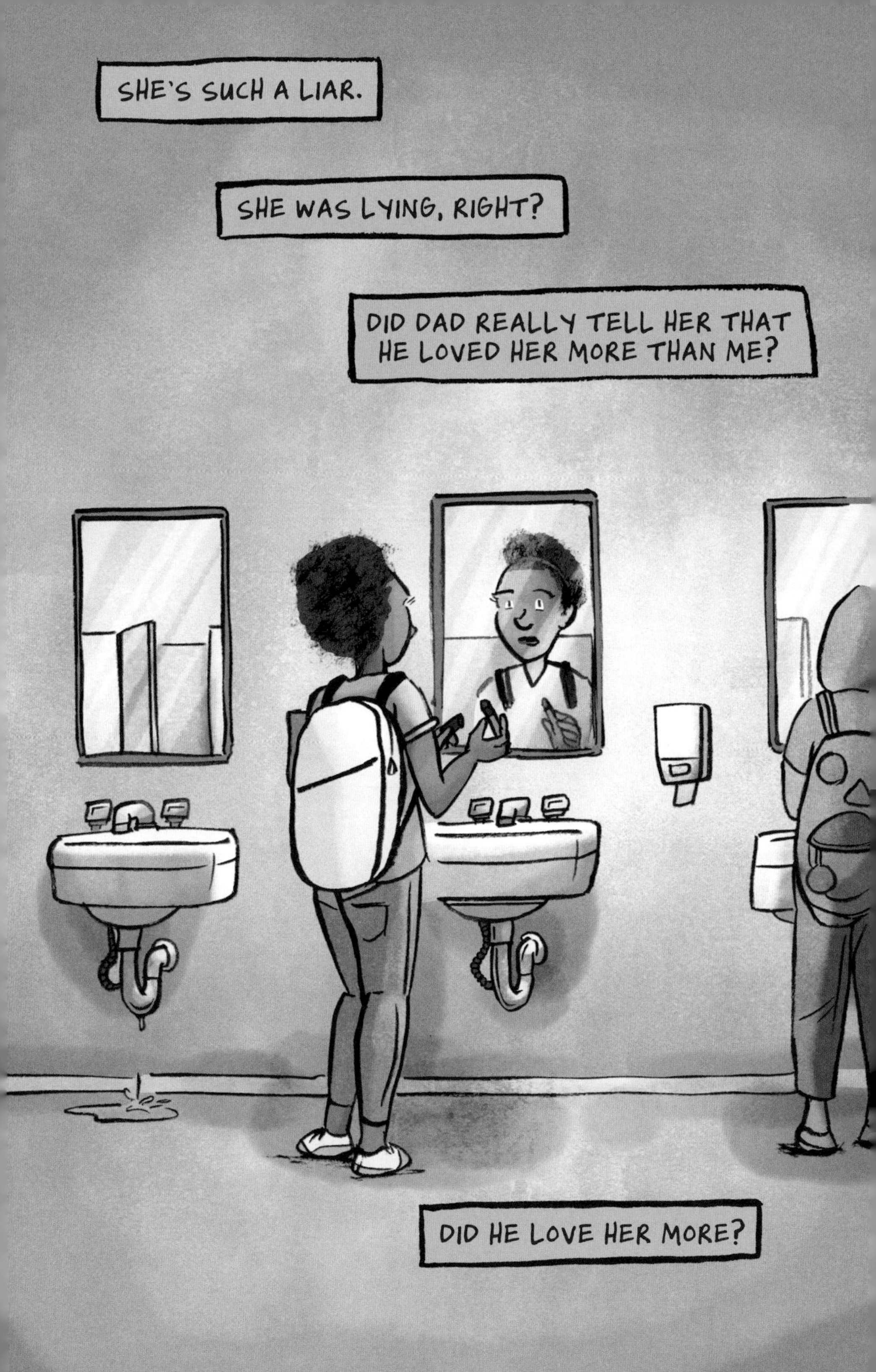
SHE'S SUCH A LIAR.
SHE WAS LYING, RIGHT?
DID DAD REALLY TELL HER THAT HE LOVED HER MORE THAN ME?
DID HE LOVE HER MORE?

Chapter 7

Retreat

The second basic move in footwork is the retreat. Your rear foot reaches backward in a naturally comfortable distance and is firmly planted. Then the front leg pushes your body weight smoothly backward into the en garde stance. The act of retreating helps you to maintain proper distance from your opponent, so they are no longer within striking distance. Maintaining the (right distance) from your opponent is key to avoiding being easily hit.

Like dancing

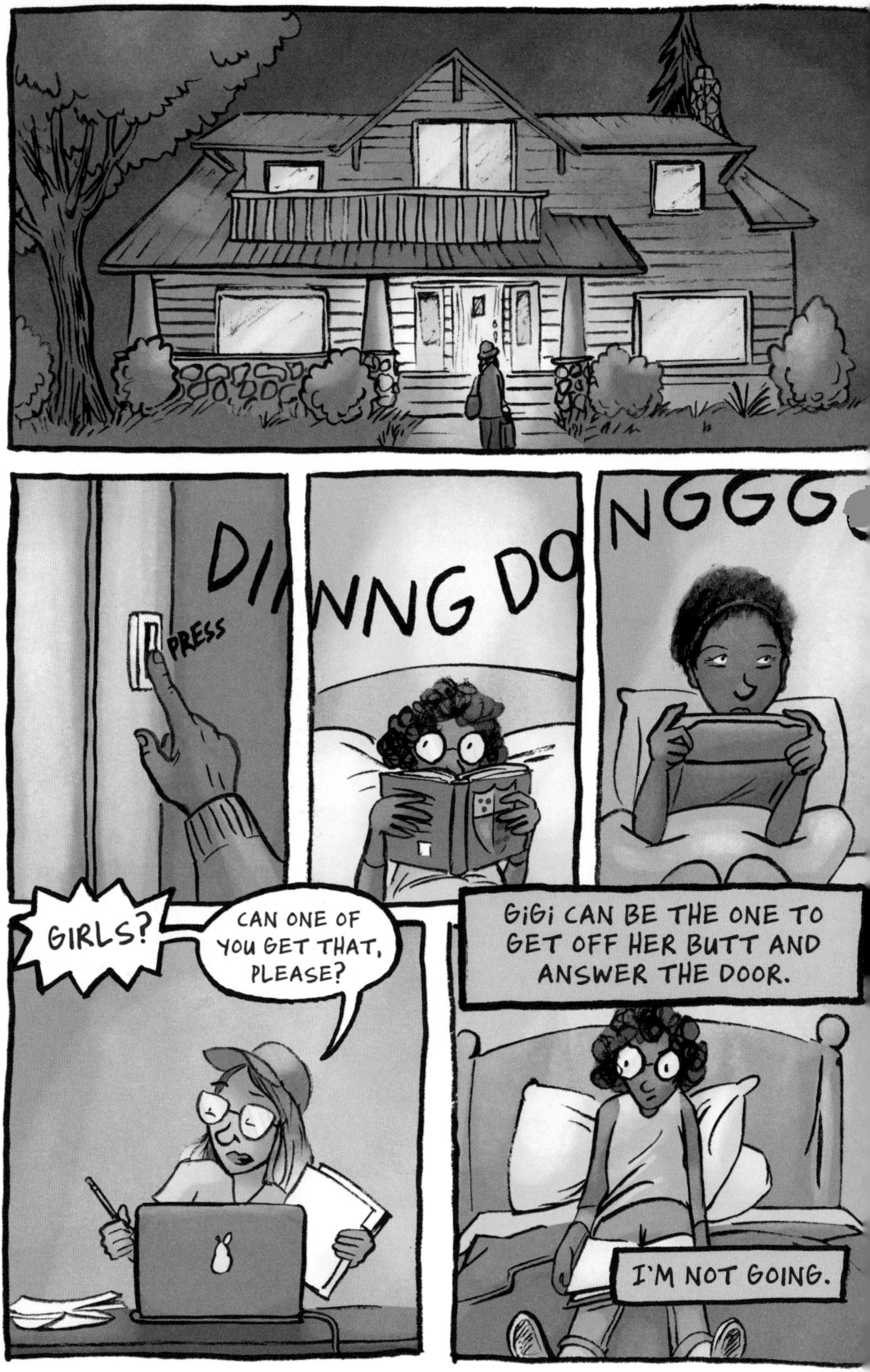

PRESS
DIIIING DONGGG
GIRLS?
CAN ONE OF YOU GET THAT, PLEASE?
GiGi CAN BE THE ONE TO GET OFF HER BUTT AND ANSWER THE DOOR.
I'M NOT GOING.

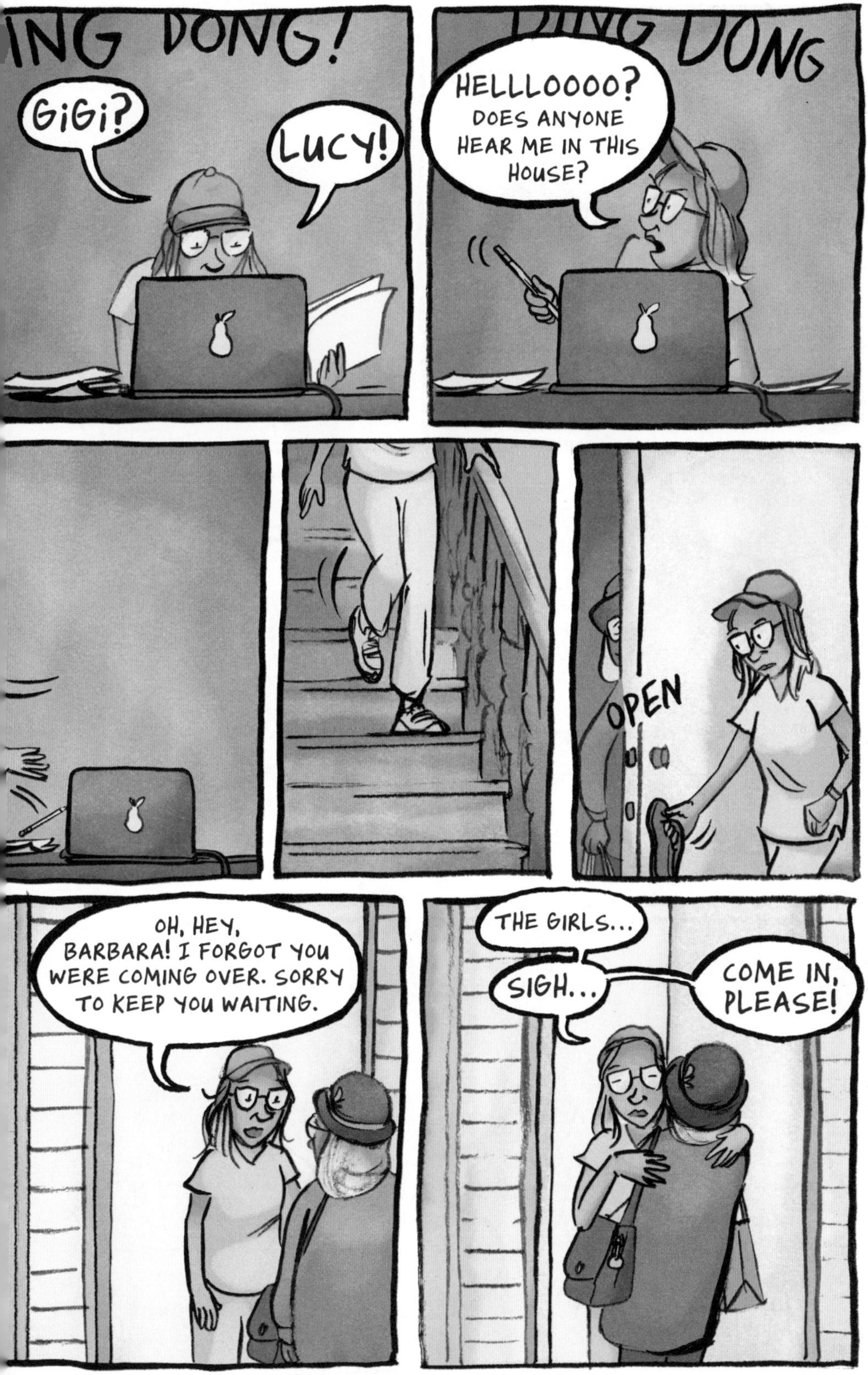
ING DONG!
GiGi?
LUCY!
DING DONG
HELLLOOOO? DOES ANYONE HEAR ME IN THIS HOUSE?
OPEN
OH, HEY, BARBARA! I FORGOT YOU WERE COMING OVER. SORRY TO KEEP YOU WAITING.
THE GIRLS...
SIGH...
COME IN, PLEASE!

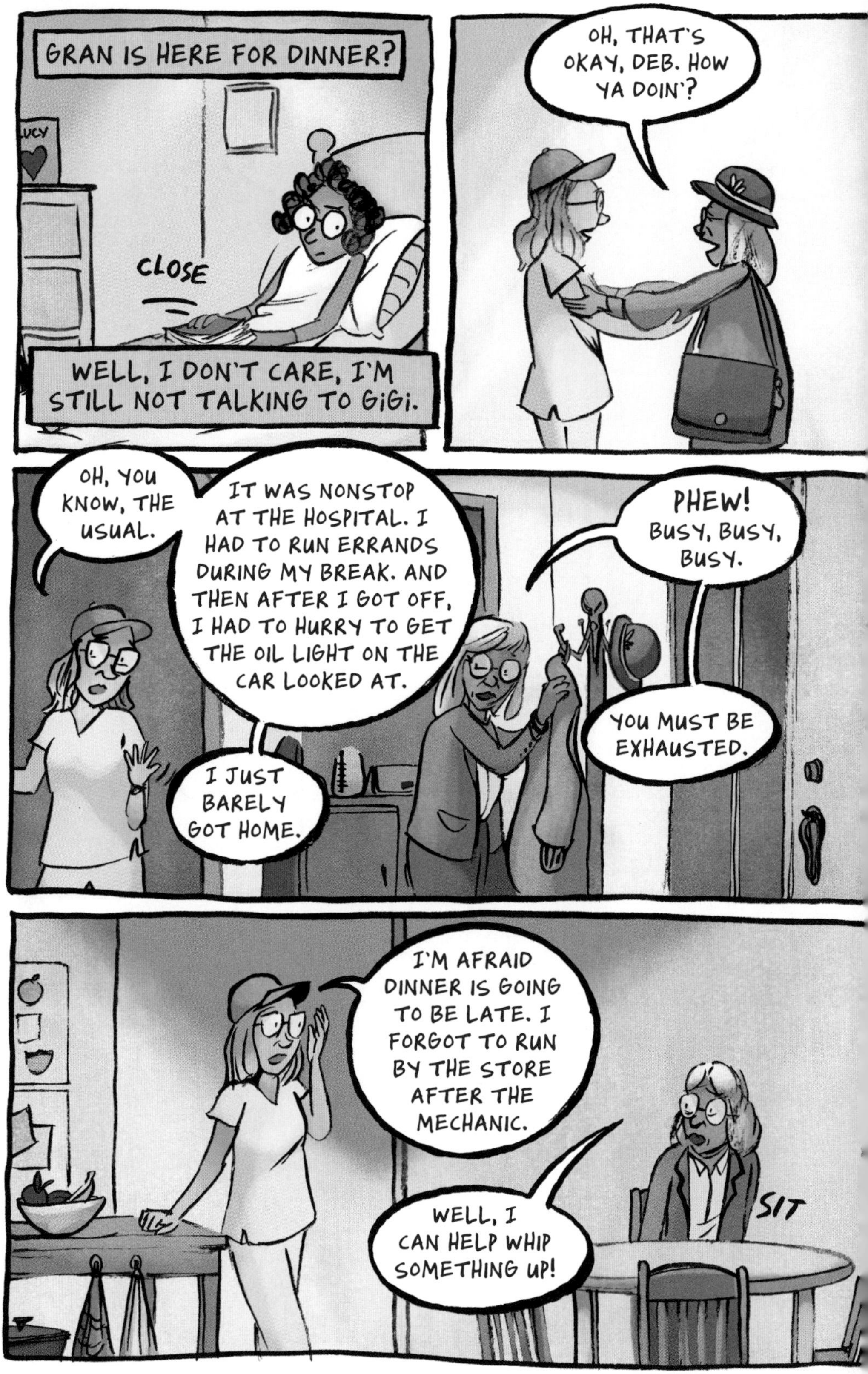
GRAN IS HERE FOR DINNER?
LUCY
CLOSE
WELL, I DON'T CARE, I'M STILL NOT TALKING TO GiGi.
OH, THAT'S OKAY, DEB. HOW YA DOIN'?
OH, YOU KNOW, THE USUAL.
IT WAS NONSTOP AT THE HOSPITAL. I HAD TO RUN ERRANDS DURING MY BREAK. AND THEN AFTER I GOT OFF, I HAD TO HURRY TO GET THE OIL LIGHT ON THE CAR LOOKED AT.
I JUST BARELY GOT HOME.
PHEW! BUSY, BUSY, BUSY.
YOU MUST BE EXHAUSTED.
I'M AFRAID DINNER IS GOING TO BE LATE. I FORGOT TO RUN BY THE STORE AFTER THE MECHANIC.
WELL, I CAN HELP WHIP SOMETHING UP!
SIT

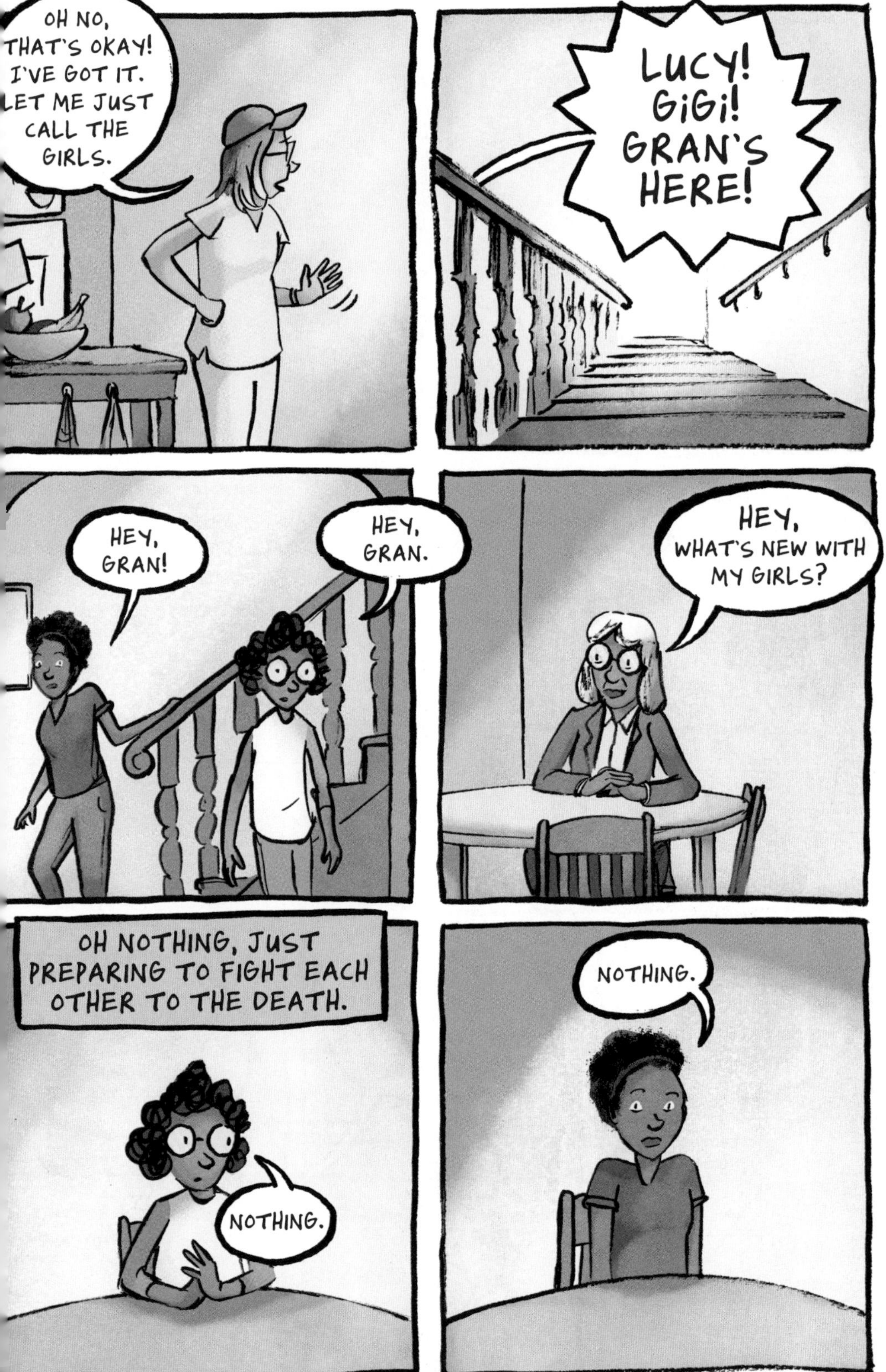
OH NO, THAT'S OKAY! I'VE GOT IT. LET ME JUST CALL THE GIRLS.
LUCY! GiGi! GRAN'S HERE!
HEY, GRAN!
HEY, GRAN.
HEY, WHAT'S NEW WITH MY GIRLS?
OH NOTHING, JUST PREPARING TO FIGHT EACH OTHER TO THE DEATH.
NOTHING.
NOTHING.

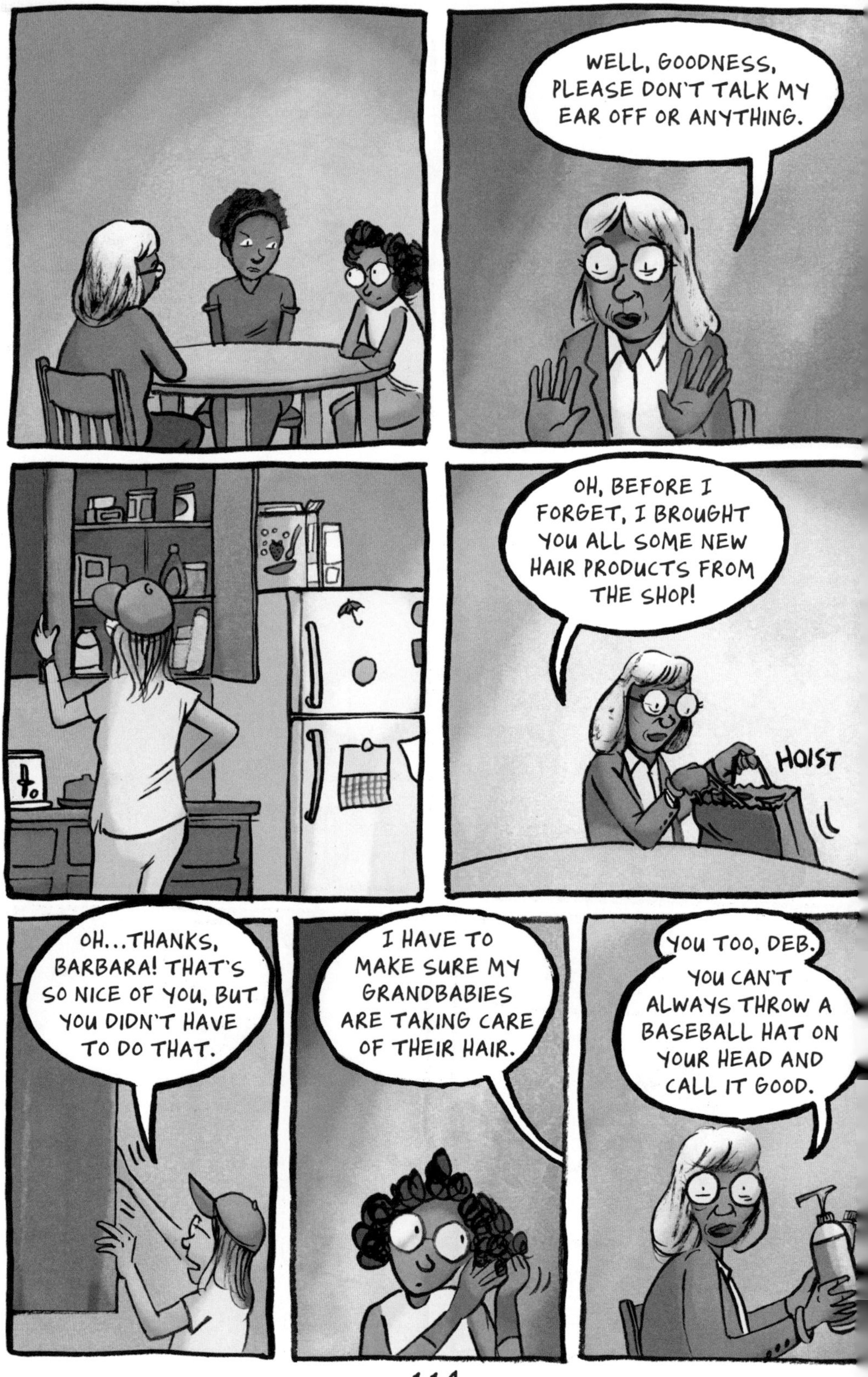
WELL, GOODNESS, PLEASE DON'T TALK MY EAR OFF OR ANYTHING.
OH, BEFORE I FORGET, I BROUGHT YOU ALL SOME NEW HAIR PRODUCTS FROM THE SHOP!
HOIST
OH...THANKS, BARBARA! THAT'S SO NICE OF YOU, BUT YOU DIDN'T HAVE TO DO THAT.
I HAVE TO MAKE SURE MY GRANDBABIES ARE TAKING CARE OF THEIR HAIR.
YOU TOO, DEB.
YOU CAN'T ALWAYS THROW A BASEBALL HAT ON YOUR HEAD AND CALL IT GOOD.

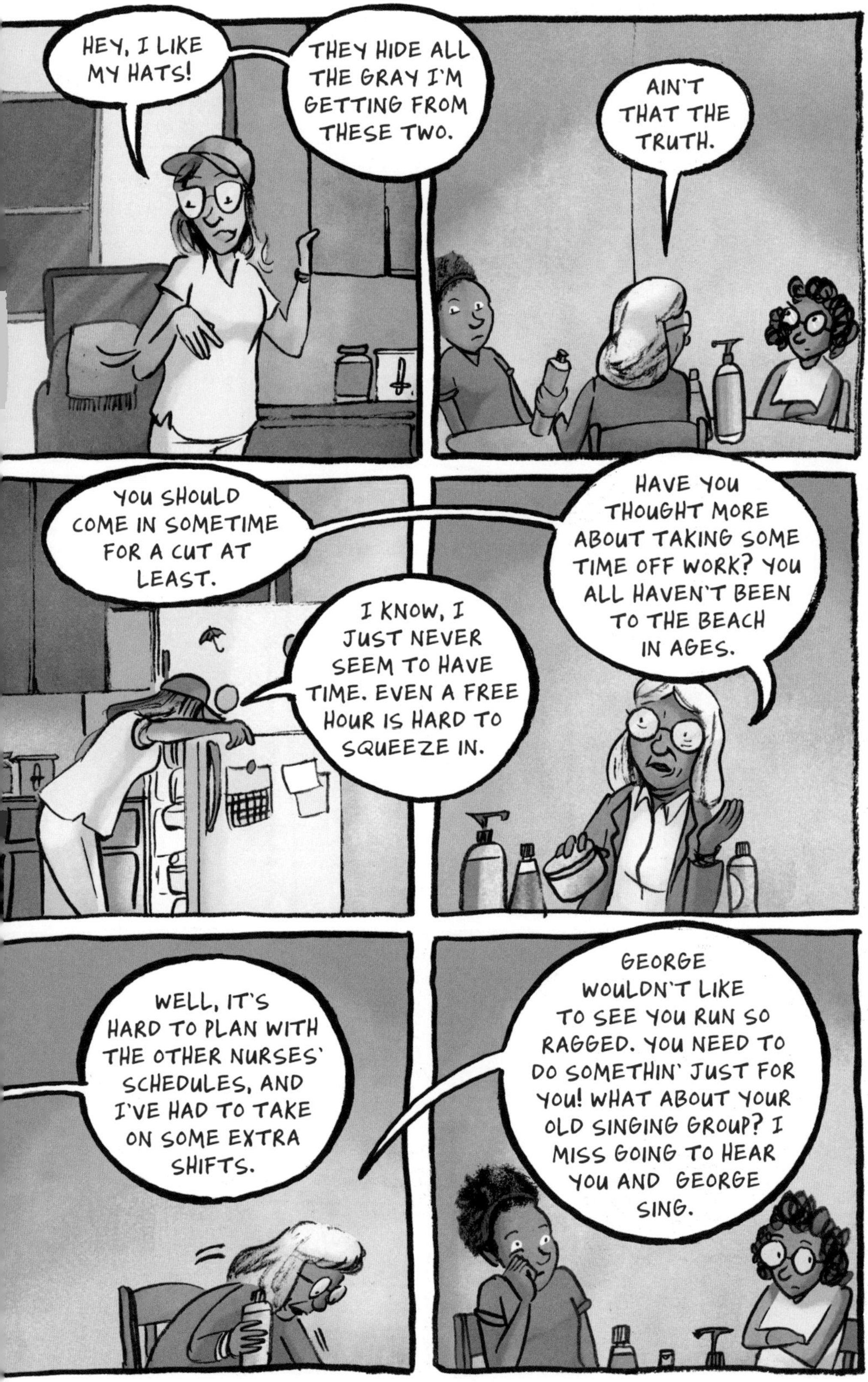
HEY, I LIKE MY HATS!
THEY HIDE ALL THE GRAY I'M GETTING FROM THESE TWO.
AIN'T THAT THE TRUTH.
YOU SHOULD COME IN SOMETIME FOR A CUT AT LEAST.
HAVE YOU THOUGHT MORE ABOUT TAKING SOME TIME OFF WORK? YOU ALL HAVEN'T BEEN TO THE BEACH IN AGES.
I KNOW, I JUST NEVER SEEM TO HAVE TIME. EVEN A FREE HOUR IS HARD TO SQUEEZE IN.
WELL, IT'S HARD TO PLAN WITH THE OTHER NURSES' SCHEDULES, AND I'VE HAD TO TAKE ON SOME EXTRA SHIFTS.
GEORGE WOULDN'T LIKE TO SEE YOU RUN SO RAGGED. YOU NEED TO DO SOMETHIN' JUST FOR YOU! WHAT ABOUT YOUR OLD SINGING GROUP? I MISS GOING TO HEAR YOU AND GEORGE SING.

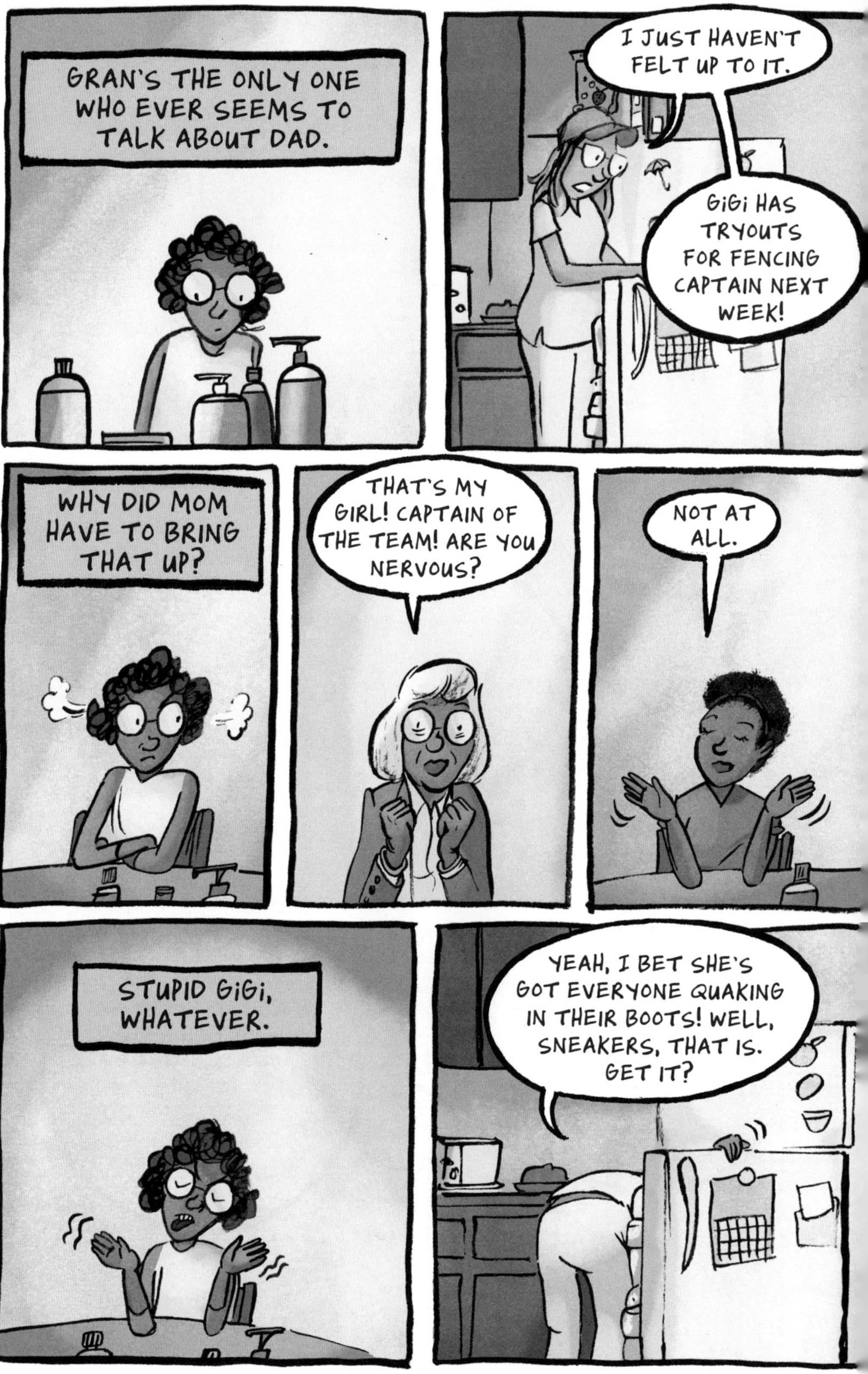
GRAN'S THE ONLY ONE WHO EVER SEEMS TO TALK ABOUT DAD.
I JUST HAVEN'T FELT UP TO IT.
GiGi HAS TRYOUTS FOR FENCING CAPTAIN NEXT WEEK!
WHY DID MOM HAVE TO BRING THAT UP?
THAT'S MY GIRL! CAPTAIN OF THE TEAM! ARE YOU NERVOUS?
NOT AT ALL.
STUPID GiGi, WHATEVER.
YEAH, I BET SHE'S GOT EVERYONE QUAKING IN THEIR BOOTS! WELL, SNEAKERS, THAT IS. GET IT?

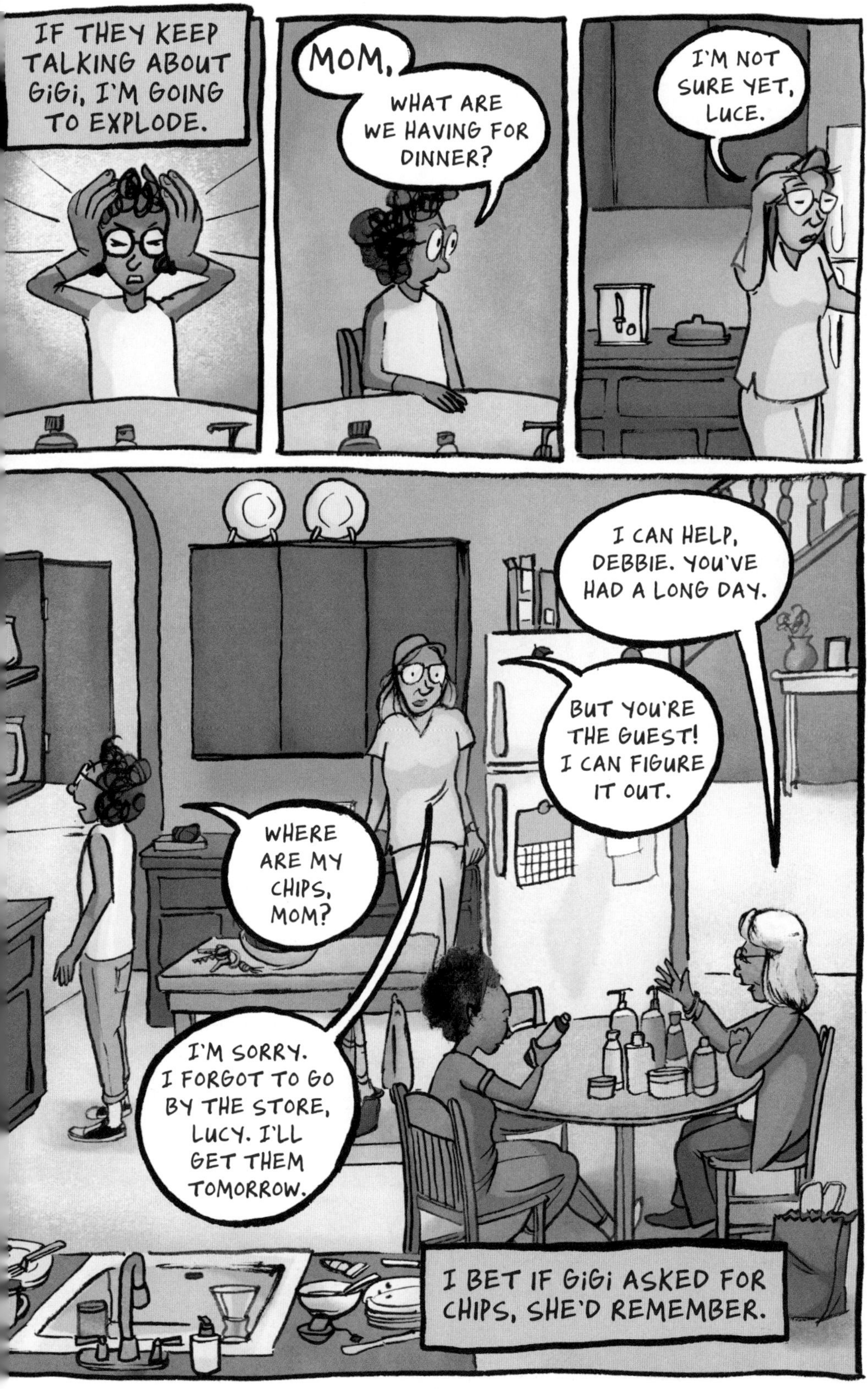
IF THEY KEEP TALKING ABOUT GiGi, I'M GOING TO EXPLODE.
MOM,
WHAT ARE WE HAVING FOR DINNER?
I'M NOT SURE YET, LUCE.
I CAN HELP, DEBBIE. YOU'VE HAD A LONG DAY.
BUT YOU'RE THE GUEST! I CAN FIGURE IT OUT.
WHERE ARE MY CHIPS, MOM?
I'M SORRY. I FORGOT TO GO BY THE STORE, LUCY. I'LL GET THEM TOMORROW.
I BET IF GiGi ASKED FOR CHIPS, SHE'D REMEMBER.

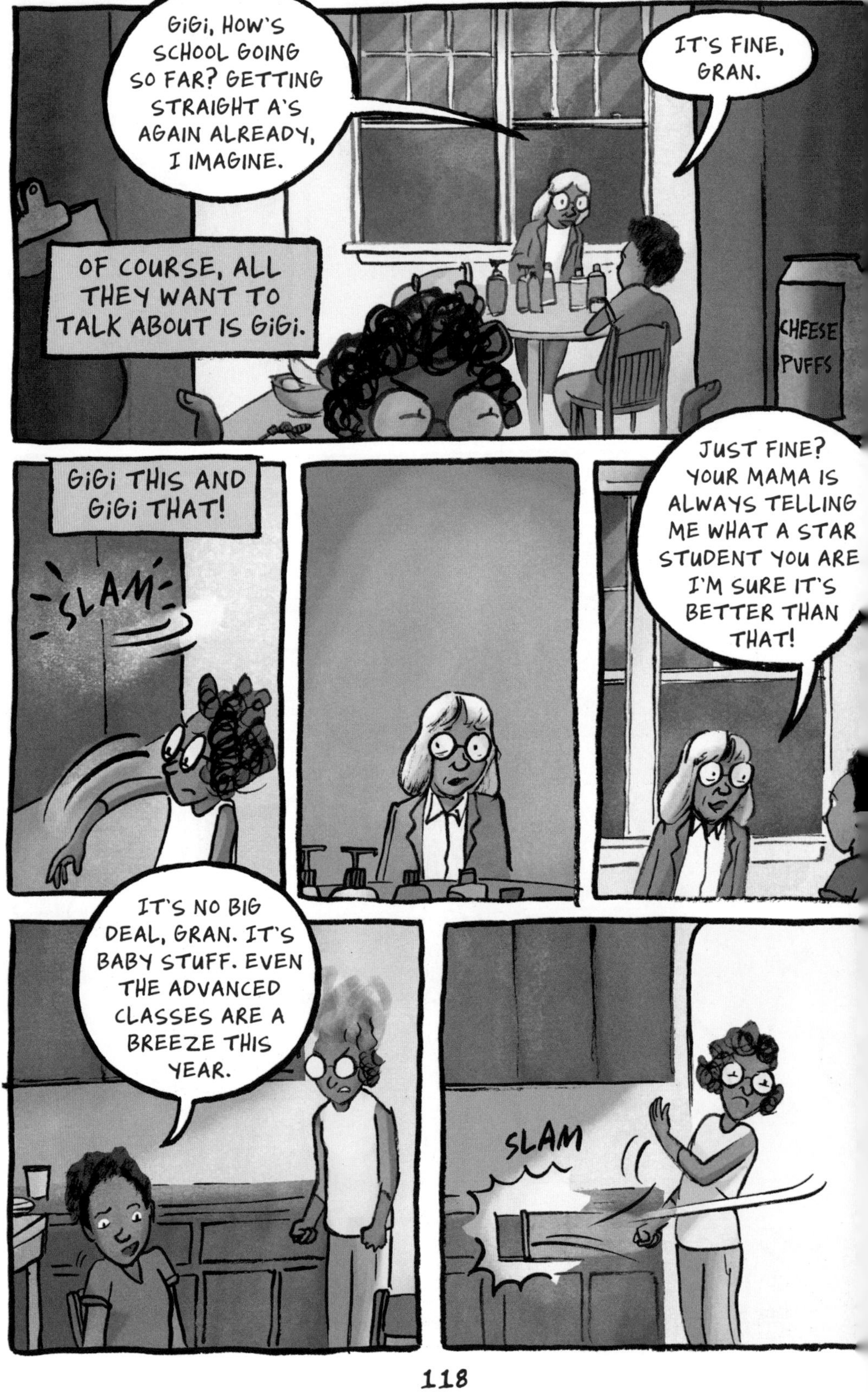
GiGi, HOW'S SCHOOL GOING SO FAR? GETTING STRAIGHT A'S AGAIN ALREADY, I IMAGINE.
IT'S FINE, GRAN.
OF COURSE, ALL THEY WANT TO TALK ABOUT IS GiGi.
CHEESE PUFFS
GiGi THIS AND GiGi THAT!
SLAM
JUST FINE? YOUR MAMA IS ALWAYS TELLING ME WHAT A STAR STUDENT YOU ARE I'M SURE IT'S BETTER THAN THAT!
IT'S NO BIG DEAL, GRAN. IT'S BABY STUFF. EVEN THE ADVANCED CLASSES ARE A BREEZE THIS YEAR.
SLAM

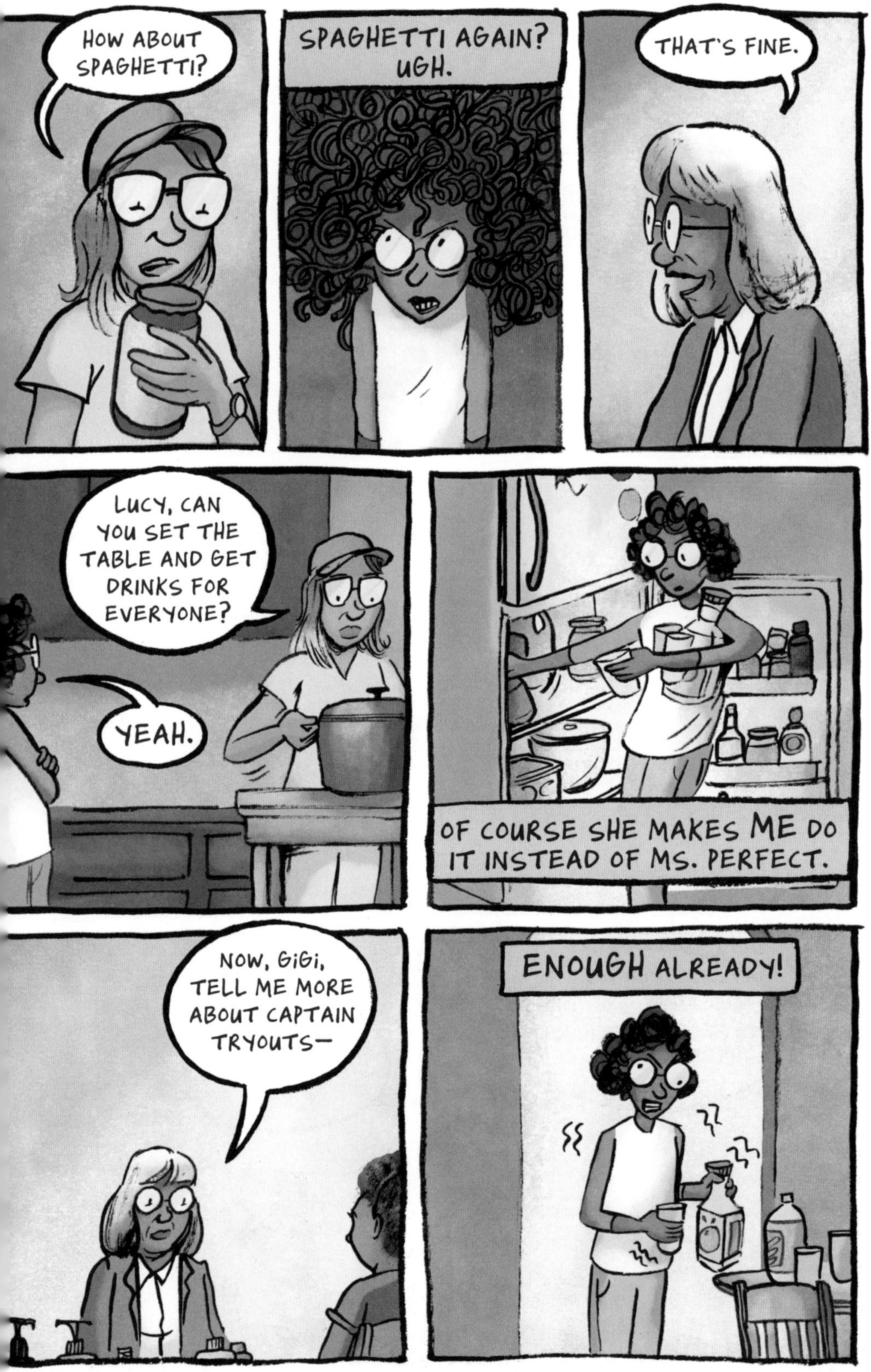
HOW ABOUT SPAGHETTI?
SPAGHETTI AGAIN? UGH.
THAT'S FINE.
LUCY, CAN YOU SET THE TABLE AND GET DRINKS FOR EVERYONE?
YEAH.
OF COURSE SHE MAKES ME DO IT INSTEAD OF MS. PERFECT.
NOW, GiGi, TELL ME MORE ABOUT CAPTAIN TRYOUTS—
ENOUGH ALREADY!

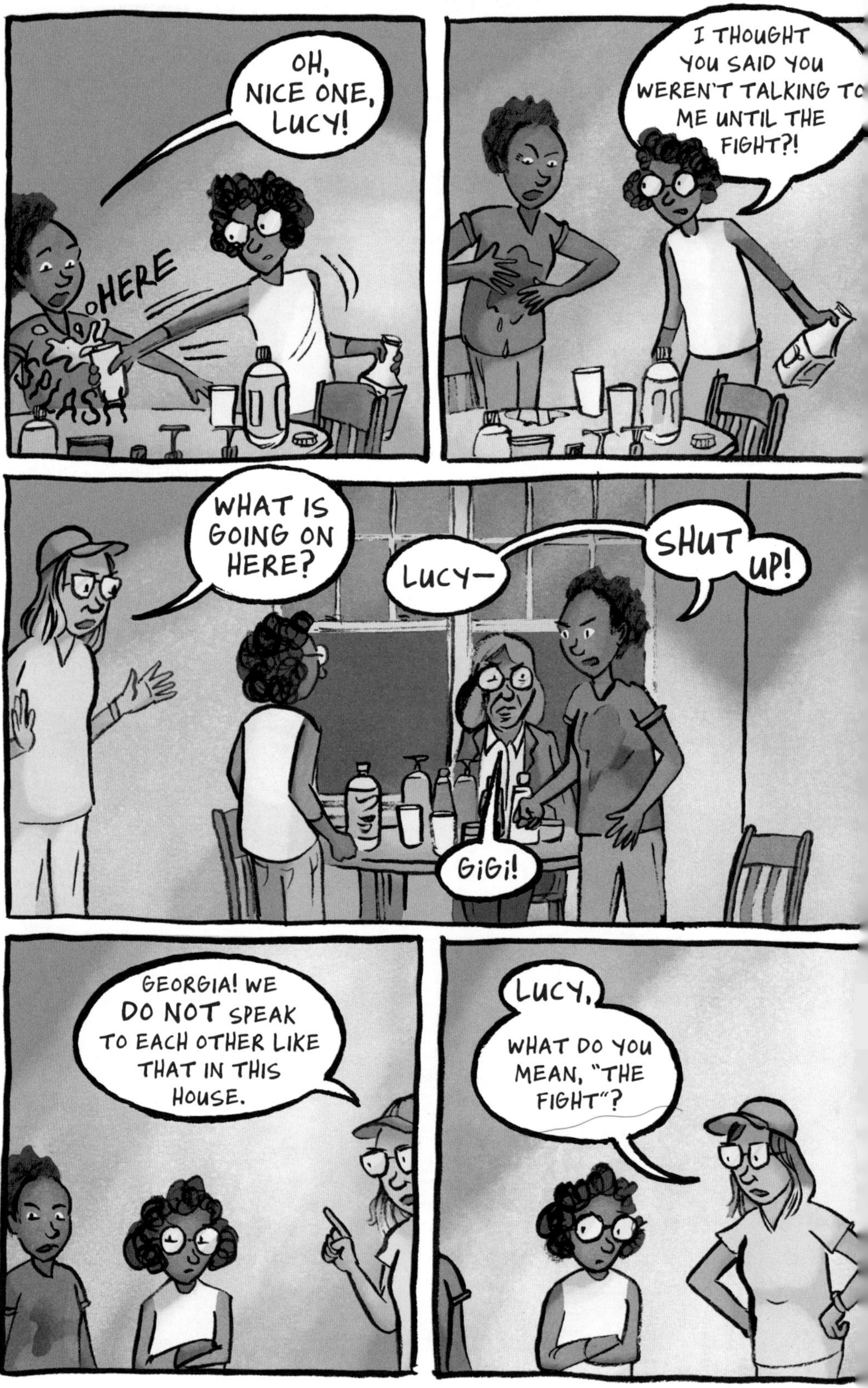
OH, NICE ONE, LUCY!
HERE
SPLASH
I THOUGHT YOU SAID YOU WEREN'T TALKING TO ME UNTIL THE FIGHT?!
WHAT IS GOING ON HERE?
LUCY—
SHUT UP!
GiGi!
GEORGIA! WE DO NOT SPEAK TO EACH OTHER LIKE THAT IN THIS HOUSE.
LUCY,
WHAT DO YOU MEAN, "THE FIGHT"?

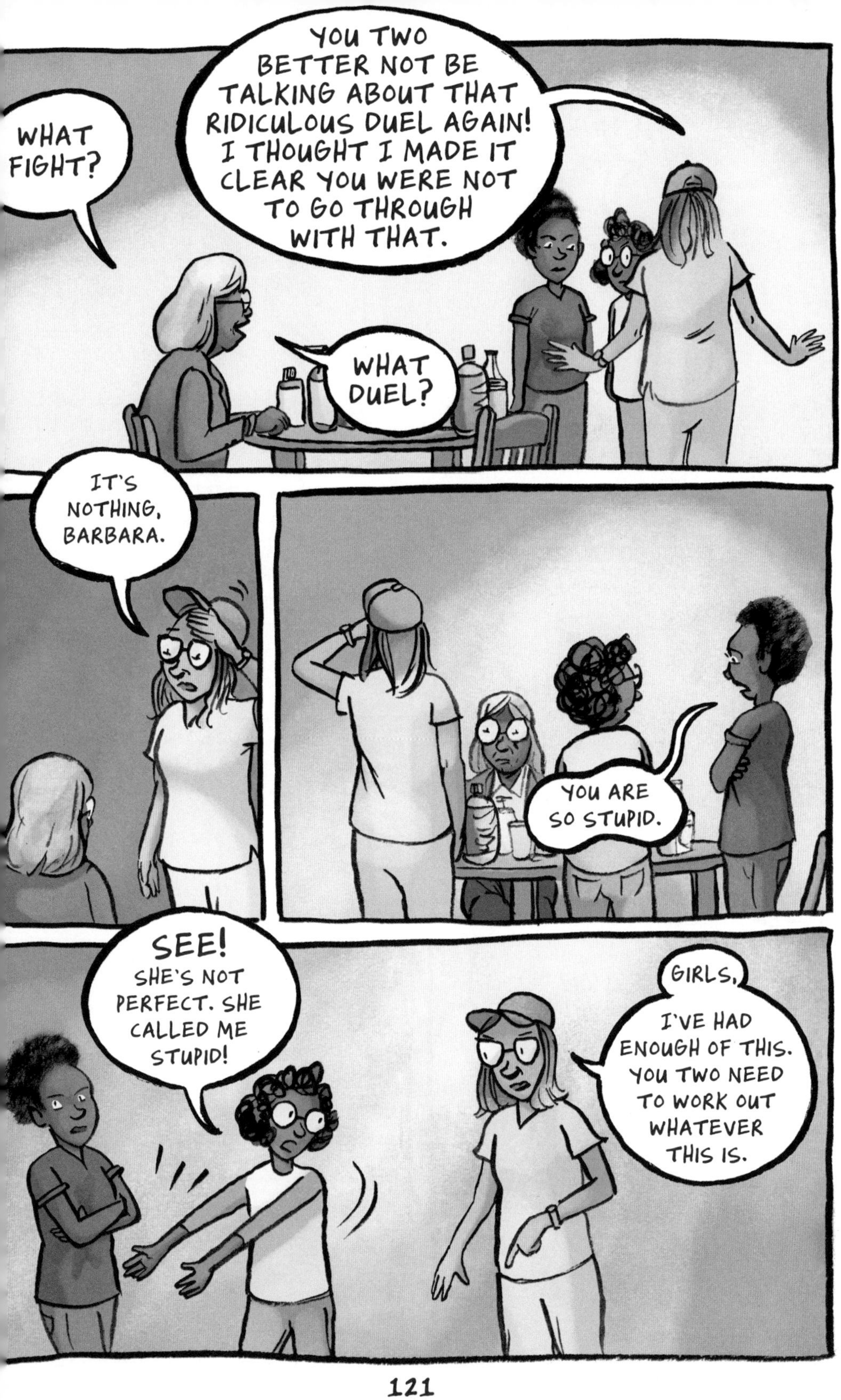
WHAT FIGHT?
YOU TWO BETTER NOT BE TALKING ABOUT THAT RIDICULOUS DUEL AGAIN! I THOUGHT I MADE IT CLEAR YOU WERE NOT TO GO THROUGH WITH THAT.
WHAT DUEL?
IT'S NOTHING, BARBARA.
YOU ARE SO STUPID.
SEE! SHE'S NOT PERFECT. SHE CALLED ME STUPID!
GIRLS,
I'VE HAD ENOUGH OF THIS. YOU TWO NEED TO WORK OUT WHATEVER THIS IS.

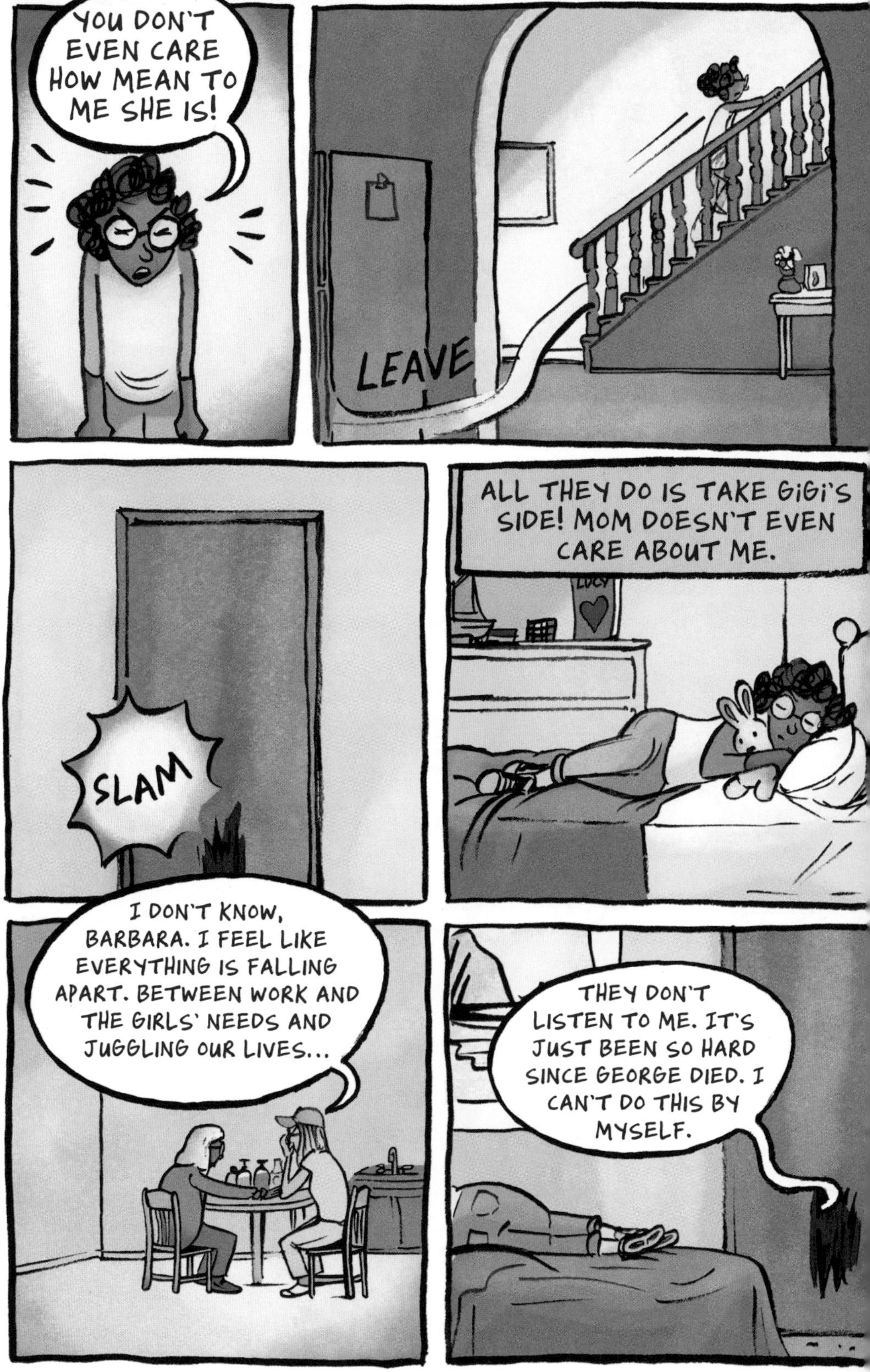
YOU DON'T EVEN CARE HOW MEAN TO ME SHE IS!
LEAVE
SLAM
ALL THEY DO IS TAKE GIGI'S SIDE! MOM DOESN'T EVEN CARE ABOUT ME.
LUCY
I DON'T KNOW, BARBARA. I FEEL LIKE EVERYTHING IS FALLING APART. BETWEEN WORK AND THE GIRLS' NEEDS AND JUGGLING OUR LIVES...
THEY DON'T LISTEN TO ME. IT'S JUST BEEN SO HARD SINCE GEORGE DIED. I CAN'T DO THIS BY MYSELF.

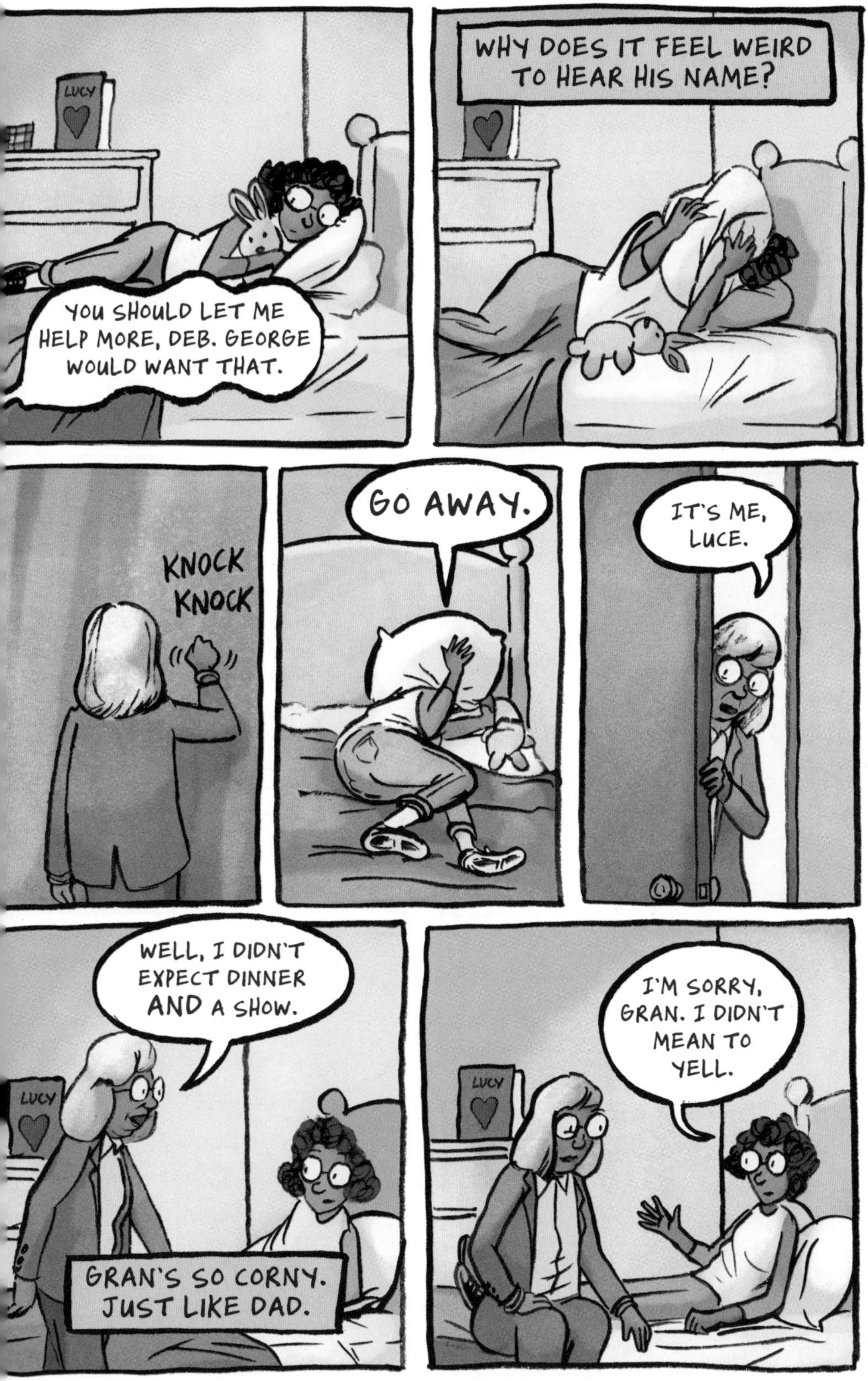
LUCY
YOU SHOULD LET ME HELP MORE, DEB. GEORGE WOULD WANT THAT.
WHY DOES IT FEEL WEIRD TO HEAR HIS NAME?
KNOCK KNOCK
GO AWAY.
IT'S ME, LUCE.
WELL, I DIDN'T EXPECT DINNER AND A SHOW.
LUCY
GRAN'S SO CORNY. JUST LIKE DAD.
LUCY
I'M SORRY, GRAN. I DIDN'T MEAN TO YELL.

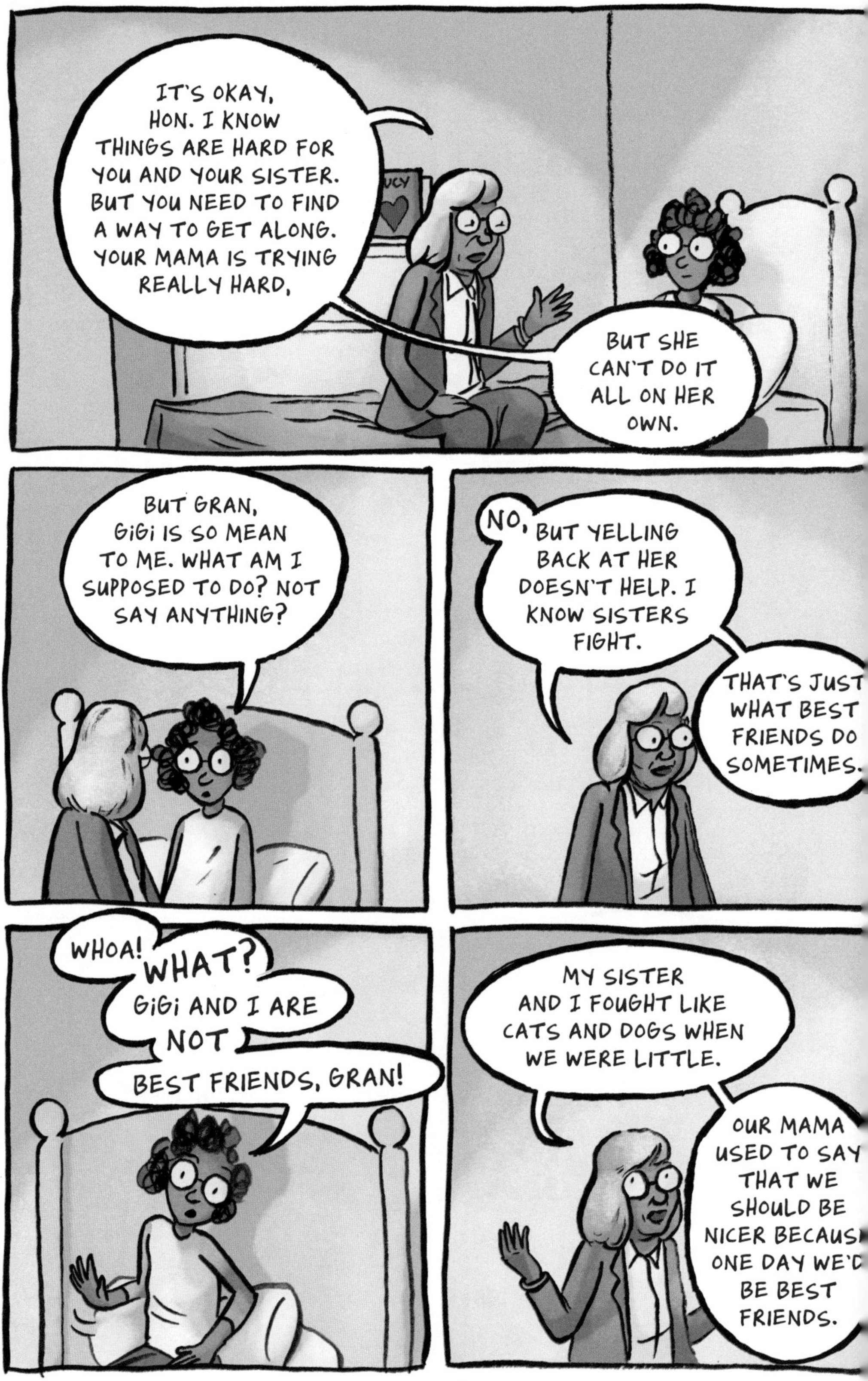
IT'S OKAY, HON. I KNOW THINGS ARE HARD FOR YOU AND YOUR SISTER. BUT YOU NEED TO FIND A WAY TO GET ALONG. YOUR MAMA IS TRYING REALLY HARD,
BUT SHE CAN'T DO IT ALL ON HER OWN.
BUT GRAN, GIGI IS SO MEAN TO ME. WHAT AM I SUPPOSED TO DO? NOT SAY ANYTHING?
NO, BUT YELLING BACK AT HER DOESN'T HELP. I KNOW SISTERS FIGHT.
THAT'S JUST WHAT BEST FRIENDS DO SOMETIMES.
WHOA! WHAT?
GIGI AND I ARE NOT
BEST FRIENDS, GRAN!
MY SISTER AND I FOUGHT LIKE CATS AND DOGS WHEN WE WERE LITTLE.
OUR MAMA USED TO SAY THAT WE SHOULD BE NICER BECAUS ONE DAY WE'D BE BEST FRIENDS.

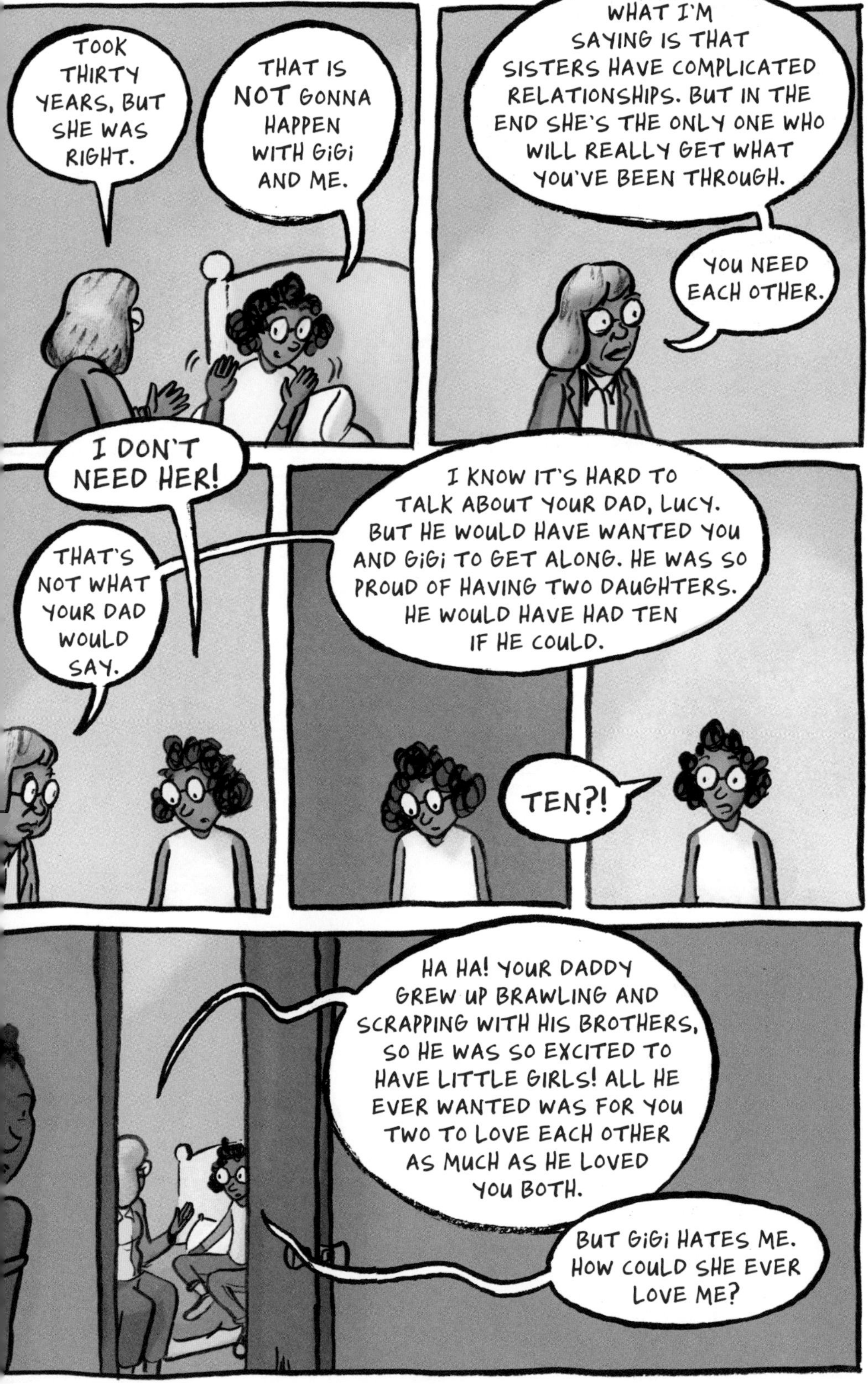
TOOK THIRTY YEARS, BUT SHE WAS RIGHT.
THAT IS NOT GONNA HAPPEN WITH GIGI AND ME.
WHAT I'M SAYING IS THAT SISTERS HAVE COMPLICATED RELATIONSHIPS. BUT IN THE END SHE'S THE ONLY ONE WHO WILL REALLY GET WHAT YOU'VE BEEN THROUGH.
YOU NEED EACH OTHER.
I DON'T NEED HER!
THAT'S NOT WHAT YOUR DAD WOULD SAY.
I KNOW IT'S HARD TO TALK ABOUT YOUR DAD, LUCY. BUT HE WOULD HAVE WANTED YOU AND GIGI TO GET ALONG. HE WAS SO PROUD OF HAVING TWO DAUGHTERS. HE WOULD HAVE HAD TEN IF HE COULD.
TEN?!
HA HA! YOUR DADDY GREW UP BRAWLING AND SCRAPPING WITH HIS BROTHERS, SO HE WAS SO EXCITED TO HAVE LITTLE GIRLS! ALL HE EVER WANTED WAS FOR YOU TWO TO LOVE EACH OTHER AS MUCH AS HE LOVED YOU BOTH.
BUT GIGI HATES ME. HOW COULD SHE EVER LOVE ME?

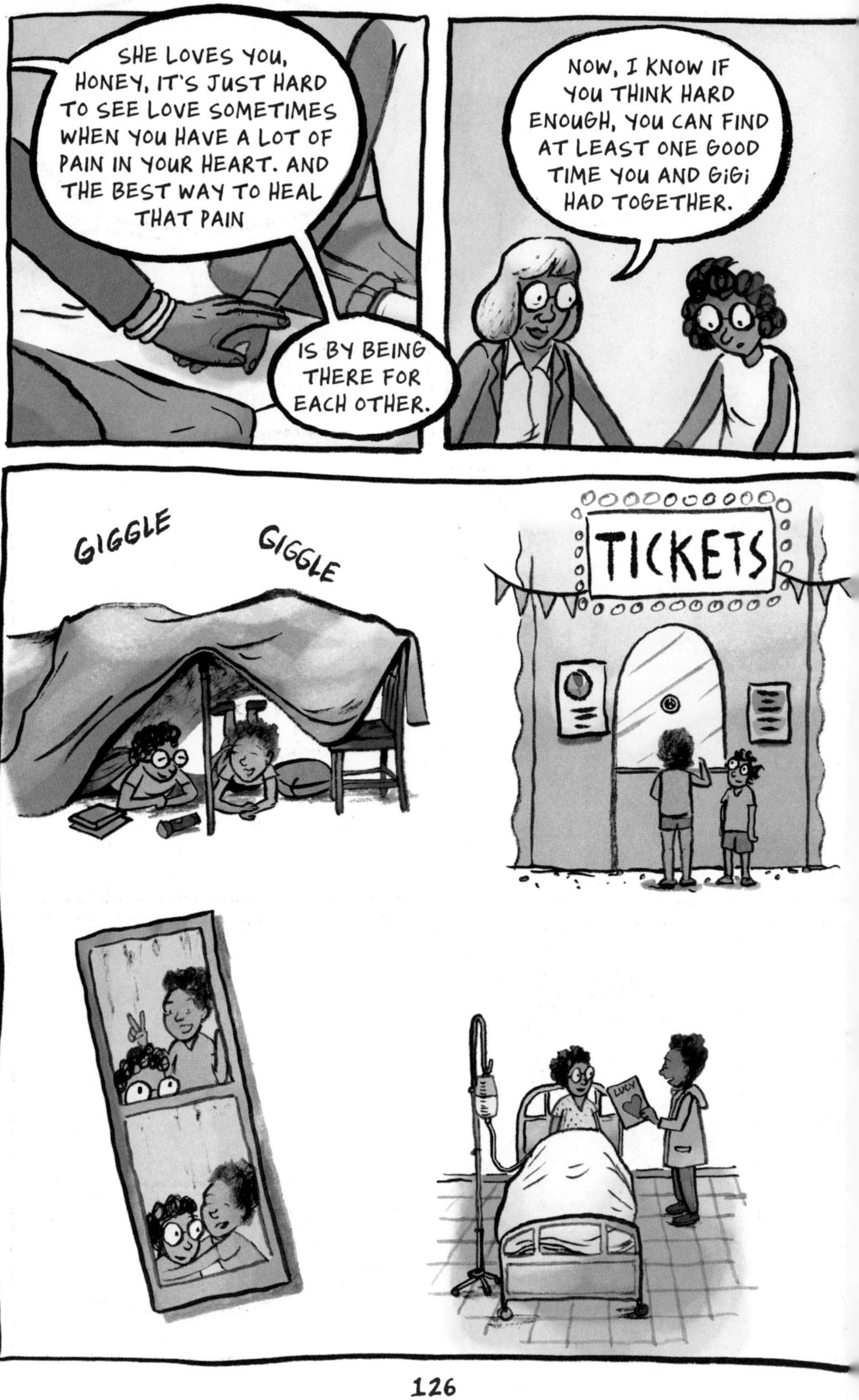
SHE LOVES YOU, HONEY, IT'S JUST HARD TO SEE LOVE SOMETIMES WHEN YOU HAVE A LOT OF PAIN IN YOUR HEART. AND THE BEST WAY TO HEAL THAT PAIN
IS BY BEING THERE FOR EACH OTHER.
NOW, I KNOW IF YOU THINK HARD ENOUGH, YOU CAN FIND AT LEAST ONE GOOD TIME YOU AND GIGI HAD TOGETHER.
GIGGLE
GIGGLE
TICKETS
LUCY

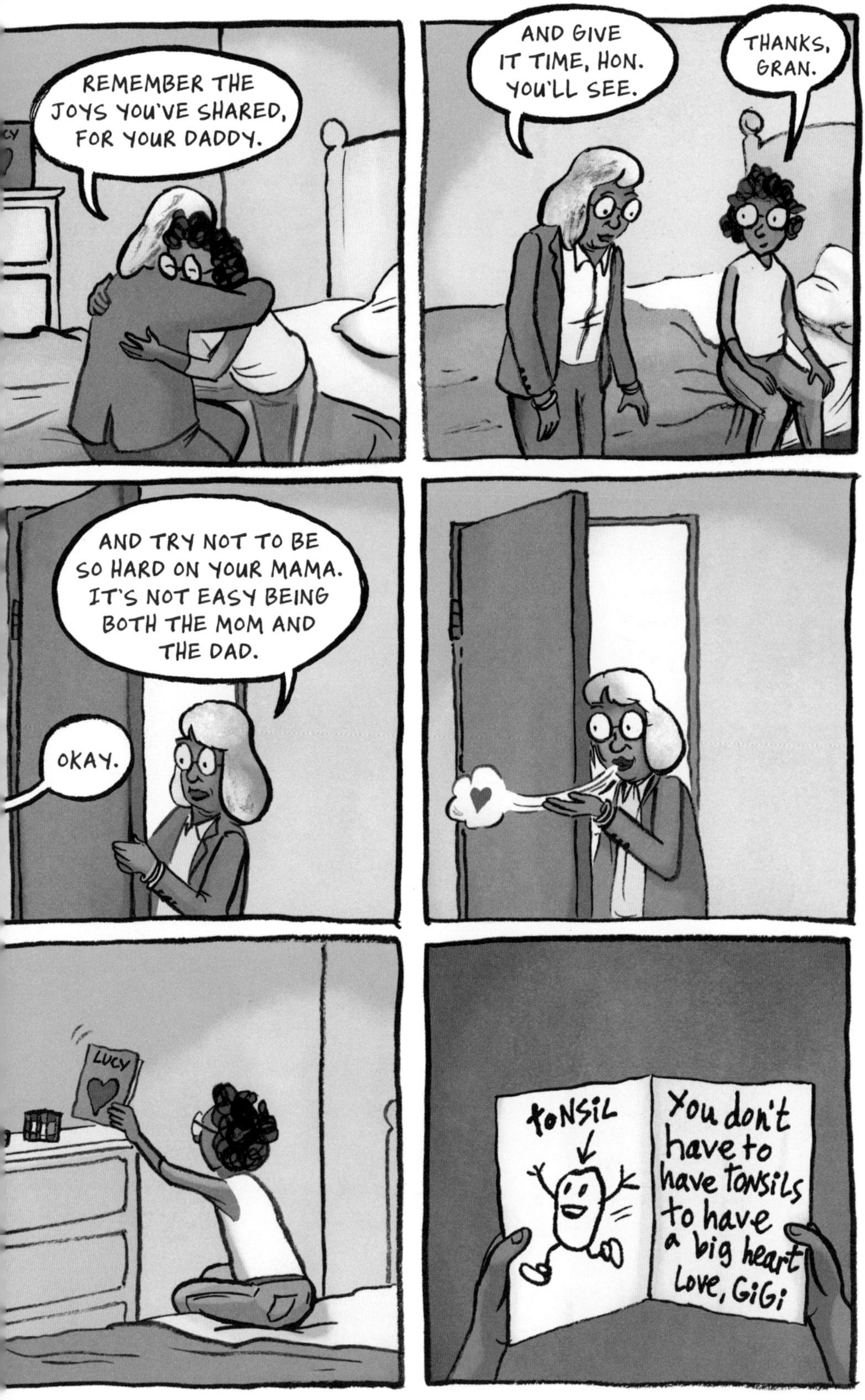
REMEMBER THE JOYS YOU'VE SHARED, FOR YOUR DADDY.
AND GIVE IT TIME, HON. YOU'LL SEE.
THANKS, GRAN.
AND TRY NOT TO BE SO HARD ON YOUR MAMA. IT'S NOT EASY BEING BOTH THE MOM AND THE DAD.
OKAY.
LUCY
TONSIL
You don't have to have TONSILS to have a big heart
Love, GiGi

Chapter 8

Attack!

An attack is made by extending your foil arm in a continuously threatening manner at a valid target of your opponent. There are various types of attacks in foil fencing. An attack must be intentional by moving toward your opponent with both the hand and feet. If done correctly, the attacking fencer gains right-of-way and hits their target and is therefore awarded the point. However, the attack may be stopped with a parry or abandoned. Attacks are most effective when they are unexpected and catch one's opponent off guard. *Important!*

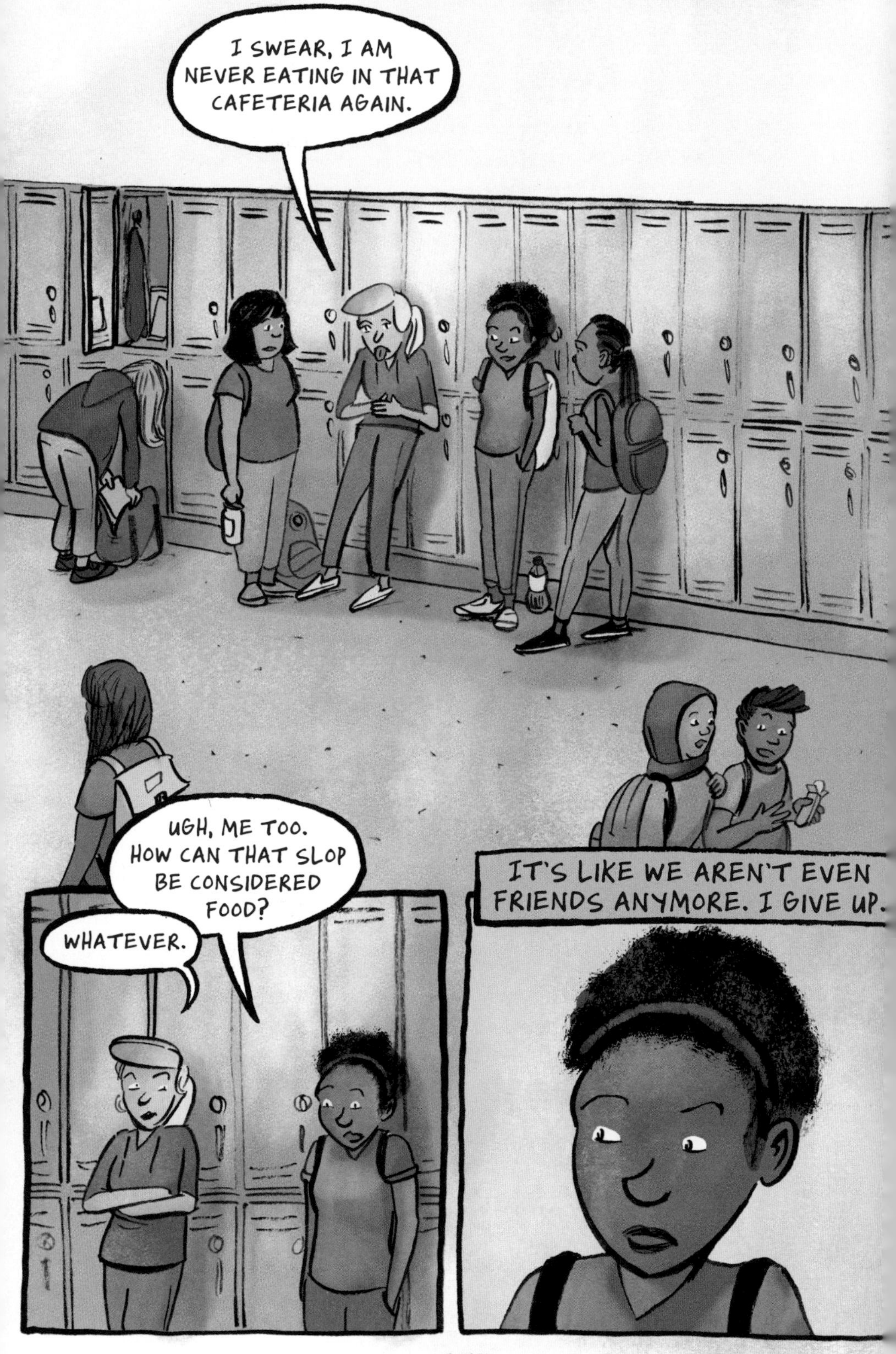
I SWEAR, I AM NEVER EATING IN THAT CAFETERIA AGAIN.
UGH, ME TOO. HOW CAN THAT SLOP BE CONSIDERED FOOD?
WHATEVER.
IT'S LIKE WE AREN'T EVEN FRIENDS ANYMORE. I GIVE UP.

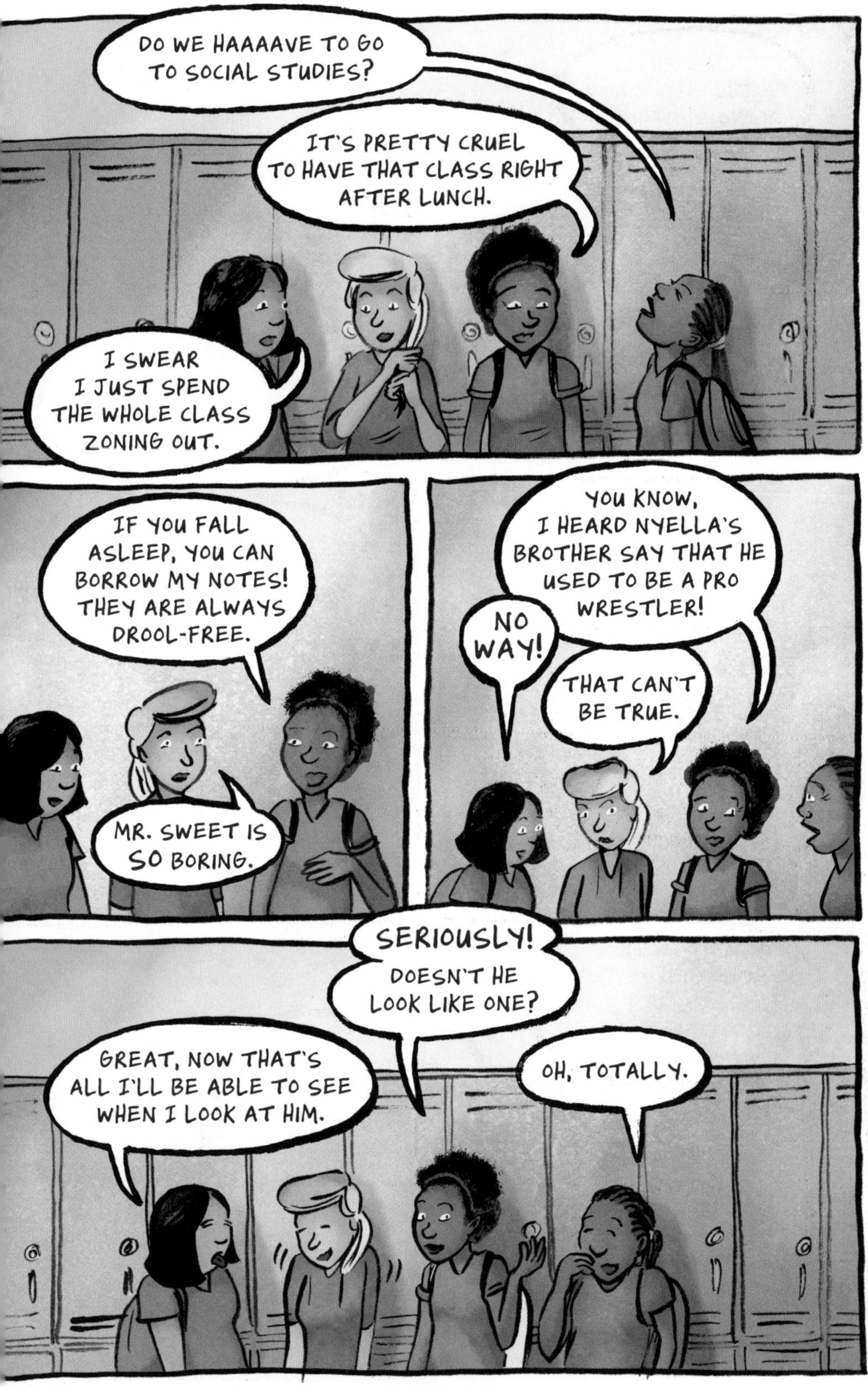
DO WE HAAAAVE TO GO TO SOCIAL STUDIES?
IT'S PRETTY CRUEL TO HAVE THAT CLASS RIGHT AFTER LUNCH.
I SWEAR I JUST SPEND THE WHOLE CLASS ZONING OUT.
IF YOU FALL ASLEEP, YOU CAN BORROW MY NOTES! THEY ARE ALWAYS DROOL-FREE.
MR. SWEET IS SO BORING.
YOU KNOW, I HEARD NYELLA'S BROTHER SAY THAT HE USED TO BE A PRO WRESTLER!
NO WAY!
THAT CAN'T BE TRUE.
SERIOUSLY!
DOESN'T HE LOOK LIKE ONE?
GREAT, NOW THAT'S ALL I'LL BE ABLE TO SEE WHEN I LOOK AT HIM.
OH, TOTALLY.

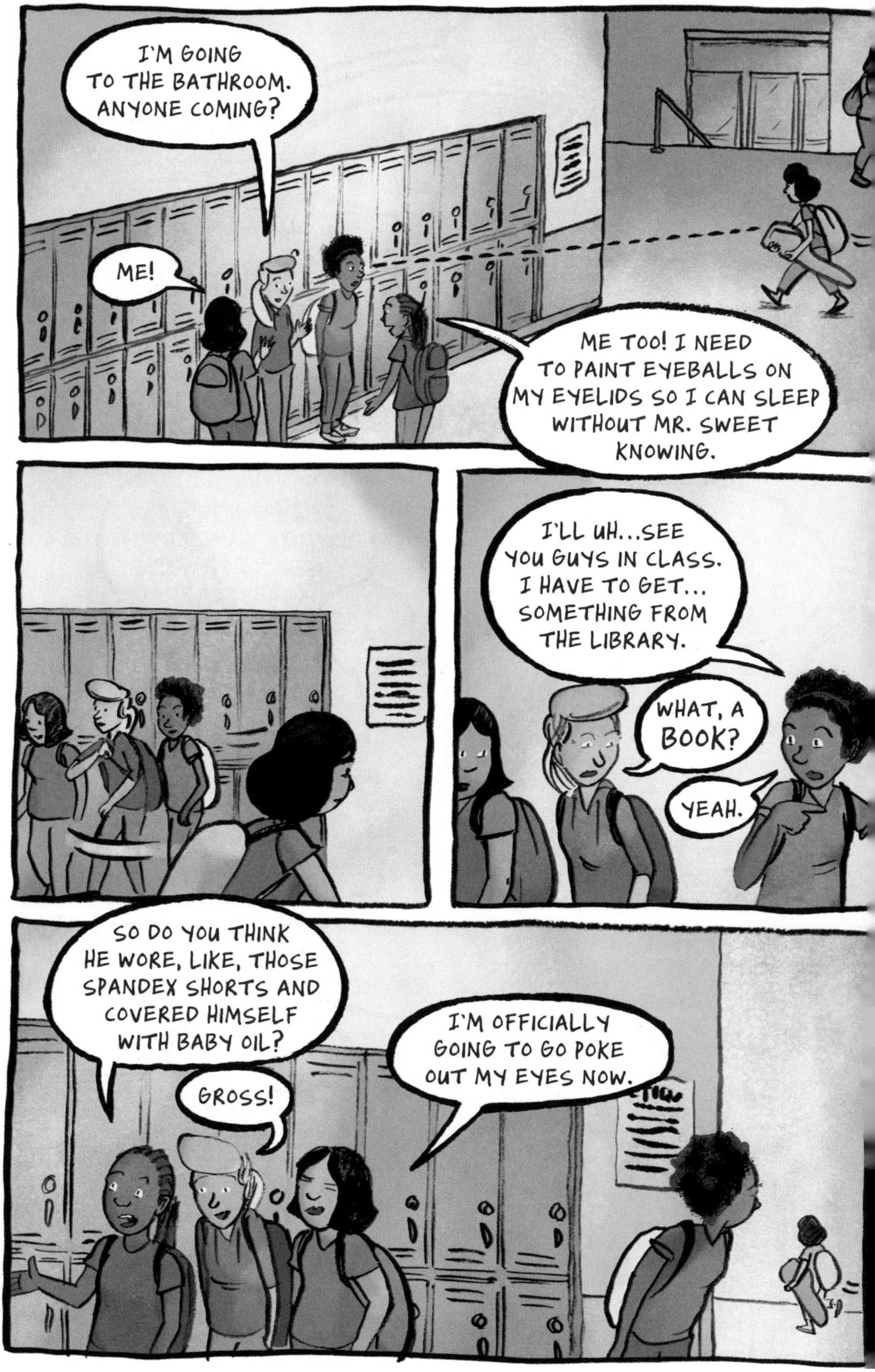
I'M GOING TO THE BATHROOM. ANYONE COMING?
ME!
ME TOO! I NEED TO PAINT EYEBALLS ON MY EYELIDS SO I CAN SLEEP WITHOUT MR. SWEET KNOWING.
I'LL UH...SEE YOU GUYS IN CLASS. I HAVE TO GET... SOMETHING FROM THE LIBRARY.
WHAT, A BOOK?
YEAH.
SO DO YOU THINK HE WORE, LIKE, THOSE SPANDEX SHORTS AND COVERED HIMSELF WITH BABY OIL?
GROSS!
I'M OFFICIALLY GOING TO GO POKE OUT MY EYES NOW.

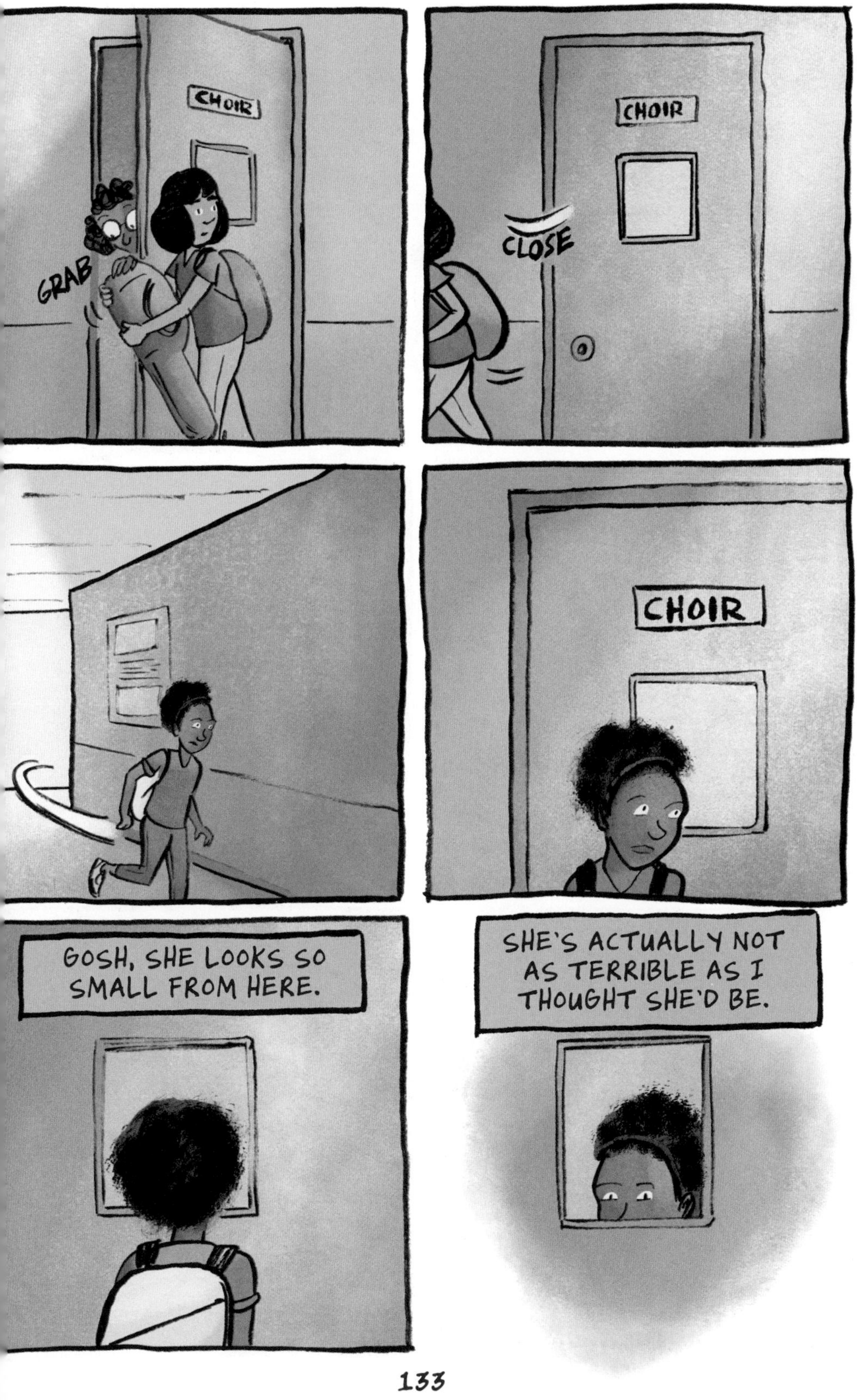

CHOIR
GRAB
CHOIR
CLOSE
CHOIR
GOSH, SHE LOOKS SO SMALL FROM HERE.
SHE'S ACTUALLY NOT AS TERRIBLE AS I THOUGHT SHE'D BE.

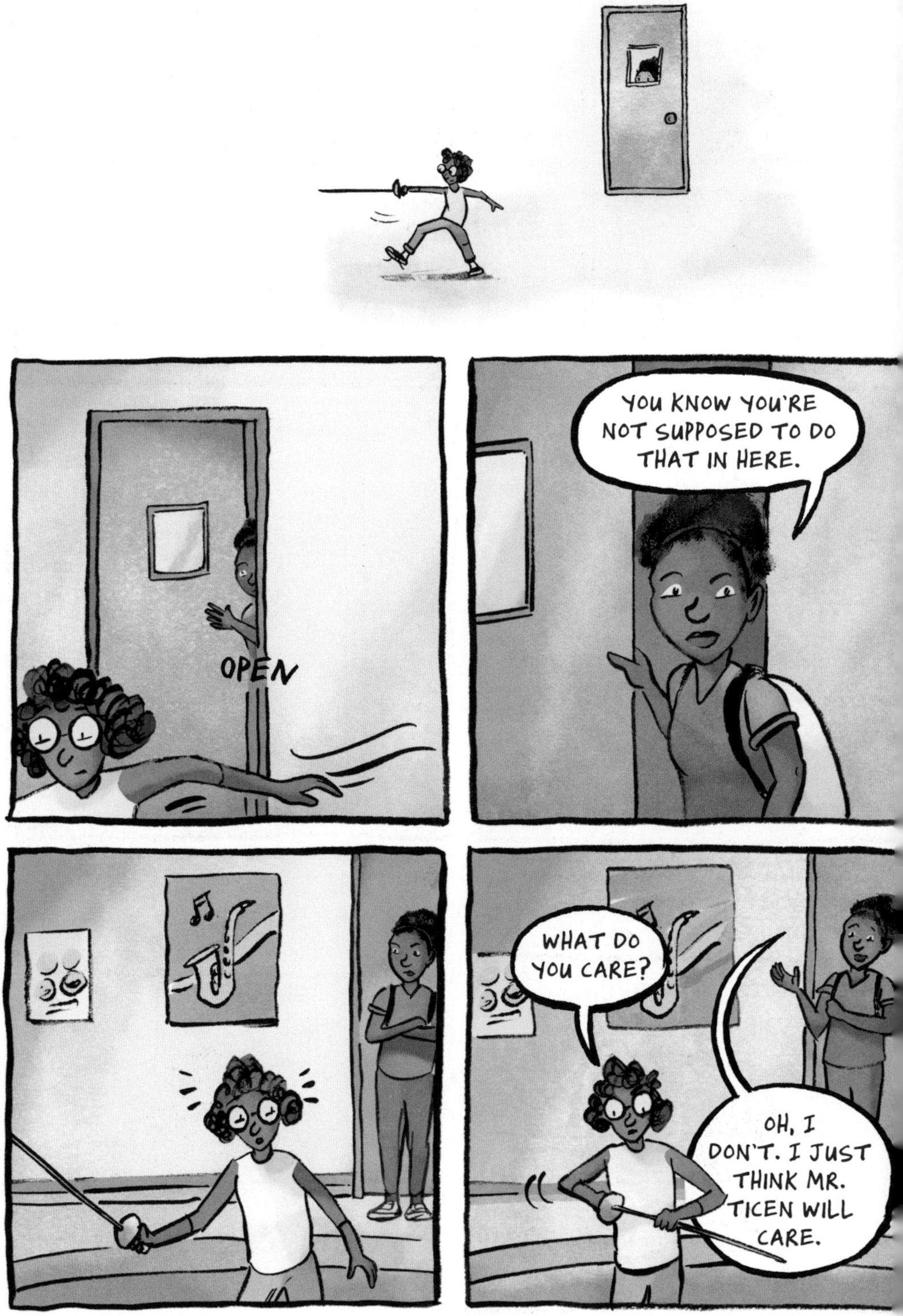
OPEN
YOU KNOW YOU'RE NOT SUPPOSED TO DO THAT IN HERE.
WHAT DO YOU CARE?
OH, I DON'T. I JUST THINK MR. TICEN WILL CARE.

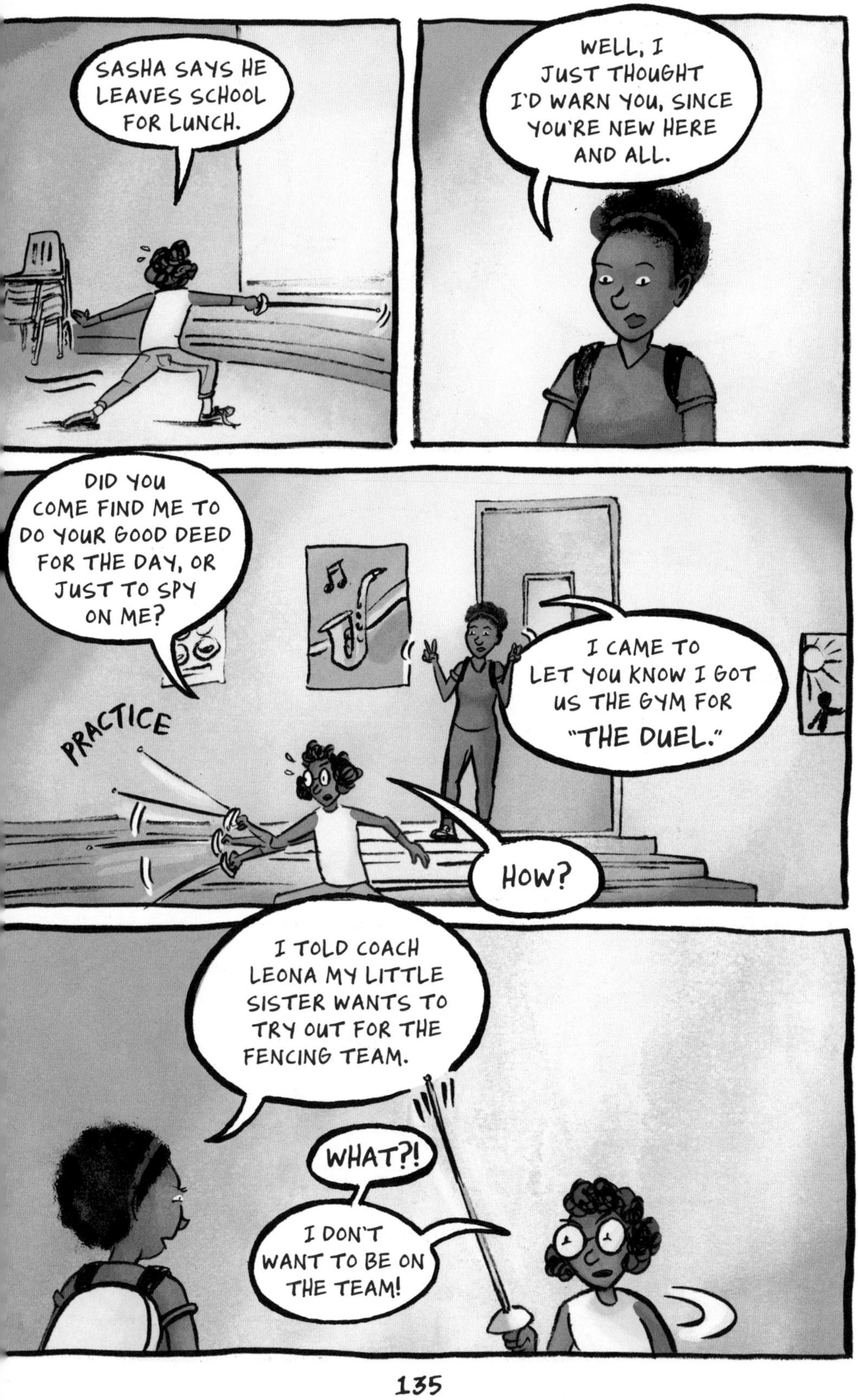
SASHA SAYS HE LEAVES SCHOOL FOR LUNCH.
WELL, I JUST THOUGHT I'D WARN YOU, SINCE YOU'RE NEW HERE AND ALL.
DID YOU COME FIND ME TO DO YOUR GOOD DEED FOR THE DAY, OR JUST TO SPY ON ME?
PRACTICE
I CAME TO LET YOU KNOW I GOT US THE GYM FOR "THE DUEL."
HOW?
I TOLD COACH LEONA MY LITTLE SISTER WANTS TO TRY OUT FOR THE FENCING TEAM.
WHAT?!
I DON'T WANT TO BE ON THE TEAM!

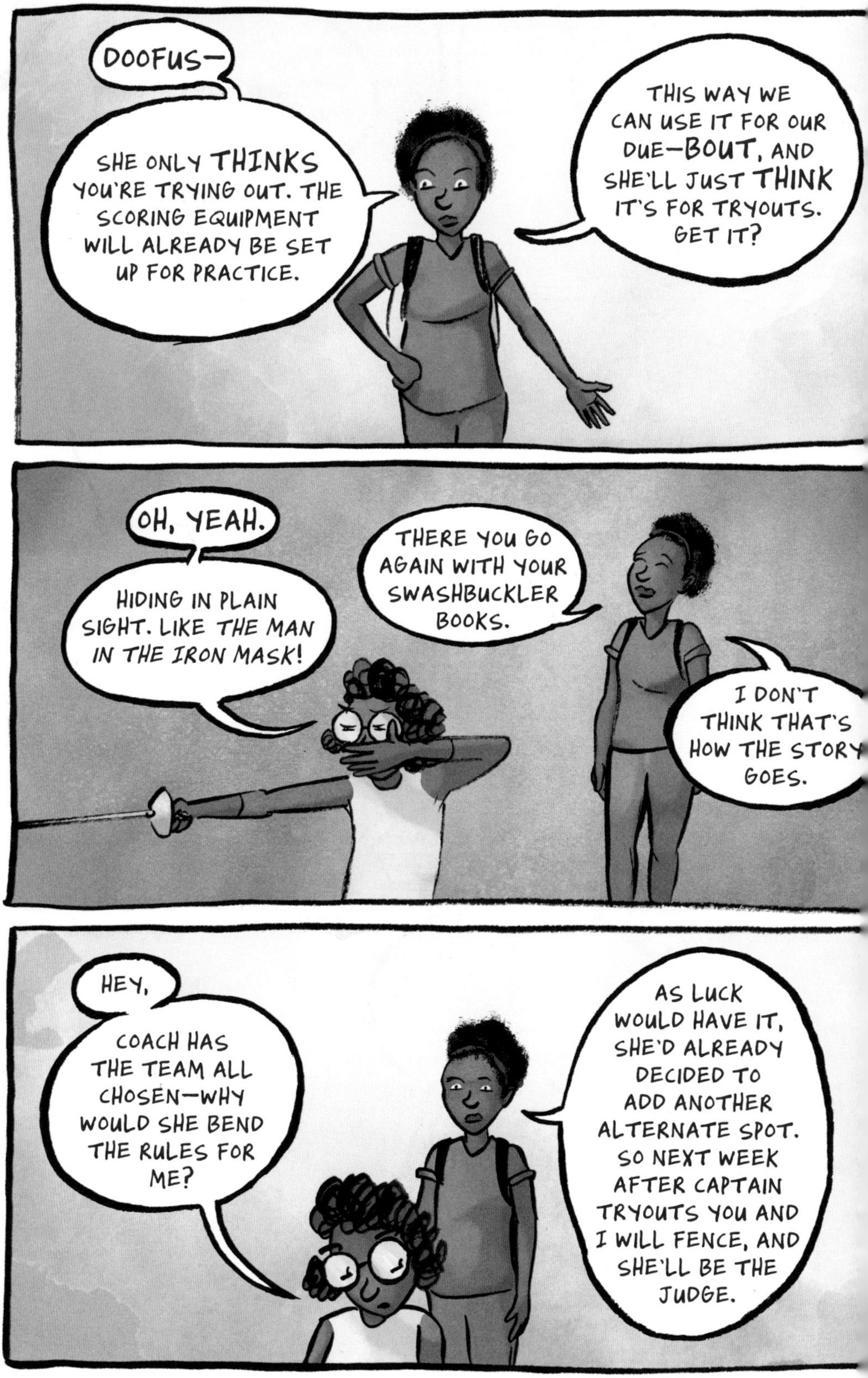
DOOFUS—
SHE ONLY THINKS YOU'RE TRYING OUT. THE SCORING EQUIPMENT WILL ALREADY BE SET UP FOR PRACTICE.
THIS WAY WE CAN USE IT FOR OUR DUE—BOUT, AND SHE'LL JUST THINK IT'S FOR TRYOUTS. GET IT?
OH, YEAH.
HIDING IN PLAIN SIGHT. LIKE THE MAN IN THE IRON MASK!
THERE YOU GO AGAIN WITH YOUR SWASHBUCKLER BOOKS.
I DON'T THINK THAT'S HOW THE STORY GOES.
HEY,
COACH HAS THE TEAM ALL CHOSEN—WHY WOULD SHE BEND THE RULES FOR ME?
AS LUCK WOULD HAVE IT, SHE'D ALREADY DECIDED TO ADD ANOTHER ALTERNATE SPOT. SO NEXT WEEK AFTER CAPTAIN TRYOUTS YOU AND I WILL FENCE, AND SHE'LL BE THE JUDGE.

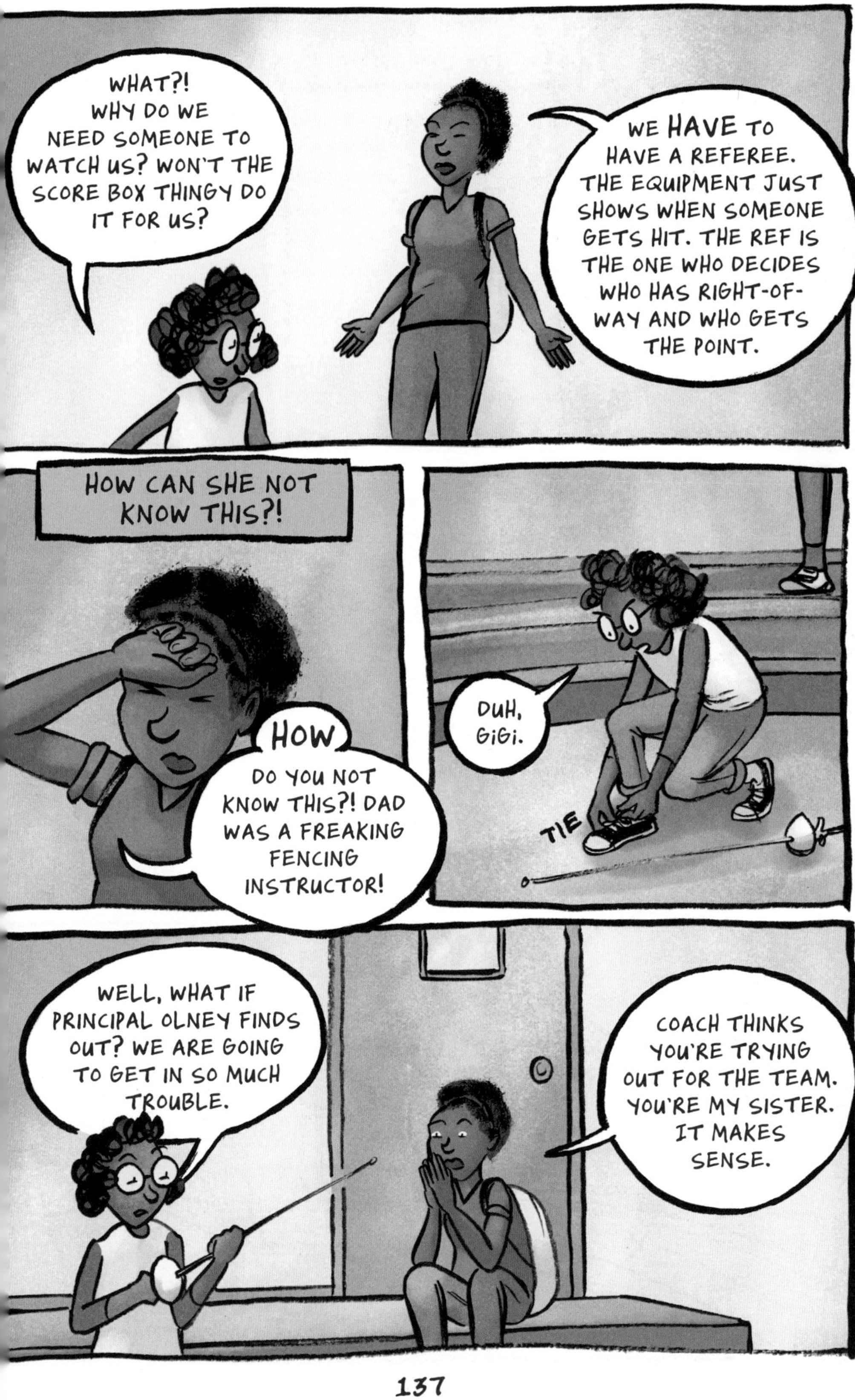
WHAT?! WHY DO WE NEED SOMEONE TO WATCH US? WON'T THE SCORE BOX THINGY DO IT FOR US?
WE HAVE TO HAVE A REFEREE. THE EQUIPMENT JUST SHOWS WHEN SOMEONE GETS HIT. THE REF IS THE ONE WHO DECIDES WHO HAS RIGHT-OF-WAY AND WHO GETS THE POINT.
HOW CAN SHE NOT KNOW THIS?!
HOW DO YOU NOT KNOW THIS?! DAD WAS A FREAKING FENCING INSTRUCTOR!
DUH, GiGi.
TIE
WELL, WHAT IF PRINCIPAL OLNEY FINDS OUT? WE ARE GOING TO GET IN SO MUCH TROUBLE.
COACH THINKS YOU'RE TRYING OUT FOR THE TEAM. YOU'RE MY SISTER. IT MAKES SENSE.

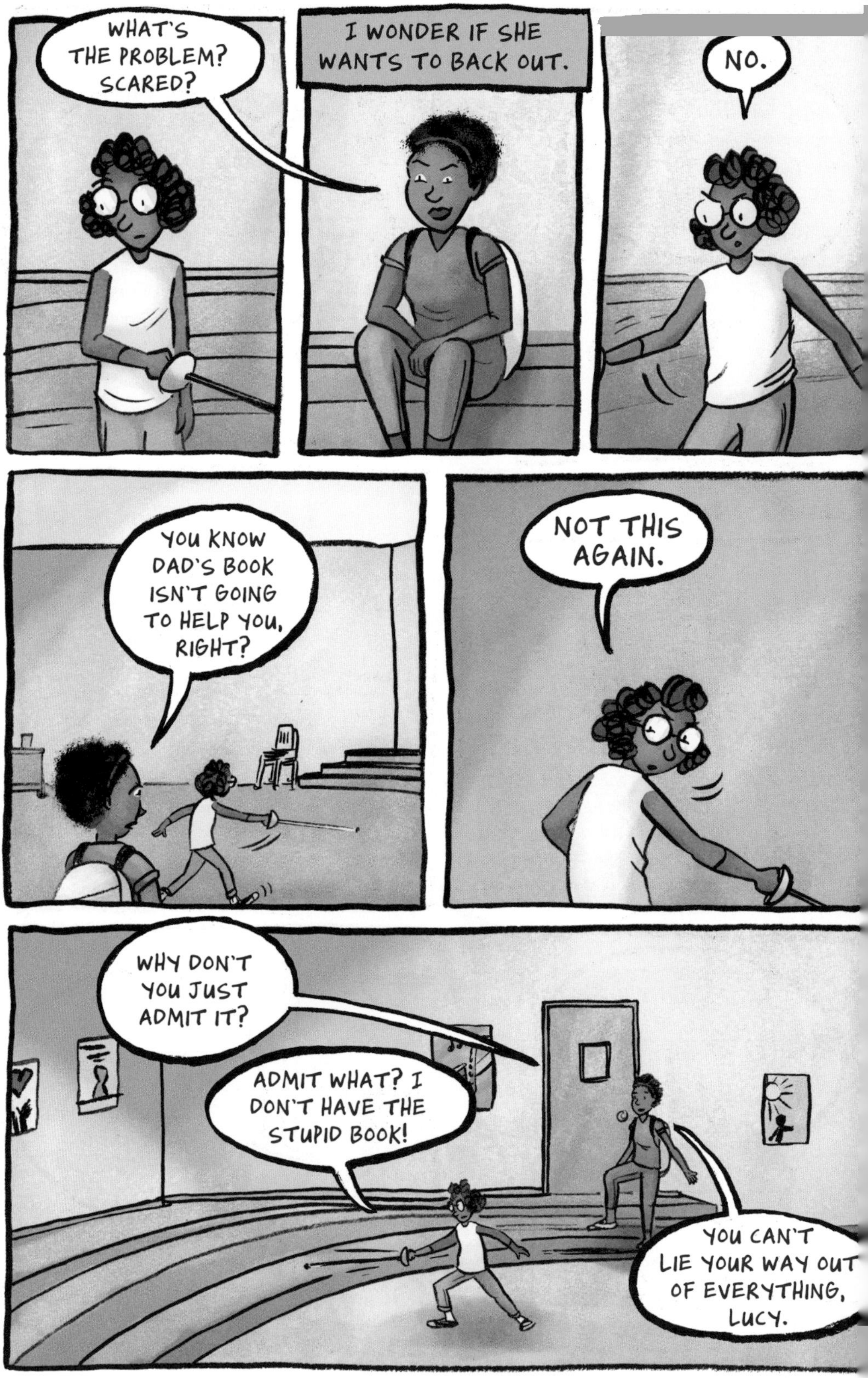
WHAT'S THE PROBLEM? SCARED?
I WONDER IF SHE WANTS TO BACK OUT.
NO.
YOU KNOW DAD'S BOOK ISN'T GOING TO HELP YOU, RIGHT?
NOT THIS AGAIN.
WHY DON'T YOU JUST ADMIT IT?
ADMIT WHAT? I DON'T HAVE THE STUPID BOOK!
YOU CAN'T LIE YOUR WAY OUT OF EVERYTHING, LUCY.

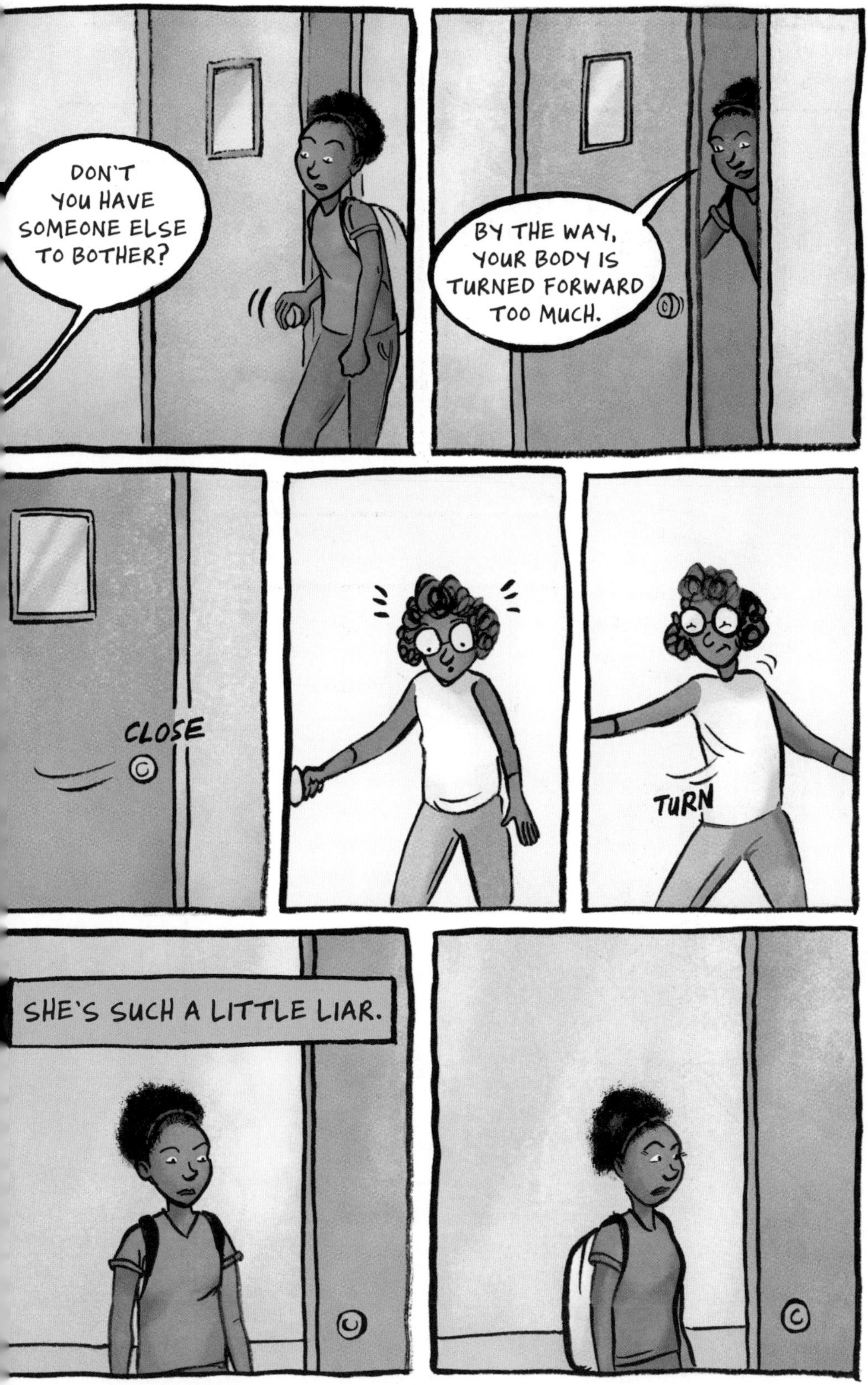
DON'T YOU HAVE SOMEONE ELSE TO BOTHER?
BY THE WAY, YOUR BODY IS TURNED FORWARD TOO MUCH.
CLOSE
TURN
SHE'S SUCH A LITTLE LIAR.

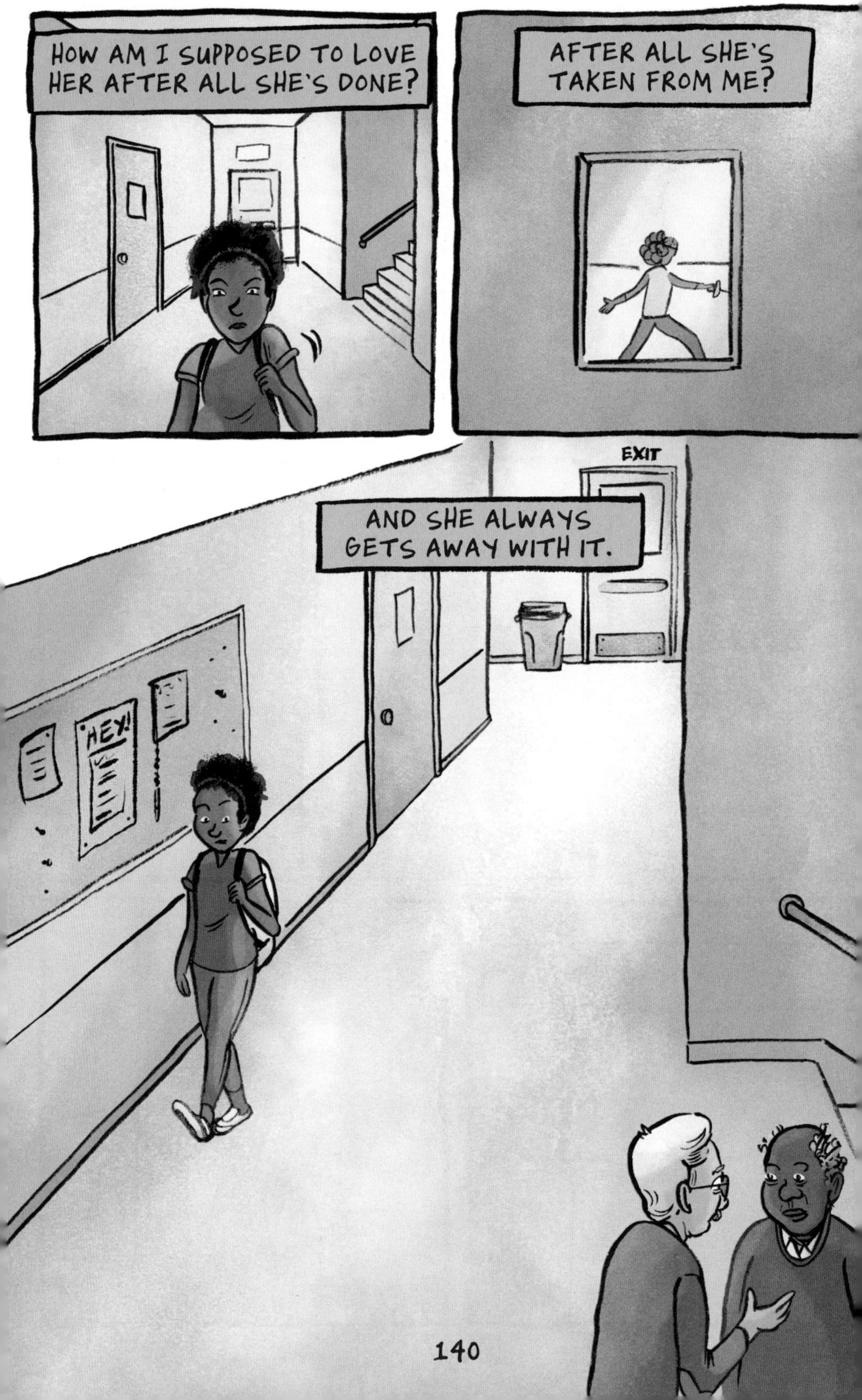
HOW AM I SUPPOSED TO LOVE HER AFTER ALL SHE'S DONE?
AFTER ALL SHE'S TAKEN FROM ME?
EXIT
AND SHE ALWAYS GETS AWAY WITH IT.
HEY!

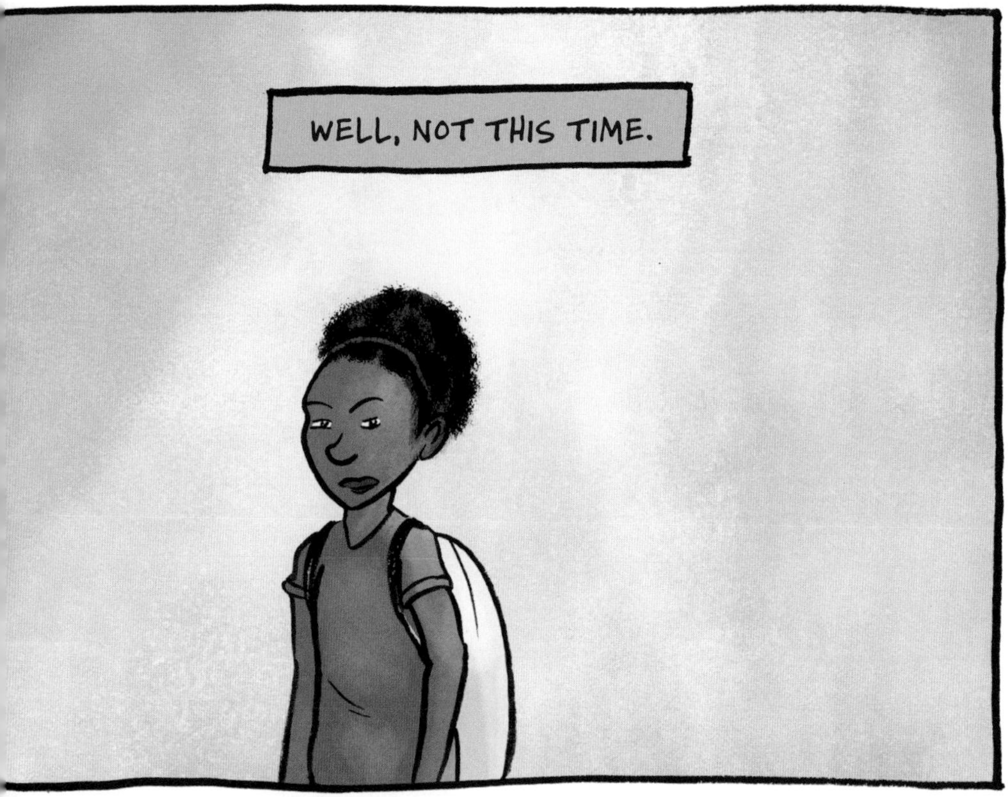
WELL, NOT THIS TIME.

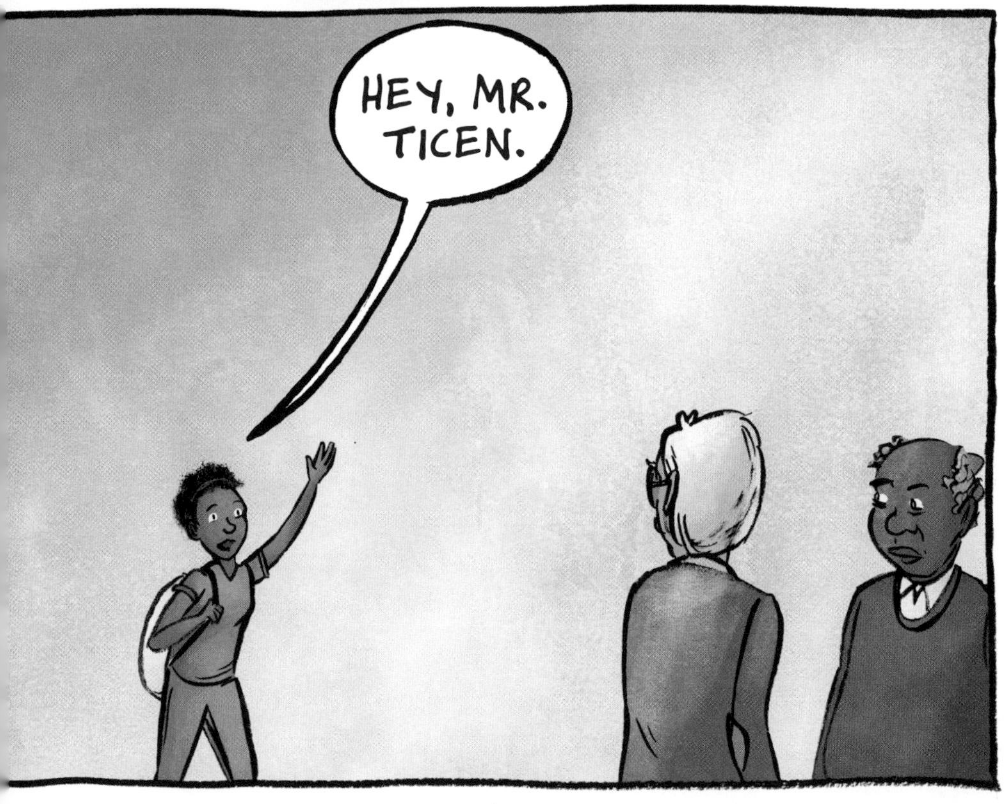
HEY, MR. TICEN.

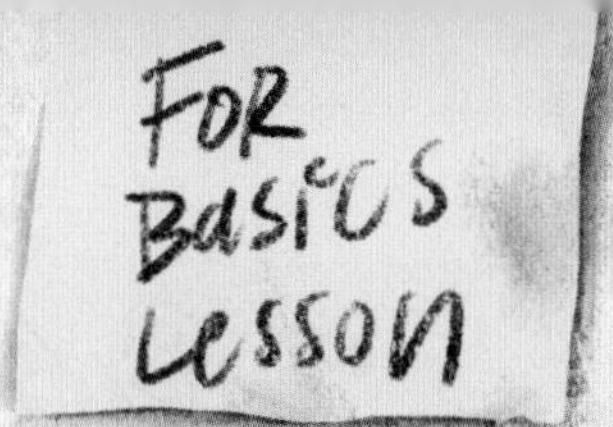
FOR BASICS LESSON

Chapter 9

Parry

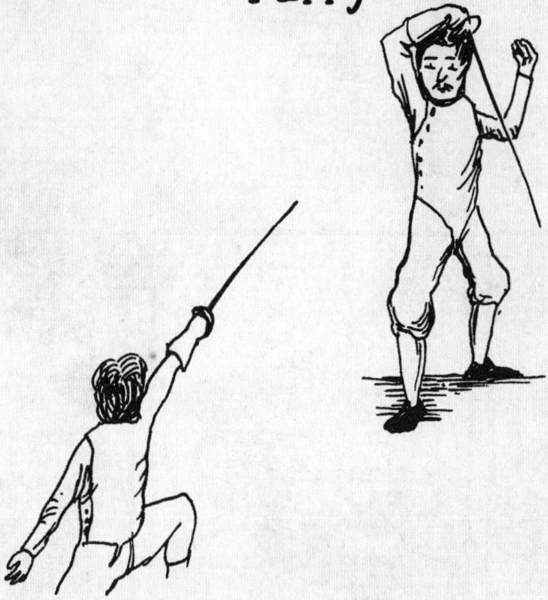

The parry is a simple defensive action designed to deflect an attack. There are eight parries in foil, each one corresponding to a section of the target. In foil, you must deflect your opponent's blade away from both the target and off-target areas. Your opponent cannot score a point if you have parried their blade—even if you get hit afterward. A proper parry will ward off an attack and cancel out your opponent's right-of-way, giving you the ability to make a countermove and score, should you choose to attack.

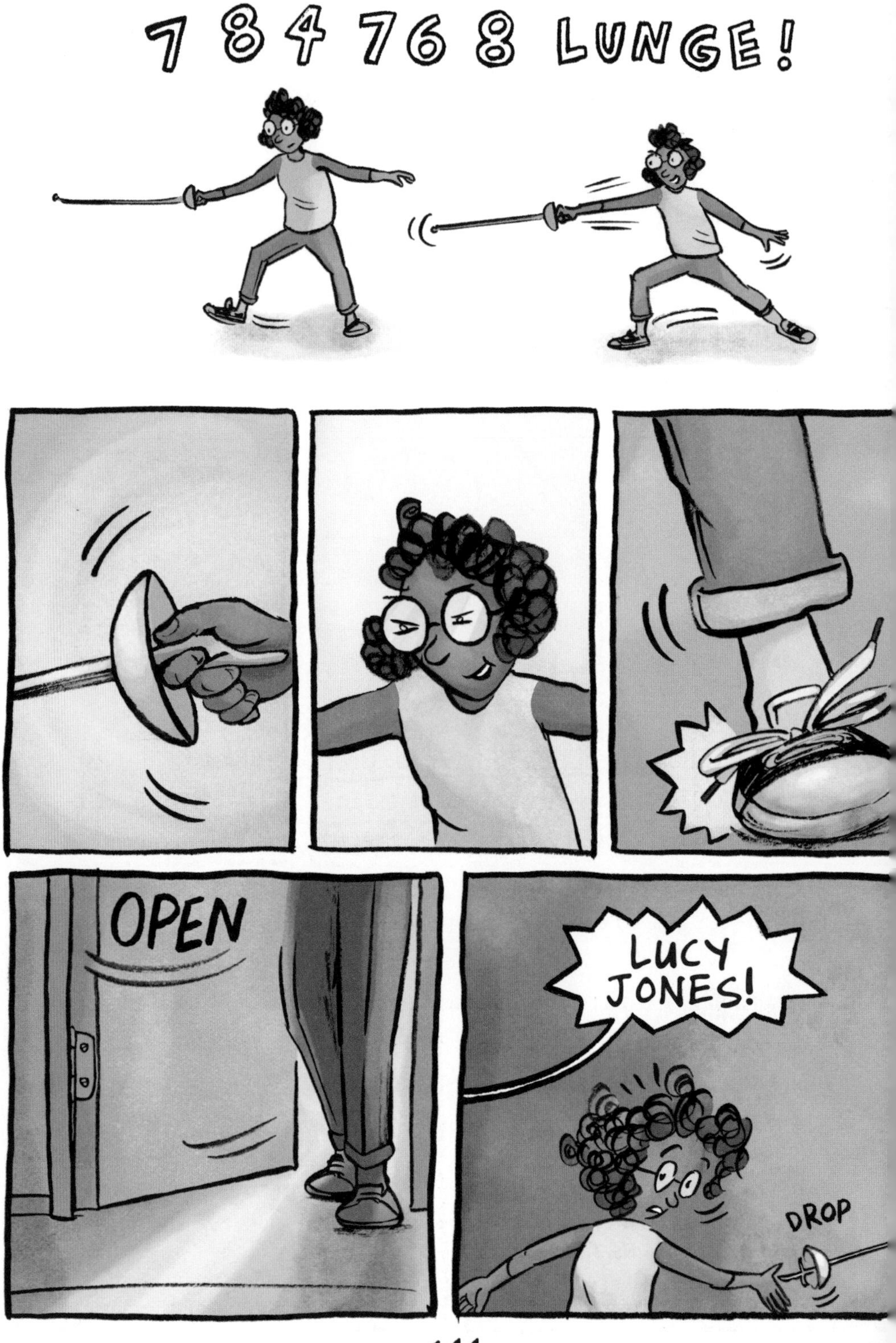
7 8 4 76 8 LUNGE!
OPEN
LUCY JONES!
DROP

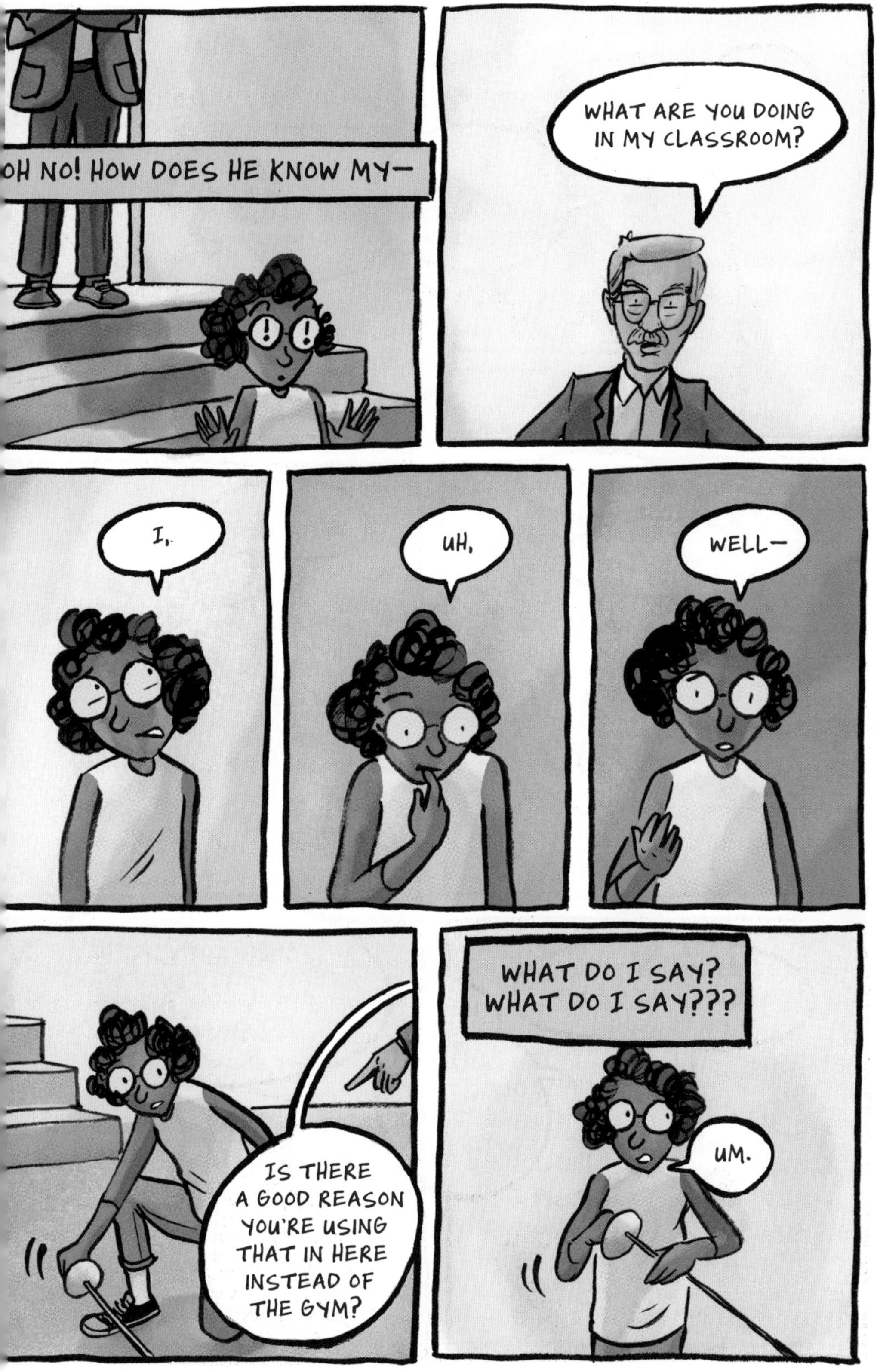
OH NO! HOW DOES HE KNOW MY—
WHAT ARE YOU DOING IN MY CLASSROOM?
I,
UH,
WELL—
IS THERE A GOOD REASON YOU'RE USING THAT IN HERE INSTEAD OF THE GYM?
WHAT DO I SAY? WHAT DO I SAY???
UM.

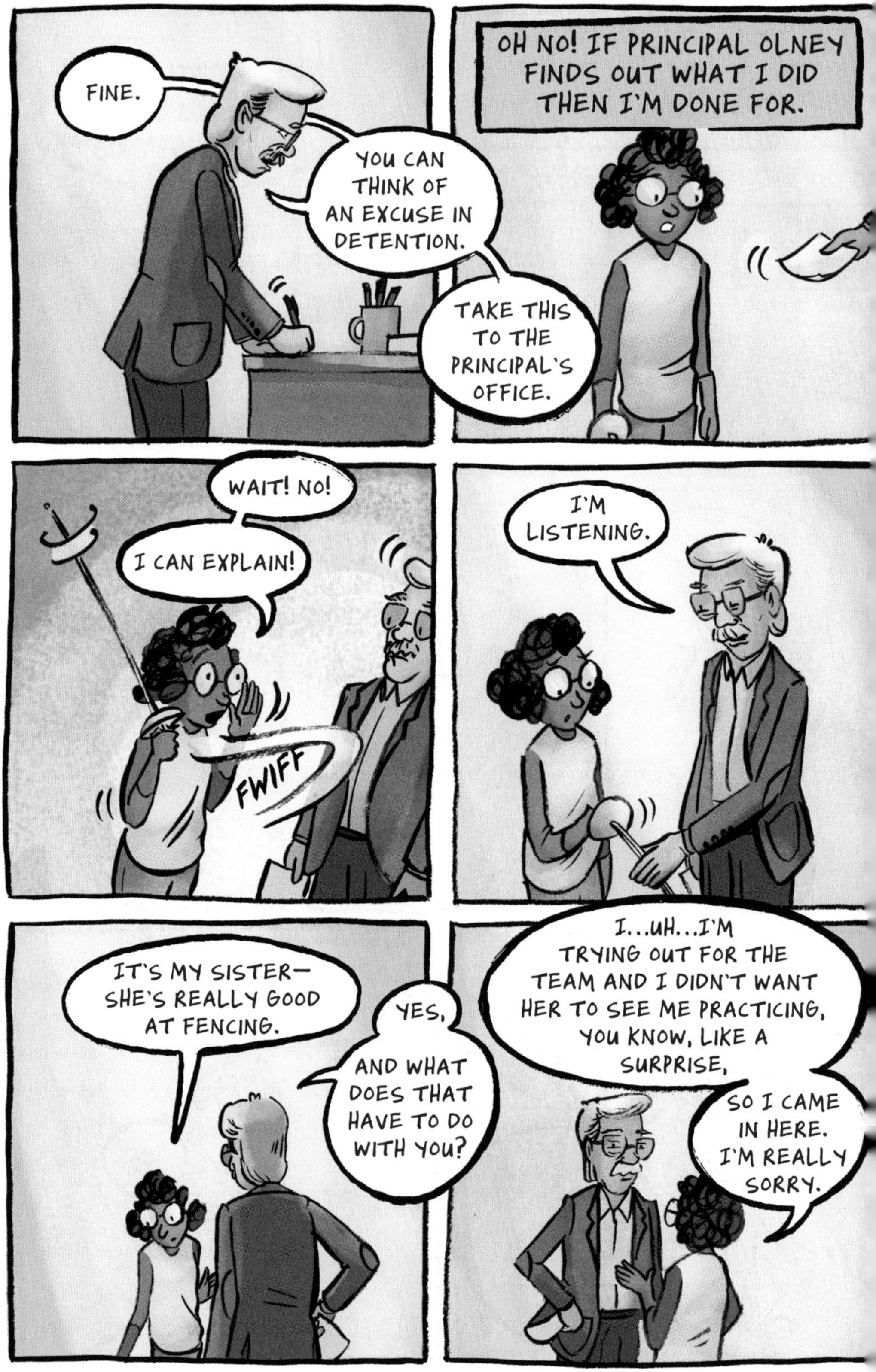
FINE.
YOU CAN THINK OF AN EXCUSE IN DETENTION.
TAKE THIS TO THE PRINCIPAL'S OFFICE.
OH NO! IF PRINCIPAL OLNEY FINDS OUT WHAT I DID THEN I'M DONE FOR.
WAIT! NO!
I CAN EXPLAIN!
FWIFF
I'M LISTENING.
IT'S MY SISTER—SHE'S REALLY GOOD AT FENCING.
YES,
AND WHAT DOES THAT HAVE TO DO WITH YOU?
I...UH...I'M TRYING OUT FOR THE TEAM AND I DIDN'T WANT HER TO SEE ME PRACTICING, YOU KNOW, LIKE A SURPRISE,
SO I CAME IN HERE. I'M REALLY SORRY.

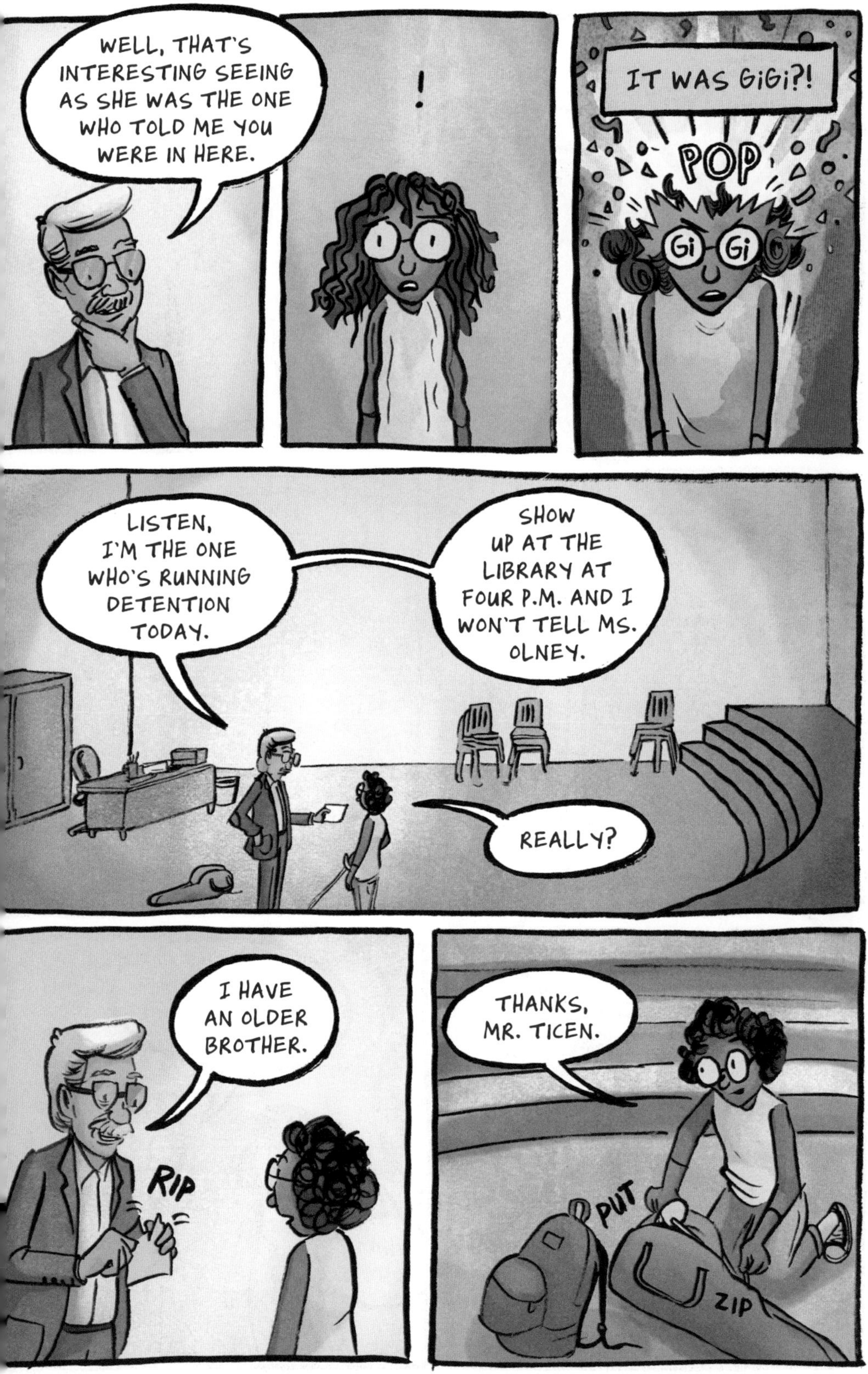
WELL, THAT'S INTERESTING SEEING AS SHE WAS THE ONE WHO TOLD ME YOU WERE IN HERE.
!
IT WAS GiGi?!
POP
Gi Gi
LISTEN, I'M THE ONE WHO'S RUNNING DETENTION TODAY.
SHOW UP AT THE LIBRARY AT FOUR P.M. AND I WON'T TELL MS. OLNEY.
REALLY?
I HAVE AN OLDER BROTHER.
RIP
THANKS, MR. TICEN.
PUT
ZIP

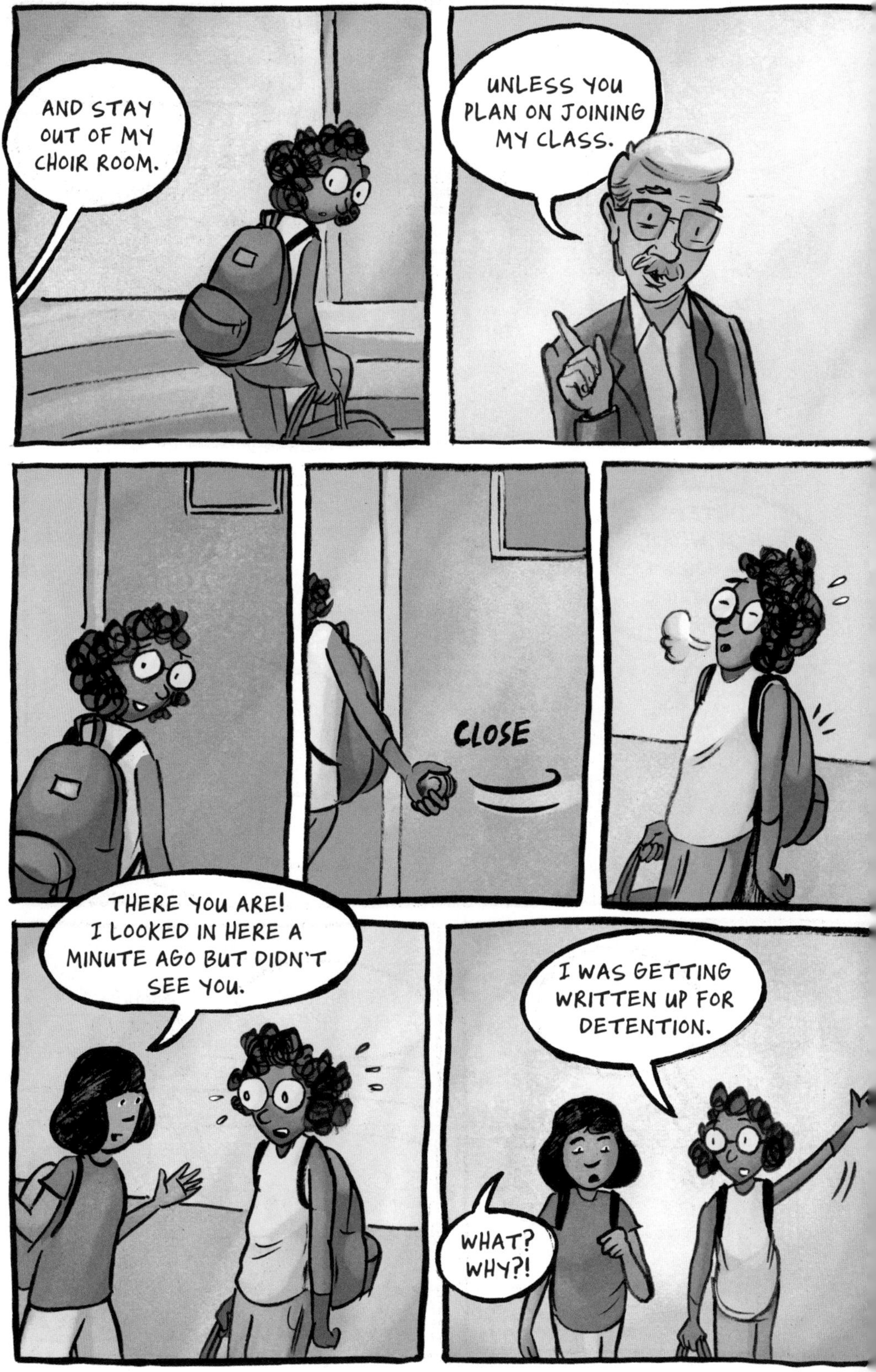
AND STAY OUT OF MY CHOIR ROOM.
UNLESS YOU PLAN ON JOINING MY CLASS.
CLOSE
THERE YOU ARE! I LOOKED IN HERE A MINUTE AGO BUT DIDN'T SEE YOU.
I WAS GETTING WRITTEN UP FOR DETENTION.
WHAT? WHY?!

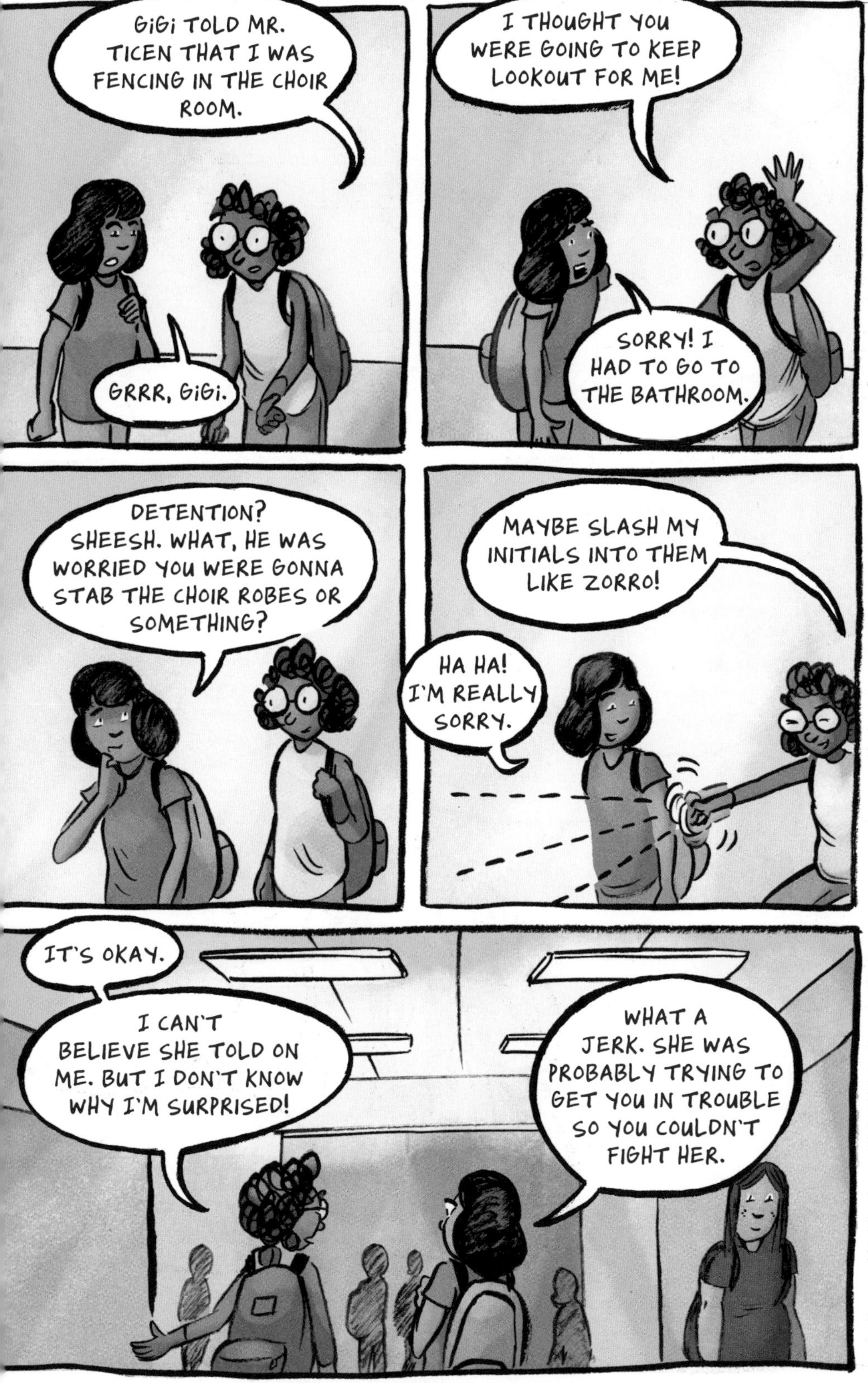
GiGi TOLD MR. TICEN THAT I WAS FENCING IN THE CHOIR ROOM.
GRRR, GiGi.
I THOUGHT YOU WERE GOING TO KEEP LOOKOUT FOR ME!
SORRY! I HAD TO GO TO THE BATHROOM.
DETENTION? SHEESH. WHAT, HE WAS WORRIED YOU WERE GONNA STAB THE CHOIR ROBES OR SOMETHING?
MAYBE SLASH MY INITIALS INTO THEM LIKE ZORRO!
HA HA! I'M REALLY SORRY.
IT'S OKAY.
I CAN'T BELIEVE SHE TOLD ON ME. BUT I DON'T KNOW WHY I'M SURPRISED!
WHAT A JERK. SHE WAS PROBABLY TRYING TO GET YOU IN TROUBLE SO YOU COULDN'T FIGHT HER.

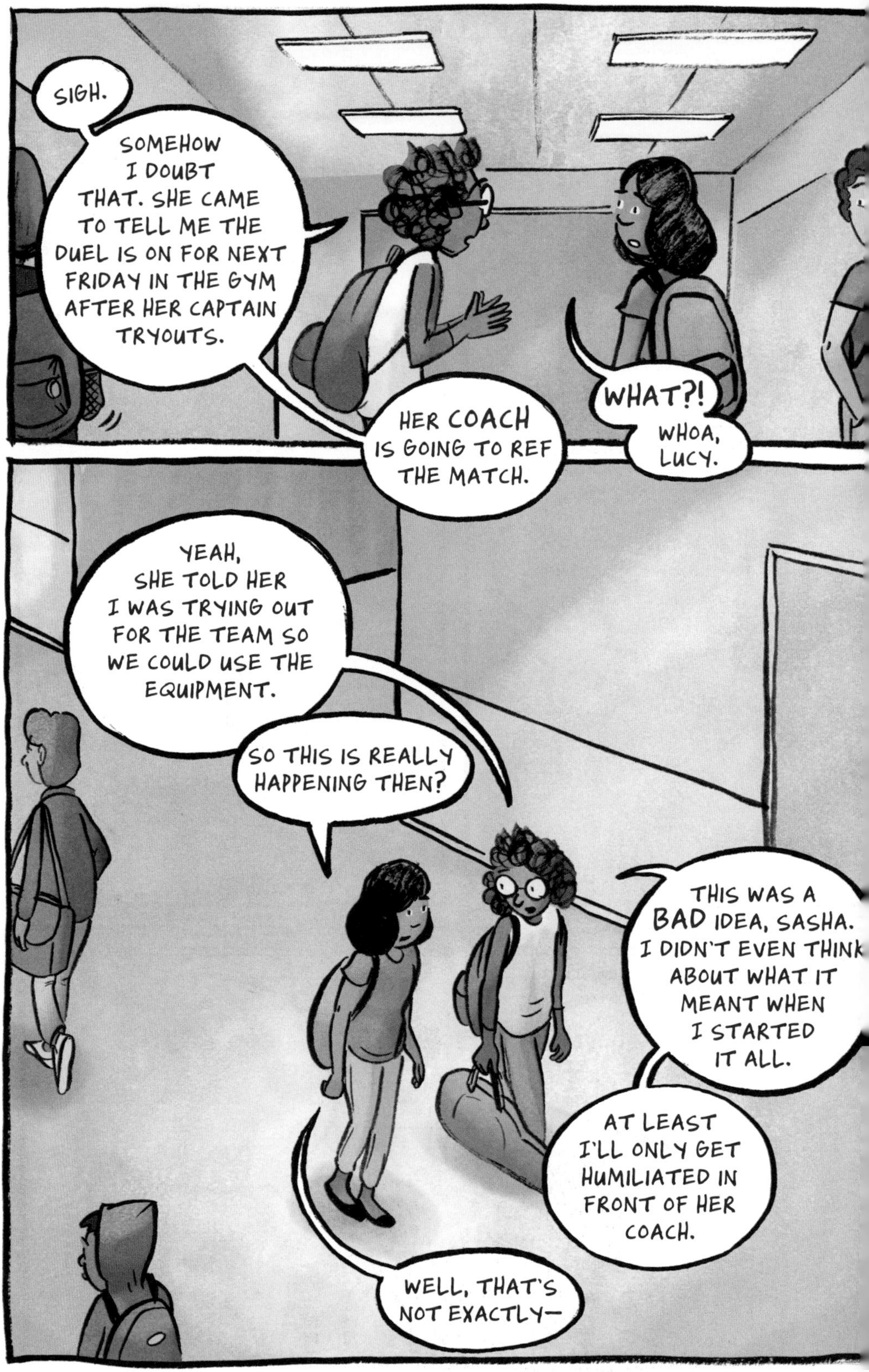
SIGH.
SOMEHOW I DOUBT THAT. SHE CAME TO TELL ME THE DUEL IS ON FOR NEXT FRIDAY IN THE GYM AFTER HER CAPTAIN TRYOUTS.
HER COACH IS GOING TO REF THE MATCH.
WHAT?! WHOA, LUCY.
YEAH, SHE TOLD HER I WAS TRYING OUT FOR THE TEAM SO WE COULD USE THE EQUIPMENT.
SO THIS IS REALLY HAPPENING THEN?
THIS WAS A BAD IDEA, SASHA. I DIDN'T EVEN THINK ABOUT WHAT IT MEANT WHEN I STARTED IT ALL.
AT LEAST I'LL ONLY GET HUMILIATED IN FRONT OF HER COACH.
WELL, THAT'S NOT EXACTLY—

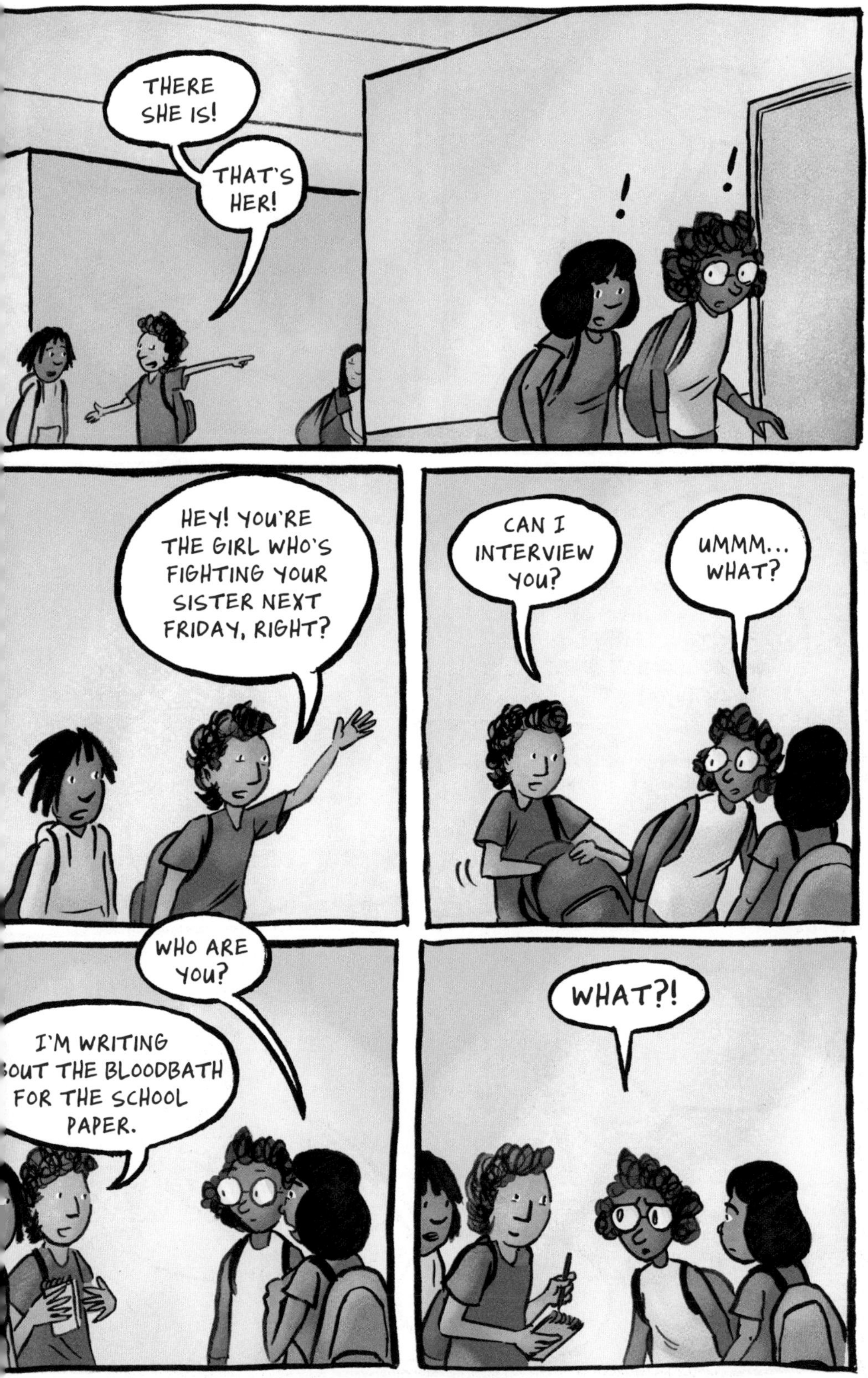
THERE SHE IS!
THAT'S HER!
HEY! YOU'RE THE GIRL WHO'S FIGHTING YOUR SISTER NEXT FRIDAY, RIGHT?
CAN I INTERVIEW YOU?
UMMM... WHAT?
WHO ARE YOU?
I'M WRITING ABOUT THE BLOODBATH FOR THE SCHOOL PAPER.
WHAT?!

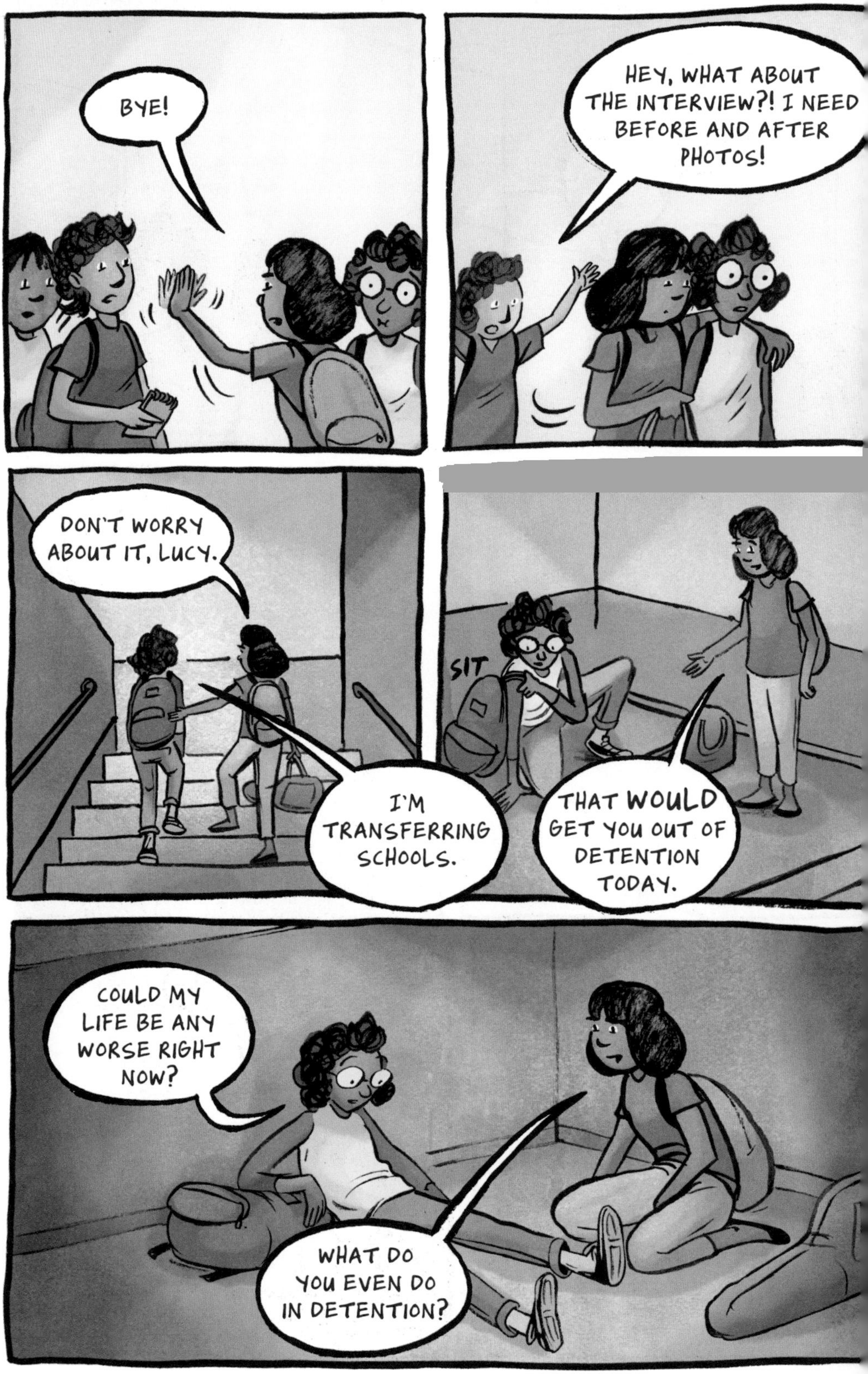
BYE!
HEY, WHAT ABOUT THE INTERVIEW?! I NEED BEFORE AND AFTER PHOTOS!
DON'T WORRY ABOUT IT, LUCY.
I'M TRANSFERRING SCHOOLS.
SIT
THAT WOULD GET YOU OUT OF DETENTION TODAY.
COULD MY LIFE BE ANY WORSE RIGHT NOW?
WHAT DO YOU EVEN DO IN DETENTION?

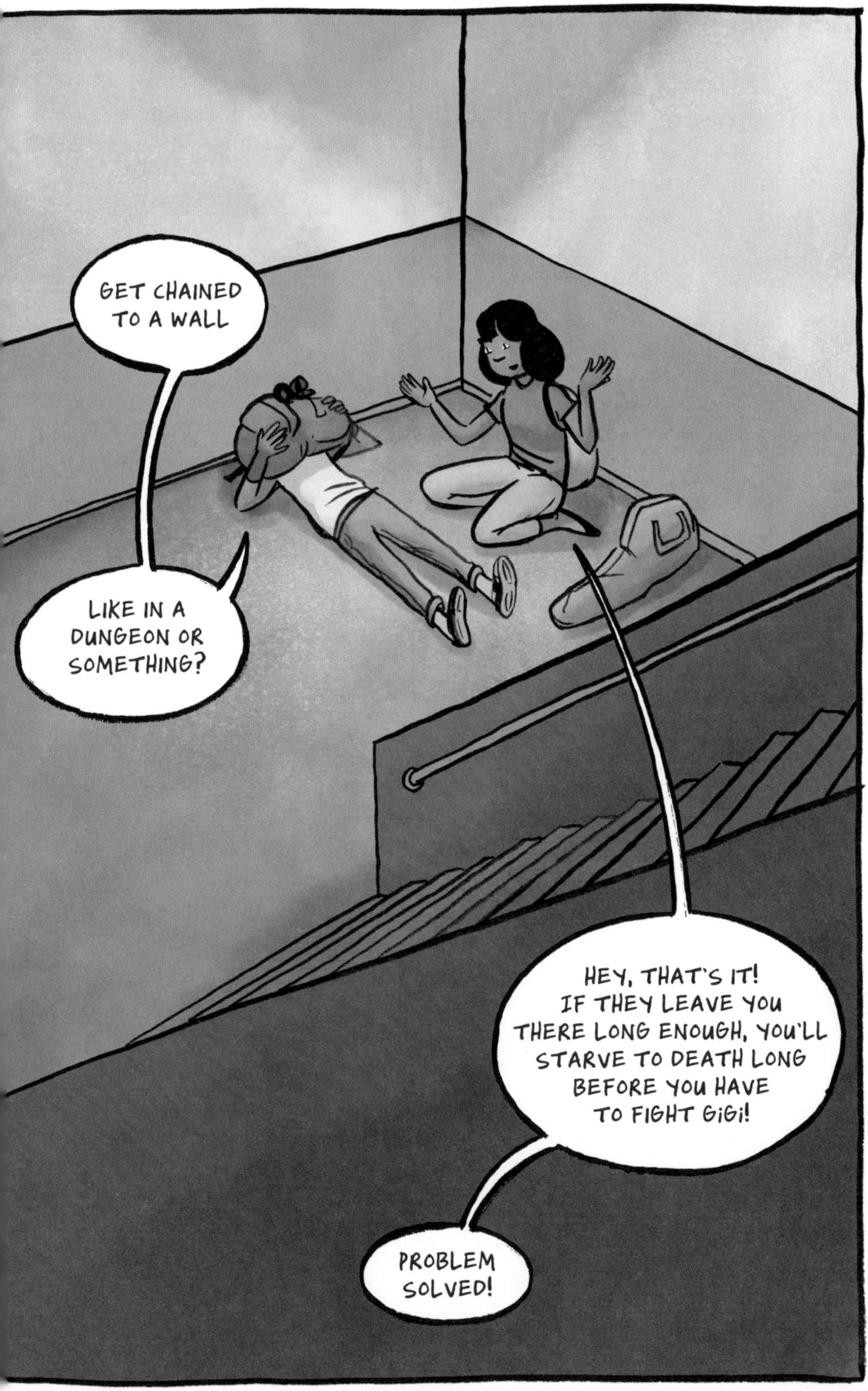
GET CHAINED TO A WALL
LIKE IN A DUNGEON OR SOMETHING?
HEY, THAT'S IT! IF THEY LEAVE YOU THERE LONG ENOUGH, YOU'LL STARVE TO DEATH LONG BEFORE YOU HAVE TO FIGHT GiGi!
PROBLEM SOLVED!

Chapter 10

Riposte

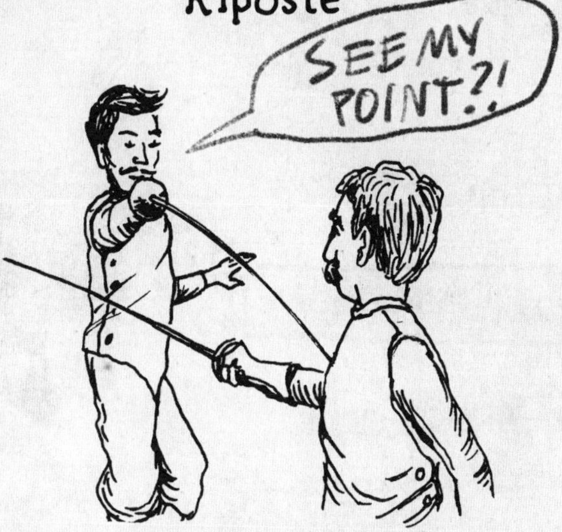
SEE MY POINT?!

One should parry with the forte (the strongest part of the blade) to the foible (the weakest part) of their opponent's blade and then commence in a riposte.

The riposte is an offensive action with the intent of hitting one's opponent, made by the fencer who has just parried an attack. If the attacker doesn't riposte after parrying, they lose the right-of-way. In everyday language, riposte refers to a quick and witty reply to an argument or an insult.

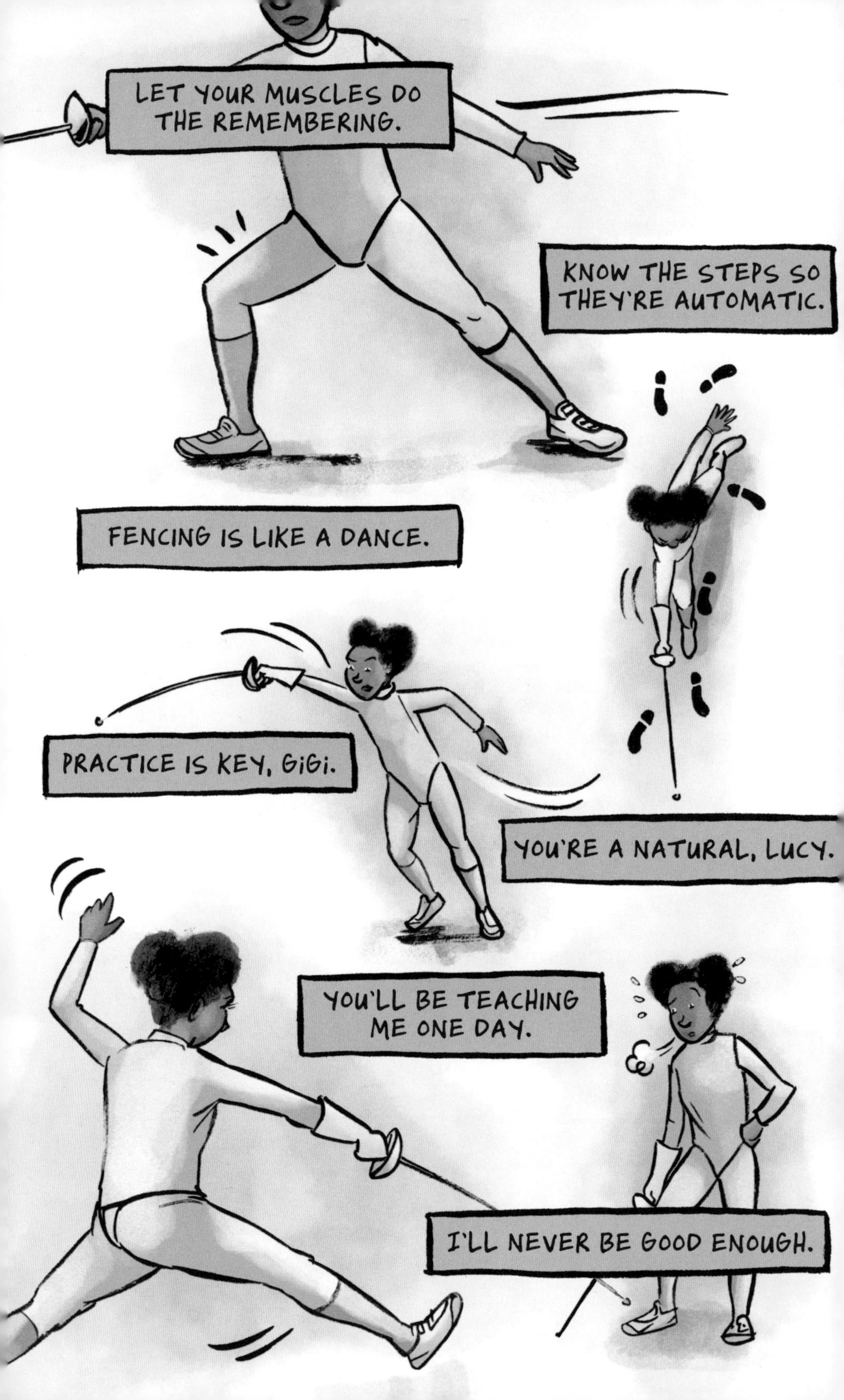
LET YOUR MUSCLES DO THE REMEMBERING.
KNOW THE STEPS SO THEY'RE AUTOMATIC.
FENCING IS LIKE A DANCE.
PRACTICE IS KEY, GiGi.
YOU'RE A NATURAL, LUCY.
YOU'LL BE TEACHING ME ONE DAY.
I'LL NEVER BE GOOD ENOUGH.

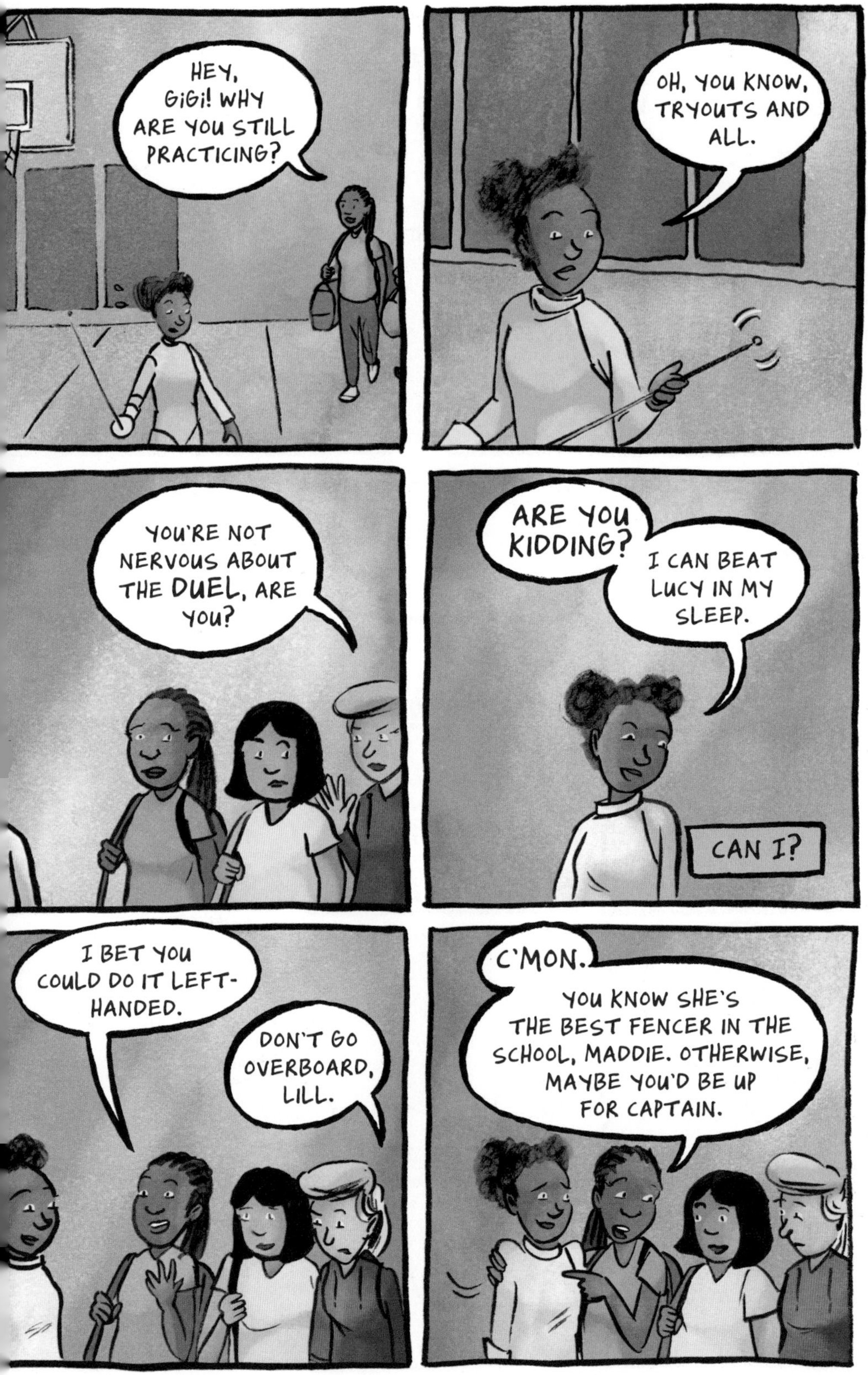
HEY, GIGI! WHY ARE YOU STILL PRACTICING?
OH, YOU KNOW, TRYOUTS AND ALL.
YOU'RE NOT NERVOUS ABOUT THE DUEL, ARE YOU?
ARE YOU KIDDING?
I CAN BEAT LUCY IN MY SLEEP.
CAN I?
I BET YOU COULD DO IT LEFT-HANDED.
DON'T GO OVERBOARD, LILL.
C'MON.
YOU KNOW SHE'S THE BEST FENCER IN THE SCHOOL, MADDIE. OTHERWISE, MAYBE YOU'D BE UP FOR CAPTAIN.

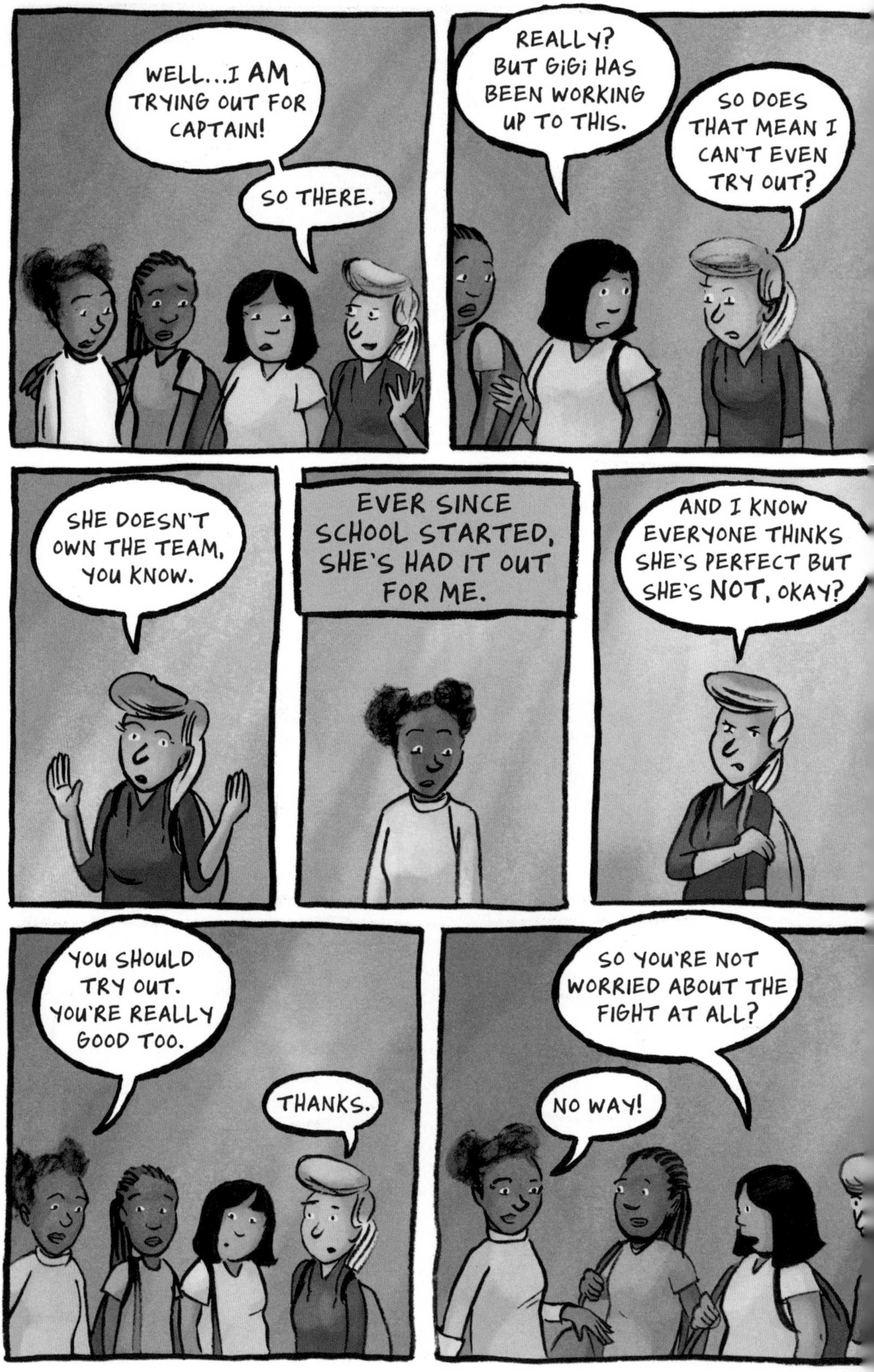
WELL...I AM TRYING OUT FOR CAPTAIN!
SO THERE.
REALLY? BUT GIGI HAS BEEN WORKING UP TO THIS.
SO DOES THAT MEAN I CAN'T EVEN TRY OUT?
SHE DOESN'T OWN THE TEAM, YOU KNOW.
EVER SINCE SCHOOL STARTED, SHE'S HAD IT OUT FOR ME.
AND I KNOW EVERYONE THINKS SHE'S PERFECT BUT SHE'S NOT, OKAY?
YOU SHOULD TRY OUT. YOU'RE REALLY GOOD TOO.
THANKS.
SO YOU'RE NOT WORRIED ABOUT THE FIGHT AT ALL?
NO WAY!

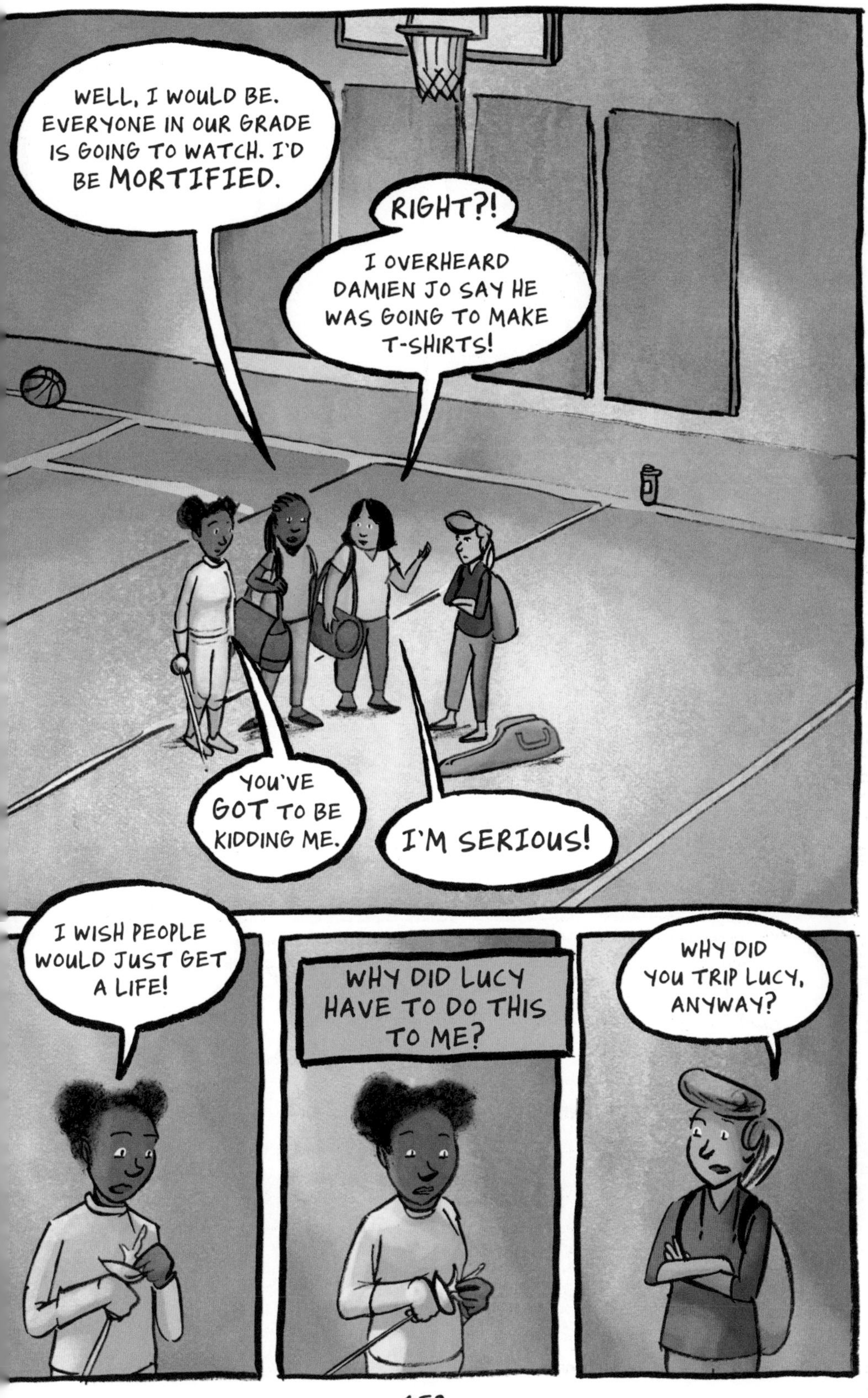
WELL, I WOULD BE. EVERYONE IN OUR GRADE IS GOING TO WATCH. I'D BE MORTIFIED.
RIGHT?!
I OVERHEARD DAMIEN JO SAY HE WAS GOING TO MAKE T-SHIRTS!
YOU'VE GOT TO BE KIDDING ME.
I'M SERIOUS!
I WISH PEOPLE WOULD JUST GET A LIFE!
WHY DID LUCY HAVE TO DO THIS TO ME?
WHY DID YOU TRIP LUCY, ANYWAY?

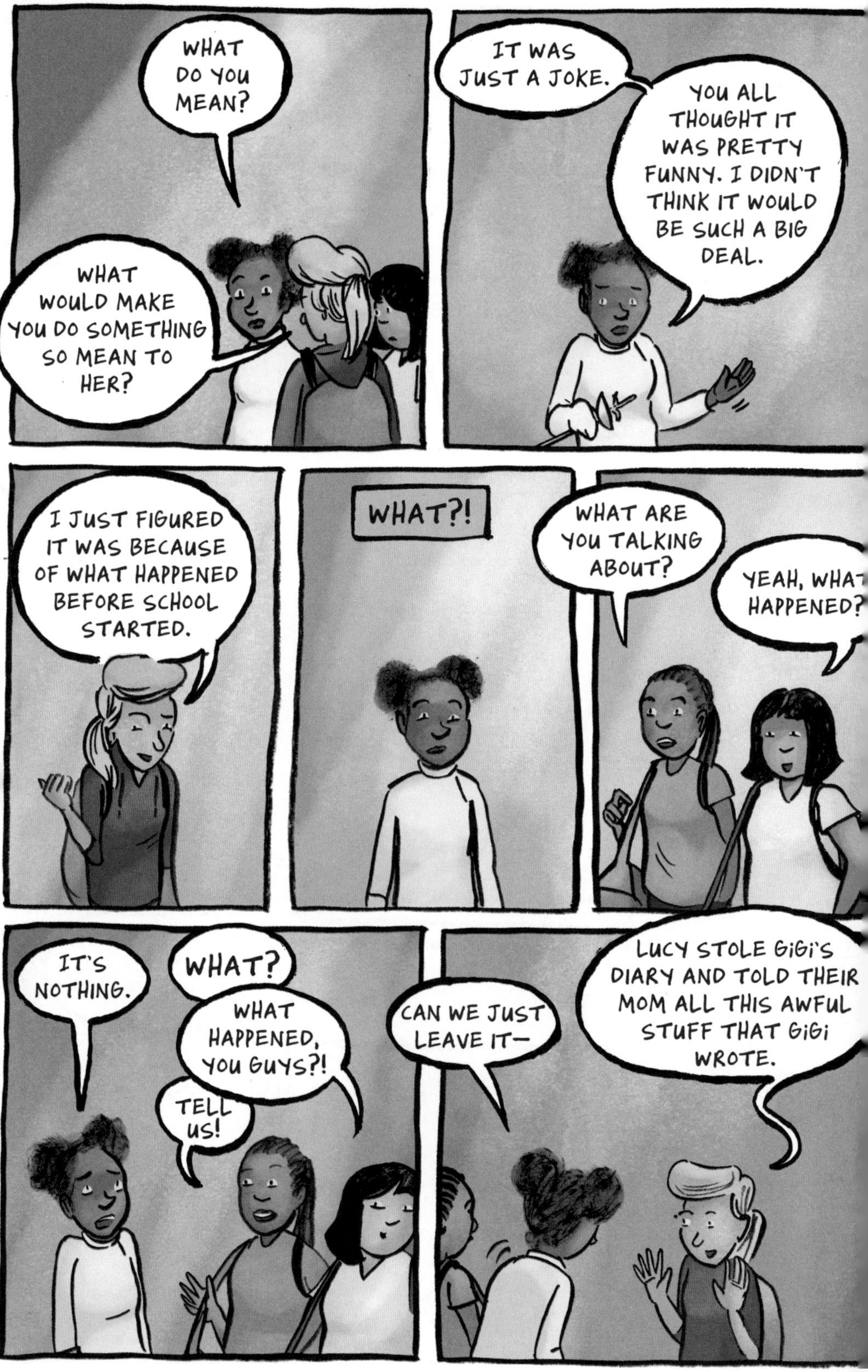
WHAT DO YOU MEAN?
WHAT WOULD MAKE YOU DO SOMETHING SO MEAN TO HER?
IT WAS JUST A JOKE.
YOU ALL THOUGHT IT WAS PRETTY FUNNY. I DIDN'T THINK IT WOULD BE SUCH A BIG DEAL.
I JUST FIGURED IT WAS BECAUSE OF WHAT HAPPENED BEFORE SCHOOL STARTED.
WHAT?!
WHAT ARE YOU TALKING ABOUT?
YEAH, WHAT HAPPENED?
IT'S NOTHING.
WHAT?
WHAT HAPPENED, YOU GUYS?!
TELL US!
CAN WE JUST LEAVE IT—
LUCY STOLE GiGi'S DIARY AND TOLD THEIR MOM ALL THIS AWFUL STUFF THAT GiGi WROTE.

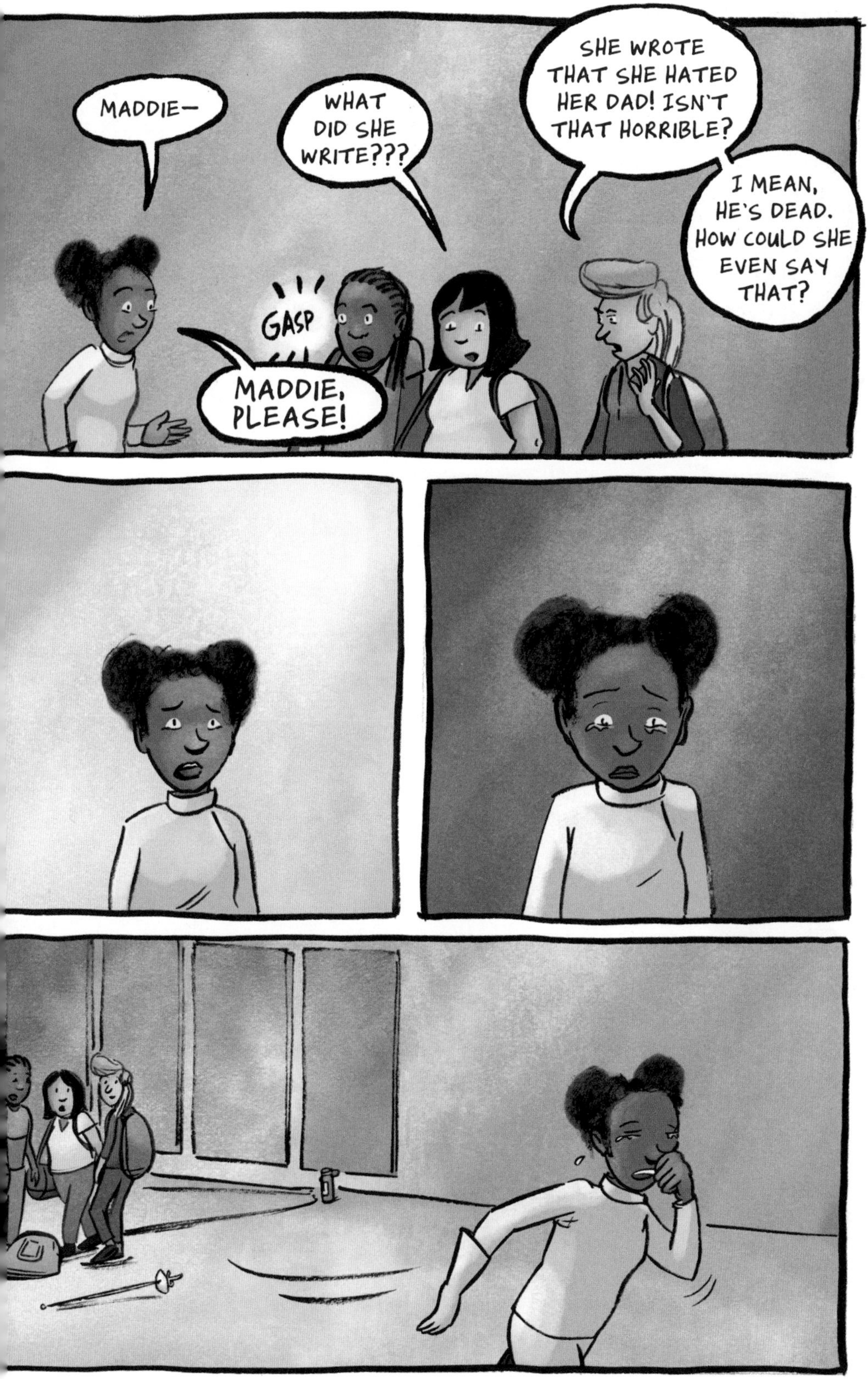
MADDIE—
WHAT DID SHE WRITE???
SHE WROTE THAT SHE HATED HER DAD! ISN'T THAT HORRIBLE?
I MEAN, HE'S DEAD. HOW COULD SHE EVEN SAY THAT?
GASP
MADDIE, PLEASE!

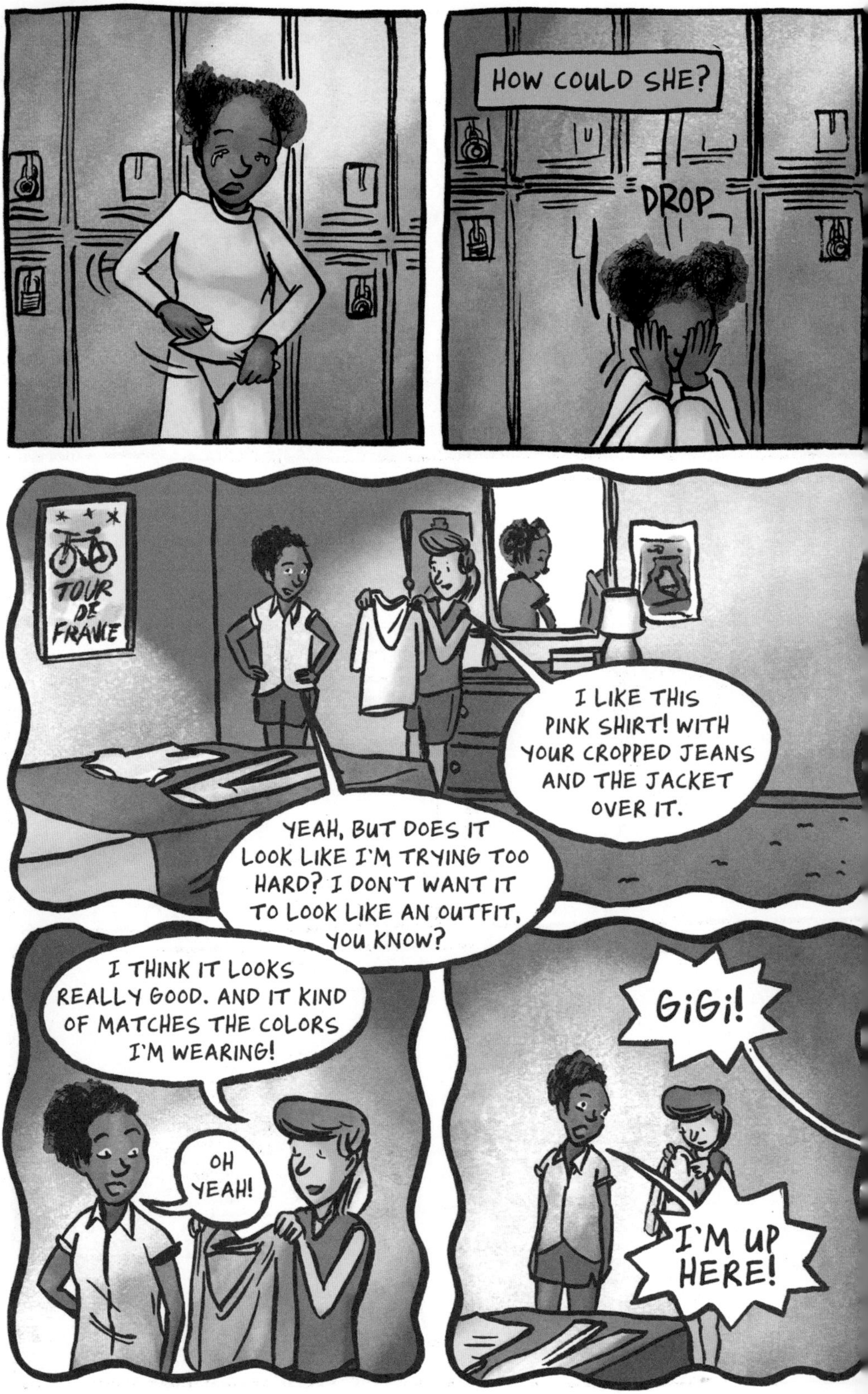
HOW COULD SHE?
DROP
TOUR DE FRANCE
I LIKE THIS PINK SHIRT! WITH YOUR CROPPED JEANS AND THE JACKET OVER IT.
YEAH, BUT DOES IT LOOK LIKE I'M TRYING TOO HARD? I DON'T WANT IT TO LOOK LIKE AN OUTFIT, YOU KNOW?
I THINK IT LOOKS REALLY GOOD. AND IT KIND OF MATCHES THE COLORS I'M WEARING!
OH YEAH!
GiGi!
I'M UP HERE!

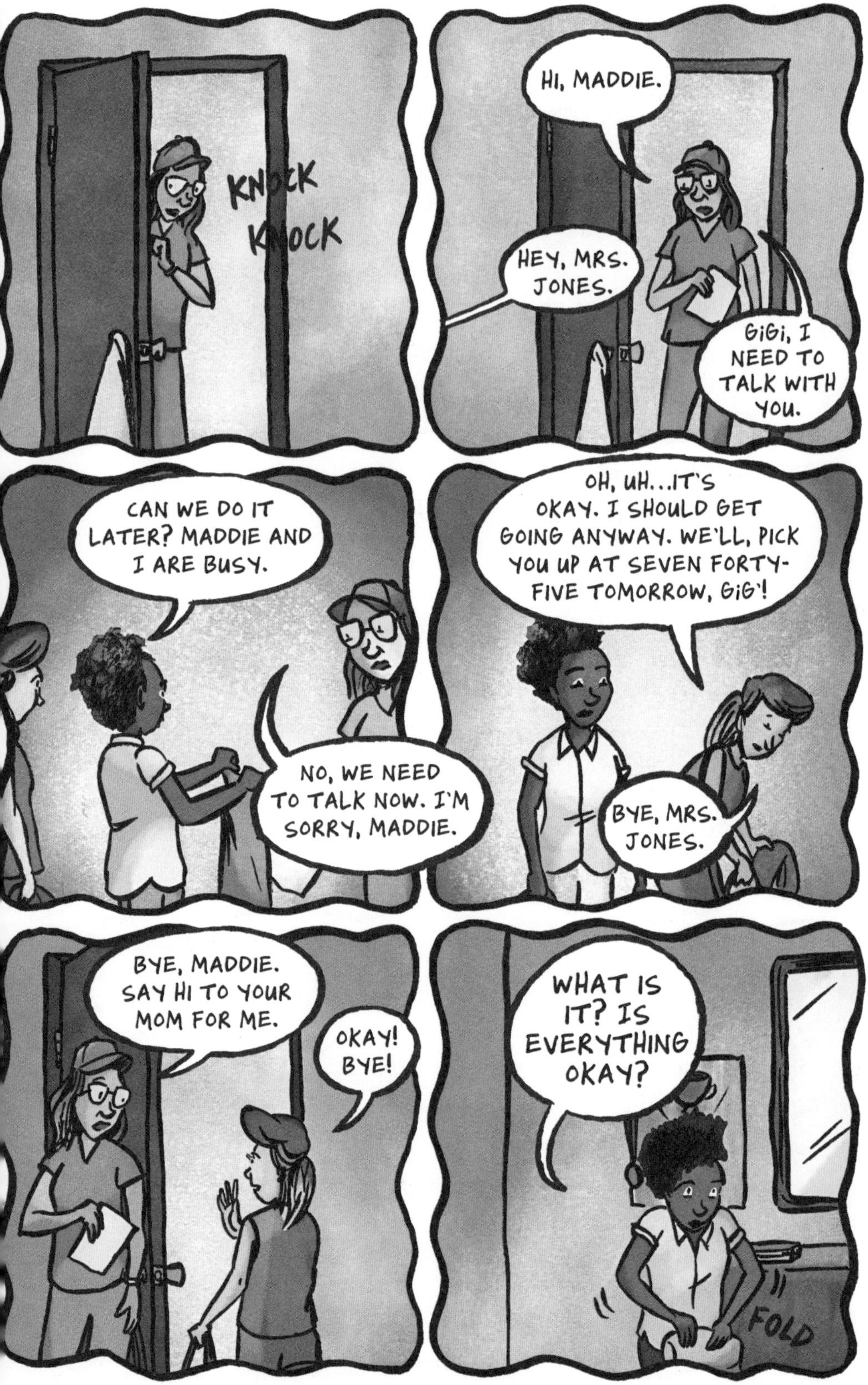
KNOCK KNOCK
HI, MADDIE.
HEY, MRS. JONES.
GiGi, I NEED TO TALK WITH YOU.
CAN WE DO IT LATER? MADDIE AND I ARE BUSY.
NO, WE NEED TO TALK NOW. I'M SORRY, MADDIE.
OH, UH...IT'S OKAY. I SHOULD GET GOING ANYWAY. WE'LL, PICK YOU UP AT SEVEN FORTY-FIVE TOMORROW, GiG'!
BYE, MRS. JONES.
BYE, MADDIE. SAY HI TO YOUR MOM FOR ME.
OKAY! BYE!
WHAT IS IT? IS EVERYTHING OKAY?
FOLD

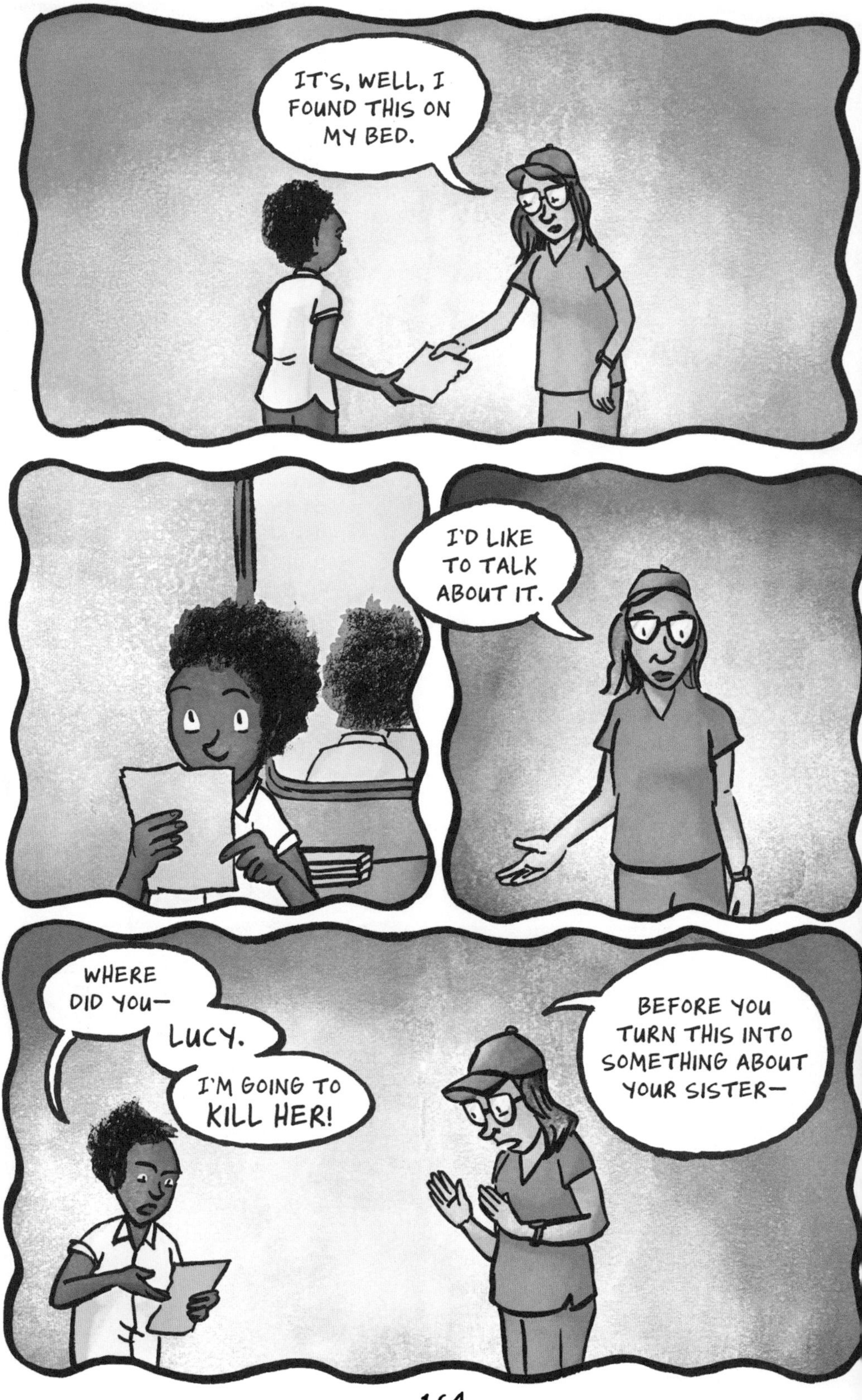
IT'S, WELL, I FOUND THIS ON MY BED.
I'D LIKE TO TALK ABOUT IT.
WHERE DID YOU—
LUCY.
I'M GOING TO KILL HER!
BEFORE YOU TURN THIS INTO SOMETHING ABOUT YOUR SISTER—

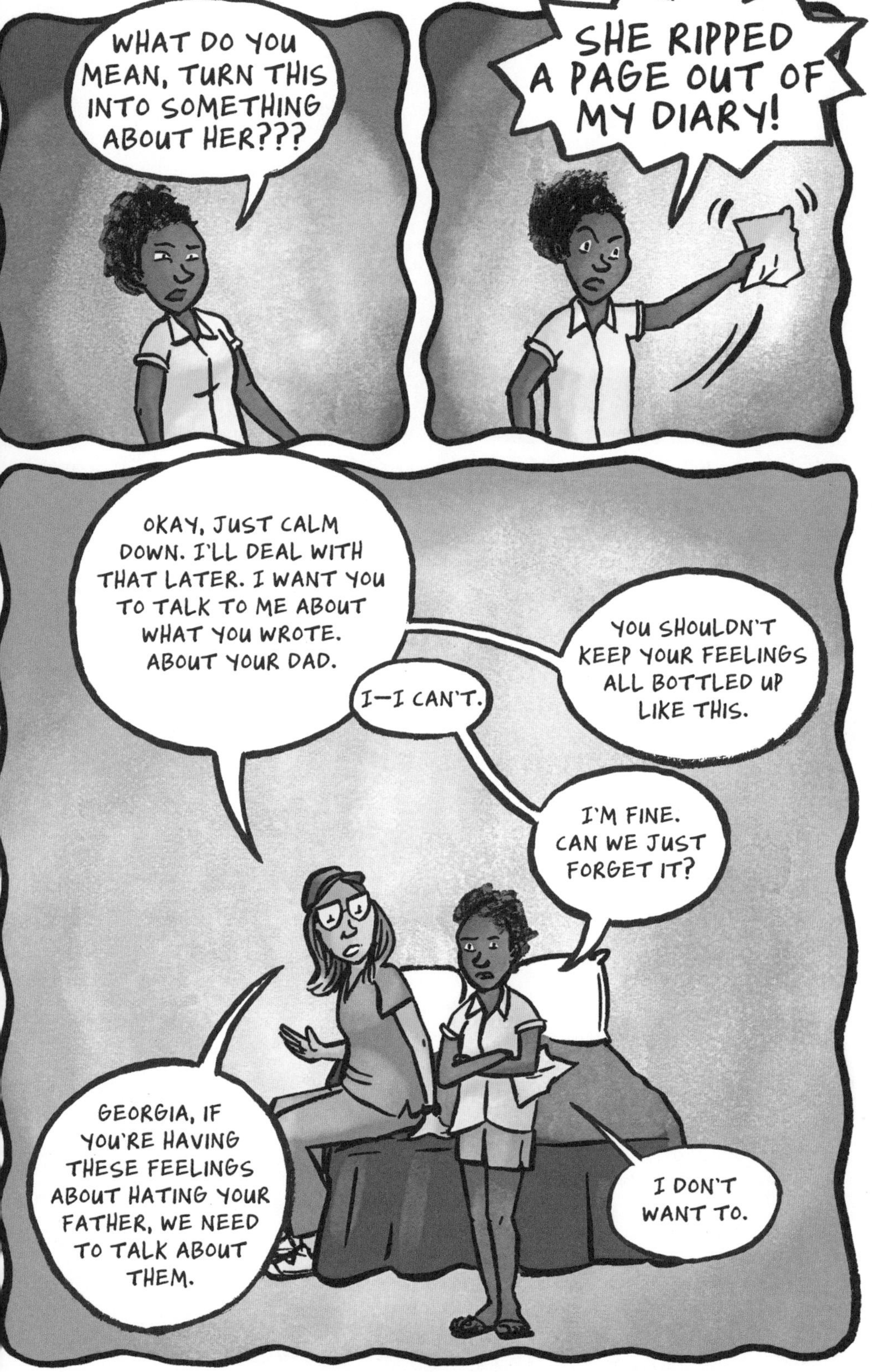
WHAT DO YOU MEAN, TURN THIS INTO SOMETHING ABOUT HER???
SHE RIPPED A PAGE OUT OF MY DIARY!
OKAY, JUST CALM DOWN. I'LL DEAL WITH THAT LATER. I WANT YOU TO TALK TO ME ABOUT WHAT YOU WROTE. ABOUT YOUR DAD.
YOU SHOULDN'T KEEP YOUR FEELINGS ALL BOTTLED UP LIKE THIS.
I—I CAN'T.
I'M FINE. CAN WE JUST FORGET IT?
GEORGIA, IF YOU'RE HAVING THESE FEELINGS ABOUT HATING YOUR FATHER, WE NEED TO TALK ABOUT THEM.
I DON'T WANT TO.

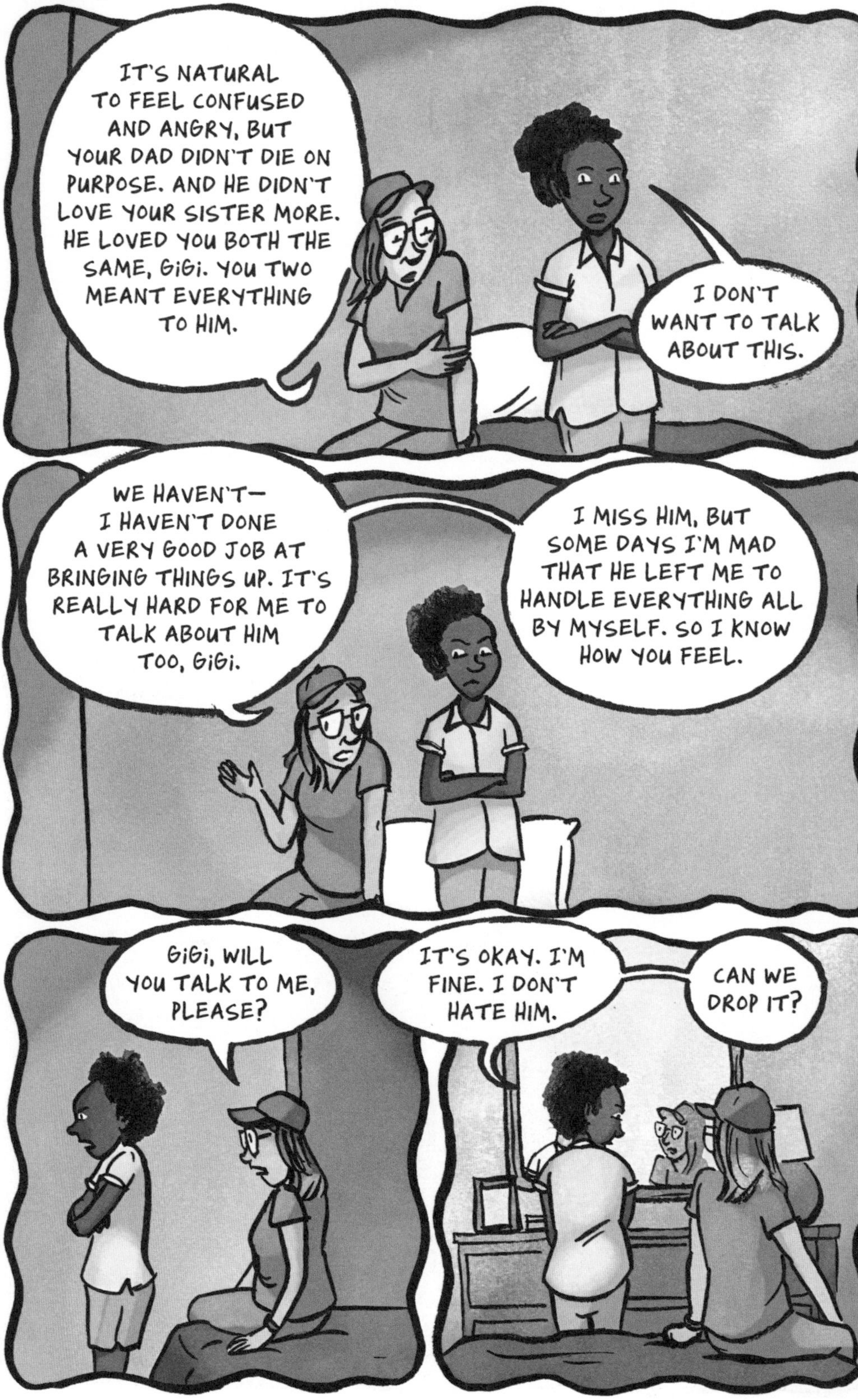
IT'S NATURAL TO FEEL CONFUSED AND ANGRY, BUT YOUR DAD DIDN'T DIE ON PURPOSE. AND HE DIDN'T LOVE YOUR SISTER MORE. HE LOVED YOU BOTH THE SAME, GiGi. YOU TWO MEANT EVERYTHING TO HIM.
I DON'T WANT TO TALK ABOUT THIS.
WE HAVEN'T— I HAVEN'T DONE A VERY GOOD JOB AT BRINGING THINGS UP. IT'S REALLY HARD FOR ME TO TALK ABOUT HIM TOO, GiGi.
I MISS HIM, BUT SOME DAYS I'M MAD THAT HE LEFT ME TO HANDLE EVERYTHING ALL BY MYSELF. SO I KNOW HOW YOU FEEL.
GiGi, WILL YOU TALK TO ME, PLEASE?
IT'S OKAY. I'M FINE. I DON'T HATE HIM.
CAN WE DROP IT?

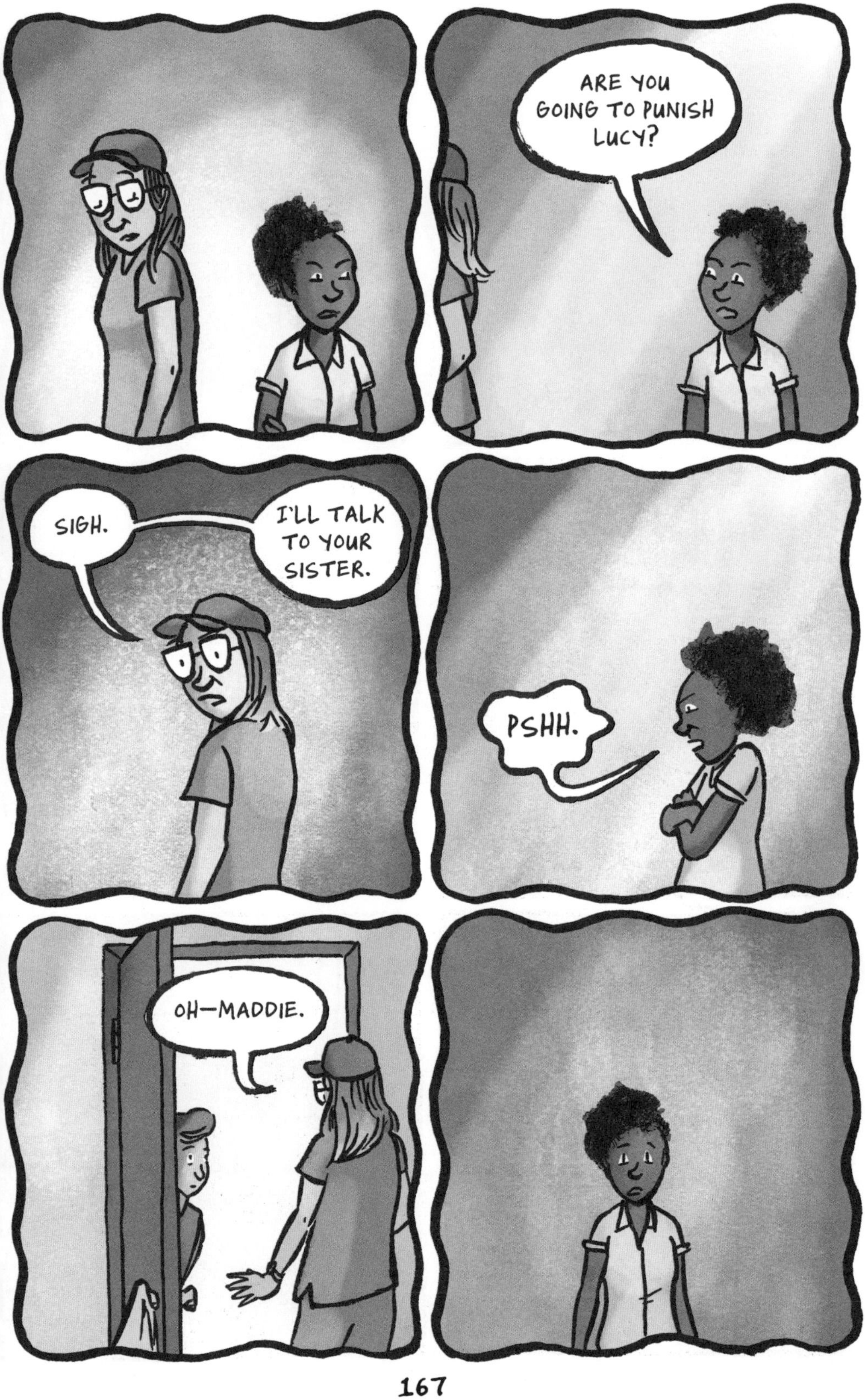
ARE YOU GOING TO PUNISH LUCY?
SIGH.
I'LL TALK TO YOUR SISTER.
PSHH.
OH—MADDIE.

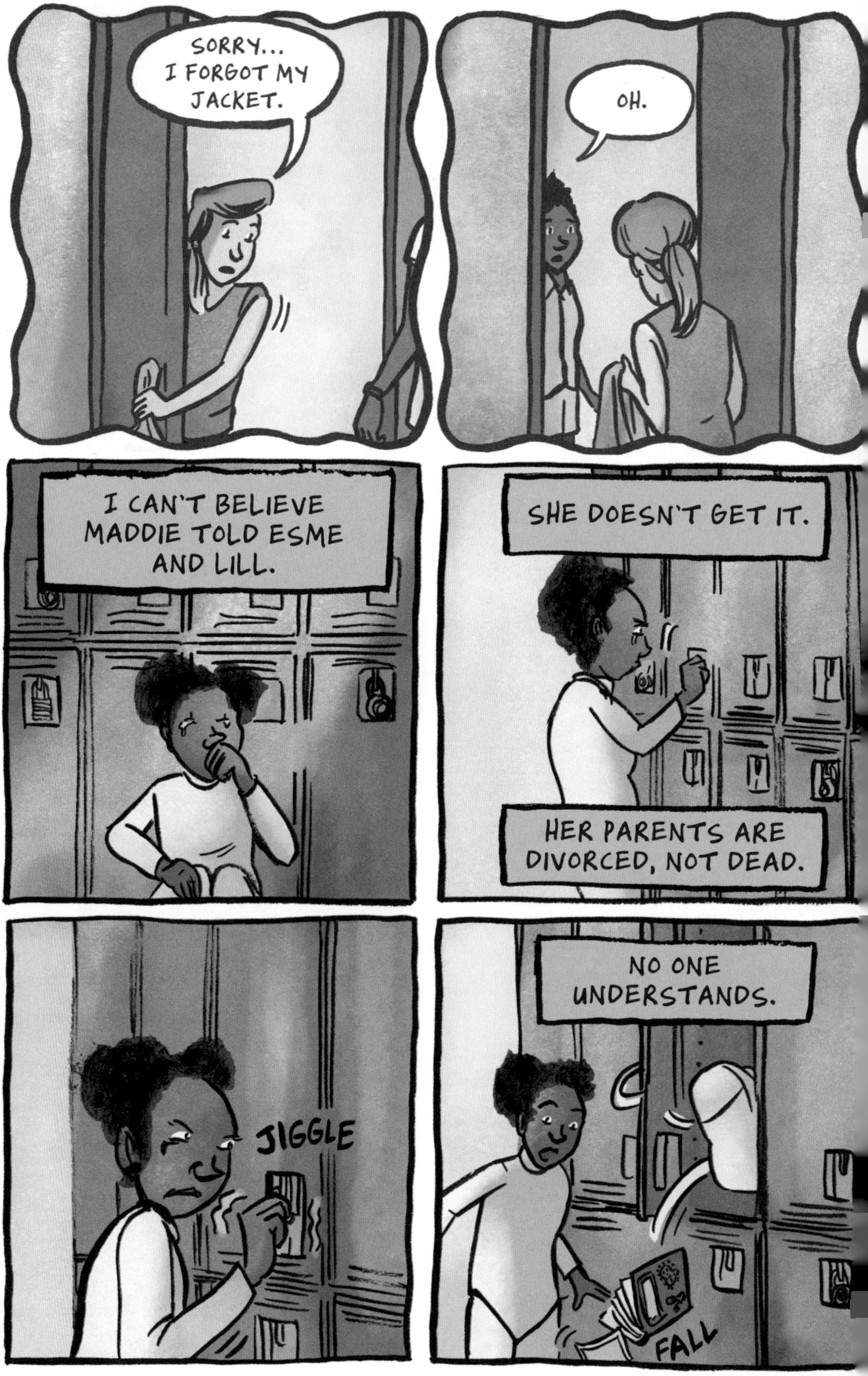
SORRY...
I FORGOT MY
JACKET.
OH.
I CAN'T BELIEVE
MADDIE TOLD ESME
AND LILL.
SHE DOESN'T GET IT.
HER PARENTS ARE
DIVORCED, NOT DEAD.
JIGGLE
NO ONE
UNDERSTANDS.
FALL

MOM'S ALWAYS BUSY AND I'M JUST LEFT WITH LUCY.

AND I CAN'T STOP MYSELF FROM BEING MEAN TO HER ALL THE TIME.

EVERYTHING IS AWFUL.

WHY DID YOU HAVE TO DIE?

Chapter 11

Engage

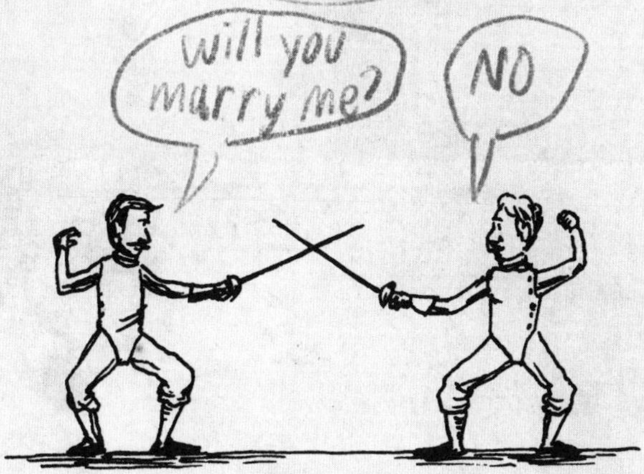
will you marry me?
NO

To engage, or the act of engagement, is when two fencers are at an appropriate distance to join their blades in contact. It can also refer to when you are in a pris de fer (taking your opponent's blade—see *bind*), attack au fer (beating or pressing your opponent's blade), or during a parry. An engagement is often a prelude to an attack.

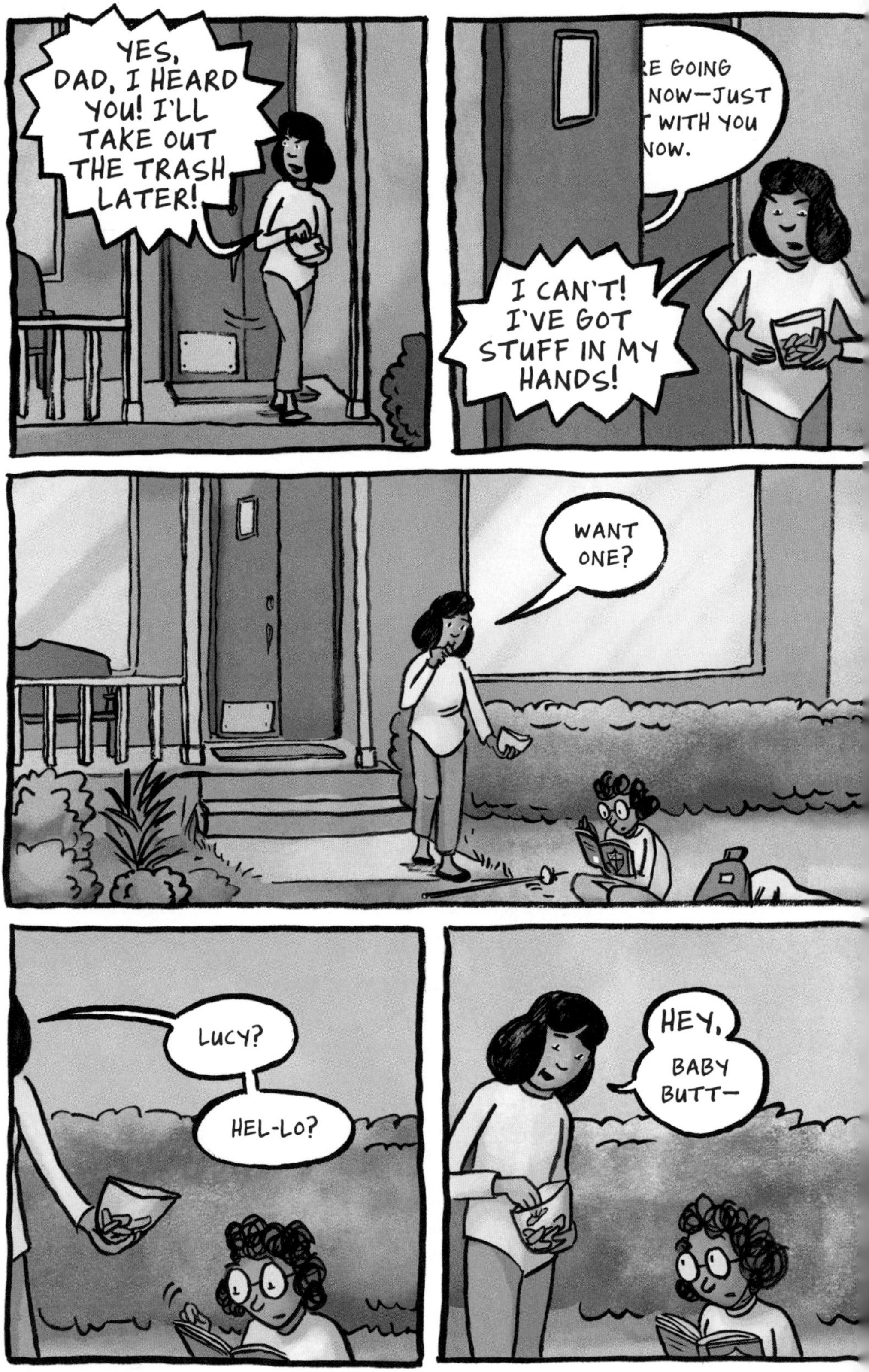
YES, DAD, I HEARD YOU! I'LL TAKE OUT THE TRASH LATER!
E GOING NOW—JUST WITH YOU NOW.
I CAN'T! I'VE GOT STUFF IN MY HANDS!
WANT ONE?
LUCY?
HEL-LO?
HEY, BABY BUTT—

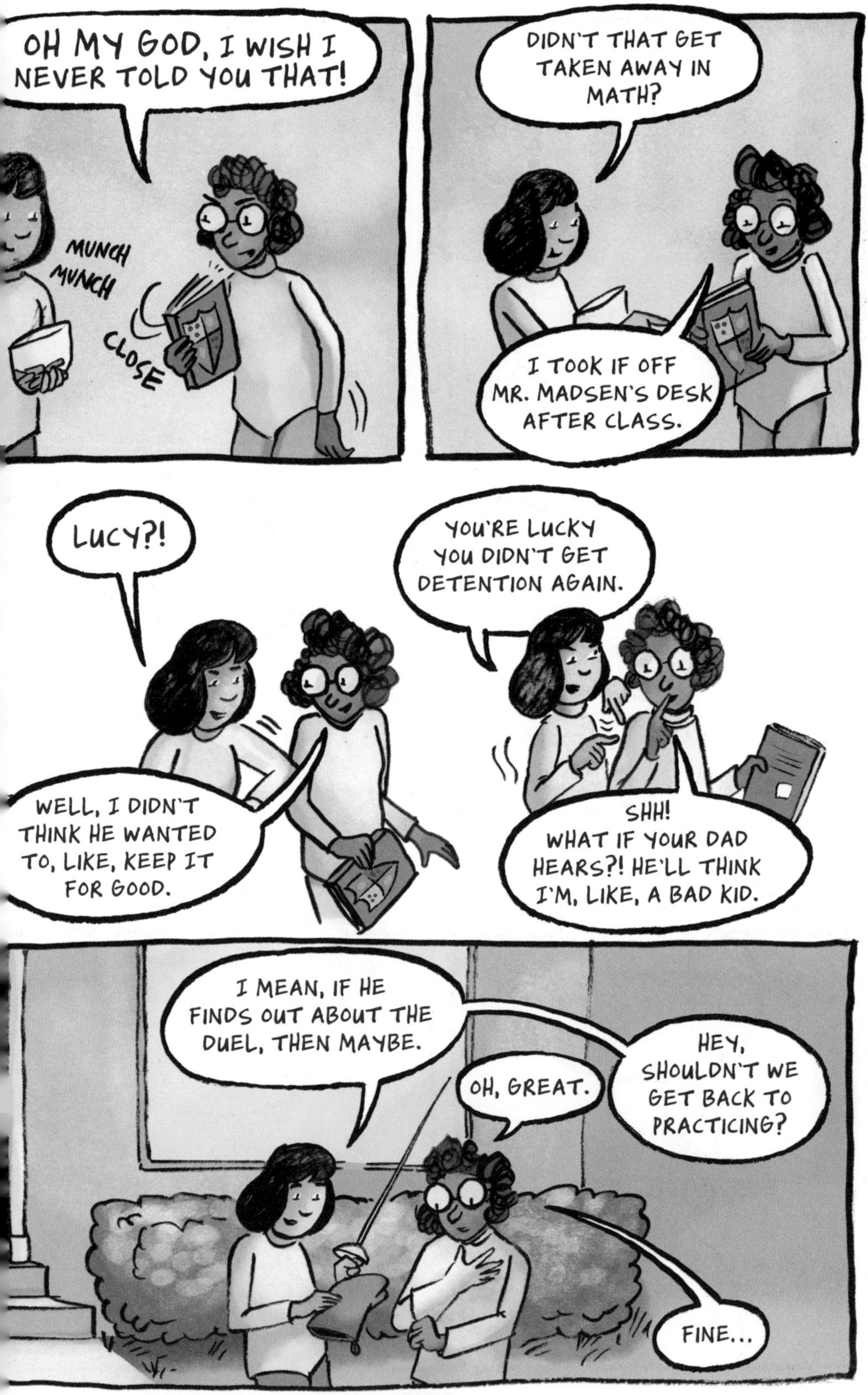
OH MY GOD, I WISH I NEVER TOLD YOU THAT!
MUNCH MUNCH
CLOSE
DIDN'T THAT GET TAKEN AWAY IN MATH?
I TOOK IF OFF MR. MADSEN'S DESK AFTER CLASS.
LUCY?!
WELL, I DIDN'T THINK HE WANTED TO, LIKE, KEEP IT FOR GOOD.
YOU'RE LUCKY YOU DIDN'T GET DETENTION AGAIN.
SHH! WHAT IF YOUR DAD HEARS?! HE'LL THINK I'M, LIKE, A BAD KID.
I MEAN, IF HE FINDS OUT ABOUT THE DUEL, THEN MAYBE.
OH, GREAT.
HEY, SHOULDN'T WE GET BACK TO PRACTICING?
FINE...

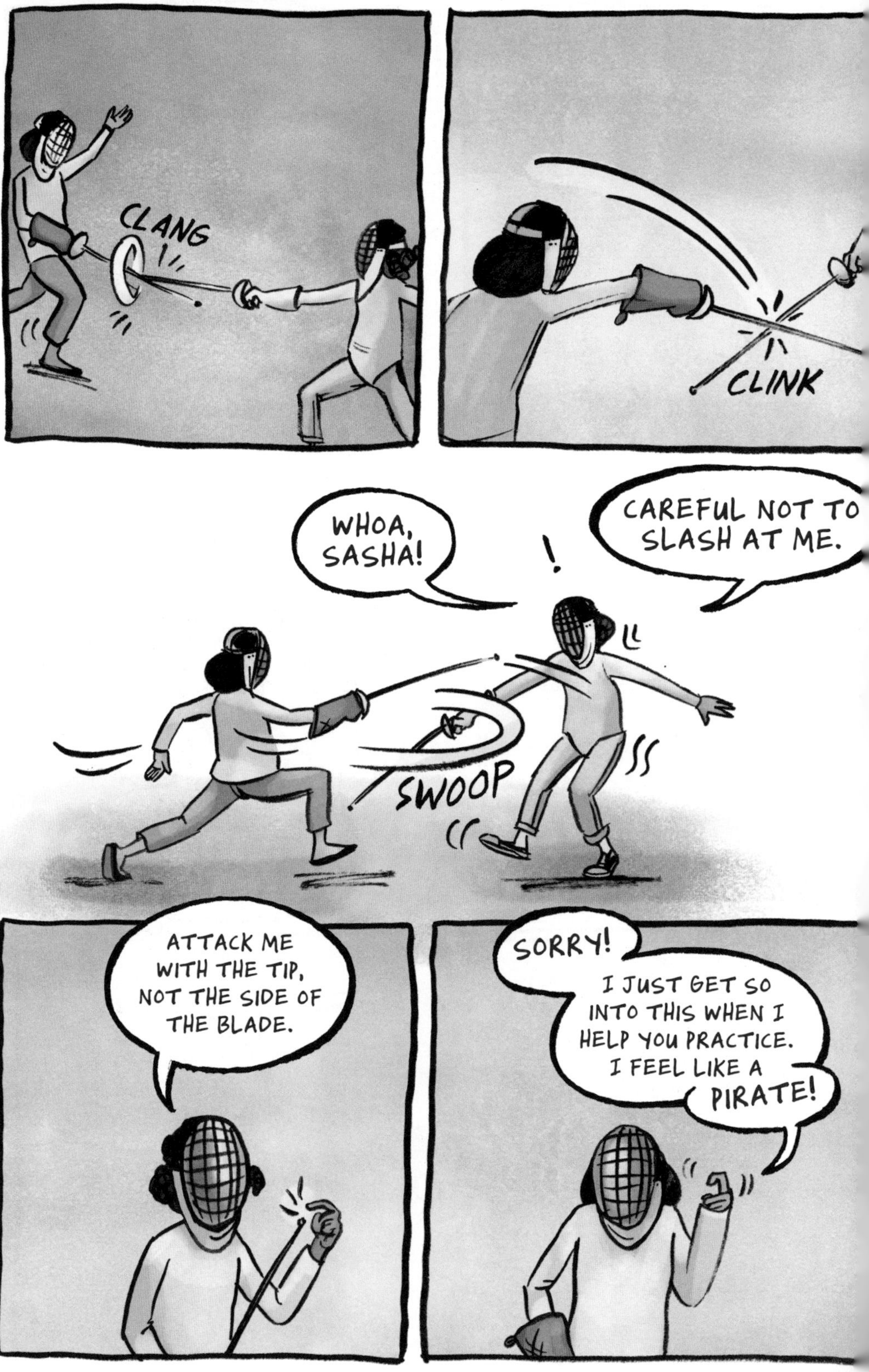
CLANG
CLINK
WHOA, SASHA!
!
CAREFUL NOT TO SLASH AT ME.
SWOOP
ATTACK ME WITH THE TIP, NOT THE SIDE OF THE BLADE.
SORRY!
I JUST GET SO INTO THIS WHEN I HELP YOU PRACTICE. I FEEL LIKE A PIRATE!

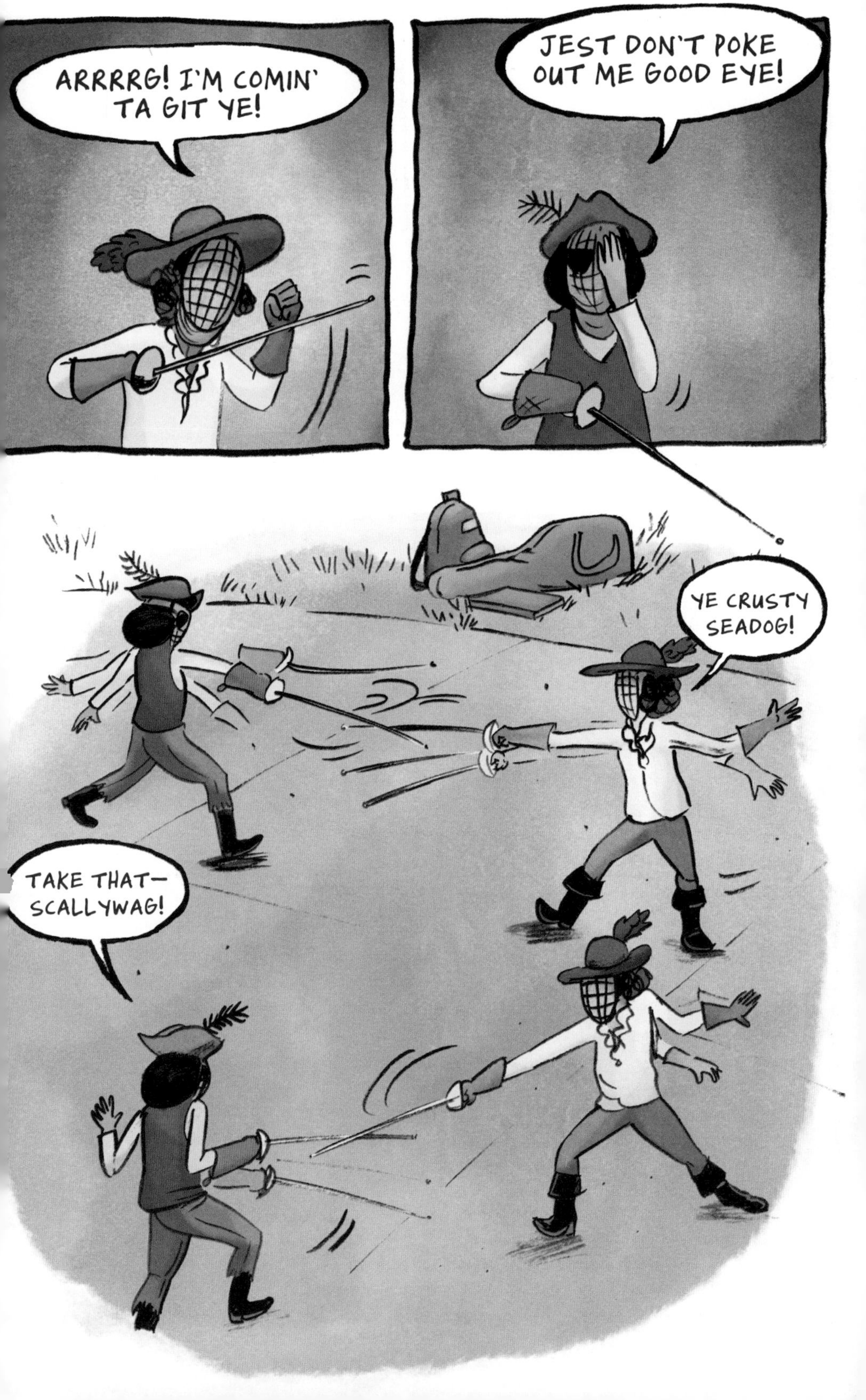
ARRRRG! I'M COMIN' TA GIT YE!
JEST DON'T POKE OUT ME GOOD EYE!
YE CRUSTY SEADOG!
TAKE THAT— SCALLYWAG!

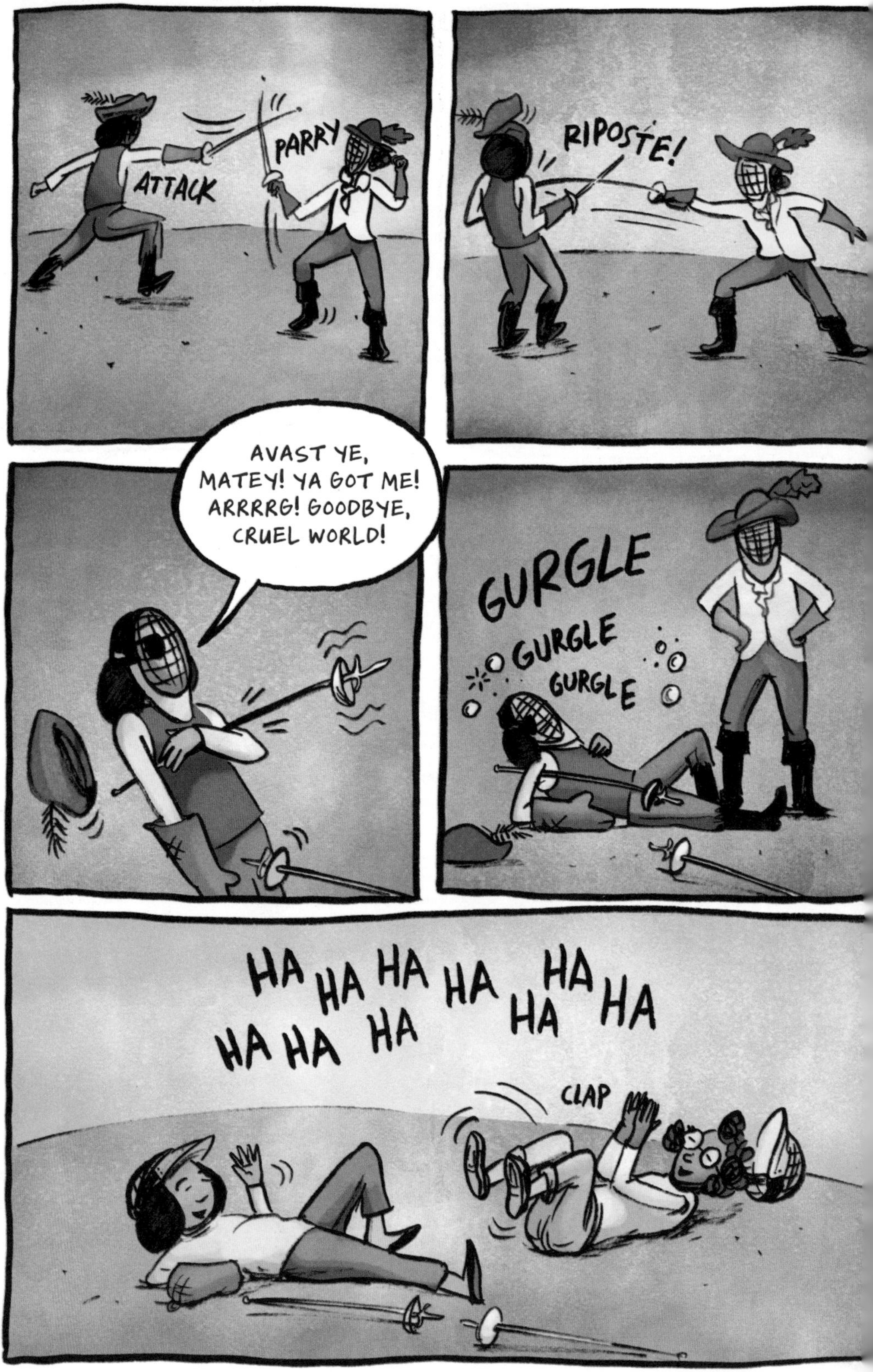
ATTACK
PARRY
RIPOSTE!
AVAST YE, MATEY! YA GOT ME! ARRRRG! GOODBYE, CRUEL WORLD!
GURGLE
GURGLE
GURGLE
HA HA HA HA HA HA HA HA HA HA HA
CLAP

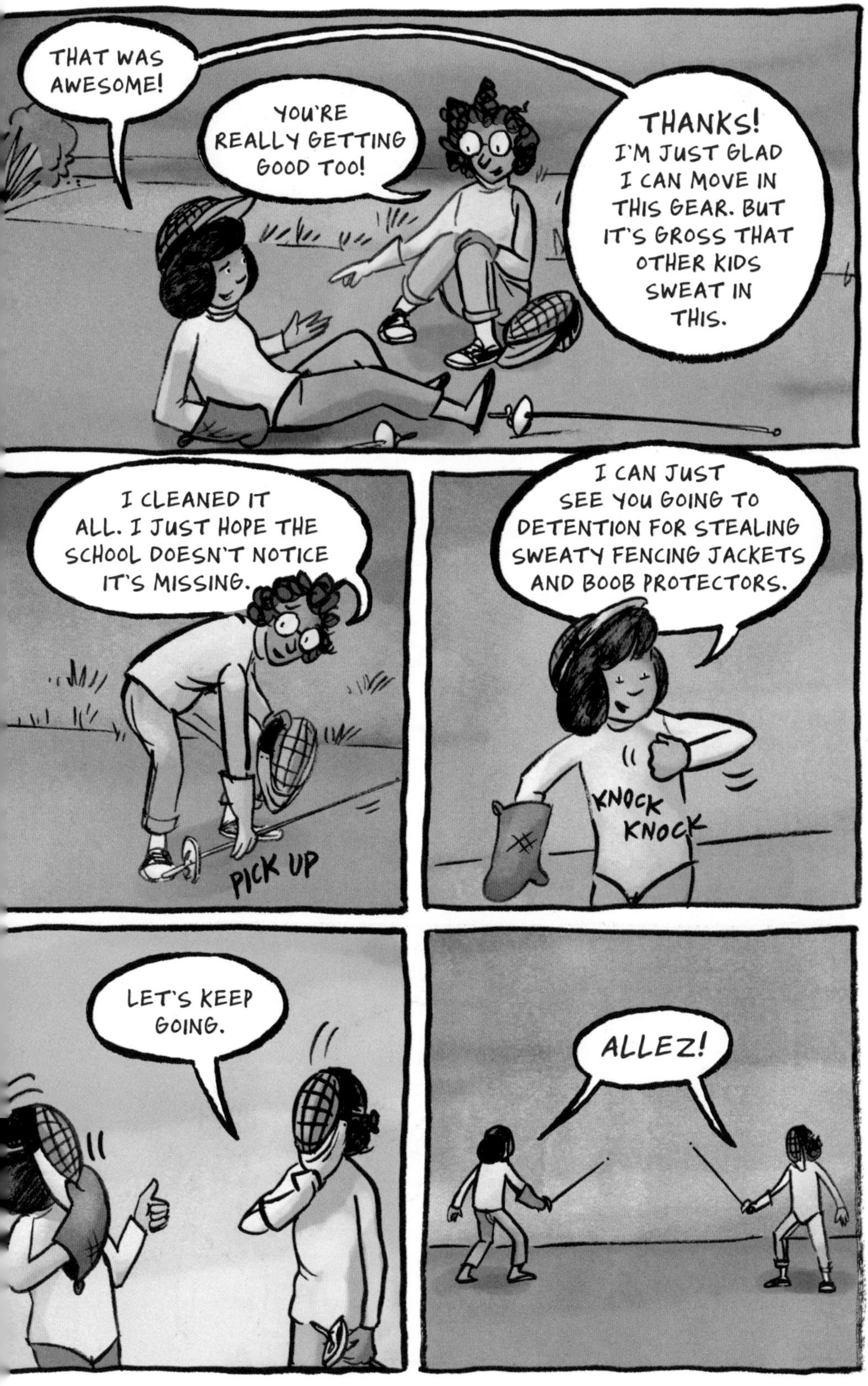
THAT WAS AWESOME!
YOU'RE REALLY GETTING GOOD TOO!
THANKS! I'M JUST GLAD I CAN MOVE IN THIS GEAR. BUT IT'S GROSS THAT OTHER KIDS SWEAT IN THIS.
I CLEANED IT ALL. I JUST HOPE THE SCHOOL DOESN'T NOTICE IT'S MISSING.
PICK UP
I CAN JUST SEE YOU GOING TO DETENTION FOR STEALING SWEATY FENCING JACKETS AND BOOB PROTECTORS.
KNOCK KNOCK
LET'S KEEP GOING.
ALLEZ!

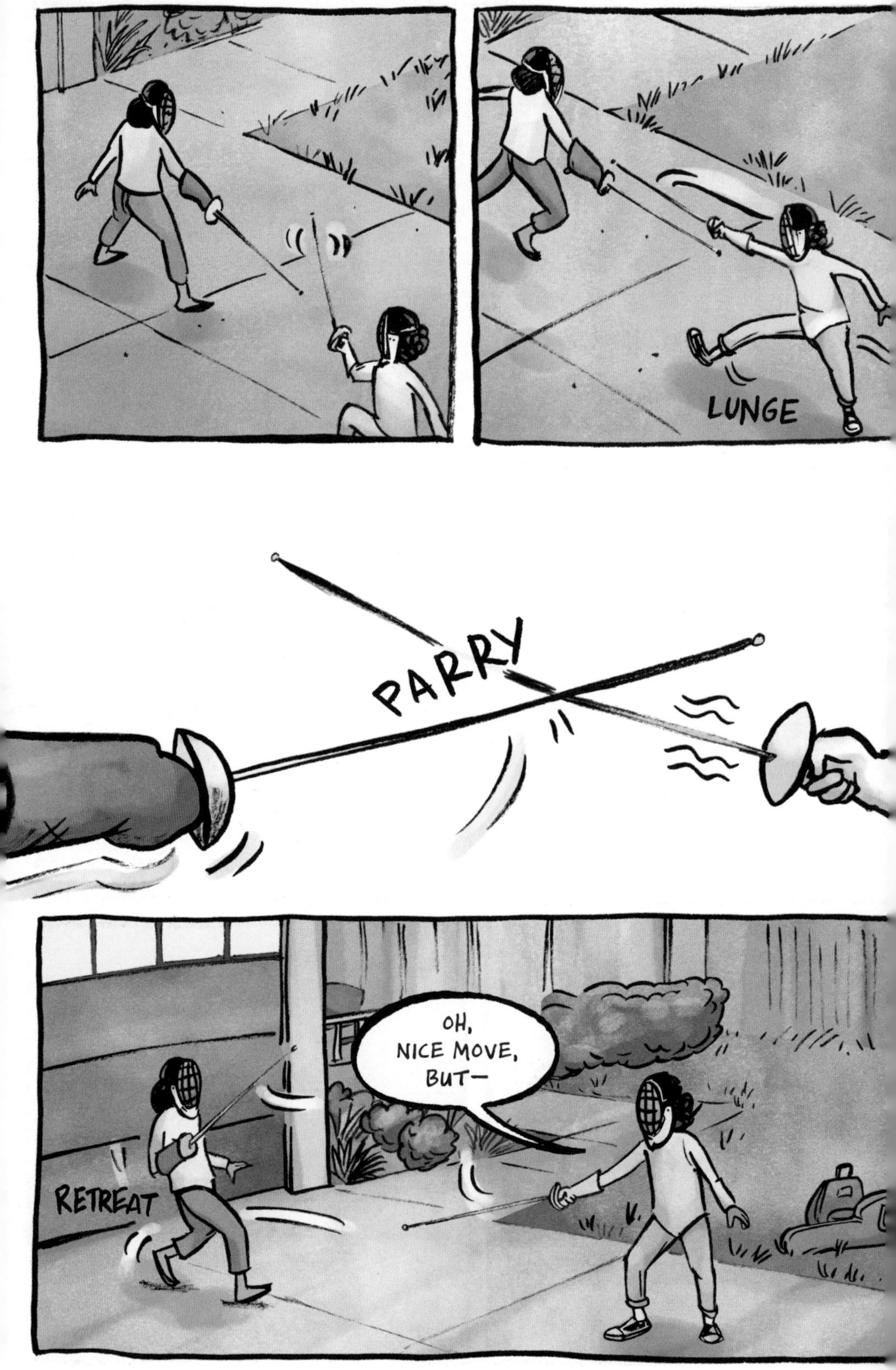
LUNGE
PARRY
RETREAT
OH, NICE MOVE, BUT—

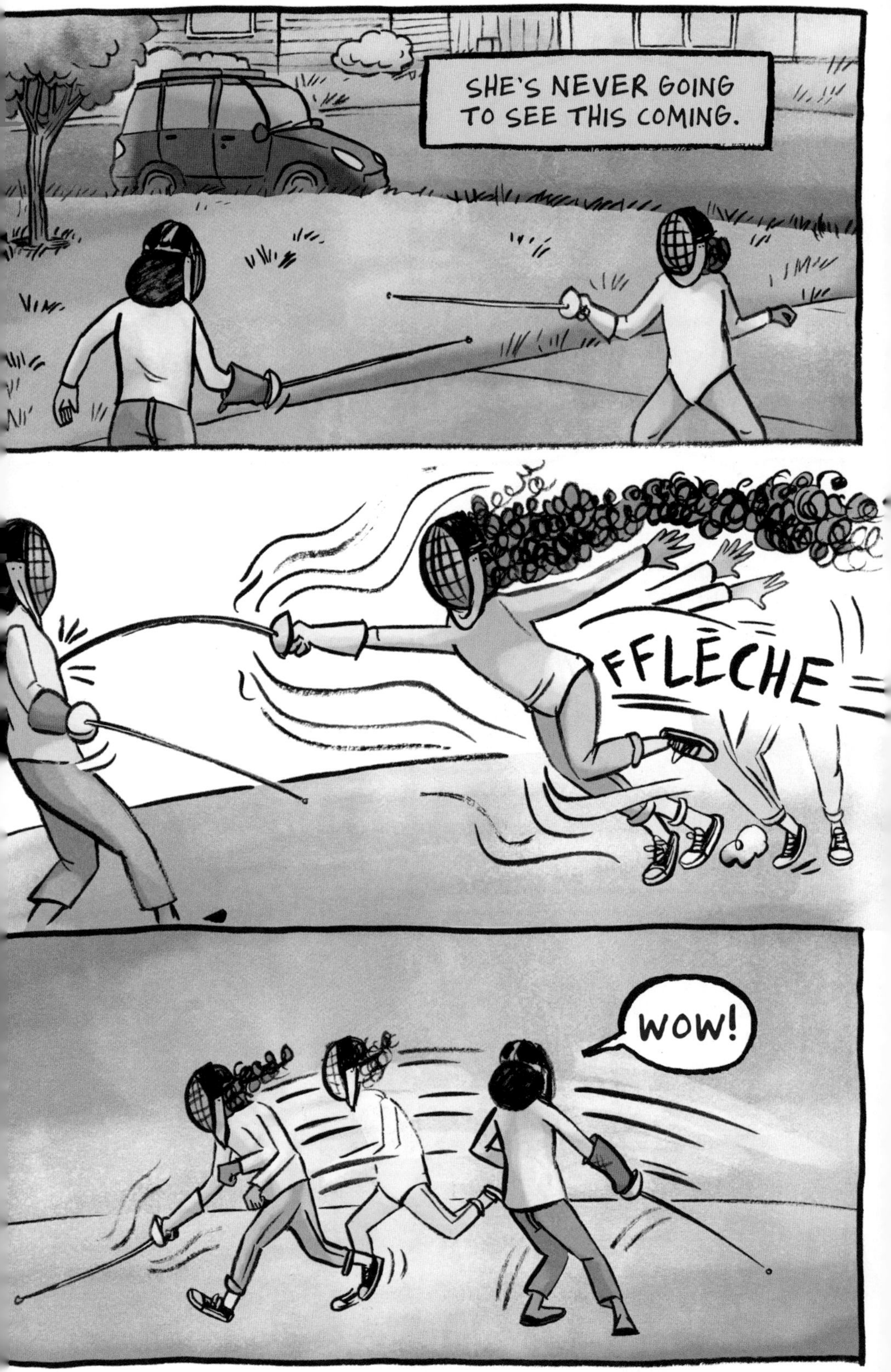
SHE'S NEVER GOING TO SEE THIS COMING.
FFLECHE
WOW!

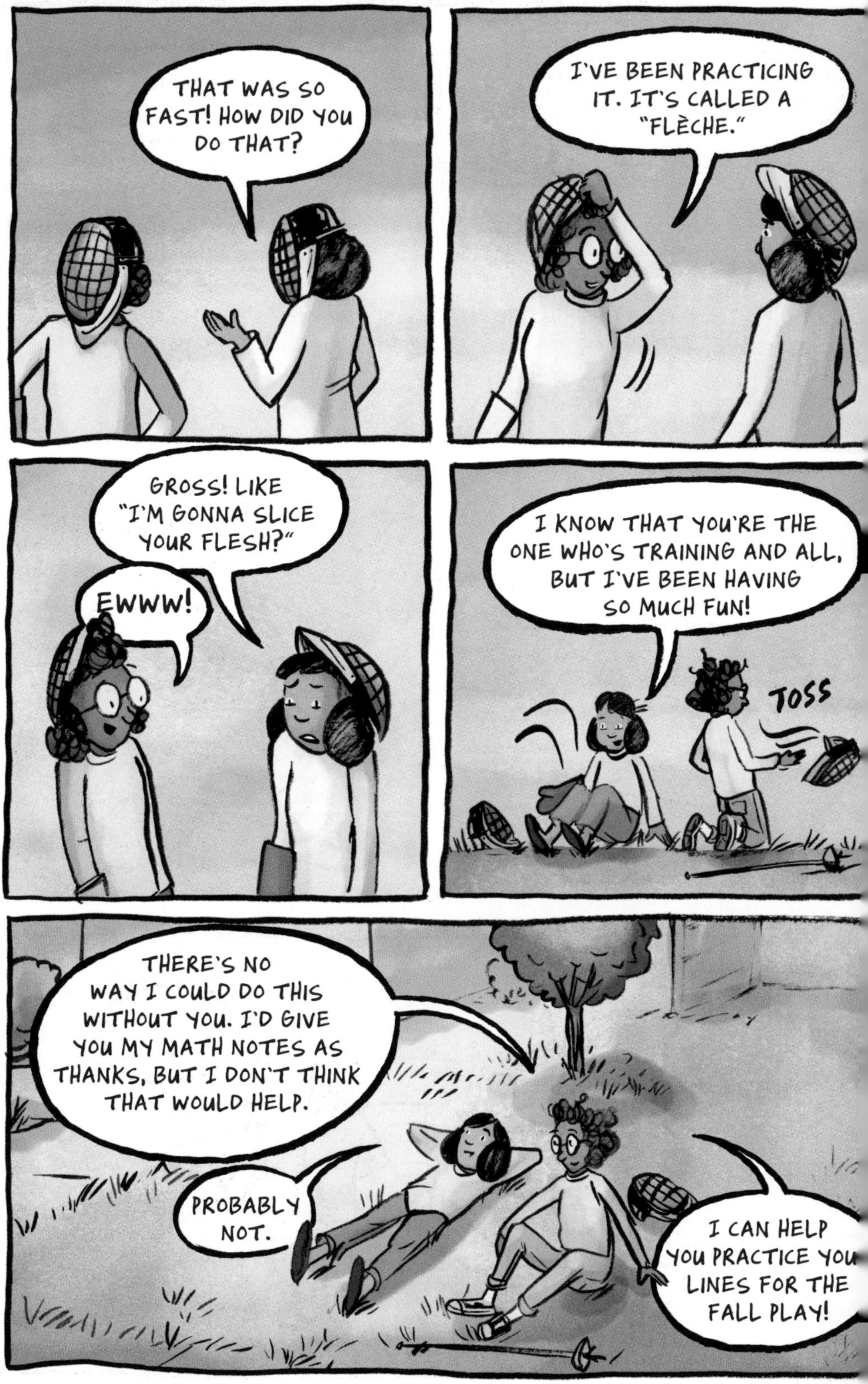
THAT WAS SO FAST! HOW DID YOU DO THAT?
I'VE BEEN PRACTICING IT. IT'S CALLED A "FLÈCHE."
GROSS! LIKE "I'M GONNA SLICE YOUR FLESH?"
EWWW!
I KNOW THAT YOU'RE THE ONE WHO'S TRAINING AND ALL, BUT I'VE BEEN HAVING SO MUCH FUN!
TOSS
THERE'S NO WAY I COULD DO THIS WITHOUT YOU. I'D GIVE YOU MY MATH NOTES AS THANKS, BUT I DON'T THINK THAT WOULD HELP.
PROBABLY NOT.
I CAN HELP YOU PRACTICE YOU LINES FOR THE FALL PLAY!

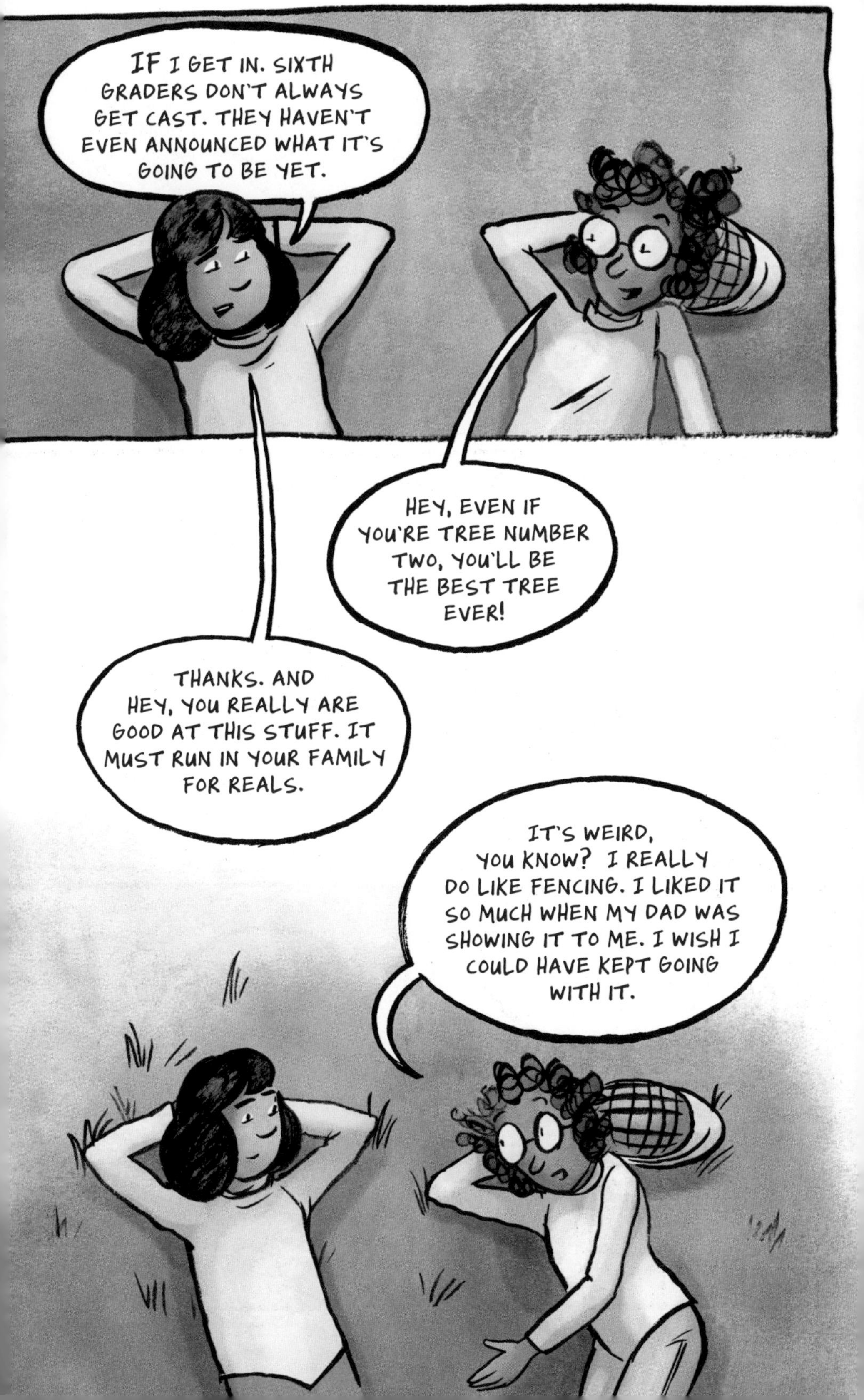
IF I GET IN. SIXTH GRADERS DON'T ALWAYS GET CAST. THEY HAVEN'T EVEN ANNOUNCED WHAT IT'S GOING TO BE YET.
HEY, EVEN IF YOU'RE TREE NUMBER TWO, YOU'LL BE THE BEST TREE EVER!
THANKS. AND HEY, YOU REALLY ARE GOOD AT THIS STUFF. IT MUST RUN IN YOUR FAMILY FOR REALS.
IT'S WEIRD, YOU KNOW? I REALLY DO LIKE FENCING. I LIKED IT SO MUCH WHEN MY DAD WAS SHOWING IT TO ME. I WISH I COULD HAVE KEPT GOING WITH IT.

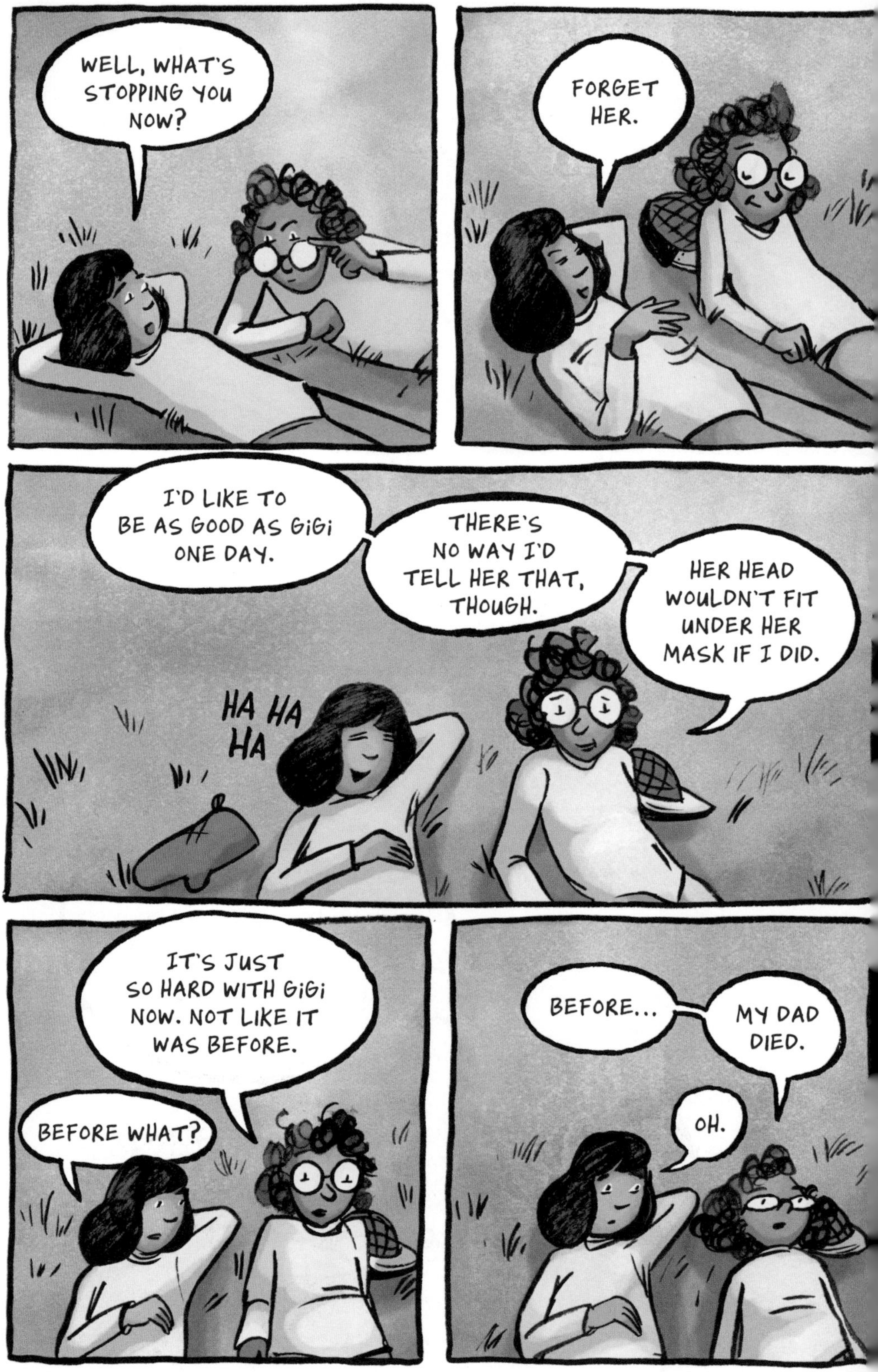
WELL, WHAT'S STOPPING YOU NOW?
FORGET HER.
I'D LIKE TO BE AS GOOD AS GiGi ONE DAY.
THERE'S NO WAY I'D TELL HER THAT, THOUGH.
HER HEAD WOULDN'T FIT UNDER HER MASK IF I DID.
HA HA HA
IT'S JUST SO HARD WITH GiGi NOW. NOT LIKE IT WAS BEFORE.
BEFORE WHAT?
BEFORE...
MY DAD DIED.
OH.

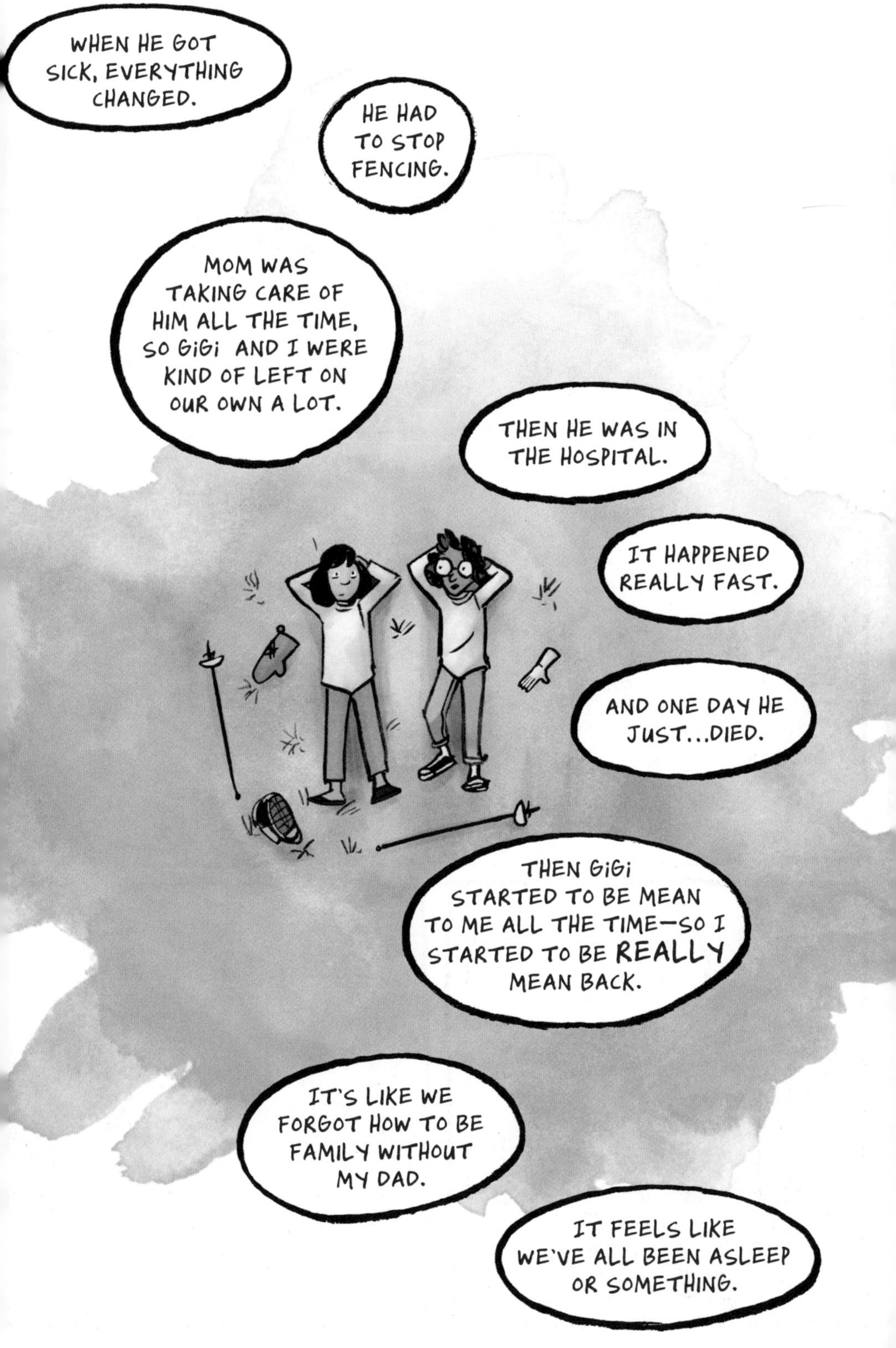
WHEN HE GOT SICK, EVERYTHING CHANGED.
HE HAD TO STOP FENCING.
MOM WAS TAKING CARE OF HIM ALL THE TIME, SO GIGI AND I WERE KIND OF LEFT ON OUR OWN A LOT.
THEN HE WAS IN THE HOSPITAL.
IT HAPPENED REALLY FAST.
AND ONE DAY HE JUST...DIED.
THEN GIGI STARTED TO BE MEAN TO ME ALL THE TIME—SO I STARTED TO BE REALLY MEAN BACK.
IT'S LIKE WE FORGOT HOW TO BE FAMILY WITHOUT MY DAD.
IT FEELS LIKE WE'VE ALL BEEN ASLEEP OR SOMETHING.

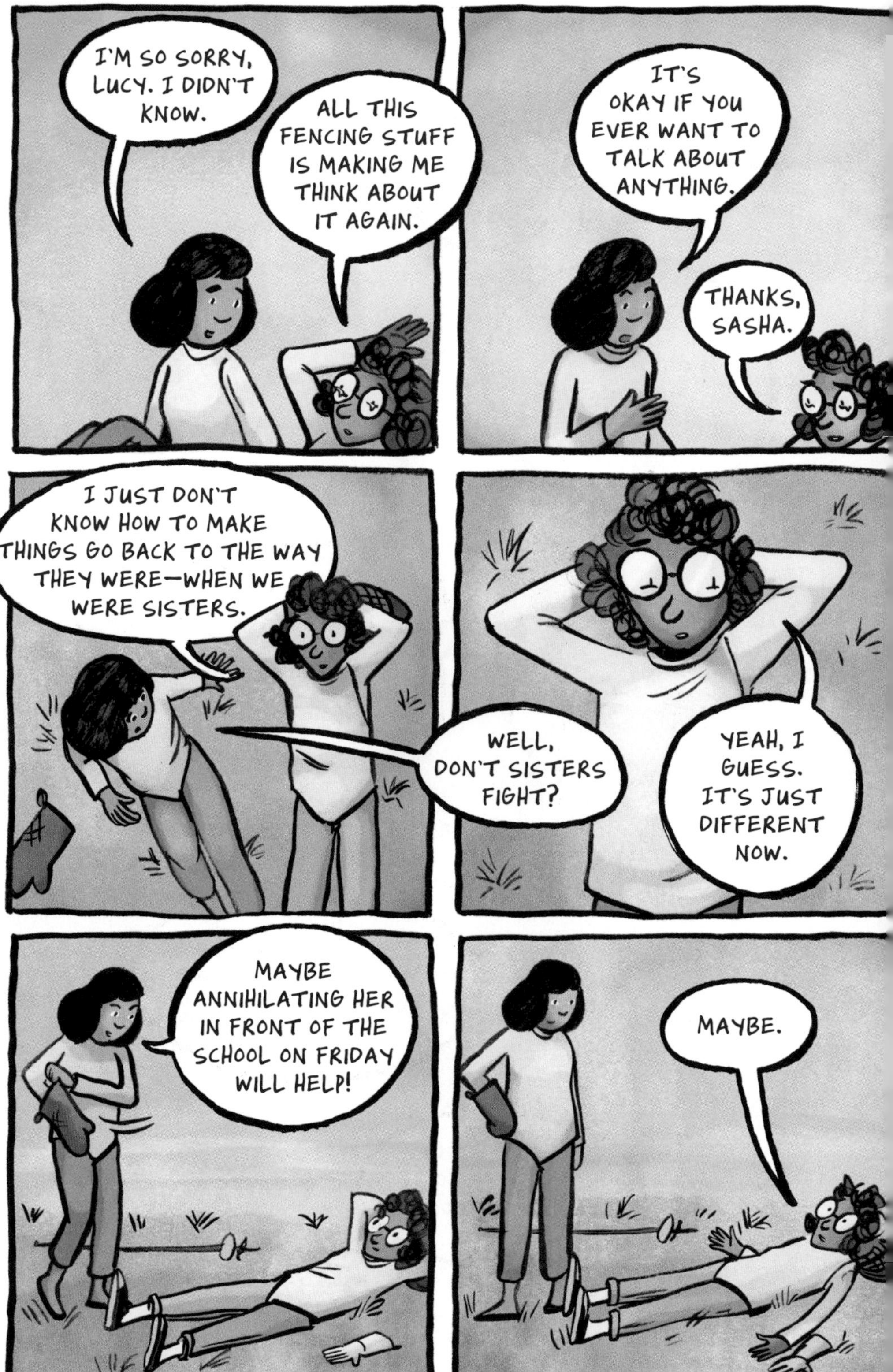
I'M SO SORRY, LUCY. I DIDN'T KNOW.
ALL THIS FENCING STUFF IS MAKING ME THINK ABOUT IT AGAIN.
IT'S OKAY IF YOU EVER WANT TO TALK ABOUT ANYTHING.
THANKS, SASHA.
I JUST DON'T KNOW HOW TO MAKE THINGS GO BACK TO THE WAY THEY WERE—WHEN WE WERE SISTERS.
WELL, DON'T SISTERS FIGHT?
YEAH, I GUESS. IT'S JUST DIFFERENT NOW.
MAYBE ANNIHILATING HER IN FRONT OF THE SCHOOL ON FRIDAY WILL HELP!
MAYBE.

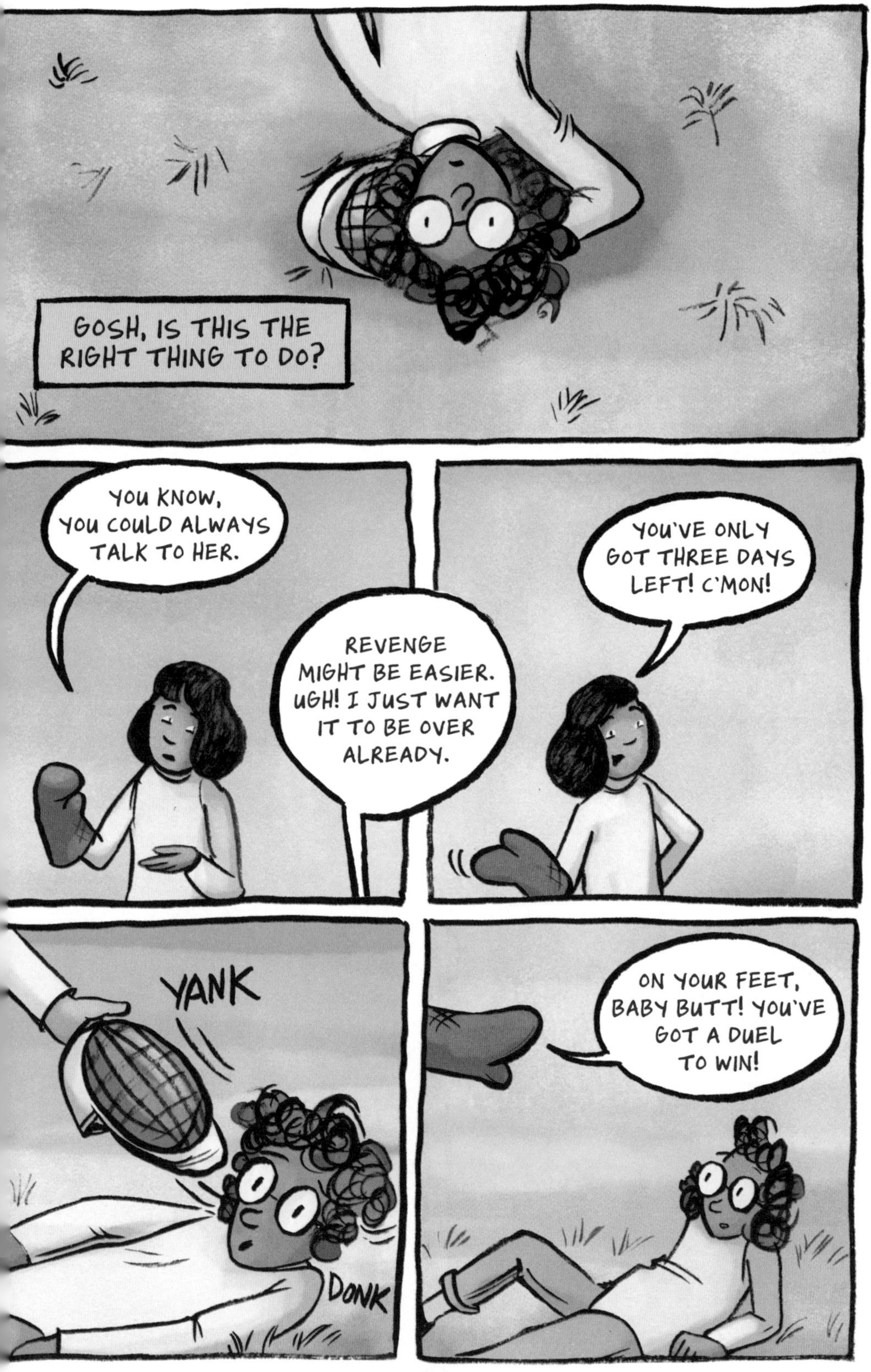
GOSH, IS THIS THE RIGHT THING TO DO?
YOU KNOW, YOU COULD ALWAYS TALK TO HER.
REVENGE MIGHT BE EASIER. UGH! I JUST WANT IT TO BE OVER ALREADY.
YOU'VE ONLY GOT THREE DAYS LEFT! C'MON!
YANK
DONK
ON YOUR FEET, BABY BUTT! YOU'VE GOT A DUEL TO WIN!

Chapter 12

Disengage

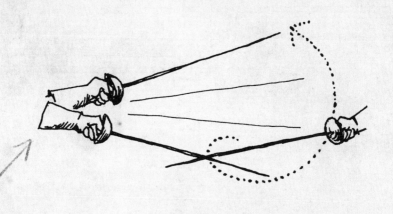

A disengage is often preceded by a beat or pressing of the opponent's blade meant to draw a reaction. Once you beat or press your opponent's blade, your opponent may reflexively react with a parry, which you can then avoid with a small circular motion, dropping the tip of your blade under the opponent's and coming back around to extend and then make your attack. To disengage in common usage can mean to stop being involved, or stop taking part in something.

Motion comes from the fingers not the wrist

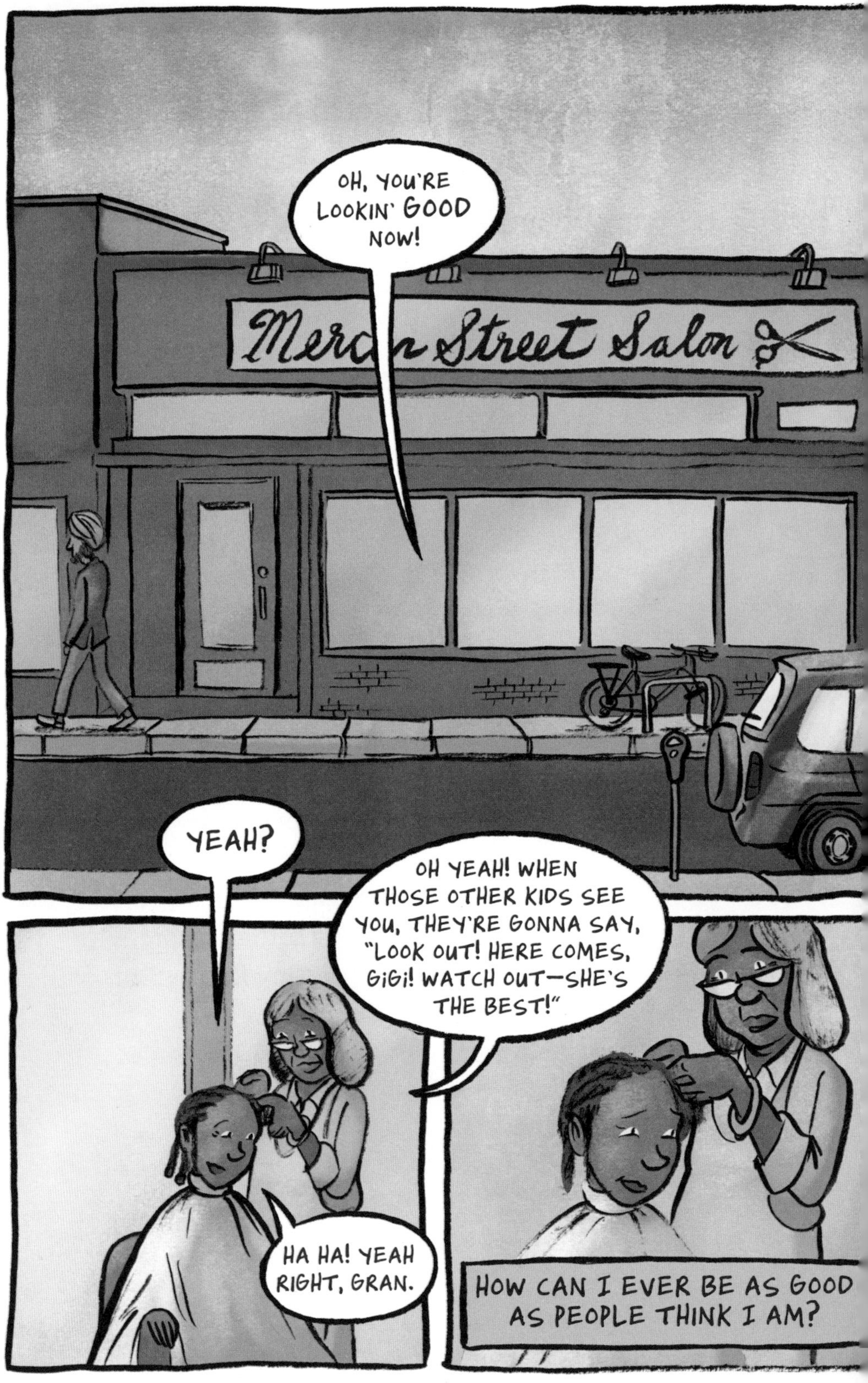

OH, YOU'RE LOOKIN' GOOD NOW!
YEAH?
OH YEAH! WHEN THOSE OTHER KIDS SEE YOU, THEY'RE GONNA SAY, "LOOK OUT! HERE COMES, GIGI! WATCH OUT—SHE'S THE BEST!"
HA HA! YEAH RIGHT, GRAN.
HOW CAN I EVER BE AS GOOD AS PEOPLE THINK I AM?

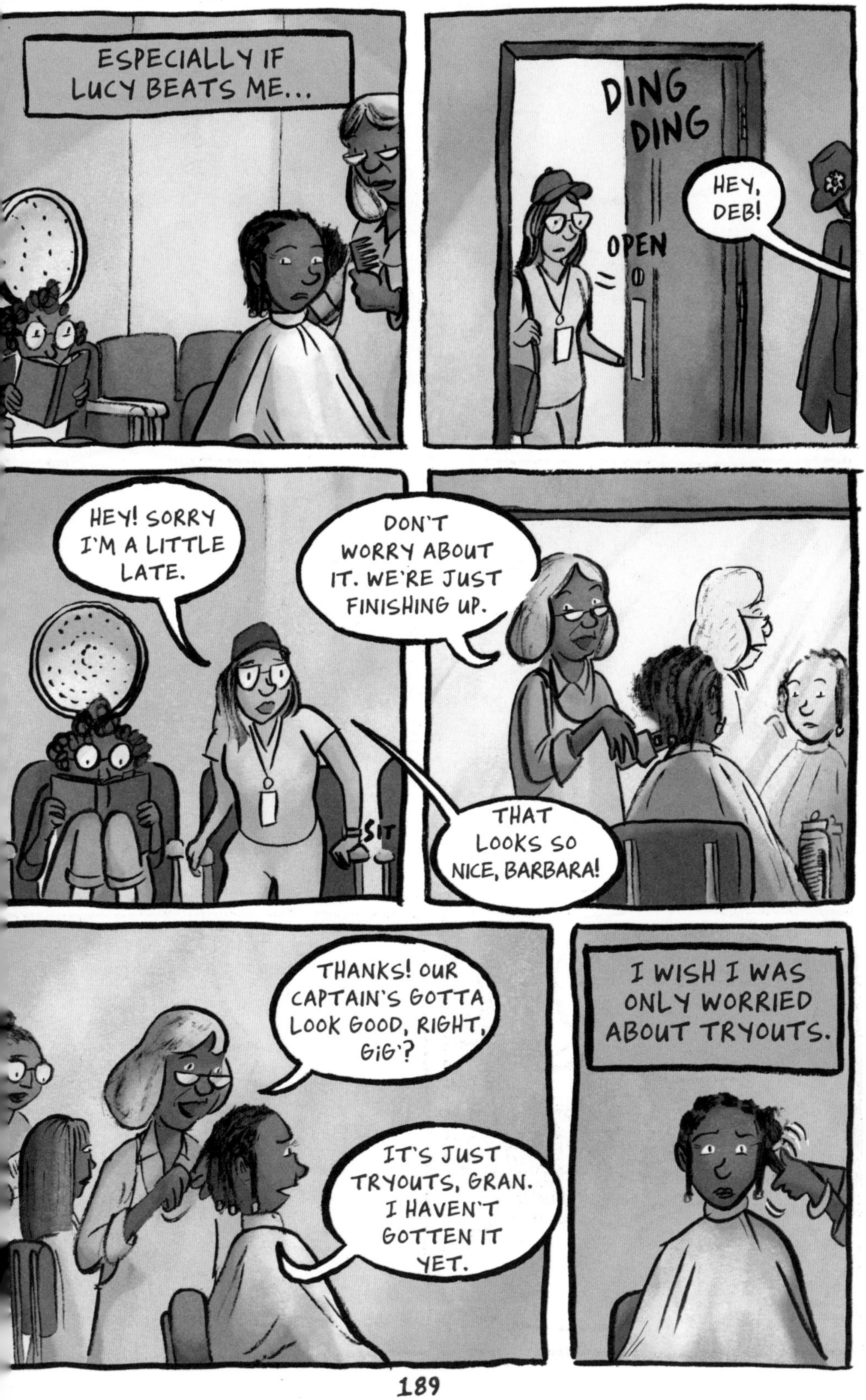
ESPECIALLY IF LUCY BEATS ME...
DING DING
OPEN
HEY, DEB!
HEY! SORRY I'M A LITTLE LATE.
DON'T WORRY ABOUT IT. WE'RE JUST FINISHING UP.
SIT
THAT LOOKS SO NICE, BARBARA!
THANKS! OUR CAPTAIN'S GOTTA LOOK GOOD, RIGHT, GIG'?
IT'S JUST TRYOUTS, GRAN. I HAVEN'T GOTTEN IT YET.
I WISH I WAS ONLY WORRIED ABOUT TRYOUTS.

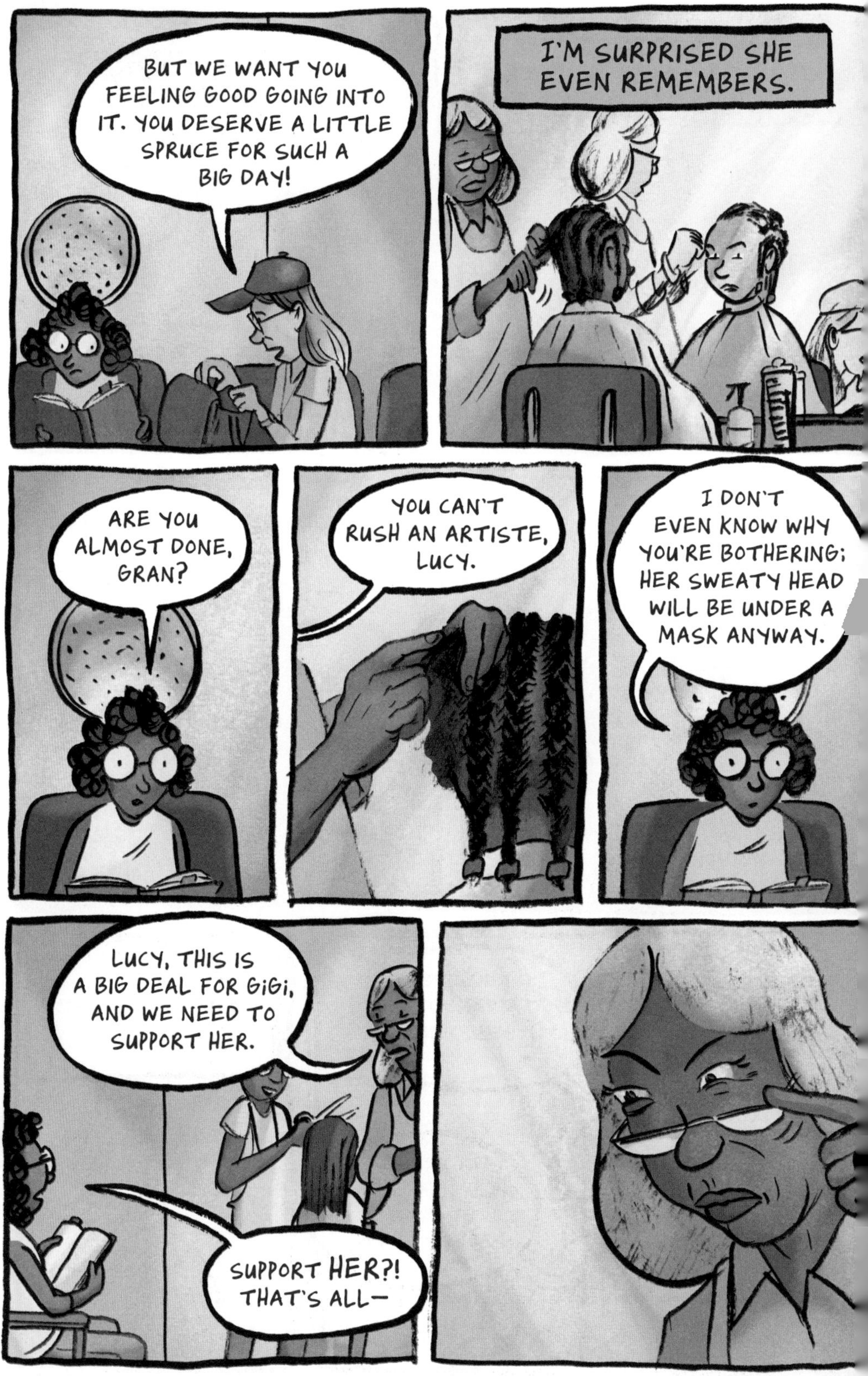
BUT WE WANT YOU FEELING GOOD GOING INTO IT. YOU DESERVE A LITTLE SPRUCE FOR SUCH A BIG DAY!
I'M SURPRISED SHE EVEN REMEMBERS.
ARE YOU ALMOST DONE, GRAN?
YOU CAN'T RUSH AN ARTISTE, LUCY.
I DON'T EVEN KNOW WHY YOU'RE BOTHERING: HER SWEATY HEAD WILL BE UNDER A MASK ANYWAY.
LUCY, THIS IS A BIG DEAL FOR GIGI, AND WE NEED TO SUPPORT HER.
SUPPORT HER?! THAT'S ALL—

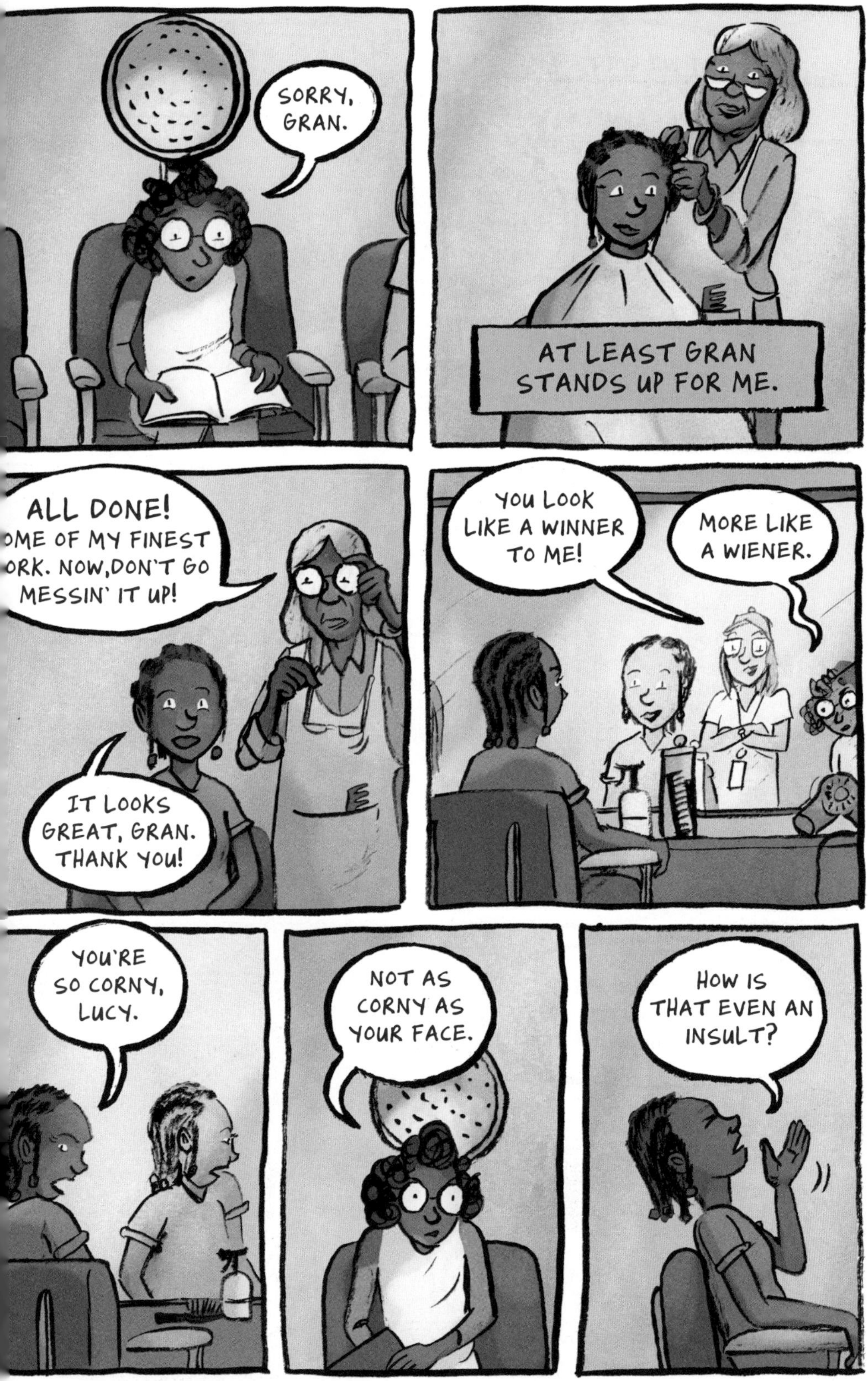
SORRY, GRAN.
AT LEAST GRAN STANDS UP FOR ME.
ALL DONE! OME OF MY FINEST ORK. NOW, DON'T GO MESSIN' IT UP!
IT LOOKS GREAT, GRAN. THANK YOU!
YOU LOOK LIKE A WINNER TO ME!
MORE LIKE A WIENER.
YOU'RE SO CORNY, LUCY.
NOT AS CORNY AS YOUR FACE.
HOW IS THAT EVEN AN INSULT?

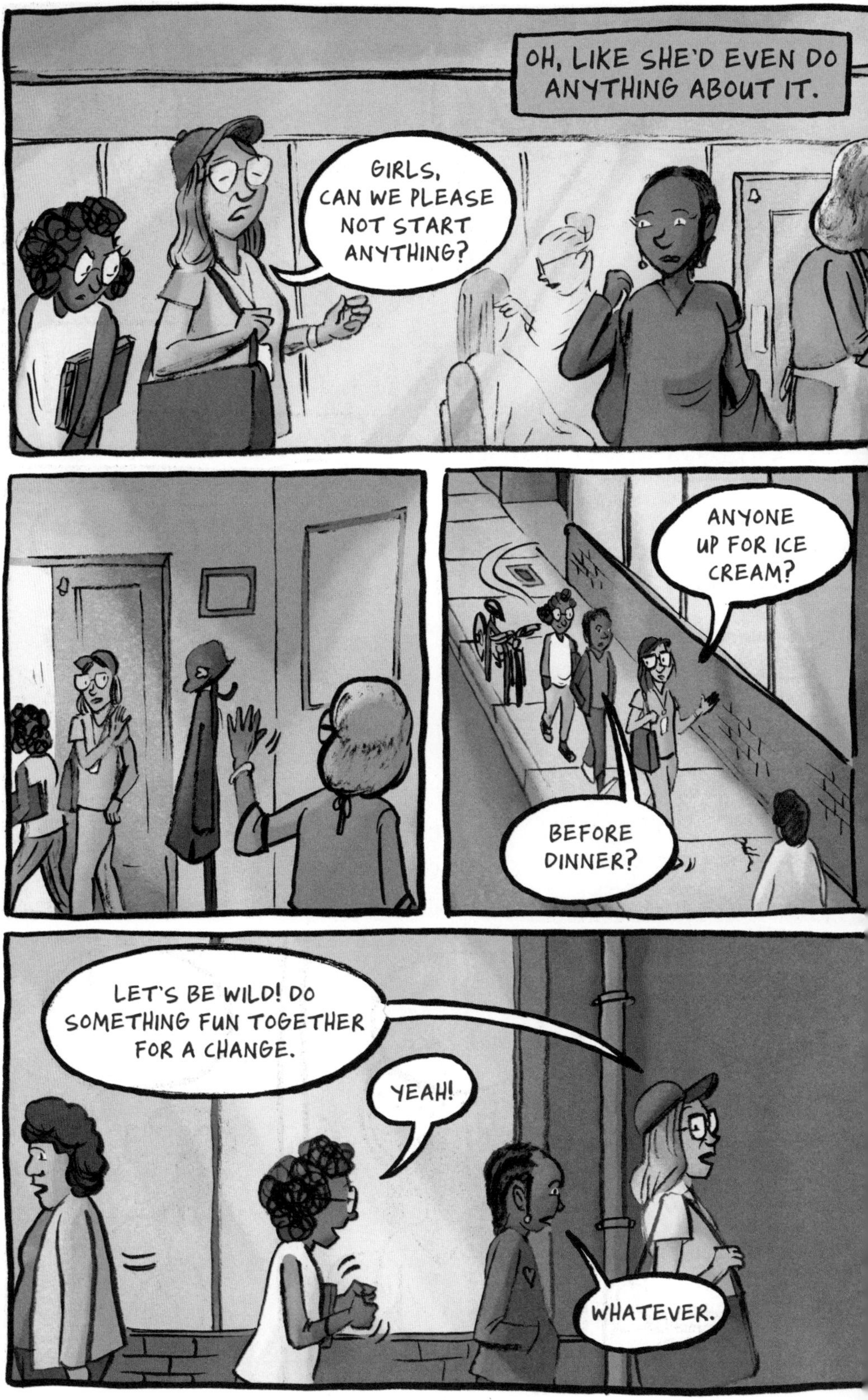
OH, LIKE SHE'D EVEN DO ANYTHING ABOUT IT.
GIRLS, CAN WE PLEASE NOT START ANYTHING?
ANYONE UP FOR ICE CREAM?
BEFORE DINNER?
LET'S BE WILD! DO SOMETHING FUN TOGETHER FOR A CHANGE.
YEAH!
WHATEVER.

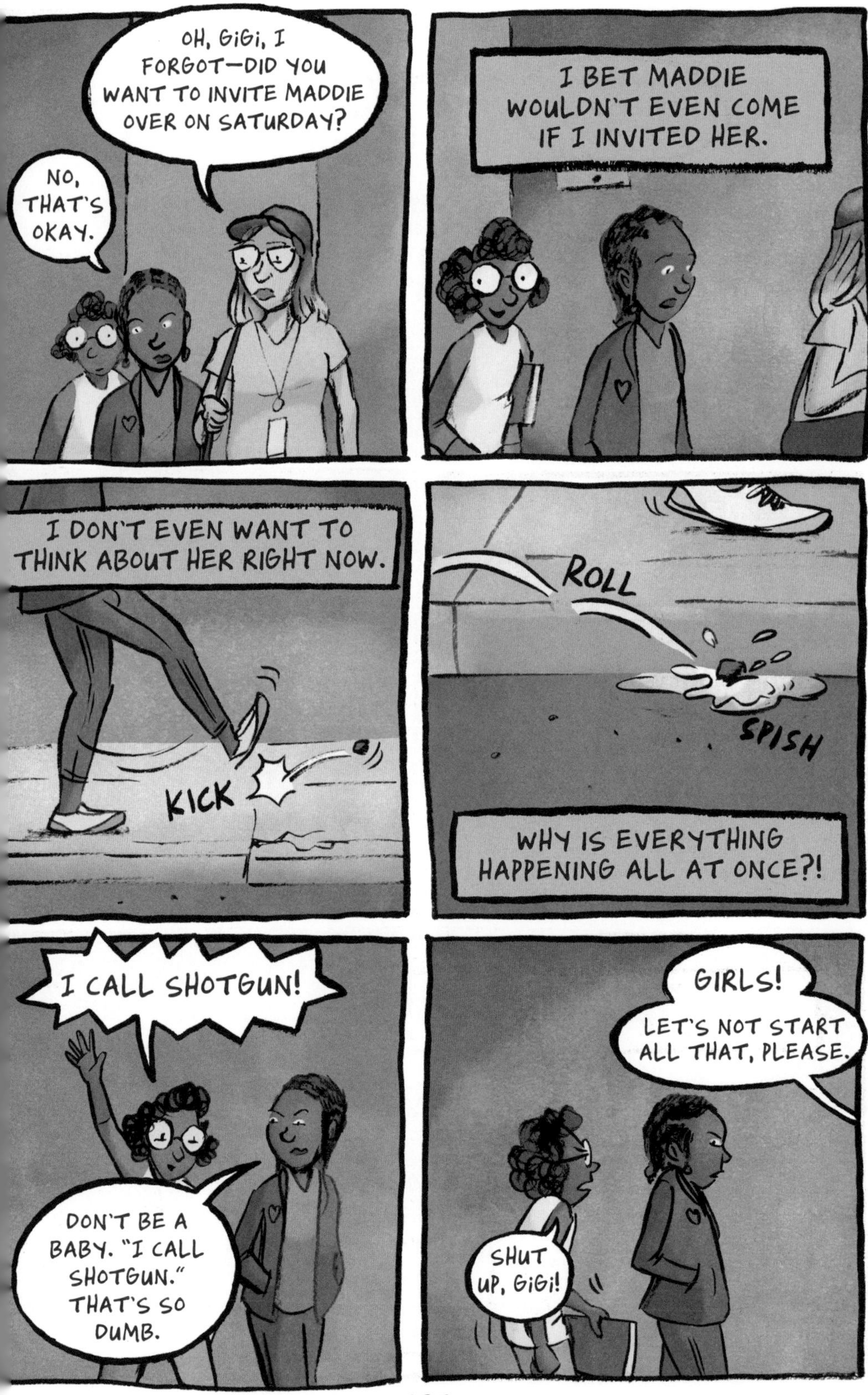
OH, GiGi, I FORGOT—DID YOU WANT TO INVITE MADDIE OVER ON SATURDAY?
NO, THAT'S OKAY.
I BET MADDIE WOULDN'T EVEN COME IF I INVITED HER.
I DON'T EVEN WANT TO THINK ABOUT HER RIGHT NOW.
KICK
ROLL
SPISH
WHY IS EVERYTHING HAPPENING ALL AT ONCE?!
I CALL SHOTGUN!
DON'T BE A BABY. "I CALL SHOTGUN." THAT'S SO DUMB.
GIRLS!
LET'S NOT START ALL THAT, PLEASE.
SHUT UP, GiGi!

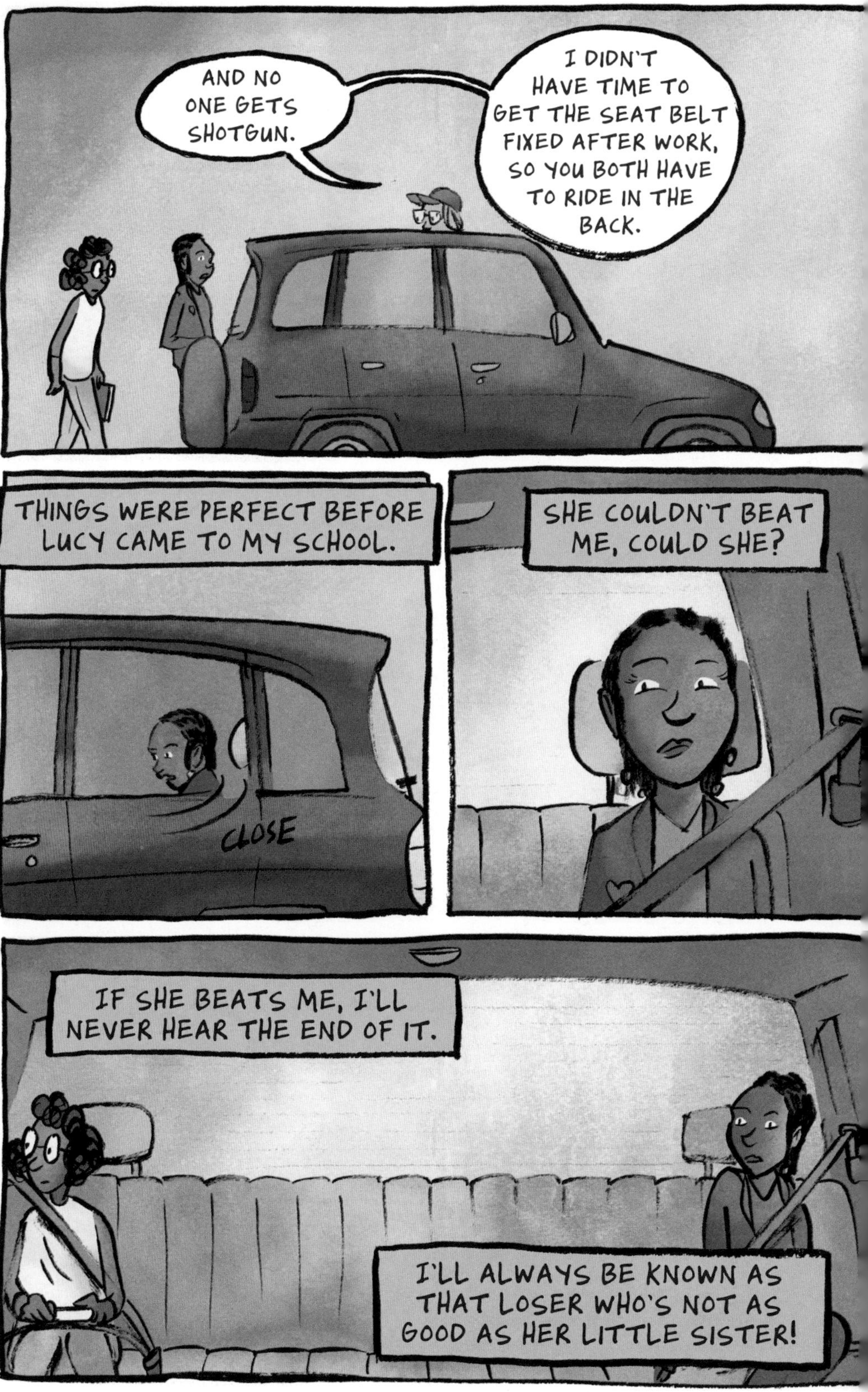
AND NO ONE GETS SHOTGUN.
I DIDN'T HAVE TIME TO GET THE SEAT BELT FIXED AFTER WORK, SO YOU BOTH HAVE TO RIDE IN THE BACK.
THINGS WERE PERFECT BEFORE LUCY CAME TO MY SCHOOL.
CLOSE
SHE COULDN'T BEAT ME, COULD SHE?
IF SHE BEATS ME, I'LL NEVER HEAR THE END OF IT.
I'LL ALWAYS BE KNOWN AS THAT LOSER WHO'S NOT AS GOOD AS HER LITTLE SISTER!

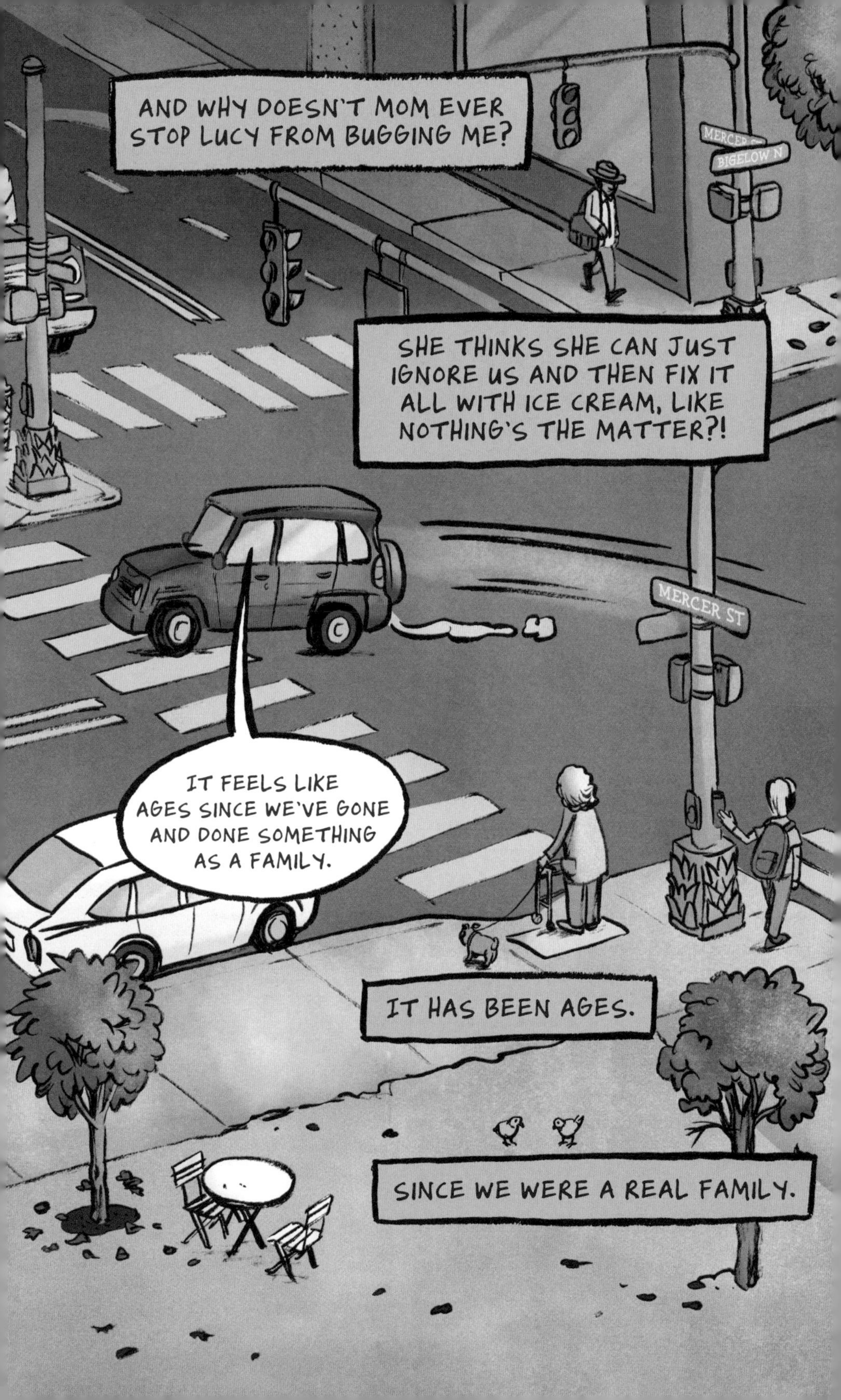
AND WHY DOESN'T MOM EVER STOP LUCY FROM BUGGING ME?
MERCER
BIGELOW N
SHE THINKS SHE CAN JUST IGNORE US AND THEN FIX IT ALL WITH ICE CREAM, LIKE NOTHING'S THE MATTER?!
MERCER ST
IT FEELS LIKE AGES SINCE WE'VE GONE AND DONE SOMETHING AS A FAMILY.
IT HAS BEEN AGES.
SINCE WE WERE A REAL FAMILY.

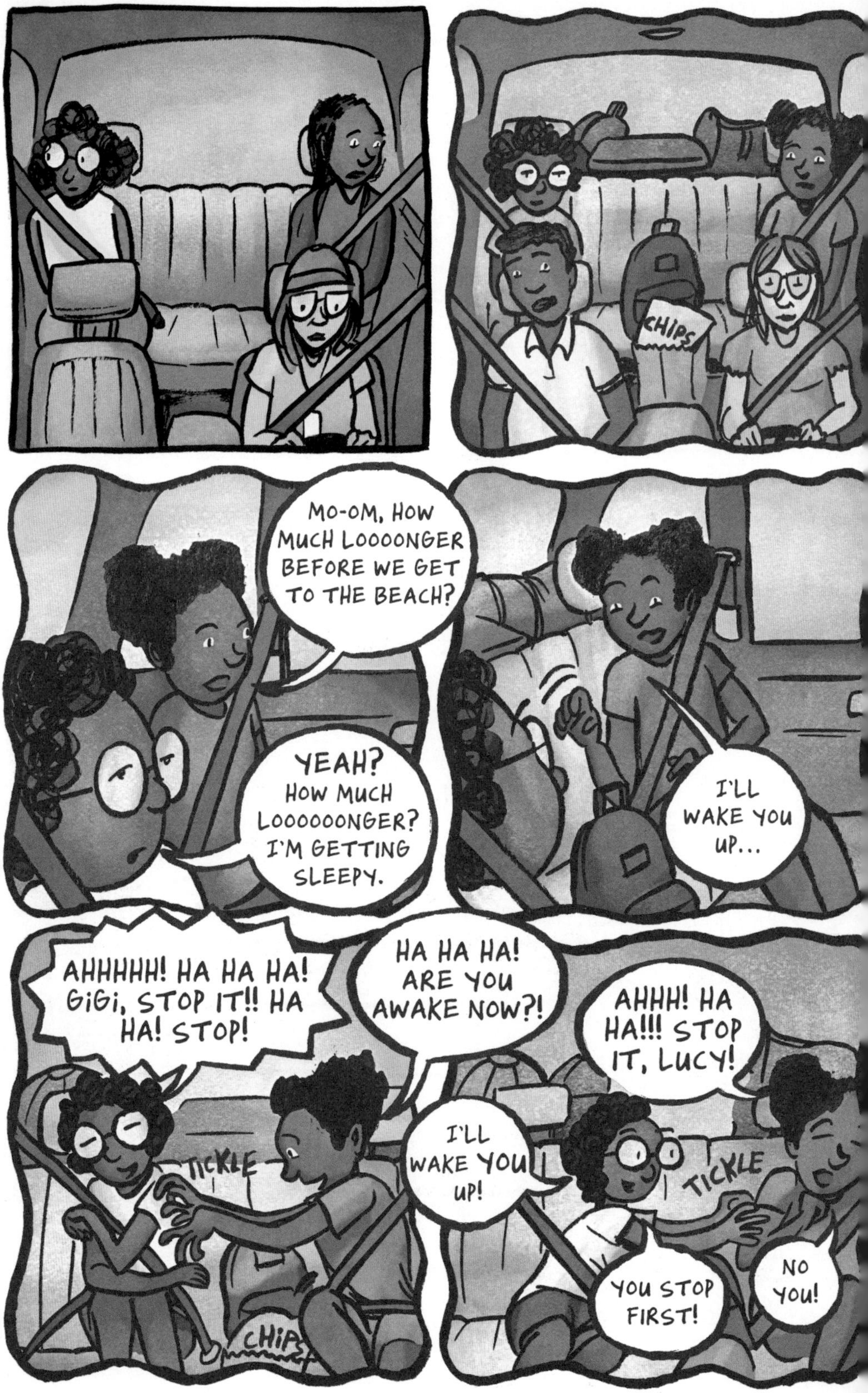

MO-OM, HOW MUCH LOOOONGER BEFORE WE GET TO THE BEACH?
YEAH? HOW MUCH LOOOOOONGER? I'M GETTING SLEEPY.
I'LL WAKE YOU UP...
AHHHHH! HA HA HA! GiGi, STOP IT!! HA HA! STOP!
HA HA HA! ARE YOU AWAKE NOW?!
TICKLE
CHIPS
AHHH! HA HA!!! STOP IT, LUCY!
I'LL WAKE YOU UP!
TICKLE
YOU STOP FIRST!
NO YOU!

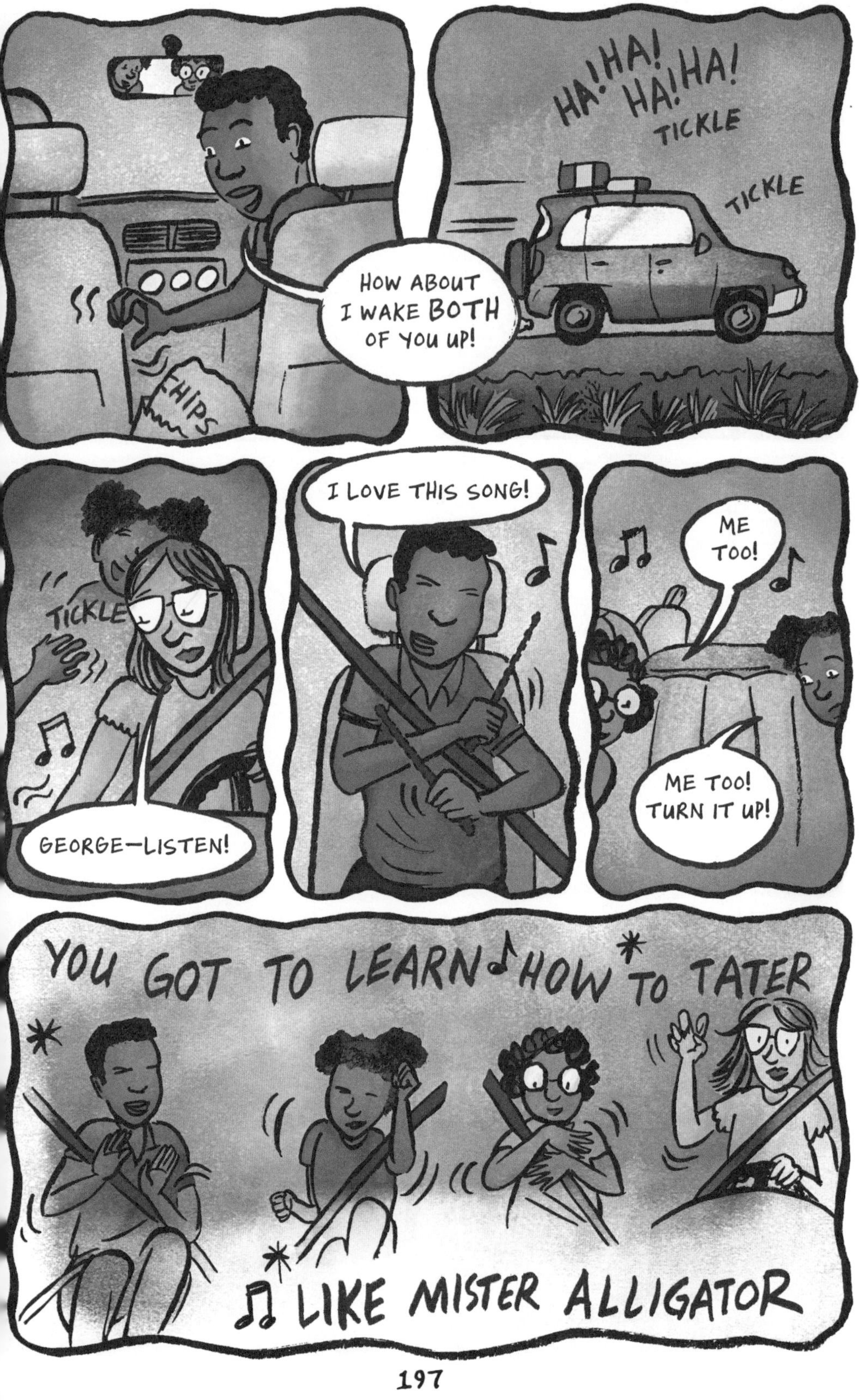
HOW ABOUT I WAKE BOTH OF YOU UP!
CHIPS
HA! HA! HA! HA!
TICKLE
TICKLE
TICKLE
GEORGE—LISTEN!
I LOVE THIS SONG!
ME TOO!
ME TOO! TURN IT UP!
YOU GOT TO LEARN HOW TO TATER
LIKE MISTER ALLIGATOR

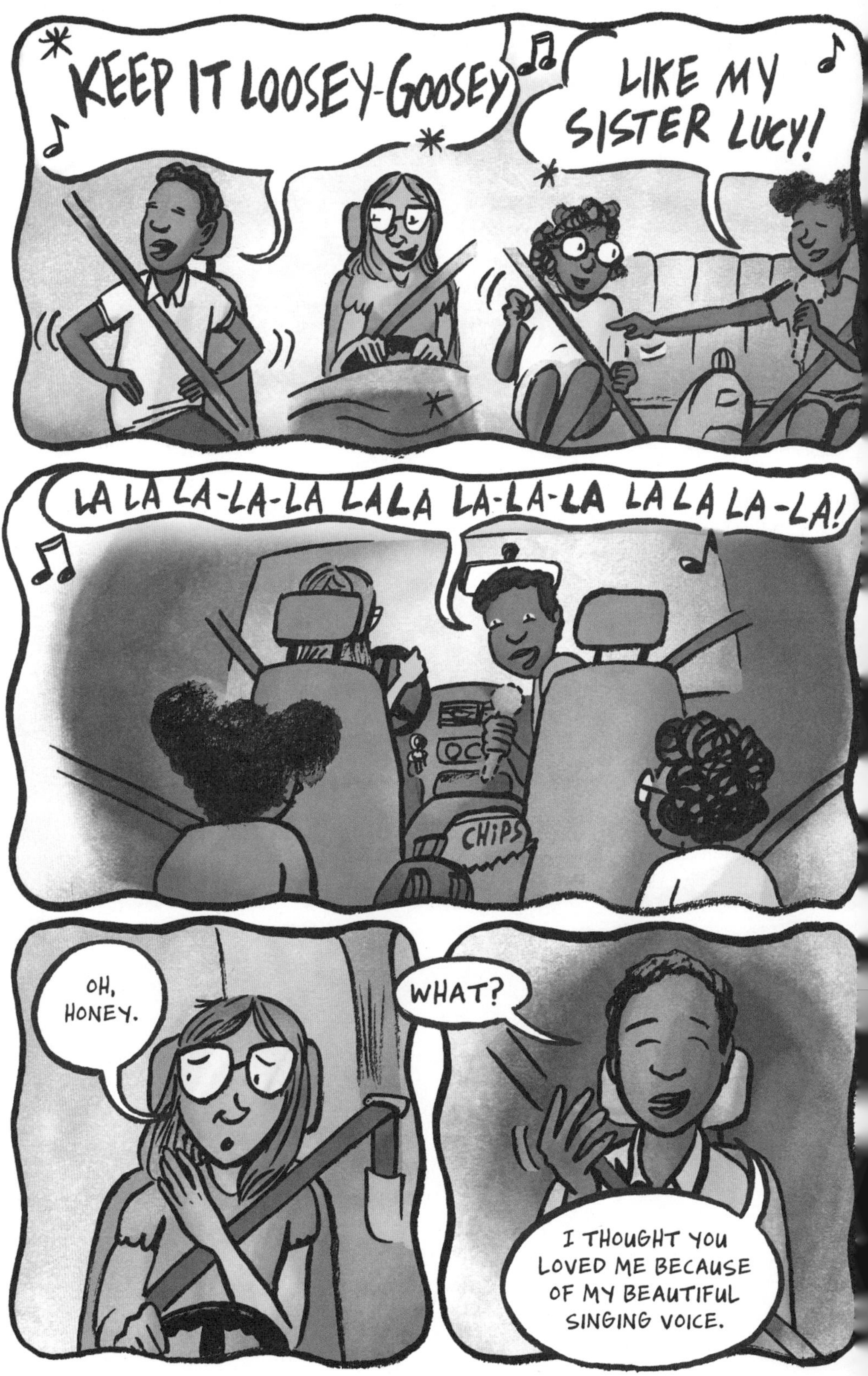
KEEP IT LOOSEY-GOOSEY
LIKE MY SISTER LUCY!
LA LA LA-LA-LA LALA LA-LA-LA LA LA LA LA-LA!
CHIPS
OH, HONEY.
WHAT?
I THOUGHT YOU LOVED ME BECAUSE OF MY BEAUTIFUL SINGING VOICE.

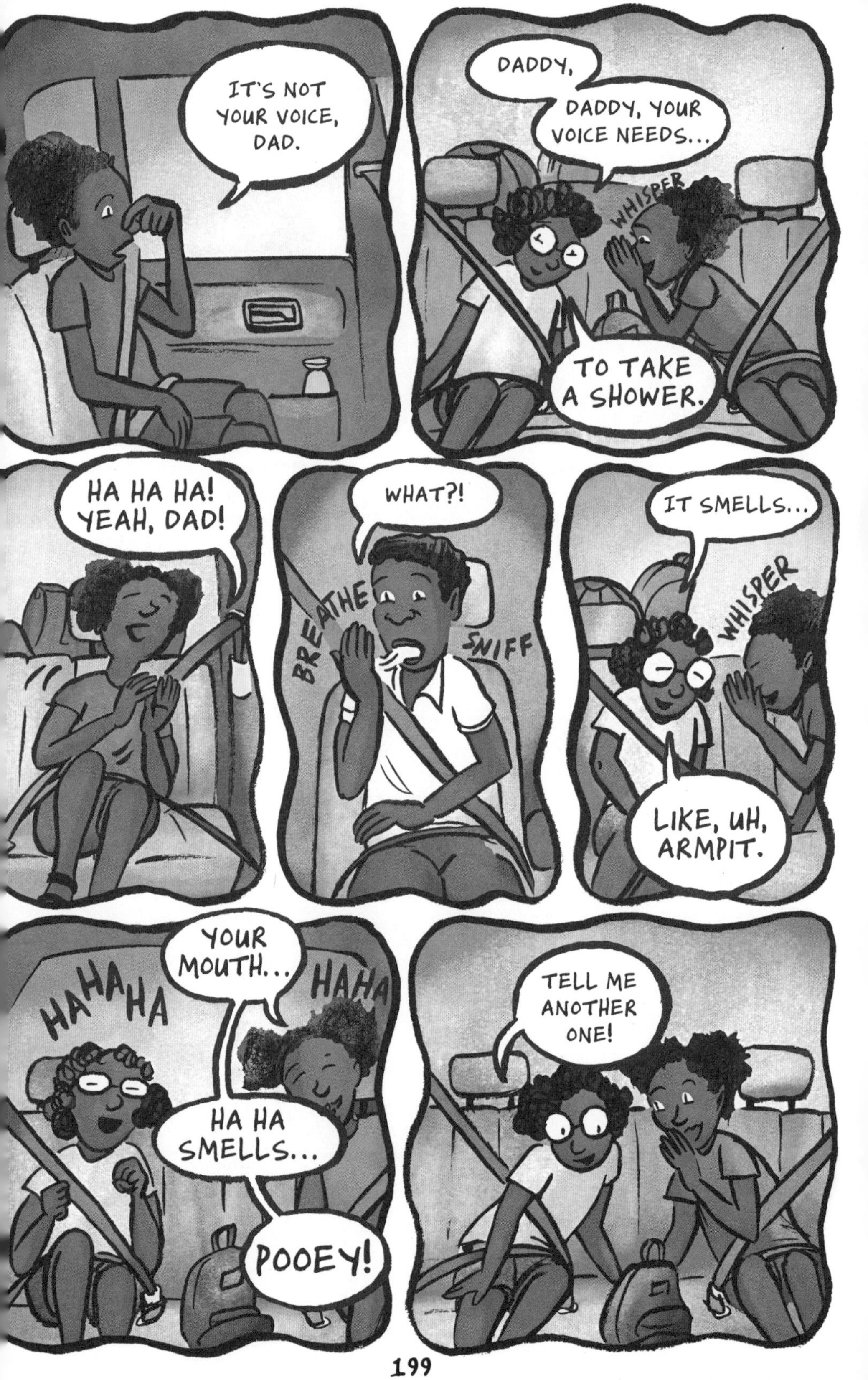
IT'S NOT YOUR VOICE, DAD.
DADDY,
DADDY, YOUR VOICE NEEDS...
WHISPER
TO TAKE A SHOWER.
HA HA HA! YEAH, DAD!
WHAT?!
BREATHE
SNIFF
IT SMELLS...
WHISPER
LIKE, UH, ARMPIT.
YOUR MOUTH...
HAHAHAHA
HAHA
HA HA SMELLS...
POOEY!
TELL ME ANOTHER ONE!

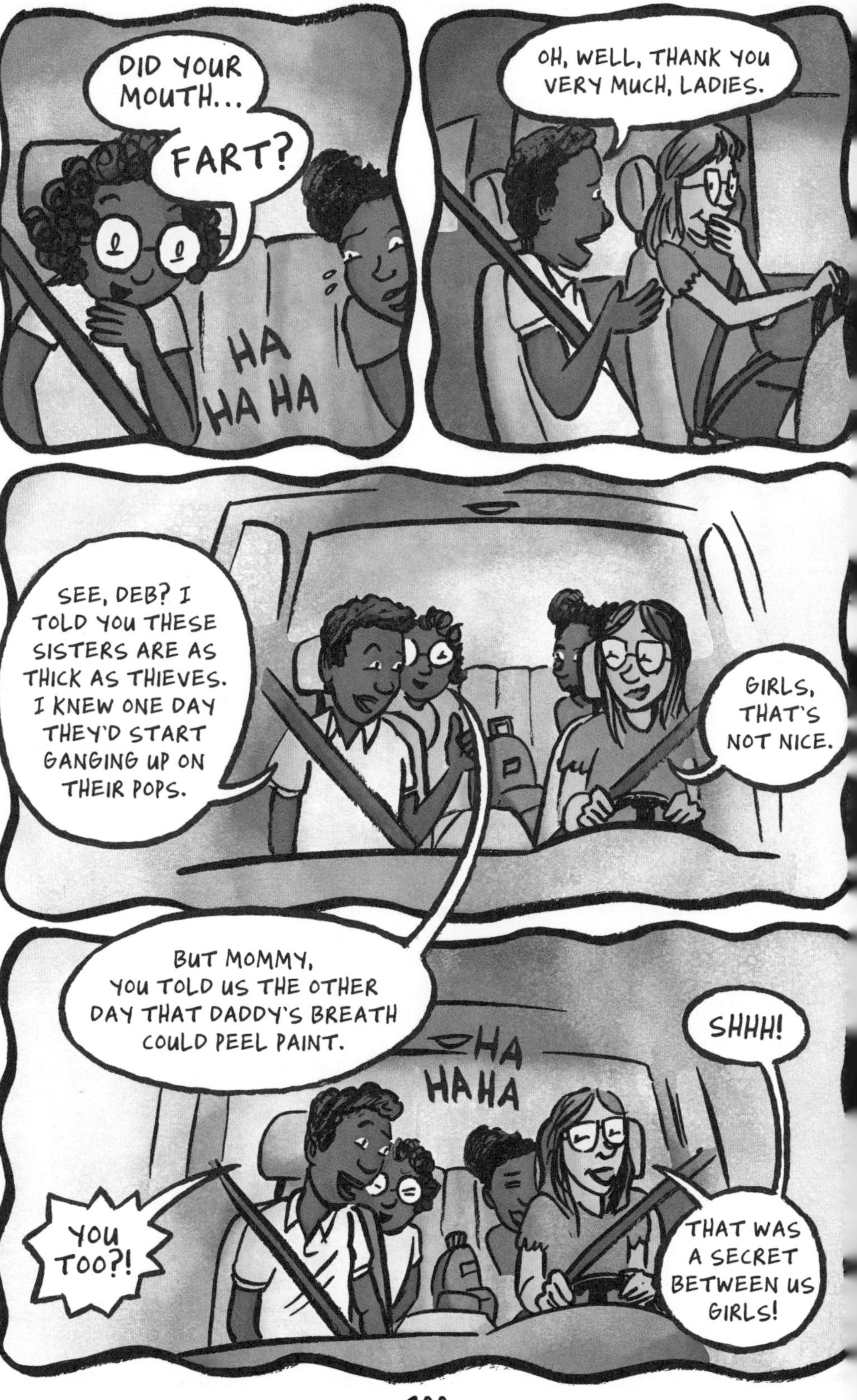
DID YOUR MOUTH...
FART?
HA HA HA
OH, WELL, THANK YOU VERY MUCH, LADIES.
SEE, DEB? I TOLD YOU THESE SISTERS ARE AS THICK AS THIEVES. I KNEW ONE DAY THEY'D START GANGING UP ON THEIR POPS.
GIRLS, THAT'S NOT NICE.
BUT MOMMY, YOU TOLD US THE OTHER DAY THAT DADDY'S BREATH COULD PEEL PAINT.
HA HAHA
SHHH!
YOU TOO?!
THAT WAS A SECRET BETWEEN US GIRLS!

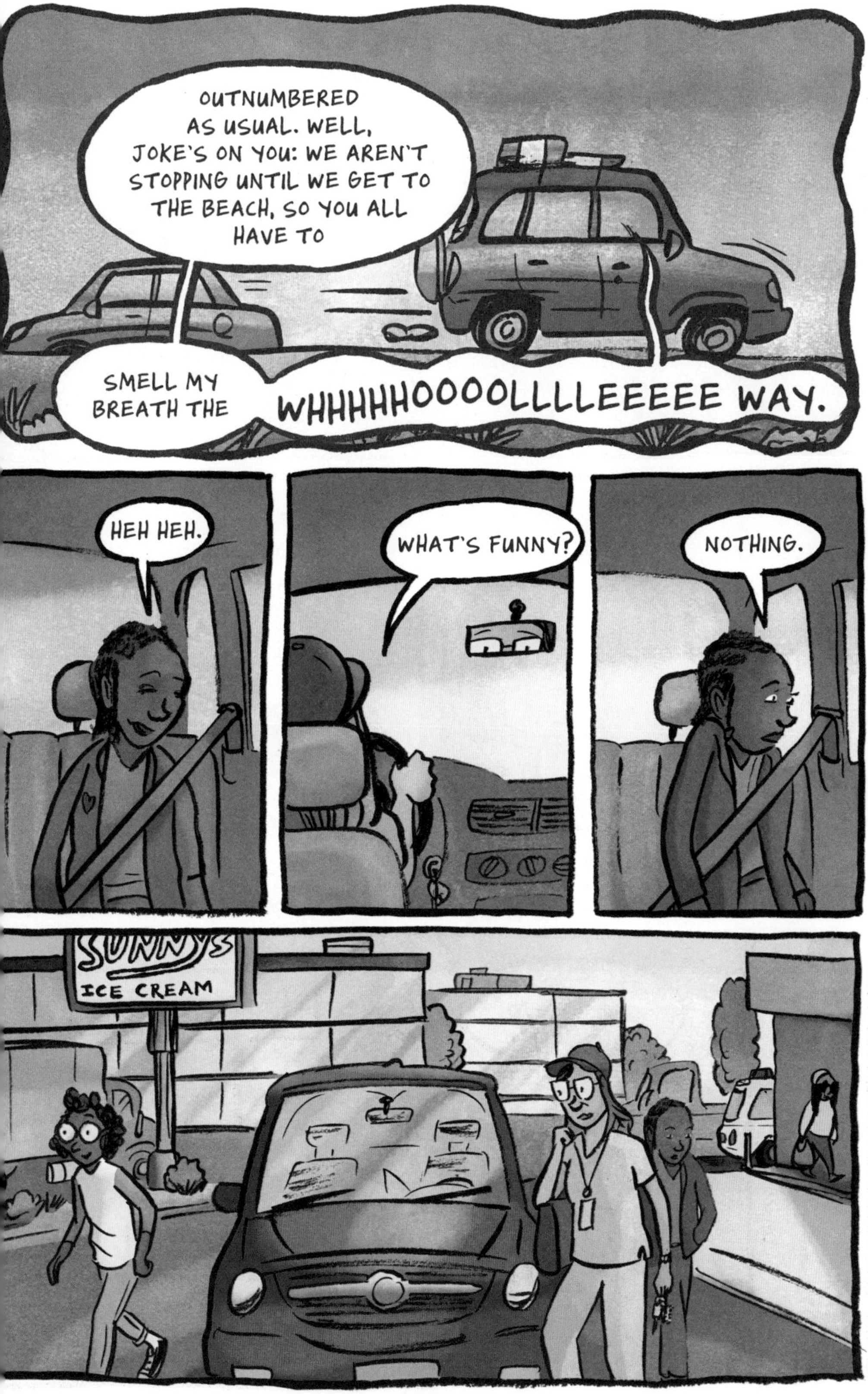
OUTNUMBERED AS USUAL. WELL, JOKE'S ON YOU: WE AREN'T STOPPING UNTIL WE GET TO THE BEACH, SO YOU ALL HAVE TO
SMELL MY BREATH THE
WHHHHHOOOOOLLLLLEEEEE WAY.
HEH HEH.
WHAT'S FUNNY?
NOTHING.
SUNNY'S
ICE CREAM

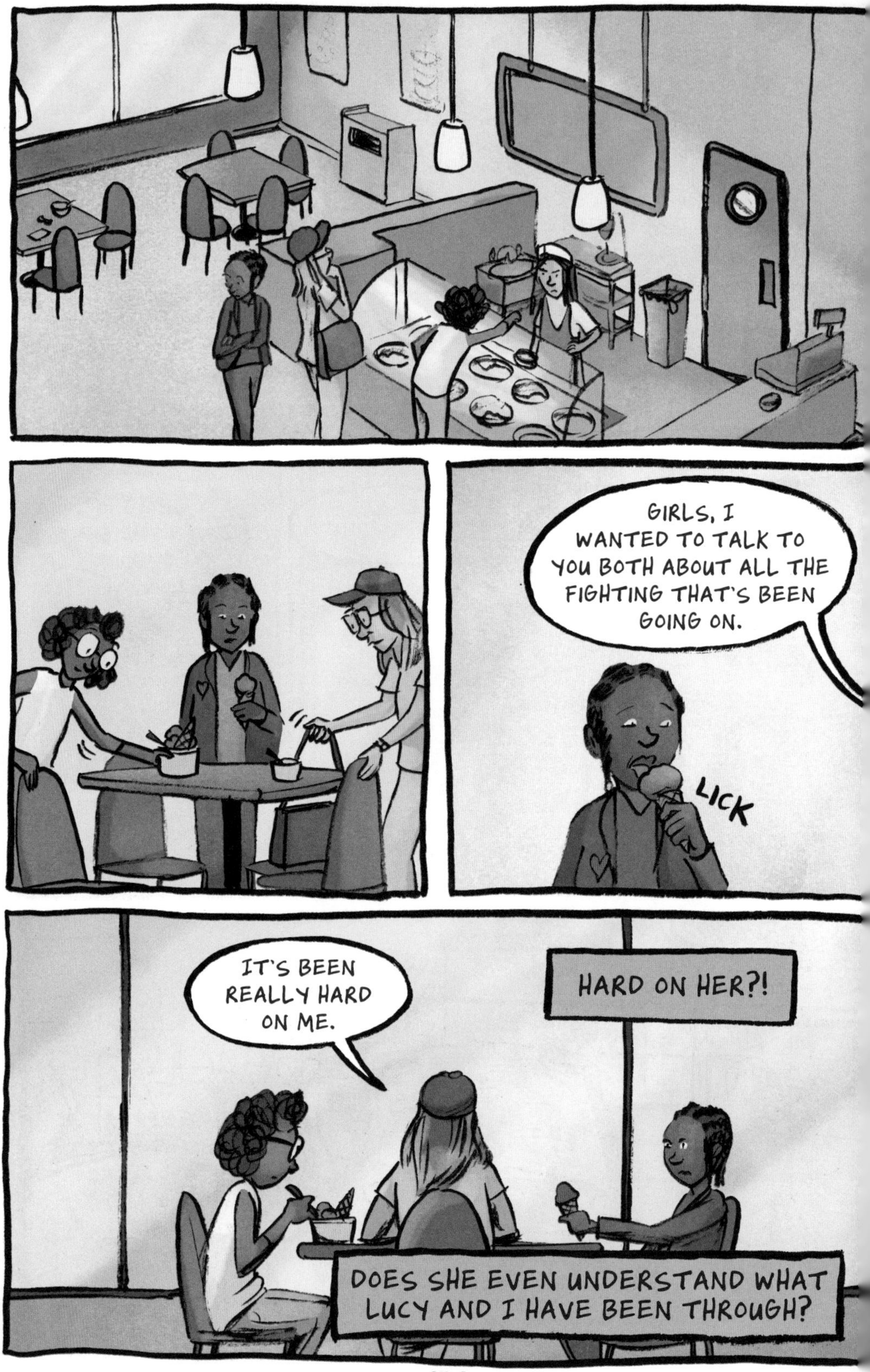
GIRLS, I WANTED TO TALK TO YOU BOTH ABOUT ALL THE FIGHTING THAT'S BEEN GOING ON.
LICK
IT'S BEEN REALLY HARD ON ME.
HARD ON HER?!
DOES SHE EVEN UNDERSTAND WHAT LUCY AND I HAVE BEEN THROUGH?

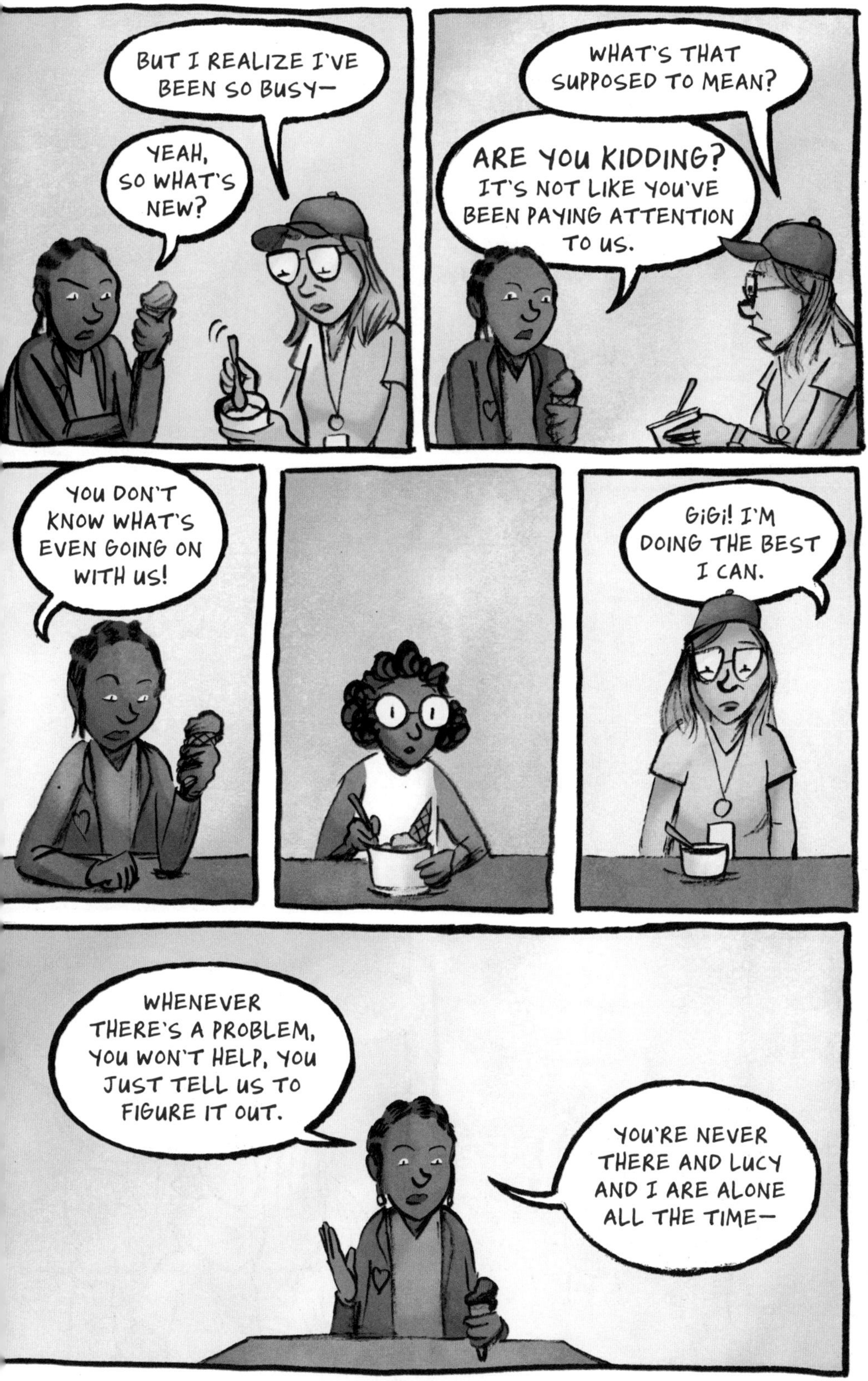
BUT I REALIZE I'VE BEEN SO BUSY—
YEAH, SO WHAT'S NEW?
WHAT'S THAT SUPPOSED TO MEAN?
ARE YOU KIDDING? IT'S NOT LIKE YOU'VE BEEN PAYING ATTENTION TO US.
YOU DON'T KNOW WHAT'S EVEN GOING ON WITH US!
GIGI! I'M DOING THE BEST I CAN.
WHENEVER THERE'S A PROBLEM, YOU WON'T HELP, YOU JUST TELL US TO FIGURE IT OUT.
YOU'RE NEVER THERE AND LUCY AND I ARE ALONE ALL THE TIME—

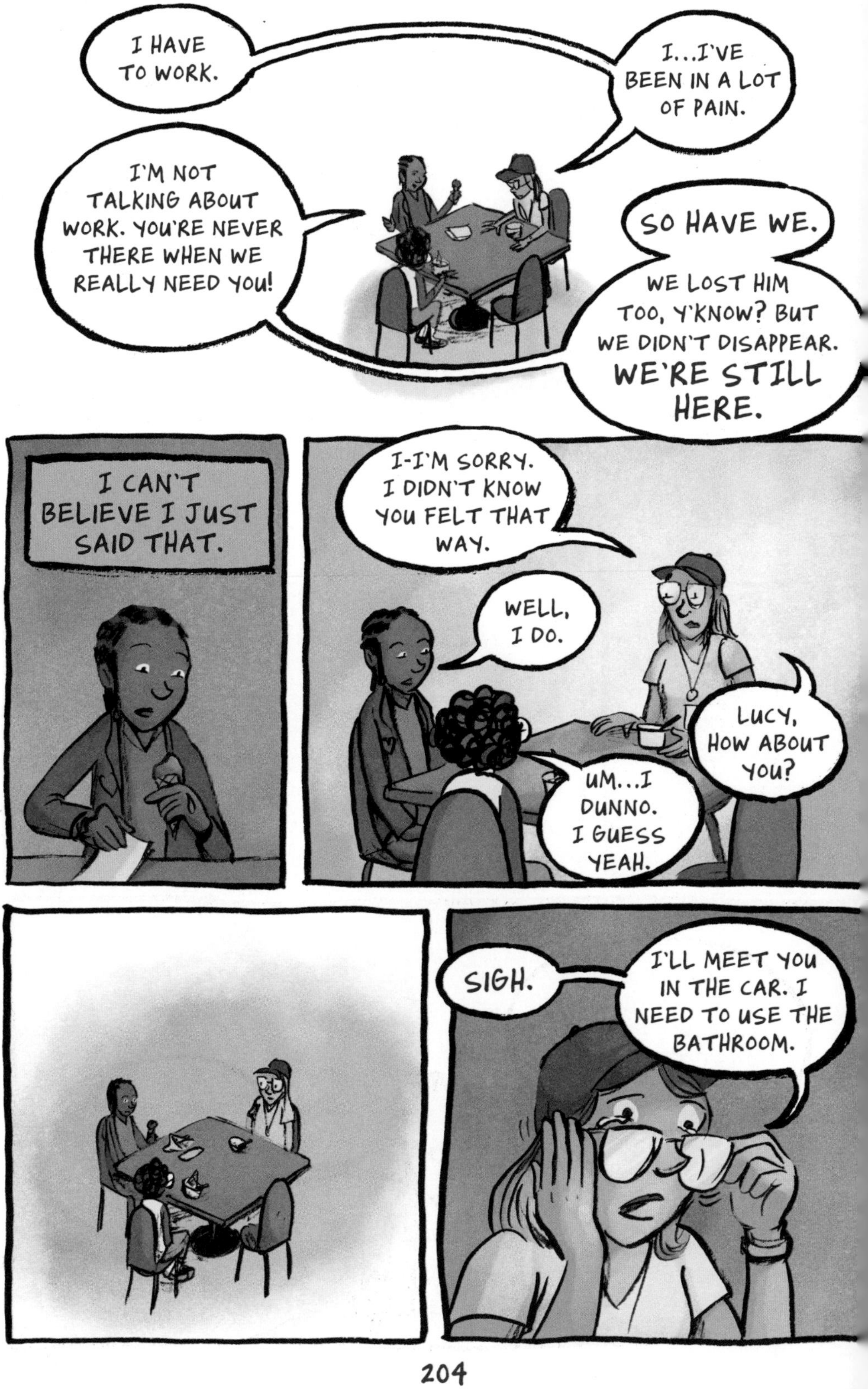

I HAVE TO WORK.
I...I'VE BEEN IN A LOT OF PAIN.
I'M NOT TALKING ABOUT WORK. YOU'RE NEVER THERE WHEN WE REALLY NEED YOU!
SO HAVE WE.
WE LOST HIM TOO, Y'KNOW? BUT WE DIDN'T DISAPPEAR. WE'RE STILL HERE.
I CAN'T BELIEVE I JUST SAID THAT.
I-I'M SORRY. I DIDN'T KNOW YOU FELT THAT WAY.
WELL, I DO.
LUCY, HOW ABOUT YOU?
UM...I DUNNO. I GUESS YEAH.
SIGH.
I'LL MEET YOU IN THE CAR. I NEED TO USE THE BATHROOM.

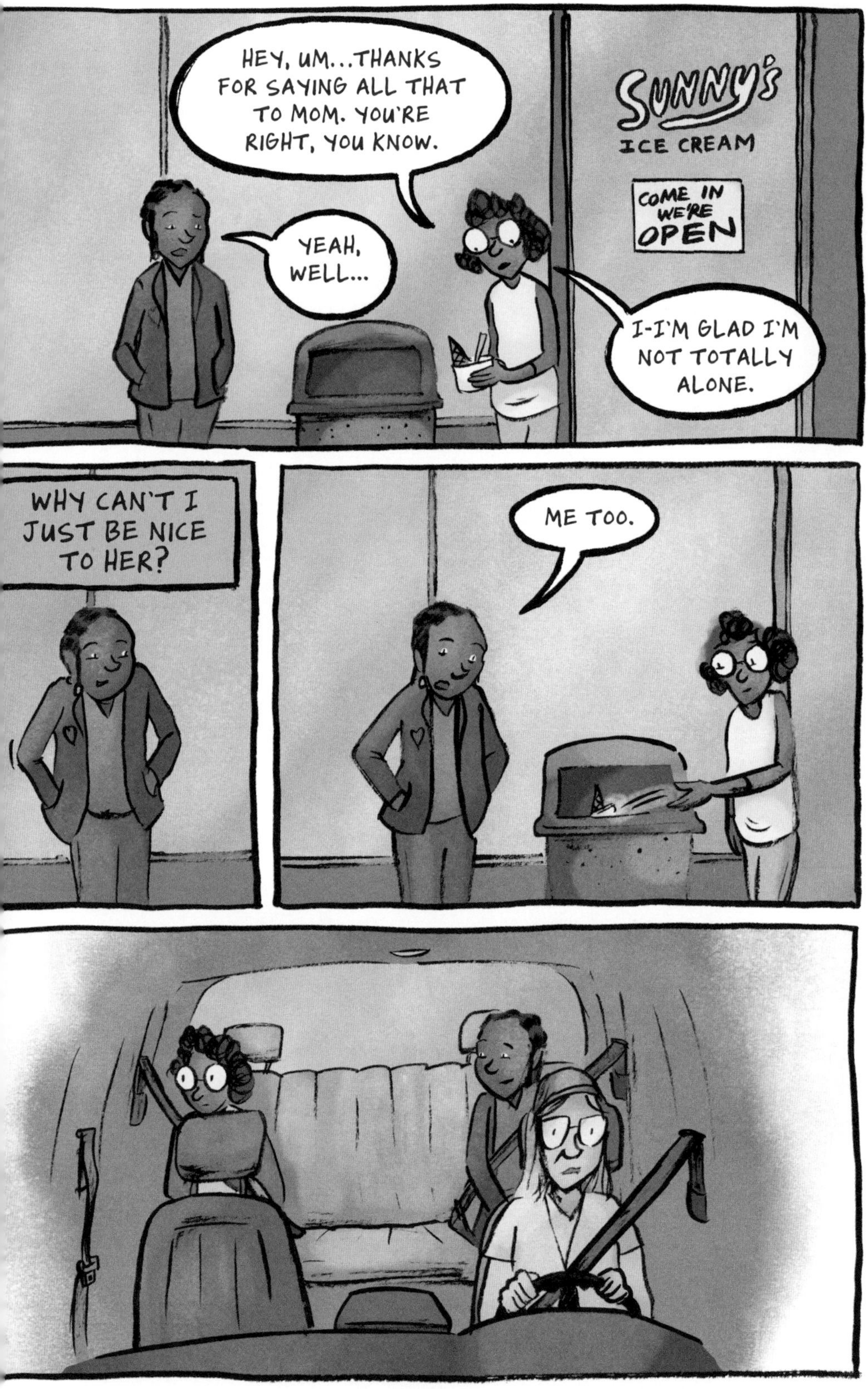
HEY, UM...THANKS FOR SAYING ALL THAT TO MOM. YOU'RE RIGHT, YOU KNOW.
SUNNY'S
ICE CREAM
COME IN WE'RE OPEN
YEAH, WELL...
I-I'M GLAD I'M NOT TOTALLY ALONE.
WHY CAN'T I JUST BE NICE TO HER?
ME TOO.

Chapter 13

Bind

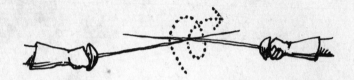

The bind, also called the pris de fer, is an action in which the fencer takes the opponent's blade into a line and holds it there in preparation to attack. When the fencer takes the opponent's blade with the strong part of their own blade (the forte), the blades become bound up with each other. There are four main binds that can be done to take control of your opponent's blade. When one is in a bind, it might seem as if there is no way out.

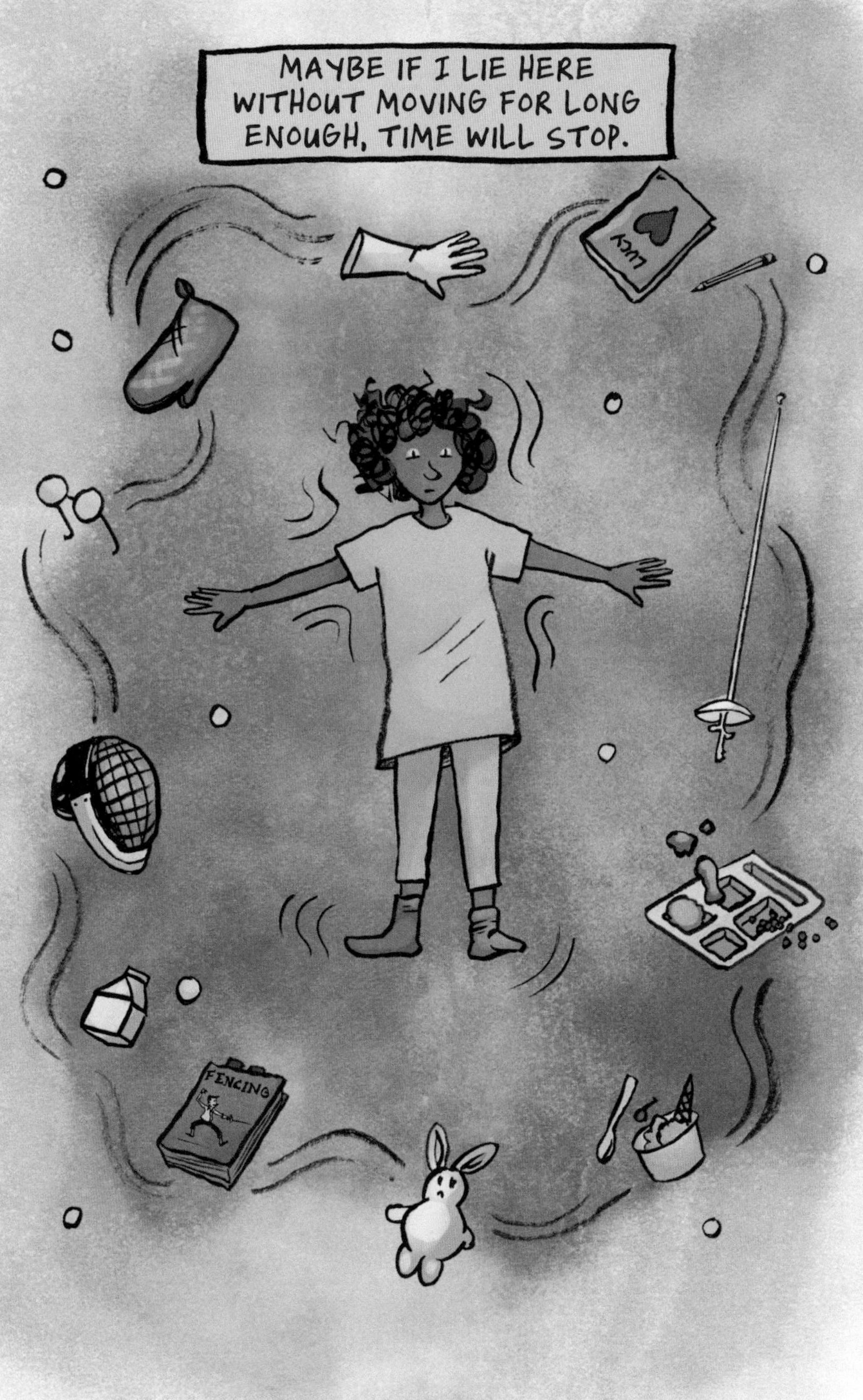
MAYBE IF I LIE HERE WITHOUT MOVING FOR LONG ENOUGH, TIME WILL STOP.
LUCY
FENCING

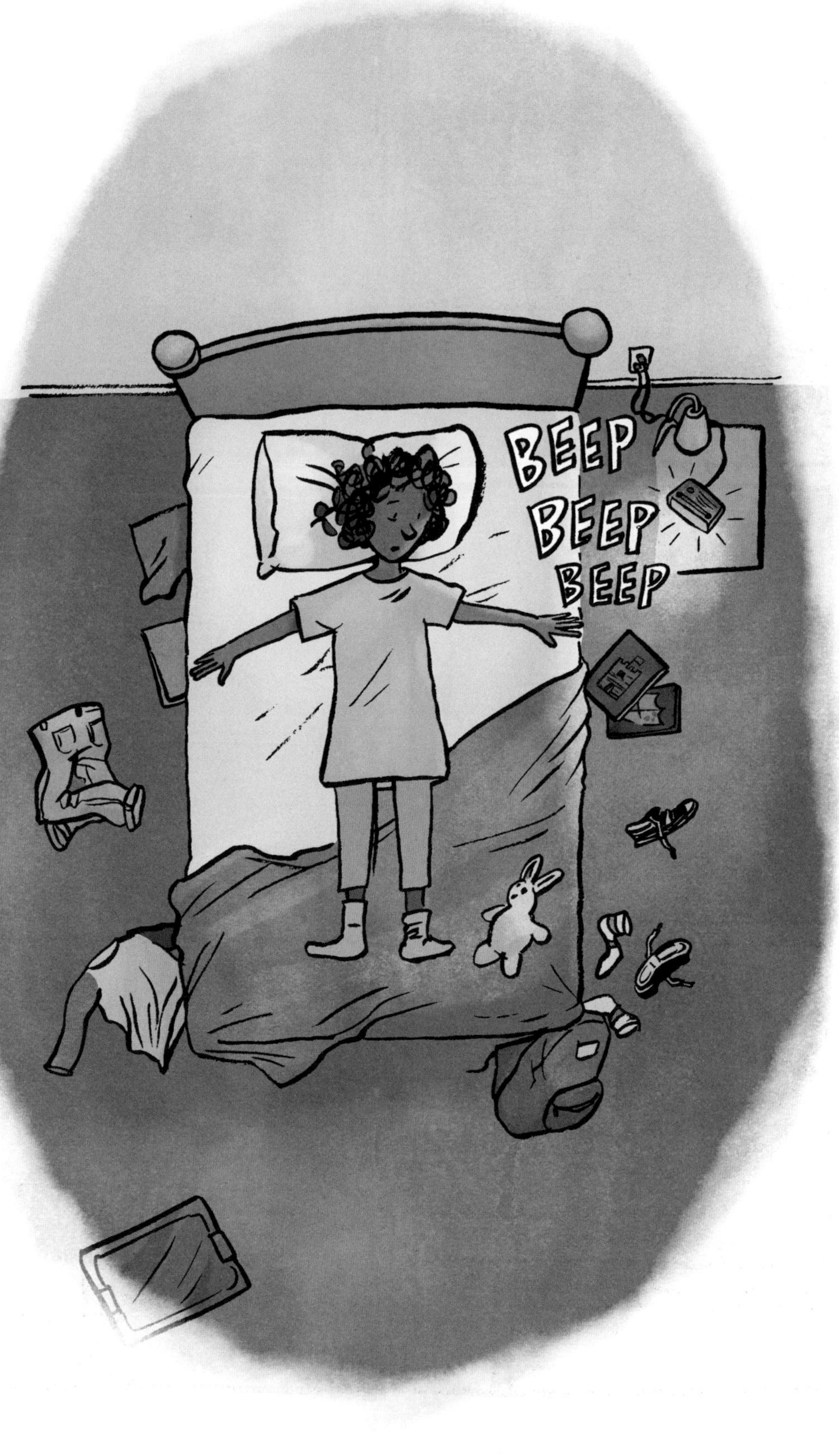
BEEP
BEEP
BEEP

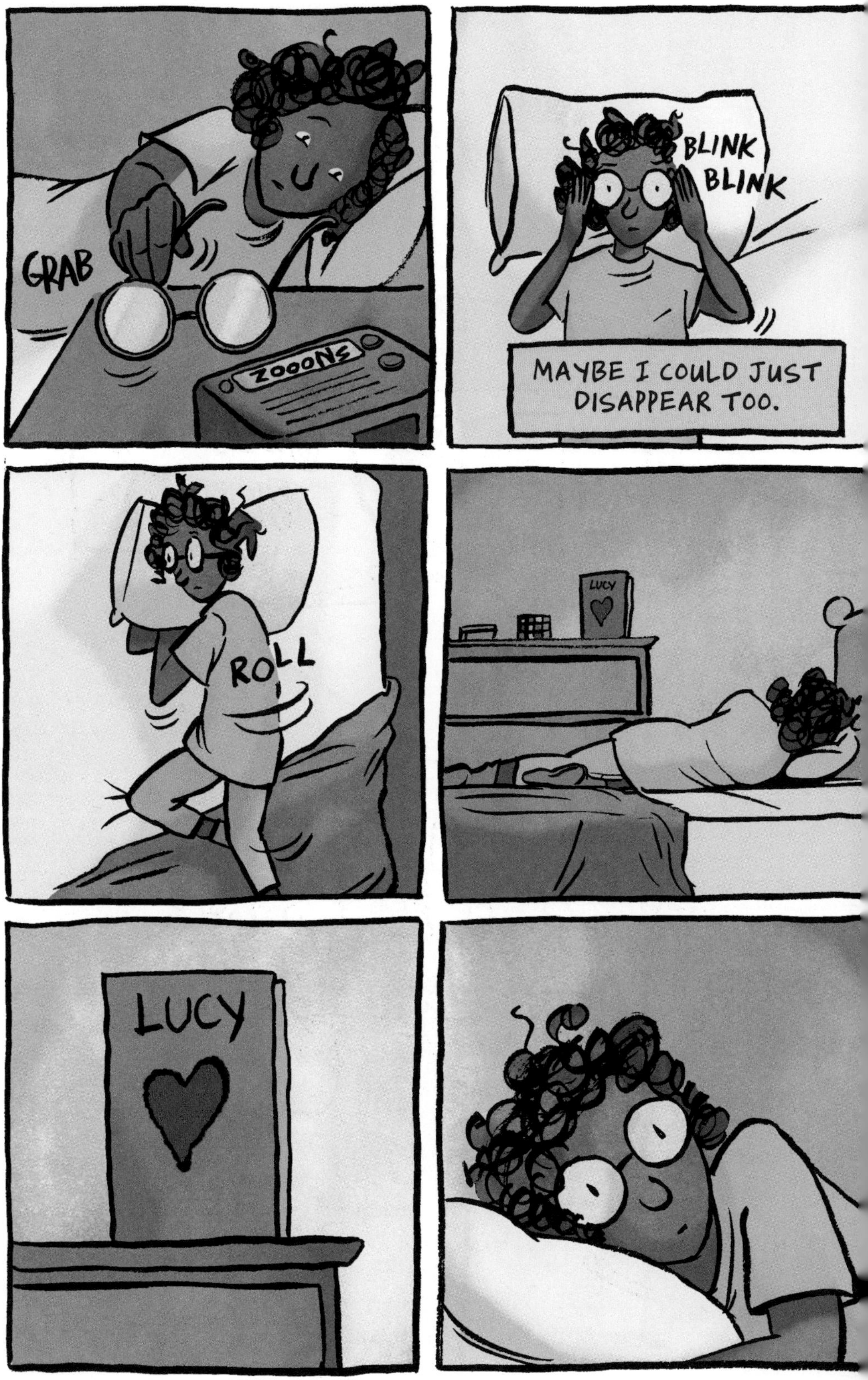
GRAB
ZOOONS
BLINK
BLINK
MAYBE I COULD JUST DISAPPEAR TOO.
ROLL
LUCY
LUCY

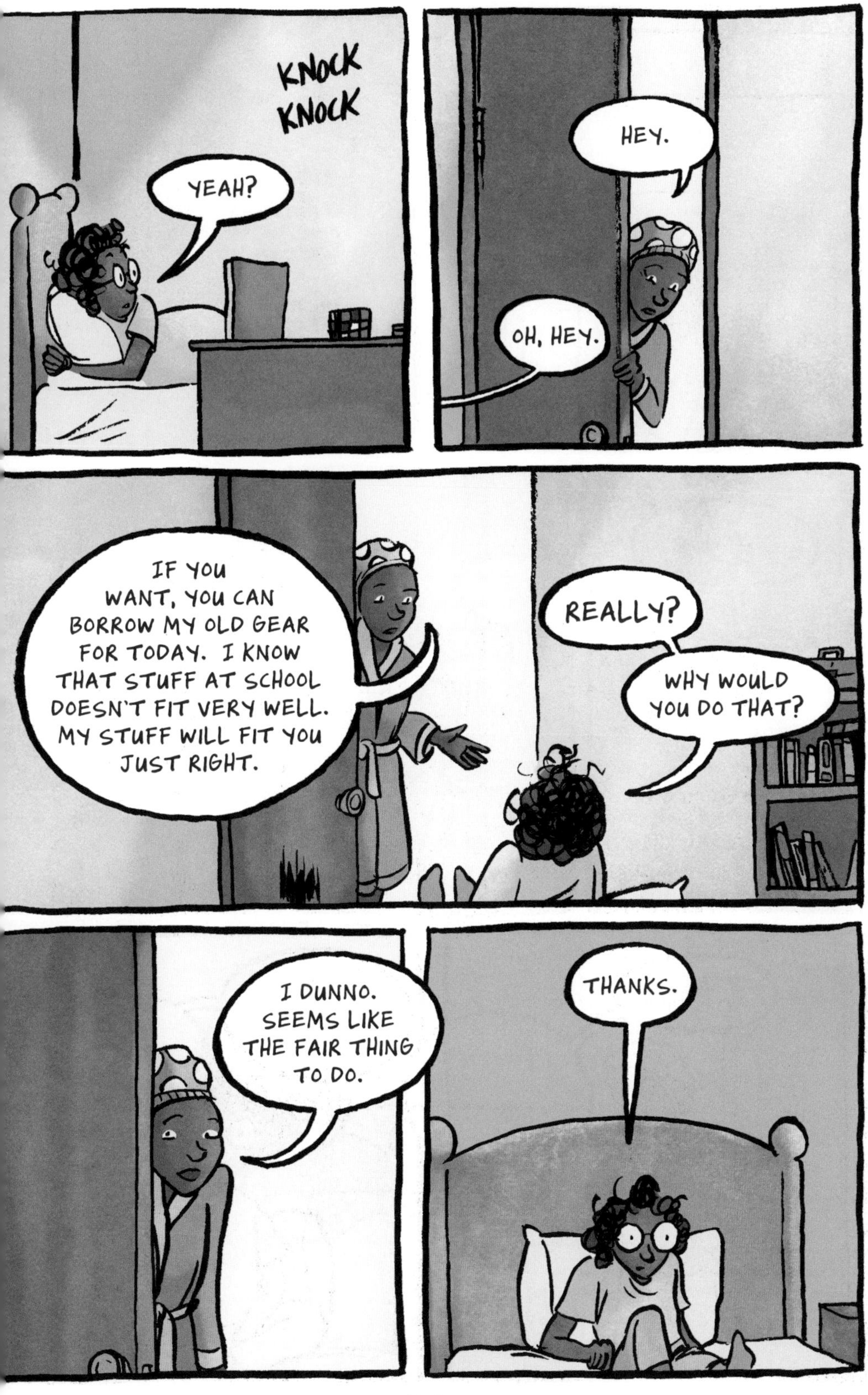
KNOCK KNOCK
YEAH?
HEY.
OH, HEY.
IF YOU WANT, YOU CAN BORROW MY OLD GEAR FOR TODAY. I KNOW THAT STUFF AT SCHOOL DOESN'T FIT VERY WELL. MY STUFF WILL FIT YOU JUST RIGHT.
REALLY?
WHY WOULD YOU DO THAT?
I DUNNO. SEEMS LIKE THE FAIR THING TO DO.
THANKS.

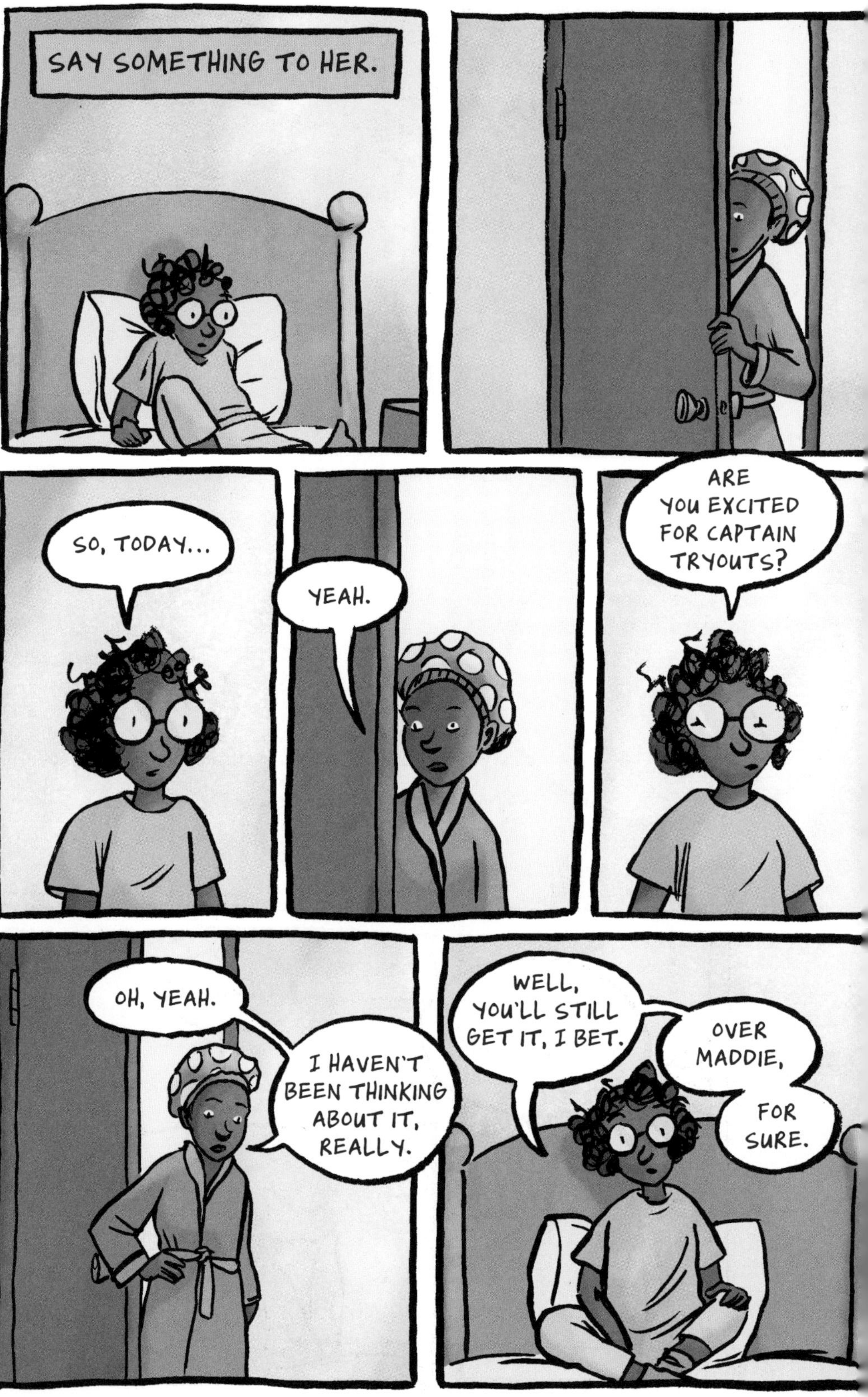
SAY SOMETHING TO HER.
SO, TODAY...
YEAH.
ARE YOU EXCITED FOR CAPTAIN TRYOUTS?
OH, YEAH.
I HAVEN'T BEEN THINKING ABOUT IT, REALLY.
WELL, YOU'LL STILL GET IT, I BET.
OVER MADDIE,
FOR SURE.

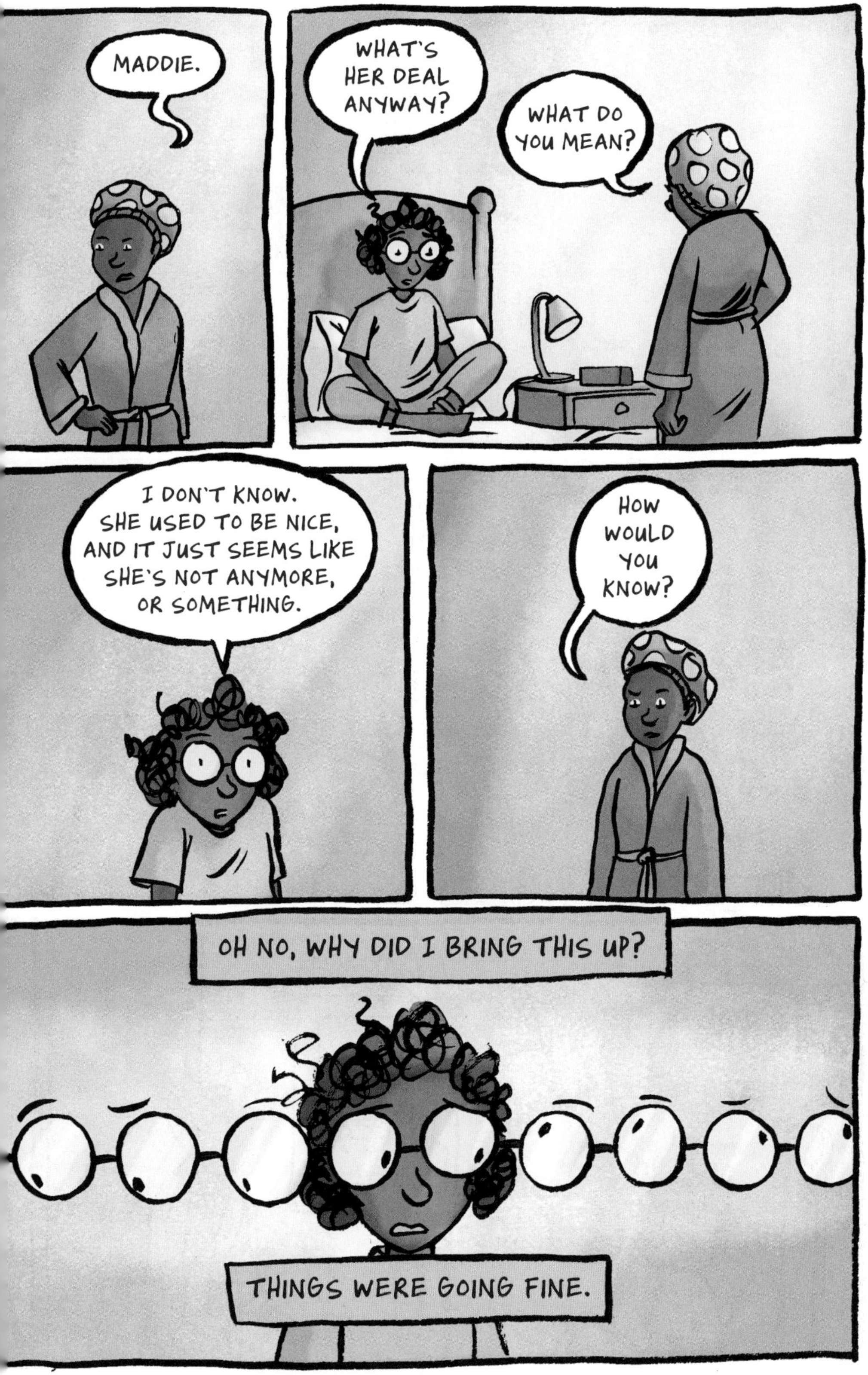

MADDIE.
WHAT'S HER DEAL ANYWAY?
WHAT DO YOU MEAN?
I DON'T KNOW. SHE USED TO BE NICE, AND IT JUST SEEMS LIKE SHE'S NOT ANYMORE, OR SOMETHING.
HOW WOULD YOU KNOW?
OH NO, WHY DID I BRING THIS UP?
THINGS WERE GOING FINE.

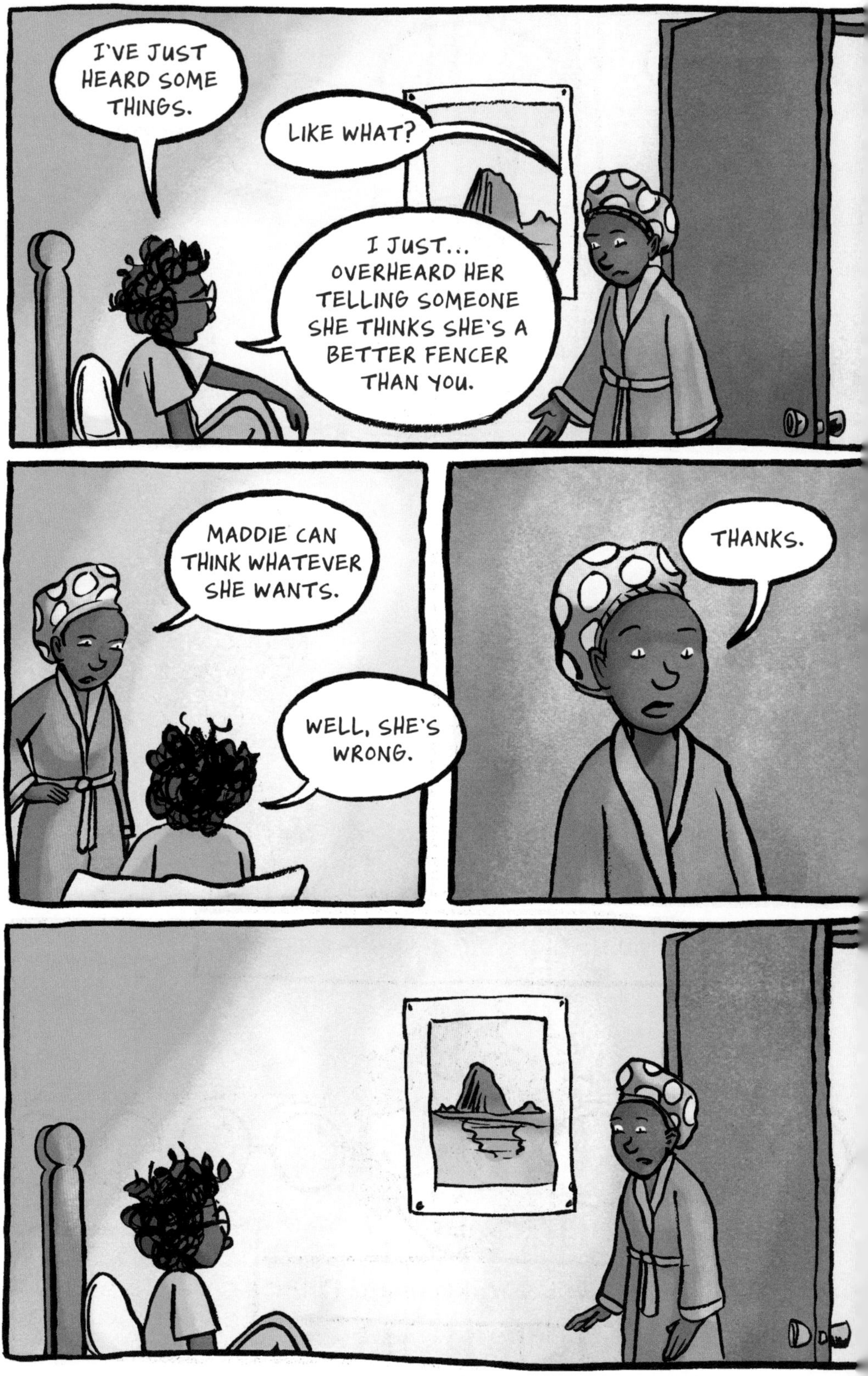
I'VE JUST HEARD SOME THINGS.
LIKE WHAT?
I JUST... OVERHEARD HER TELLING SOMEONE SHE THINKS SHE'S A BETTER FENCER THAN YOU.
MADDIE CAN THINK WHATEVER SHE WANTS.
WELL, SHE'S WRONG.
THANKS.

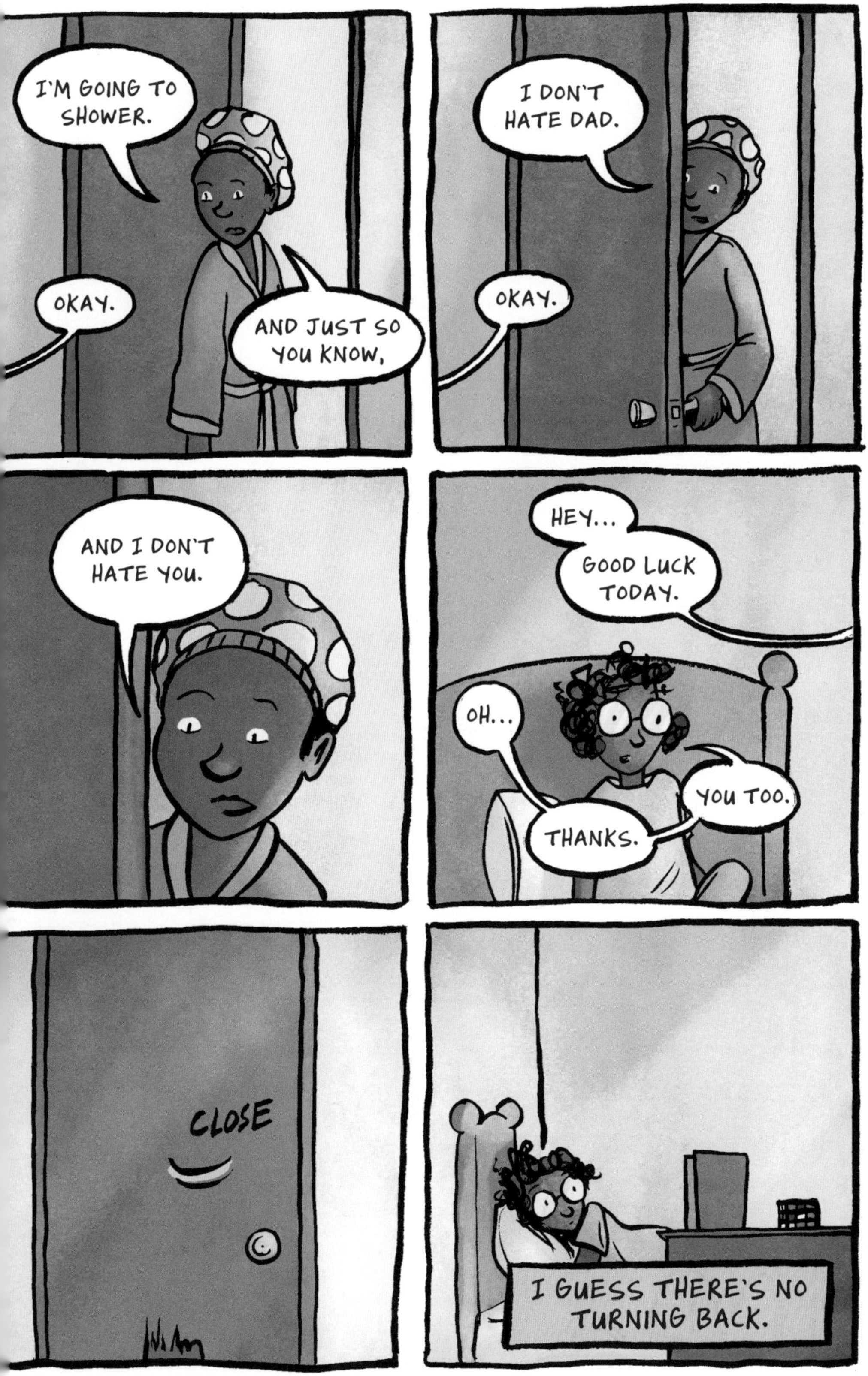
I'M GOING TO SHOWER.
OKAY.
AND JUST SO YOU KNOW,
I DON'T HATE DAD.
OKAY.
AND I DON'T HATE YOU.
HEY...
GOOD LUCK TODAY.
OH...
THANKS.
YOU TOO.
CLOSE
I GUESS THERE'S NO TURNING BACK.

Chapter 14

Halt!

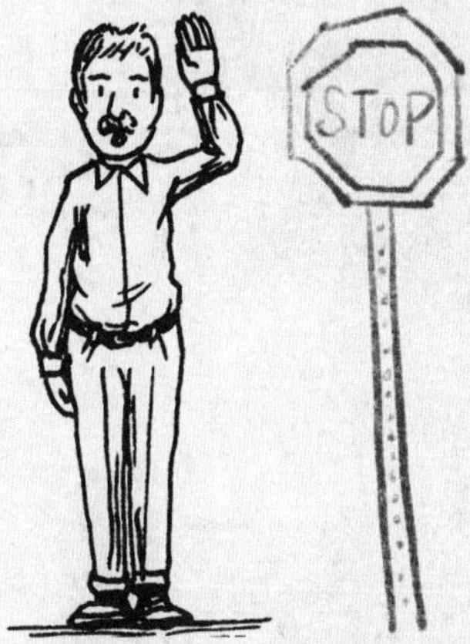
STOP

At any time during a bout, the referee can call for a halt. The command instructs the fencers to cease fighting. The referee could call a halt to address an error of any kind, such as an improper start, to issue a penalty, problems with equipment, or to realign the fencers if one of them has gone out of bounds. By holding up their weapon and tapping the ground with their front leg, a fencer can signal the referee to halt the bout. The fencer can request to stop for many reasons.

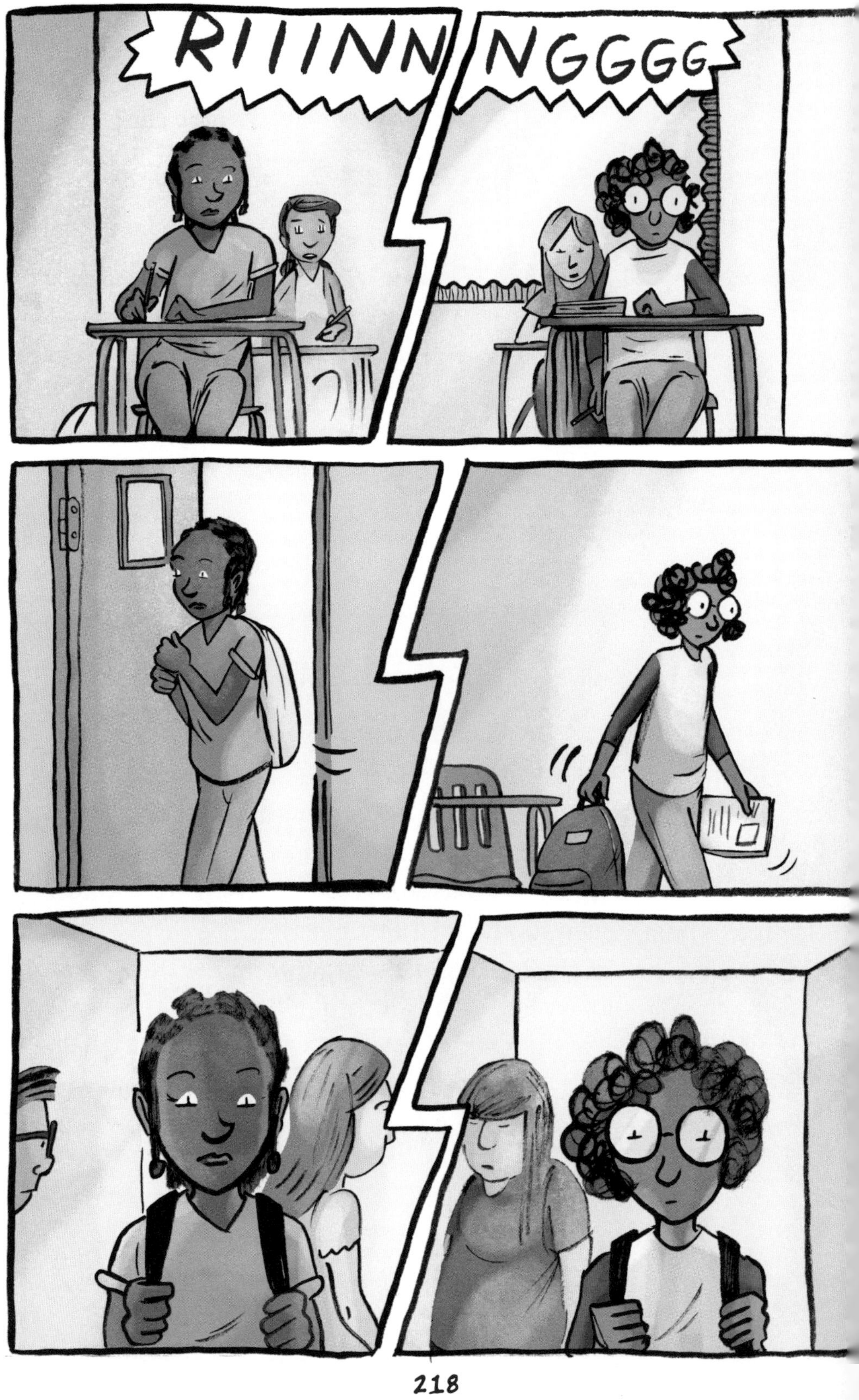
RIIINN NGGGG

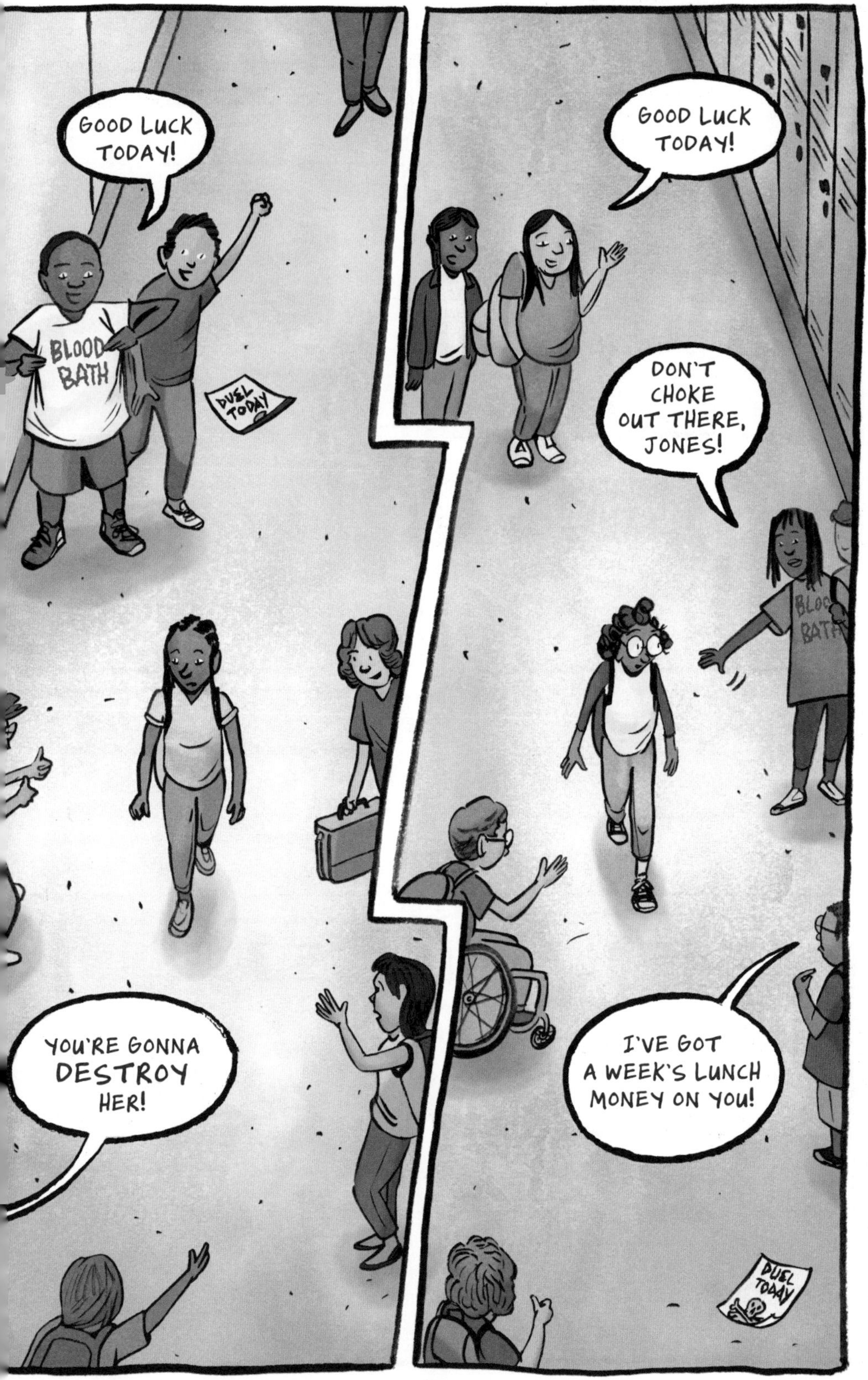
GOOD LUCK TODAY!
BLOOD BATH
DUEL TODAY
GOOD LUCK TODAY!
DON'T CHOKE OUT THERE, JONES!
BLOOD BATH
YOU'RE GONNA DESTROY HER!
I'VE GOT A WEEK'S LUNCH MONEY ON YOU!
DUEL TODAY

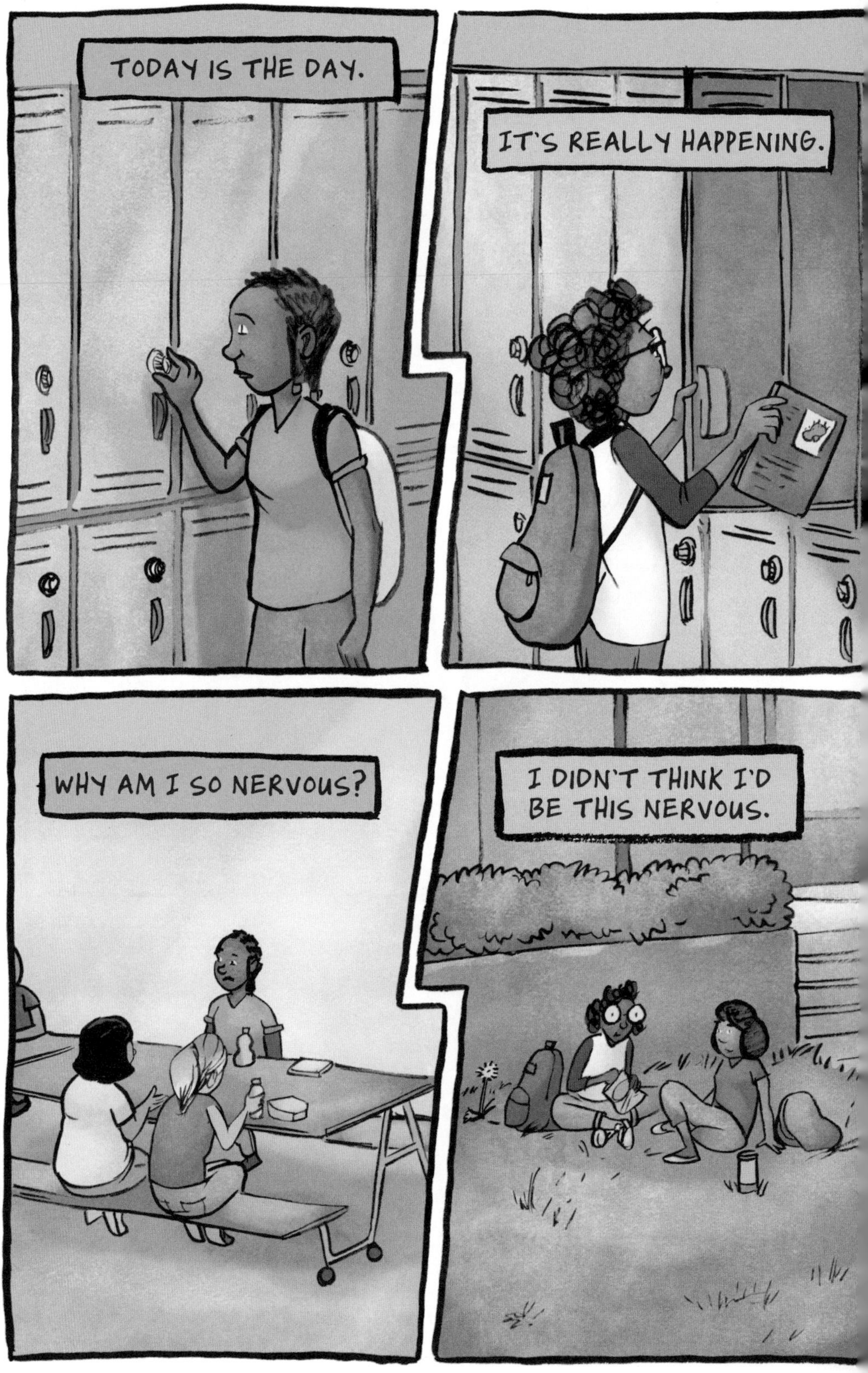
TODAY IS THE DAY.
IT'S REALLY HAPPENING.
WHY AM I SO NERVOUS?
I DIDN'T THINK I'D BE THIS NERVOUS.

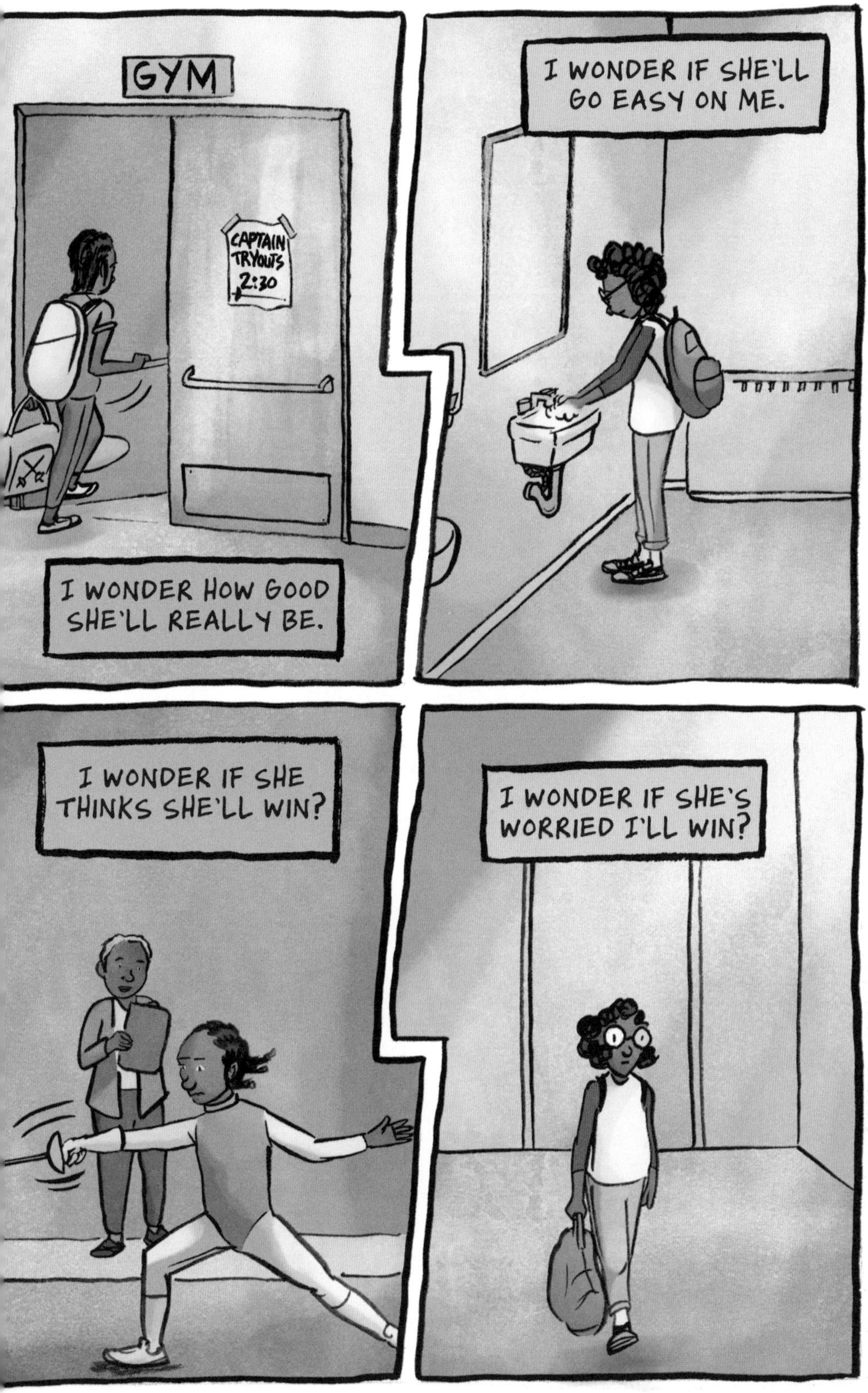
GYM
CAPTAIN TRYOUTS 2:30
I WONDER HOW GOOD SHE'LL REALLY BE.
I WONDER IF SHE'LL GO EASY ON ME.
I WONDER IF SHE THINKS SHE'LL WIN?
I WONDER IF SHE'S WORRIED I'LL WIN?

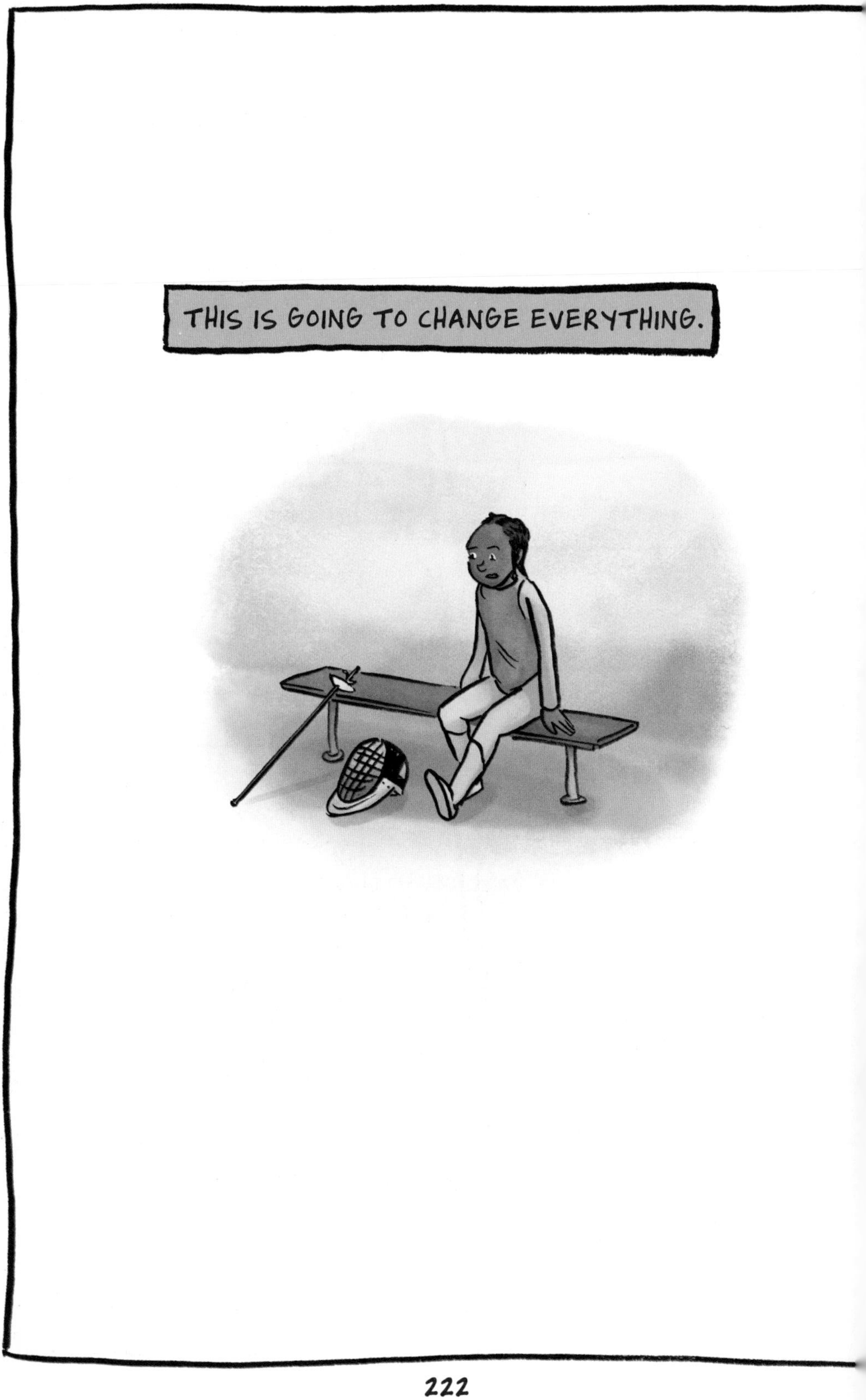
THIS IS GOING TO CHANGE EVERYTHING.

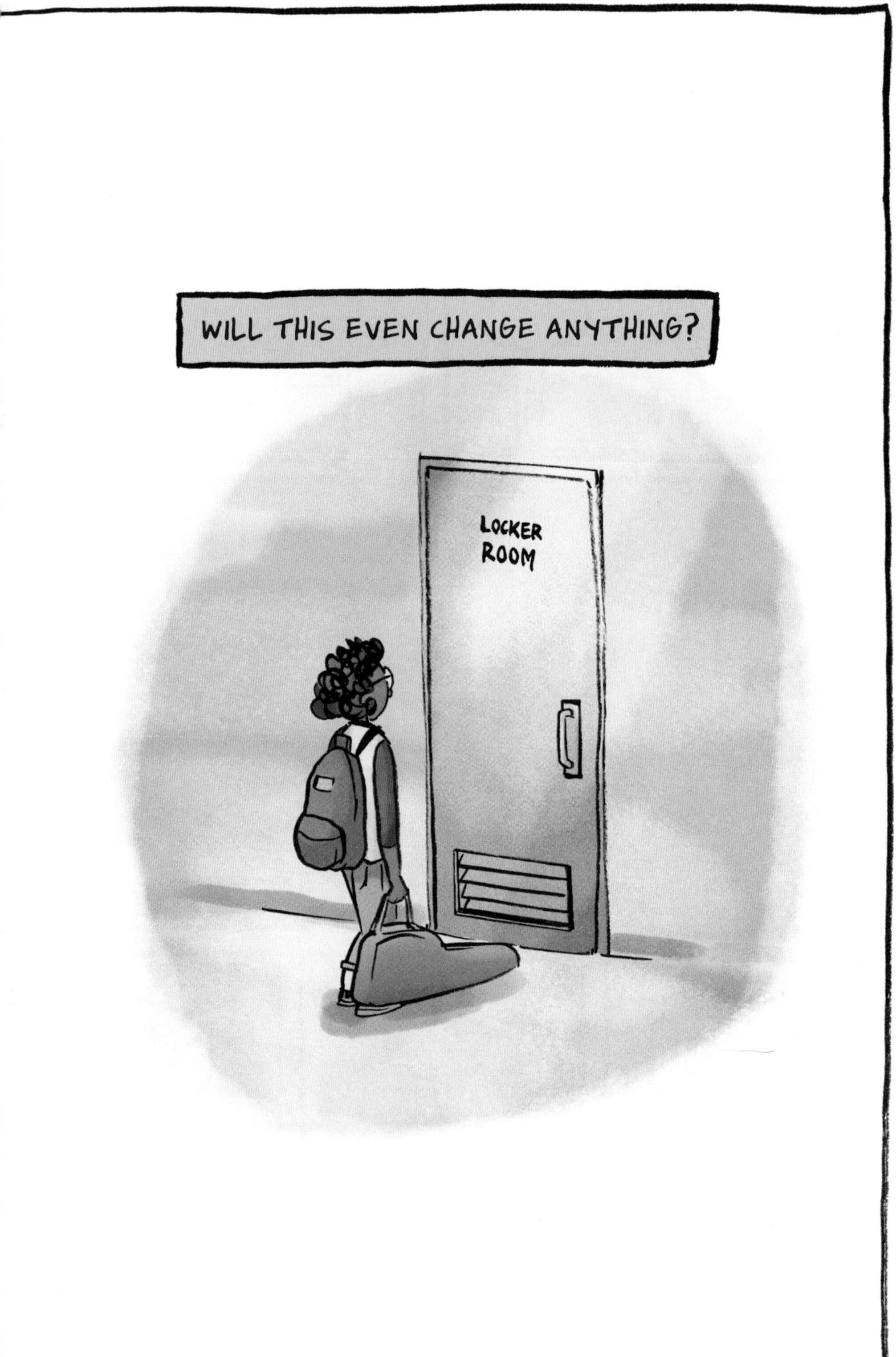
WILL THIS EVEN CHANGE ANYTHING?
LOCKER ROOM

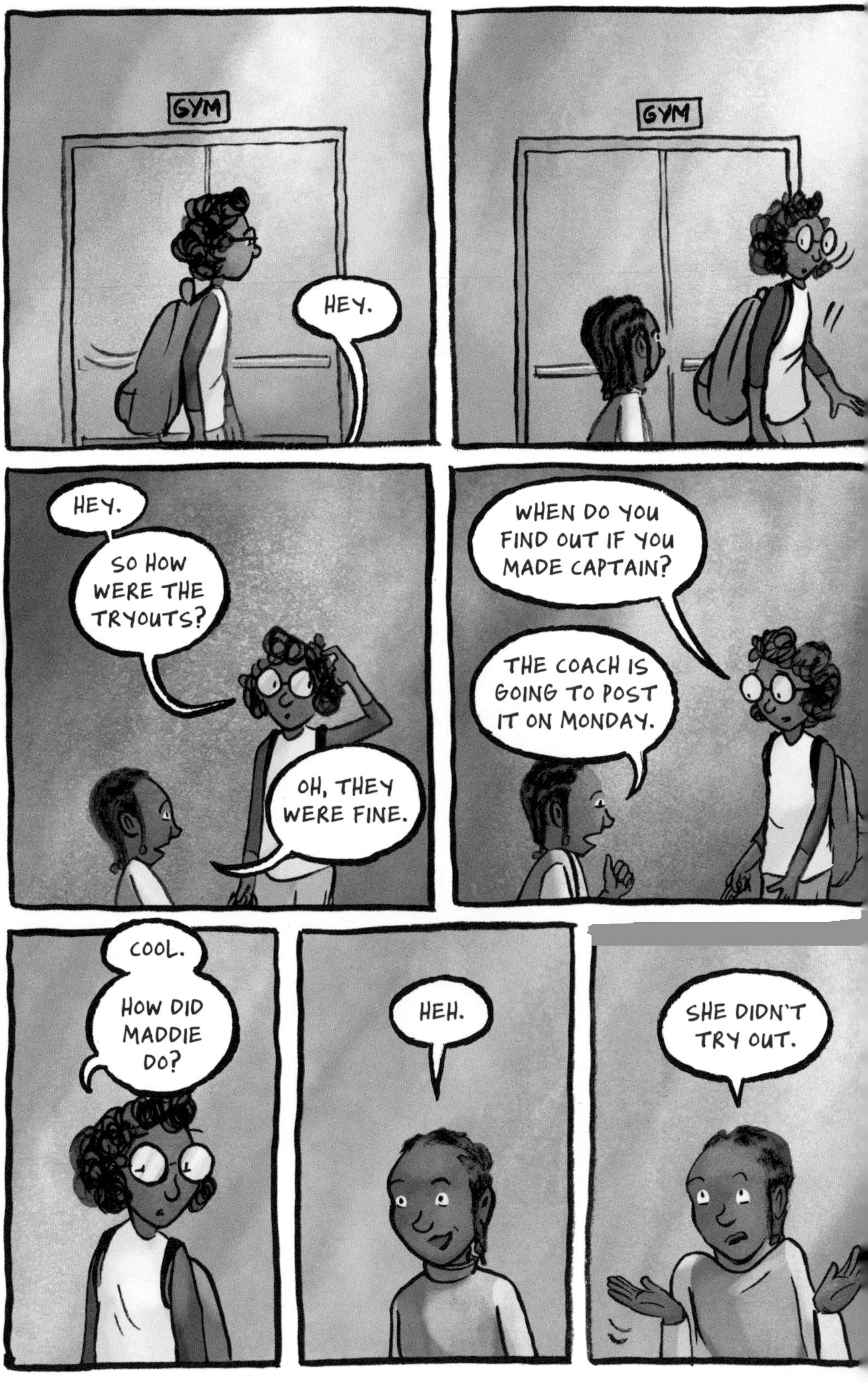
GYM
HEY.
GYM
HEY.
SO HOW WERE THE TRYOUTS?
OH, THEY WERE FINE.
WHEN DO YOU FIND OUT IF YOU MADE CAPTAIN?
THE COACH IS GOING TO POST IT ON MONDAY.
COOL.
HOW DID MADDIE DO?
HEH.
SHE DIDN'T TRY OUT.

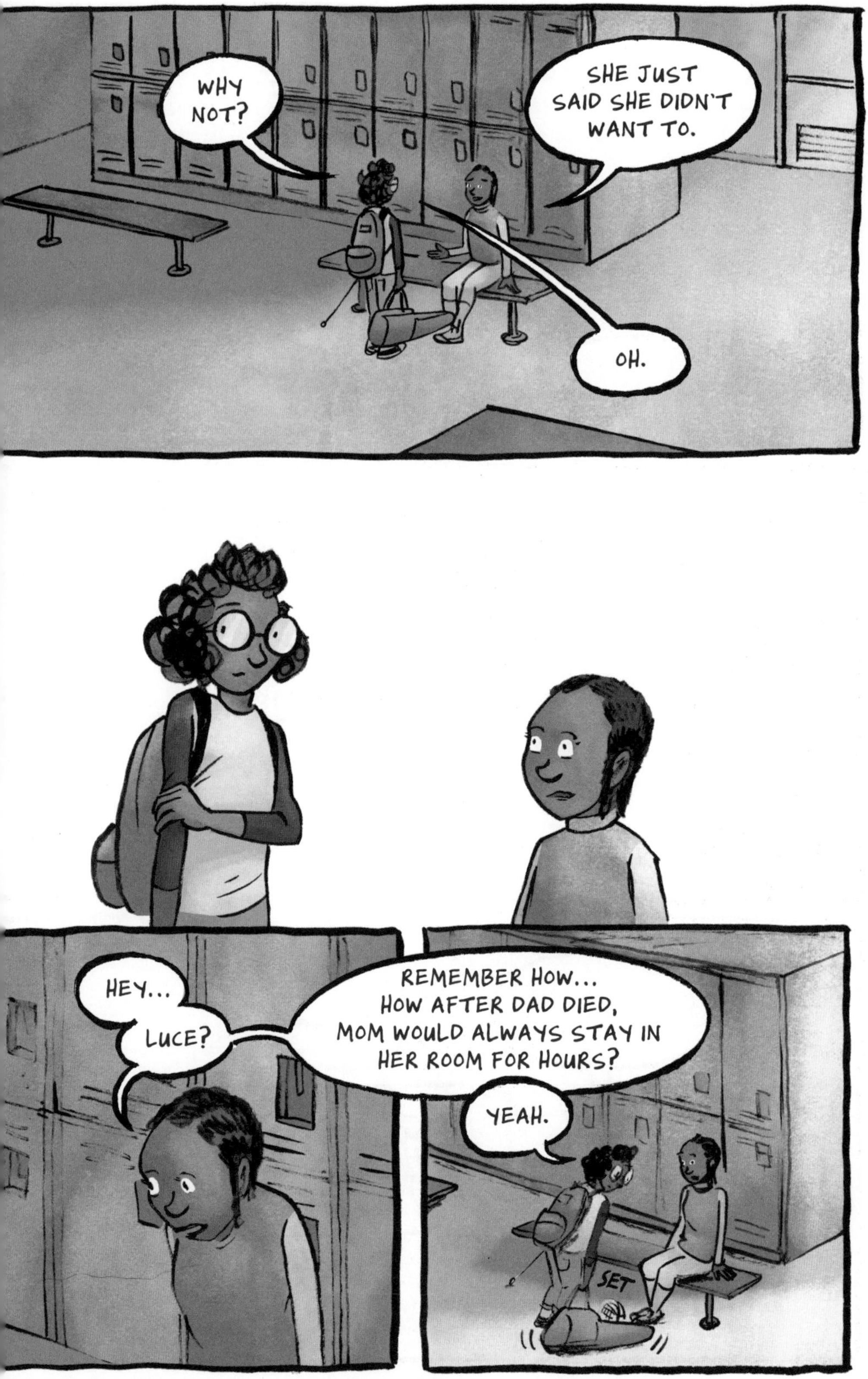
WHY NOT?
SHE JUST SAID SHE DIDN'T WANT TO.
OH.
HEY...
LUCE?
REMEMBER HOW... HOW AFTER DAD DIED, MOM WOULD ALWAYS STAY IN HER ROOM FOR HOURS?
YEAH.
SET

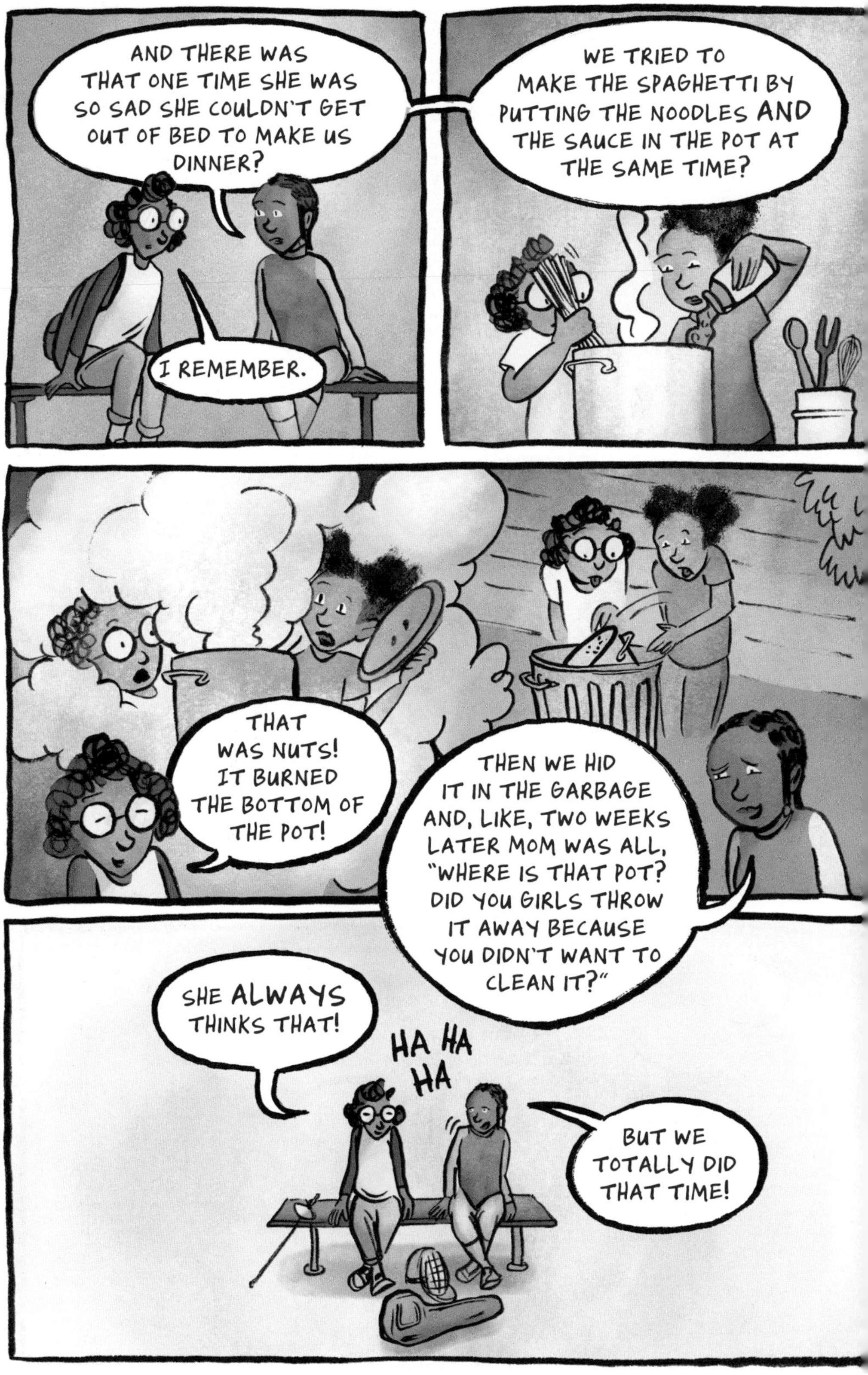
AND THERE WAS THAT ONE TIME SHE WAS SO SAD SHE COULDN'T GET OUT OF BED TO MAKE US DINNER?
I REMEMBER.
WE TRIED TO MAKE THE SPAGHETTI BY PUTTING THE NOODLES AND THE SAUCE IN THE POT AT THE SAME TIME?
THAT WAS NUTS! IT BURNED THE BOTTOM OF THE POT!
THEN WE HID IT IN THE GARBAGE AND, LIKE, TWO WEEKS LATER MOM WAS ALL, "WHERE IS THAT POT? DID YOU GIRLS THROW IT AWAY BECAUSE YOU DIDN'T WANT TO CLEAN IT?"
SHE ALWAYS THINKS THAT!
HA HA HA
BUT WE TOTALLY DID THAT TIME!

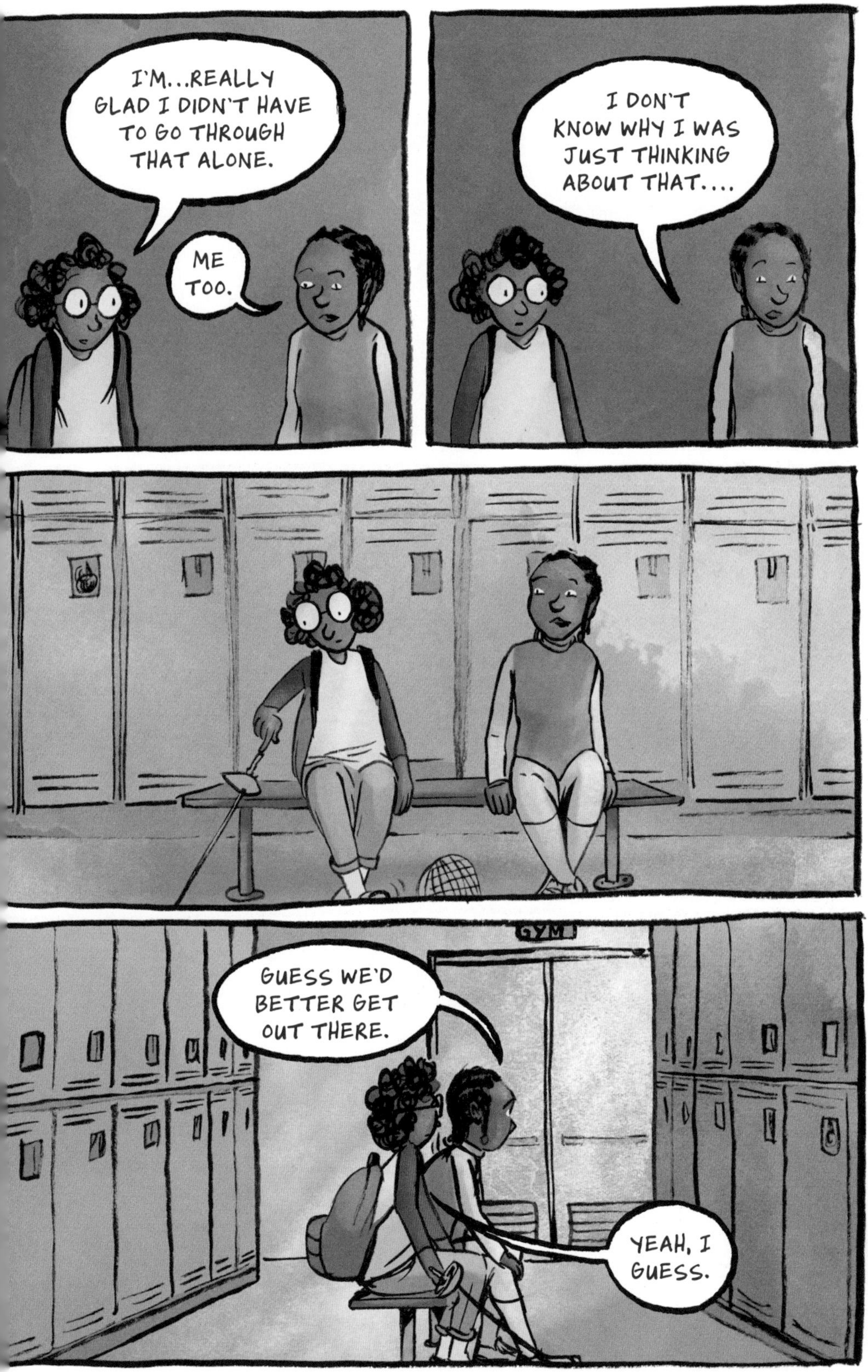
I'M...REALLY GLAD I DIDN'T HAVE TO GO THROUGH THAT ALONE.
ME TOO.
I DON'T KNOW WHY I WAS JUST THINKING ABOUT THAT....
GYM
GUESS WE'D BETTER GET OUT THERE.
YEAH, I GUESS.

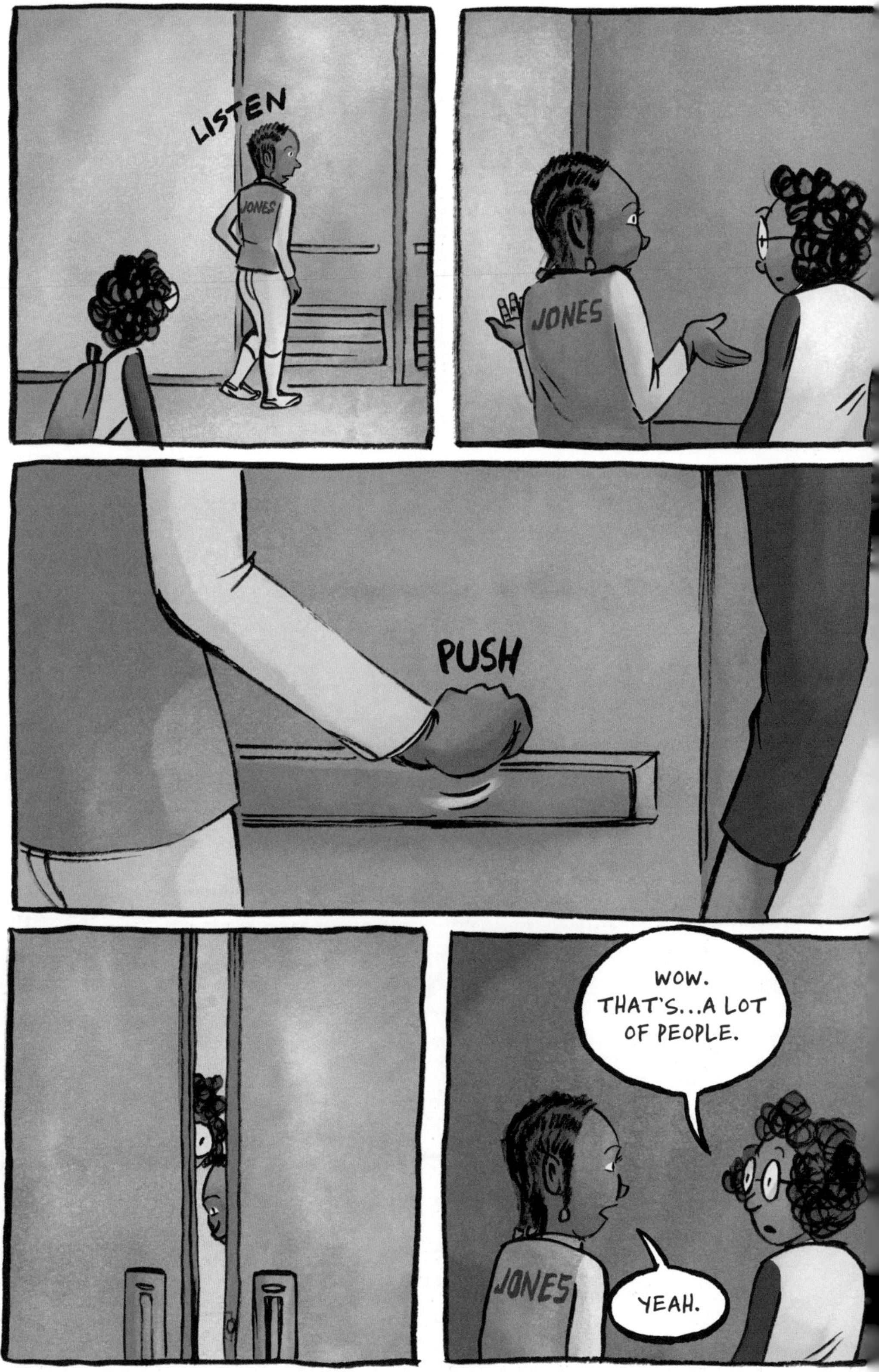
LISTEN
JONES
JONES
PUSH
WOW.
THAT'S...A LOT
OF PEOPLE.
JONES
YEAH.

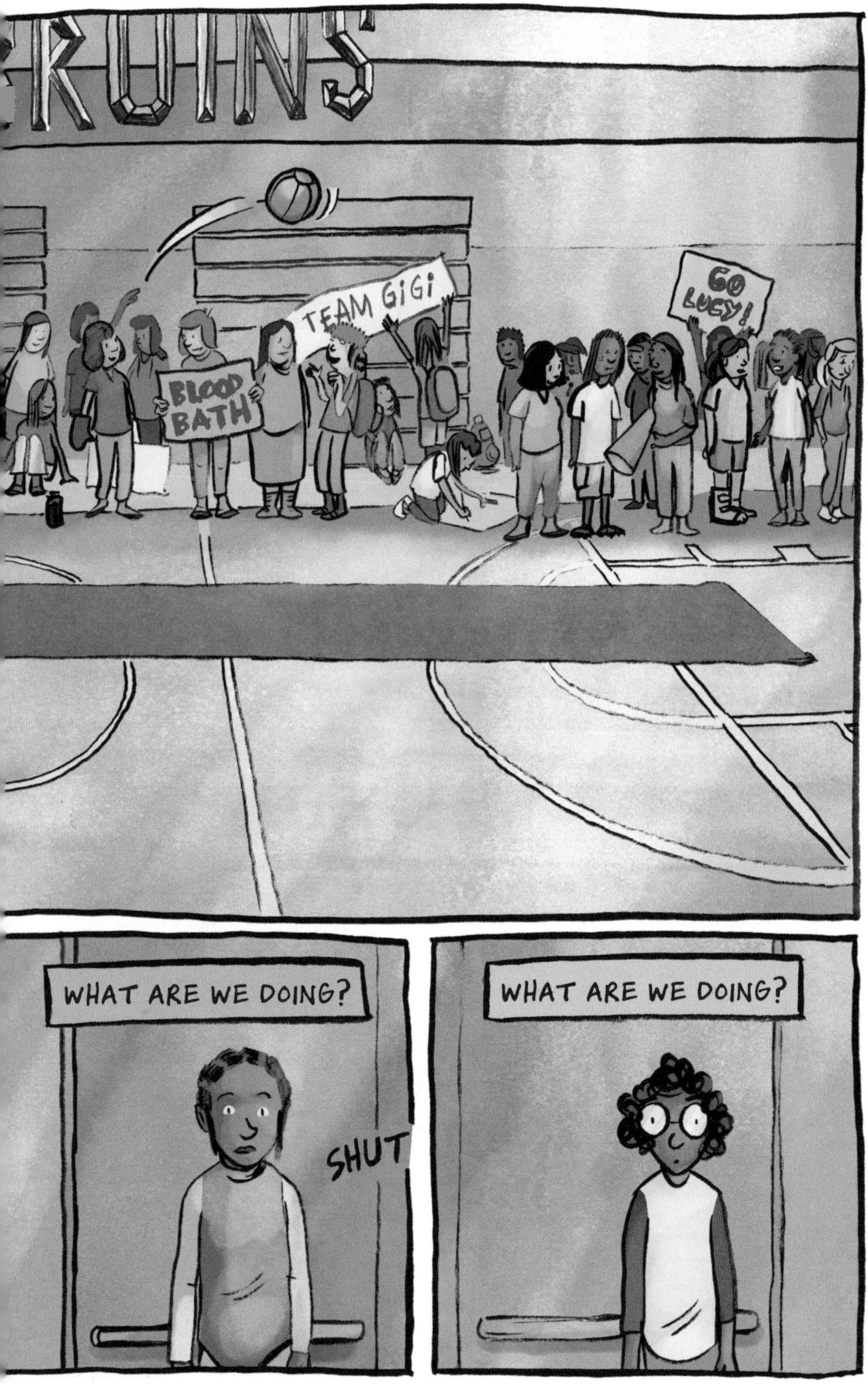
BRUINS
BLOOD BATH
TEAM GIGI
GO LUCY!
WHAT ARE WE DOING?
SHUT
WHAT ARE WE DOING?

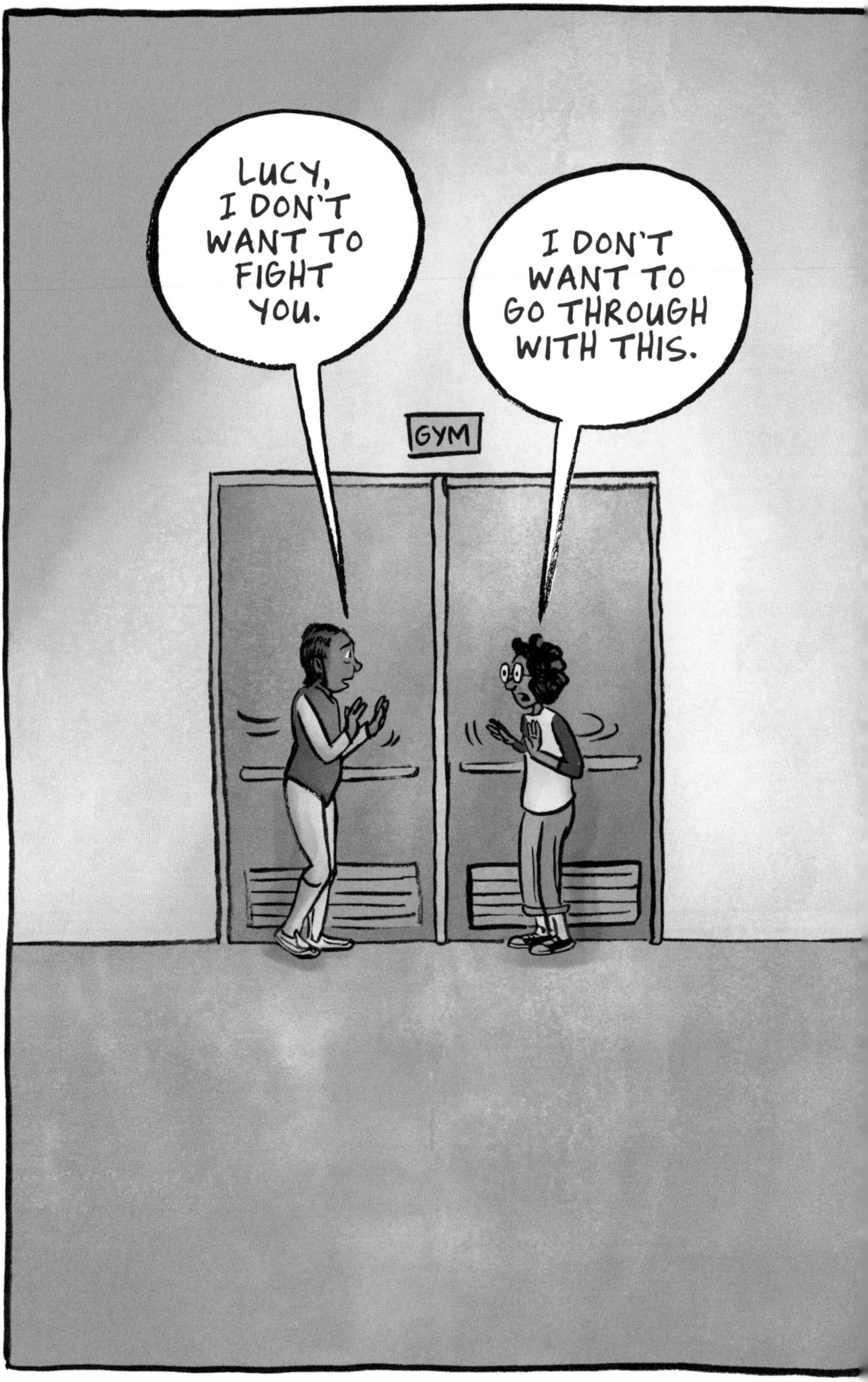
LUCY, I DON'T WANT TO FIGHT YOU.
I DON'T WANT TO GO THROUGH WITH THIS.
GYM

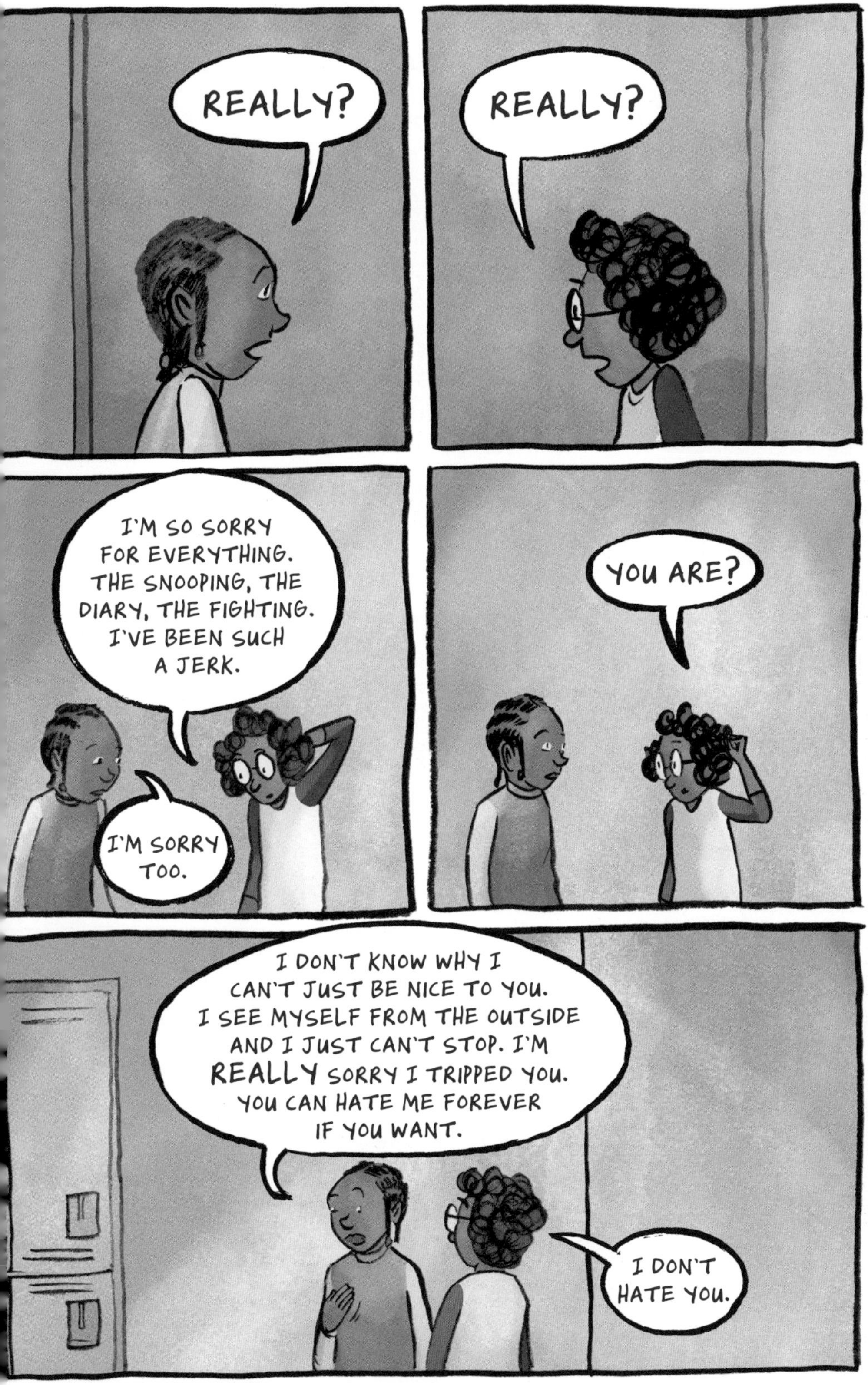
REALLY?
REALLY?
I'M SO SORRY FOR EVERYTHING. THE SNOOPING, THE DIARY, THE FIGHTING. I'VE BEEN SUCH A JERK.
I'M SORRY TOO.
YOU ARE?
I DON'T KNOW WHY I CAN'T JUST BE NICE TO YOU. I SEE MYSELF FROM THE OUTSIDE AND I JUST CAN'T STOP. I'M REALLY SORRY I TRIPPED YOU. YOU CAN HATE ME FOREVER IF YOU WANT.
I DON'T HATE YOU.

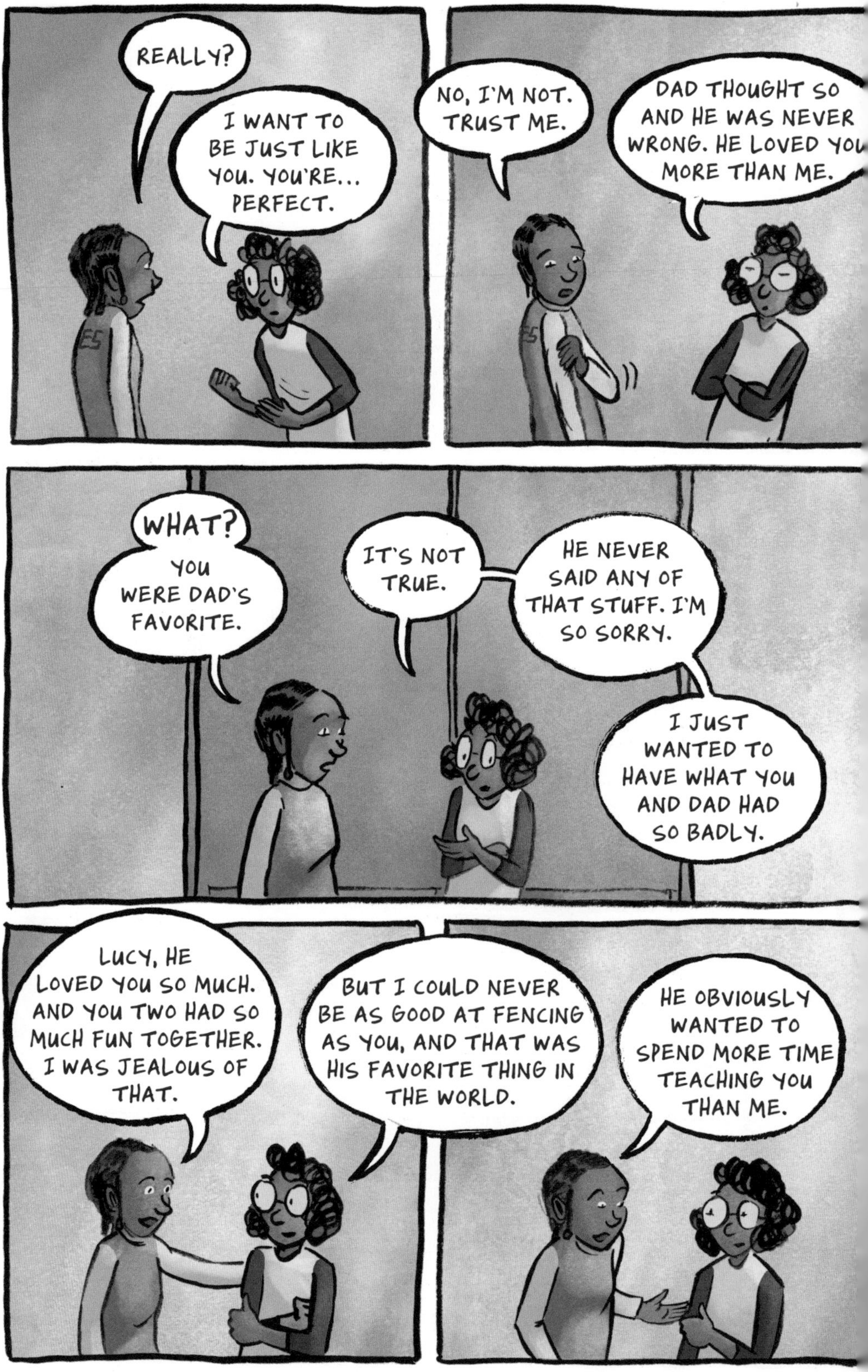

REALLY?
I WANT TO BE JUST LIKE YOU. YOU'RE... PERFECT.
NO, I'M NOT. TRUST ME.
DAD THOUGHT SO AND HE WAS NEVER WRONG. HE LOVED YOU MORE THAN ME.
WHAT?
YOU WERE DAD'S FAVORITE.
IT'S NOT TRUE.
HE NEVER SAID ANY OF THAT STUFF. I'M SO SORRY.
I JUST WANTED TO HAVE WHAT YOU AND DAD HAD SO BADLY.
LUCY, HE LOVED YOU SO MUCH. AND YOU TWO HAD SO MUCH FUN TOGETHER. I WAS JEALOUS OF THAT.
BUT I COULD NEVER BE AS GOOD AT FENCING AS YOU, AND THAT WAS HIS FAVORITE THING IN THE WORLD.
HE OBVIOUSLY WANTED TO SPEND MORE TIME TEACHING YOU THAN ME.

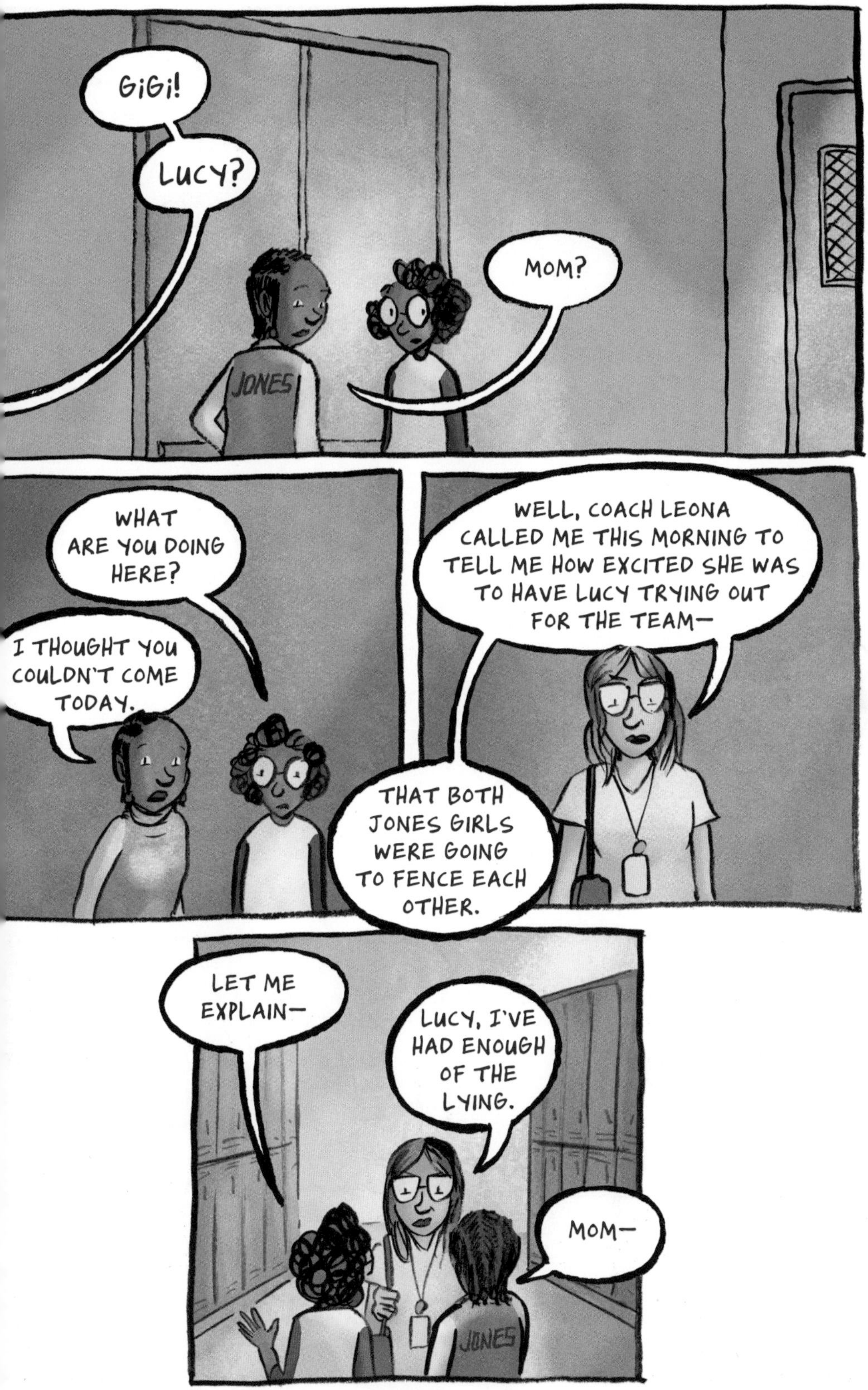
GiGi!
LUCY?
MOM?
JONES
WHAT ARE YOU DOING HERE?
I THOUGHT YOU COULDN'T COME TODAY.
WELL, COACH LEONA CALLED ME THIS MORNING TO TELL ME HOW EXCITED SHE WAS TO HAVE LUCY TRYING OUT FOR THE TEAM—
THAT BOTH JONES GIRLS WERE GOING TO FENCE EACH OTHER.
LET ME EXPLAIN—
LUCY, I'VE HAD ENOUGH OF THE LYING.
MOM—
JONES

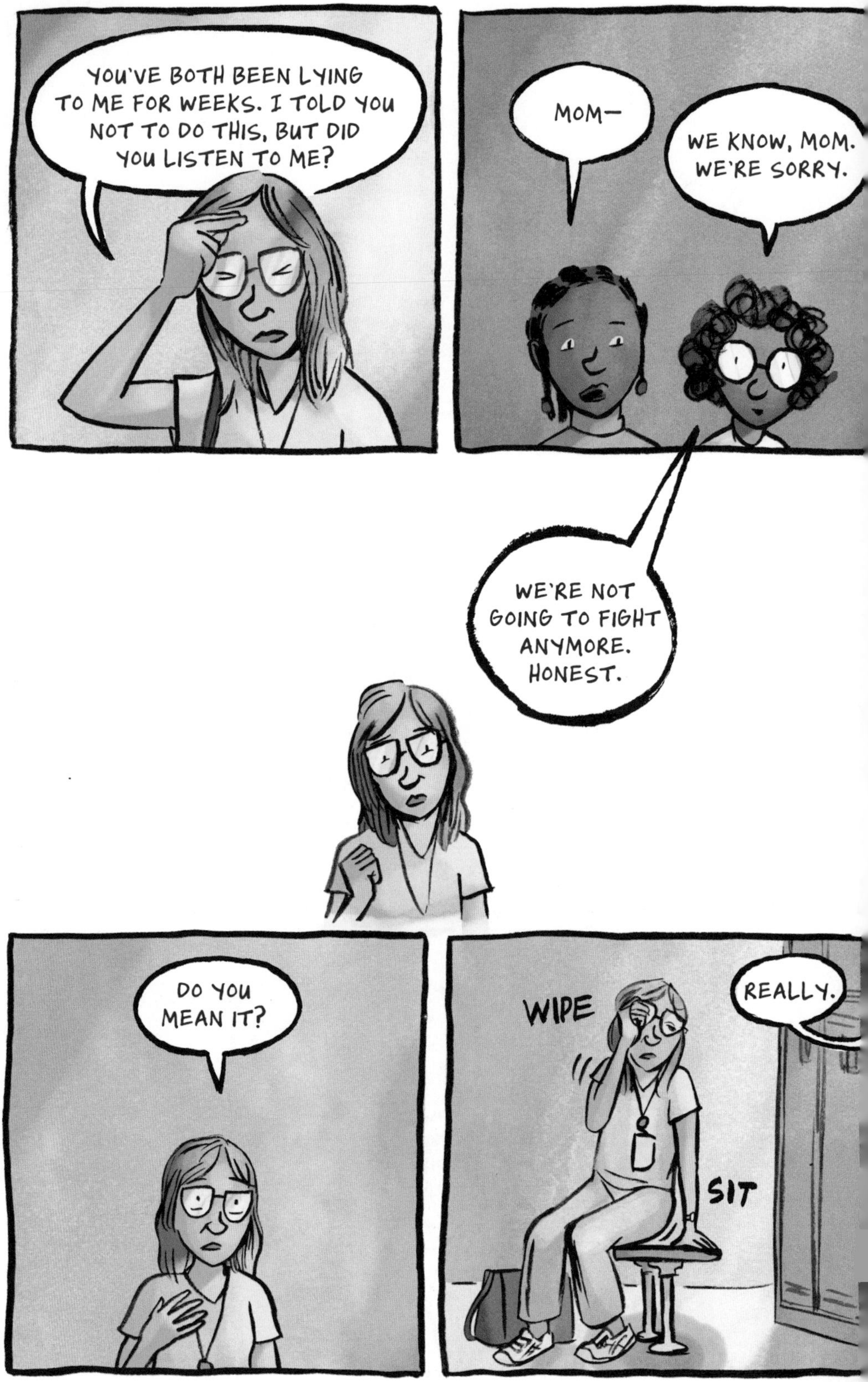
YOU'VE BOTH BEEN LYING TO ME FOR WEEKS. I TOLD YOU NOT TO DO THIS, BUT DID YOU LISTEN TO ME?
MOM—
WE KNOW, MOM. WE'RE SORRY.
WE'RE NOT GOING TO FIGHT ANYMORE. HONEST.
DO YOU MEAN IT?
WIPE
REALLY.
SIT

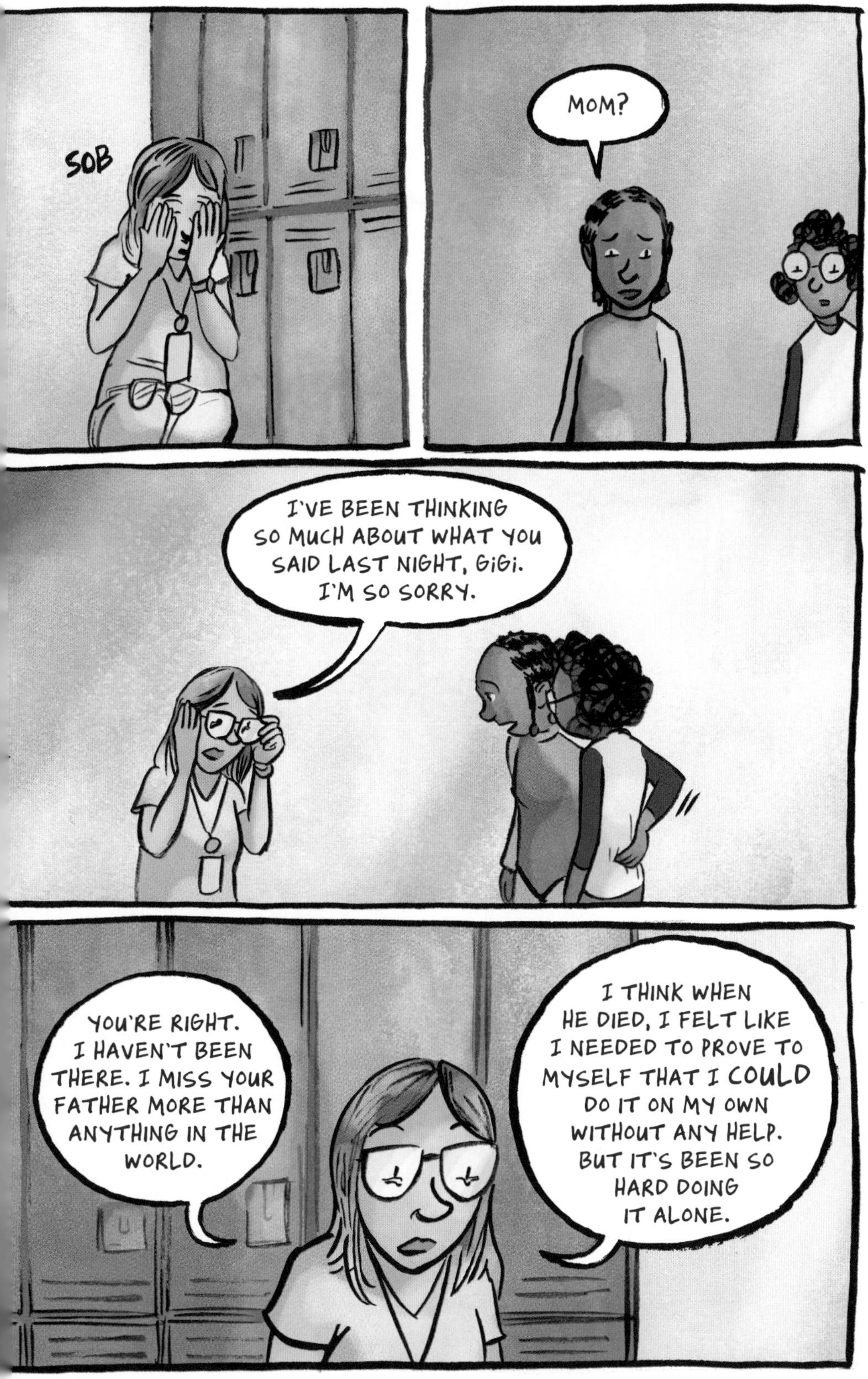
SOB
MOM?
I'VE BEEN THINKING SO MUCH ABOUT WHAT YOU SAID LAST NIGHT, GIGI. I'M SO SORRY.
YOU'RE RIGHT. I HAVEN'T BEEN THERE. I MISS YOUR FATHER MORE THAN ANYTHING IN THE WORLD.
I THINK WHEN HE DIED, I FELT LIKE I NEEDED TO PROVE TO MYSELF THAT I COULD DO IT ON MY OWN WITHOUT ANY HELP. BUT IT'S BEEN SO HARD DOING IT ALONE.

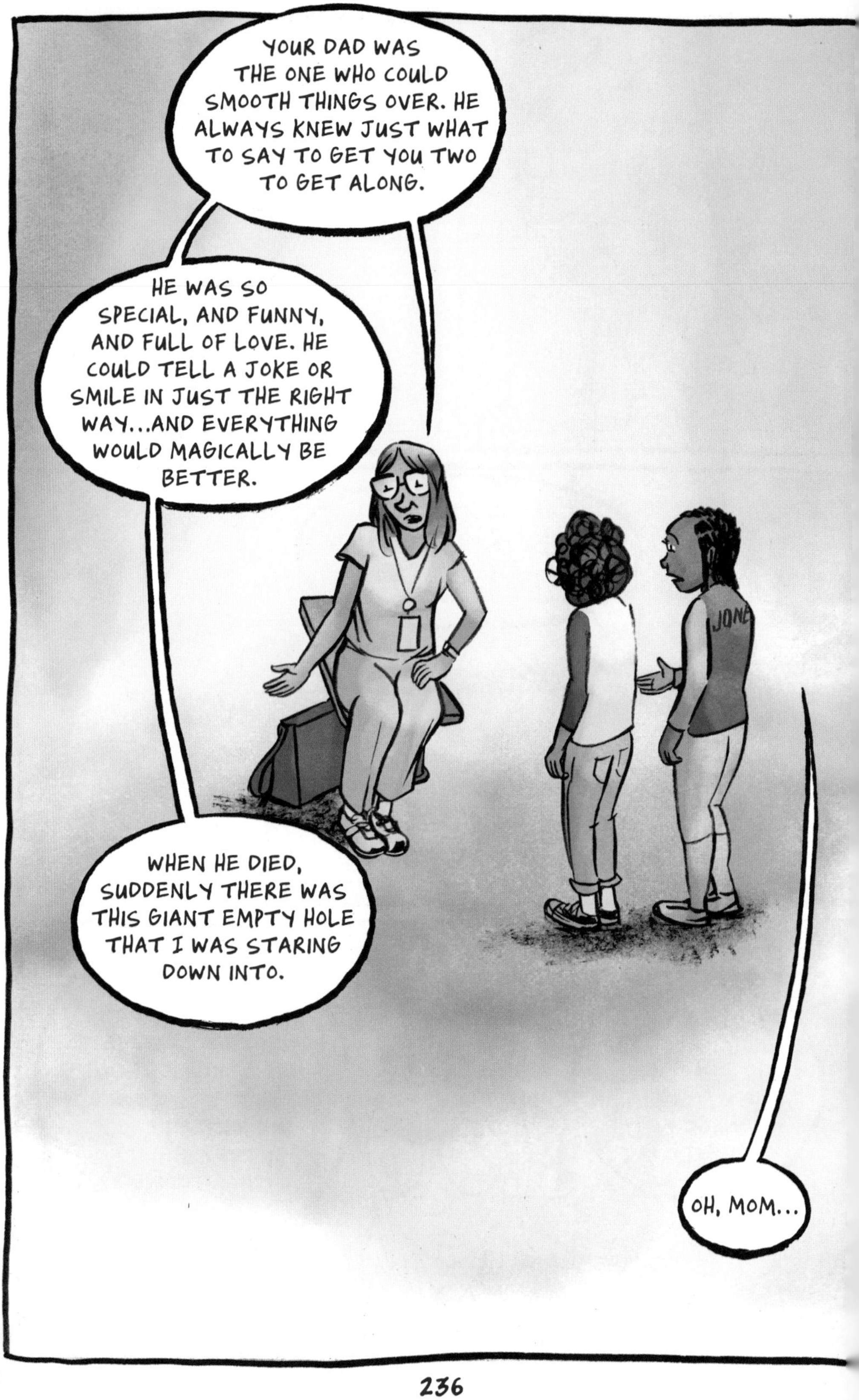

YOUR DAD WAS THE ONE WHO COULD SMOOTH THINGS OVER. HE ALWAYS KNEW JUST WHAT TO SAY TO GET YOU TWO TO GET ALONG.
HE WAS SO SPECIAL, AND FUNNY, AND FULL OF LOVE. HE COULD TELL A JOKE OR SMILE IN JUST THE RIGHT WAY...AND EVERYTHING WOULD MAGICALLY BE BETTER.
WHEN HE DIED, SUDDENLY THERE WAS THIS GIANT EMPTY HOLE THAT I WAS STARING DOWN INTO.
OH, MOM...

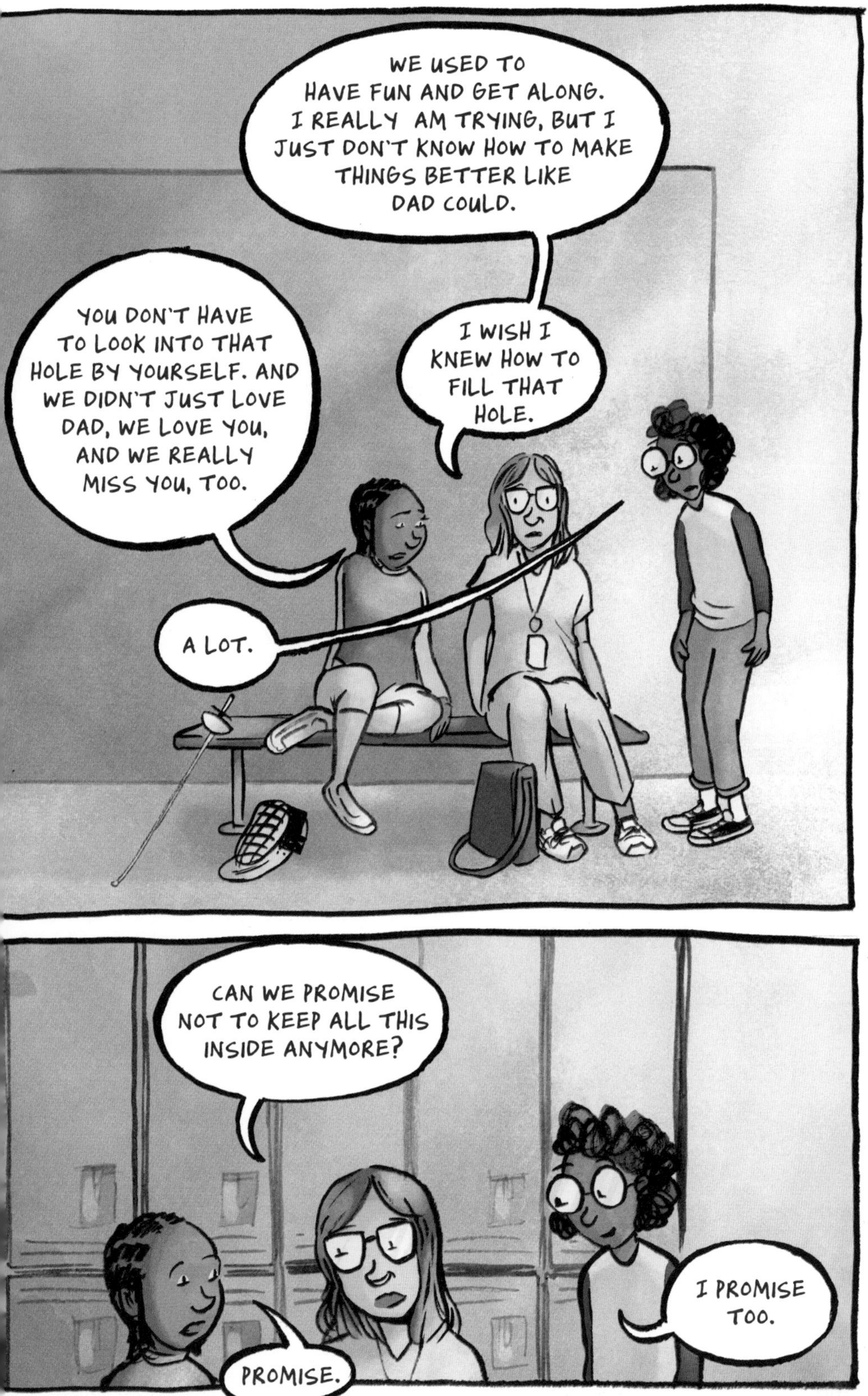
WE USED TO HAVE FUN AND GET ALONG. I REALLY AM TRYING, BUT I JUST DON'T KNOW HOW TO MAKE THINGS BETTER LIKE DAD COULD.
I WISH I KNEW HOW TO FILL THAT HOLE.
YOU DON'T HAVE TO LOOK INTO THAT HOLE BY YOURSELF. AND WE DIDN'T JUST LOVE DAD, WE LOVE YOU, AND WE REALLY MISS YOU, TOO.
A LOT.
CAN WE PROMISE NOT TO KEEP ALL THIS INSIDE ANYMORE?
PROMISE.
I PROMISE TOO.

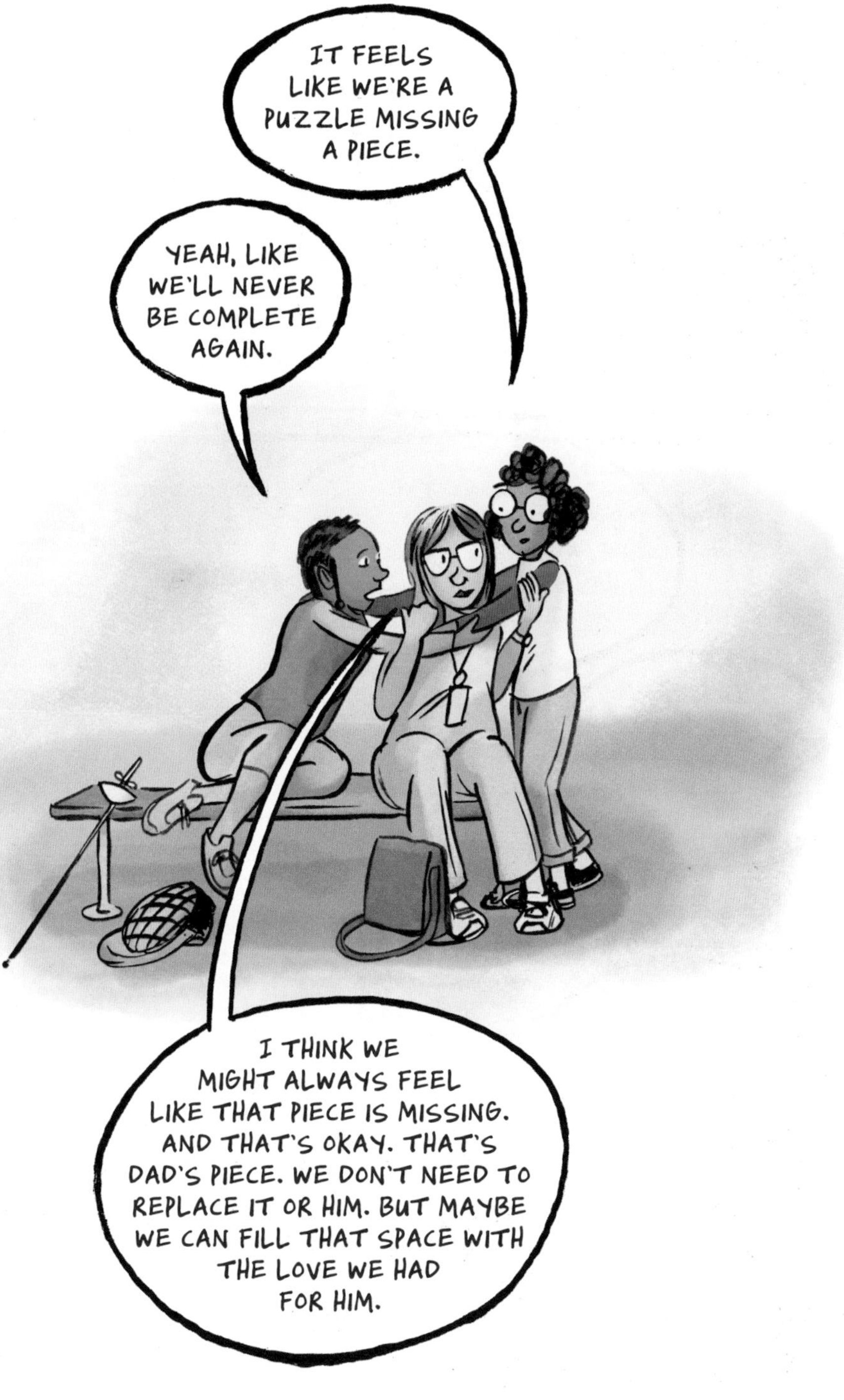
IT FEELS LIKE WE'RE A PUZZLE MISSING A PIECE.
YEAH, LIKE WE'LL NEVER BE COMPLETE AGAIN.
I THINK WE MIGHT ALWAYS FEEL LIKE THAT PIECE IS MISSING. AND THAT'S OKAY. THAT'S DAD'S PIECE. WE DON'T NEED TO REPLACE IT OR HIM. BUT MAYBE WE CAN FILL THAT SPACE WITH THE LOVE WE HAD FOR HIM.

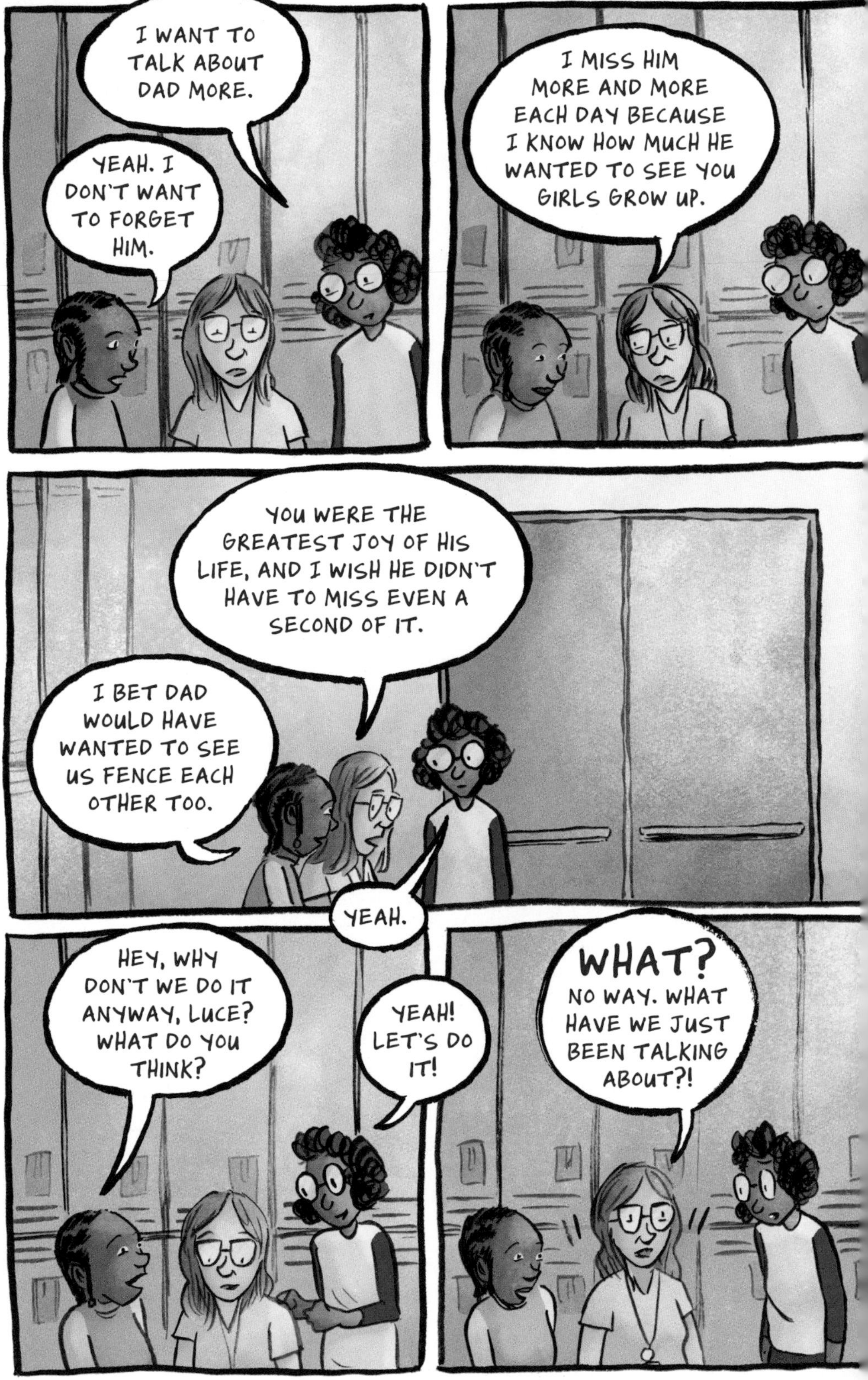
I WANT TO TALK ABOUT DAD MORE.
YEAH. I DON'T WANT TO FORGET HIM.
I MISS HIM MORE AND MORE EACH DAY BECAUSE I KNOW HOW MUCH HE WANTED TO SEE YOU GIRLS GROW UP.
YOU WERE THE GREATEST JOY OF HIS LIFE, AND I WISH HE DIDN'T HAVE TO MISS EVEN A SECOND OF IT.
I BET DAD WOULD HAVE WANTED TO SEE US FENCE EACH OTHER TOO.
YEAH.
HEY, WHY DON'T WE DO IT ANYWAY, LUCE? WHAT DO YOU THINK?
YEAH! LET'S DO IT!
WHAT? NO WAY. WHAT HAVE WE JUST BEEN TALKING ABOUT?!

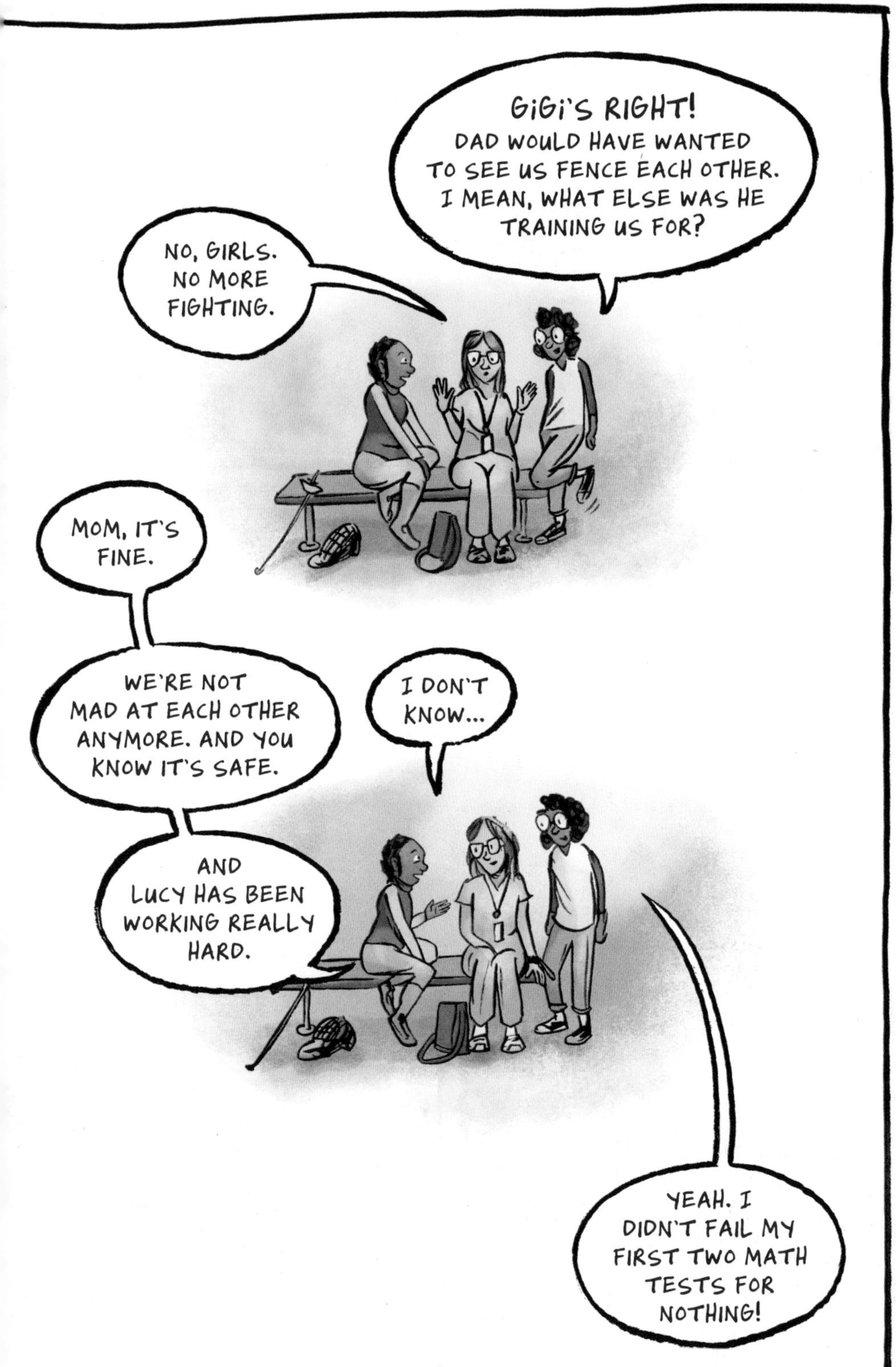
GiGi'S RIGHT! DAD WOULD HAVE WANTED TO SEE US FENCE EACH OTHER. I MEAN, WHAT ELSE WAS HE TRAINING US FOR?
NO, GIRLS. NO MORE FIGHTING.
MOM, IT'S FINE.
WE'RE NOT MAD AT EACH OTHER ANYMORE. AND YOU KNOW IT'S SAFE.
AND LUCY HAS BEEN WORKING REALLY HARD.
I DON'T KNOW...
YEAH. I DIDN'T FAIL MY FIRST TWO MATH TESTS FOR NOTHING!

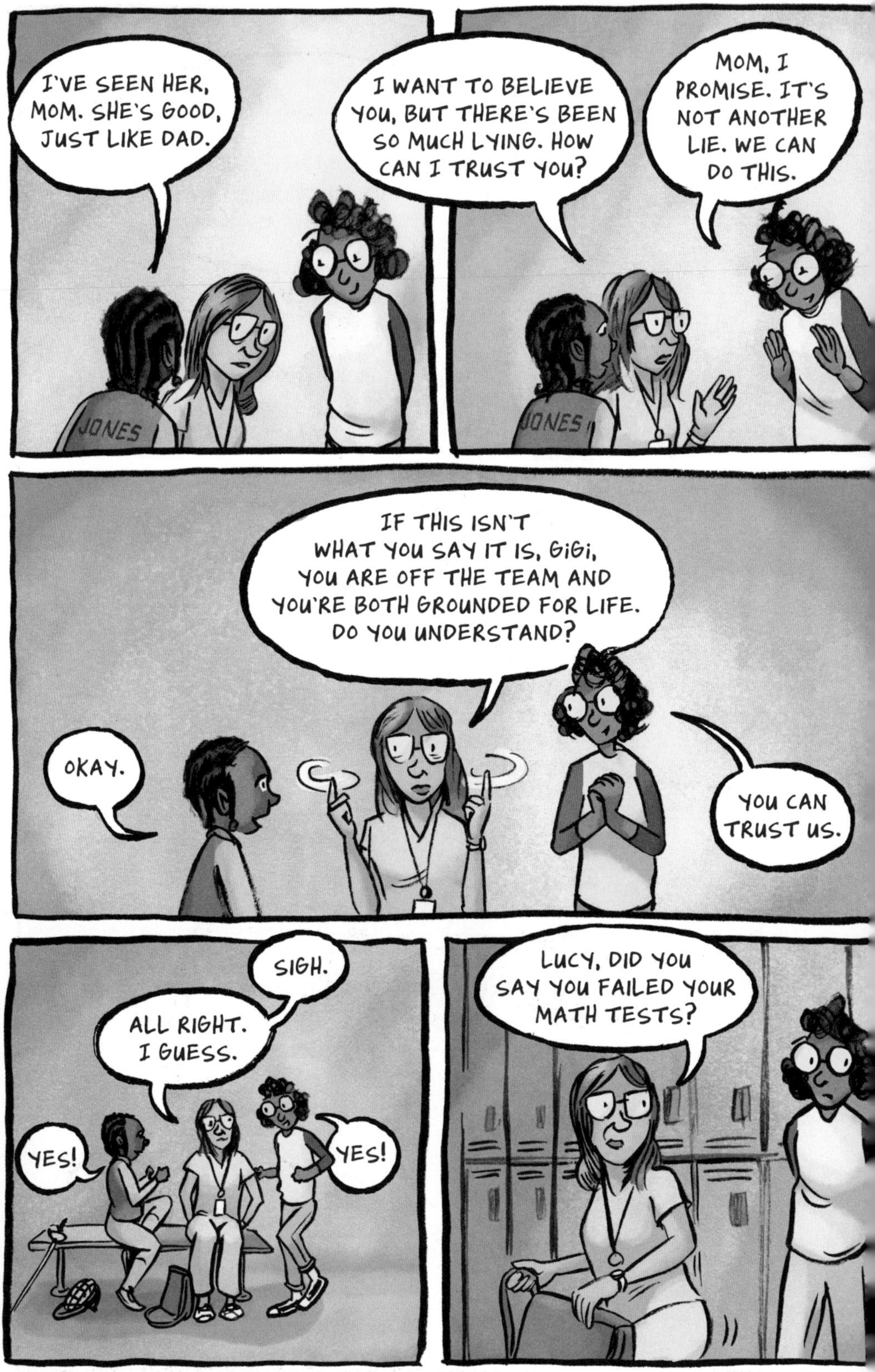
I'VE SEEN HER, MOM. SHE'S GOOD, JUST LIKE DAD.
JONES
I WANT TO BELIEVE YOU, BUT THERE'S BEEN SO MUCH LYING. HOW CAN I TRUST YOU?
MOM, I PROMISE. IT'S NOT ANOTHER LIE. WE CAN DO THIS.
JONES
IF THIS ISN'T WHAT YOU SAY IT IS, GIGI, YOU ARE OFF THE TEAM AND YOU'RE BOTH GROUNDED FOR LIFE. DO YOU UNDERSTAND?
OKAY.
YOU CAN TRUST US.
SIGH.
ALL RIGHT. I GUESS.
YES!
YES!
LUCY, DID YOU SAY YOU FAILED YOUR MATH TESTS?

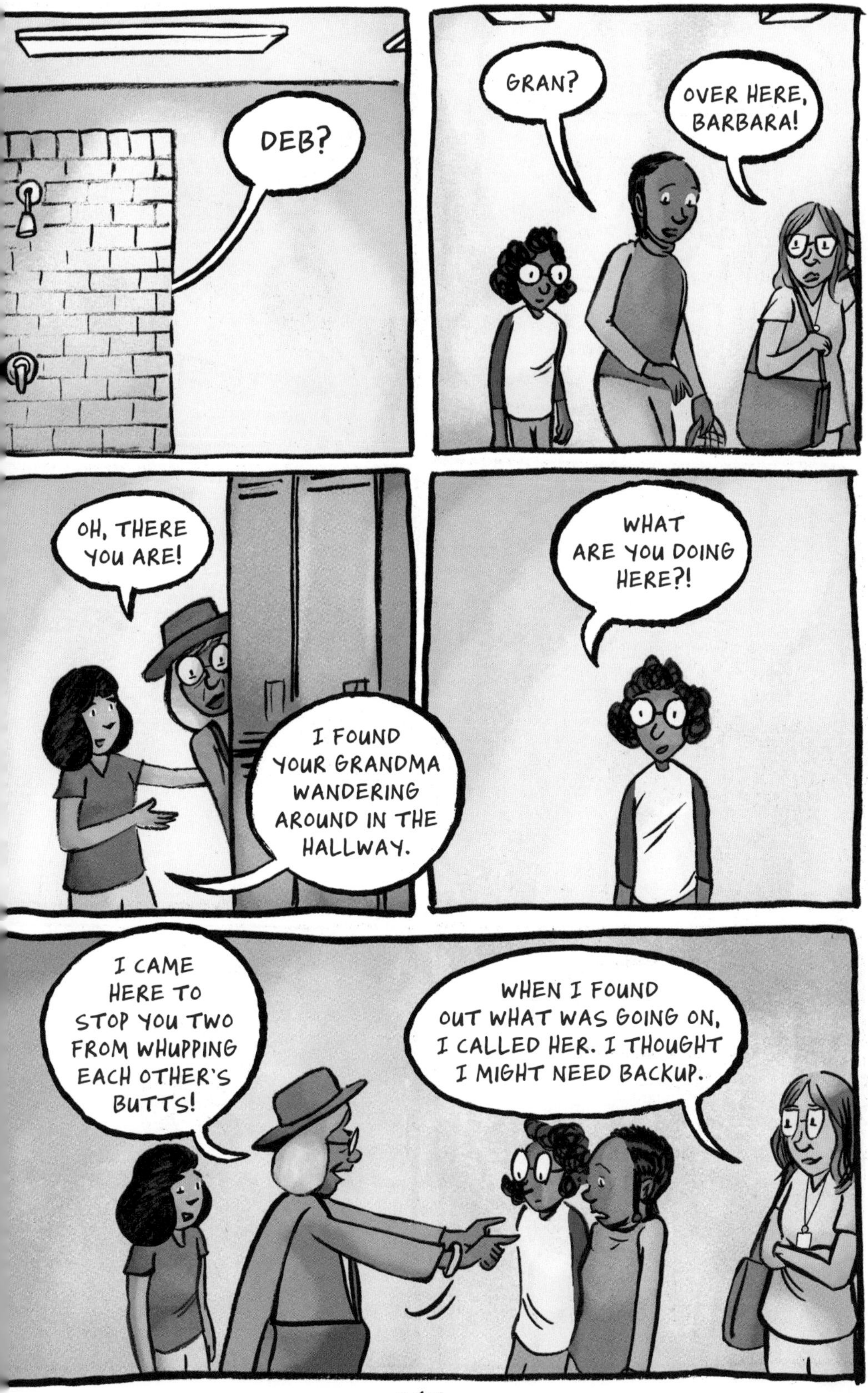
DEB?
GRAN?
OVER HERE, BARBARA!
OH, THERE YOU ARE!
I FOUND YOUR GRANDMA WANDERING AROUND IN THE HALLWAY.
WHAT ARE YOU DOING HERE?!
I CAME HERE TO STOP YOU TWO FROM WHUPPING EACH OTHER'S BUTTS!
WHEN I FOUND OUT WHAT WAS GOING ON, I CALLED HER. I THOUGHT I MIGHT NEED BACKUP.

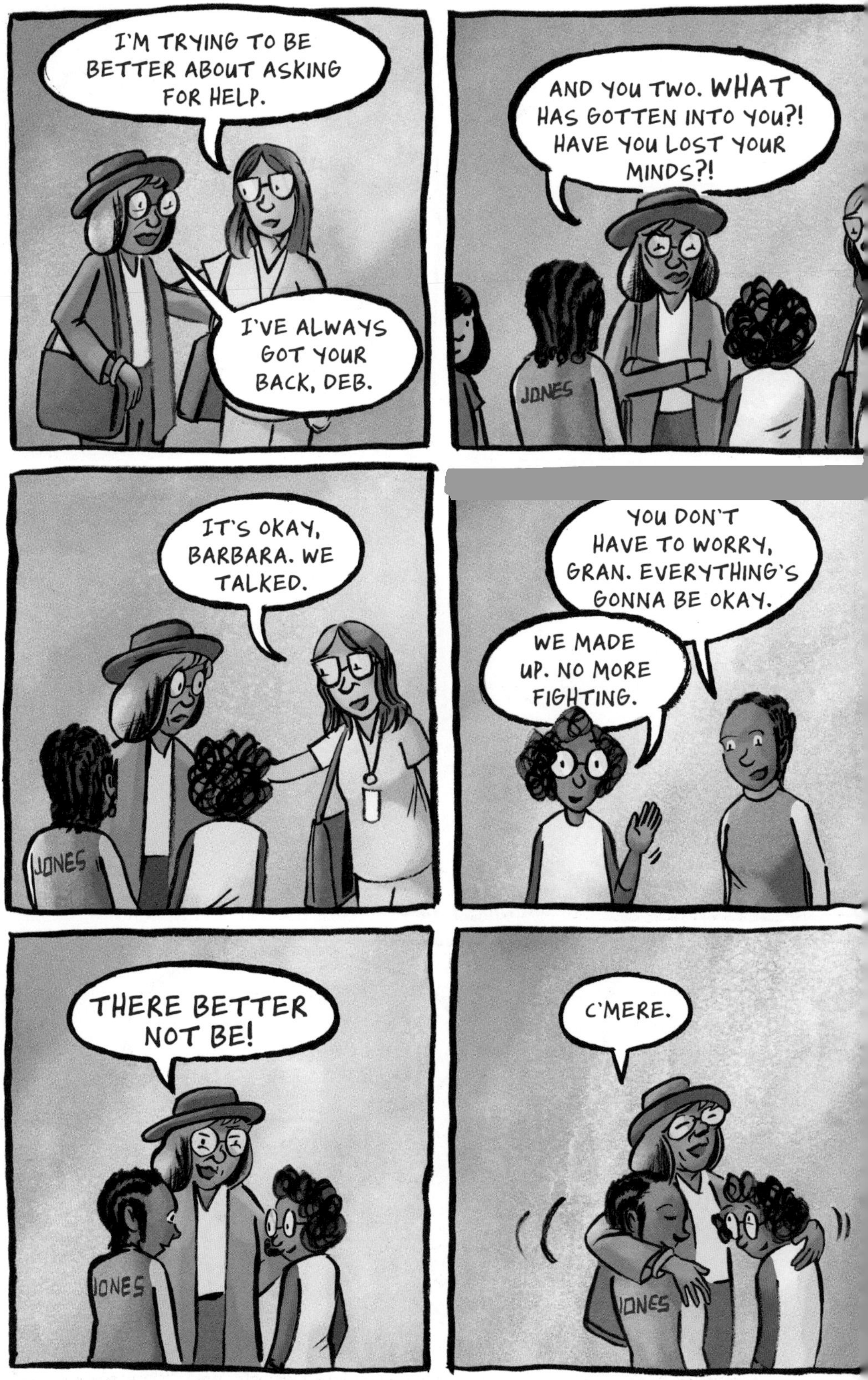
I'M TRYING TO BE BETTER ABOUT ASKING FOR HELP.
I'VE ALWAYS GOT YOUR BACK, DEB.
AND YOU TWO. WHAT HAS GOTTEN INTO YOU?! HAVE YOU LOST YOUR MINDS?!
JONES
IT'S OKAY, BARBARA. WE TALKED.
JONES
YOU DON'T HAVE TO WORRY, GRAN. EVERYTHING'S GONNA BE OKAY.
WE MADE UP. NO MORE FIGHTING.
THERE BETTER NOT BE!
JONES
C'MERE.
JONES

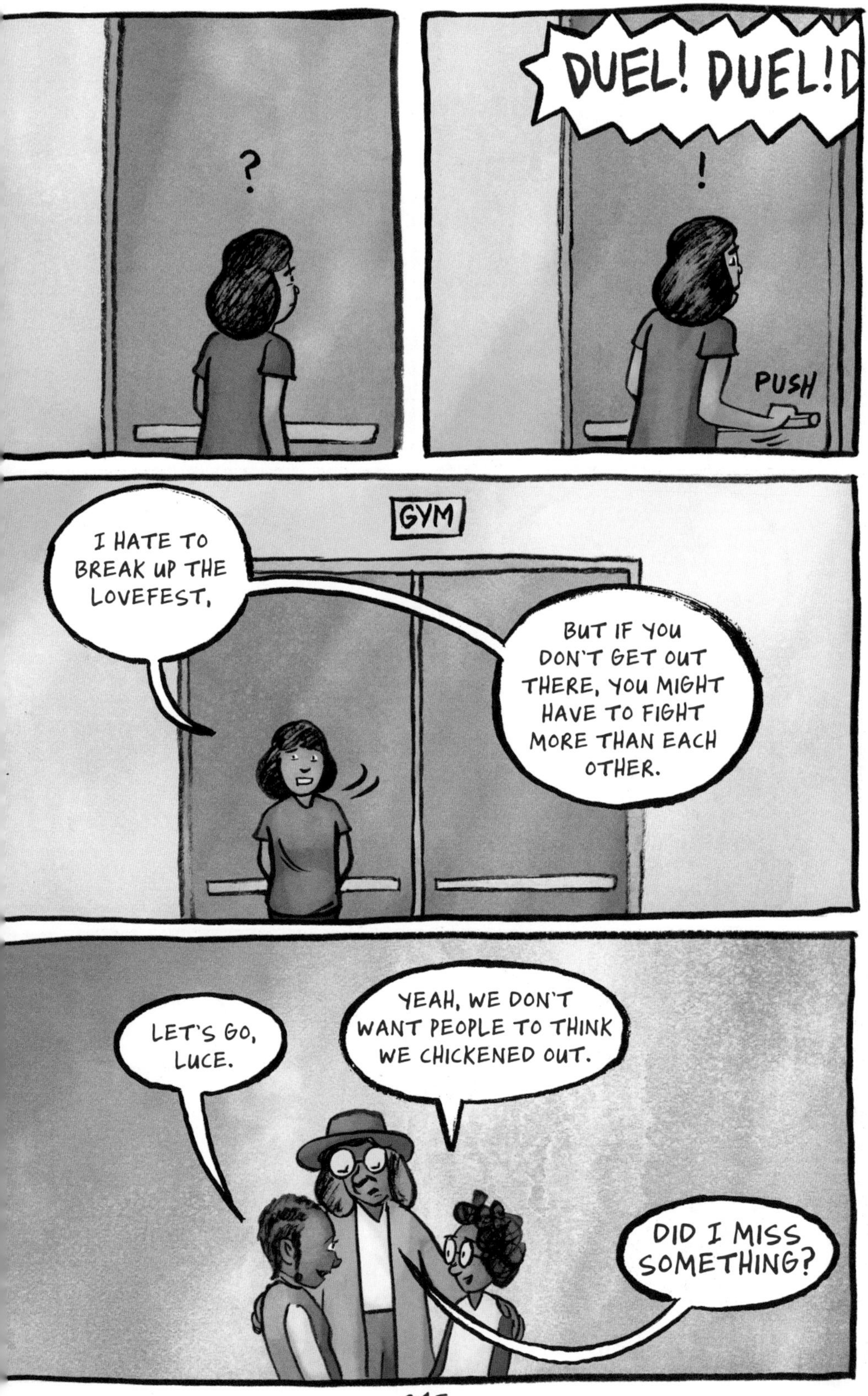
?
DUEL! DUEL! D
!
PUSH
GYM
I HATE TO BREAK UP THE LOVEFEST,
BUT IF YOU DON'T GET OUT THERE, YOU MIGHT HAVE TO FIGHT MORE THAN EACH OTHER.
LET'S GO, LUCE.
YEAH, WE DON'T WANT PEOPLE TO THINK WE CHICKENED OUT.
DID I MISS SOMETHING?

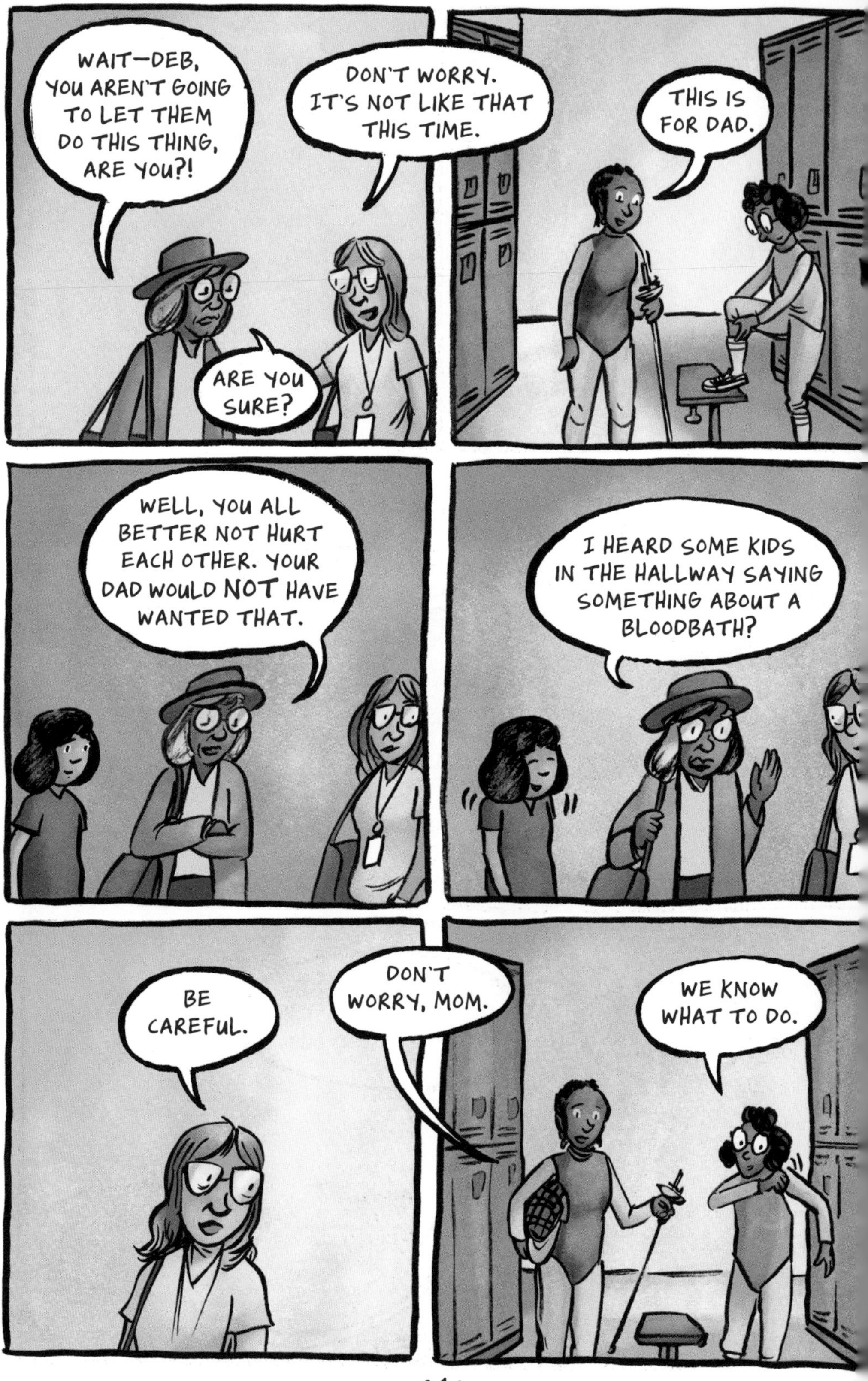
WAIT—DEB, YOU AREN'T GOING TO LET THEM DO THIS THING, ARE YOU?!
DON'T WORRY. IT'S NOT LIKE THAT THIS TIME.
ARE YOU SURE?
THIS IS FOR DAD.
WELL, YOU ALL BETTER NOT HURT EACH OTHER. YOUR DAD WOULD NOT HAVE WANTED THAT.
I HEARD SOME KIDS IN THE HALLWAY SAYING SOMETHING ABOUT A BLOODBATH?
BE CAREFUL.
DON'T WORRY, MOM.
WE KNOW WHAT TO DO.

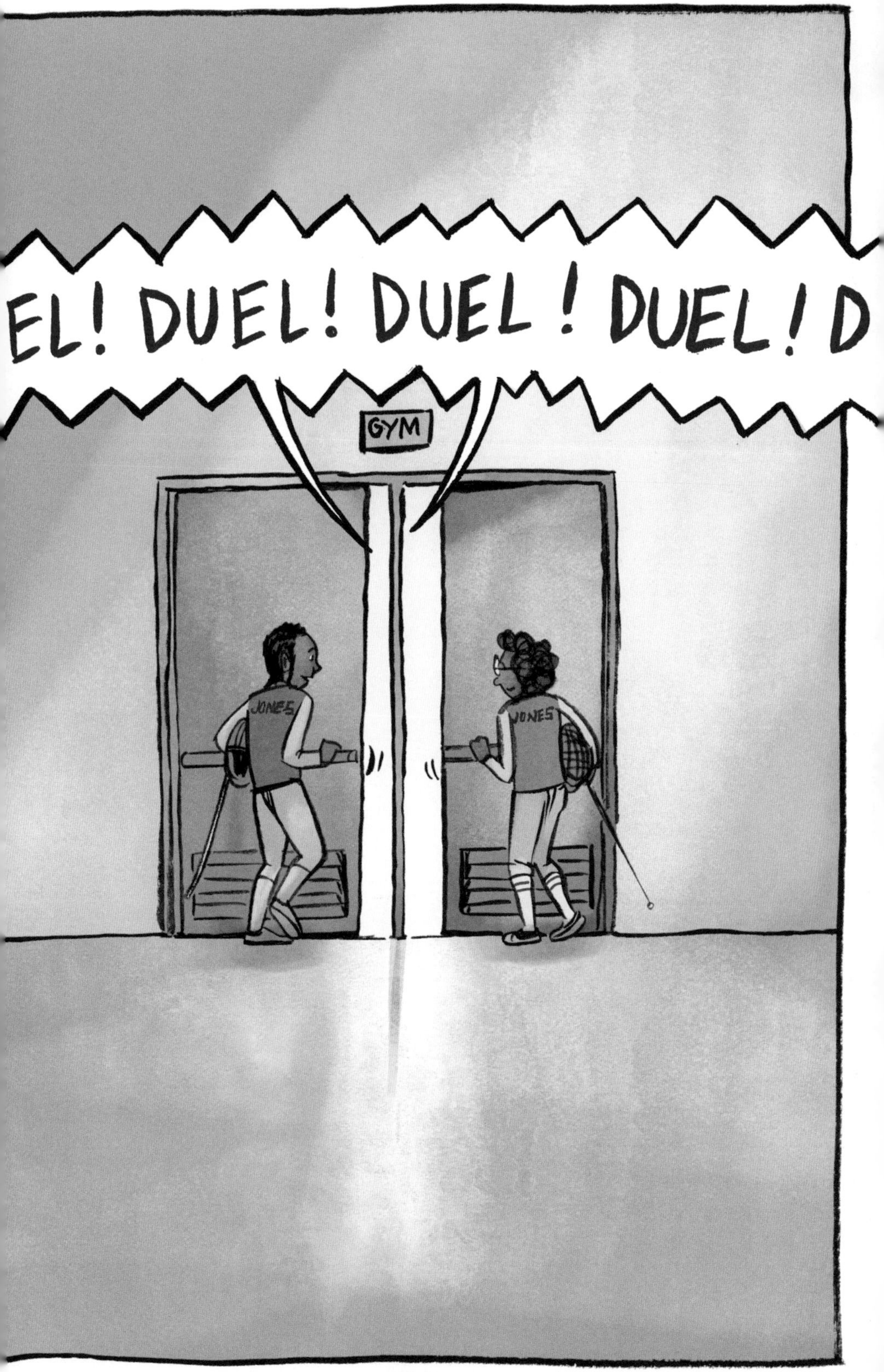
EL! DUEL! DUEL! DUEL! D
GYM
JONES
JONES

Chapter 15

Lunge

The lunge is one of the most common attacking techniques in all three weapons of fencing. To execute the lunge, you launch yourself at your opponent by kicking forward with your front foot and pushing off from the back leg while the back foot stays in place. When in a proper lunge position, you are using your full body length and that extension of your blade to reach the target. The lunge is meant to be an explosive forward action that delivers a solid attack to the opponent. While it is a fundamental maneuver, it is not, however, the only offensive attack in fencing.

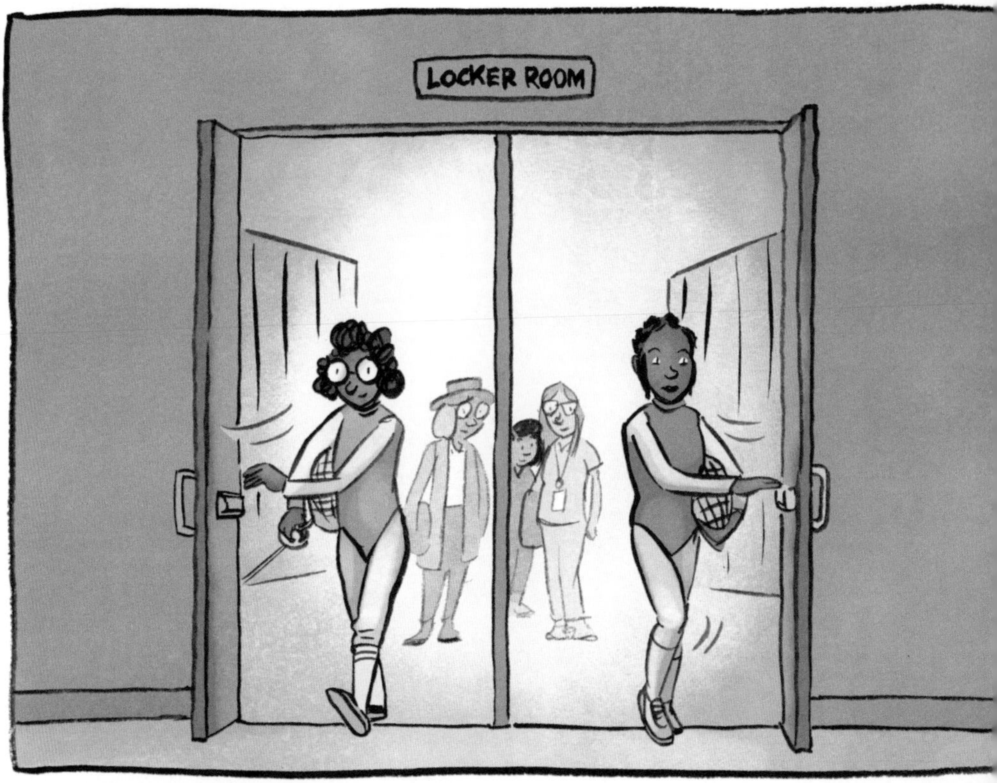
LOCKER ROOM

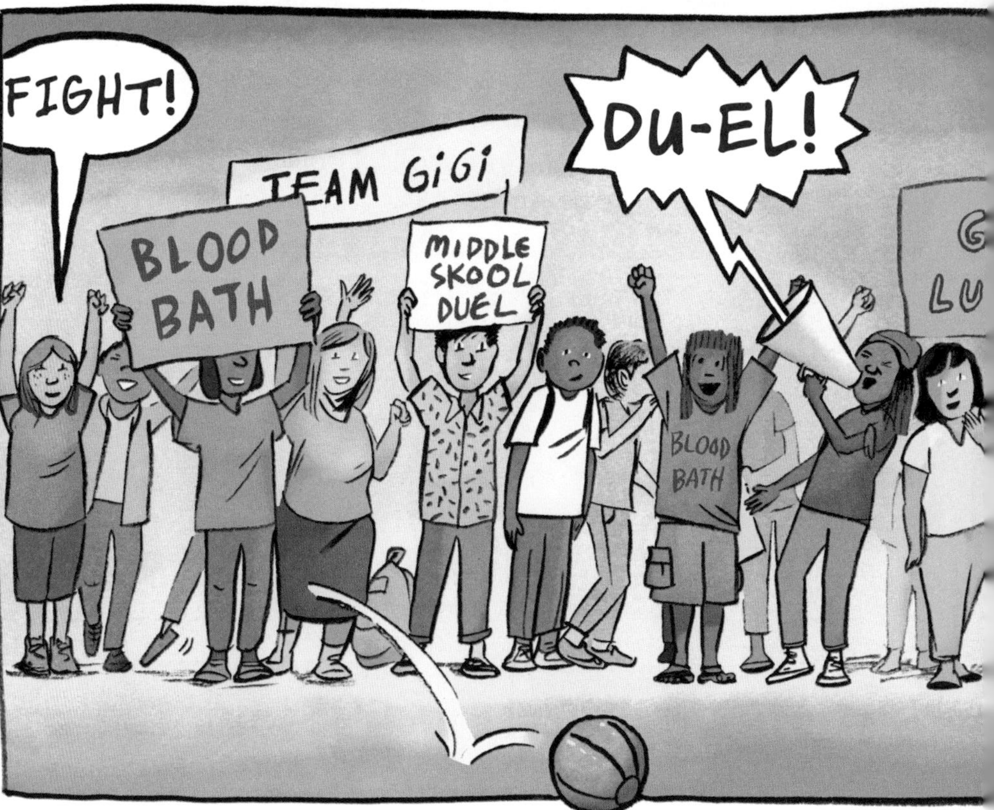
FIGHT!
TEAM GiGi
BLOOD BATH
MIDDLE SKOOL DUEL
DU-EL!
BLOOD BATH

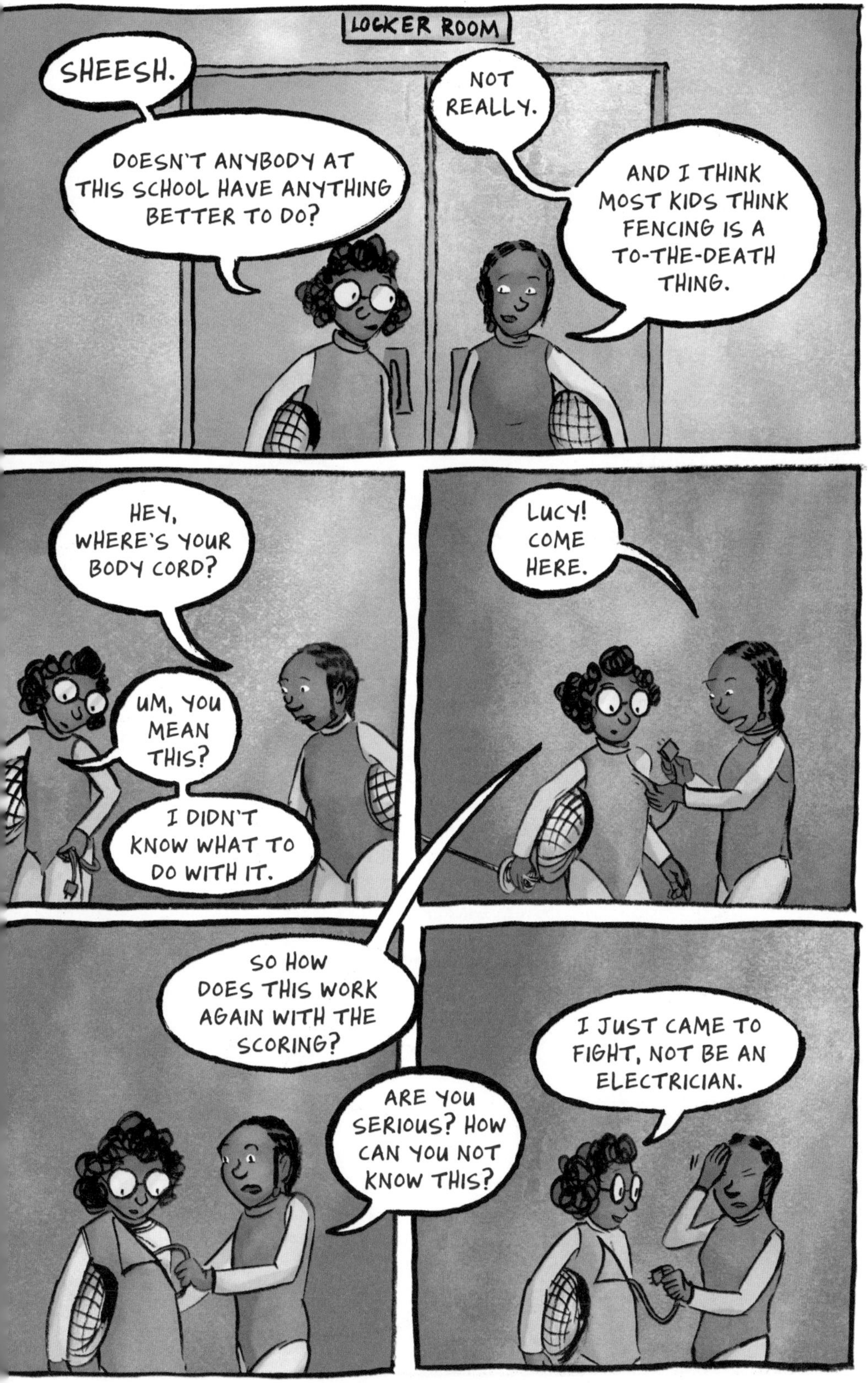
LOCKER ROOM
SHEESH.
DOESN'T ANYBODY AT THIS SCHOOL HAVE ANYTHING BETTER TO DO?
NOT REALLY.
AND I THINK MOST KIDS THINK FENCING IS A TO-THE-DEATH THING.
HEY, WHERE'S YOUR BODY CORD?
UM, YOU MEAN THIS?
I DIDN'T KNOW WHAT TO DO WITH IT.
LUCY! COME HERE.
SO HOW DOES THIS WORK AGAIN WITH THE SCORING?
ARE YOU SERIOUS? HOW CAN YOU NOT KNOW THIS?
I JUST CAME TO FIGHT, NOT BE AN ELECTRICIAN.

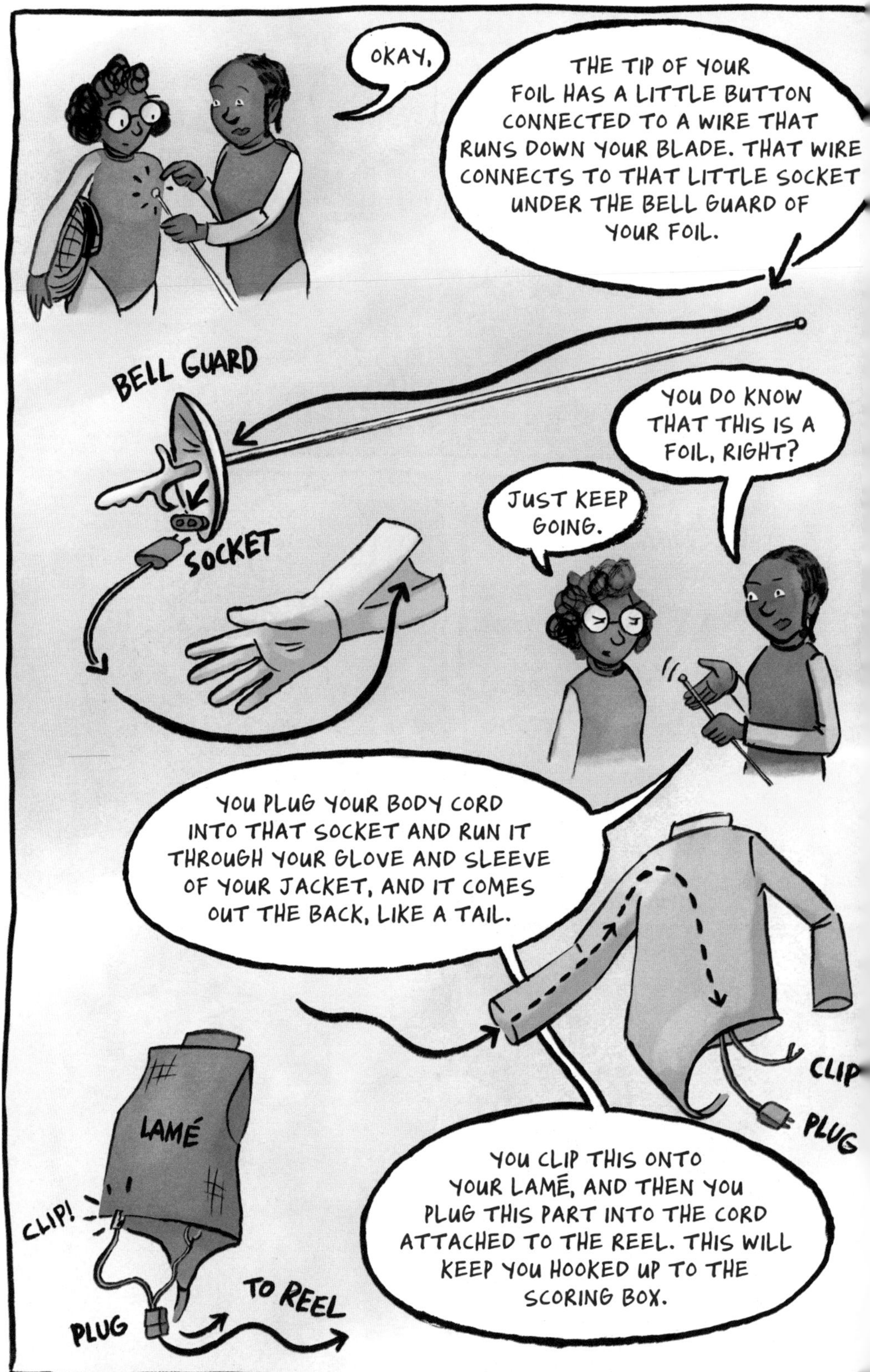
OKAY,
THE TIP OF YOUR FOIL HAS A LITTLE BUTTON CONNECTED TO A WIRE THAT RUNS DOWN YOUR BLADE. THAT WIRE CONNECTS TO THAT LITTLE SOCKET UNDER THE BELL GUARD OF YOUR FOIL.
BELL GUARD
SOCKET
YOU DO KNOW THAT THIS IS A FOIL, RIGHT?
JUST KEEP GOING.
YOU PLUG YOUR BODY CORD INTO THAT SOCKET AND RUN IT THROUGH YOUR GLOVE AND SLEEVE OF YOUR JACKET, AND IT COMES OUT THE BACK, LIKE A TAIL.
CLIP
PLUG
LAMÉ
CLIP!
PLUG
TO REEL
YOU CLIP THIS ONTO YOUR LAMÉ, AND THEN YOU PLUG THIS PART INTO THE CORD ATTACHED TO THE REEL. THIS WILL KEEP YOU HOOKED UP TO THE SCORING BOX.

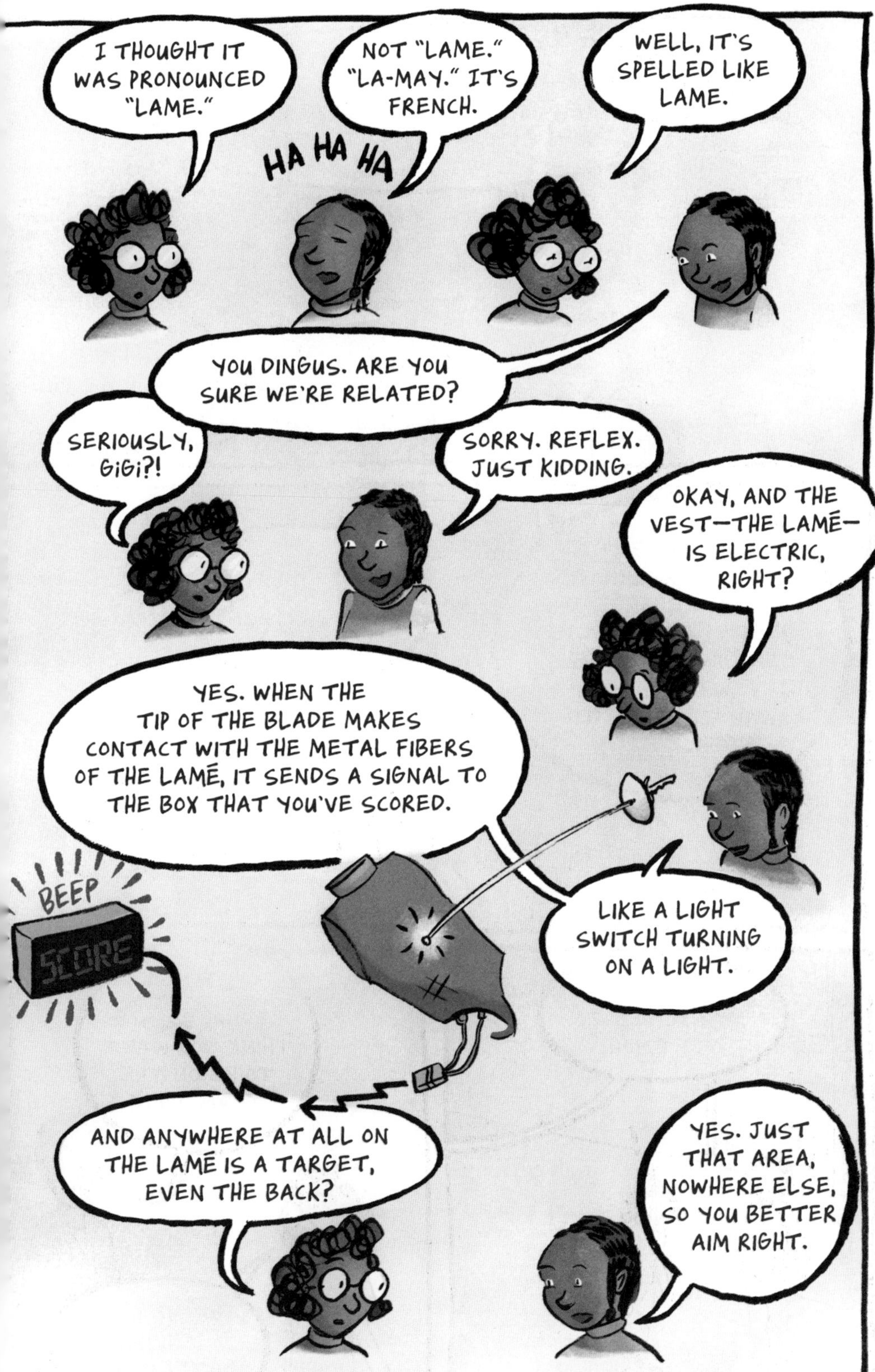
I THOUGHT IT WAS PRONOUNCED "LAME."
HA HA HA
NOT "LAME." "LA-MAY." IT'S FRENCH.
WELL, IT'S SPELLED LIKE LAME.
YOU DINGUS. ARE YOU SURE WE'RE RELATED?
SERIOUSLY, GIGI?!
SORRY. REFLEX. JUST KIDDING.
OKAY, AND THE VEST—THE LAMÉ—IS ELECTRIC, RIGHT?
YES. WHEN THE TIP OF THE BLADE MAKES CONTACT WITH THE METAL FIBERS OF THE LAMÉ, IT SENDS A SIGNAL TO THE BOX THAT YOU'VE SCORED.
BEEP
SCORE
LIKE A LIGHT SWITCH TURNING ON A LIGHT.
AND ANYWHERE AT ALL ON THE LAMÉ IS A TARGET, EVEN THE BACK?
YES. JUST THAT AREA, NOWHERE ELSE, SO YOU BETTER AIM RIGHT.

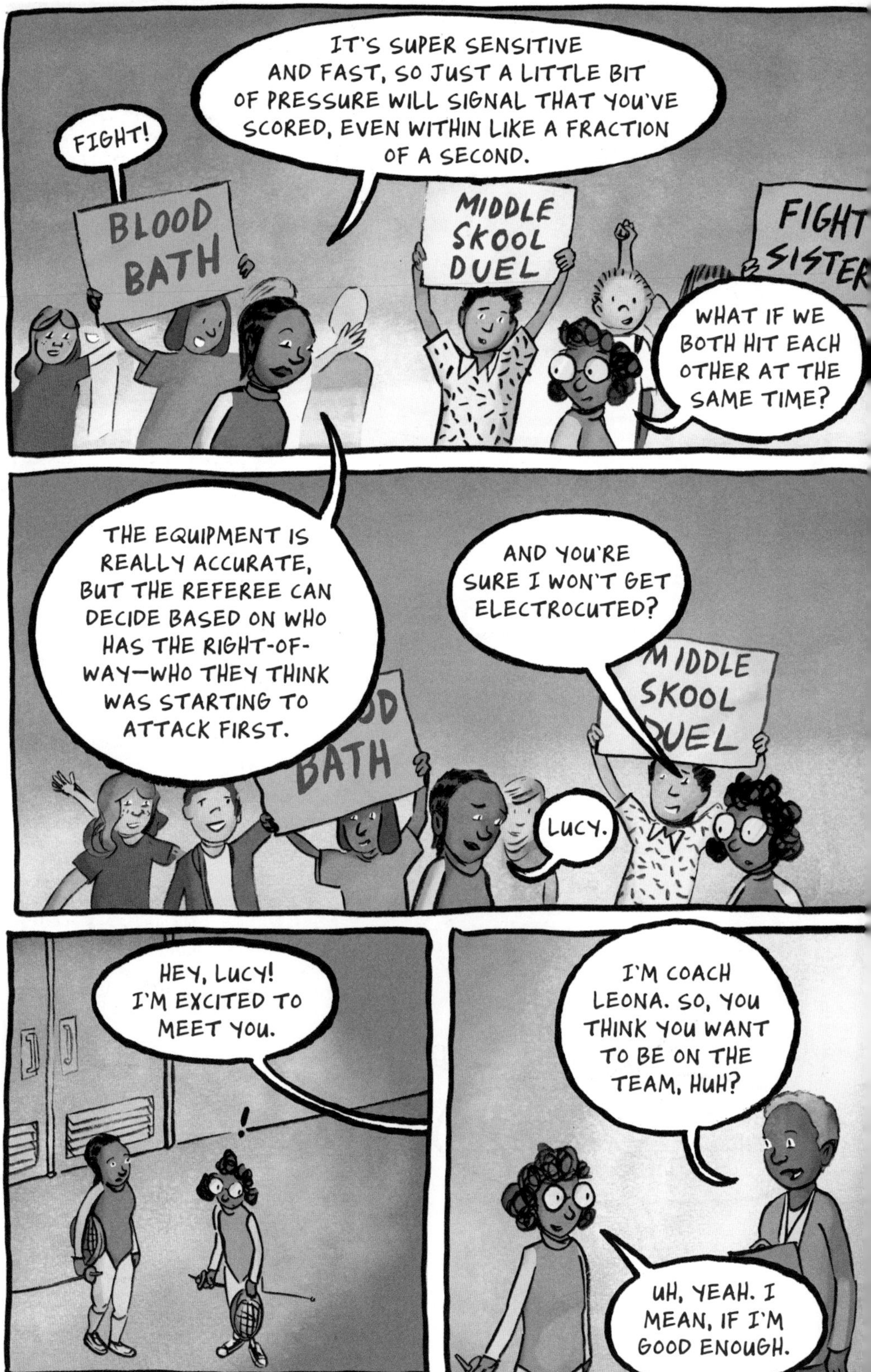
FIGHT!
IT'S SUPER SENSITIVE AND FAST, SO JUST A LITTLE BIT OF PRESSURE WILL SIGNAL THAT YOU'VE SCORED, EVEN WITHIN LIKE A FRACTION OF A SECOND.
BLOOD BATH
MIDDLE SKOOL DUEL
FIGHT SISTER
WHAT IF WE BOTH HIT EACH OTHER AT THE SAME TIME?
THE EQUIPMENT IS REALLY ACCURATE, BUT THE REFEREE CAN DECIDE BASED ON WHO HAS THE RIGHT-OF-WAY—WHO THEY THINK WAS STARTING TO ATTACK FIRST.
AND YOU'RE SURE I WON'T GET ELECTROCUTED?
MIDDLE SKOOL DUEL
BATH
LUCY.
HEY, LUCY! I'M EXCITED TO MEET YOU.
!
I'M COACH LEONA. SO, YOU THINK YOU WANT TO BE ON THE TEAM, HUH?
UH, YEAH. I MEAN, IF I'M GOOD ENOUGH.

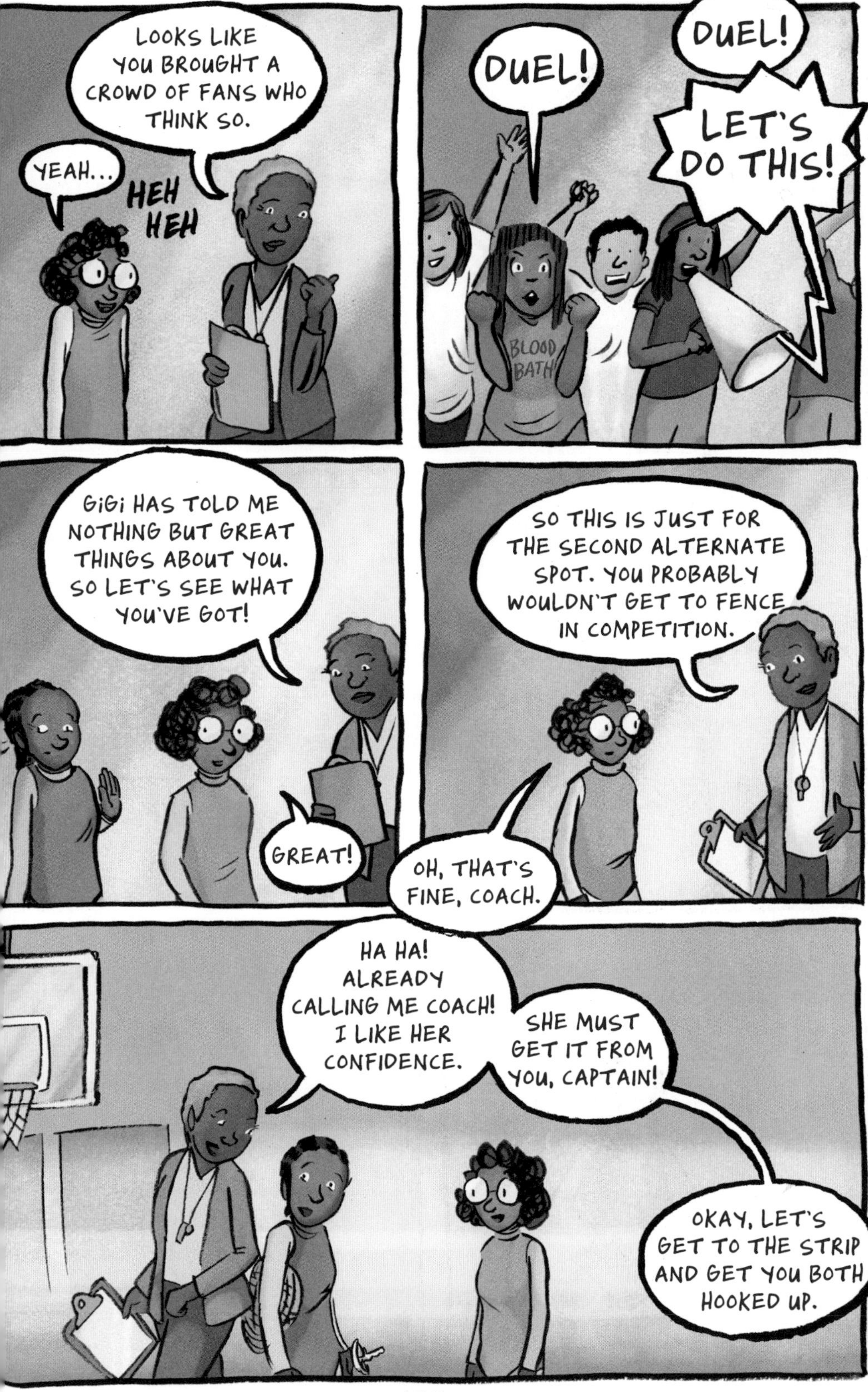
LOOKS LIKE YOU BROUGHT A CROWD OF FANS WHO THINK SO.
YEAH...
HEH HEH
DUEL!
DUEL!
LET'S DO THIS!
BLOOD BATH
GIGI HAS TOLD ME NOTHING BUT GREAT THINGS ABOUT YOU. SO LET'S SEE WHAT YOU'VE GOT!
GREAT!
SO THIS IS JUST FOR THE SECOND ALTERNATE SPOT. YOU PROBABLY WOULDN'T GET TO FENCE IN COMPETITION.
OH, THAT'S FINE, COACH.
HA HA! ALREADY CALLING ME COACH! I LIKE HER CONFIDENCE.
SHE MUST GET IT FROM YOU, CAPTAIN!
OKAY, LET'S GET TO THE STRIP AND GET YOU BOTH HOOKED UP.

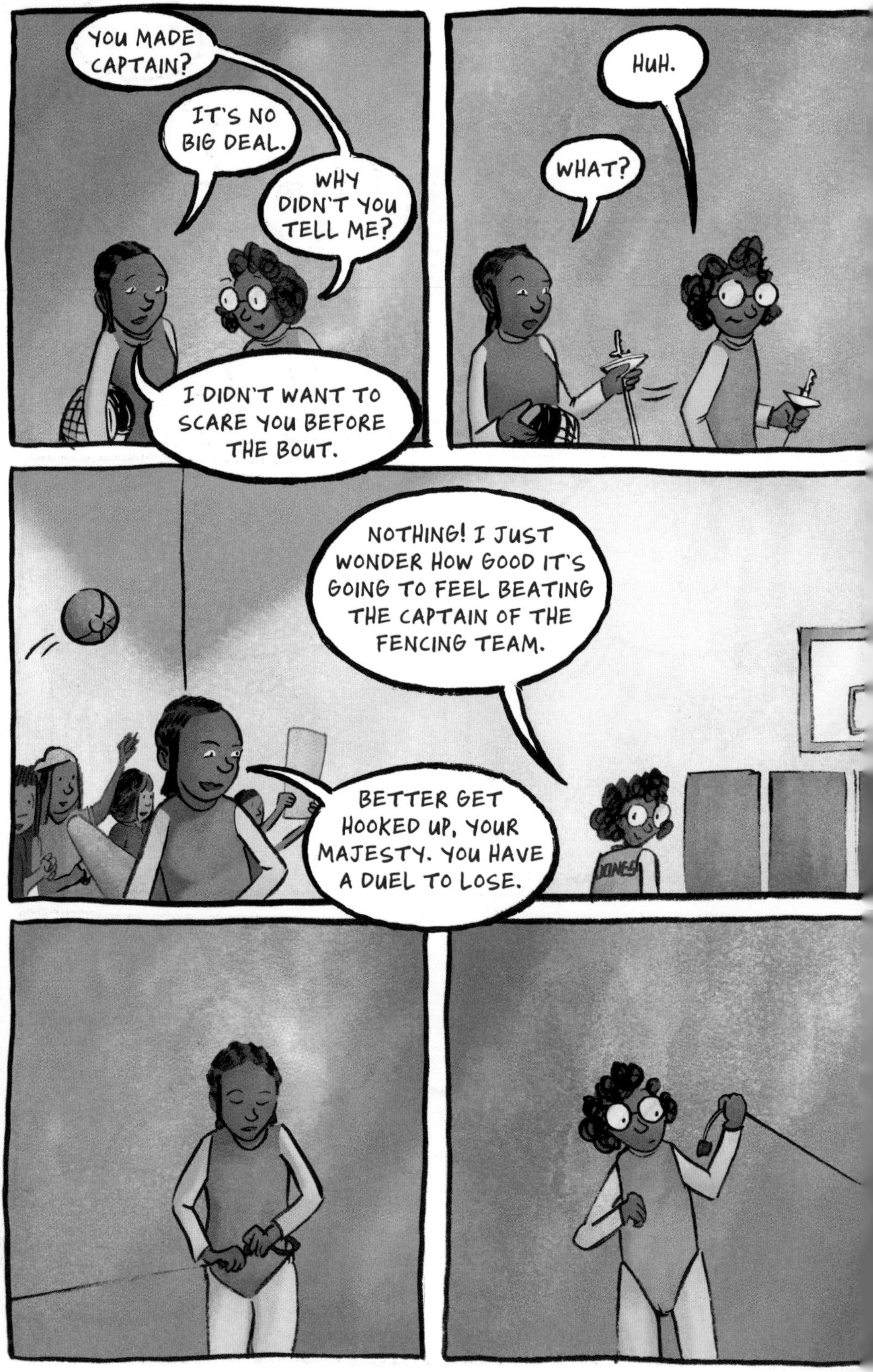
YOU MADE CAPTAIN?
IT'S NO BIG DEAL.
WHY DIDN'T YOU TELL ME?
I DIDN'T WANT TO SCARE YOU BEFORE THE BOUT.
HUH.
WHAT?
NOTHING! I JUST WONDER HOW GOOD IT'S GOING TO FEEL BEATING THE CAPTAIN OF THE FENCING TEAM.
BETTER GET HOOKED UP, YOUR MAJESTY. YOU HAVE A DUEL TO LOSE.

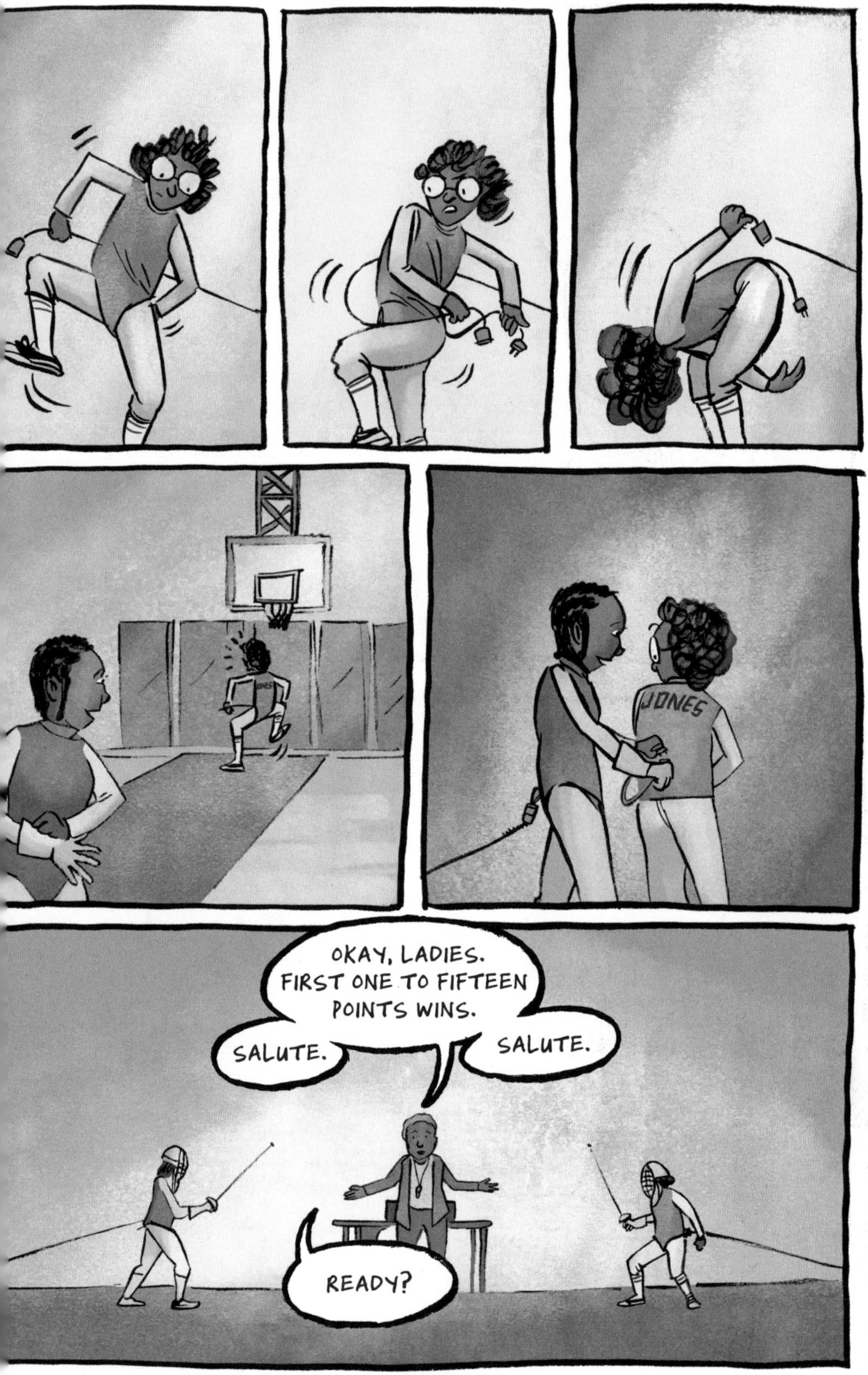
JONES
JONES
OKAY, LADIES.
FIRST ONE TO FIFTEEN
POINTS WINS.
SALUTE.
SALUTE.
READY?

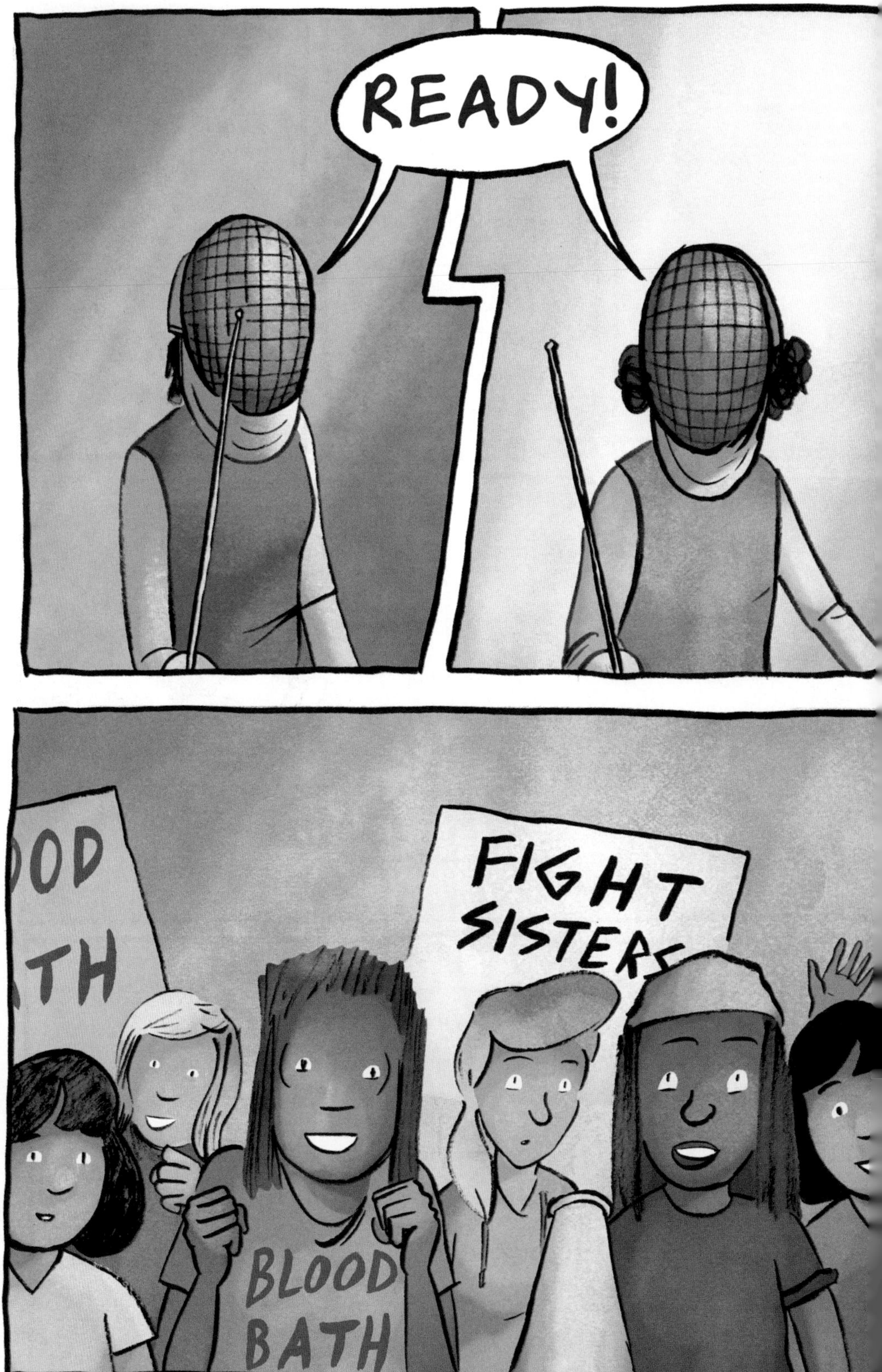
READY!
OOD
TH
FIGHT
SISTERS
BLOOD
BATH

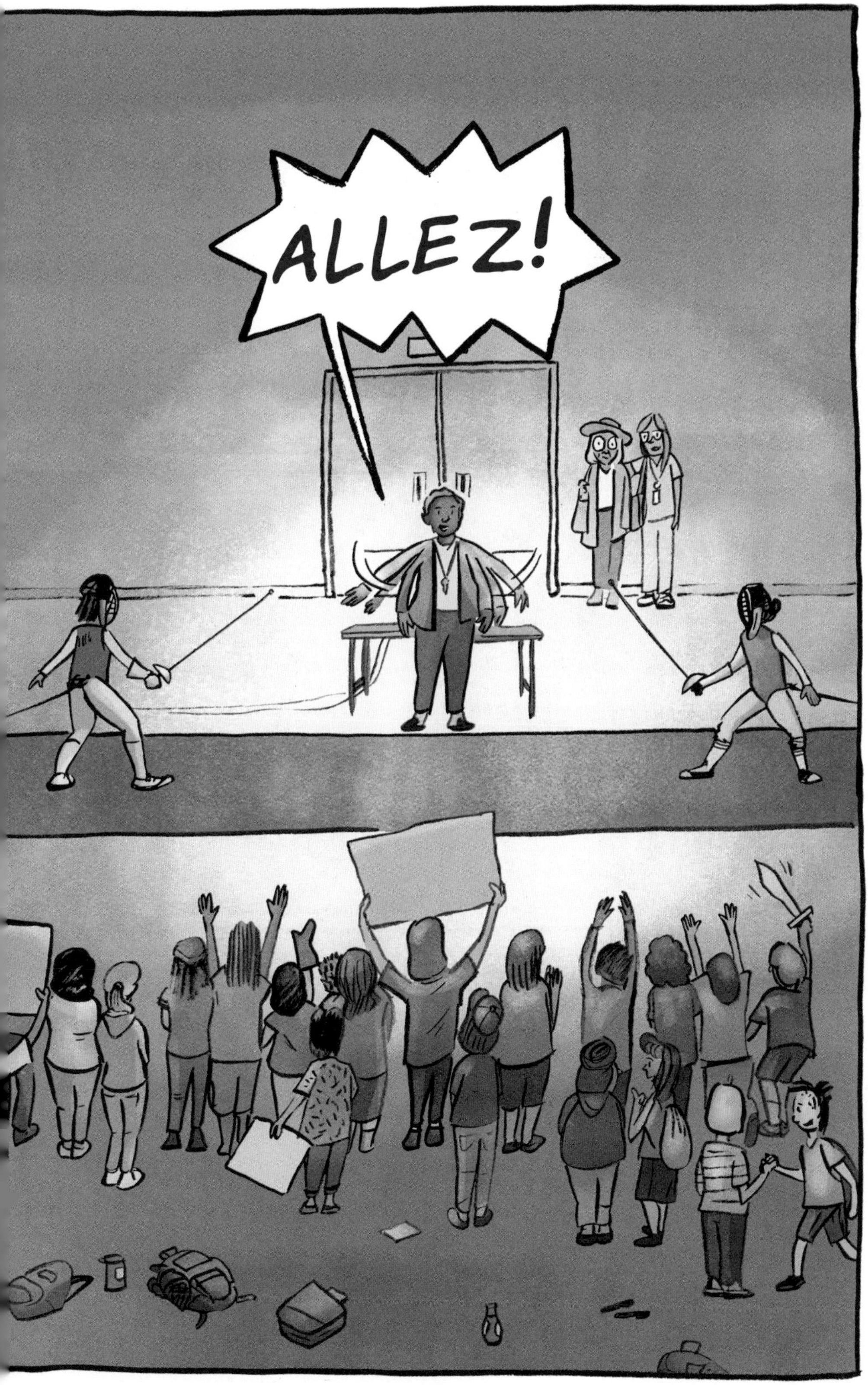
ALLEZ!

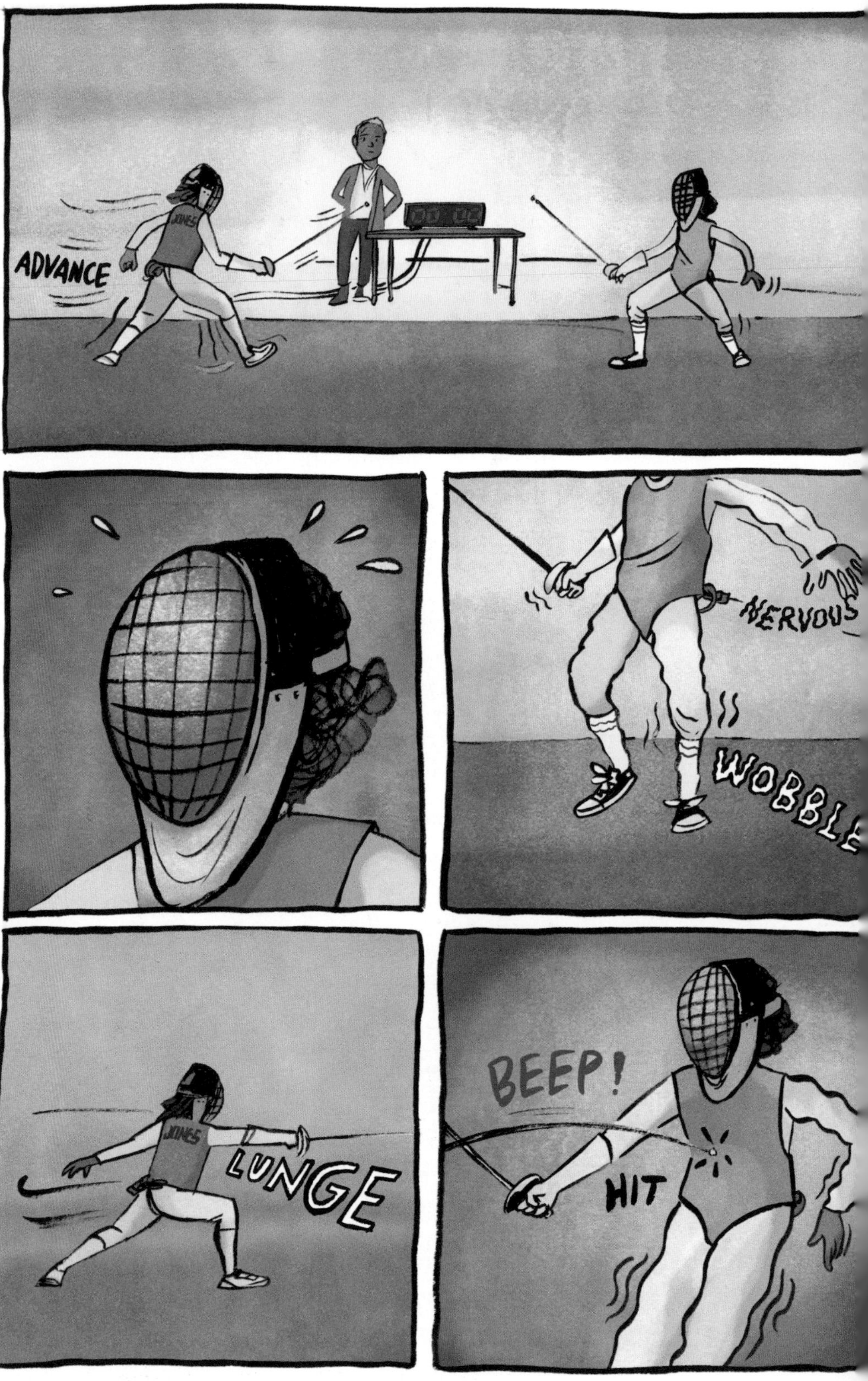
ADVANCE
NERVOUS
WOBBLE
LUNGE
BEEP!
HIT

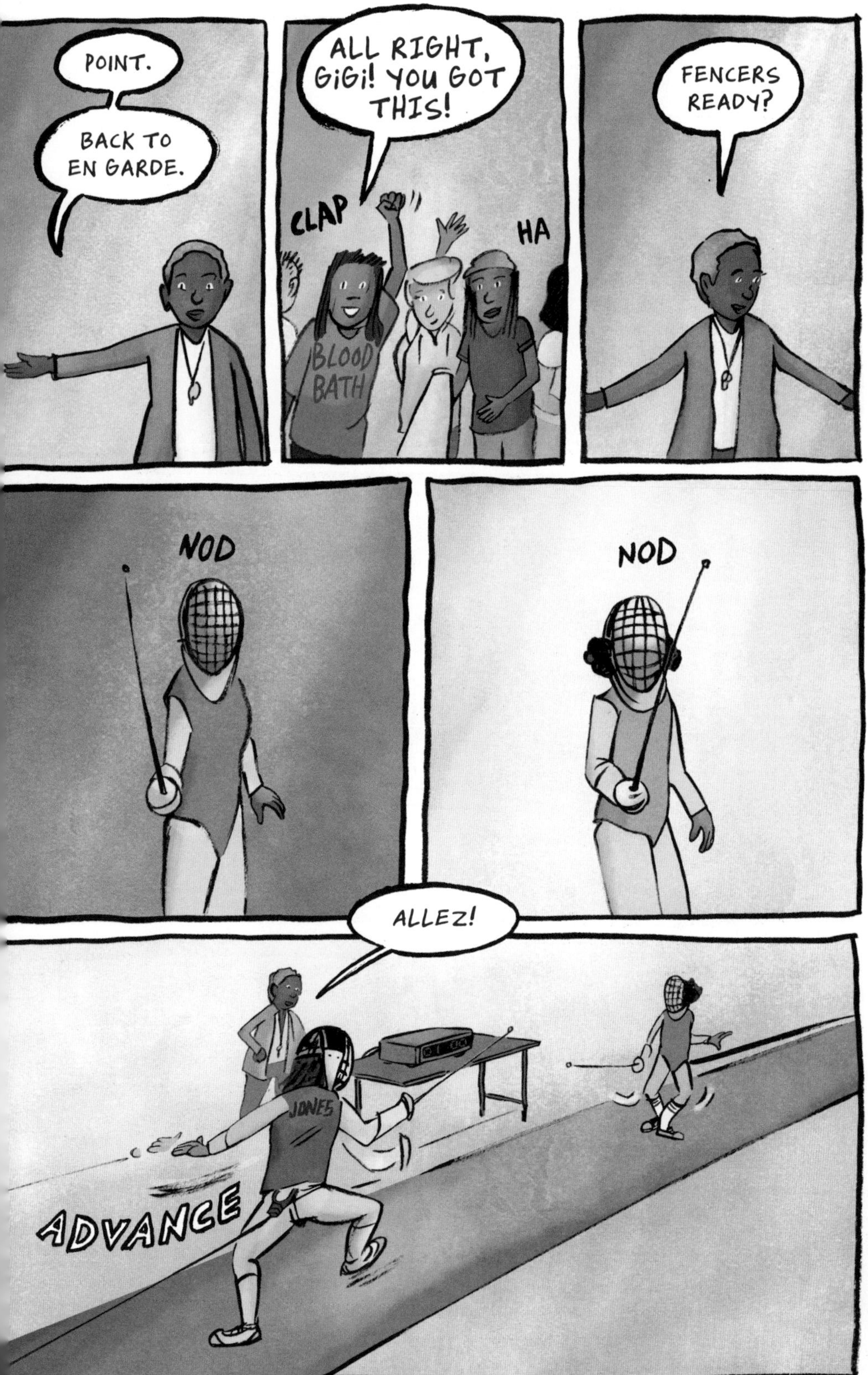
POINT.
BACK TO EN GARDE.
ALL RIGHT, GIGI! YOU GOT THIS!
CLAP
HA
BLOOD BATH
FENCERS READY?
NOD
NOD
ALLEZ!
JONES
ADVANCE

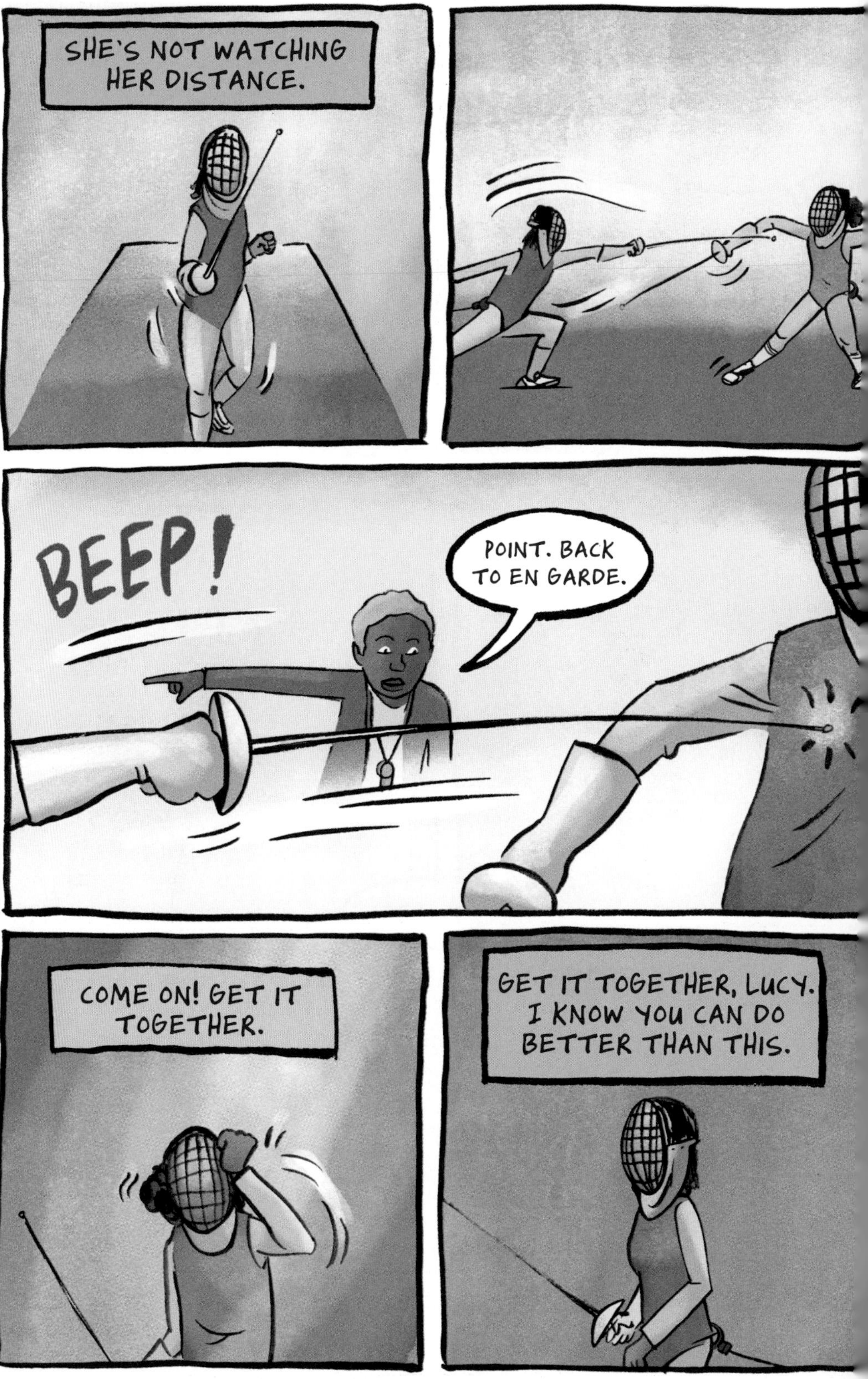
SHE'S NOT WATCHING HER DISTANCE.
BEEP!
POINT. BACK TO EN GARDE.
COME ON! GET IT TOGETHER.
GET IT TOGETHER, LUCY. I KNOW YOU CAN DO BETTER THAN THIS.

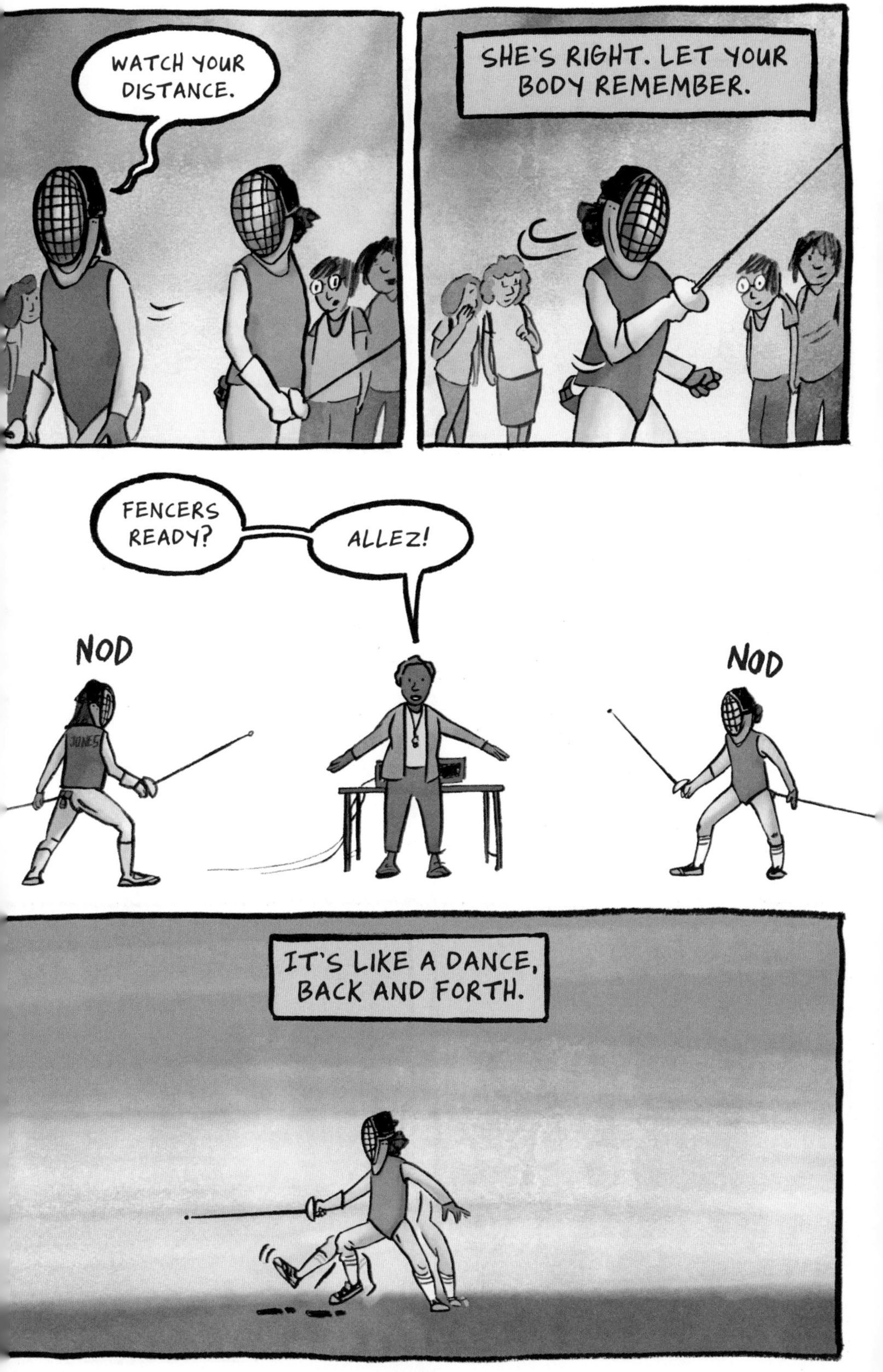
WATCH YOUR DISTANCE.
SHE'S RIGHT. LET YOUR BODY REMEMBER.
FENCERS READY?
ALLEZ!
NOD
JONES
NOD
IT'S LIKE A DANCE, BACK AND FORTH.

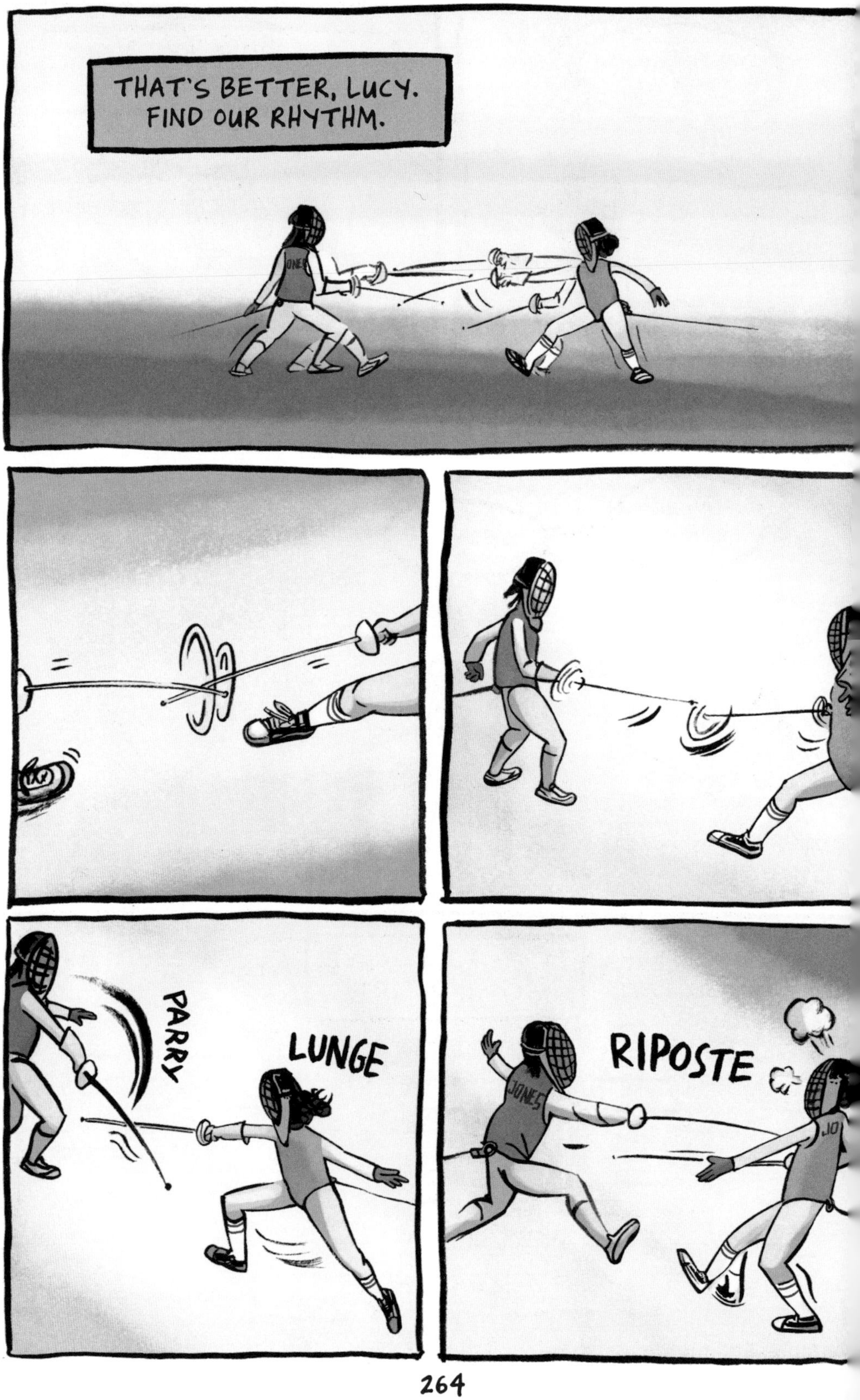
THAT'S BETTER, LUCY.
FIND OUR RHYTHM.
PARRY
LUNGE
RIPOSTE

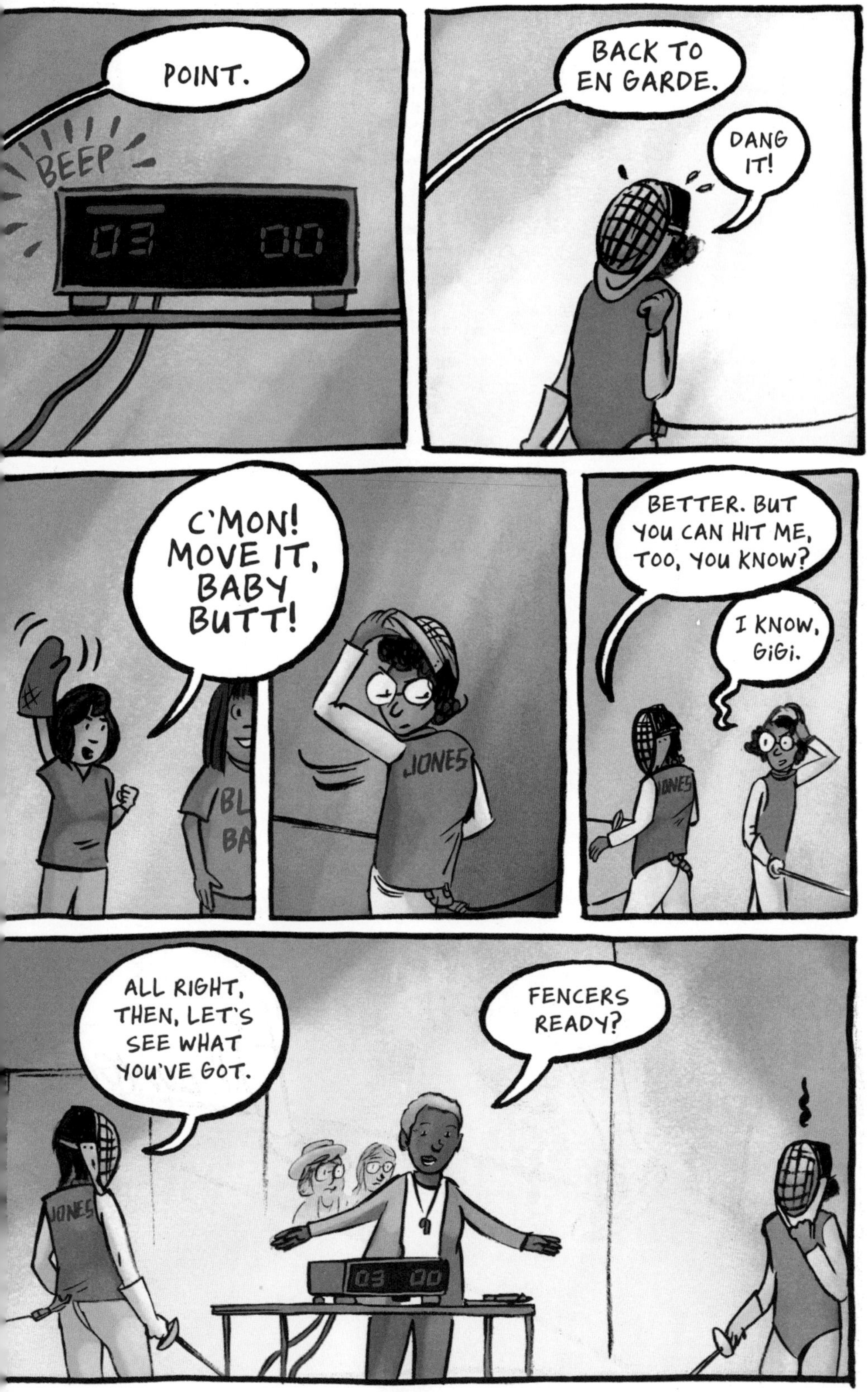

POINT.
BEEP
03
00
BACK TO EN GARDE.
DANG IT!
C'MON! MOVE IT, BABY BUTT!
JONES
BETTER. BUT YOU CAN HIT ME, TOO, YOU KNOW?
I KNOW, GiGi.
ALL RIGHT, THEN, LET'S SEE WHAT YOU'VE GOT.
FENCERS READY?

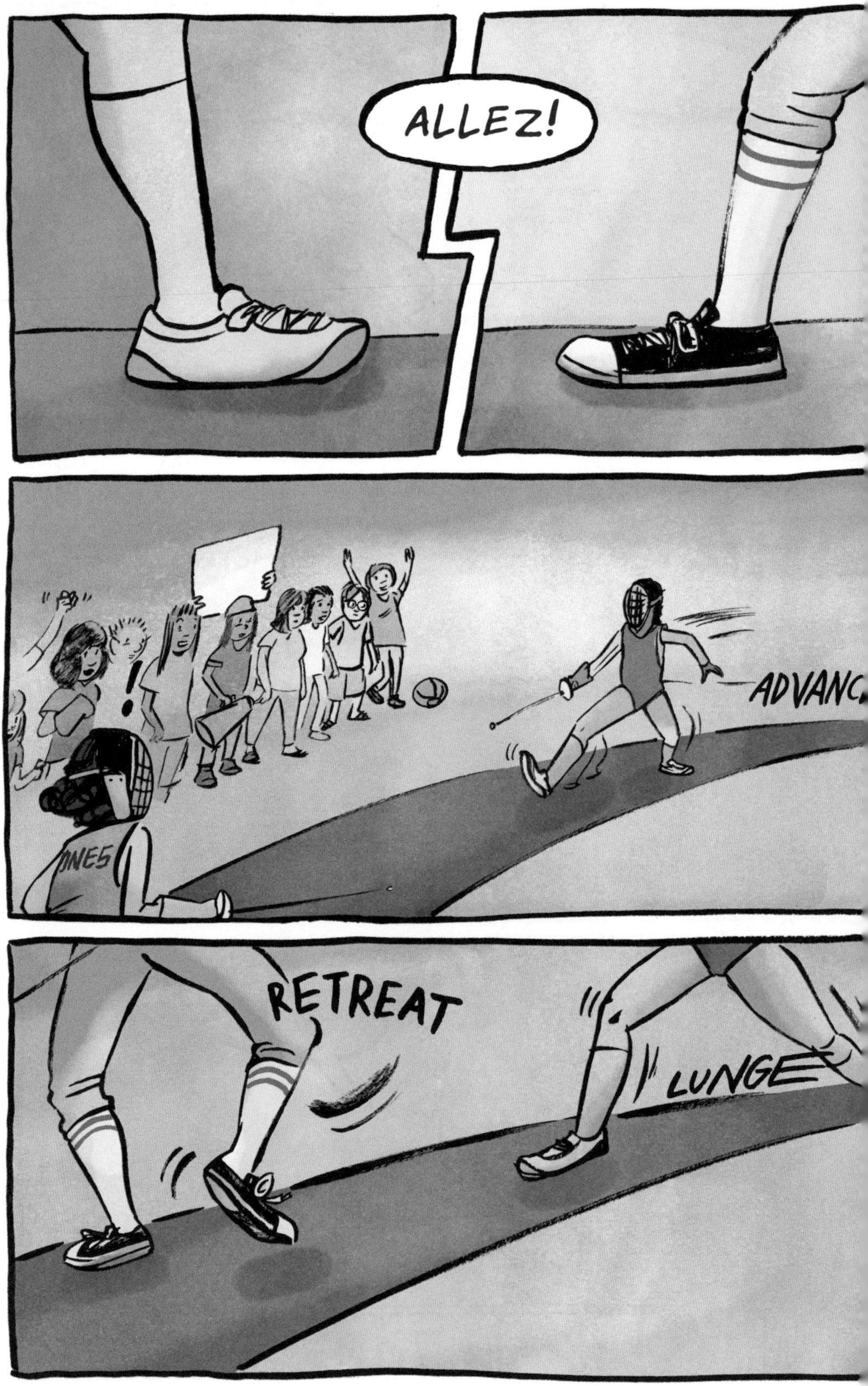
ALLEZ!
ADVANC
RETREAT
LUNGE

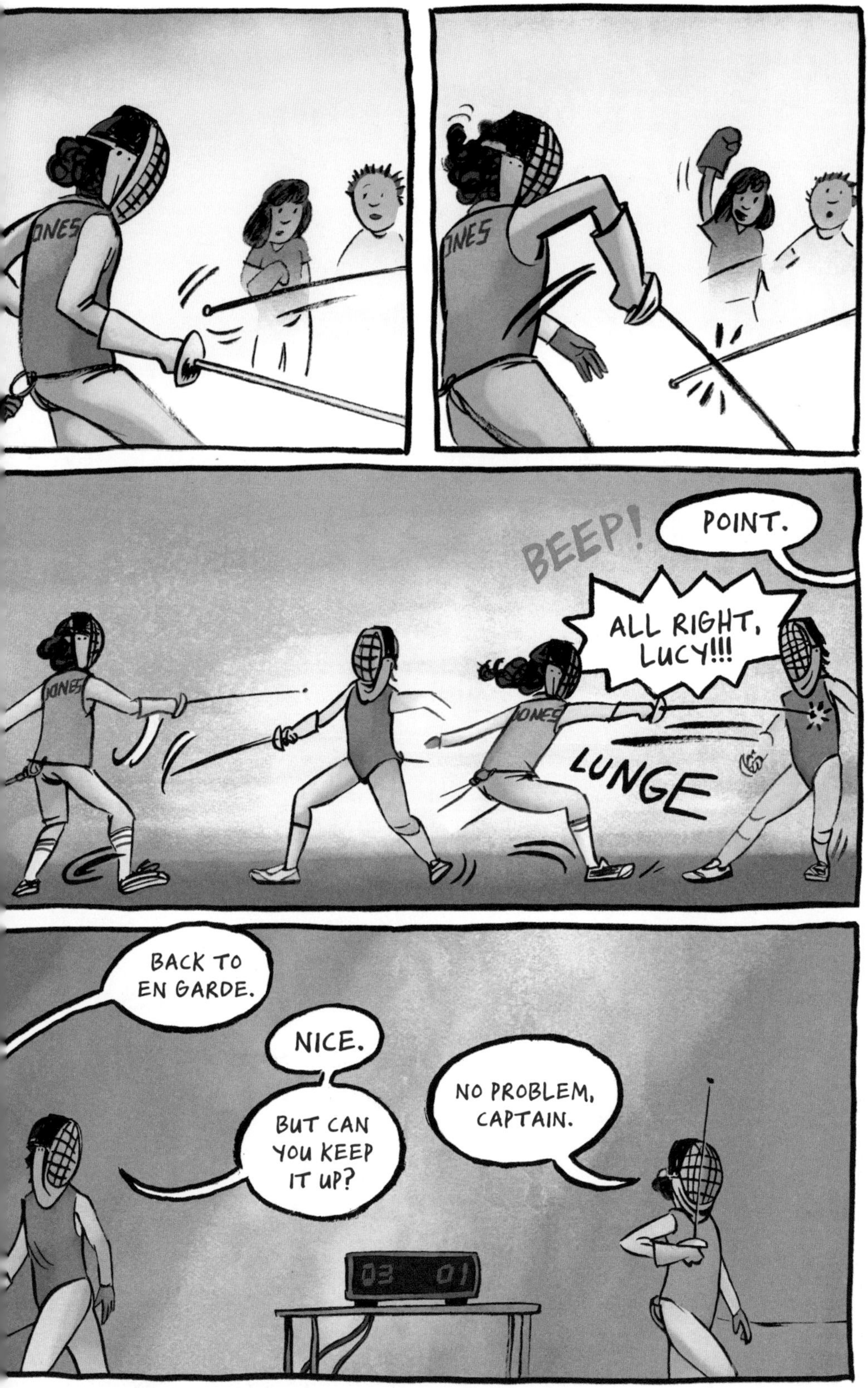
JONES
JONES
BEEP!
POINT.
ALL RIGHT, LUCY!!!
JONES
JONES
LUNGE
BACK TO EN GARDE.
NICE.
BUT CAN YOU KEEP IT UP?
NO PROBLEM, CAPTAIN.
03 01

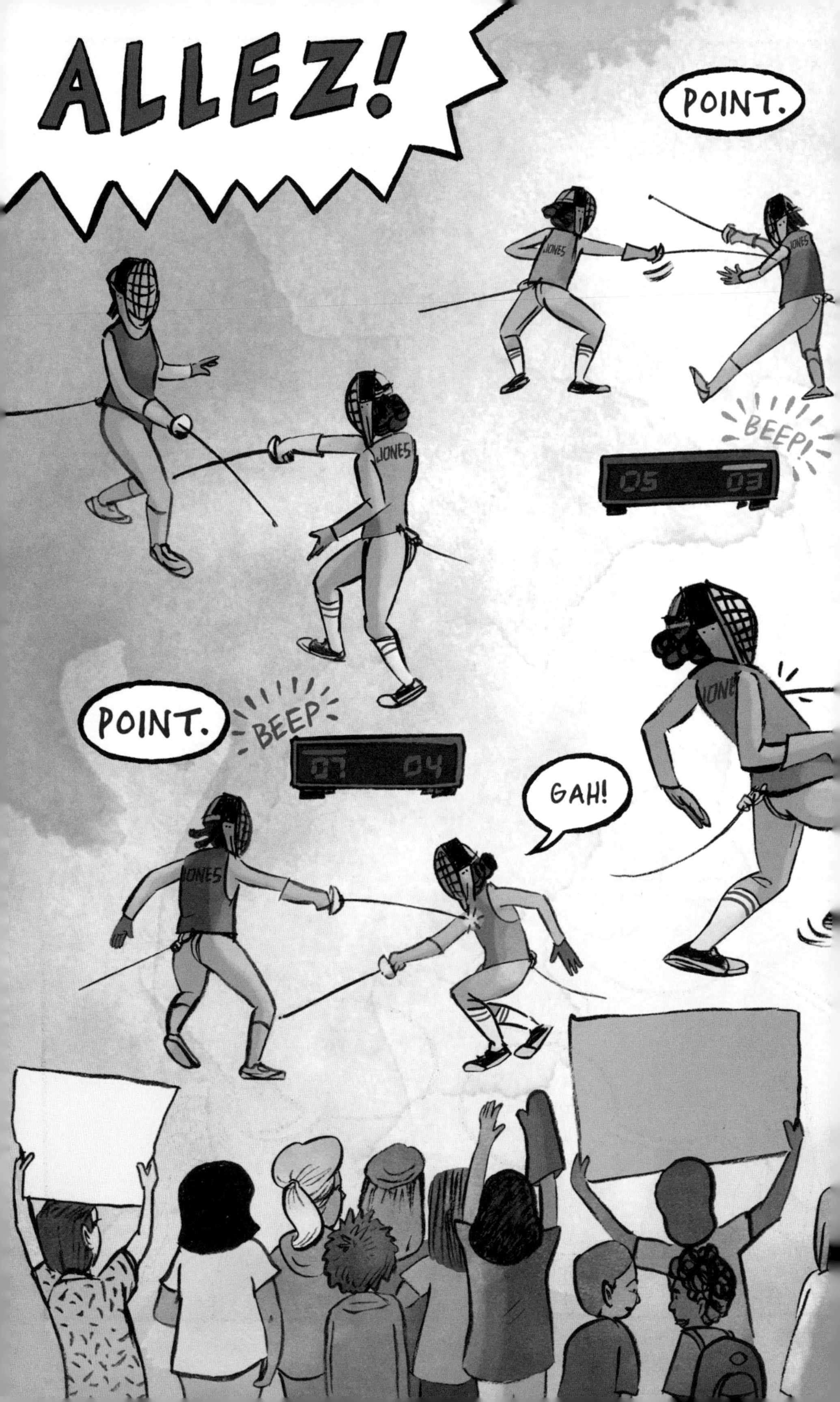

ALLEZ!
POINT.
JONES
JONES
JONES
BEEP!
05 03
POINT.
BEEP
07 04
JONES
GAH!
JONES

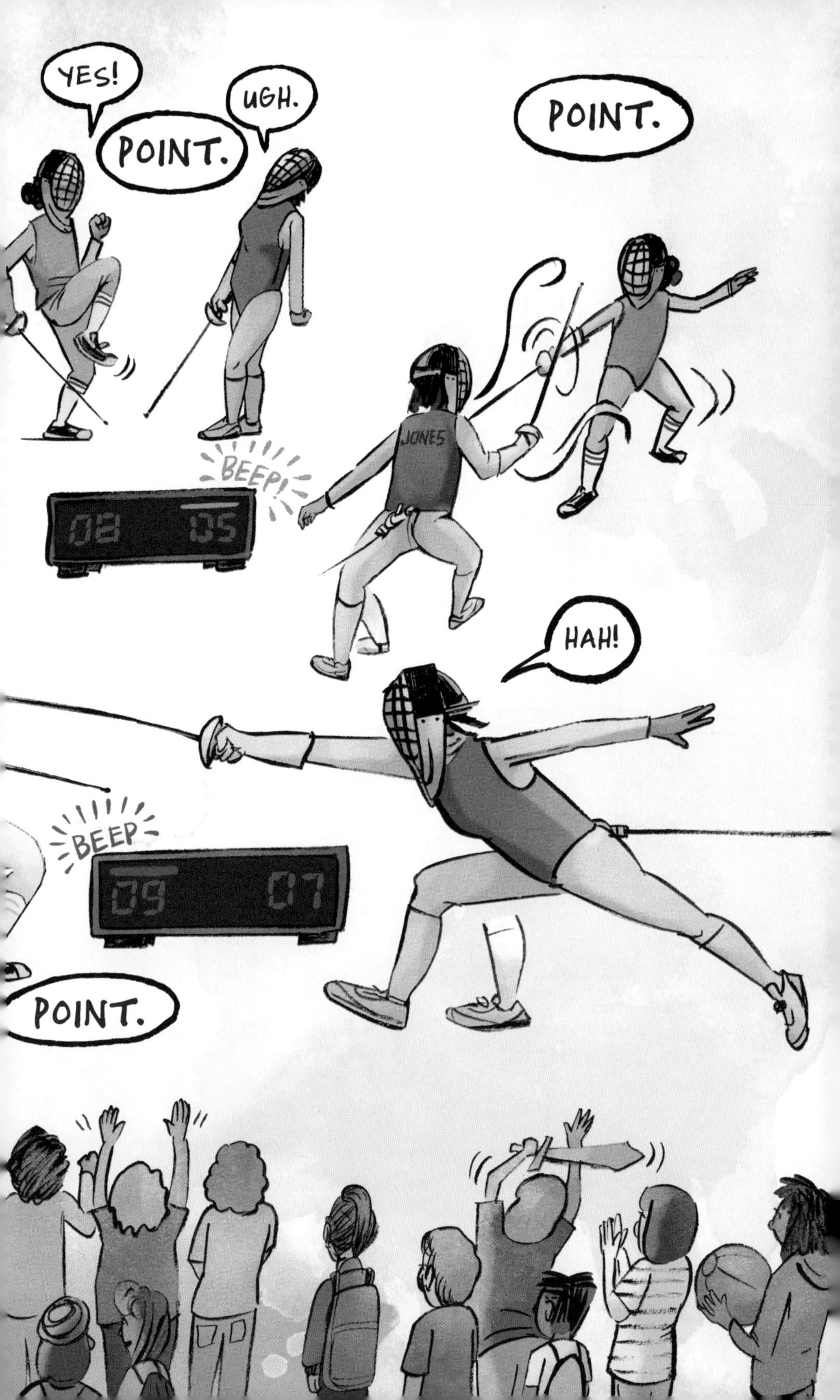
YES!
POINT.
UGH.
POINT.
BEEP!
JONES
HAH!
BEEP
POINT.

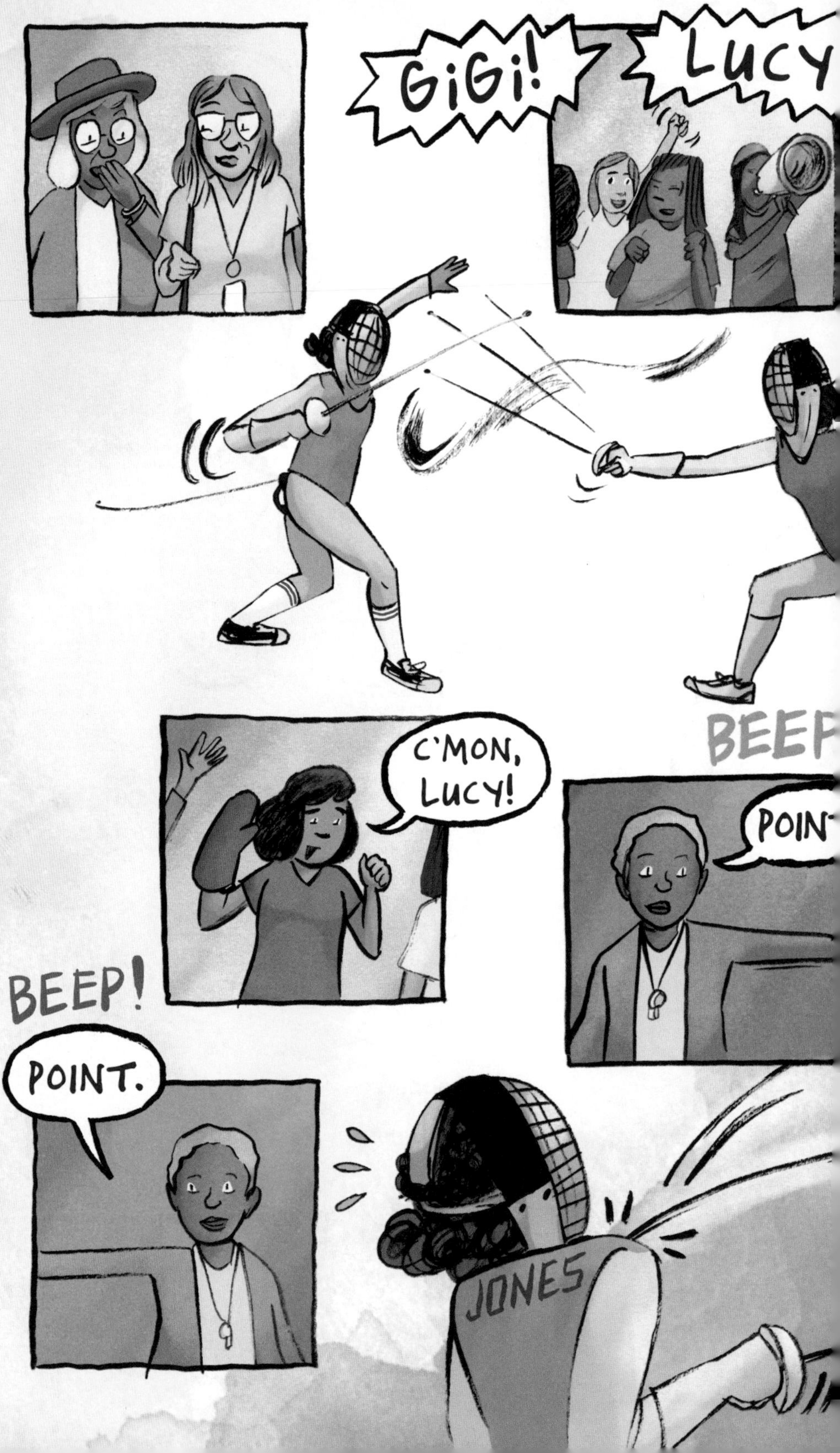
GiGi!
LUCY
C'MON, LUCY!
BEEP
POIN
BEEP!
POINT.
JONES

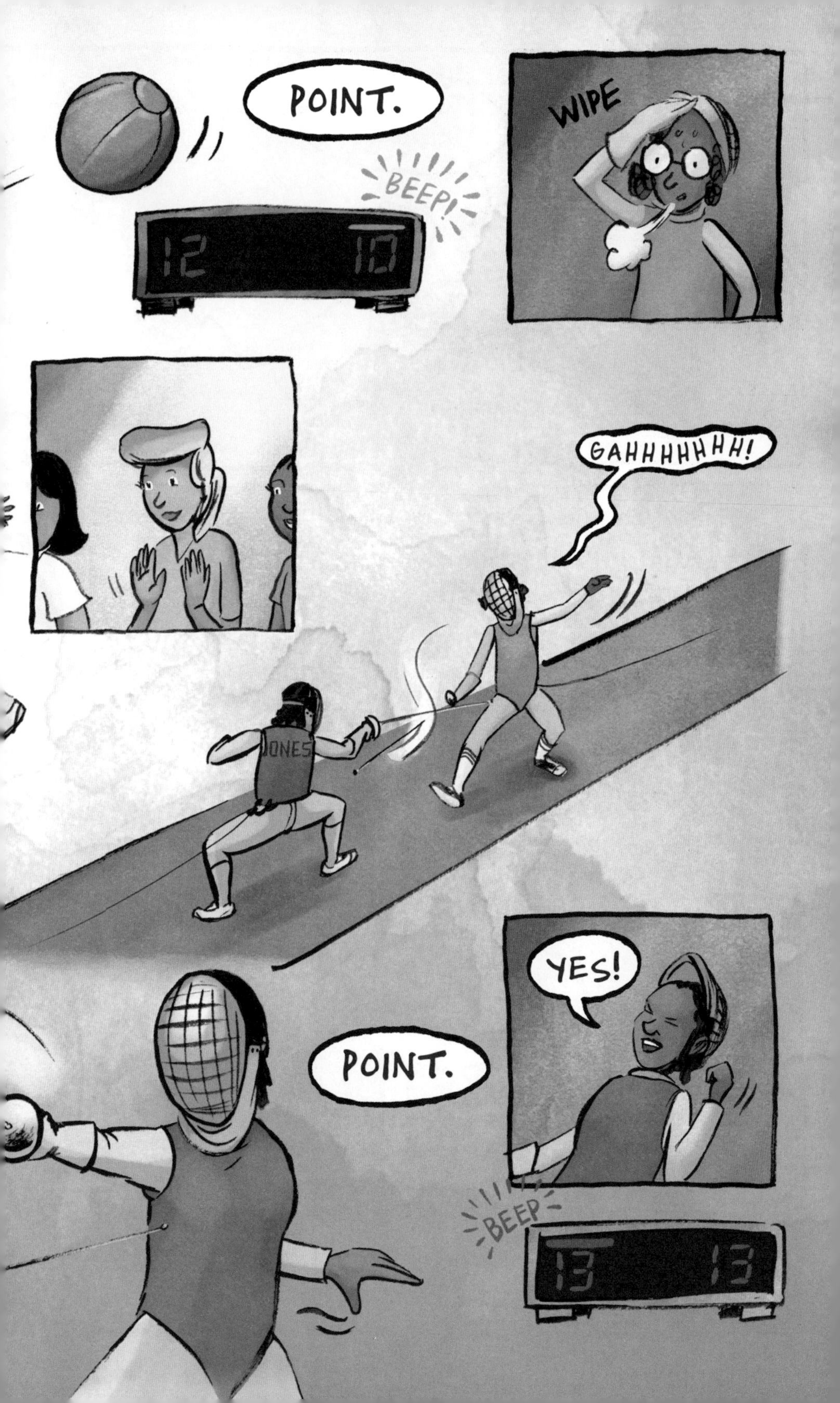
POINT.
BEEP!
12
10
WIPE
GAHHHHHHH!
JONES
POINT.
YES!
BEEP
13
13

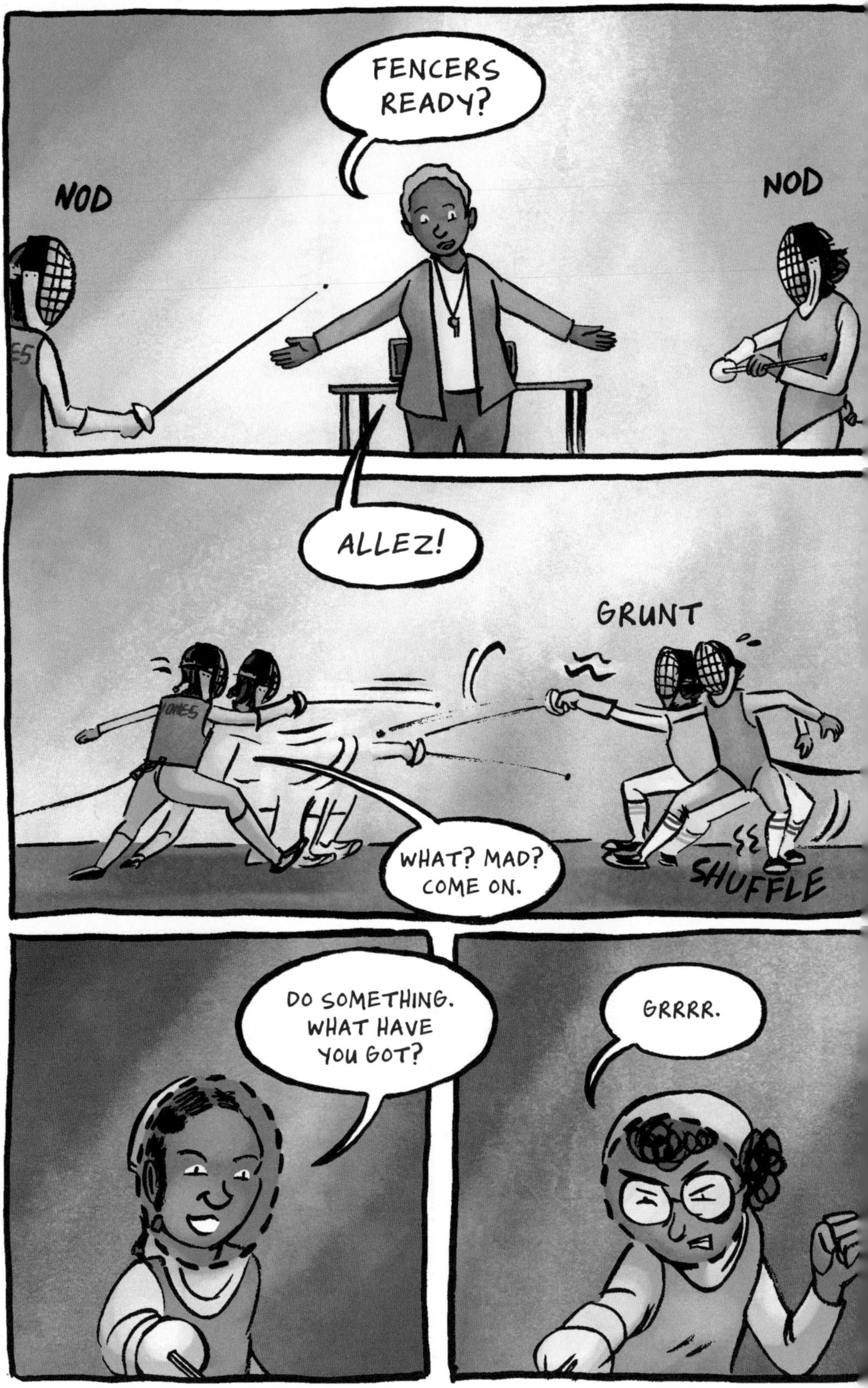
FENCERS READY?
NOD
NOD
ALLEZ!
GRUNT
SHUFFLE
WHAT? MAD? COME ON.
DO SOMETHING. WHAT HAVE YOU GOT?
GRRRR.

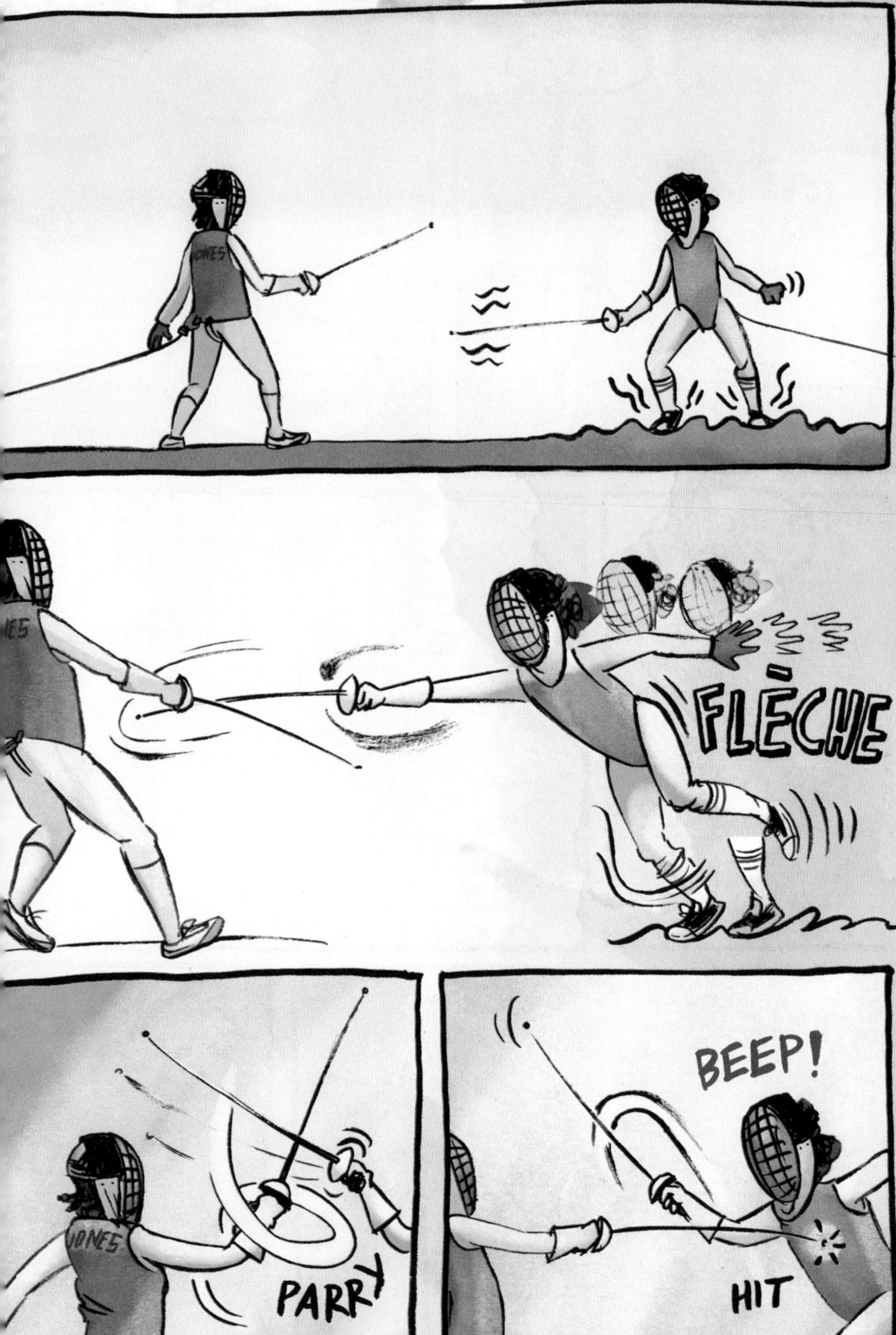
JONES
FLÈCHE
JONES
PARRY
BEEP!
HIT

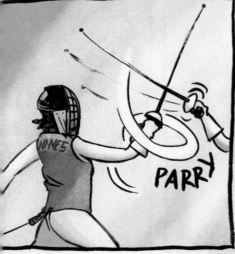

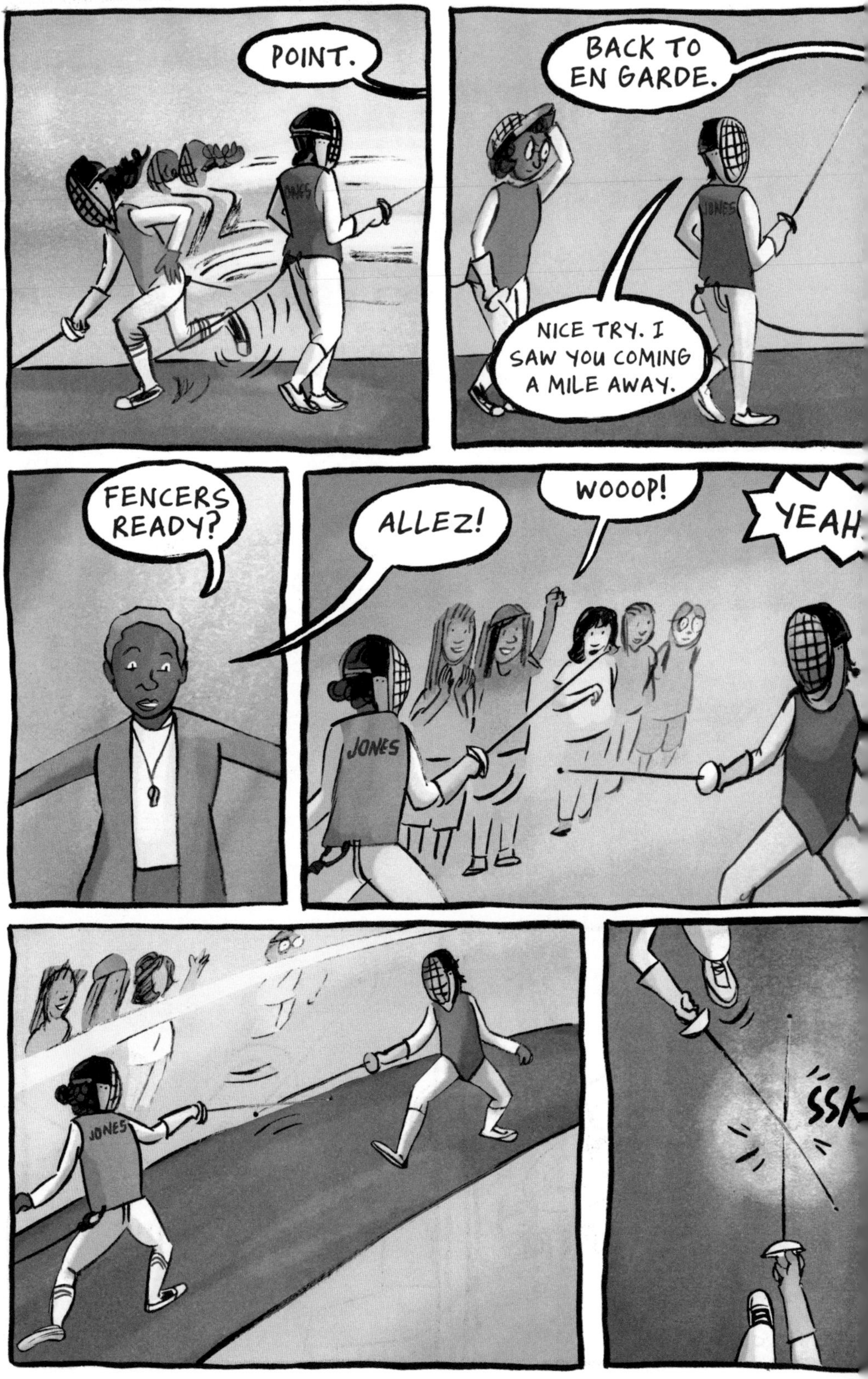

POINT.
BACK TO EN GARDE.
NICE TRY. I SAW YOU COMING A MILE AWAY.
FENCERS READY?
ALLEZ!
WOOOP!
YEAH
JONES
SSK

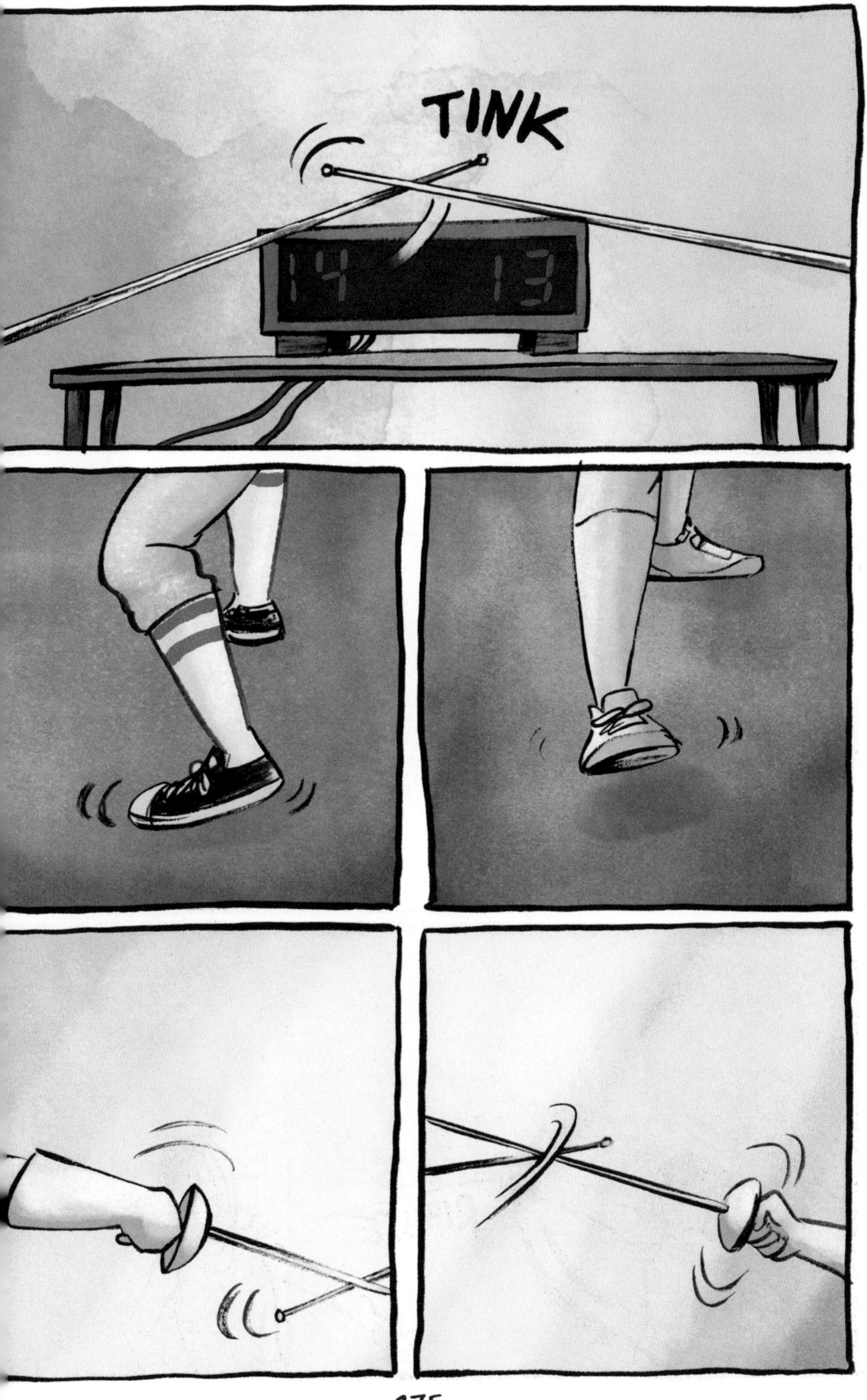
TINK
14
13

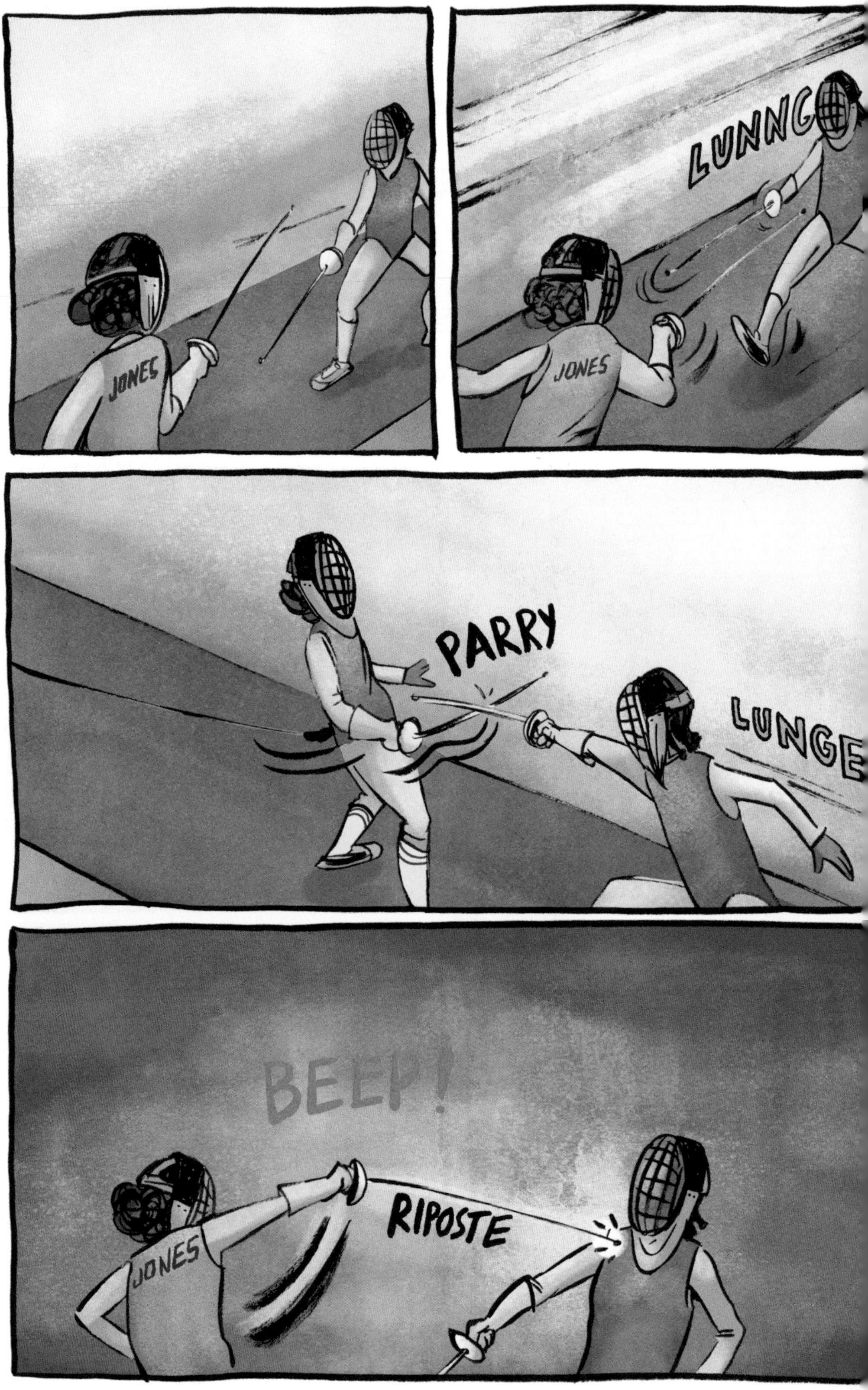
JONES
LUNNG
JONES
PARRY
LUNGE
BEEP!
RIPOSTE
JONES

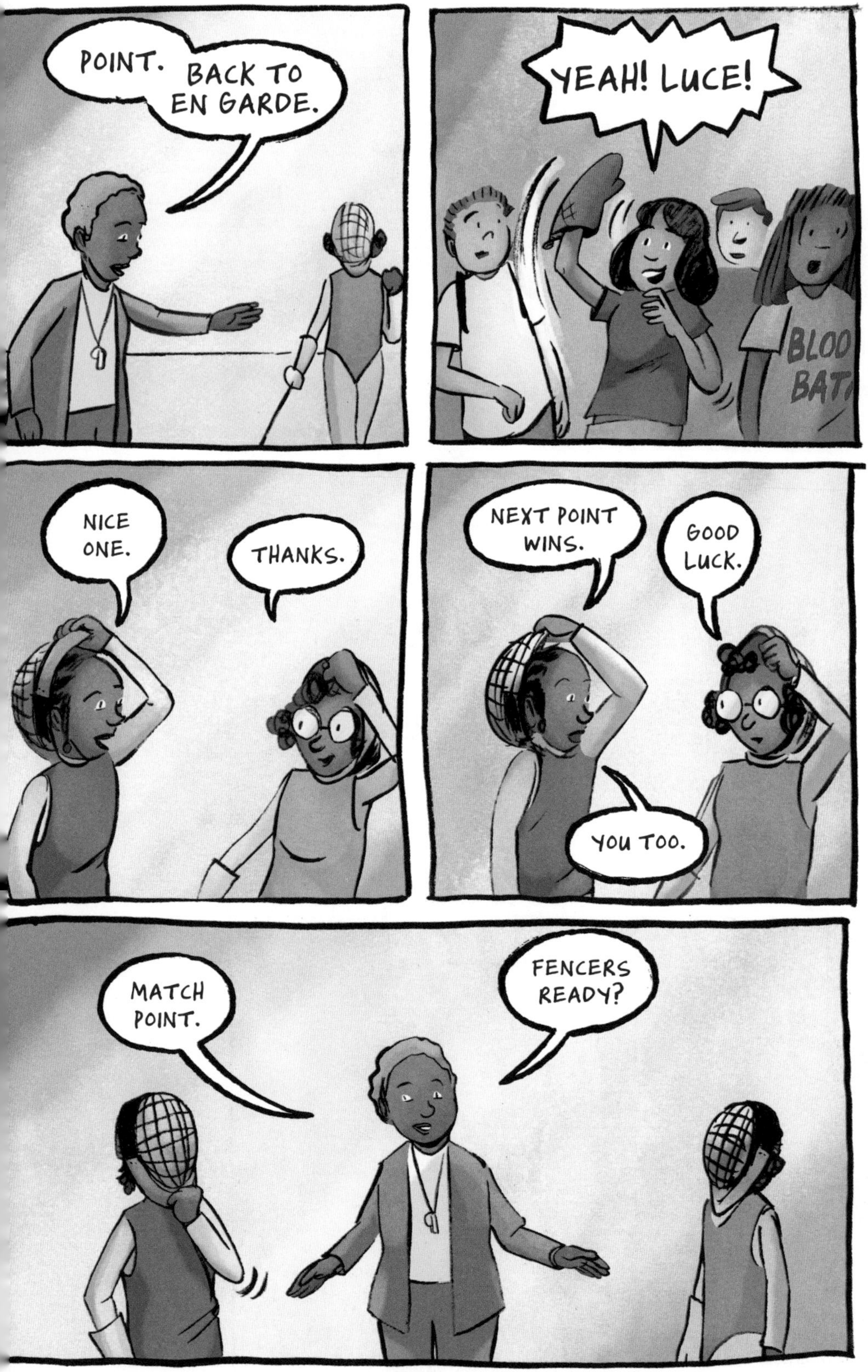
POINT. BACK TO EN GARDE.
YEAH! LUCE!
BLOO BAT
NICE ONE.
THANKS.
NEXT POINT WINS.
GOOD LUCK.
YOU TOO.
MATCH POINT.
FENCERS READY?

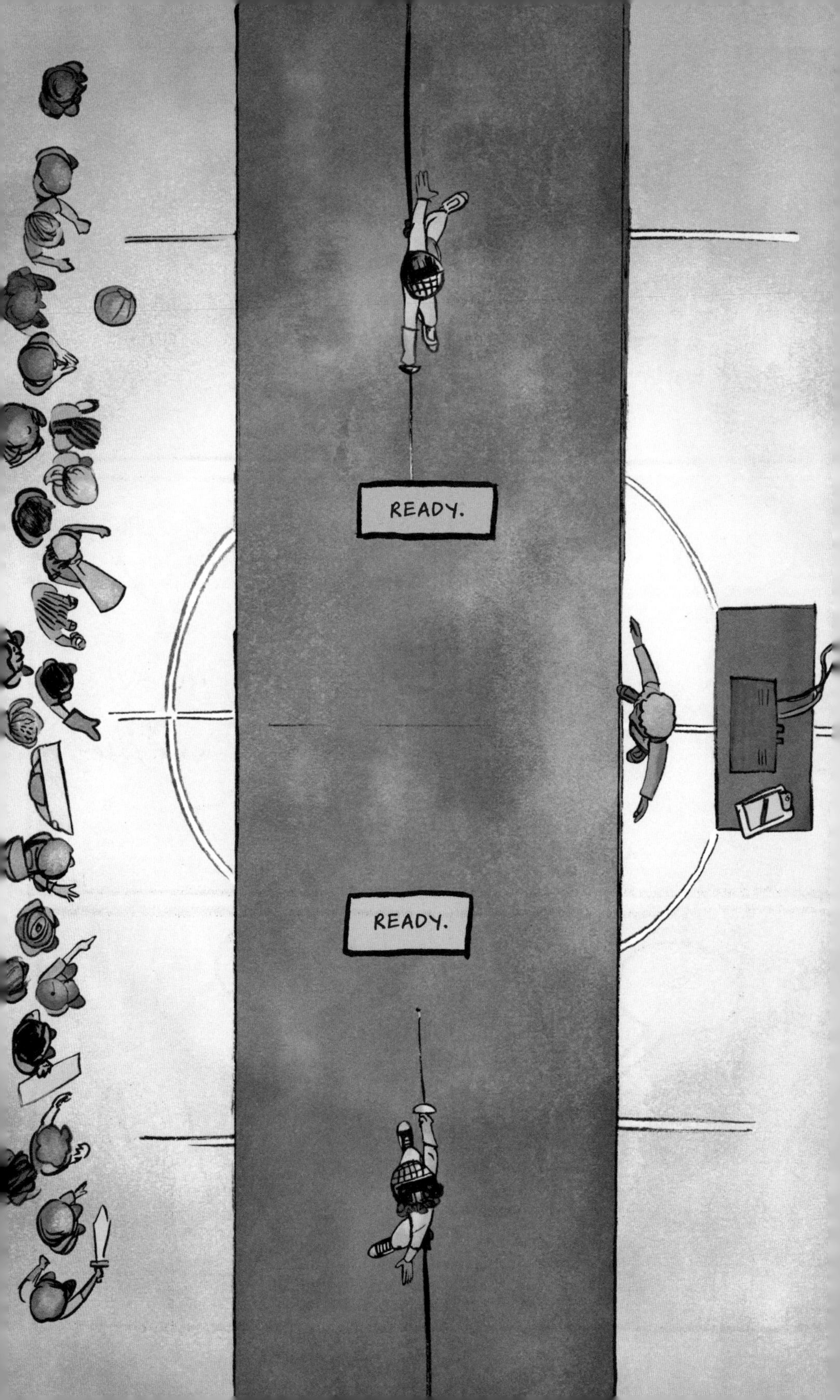
READY.
READY.

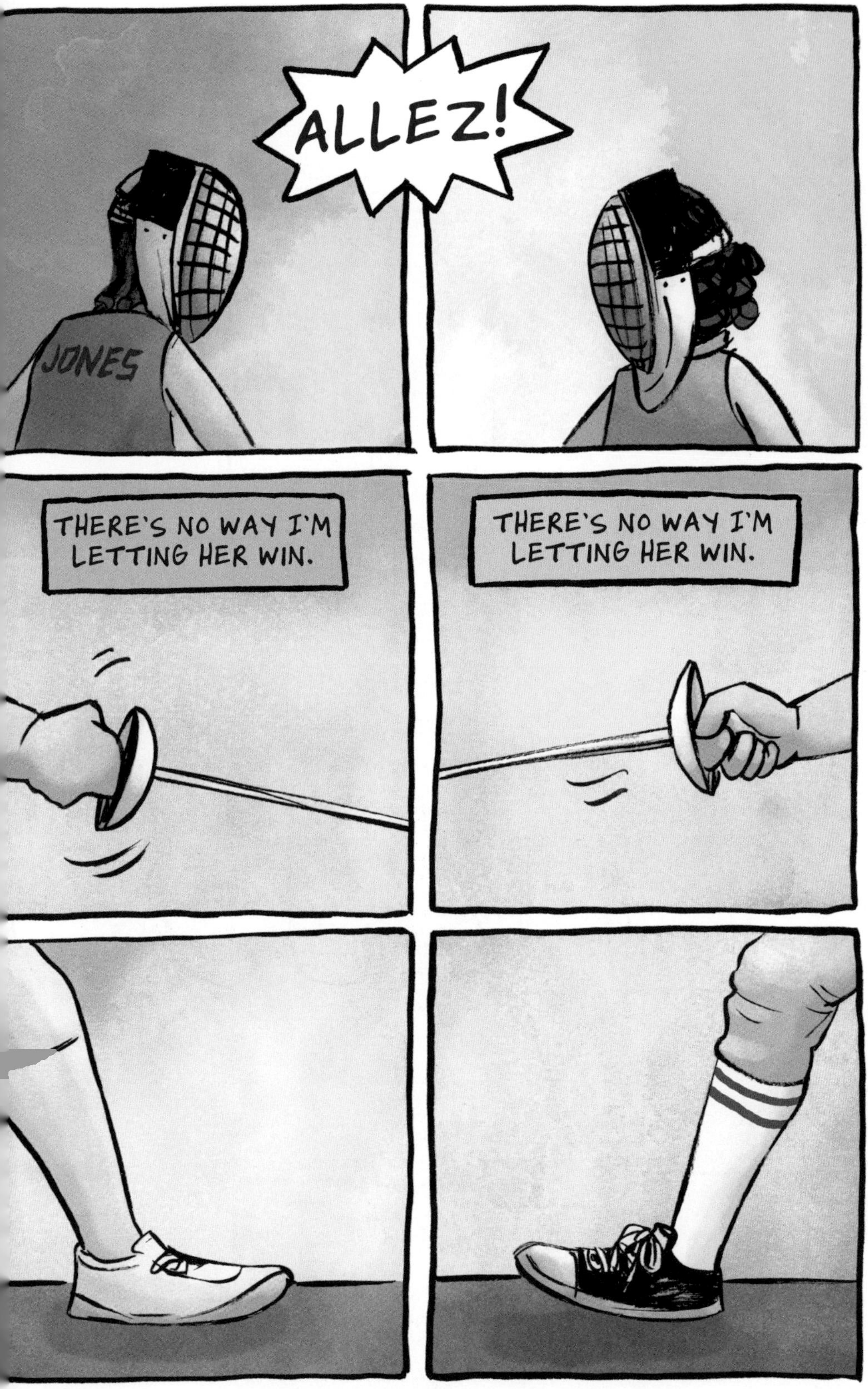
ALLEZ!
JONES
THERE'S NO WAY I'M LETTING HER WIN.
THERE'S NO WAY I'M LETTING HER WIN.

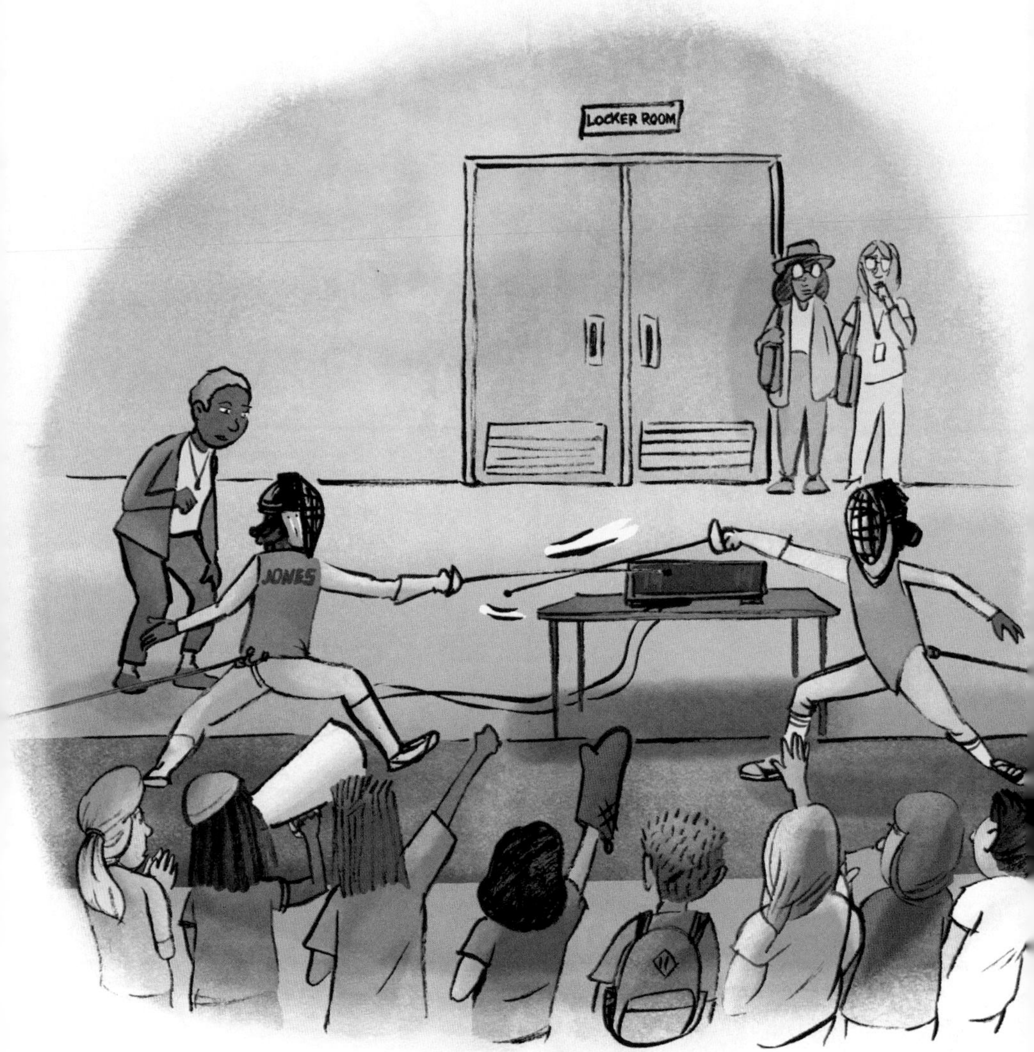

LOCKER ROOM
JONES

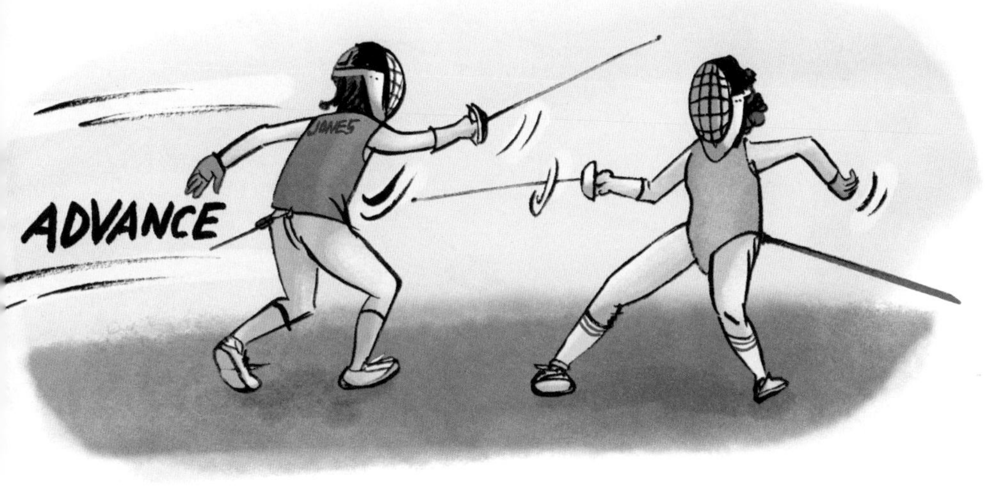
ADVANCE
JONES

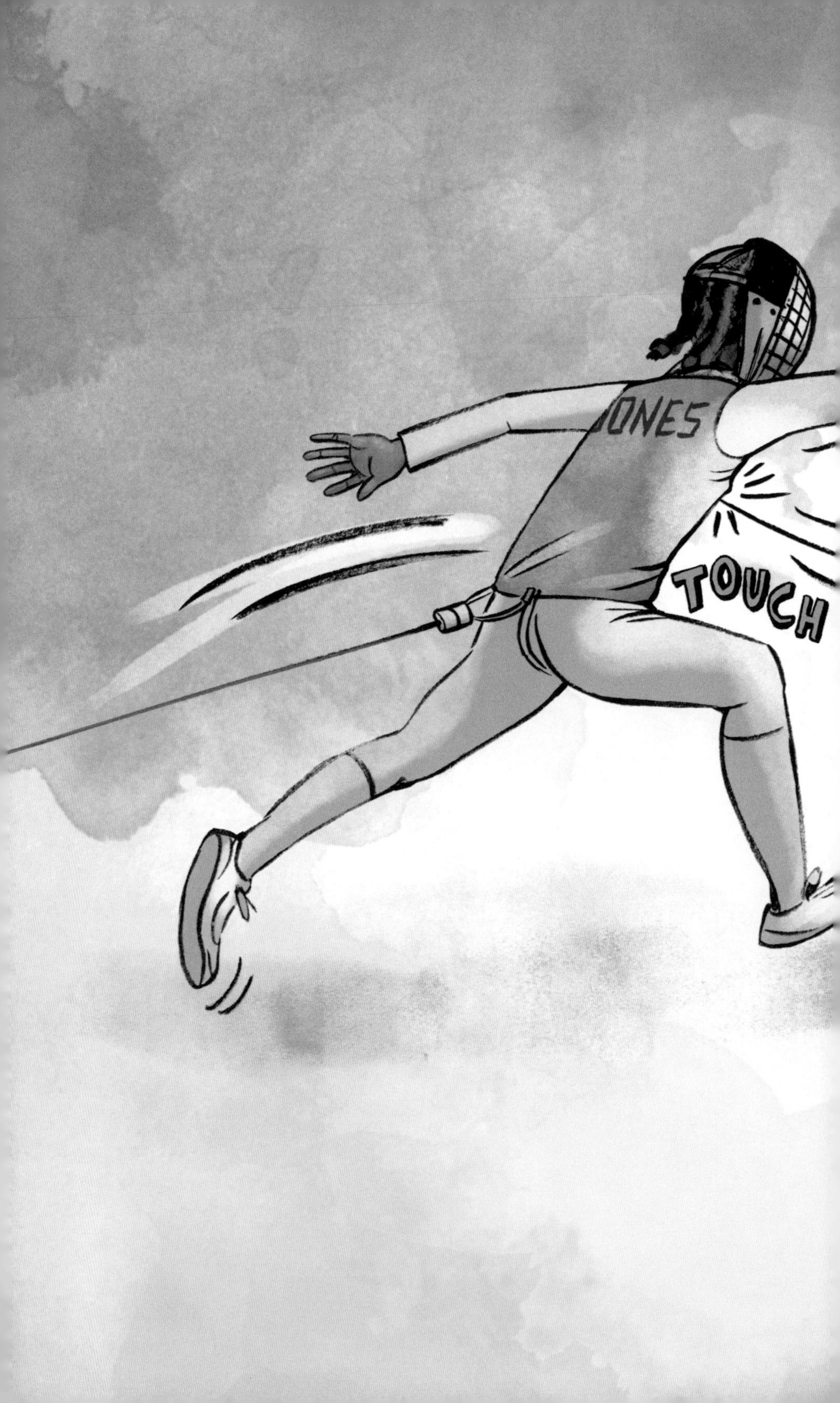
JONES
TOUCH

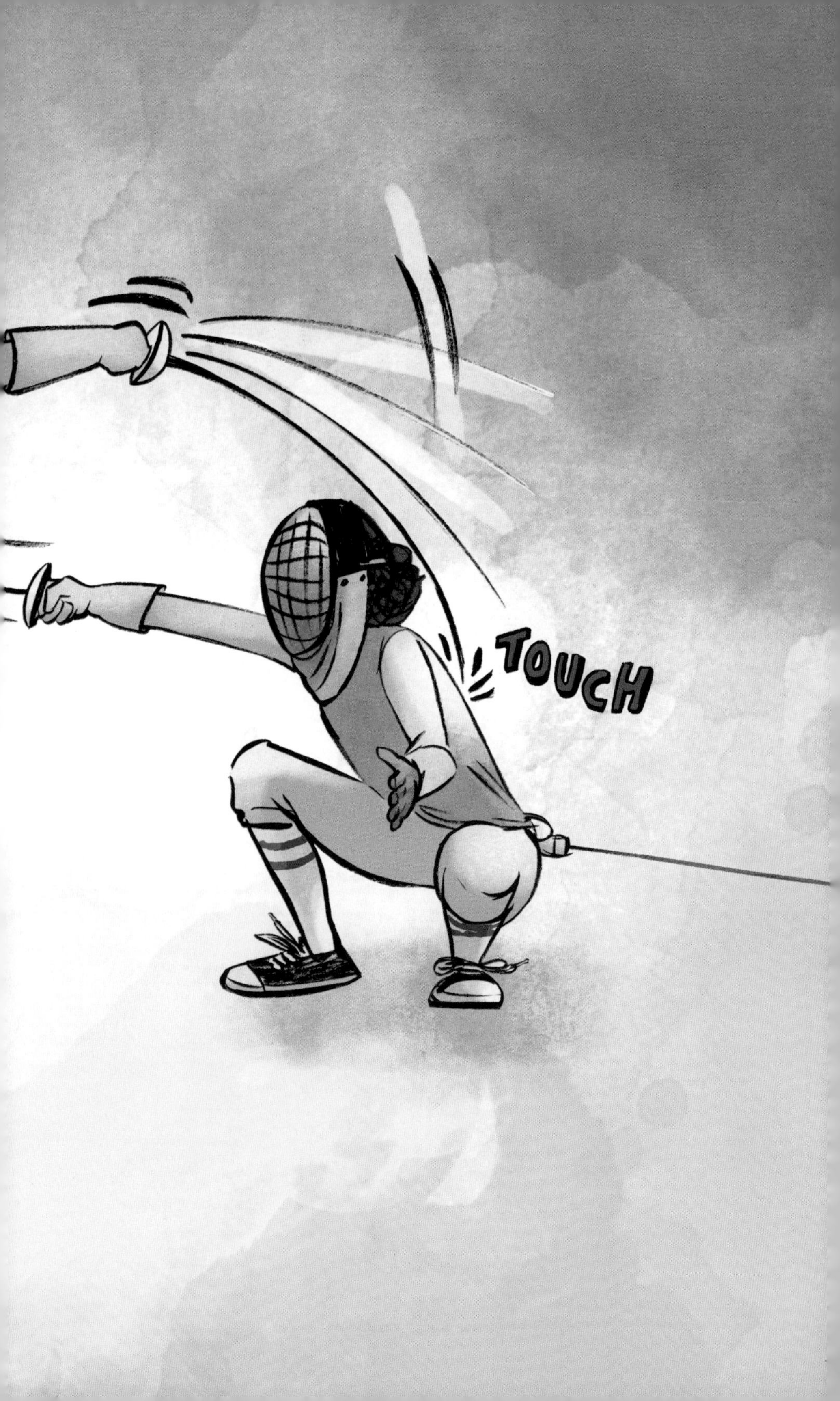
TOUCH

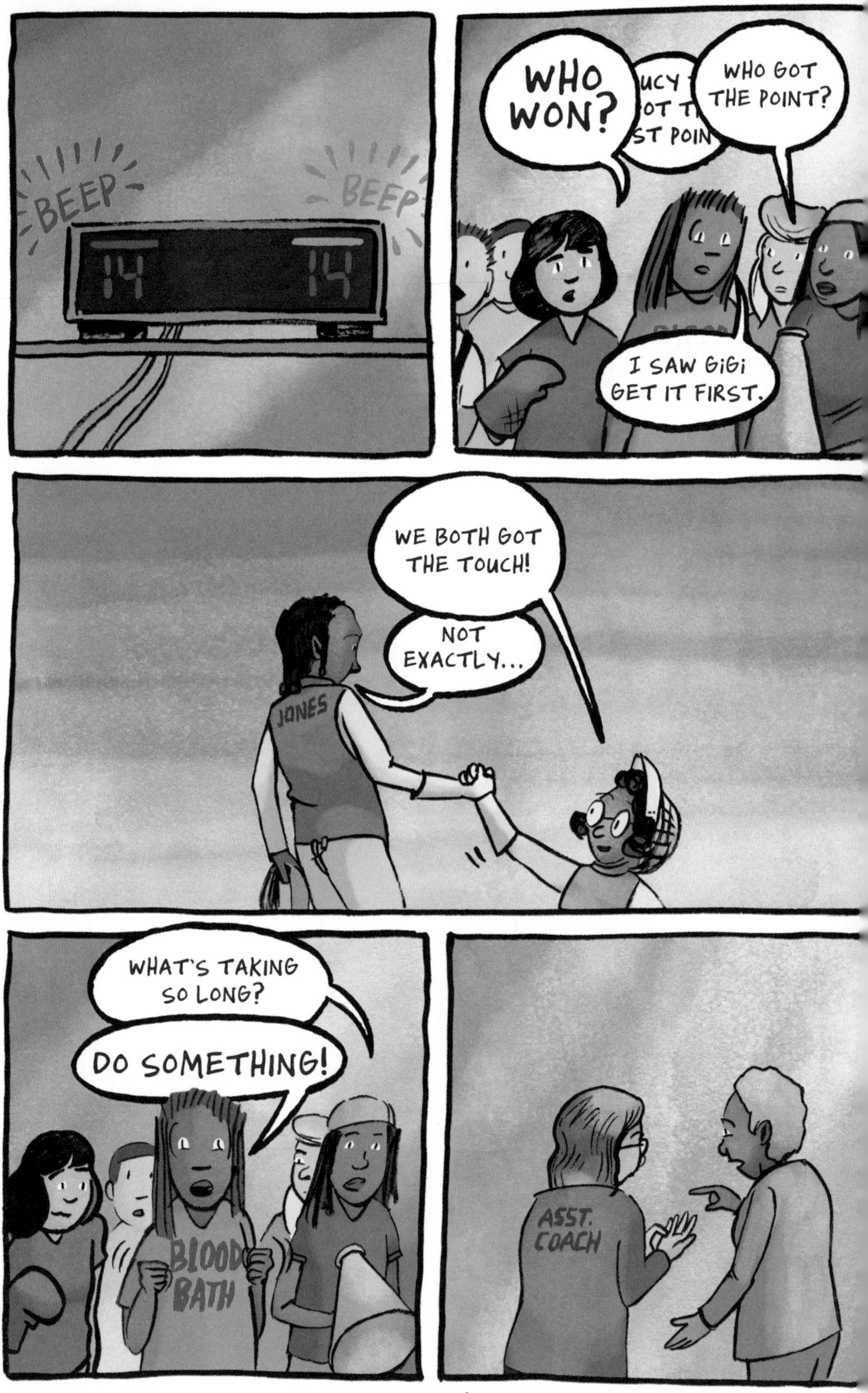
BEEP
BEEP
14
14
WHO WON?
WHO GOT THE POINT?
I SAW GIGI GET IT FIRST.
WE BOTH GOT THE TOUCH!
NOT EXACTLY...
JONES
WHAT'S TAKING SO LONG?
DO SOMETHING!
BLOOD BATH
ASST. COACH

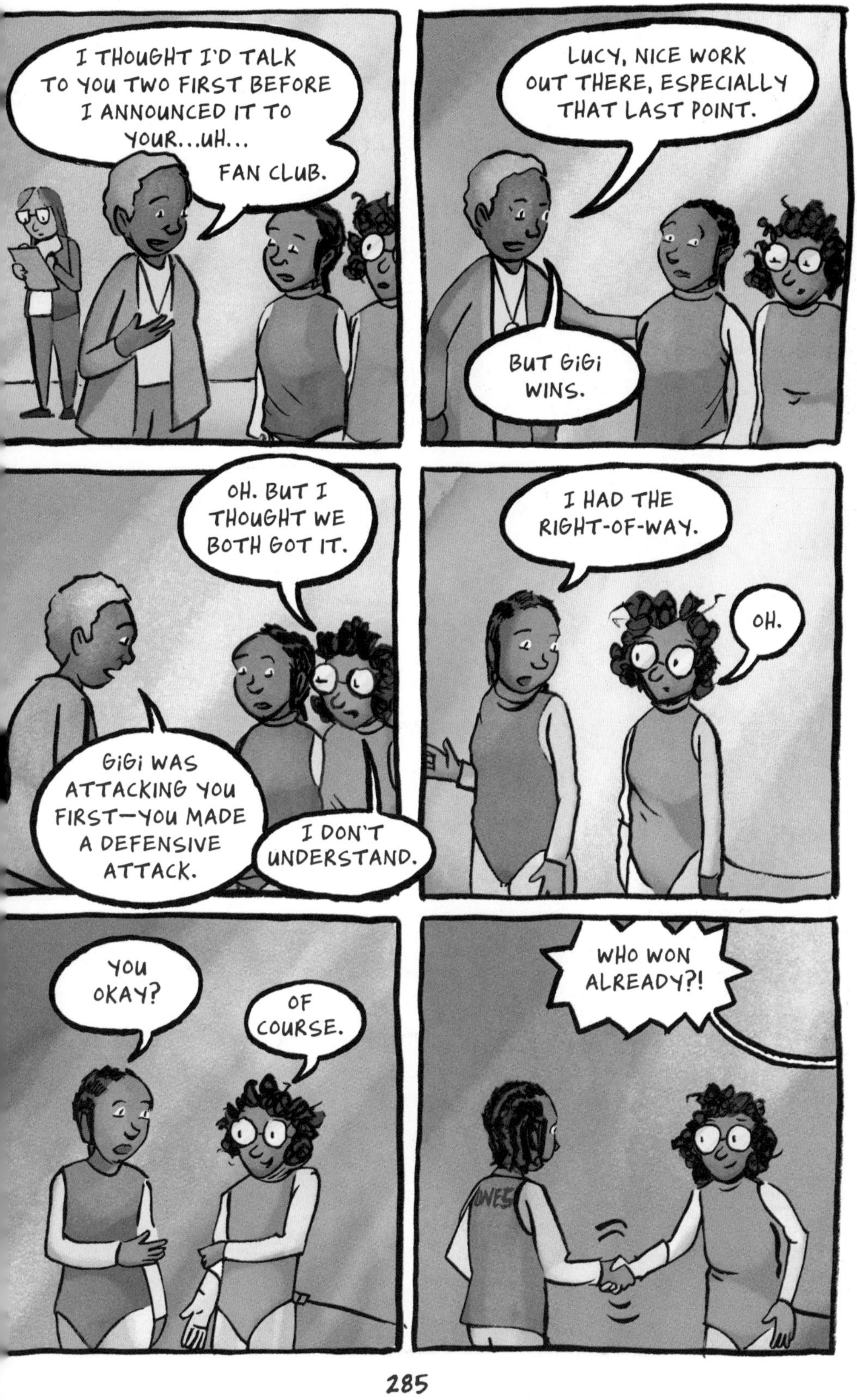
I THOUGHT I'D TALK TO YOU TWO FIRST BEFORE I ANNOUNCED IT TO YOUR...UH...
FAN CLUB.
LUCY, NICE WORK OUT THERE, ESPECIALLY THAT LAST POINT.
BUT GIGI WINS.
OH. BUT I THOUGHT WE BOTH GOT IT.
GIGI WAS ATTACKING YOU FIRST—YOU MADE A DEFENSIVE ATTACK.
I DON'T UNDERSTAND.
I HAD THE RIGHT-OF-WAY.
OH.
YOU OKAY?
OF COURSE.
WHO WON ALREADY?!

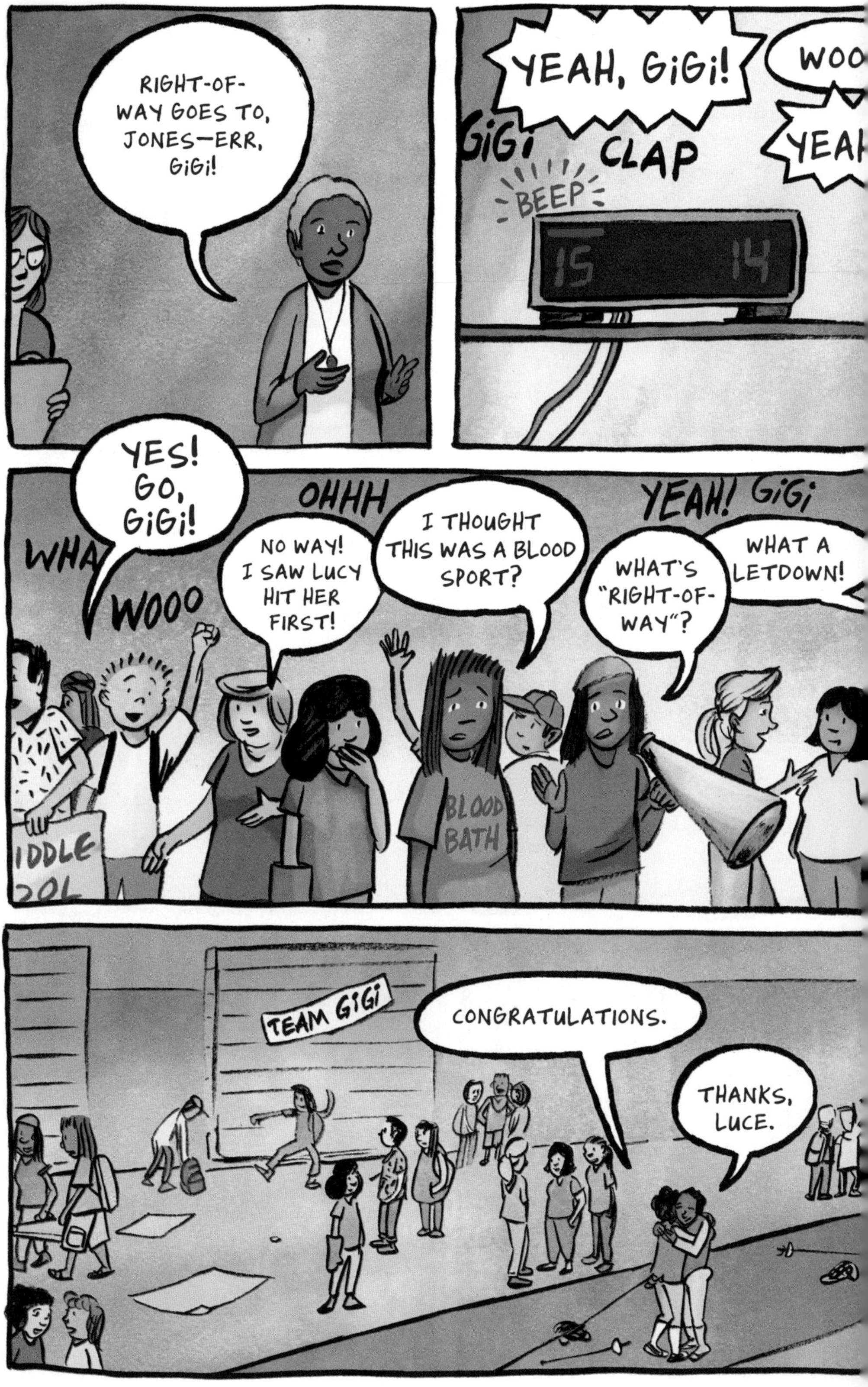
RIGHT-OF-WAY GOES TO, JONES—ERR, GiGi!
YEAH, GiGi!
WOO
GiGi
CLAP
YEAH
BEEP
15
14
YES! GO, GiGi!
OHHH
WHA
WOOO
NO WAY! I SAW LUCY HIT HER FIRST!
I THOUGHT THIS WAS A BLOOD SPORT?
YEAH! GiGi
WHAT'S "RIGHT-OF-WAY"?
WHAT A LETDOWN!
BLOOD BATH
TEAM GiGi
CONGRATULATIONS.
THANKS, LUCE.

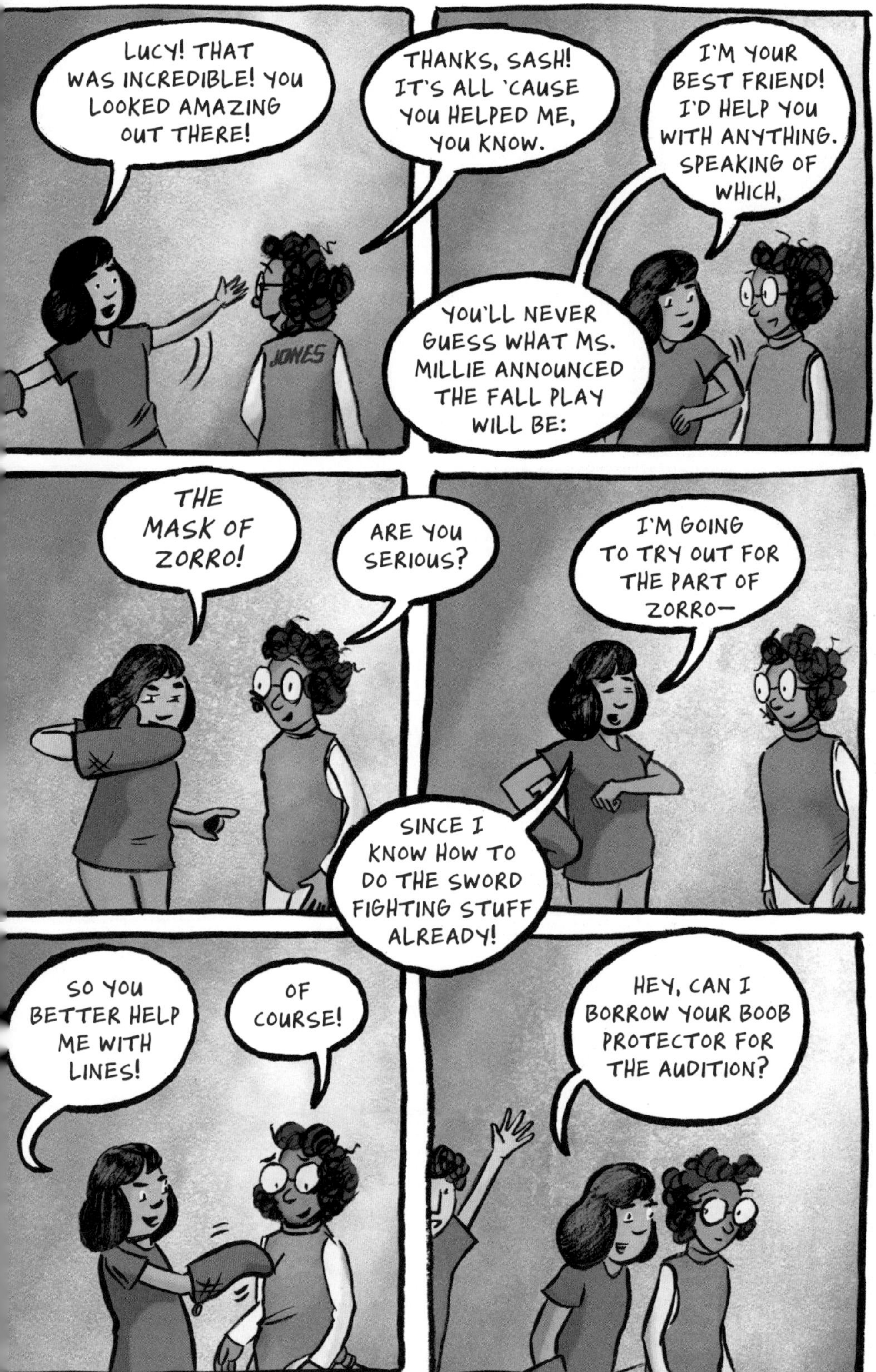
LUCY! THAT WAS INCREDIBLE! YOU LOOKED AMAZING OUT THERE!
THANKS, SASH! IT'S ALL 'CAUSE YOU HELPED ME, YOU KNOW.
JONES
I'M YOUR BEST FRIEND! I'D HELP YOU WITH ANYTHING. SPEAKING OF WHICH,
YOU'LL NEVER GUESS WHAT MS. MILLIE ANNOUNCED THE FALL PLAY WILL BE:
THE MASK OF ZORRO!
ARE YOU SERIOUS?
I'M GOING TO TRY OUT FOR THE PART OF ZORRO—
SINCE I KNOW HOW TO DO THE SWORD FIGHTING STUFF ALREADY!
SO YOU BETTER HELP ME WITH LINES!
OF COURSE!
HEY, CAN I BORROW YOUR BOOB PROTECTOR FOR THE AUDITION?

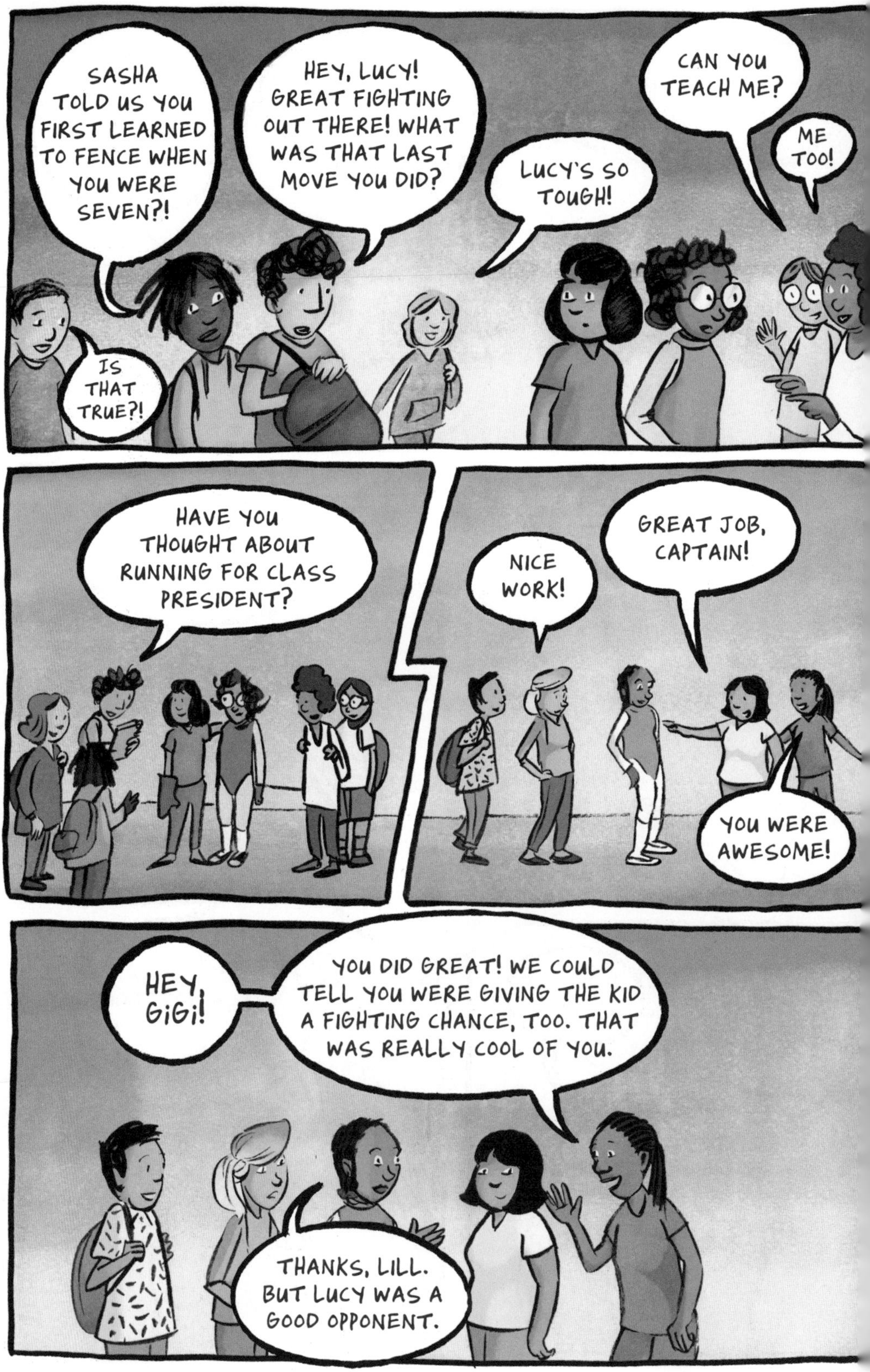
SASHA TOLD US YOU FIRST LEARNED TO FENCE WHEN YOU WERE SEVEN?!
IS THAT TRUE?!
HEY, LUCY! GREAT FIGHTING OUT THERE! WHAT WAS THAT LAST MOVE YOU DID?
LUCY'S SO TOUGH!
CAN YOU TEACH ME?
ME TOO!
HAVE YOU THOUGHT ABOUT RUNNING FOR CLASS PRESIDENT?
NICE WORK!
GREAT JOB, CAPTAIN!
YOU WERE AWESOME!
HEY, GIGI!
YOU DID GREAT! WE COULD TELL YOU WERE GIVING THE KID A FIGHTING CHANCE, TOO. THAT WAS REALLY COOL OF YOU.
THANKS, LILL. BUT LUCY WAS A GOOD OPPONENT.

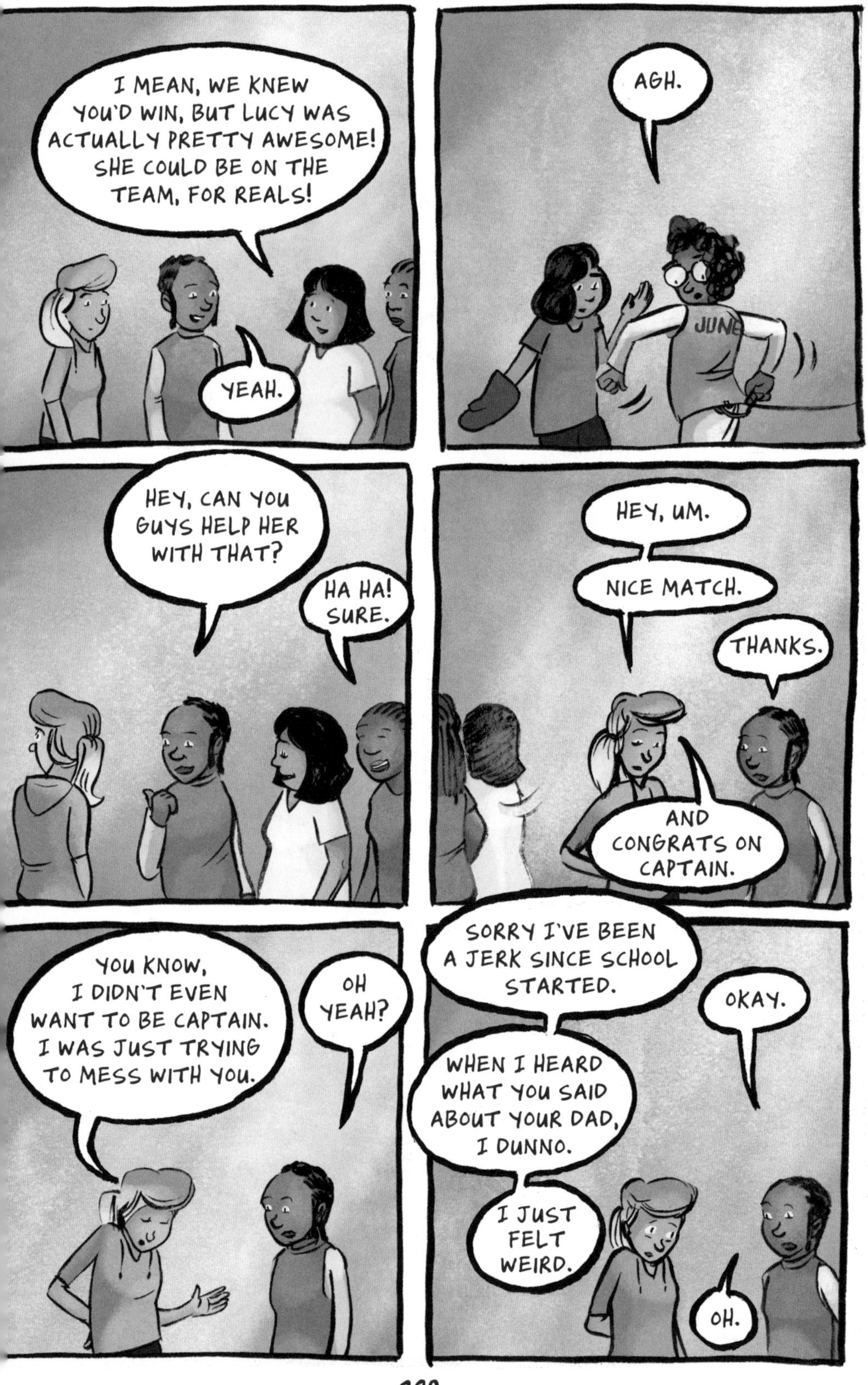
I MEAN, WE KNEW YOU'D WIN, BUT LUCY WAS ACTUALLY PRETTY AWESOME! SHE COULD BE ON THE TEAM, FOR REALS!
YEAH.
AGH.
JUNE
HEY, CAN YOU GUYS HELP HER WITH THAT?
HA HA! SURE.
HEY, UM.
NICE MATCH.
THANKS.
AND CONGRATS ON CAPTAIN.
YOU KNOW, I DIDN'T EVEN WANT TO BE CAPTAIN. I WAS JUST TRYING TO MESS WITH YOU.
OH YEAH?
SORRY I'VE BEEN A JERK SINCE SCHOOL STARTED.
OKAY.
WHEN I HEARD WHAT YOU SAID ABOUT YOUR DAD, I DUNNO.
I JUST FELT WEIRD.
OH.

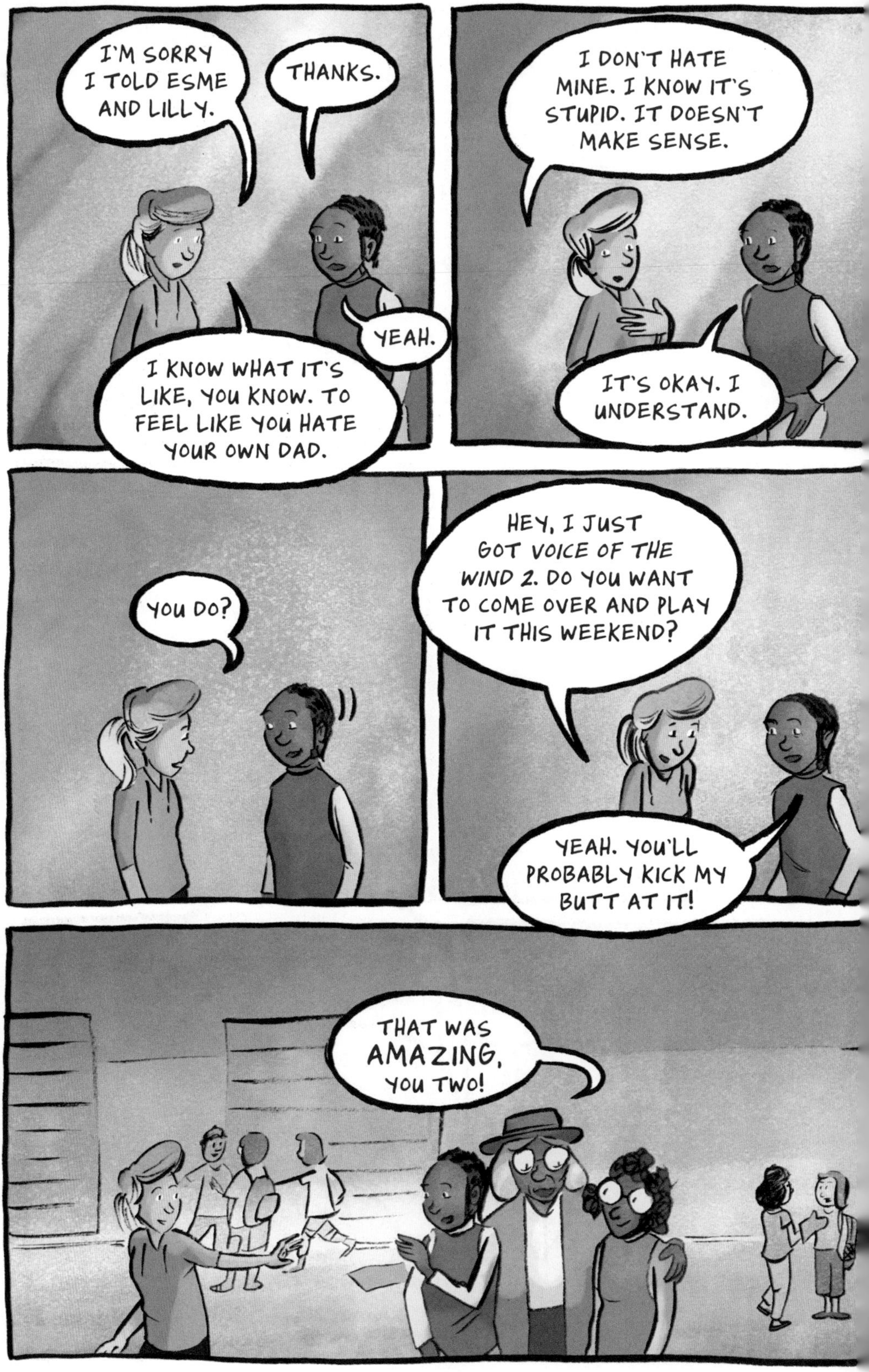
I'M SORRY I TOLD ESME AND LILLY.
THANKS.
I KNOW WHAT IT'S LIKE, YOU KNOW. TO FEEL LIKE YOU HATE YOUR OWN DAD.
YEAH.
I DON'T HATE MINE. I KNOW IT'S STUPID. IT DOESN'T MAKE SENSE.
IT'S OKAY. I UNDERSTAND.
YOU DO?
HEY, I JUST GOT VOICE OF THE WIND 2. DO YOU WANT TO COME OVER AND PLAY IT THIS WEEKEND?
YEAH. YOU'LL PROBABLY KICK MY BUTT AT IT!
THAT WAS AMAZING, YOU TWO!

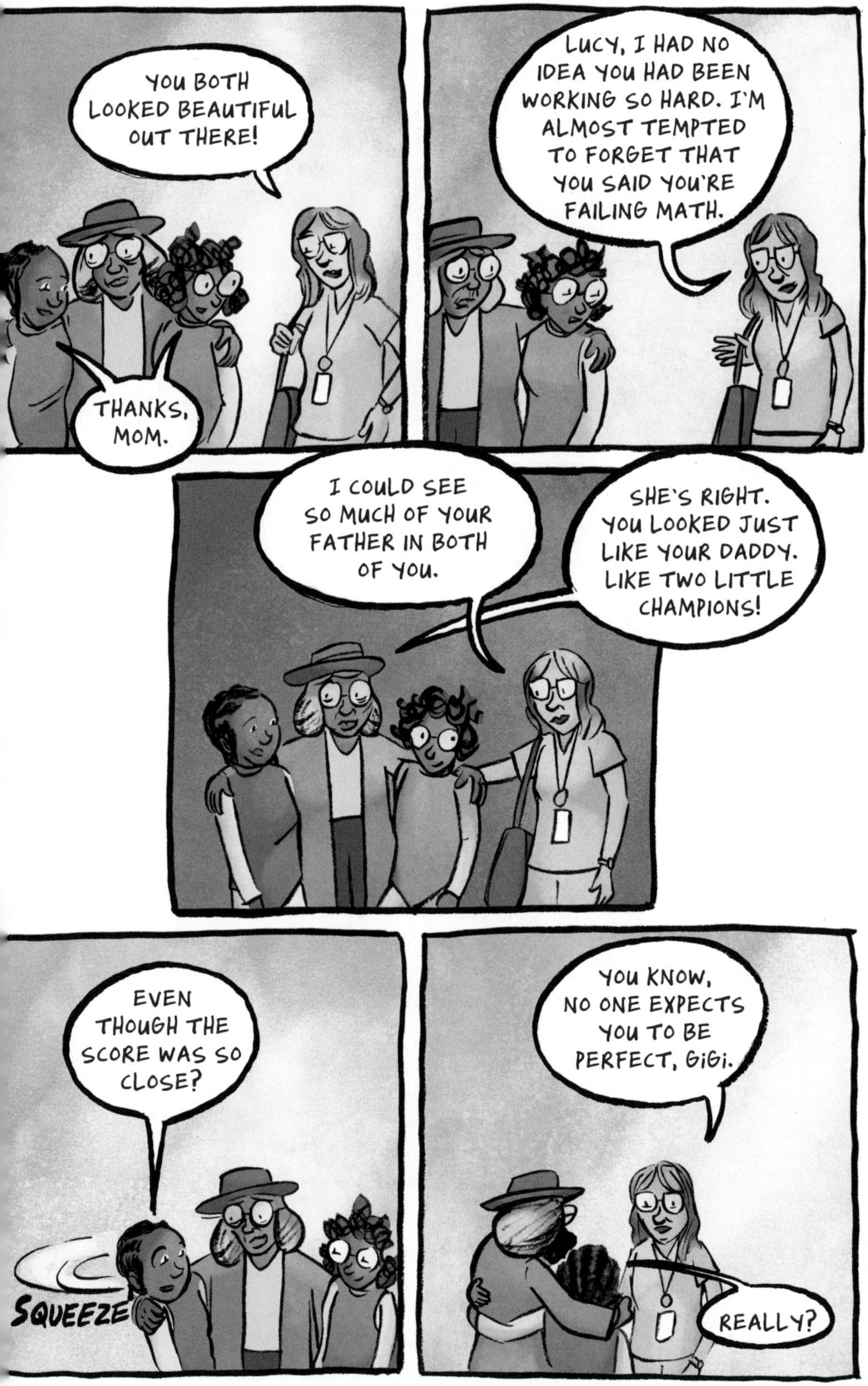
YOU BOTH LOOKED BEAUTIFUL OUT THERE!
THANKS, MOM.
LUCY, I HAD NO IDEA YOU HAD BEEN WORKING SO HARD. I'M ALMOST TEMPTED TO FORGET THAT YOU SAID YOU'RE FAILING MATH.
I COULD SEE SO MUCH OF YOUR FATHER IN BOTH OF YOU.
SHE'S RIGHT. YOU LOOKED JUST LIKE YOUR DADDY. LIKE TWO LITTLE CHAMPIONS!
EVEN THOUGH THE SCORE WAS SO CLOSE?
SQUEEZE
YOU KNOW, NO ONE EXPECTS YOU TO BE PERFECT, GIGI.
REALLY?

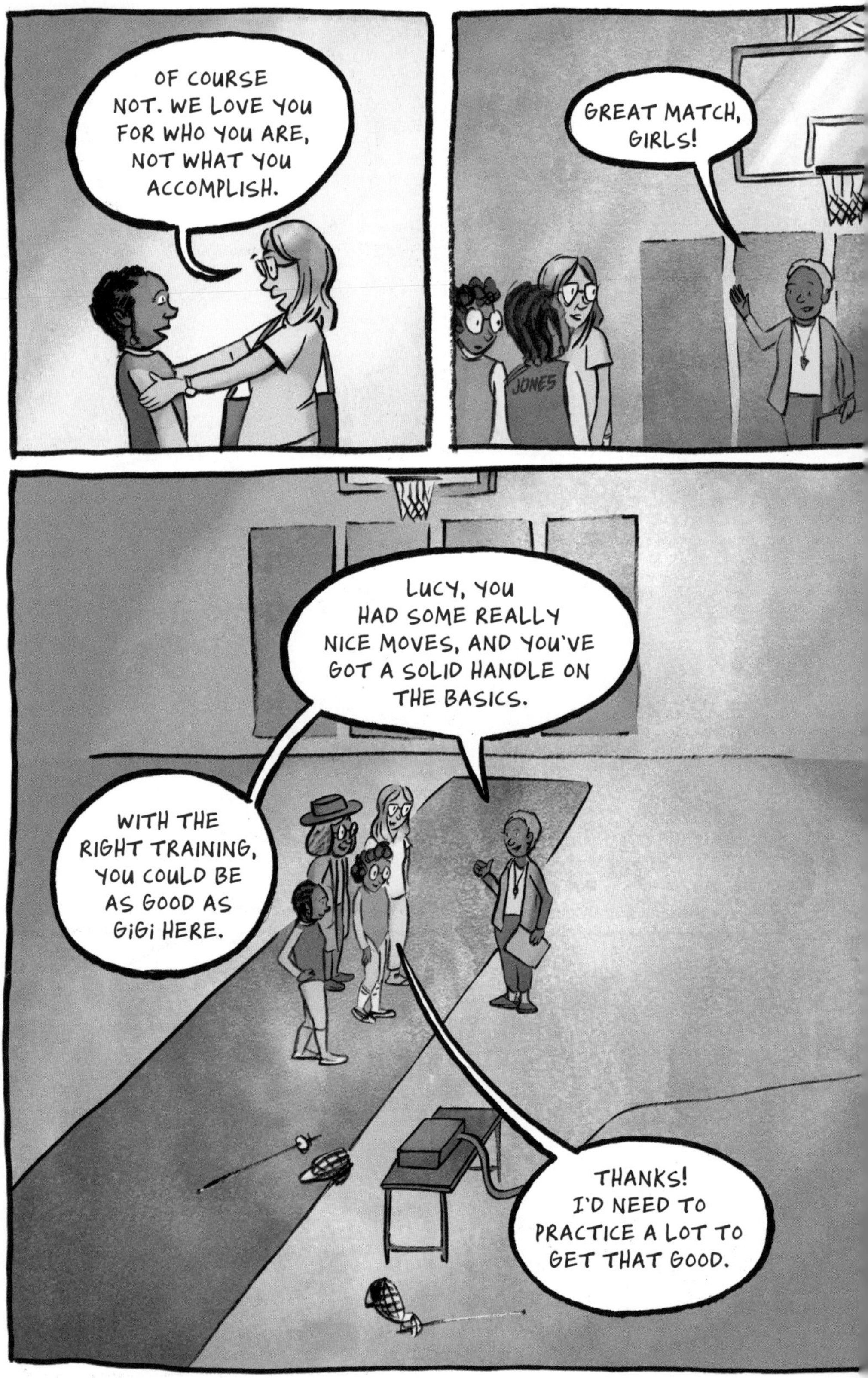
OF COURSE NOT. WE LOVE YOU FOR WHO YOU ARE, NOT WHAT YOU ACCOMPLISH.
GREAT MATCH, GIRLS!
JONES
LUCY, YOU HAD SOME REALLY NICE MOVES, AND YOU'VE GOT A SOLID HANDLE ON THE BASICS.
WITH THE RIGHT TRAINING, YOU COULD BE AS GOOD AS GiGi HERE.
THANKS! I'D NEED TO PRACTICE A LOT TO GET THAT GOOD.

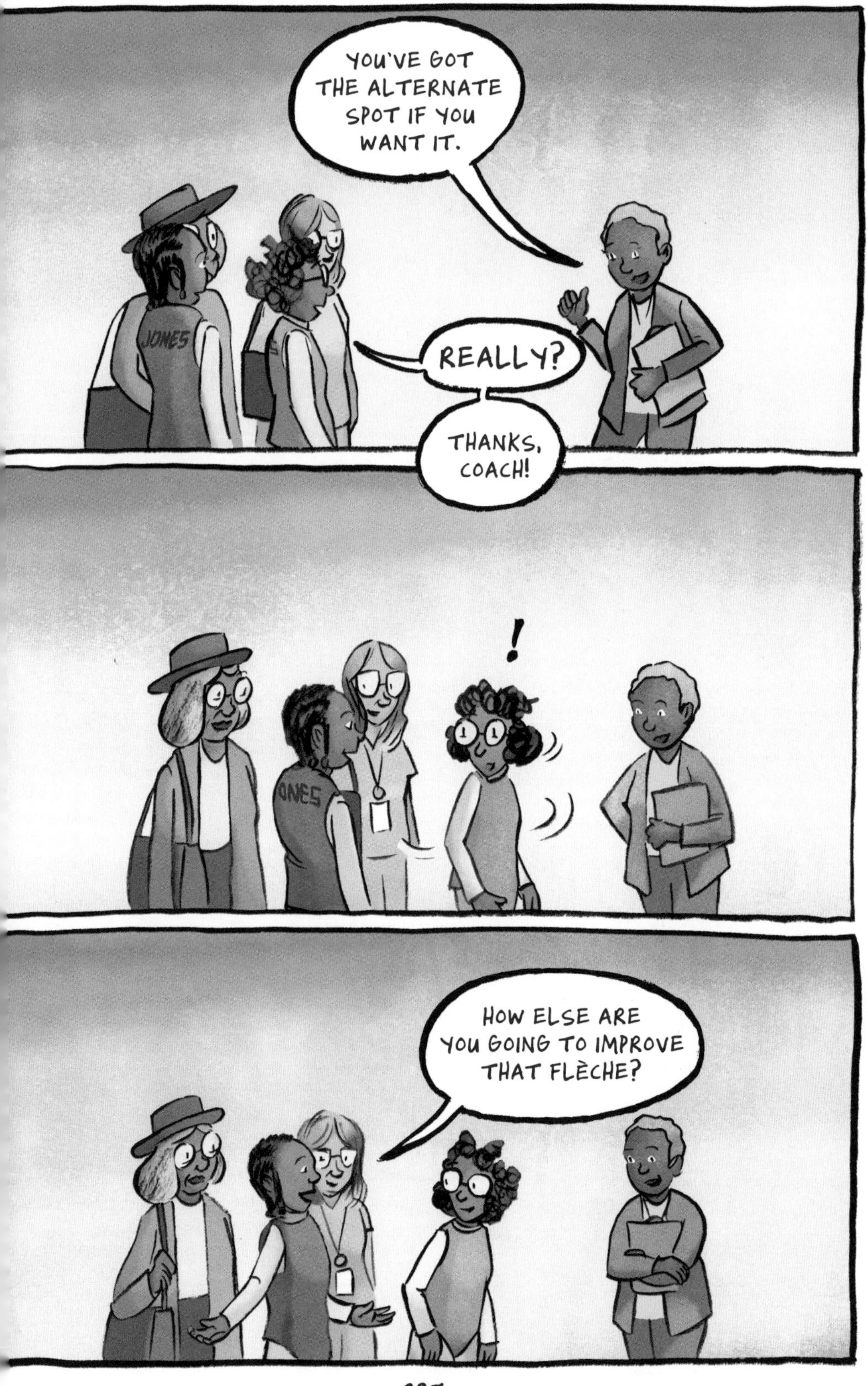
YOU'VE GOT THE ALTERNATE SPOT IF YOU WANT IT.
JONES
REALLY?
THANKS, COACH!
!
HOW ELSE ARE YOU GOING TO IMPROVE THAT FLÈCHE?

Epilogue

Épée-log Ha! Ha!

LEAVE
YOUR
SWORDS
AT THE
DOOR.

In medieval times, public gathering spaces such churches or pubs often posted signs at the front of the building asking guests to leave their weapons outside before entering. The three weapons in modern-day fencing—foil, épée, and sabre—are typically not referred to as swords in the parlance of American competitive sport fencing, though in some regions, such as the United Kingdom, the term "swords" is often used interchangeably. Figuratively, to leave your sword at the door would mean putting grievances aside and making peace with a former opponent.

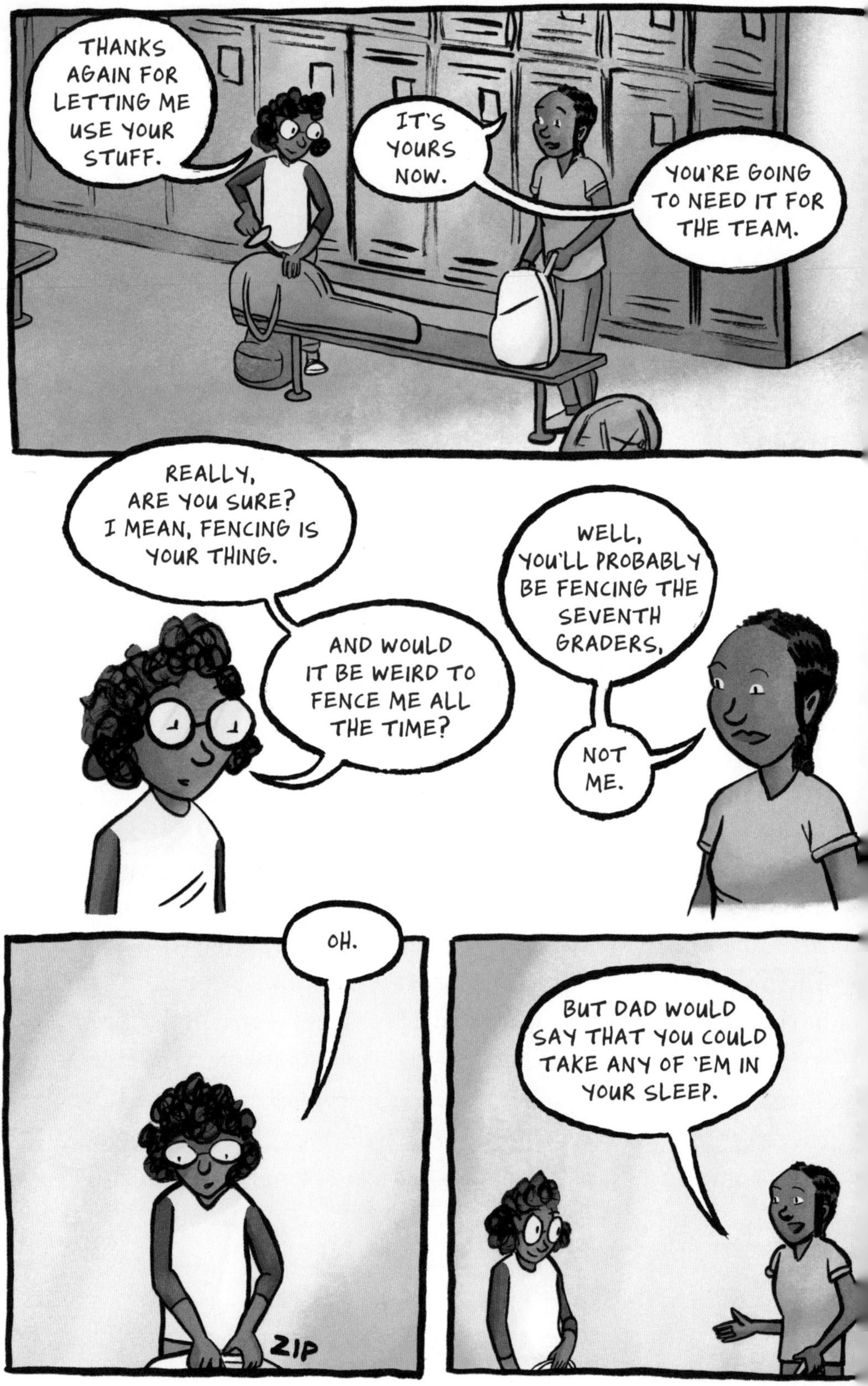
THANKS AGAIN FOR LETTING ME USE YOUR STUFF.
IT'S YOURS NOW.
YOU'RE GOING TO NEED IT FOR THE TEAM.
REALLY, ARE YOU SURE? I MEAN, FENCING IS YOUR THING.
AND WOULD IT BE WEIRD TO FENCE ME ALL THE TIME?
WELL, YOU'LL PROBABLY BE FENCING THE SEVENTH GRADERS,
NOT ME.
OH.
ZIP
BUT DAD WOULD SAY THAT YOU COULD TAKE ANY OF 'EM IN YOUR SLEEP.

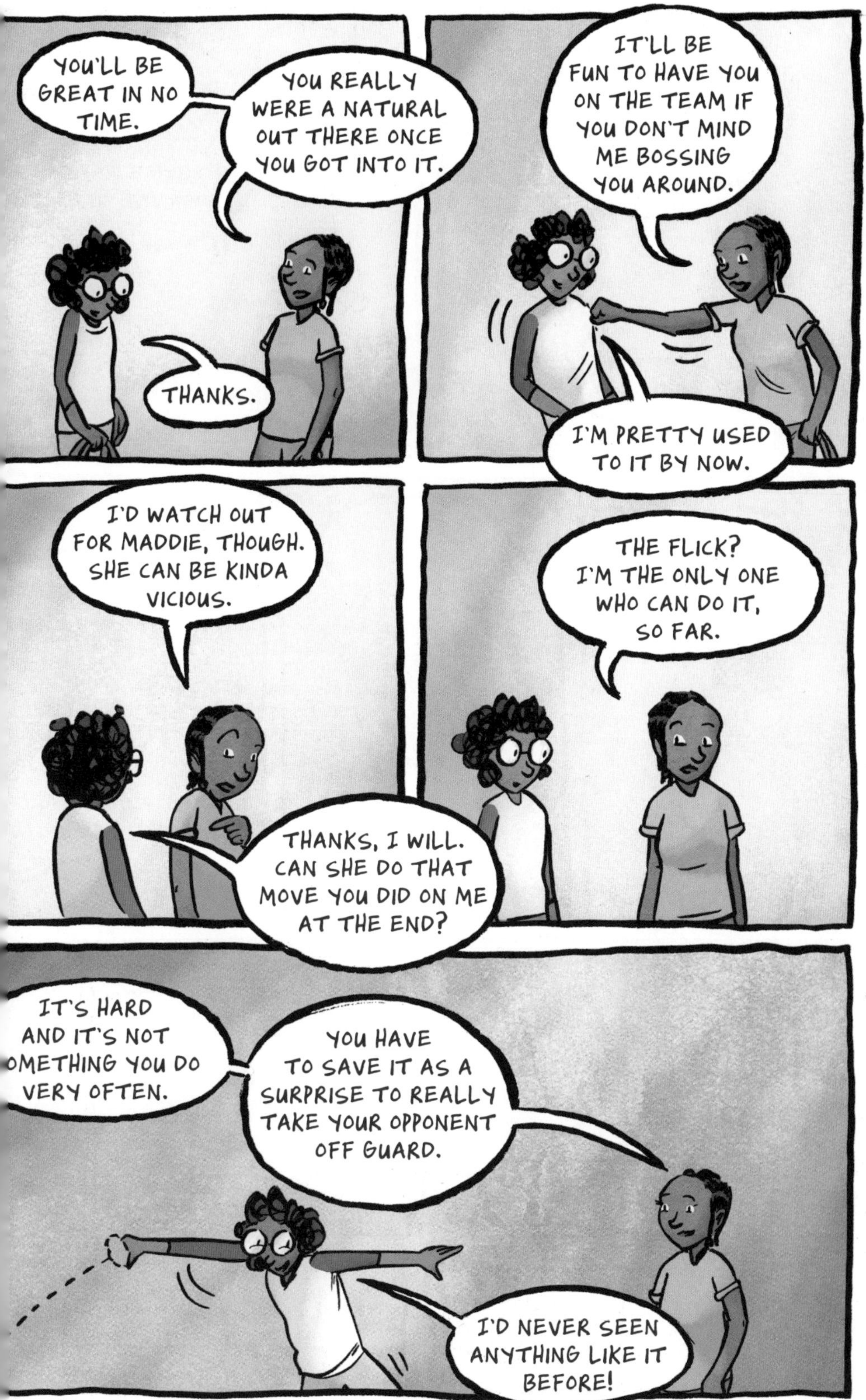

YOU'LL BE GREAT IN NO TIME.
YOU REALLY WERE A NATURAL OUT THERE ONCE YOU GOT INTO IT.
THANKS.
IT'LL BE FUN TO HAVE YOU ON THE TEAM IF YOU DON'T MIND ME BOSSING YOU AROUND.
I'M PRETTY USED TO IT BY NOW.
I'D WATCH OUT FOR MADDIE, THOUGH. SHE CAN BE KINDA VICIOUS.
THANKS, I WILL. CAN SHE DO THAT MOVE YOU DID ON ME AT THE END?
THE FLICK? I'M THE ONLY ONE WHO CAN DO IT, SO FAR.
IT'S HARD AND IT'S NOT OMETHING YOU DO VERY OFTEN.
YOU HAVE TO SAVE IT AS A SURPRISE TO REALLY TAKE YOUR OPPONENT OFF GUARD.
I'D NEVER SEEN ANYTHING LIKE IT BEFORE!

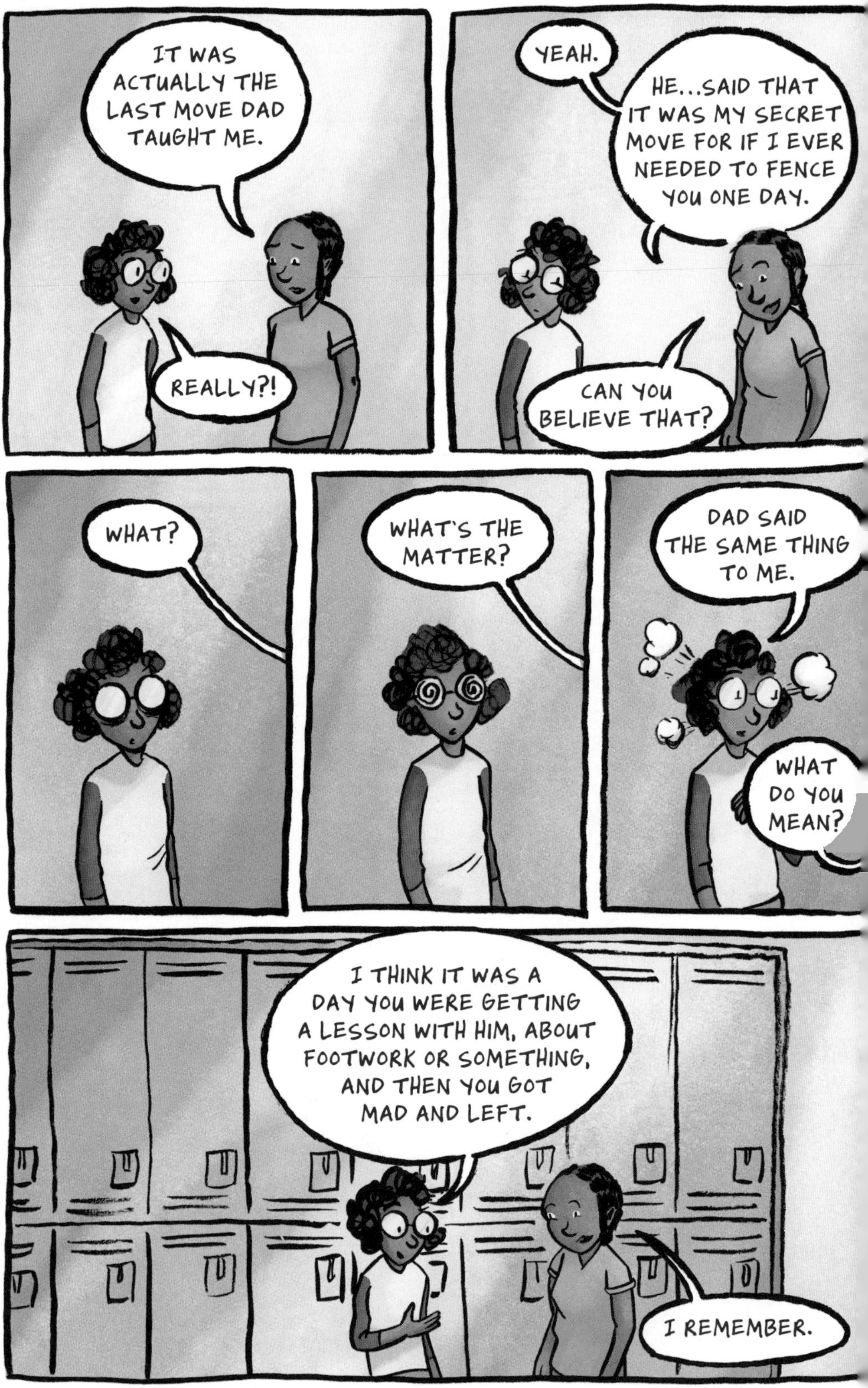
IT WAS ACTUALLY THE LAST MOVE DAD TAUGHT ME.
REALLY?!
YEAH.
HE...SAID THAT IT WAS MY SECRET MOVE FOR IF I EVER NEEDED TO FENCE YOU ONE DAY.
CAN YOU BELIEVE THAT?
WHAT?
WHAT'S THE MATTER?
DAD SAID THE SAME THING TO ME.
WHAT DO YOU MEAN?
I THINK IT WAS A DAY YOU WERE GETTING A LESSON WITH HIM, ABOUT FOOTWORK OR SOMETHING, AND THEN YOU GOT MAD AND LEFT.
I REMEMBER.

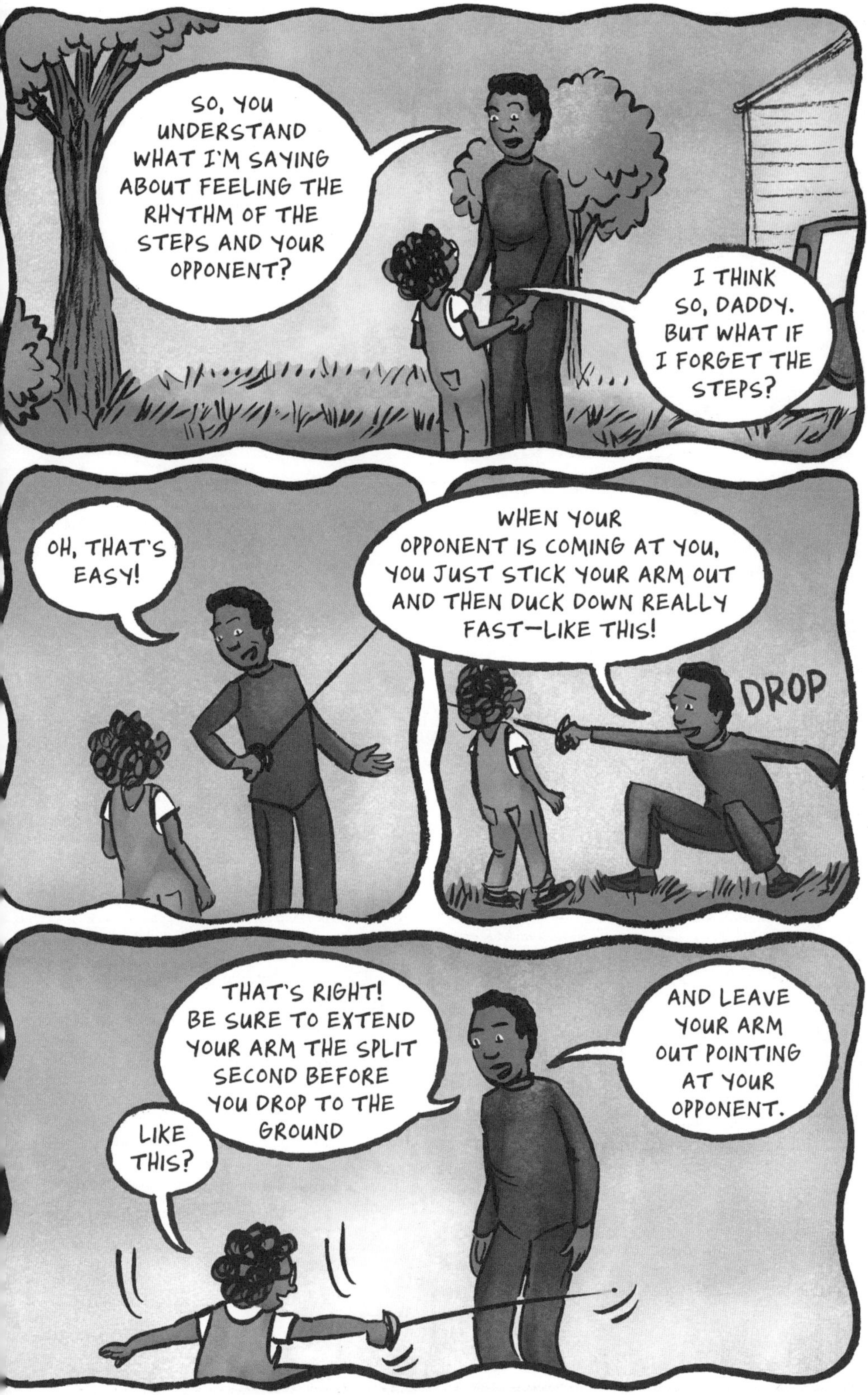

SO, YOU UNDERSTAND WHAT I'M SAYING ABOUT FEELING THE RHYTHM OF THE STEPS AND YOUR OPPONENT?
I THINK SO, DADDY. BUT WHAT IF I FORGET THE STEPS?
OH, THAT'S EASY!
WHEN YOUR OPPONENT IS COMING AT YOU, YOU JUST STICK YOUR ARM OUT AND THEN DUCK DOWN REALLY FAST—LIKE THIS!
DROP
THAT'S RIGHT! BE SURE TO EXTEND YOUR ARM THE SPLIT SECOND BEFORE YOU DROP TO THE GROUND
AND LEAVE YOUR ARM OUT POINTING AT YOUR OPPONENT.
LIKE THIS?

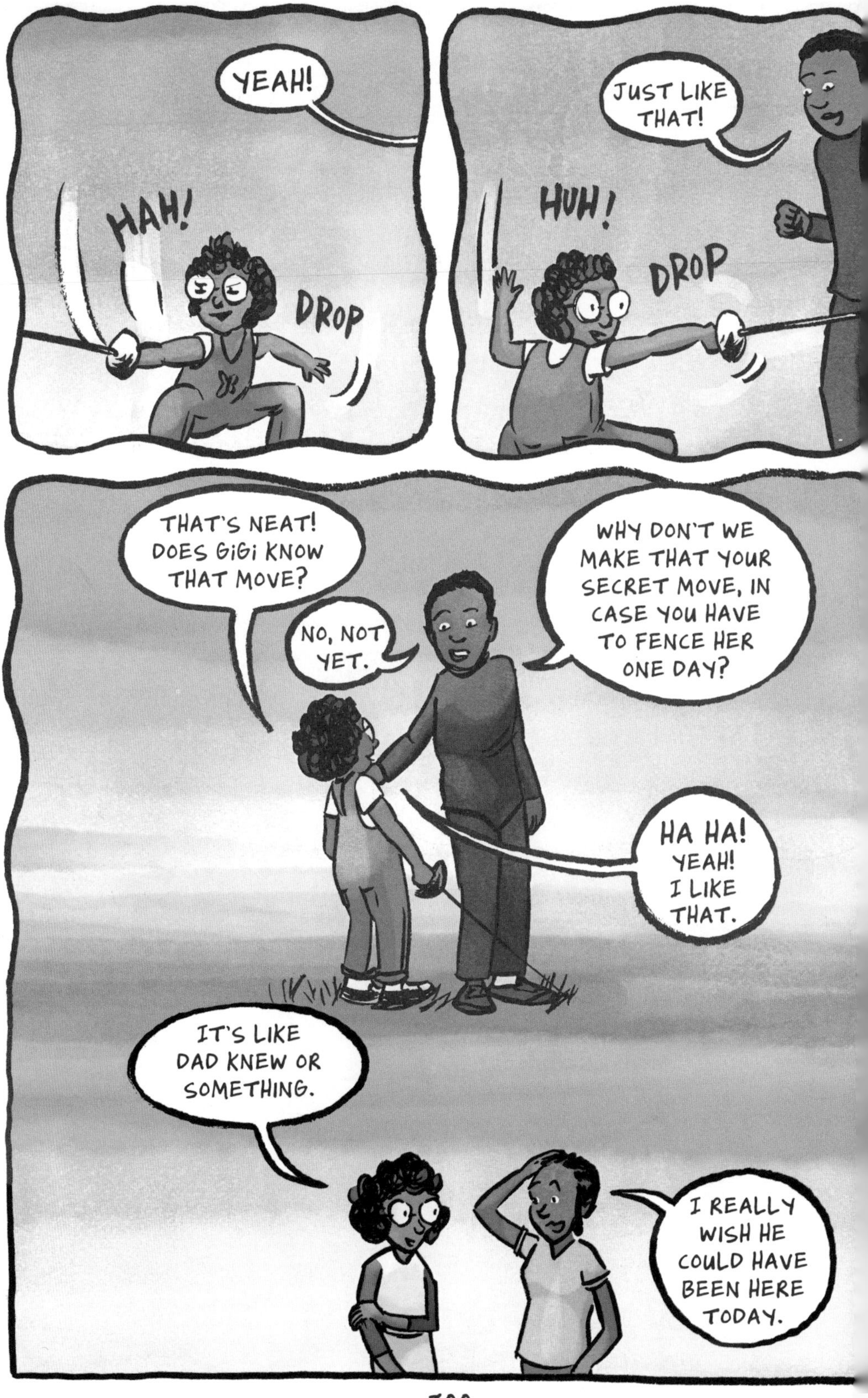
YEAH!
HAH!
DROP
JUST LIKE THAT!
HUH!
DROP
THAT'S NEAT! DOES GIGI KNOW THAT MOVE?
NO, NOT YET.
WHY DON'T WE MAKE THAT YOUR SECRET MOVE, IN CASE YOU HAVE TO FENCE HER ONE DAY?
HA HA! YEAH! I LIKE THAT.
IT'S LIKE DAD KNEW OR SOMETHING.
I REALLY WISH HE COULD HAVE BEEN HERE TODAY.

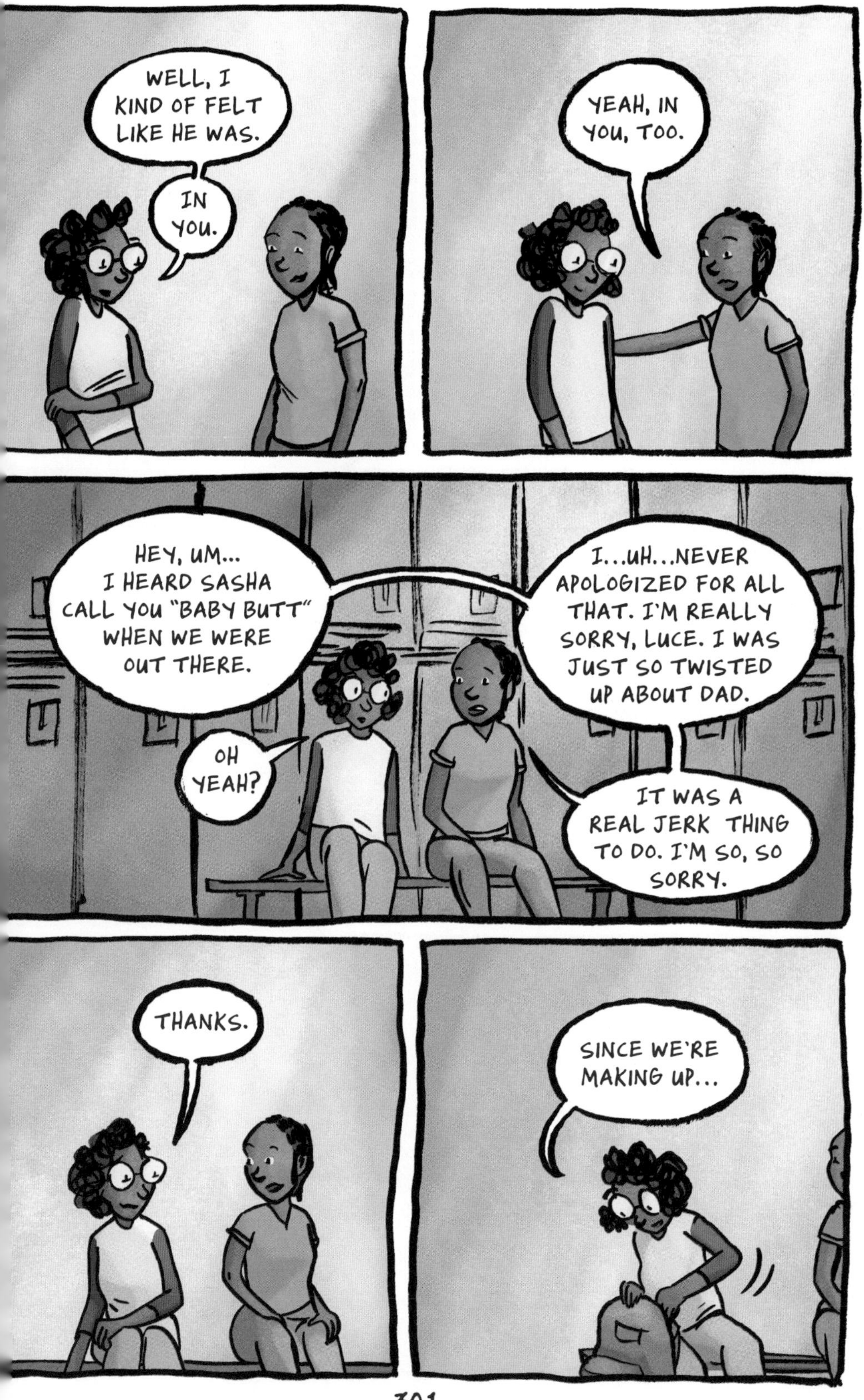
WELL, I KIND OF FELT LIKE HE WAS.
IN YOU.
YEAH, IN YOU, TOO.
HEY, UM... I HEARD SASHA CALL YOU "BABY BUTT" WHEN WE WERE OUT THERE.
OH YEAH?
I...UH...NEVER APOLOGIZED FOR ALL THAT. I'M REALLY SORRY, LUCE. I WAS JUST SO TWISTED UP ABOUT DAD.
IT WAS A REAL JERK THING TO DO. I'M SO, SO SORRY.
THANKS.
SINCE WE'RE MAKING UP...

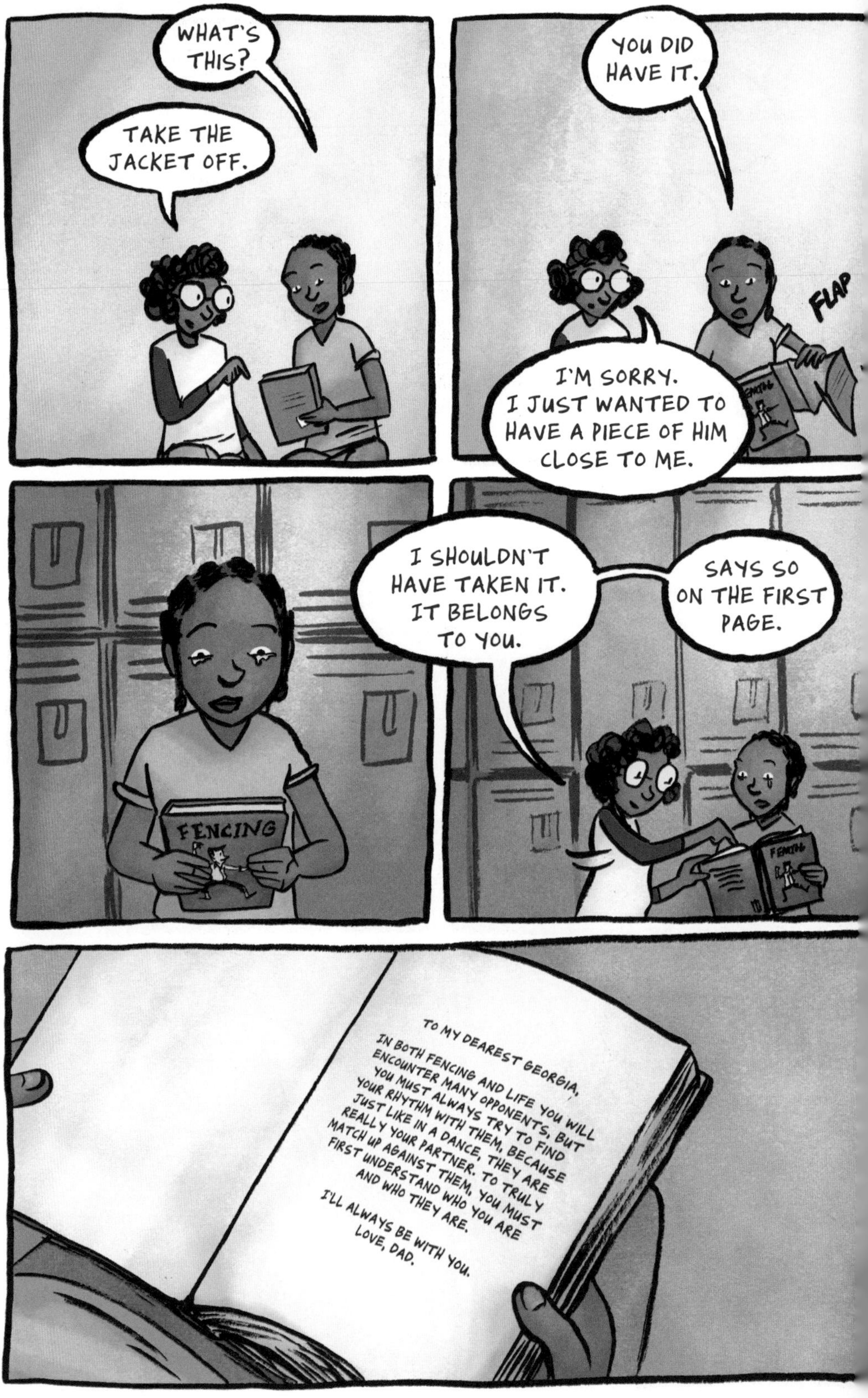

WHAT'S THIS?
TAKE THE JACKET OFF.
YOU DID HAVE IT.
FLAP
I'M SORRY. I JUST WANTED TO HAVE A PIECE OF HIM CLOSE TO ME.
FENCING
I SHOULDN'T HAVE TAKEN IT. IT BELONGS TO YOU.
SAYS SO ON THE FIRST PAGE.
TO MY DEAREST GEORGIA,
IN BOTH FENCING AND LIFE YOU WILL ENCOUNTER MANY OPPONENTS, BUT YOU MUST ALWAYS TRY TO FIND YOUR RHYTHM WITH THEM, BECAUSE JUST LIKE IN A DANCE, THEY ARE REALLY YOUR PARTNER. TO TRULY MATCH UP AGAINST THEM, YOU MUST FIRST UNDERSTAND WHO YOU ARE AND WHO THEY ARE.
I'LL ALWAYS BE WITH YOU.
LOVE, DAD.

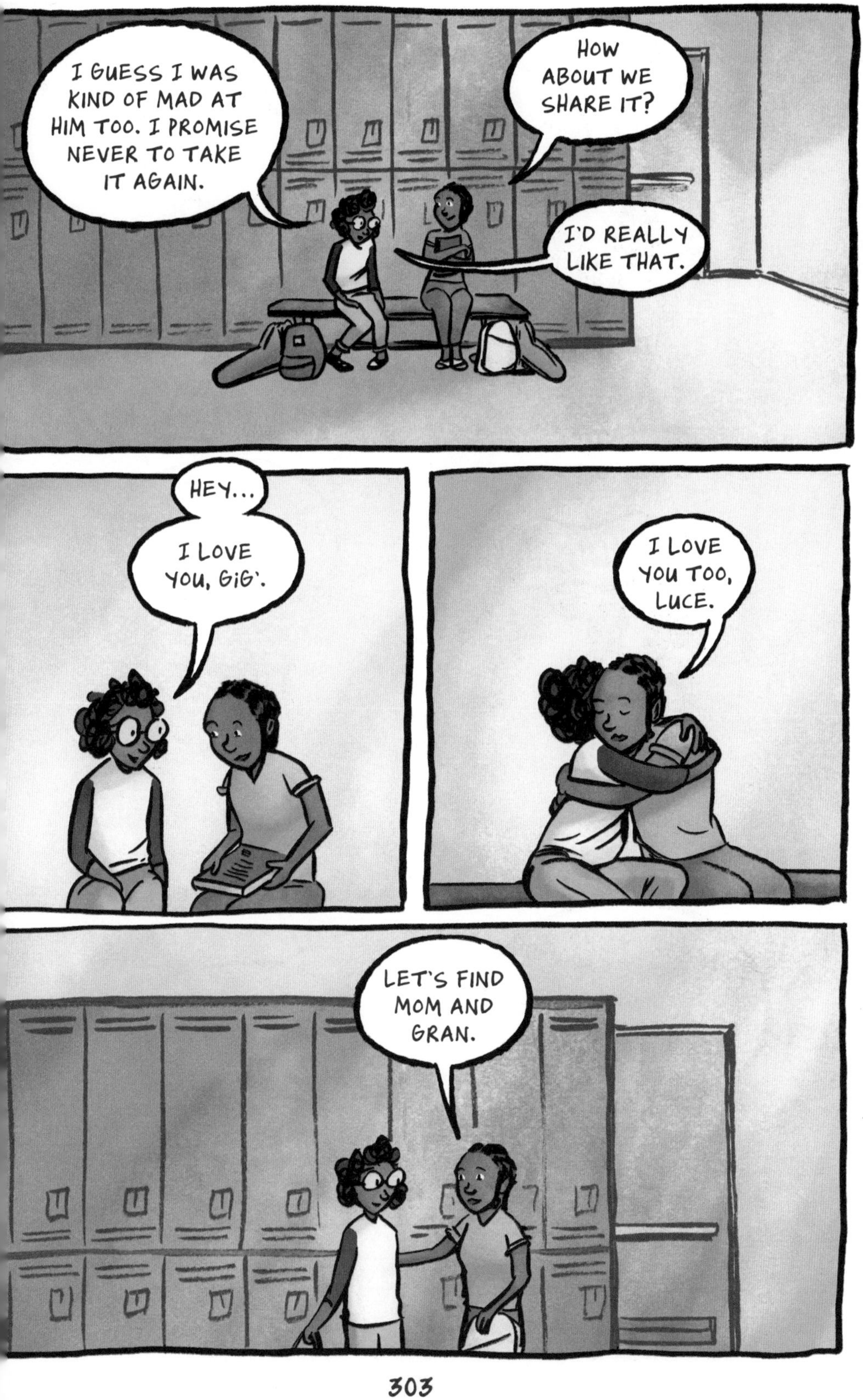
I GUESS I WAS KIND OF MAD AT HIM TOO. I PROMISE NEVER TO TAKE IT AGAIN.
HOW ABOUT WE SHARE IT?
I'D REALLY LIKE THAT.
HEY...
I LOVE YOU, GIG'.
I LOVE YOU TOO, LUCE.
LET'S FIND MOM AND GRAN.

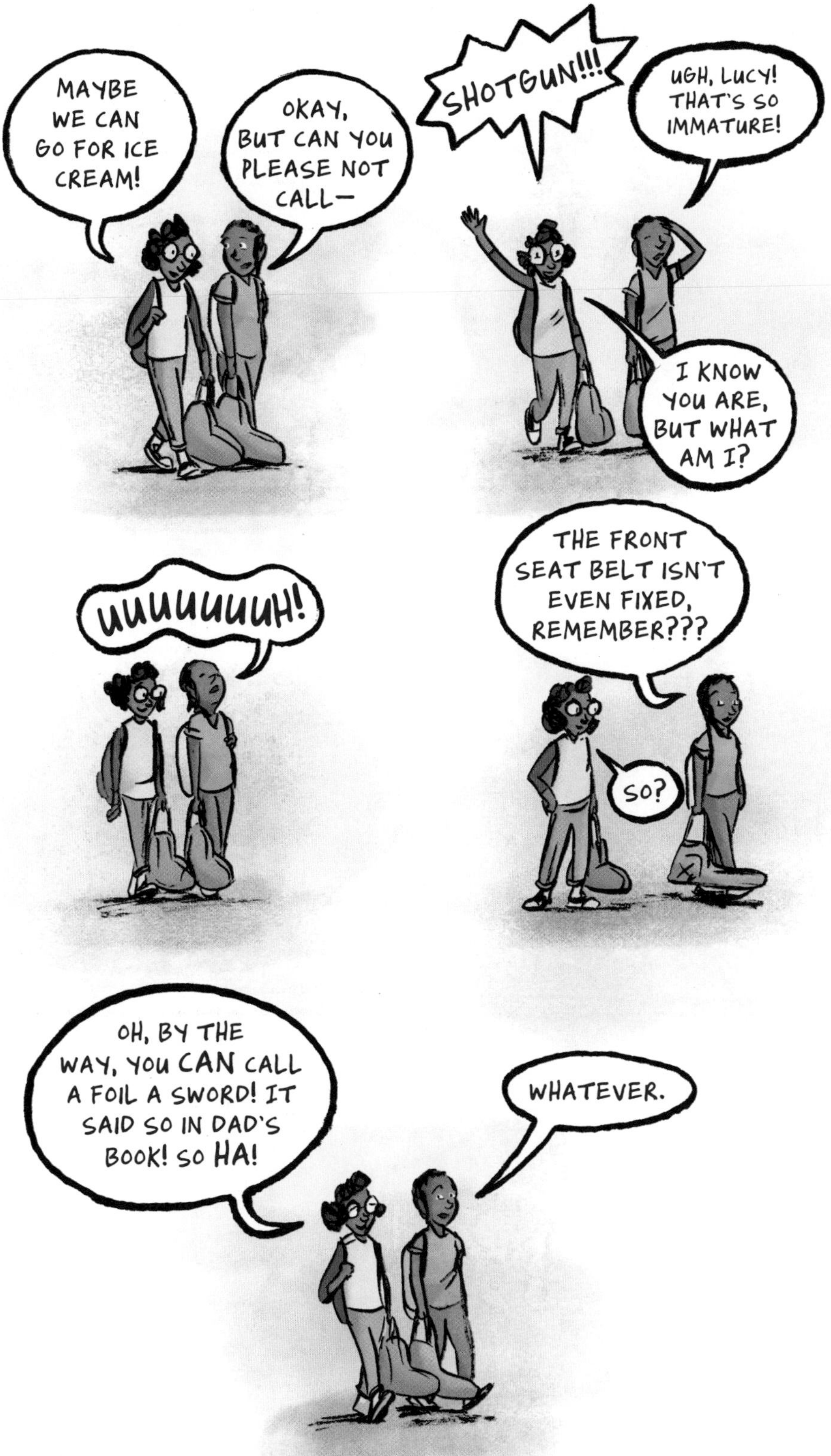

MAYBE WE CAN GO FOR ICE CREAM!
OKAY, BUT CAN YOU PLEASE NOT CALL—
SHOTGUN!!!
UGH, LUCY! THAT'S SO IMMATURE!
I KNOW YOU ARE, BUT WHAT AM I?
UUUUUUUH!
THE FRONT SEAT BELT ISN'T EVEN FIXED, REMEMBER???
SO?
OH, BY THE WAY, YOU CAN CALL A FOIL A SWORD! IT SAID SO IN DAD'S BOOK! SO HA!
WHATEVER.

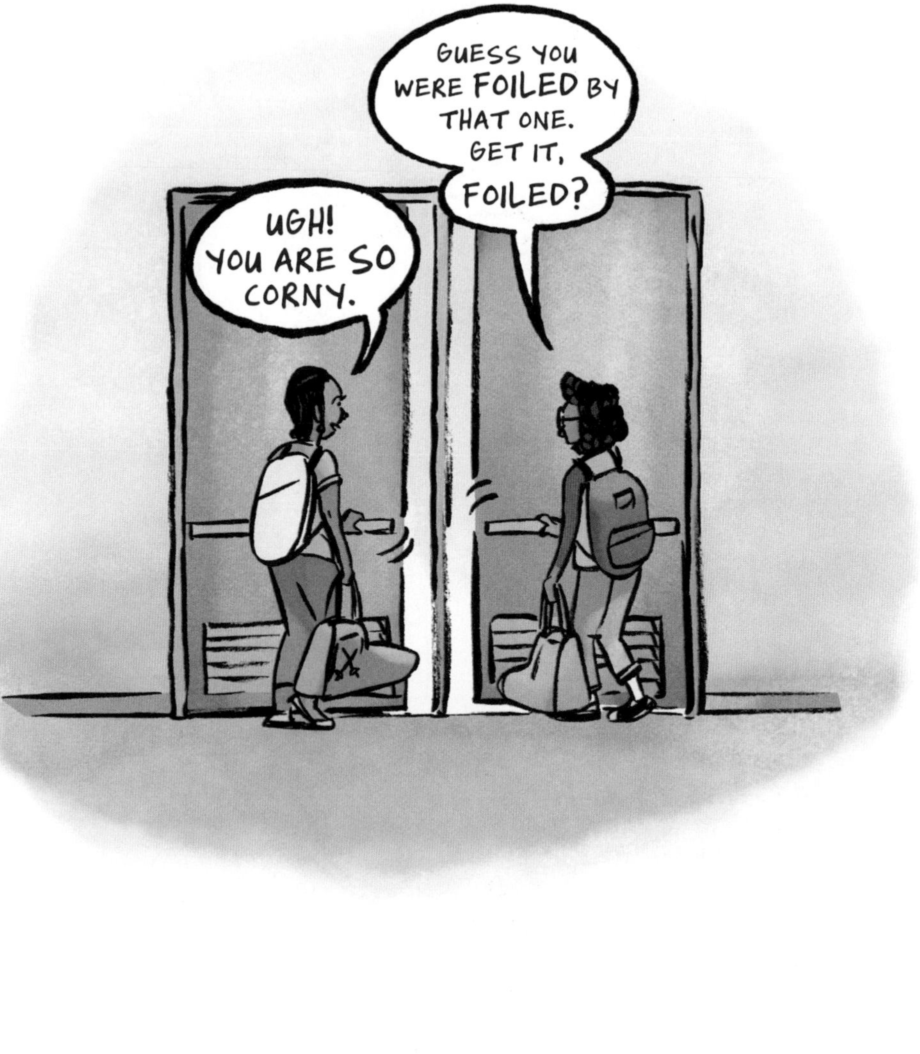
GUESS YOU WERE FOILED BY THAT ONE. GET IT, FOILED?
UGH! YOU ARE SO CORNY.

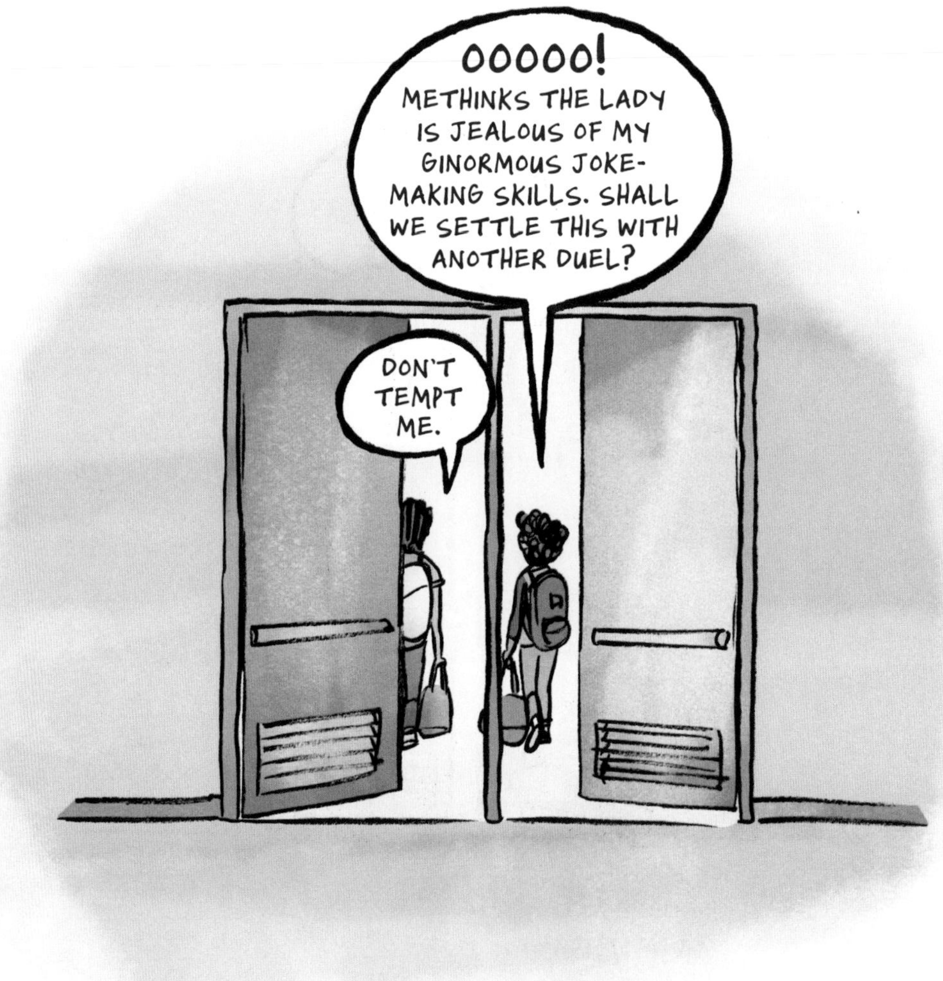
OOOOO! METHINKS THE LADY IS JEALOUS OF MY GINORMOUS JOKE-MAKING SKILLS. SHALL WE SETTLE THIS WITH ANOTHER DUEL?
DON'T TEMPT ME.

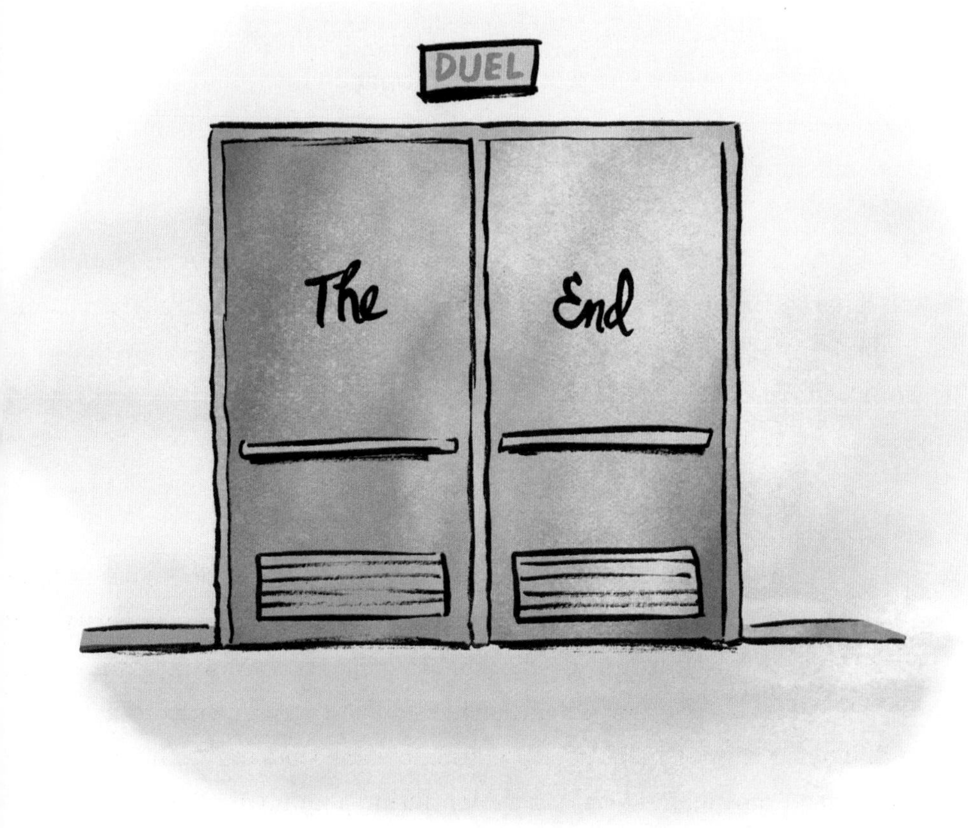
DUEL
The
End

Author's Note

What first inspired *Duel* was my love for the sport of fencing. I started fencing in college, and both my mother and sister had taken some classes for fun at different points in their lives. I instantly fell in love with foil and fenced off and on for a few years. But a series of injuries made it hard for me to keep fencing. Writing *Duel* was the perfect way to bring it back into my life. I also learned that fencing as a Black woman is not something so traditional to the sport. While there is fencing all over the world, the fencing community has a long history of excluding people of color and the racism that goes with that. I was *so* excited to find out about other Black fencers when creating this book! These are just *some* of the incredible (growing) roster of the Black athletes who have blazed a trail in the sport: Nikki Franke, Ruth White, Peter Westbrook, Sharon Monplaisir, Keeth Smart, Erinn Smart, Ibtihaj Muhammad, Jason Pryor, Daryl Homer, and Nzingha Prescod. Here are a couple of incredible organizations dedicated to teaching and providing access to fencing for underrepresented and under-resourced youth:

The Peter Westbrook Foundation: peterwestbrook.org

The Piste Fencing Academy: pisteacademy.org

My other inspiration for *Duel* was my family. A lot in the book is based on or inspired by real parts of my life, and a lot is fiction. The core dynamic between Lucy and GiGi is based on my relationship growing up with my older sister, SiSi. In real life, SiSi is seven years older than me. I played around with our memories (like SiSi never tripped me) but stayed true to some (like our grandma being a hairdresser, or me kicking a hole in a door during a fight with SiSi).

With *Duel*, I had the chance to explore my childhood relationship with my sister while thinking about what things might have been like from her point of view. In the moment, it's so easy to focus on your version of things and your own feelings, but in every situation, there's another side to the story. Writing *Duel* let me go back and give my sister a chance to tell her version of things.

My own father, Eddie, died when I was seventeen. The way we moved through the grief as a family was different (at times) from how the Jones family does in the book. Grief is a very strange thing. It comes at you in waves of numbness, pain, regret, sadness, anger, joy. And it takes its own length of time and is experienced differently from one person to the next. I didn't understand many parts of losing my father until I was in my thirties. Writing *Duel* brought up a lot of feelings that I hadn't felt for a long time. And when I saw how Aaron drew the story, looking at the art brought up old and new feelings attached to that grief. I've learned that losing someone isn't linear and it has no clear ending. But that is okay. That is what it means to feel and that is what it means to remember. And remembering is an important part of healing.

Loss can be a rocky sea to navigate alone so talking about your feelings is important. If you or someone you know needs extra support with a loss, please reach out to your network of friends, family, or doctors as well as organizations like Dougy Center (dougy.org) for help.

I hope this book can both inspire you to find a love for fencing like I did, no matter your race or economic background, and help you to know you are not alone if you have experienced loss.

—Jessixa Bagley

JESSIXA FENCING AND WITH HER FAMILY

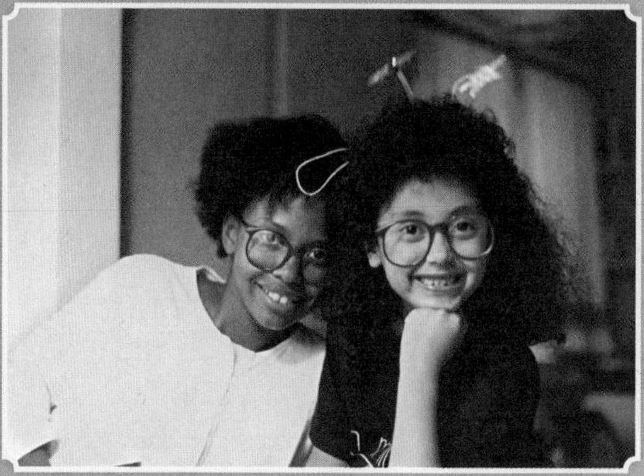

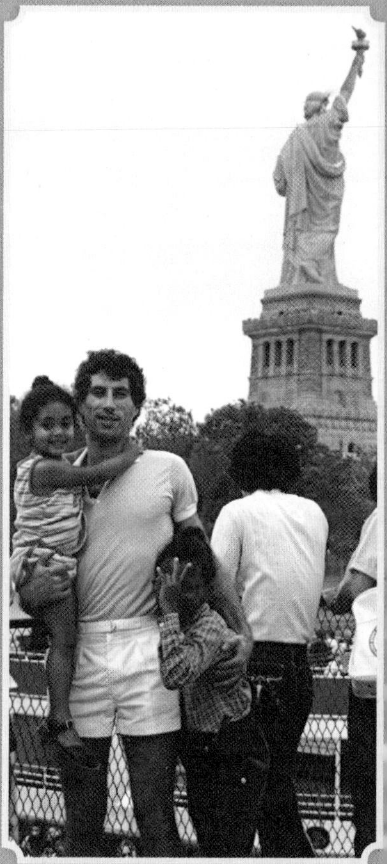

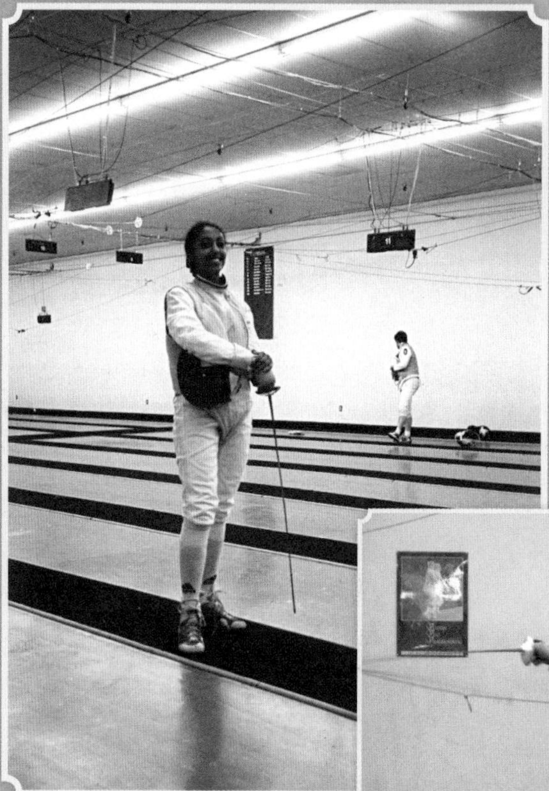

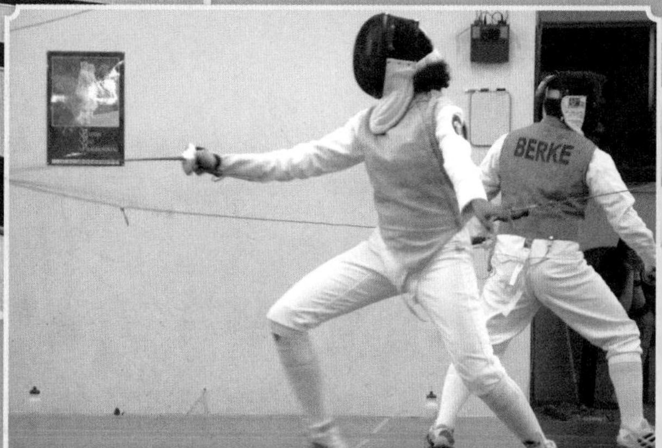
BERKE

THIS IS THE COVER OF THE *DUEL* NOTEBOOK. INSIDE THIS BOOK YOU'LL FIND THUMBNAILS, FLOOR PLANS OF THE JONES HOME AND THE MIDDLE SCHOOL, CHARACTER SKETCHES, THE FONT I CREATED FOR THE WORD BUBBLES, AND MORE! I WANTED TO MAKE IT FEEL LIKE A NOTEBOOK THAT LUCY WOULD USE FOR SCHOOL.

—AARON BAGLEY

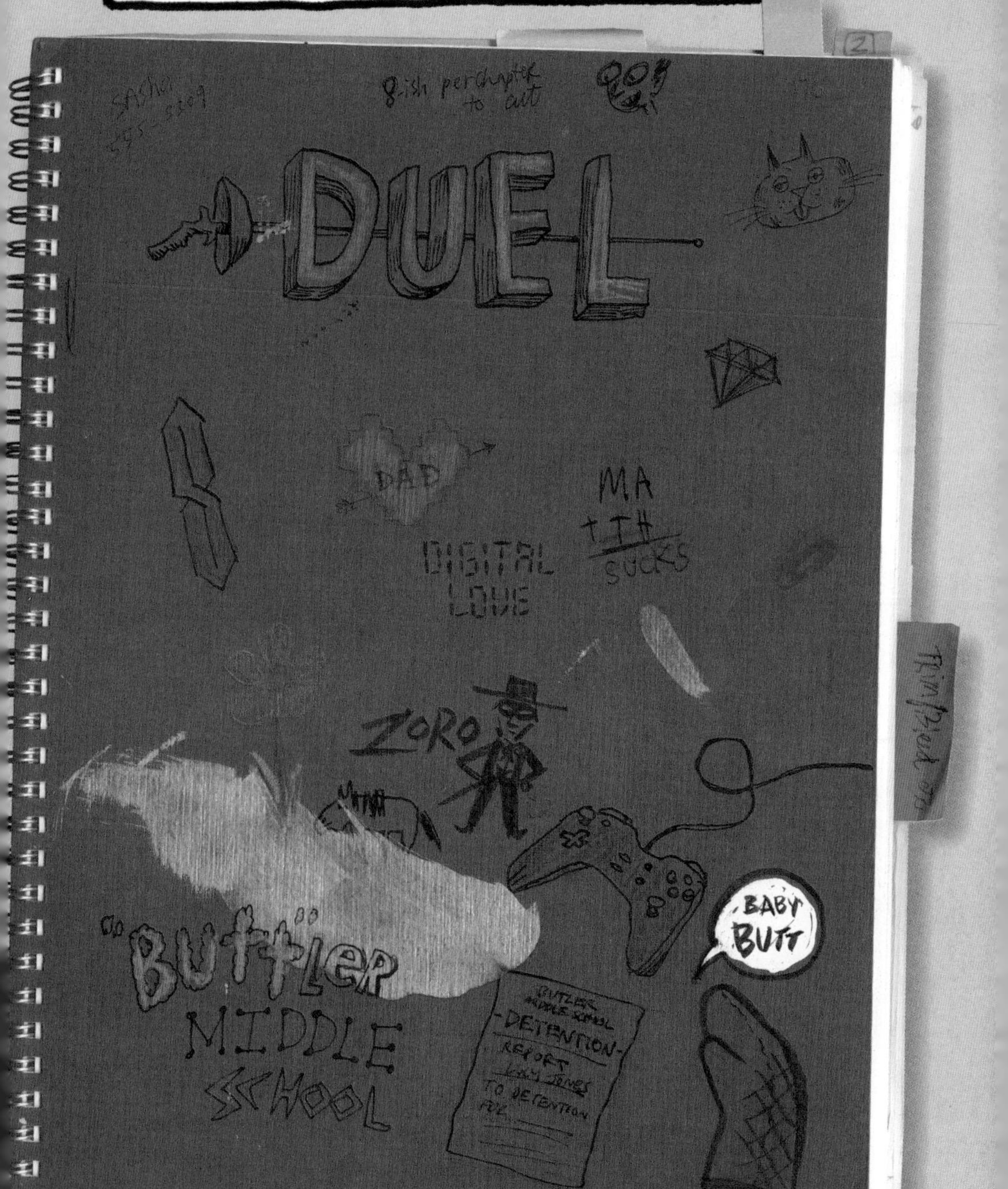
8-ish per chapter to cut
DUEL
DAD
MA TH SUCKS
DIGITAL LOVE
ZORO
BABY BUTT
BUTTLER MIDDLE SCHOOL
BUTLER MIDDLE SCHOOL -DETENTION- REPORT

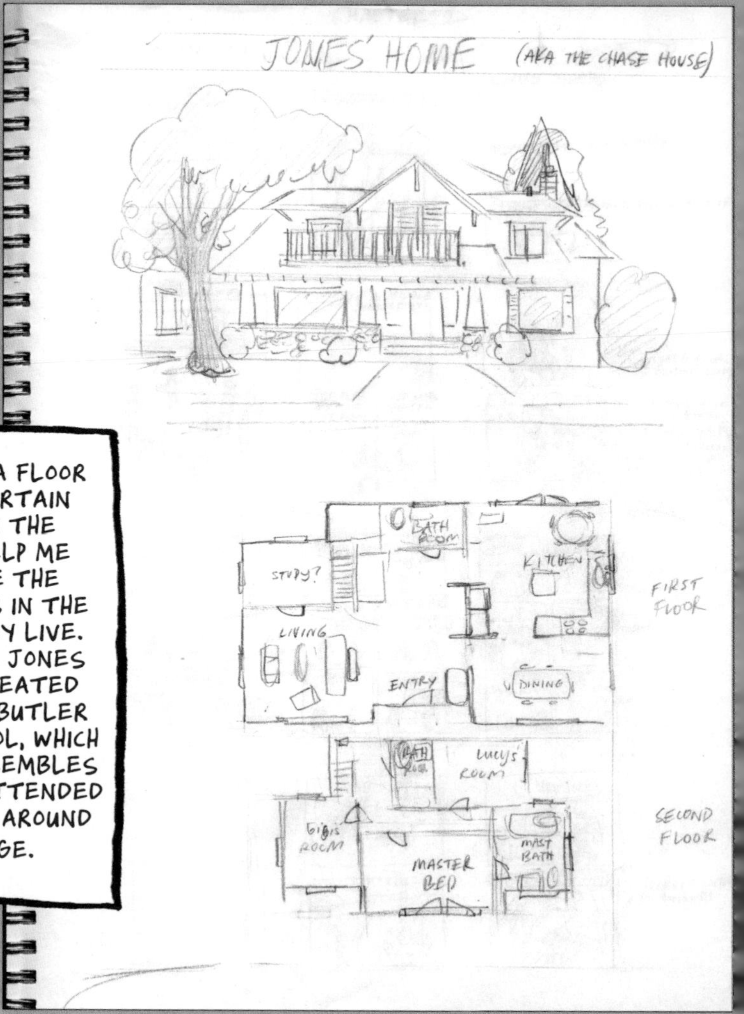
JONES' HOME (AKA THE CHASE HOUSE)
BATH ROOM
KITCHEN
STUDY?
LIVING
ENTRY
DINING
FIRST FLOOR
BATH ROOM
LUCY'S ROOM
GIGI'S ROOM
MASTER BED
MAST BATH
SECOND FLOOR

I CREATED A FLOOR PLAN OF CERTAIN PLACES IN THE BOOK TO HELP ME VISUALIZE THE CHARACTERS IN THE SPACES THEY LIVE. HERE IS THE JONES HOUSE. I CREATED ONE OF THE BUTLER MIDDLE SCHOOL, WHICH CLOSELY RESEMBLES A SCHOOL I ATTENDED WHEN I WAS AROUND GiGi'S AGE.

AFTER I FINISHED INKING, I CREATED A CHARACTER COLOR KEY TO HELP THE COLORIST KNOW HOW I WANTED THE CHARACTERS TO LOOK. I COLORED THESE WITH WATERCOLOR. GUY, THE COLORIST, DID THE COLORING DIGITALLY.

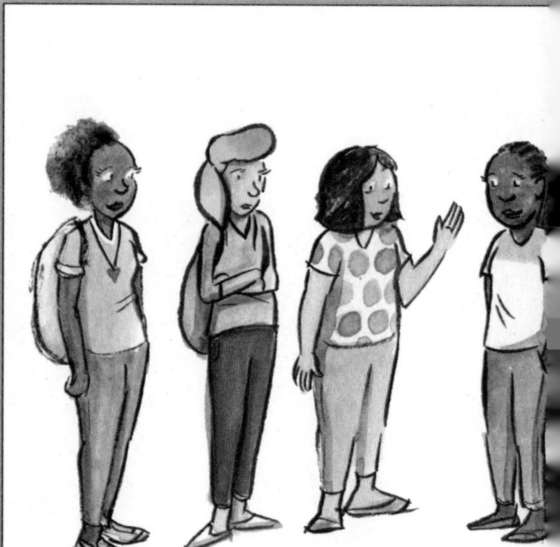

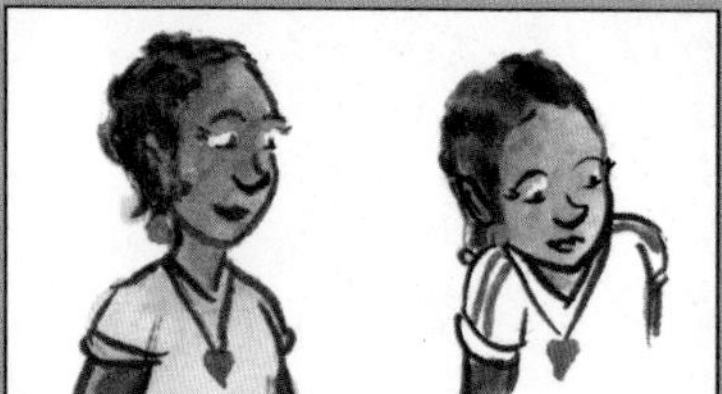

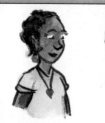

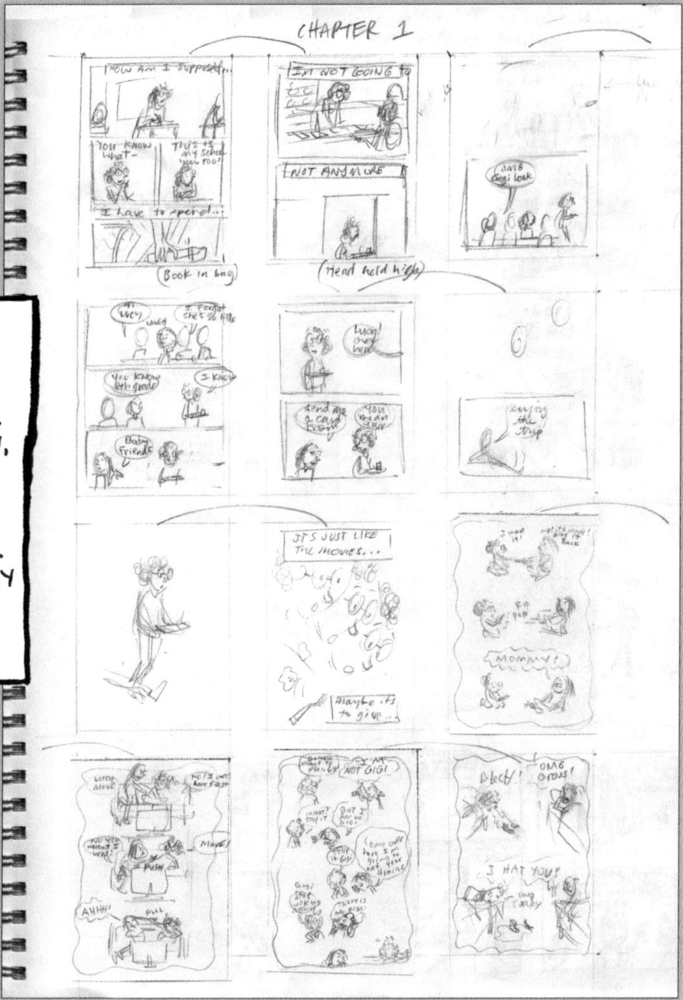
CHAPTER 1
How am I supposed...
I have to spend...
(Book in bag)
I'M NOT GOING TO
NOT ANYMORE
(Head held high)
OMG Gigi look
IT'S JUST LIKE THE MOVIES...
Maybe it's to give...
MOMMY!
MOVE!
PUSH
AHHH!
PULL
I'M NOT GIGI
Blech!
OMG Gross!
I HAT YOU!

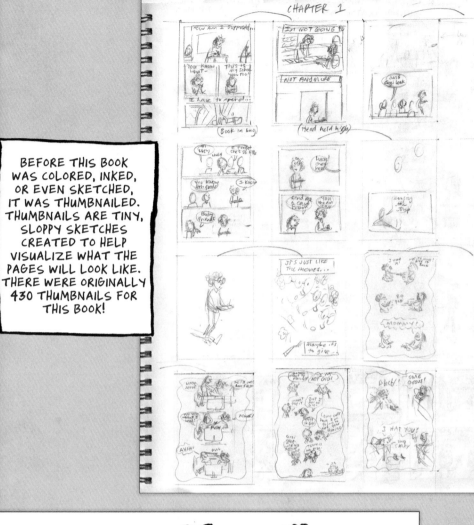

BEFORE THIS BOOK WAS COLORED, INKED, OR EVEN SKETCHED, IT WAS THUMBNAILED. THUMBNAILS ARE TINY, SLOPPY SKETCHES CREATED TO HELP VISUALIZE WHAT THE PAGES WILL LOOK LIKE. THERE WERE ORIGINALLY 430 THUMBNAILS FOR THIS BOOK!

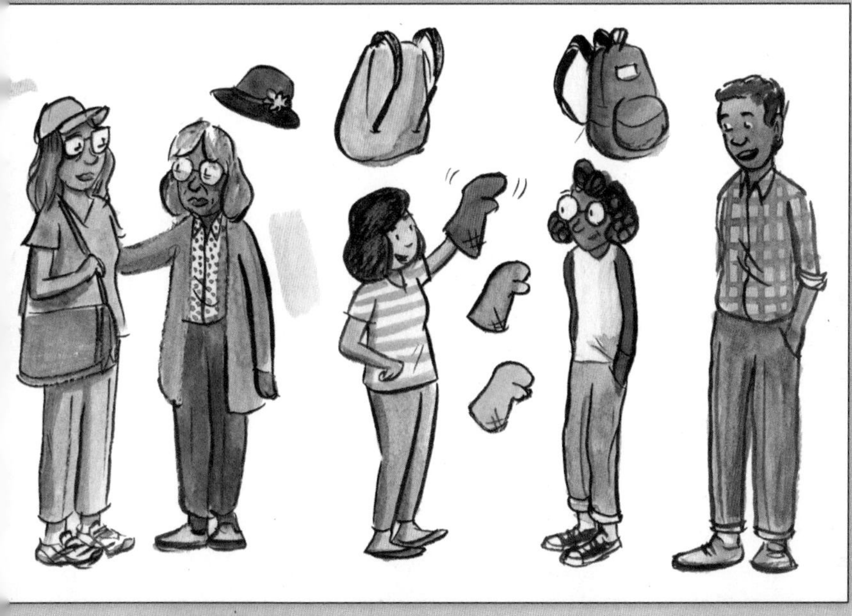

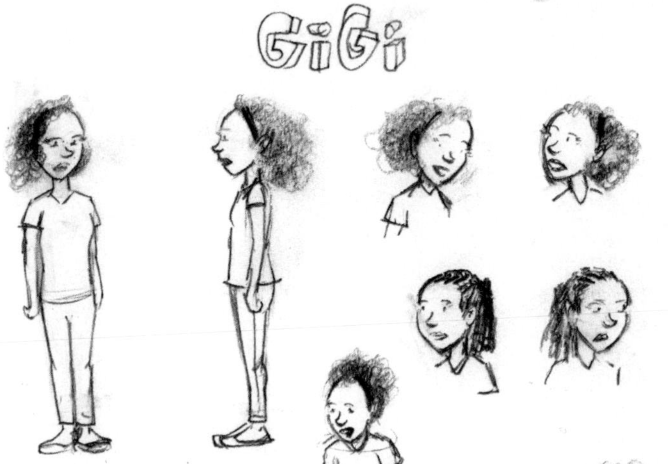
GiGi

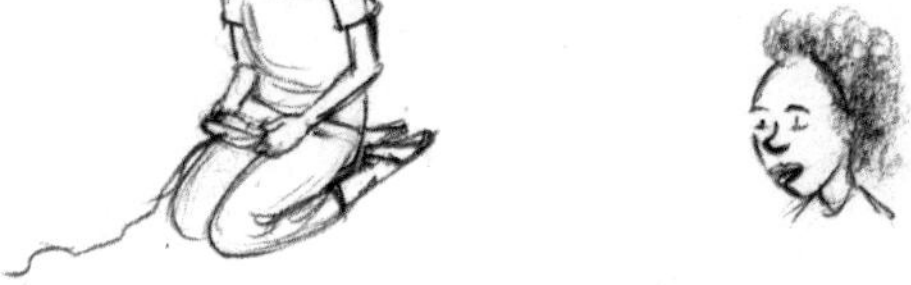

IT TOOK A LOT OF WORK TO GET THE FENCING GEAR DRAWN CORRECTLY. HERE ARE SOME SKETCHES FROM THE *DUEL* NOTEBOOK.

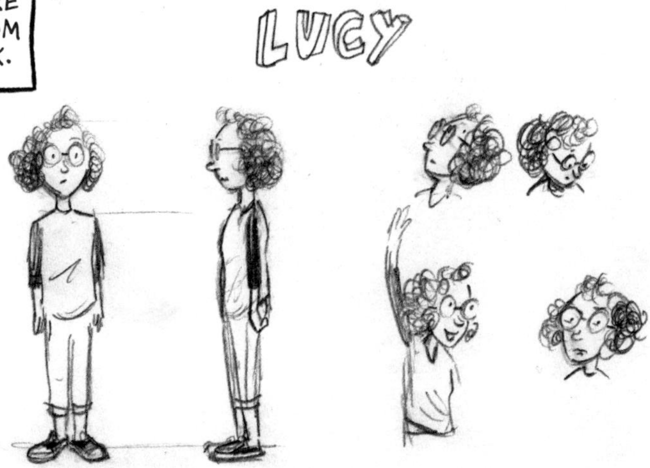
LUCY

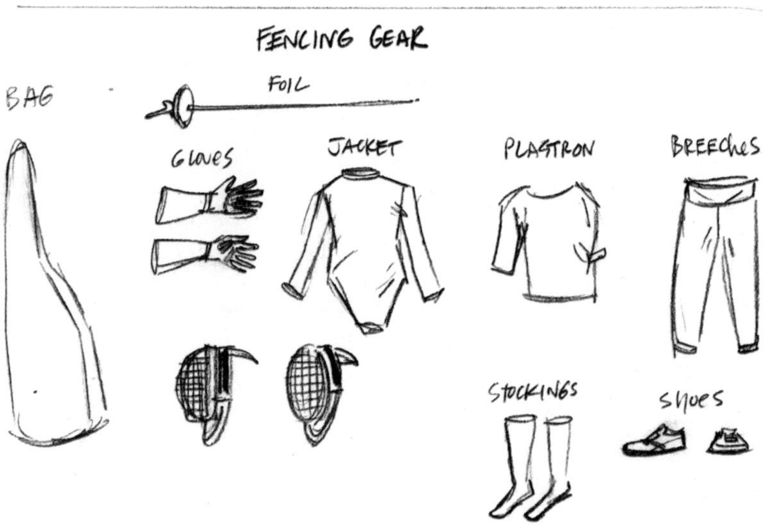
FENCING GEAR
BAG
FOIL
GLOVES
JACKET
PLASTRON
BREECHES
STOCKINGS
SHOES

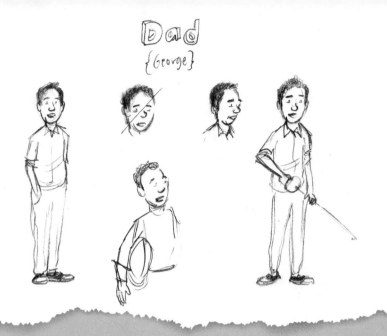

Dad
{George}

Acknowledgments

I would like to acknowledge that *Duel* was written and illustrated on the traditional land of the first people of Seattle, the Duwamish people past and present. We give gratitude to the land and the Duwamish Tribe as they continue to thrive and honor their ancient heritage.

Books take a lot of hands and hearts to make! So, I want to thank as many of those hearts as I possibly can:

Thank you to Alexandra Penfold for lighting that initial fire under me and for the constant support and hard work it took to get us here!

Endless thanks to my dear husband and creative collaborator, Aaron Bagley, without whom this book would not be the same. Aaron was the perfect person to bring it to life. Not only is he my family (and someone who understands my family intimately), his talent, creativity, and sensitivity to the comics form made him the only person I could trust my memories with.

Thank you to entire team at Simon & Schuster, especially Kendra Levin and Chloë Foglia! Special thanks to Kendra, our editor, for helping me write a better book, then a better book, then a better book. Chloë, I am grateful for your patience and support through this roller coaster of a process.

Thank you SO MUCH to Guy Major for coming in before the stroke of midnight with your amazing coloring talents!

Thank you, Sagen Shuler family (Darin, Erin, Laura, Sunny, Story), for letting me live in your magical cottage so I could write my first draft!

HUGE thanks to my awesome book community, especially Mike Curato, Victoria Jamieson, and Suzanne Kaufman for all your time spent sending me pro tips on everything from submitting a graphic novel dummy to insights on emotional teens.

Thank you SO VERY MUCH to my friend and fencing coach, Peet Sasaki, for teaching me how to fence and for being our amazing consultant on the fencing details for this book. And to Salle Auriol Seattle, for being my original fencing home (salleauriol.com)!

Thank you to my mom for being there for me all the way through my growing up. I know it wasn't easy doing it alone. You always did the best you could and that's something I take with me in all things from work to motherhood.

To my dad, Eddie, who didn't fence, but who loved running, and *Jeopardy!*, and being Jewish, and having daughters. I give thanks for my life and for being the love of Mom's life, even after you divorced, and even after you were gone. I know she misses you every day. We all miss you every day.

And of course, thank you to my sister, SiSi. Thank you for letting me make a book about our childhood. I know it's not an exact reflection, but I hope this book shows that you had a story to tell, too. I'm sorry for being a jerk at times. Even though we fought a lot, I also remember racing to the couch to watch *The Smurfs* on Saturday morning, you reading Shel Silverstein to me, and wishing I could draw castles like you. Thanks for helping me understand our family and for being my sister. I love you. —J. B.

Thanks to Jessixa, Alexandra, Kendra, Chloë, Tom, Paul Z., Steve L., Guy, fencing GIFs, the entire S&S team, and of course my family and friends. Special thanks to all the audio stimulation that inspired this work, including but not limited to Metallica, Sun Ra, Kate Bush, Cola Boyy, Pond, The Weeknd, Guns N' Roses, and all the radio hits from 1994 to 1995. —A. B.